THE END OF MY TETHER

NEIL ASTLEY has been editor of poetry publishers Bloodaxe Books for as long as anyone can remember, but his other lives have included spells as a court reporter, ice cream publicist, blood banker, bus conductor and singing waiter. As a journalist he once wrote a 24-page feature supplement on beef cattle in Australia's Northern Territory in two days to win a bet. His former life as an antipodean hack came to an abrupt end when he was buried under a house in the Darwin cyclone disaster.

Since reinventing himself, he has edited several anthologies, including *Poetry with an Edge*, *New Blood, Staying Alive: real poems for unreal times*, and *Pleased to See Me: 69 very sexy poems*. He won an Eric Gregory Award for his poetry, and has published two collections, *Darwin Survivor* (Poetry Book Society Recommendation) and *Biting My Tongue*. He received a D.Litt from Newcastle University for his work with Bloodaxe Books, which he founded. He lives in the Tarset valley in Northumberland.

The End of My Tether, his first novel, was written with the assistance of several animals.

THE END OF MY TETHER

NEIL ASTLEY

Scribner

First published in Great Britain by Flambard Press, 2002
This edition published by Scribner, 2003
An imprint of Simon & Schuster UK Ltd
A Viacom Company

1 3 5 7 9 10 8 6 4 2

Simon & Schuster UK Ltd
Africa House
64-78 Kingsway
London WC2B 6AH

www.simonsays.co.uk

Simon & Schuster Australia
Sydney

A CIP catalogue record for this book
is available from the British Library

ISBN 0-7432-4838-4

Printed and bound in Great Britain by
Cox & Wyman Ltd, Reading, Berks

A man can be alive in 1860 and in 1830
at the same time. Bodily I may be in 1860,
inert, silent, torpid; but in the spirit I am
walking about in 1828, let us say;– in a
blue dress-coat and brass buttons.

– WILLIAM MAKEPEACE THACKERAY

To love is to accept that one might die
another death before one dies one's own.

– MARIANNE WIGGINS

In this land of milk and money…
England has been bleeding…
So let's dance for our lives, boys,
in this vaudeville show.
Take your time and take a bow,
this place is gonna blow.

– THEA GILMORE

This book is dedicated to the memory of
the two and a half million cattle needlessly
slaughtered in the 1996-98 Beef War
as well as the 120 people so far known
to have died from new variant Creutzfeld-Jakob Disease.
Written before the outbreak of Foot and Mouth Disease
in England in 2001, it is also dedicated to the memory
of the six million sheep, cattle and pigs who
lost their lives during that later conflict.

CONTENTS

The End of My Tether

A MYTH OF ENGLAND IN 28 LUNAR CHAPTERS

PROLOGUE

An Inch of My Life

SAMHAIN: OCTOBER 31ST – NOVEMBER 1ST

Peering into the darkness of the garden, Kernan saw that the man was still hanging there, the rope creaking as the wind swung him back and forth.

The rope keened like an aching tree.

The hammering in his head grew more unbearable.

Taking the bread-knife from the cutlery drawer, he went outside, the moment he always dreaded. He knew that when he reached the ash tree, the hanging man would point to the wound in his side, as if he were to blame. Then he would berate him.

– You left me hanging here for nine nights.

– You did it to yourself, Kernan replied. A rope and butter: if one slip, t'other will hold.

– I offered myself to myself.

– If I be hanged, I'll choose my gallows, be it Tyburn tippet or Bridport dagger.

– I did it for you.

– He pulls with a long rope that waits for another's death.

– Cut me down then.

As Kernan started sawing, he felt the rope tighten round his own neck. For an instant he was hanging within an inch of his life, his own body about to kill him with its weight, until the bough above him broke instead, and he fell.

And kept falling. Down, down.

His guts were going the other way, heading for his head.

He knew this was the dream, the same dream, even as he dreamed it. Or it dreamed him. Yet this knowledge that he would wake did not allay the terror he felt. A terror like the war.

He had once seen a man throw himself from a building. All the time he was falling, Kernan felt he was that man, and the falling went on for ever. It was worse than the moment of impact.

When he hit the ground, Kernan found he was lying in a field as he had expected. It was still night. There was a cow nearby, her flanks glistening white in the moonlight. He heard her tearing at the wet grass. She seemed high up. He did not know why.

He knew she would have red ears, and would be tethered, separate from the rest of the herd, a cow in a fremit loaning.

The cow did not try to move away when he approached. She looked up, and chewed. He recognised the rope. She carried on chewing the cud, seemingly oblivious of his presence.

He stood in front of her then, feeling her hot grassy breath in his face. She gave a dullish low, almost a rumble, like distant thunder. Then another, louder. And a third, more threatening. Kernan counted, as if waiting for a storm flash:

– *Yan…tan…tethera*; and at the third low, untied the rope from its wooden stake. Taking the end of the tether, he walked slowly away from the cow, until the rope swayed almost taut between them. Then he passed it round his waist and secured himself with a knot like a figure eight.

It was then that he saw Diana standing at the edge of the field, mouthing something he could not hear. Motioning to her not to alarm the cow, he was suddenly gripped by a sense of panic which was new. She shouldn't be there. There was only ever him and the cow, man and beast, no one else. Something was wrong. This time something was out of step, something he couldn't put his finger on. He felt his stomach tighten, as if sensing an unknown threat. It wasn't just Diana. He knew there were others too, waiting.

But he'd already started running. The cow stood still as he circled, tied to the end of her tether, like the hand of a clock, but going backwards. Anti-clockwise. Withershins. The wrong way.

Each time he passed the stake, he counted.

– *Yan*, for the first.

– *Tan*, for two circuits.

– *Tethera*, for three.

With each circuit running faster.

– *Methera*, he gasped.

– *Pimp*. Five circuits of the track. The old hand now Kernan the young athlete.

– *Sethera*. Six. They couldn't touch him now, his pursuers, wherever they were.

– *Lethera*, after the seventh, always the toughest circuit; the cow still unmoving, like the dark bulk of a standing stone.

– *Hovera*, he cried. And still she took the strain while Kernan ran his circle, his legs pumping, his whole body fired with adrenaline. He was winning. He was in the lead.

– *Dovera*. No one could catch him now. Not even them.

– *Dik!* He was lapping himself. Ten circuits.

– *Yan dik! Yan dik!* Nearly there, only two to go. But now the cow was pulling. That was odd. Yet she wasn't shifting from the centre.

– *Tan dik!* Twelve. He'd never done twelve before. He'd always broken down, come round in a sweat. *Yan dik, yan dik*, was his cue to collapse. It was *tan dik* now. *Tan dik, tan dik*, he chanted at the milk-white cow shining in the dark field like the moon above them. The cow that seemed to be drawing him towards her, even as he ran his orbit at the end of his tether.

– *Tethera dik! Tethera dik!* So he'd done it, for the first time, all thirteen.

And kept running, for he couldn't stop. Yet the rope was getting shorter, he was being pulled into the cow at the same time as he was flying away from her, like a satellite falling to earth, burning up in the atmosphere. He thought of Hippolytus, torn apart by his two terrified horses.

Some massive centrifugal force was tearing him limb from limb, violently but without pain. He was separating, spirit from body, leaving the dream yet not waking, but being hauled backwards, as if the rope were his umbilical cord reclaiming him, and the moon-white cow his mother.

He heard Diana, calling as if from a long way off.

– *Kernan, where are you? What's happening?*

But he was being swallowed, and she was growing fainter by the second.

– *Kernan, where have you gone? Please, oh please say where...* Her voice died away.

Now he was inside the cow. And he was falling, falling like before. Down, down. Falling.

This time he would not wake.

BOOK I

SAMHAIN

NOVEMBER – JANUARY

When I was a boy, and a farmer's boy
I looked after my father's cows
With a cow a-boo-ing here
And another a-boo-ing there,
Here a-boo-ing, there a-boo-ing,
Boo-ing everywhere.
And a horse a-gee-a-woo-ing here
And another gee-a-woo-ing there,
Here a-gee-ing, there a-gee-ing,
Gee-ing everywhere.
And to plough and sow
To reap and mow
And to be a farmer's boy.

CHAPTER ONE

Showing Them the Ropes

SAMHAIN: OCTOBER 31ST – NOVEMBER 1ST

To avoid the curse of lumbago, replace your belt with a length of hempen rope. To cure headaches, make your belt of hangman's rope.

D*ik. Dik. Dik…*

– Dick Who?

– *Dik…* Kernan was muttering. Then looked up from the armchair. It was Diana Hunter, the new girl. Standing above him like a vision, the angel of the Annunciation.

Diana. This apparition with red hair. Outspoken, strong-willed, yet also vulnerable. With those dark green eyes all the Hunters had. He knew the family of old, had always been entranced by their eyes. But Diana was unaware of this connection; that her eyes gave her an advantage, even a hold, over Inspector Kernan.

– Hang on while I write something down, said Kernan. He took out a blue marble-patterned notebook, hunched over it and wrote quickly.

– What are you doing? she asked, ignoring his gesture of privacy. For there was nothing she wouldn't ask. She put the fear of God into the others at the station. No woolly thinking with *Her*, as she was quickly named: I'm out on patrol with *Her* was a statement guaranteed to elicit instant sympathy in the canteen. Many had been stung by her sharp responses: you have to be on your toes when *PC* Hunter's on the prowl, they would say, emphasising the initials to show disapproval of her admonishments as well as disgust at her too quick promotion to plainclothes. That she was usually right was not something they would dispute to her face, yet they would nurse it as a grievance, something else to be chewed over in the pub, and spat out like the word *feminist*.

– Just let me finish and I'll tell you, said Kernan.

– All right. She tried to read over his shoulder, but he sensed this, and shifted himself slightly to obscure the book from her view. Diana knew she was being forward, but that was her way. And if men didn't like it, that was their problem.

Yet if they did but know it, Diana Hunter was letting them off lightly. For she was ambitious for advancement in the force, and didn't rout her detractors as mercilessly as she was capable of doing. She'd leave that for later, when she had the whip hand. For now she was happy merely to make them feel uncomfortable.

– Nearly finished, said Kernan, looking up.

Ah, so he has some sense of courtesy after all, thought Diana, momentarily surprised. Finding him slumped asleep in his chair, his body jerking like an old dog's, she had stood for a full minute watching him off in another world, this boss she'd been lumbered with. All week she had resented him, thinking him as surly as the rest, cursing the whole pack of them. And not just the police: what was that saying? *Loamshire born and Loamshire bred, strong i' the arm and weak i' the head.* Weren't all Loamshire men uncommunicative with women, and suspicious of anything different or new, except for the farmers with their pesticides?

– You didn't knock, said Kernan, firmly, putting his book down, putting her in her place.

– There was no reply, she said. The door wasn't locked, so I came in. You were asleep, dozing in that chair.

– I never lock the door, said Kernan. There's no need round here. Kernan's first instinct was to attack, as he'd done in their scraps in the office, in this first week of her attachment to him. But at home he felt easier with her, even though she had just marched into his living-room. Invaded his space.

– But sit down. Move some of those books.

– You feel that sure of people here? asked Diana. She was looking round the room as she tried to make herself comfortable in an old chair whose springs seemed to have a life of their own. This was the first time she'd been to Kernan's house. He'd been a hard taskmaster at the station, yet she'd respected the thoroughness he'd displayed in showing her the ropes. And the fact that he hadn't once said anything she'd found objectionable, unlike most of his colleagues. Their antipathy towards him was another point in his favour, though she feared her association with someone they all distrusted might not help her prospects. Now she saw one of the main sources of their suspicion. Books. Thousands of books, lining every wall; books scattered across the floor and stacked in precarious piles on chairs. Books that someone was reading, his places marked with cards, leaves, scraps of paper and articles torn from newspapers. She remembered then how her mother had talked about a house of books in Loamfield, years ago, before her illness, and something about the man who lived there.

– I know everything that goes on in this village, said Kernan. He watched her green eyes scanning the spines of his books, and did not mind her intrusion now. Her curiosity aroused him. It was as if he lay there naked, and she were examining his body. He turned away; hoping his reddening face did not betray him in the half-light of the lamp-lit room. His shame.

– What's this? she asked, holding a book which bore his name, George Kernan.

– That's my book of Loamshire lore. *Lore*, not law, he added, seeing her look of puzzlement.

She read out the phrase 'Antiquarian Society' and 'Volume II' with a sense of wonderment or unfamiliarity.

– But it says here: *first published for the members of the Society in 1947.*

– I meant my father's book, Kernan said, rather too quickly. But I think of it as mine because I've continued his work. The third volume is mine.

His voice settled; the momentary panic under control.

– We're all Georges, us Kernans, he said, recovering. I was called George after my father, as he was after *his* father. My great-grandfather was George too, and his father, and so on back. I couldn't escape the name. It ties me to them.

She sensed his discomfort, that there were secrets here, and to help him recover, did not look him in the face, which was still faintly flushed, but let her eyes wander round him as she spoke, taking in more words from the walls of books, gathering more information on someone she still considered her antagonist, a man she had to know if she was to beat him at his game of cat and mouse. All men had their weaknesses: what was *his* Achilles' heel? Assigning her to Kernan, Superintendent Goodman had damned him with faint praise.

– You'll learn a lot from Kernan. He knows this county like the back of his hand. There's no villain can pull anything round here without our Inspector Kernan knowing something about it.

Here he had paused, his look telling her his enmity towards Kernan was no petty rivalry, but something deeper, almost primal.

– How he does it, I don't like to ask. Best conviction rate in the force, even if it has slipped a bit lately.

She noticed that Goodman's eyebrows almost met in the middle; his eyes were so dark they seemed like bottomless pits of blackness. He was trying to fix her with a vulpine stare, and her first instinct was to turn away, yet she felt compelled to respond to his predatory look, and smiled weakly, not avoiding his eyes but showing in her uneasy response that she found him both attractive and totally untrustworthy. Goodman snorted gleefully, pleased that she had not ducked his commanding leer.

Diana felt exposed, sensing that these two men were drawing at the cat's harrow. She'd have to tread carefully or she'd find herself standing between two bulls. Sitting now in the lion's den, she felt uneasy, for his books posed more questions than they answered. They showed he was obsessive, and clearly not just with folklore. There was a whole wall of books devoted to magic, superstition and – she noted – children's fairy tales, something which surprised her, for there was no other evidence in the house of children, not even pictures of grandchildren or other relatives.

– You look as though you're about to say what they all say, said Kernan.

– What's that?

– *Have you read all these books?*

– I wouldn't be so predictable. There's a less obvious question I'd ask if I were investigating you…

– Do I have to help you with your enquiries?

– You seem to read everything, but I can't see any books here on science, or criminology, psychology, sociology…

– Not my field.

– Crime?

– Crime's my job, what I do at work: I leave it behind when I walk in here. I don't need books to do the job. I just do it.

– What about the old saying: *A policeman's never off duty?*

– When I'm off duty, I'm not D.I. Kernan, I'm someone else. Yet I'm still enquiring, looking for clues, but I may never solve these cases. Searching for things that elude my understanding.

– What kind of things?

– I think I may even hold the key, but I don't know it's the key. I can't recognise it but I know it's there somewhere, probably right in front of my nose, only I'm too earthbound to see it. I've tied myself in knots hunting for it. It's the one riddle I can't crack, and it bothers me no end… As Kernan's voice trailed off into mumbling, Diana fired a question back into the fray.

– Never mind riddles, she said, aiming to score a direct hit now she had him in her sights.

He looked momentarily startled, setting his jaw to receive whatever she was going to throw at him.

– I'll tell you one which bothers me, she said. Why were you such a shit to me all last week, yet now I find you may be human after all? Or are you?

– A human being? I'm not so sure about that either. A shit, some think me that, because I get in their way. Because I know their game before they know it themselves. I taunt them as a way of amusing myself in an otherwise humdrum life, which makes them hate me all the more, cops and robbers. But they can't touch me, they've nothing on me. Not the cops: I keep solving their cases with tiresome regularity. Nor the robbers: I keep them dangling, then pull them in. But not all of them. It wouldn't look good to be *too* good, so I just do enough, but better than anyone else. And they hate that.

– Come on. Why be a shit to me then, why not help me in my first week? A damsel in distress…

– You know how to look after yourself, you're no damsel. That's your problem, you won't let anyone else help you. I was testing you, finding out where you're coming from. If we're to be a team, I have to be sure of you, regardless of what you think of me.

– And are you sure?

– Not yet, but I'm getting there. Goodman usually tries to lumber me with incompetents, no-goods who'll spy on me and sabotage my work. You're very bright, so the men will find it difficult to work with you. I don't have their problems but Goodman knows there's likely to be a clash of wills between us: you with your new ideas and scientific training, me with my old methods, hunches, instincts, age-old knowledge of my patch. A recipe for chaos, pure devilment: all he has to do is stand back and wait for it to happen. You can see all that coming, can't you, and neither of us will be able to prevent it; I'll try to control it, but you'll buck against my authority in your headstrong way. He's not stupid, old Nick Goodman. And he doesn't like it that I'm a better detective than he is. Now he has devised this perfectly plotted means of obstructing me.

– *Obstruct?* Diana queried, remembering how Goodman had used the same word, but with duplicity. Kernan's use of it was so direct it was almost paranoid. And *sabotage*? she repeated: Isn't that a bit of an overstatement?

– Not at all. I'd find they'd been going through files that didn't concern them. They were checking up on me, looking for clues. They found nothing of course, as if I'd leave anything on record which he could use against me, but he doesn't let up. He has them follow me when I'm off-duty. They watch me all the time.

– Do I watch you?

– Yes, but in a different way. Your watching is curious, not devious. At first you were suspicious, but you quickly realised I wasn't bent. I looked you straight in the eye. I saw you knew that Goodman was the one you should be watching, not me.

– I'm not stupid. I knew him from a black sheep.

– A black sheep is a biting beast.

– A shrew can better a sheep, she responded, laughing.

This was the first time Kernan had heard Diana laugh, and it took him aback at the same time as it delighted him. When she wasn't being serious, her voice was so like her grandmother's in its light tone, with its shire inflections; it had that same lilt and music as Phoebe's. She was just as stubborn too, wouldn't let anything drop. He was not surprised when she stifled her laughter, as if it had been a lapse of decorum, and reverted to her earlier shrewish, inquisitorial manner.

– What were you writing then?

– My dream, said Kernan, resolving to be direct. I write my dreams down. Not that I needed to write this one out, but I felt I had to, in case I remembered anything that was different. But this one is always the same. He picked up the book and read.

– *Peering into the darkness of the garden, Kernan saw that the man was still hanging there, the rope creaking as the wind swung him back and forth.*

– You write about yourself in the third person?

– It is me, and it isn't me. It's me in the other world of the dream, and I find I can tease out those extra tiny details by writing about the me in the dream as if I were someone else.

– *Curiouser and curiouser*, said Diana. And this other you: how often does he dream about this hanging man?

– Every year on my birthday, said Kernan.

– Today's your birthday?

– Tonight it is.

– Many happy returns. And it's Hallowe'en, how spooky.

– Samhain in the Celtic calendar, the first night of the new year. And I was born on the stroke of midnight. It's said that someone born then can see passing souls.

– You don't really believe all that stuff?

– Of course. But I have a double burden to bear. When I was delivered, the umbilical cord was wrapped round my neck...

– And that means something? asked Diana, incredulous.

– *Oooh ahh*, said Kernan, mimicking a thick Loamshire accent. *A choild boorn loik that'll be carnstantly bownd throoghowt its loif, not jus to is fammly but takkin on isself the woorries an aard taasks ov oothers. Hey-diddly-dingo. Hey-diddly-ding.*

– You're turning it into a joke, but you take it seriously...

– Many people in the village still hold to what they call the old ways. They tell me stories I used to hear from my mother, which she in turn heard from her mother. A lot of it is practical wisdom handed down through generations. I write it all down.

– But you've no family to be bound to, have you? I don't see pictures of them here. Not even your mother and father.

– Kernans never liked being photographed. And anyway, I don't need to look at pictures of my father. I see him every time I look in the mirror. People say I'm the dead spit of him.

– And in the dream, asked Diana, who's the hanging man? Someone you've known or put inside, who's swung for it?

– Someone I've put inside perhaps. When I cut him down the man is me, but when he's swinging in the storm it's Odin, the Norse God. It's a re-run of the sacrifice of Odin, the dream is like a memory that won't let me escape.

– I suppose you must get dreams like that if you're into myths. Those kind of stories used to haunt me as a child.

– The dreams came first. This one was my father's, he described it to me. When he didn't return from the war, I started having the same dream.

– You started having his dreams?

– Dreams are like myths, they exist already, and we tune into them. They are the land's songs which we overhear. *Fol-the-rol-the-diddle-diddle.* My father's dream was out there, somewhere, and I heard it. *Whack-fol-the-day.* Or it found me more like. *Fol-the-rol-the-diddle-diddle, whack-fol-the-day.*

Diana looked at Kernan, waving his arms as he explained his theories, between babbling refrains of gibberish. He keeps confounding me, she thought. Every minute I've been here, I've changed my view of him. First he was a pig. Then he turned into an eccentric scholar. Switching from Jekyll to Hyde, then from paranoid to paranormal. He knows Goodman's been after me, that he can't feel sure he's safe with me, yet he reveals far more than he needs to. There's a show-off aspect to his candour too, like a child home from school, but he's also cagey. Sometimes I think I've caught him off his guard, or does he just want to give that impression? He's completely barking, of course.

– ...Until the 20th century our relationship with the earth was preserved in stories which everyone knew, in proverbs, sayings and practical knowledge passed on, in patterns of nature...

– What kind of knowledge? How practical? Diana interposed, back with her questions. Kernan hadn't noticed she'd been away.

– You're dubious aren't you?

– I'm used to dealing with evidence, scientific proof.

– All right then, take this time of year. Samhain. Time to

bring the animals into the homestead for winter. And when winters were cold, really cold, centuries ago, how could you tell how long you're likely to be snowed in, cut off?

– I don't know. The long-range weather forecast?

– The pig told you. *With a too-ral-i-day, too-ral-i-day, too-ral-i-addy-i-day.* The pig or the cock.

– The pig? cried Diana. This was really too much.

– At Samhain you slaughtered the pig. You salted the meat, and hung it from the roof, away from the dogs, to keep you through the winter.

– And what did the pig say when you slit its throat?

– You looked at its spleen when you cut it open. The Russians call the pig's spleen its *winter*. Its shape tells the farmer the shape of the winter. *What's the winter look like?* they'd ask. The pig's spleen is usually just a couple of inches long, and it changes shape from year to year, before the winter. When the spleen's wide at the base, where it's attached to the liver, but then narrows sharply, that means the winter will start cold and hard, and then – because the spleen suddenly narrows – it will be milder later on. Wherever the spleen bulges, that's the heavy part of the winter.

– So?

– The pig sees the wind, it knows the weather ahead of time, just as birds fly off to shelter and asses bray before we're aware there's bad weather on the way. It is time to cock your hay and corn when the old donkey blows his horn. If the cock crows on going to bed, he's sure to rise with a watery head.

> But if the cock moult before the hen
> we shall have weather thick and thin:
> but if the hen moult before the cock,
> we shall have weather hard as a block.

So a tapering melt points to an early spring. Coming events cast their shadows before them. These things are out there, but we're cutting ourselves off from them, not just from our past, but from the earth, which is its record. My dog knows all this, don't you?

Unnoticed by Diana, a Newfoundland dog had entered the room, and now stood in front of Kernan, her tail wagging furiously, panting as if from a long run, and grinning undisguised worship of its master.

– This is Bella, Kernan said. Short for Bellatrix.

– The star?

– And because she does beautiful tricks, don't you, Bella? With her long *fol-the-riddle-i-do,* wagging all the day. Orion's shoulder star; the great hunter surrounded by his dogs and animals… *Bella, Bella,* he called to her in a low voice. And then barked at her, or gave a very good imitation of a dog's bark.

Bella trotted off, quickly returning with a bunch of keys between her teeth. She dropped them at Kernan's feet, and he patted her on the head, barking as he did so, less loud this time; more of a low affectionate growl. The dog returned his growl.

In Hangman's Wood five dark-coated figures sat around a blazing fire, watching two skewered rabbits start to blacken in the flames.

– Looks like they're nearly ready, said Herne, who had shot the two bucks with his ashwood bow. Herne had lived off the land for as long as anyone could remember, the farmers and gamekeepers turning a blind eye to his poaching, as long as he stuck to pests. In the village of Loamfield he was respected for his knowledge of the land; he could tell you the names of all the plants and animals in the shire, as well as where to find them. The women would present him with gifts of bread and cheese, or fruit or a bottle of milk, when they saw him resting by the roadside, just as their mothers had done, for giving food to Herne was said to bring good luck. The men were more grudging, regarding him suspiciously when they passed in the road, almost fearful of the old canvas knapsack he always carried. They would try not to look directly at the bag, as if it contained whatever Herne had left of himself in France when he'd returned shell-shocked from the war, or so the story went; as if they were somehow implicated in his sacrifice because their fathers and grandfathers – a few of them – had come back to lead "normal" lives, while Herne had been left twelve pence short of a shilling.

But if Herne was hare-brained, as the men said, the condition gave him a helpful affinity with his prey. That morning, setting out across the fields, he soon spotted his dinner, and despite his age, his gnarled fingers were as nimble as if they had been a young man's, holding the string taut and the arrow level. He took careful aim, and shot a grey buck with his first arrow. The second rabbit did not run away, but stood stockstill, as if waiting for Herne to claim it.

Lying at his feet, the felled rabbit had looked up at its killer, recognising the tall, bearded hunter with his birdnest hair and dark-green trenchcoat:

– Ah, Herne. I'm glad it's you. I can't think of a better person to take my body from me.

– I thank you for it, said Herne.

– But why take my brother's too. Would one of us not be enough to feed you?

– I'm hunting for my friends also, said Herne. I never take more than I need. Now go in peace. May you come back soon.

Herne waited until the rabbit's last breath had left it, then stooped and laid the bodies of the two creatures side by side in his knapsack, stroking their heads reverentially and humming softly as he did so, showing his respect for the two animals he had just killed.

Now he would share his food with the others. Normally he wandered the woods and lanes alone, but at Hallowe'en, and in November especially, he would seek out the company of other outcasts.

Breaking off the hind leg of one of the rabbits, he handed it to Muffy.

– Thank you rabbit, for giving us your meat, said Muffy, crossing herself in mock grace. Hedgerow mutton, that's what my mother called them, the rabbits we trapped with our wire loops. She used to bake a lovely rook and rabbit pie.

Muffy was Herne's favourite, a traveller's daughter well versed in the old lore who had lived in a caravan down by the river at Duckwidge Ditch until her husband Charlie died, poisoned by evil in the water, she said. The village women came to her for herbal remedies, to have their fortunes told or their rivals cursed.

While she was at Charlie's funeral, council workmen had towed their caravan away, claiming it was a health hazard. All their possessions had been heaped in a pile, like old rubbish, Muffy said, and she left them there, taking up wandering from that day. She cursed the council for dispossessing her, and the water board for the demons in the river; and the heads of both bodies were dead too within the month, a heart attack felling the water board chairman, and gangrene taking first a foot, then a leg, then the whole body of the district council leader.

Since then, Muffy had slept where she pleased: in summer, she favoured derelict cottages and haylofts, places with a bit of fresh air in them; in winter, the boarded-up houses on the Newlands council estate on the north side of Loamfield, where she kept warm by dismantling and burning most of the house around her, and no official would dare evict her. Sometimes she couldn't avoid sleeping in damp places, and was consequently troubled by lumbago, which she kept in check by wearing a length of hempen rope in place of a belt around her waist.

Feeling a twinge in her back, Muffy tugged at her rope-belt, and chanted over the bonfire:

A rope, a rope to burn the Pope,
A piece of cheese to toast him,
A barrel of beer to drink his health,
And a right good fire to roast him.

– *I've the rope and you've the beer*, she called across to Gubbins. *I've no cheese, but you've got fleas:* gesturing to O'Scrapie, to his annoyance. *No cheese in rarebit, just Jack Rabbit. A rope, a rope to burn the Pope*, do you hear me Mr Gubbins? If this here scrawny rabbit were a plump chicken, you could have the Pope's Nose to chew on, the Pope's Nose. Though being a Catholic you'd call it the Parson's Nose, I'm sure. But what I'd like to know is: what all these clerics have been doing, sticking their noses up chicken's arses…

– Give me the Parson's Nose, said Gubbins, who had bats in his belfry. Everything about him was batty, particularly his horse-piss smell, which bats alone found attractive. There was often a bat to be seen feasting on his yeasty sweat, or hooked upside-down to the hem of his coat by its prehensile paws.

– Ain't no Parson's or Pope's Nose on a rabbit, I told you that.

– Then give me the Archconey's Nose, he guffawed, taking a swig from a bottle of lager he did not offer round, to everyone's relief, for the foam of the beer was indistinguishable from the dribble he deposited around the neck as he sucked the drink noisily through the two worms of his lips.

– *This ain't the nose, but look how it glows*, said Muffy, handing him a stick on the end of which was a strange-looking piece of meat, an organ of some description, which Gubbins took, chewed quickly – for it was hot – then swallowed. And wished he hadn't, for it was a rabbit's brain.

He emptied the bottle down his neck, hoping to wipe out whatever it was he had just eaten which was still burning his throat. A lager-pickled agave worm from the bottle joined the fiery morsel in the upper part of his stomach, setting off an obscure chemical reaction which was to have grave consequences on his wife's bed linen.

The chemical reaction took an undocumented turn; hydrogen and sulphur exchanged molecules, nitrogen went for a short spin, methane was produced. Gubbins belched, giving Muffy a reproachful look, and a cloud of yellow gas burst forth like dragon's smoke from his surprised mouth. It floated for a moment above the fire before exploding like a balloon, leaving behind a smell like bad eggs which made the others want to retch.

– I really shouldn't be out tonight, he told them yet again. But I said to Mrs Gubbins I need some air, I said, and I'm not getting any air at home, I said, and I've had it up to here with that washbasin of yours.

He belched again, suffering this time an attack of bile which plastered the back of his throat with a greenish-yellow substance whose acid taste resembled bat vomit.

– You've eaten the hen's rump, Gubbins, said O'Scrapie, scowling to reiterate his disbelief in the washbasin story. He had been pretending to understand the workings of a walkie-talkie as he explained its use to the boy Flea, who was lookout.

– Can't you check that out in the instructions? Flea was asking.

– There ain't no instructions, stupid. It's stolen. I wasn't going to walk up to Jakes and say, please Constable Jakes, I've just nicked your walkie-talkie but there ain't no instructions with it. Would you be so kind as to find some for me, was I, Pigshit-for-Brains?

– You could have bribed him, like you do PC Clegg.

– Jakes isn't Clegg. Clegg would sell his mother for a pound of fish if he thought no one would notice the difference.

Across the fire, he saw Herne watching, and felt immediately uncomfortable, as if recognising he had him at a disadvantage; that he, O'Scrapie, was someone else's prey. Still, he liked to call himself Herne's opposite. It was a kind of joke between them.

While Herne was respected by all except his opposite number, O'Scrapie was disliked, and had consequently been able to assert himself as their leader, lord of their misrule, architect of crimes such as burglary, theft and poaching. He knew to defer to Herne's ground-knowledge if the old hunter was one of a poaching party, but suspected their many failures must be due to Herne somehow sabotaging his plans, which should otherwise be fool-proof with the master woodsman in the team. They had never managed to take a deer, despite Herne's skills in tracking game, and they only ever ended up with enough pheasants or rabbits for their own pot, leading him to believe that old HH must be in league with their quarry, tipping the buggers off. So he and Herne kept their distance, the one always watching the other, but with Herne always one step ahead of the younger man.

A tinny voice crackled above the bonfire's roar: *Come in Scrapie, come in O'Scrapie. This is Dogbreath. Are you readin' me, over?*

– I read you, Dogbreath, but you're not meant to use my name. I told you to use the codename, Snakecharm. Over.

– *My name's not Snakecharm. I don't want no codenames. I'll stick to Dogbreath, thank you very much. Cow's arse. Over.*

– No, I'm Snakecharm, you stupid fuckwit. Over.

– *Roger, O'Scrapie. So now you've just told anyone who's listening that Snakecharm is O'Scrapie's codename. Now who's stupid? And fuckwit to you. Over. Shitface. Horse's arse. Over again. Over.*

Kernan pulled up in a layby, picking out a small black shape with his lights. Another dead rabbit. He switched off the engine.

– Now we wait. We move in when Clegg gives the signal.

– But you think he won't show? Diana asked.

– That's right.

– Then why are we here?

– Goodman's theory. Whoever killed Tench thrust a spike into his skull before cutting his throat. We have the knife but not the spike, but in the paper we said no murder weapon had been found. Goodman thinks the killer will fly with the owl, go back to the farm to retrieve the knife he thinks is still there. The dog returns to his vomit.

– Why tonight?

– Because it's Hallowe'en. He knows the villagers will stay indoors tonight. Only the poachers will be out, taking advantage of this otherworldly cover for their activities. The moon will help: see, it's nearly full. Kernan dropped his voice to a conspiratorial whisper.

– This is the night when beasts and men go missing, whisked into the other world. Or poached, who knows? But tomorrow the farmers will wake to find a sheep has gone AWOL, or a cow. And the woodmen discover there are fewer deer. Where have they gone? Is it the Prince of Darkness calling in his debts? *To my fal-de-ral little law-day...*

– Come on, said Diana, you can't scare me with all that nonsense. And I'm sure Goodman doesn't set much store by it.

– Maybe not, but he knows the village does. And no one hearing anything strange tonight will go outside to investigate. It's the killer's best chance of coming back unseen.

– You don't think he will?

– No, it's a false trail. And I don't think Brock did it.

– What about the evidence you found?

– All circumstantial. Brock said he was tucked him in bed with the missus. Not much of an alibi, but probably the truth.

– You don't think you got enough on him then?

– Not to secure a conviction. That's why Goodman wants more, why he let him go. But I think Brock's innocent. And he'll know he's being watched. Of course he was pissed off when he lost his herd, but so were all the others. He didn't have a strong enough motive for killing Tench. He's not that kind of man, Brock. I've known the family for years, and they're all straight. Solid yeoman stock, the Brocks: you know, Brock the badger.

– Don't badgers spread diseases? said Diana.

– That tale has cost many a badger its life. Cattlemen blame them for the spread of bovine tuberculosis, and poison or trap them. Like Goodman's trying to do. But he's after the wrong man.

– Who did it then?

– I don't know, said Kernan. And looked worried.

– I thought you knew everything that went on round here?

– When it's someone from here, because they all have their ways of working, and I usually know what they've been up to. And if I don't, I have ways of finding out. But if it's someone from outside, that's different. Or if Goodman's involved. He has his own agenda.

– Which is?

– Connections. With the estates, with some of the farmers. With politicians and big business. He can't rock the boat. But sometimes he has to edge it into the current, without anyone noticing. Remember, he has his evil eye on the ACC job, then who knows, Chief Constable? He can't afford to have upsets.

– But what about an unsolved murder? Isn't that bad for him?

– A trial might be worse.

– Meaning?

– Tench had many enemies in the farming community. He rubbed people up the wrong way. An odd fish: he used to be a scientist with Eurochimique, but couldn't stand the rat race, took early retirement and bought the farm. None of the locals liked it that he got compensation for cows he should never have bought, and they ended up having their herds slaughtered.

– But they got compensated too.

– No farmer likes having his cattle slaughtered, especially when they may be healthy beasts. He puts a lot into raising them, there's a lot of investment too which the compensation doesn't cover. Tench didn't lay out anything. All he did was check out the cattle in the market, and buy any which showed early signs of BSE. He was very good at that, spotting them. Better than the vets, he seemed to have a sixth sense for it.

– And did everyone a favour. If he hadn't spotted them, they'd have gone for slaughter, gone into the food chain.

– The farmers didn't see it that way. They called him a troublemaker. Tench took their cattle back to his farm, got the vet to confirm the beasts were infected, then filled in the forms. He'd sold off his own stock after some row with the Ministry. But the original farmer got the whole works: herd condemned and slaughtered, livelihood wrecked, the long drawn-out arguments over compensation. There's a kind of shame in it too, and they feel a strong sense of injustice. And they don't believe there's any link between BSE and CJD, so the animals are all being slaughtered for nothing as far as they're concerned. There's strain as well: marriages break up over it, one farmer hung himself in the byre after his cattle had been taken away.

– What's happened to Hogsback now? Diana asked, looking out of the car window, trying to register the dark shapes of the buildings up Hogsback Hill.

– Tench's son inherited. But he doesn't farm it, he lets out the fields and just lives there, in the house. He's what they call a country musician, and he's away playing a concert. Not what I'd call country music, it's that American hillbilly stuff, though the rednecks who sing it are English.

They waited for an hour, but no signal came. Clegg was to flash a light to the right of the barn. Kernan leant forward, pressing a button to wind down the window. He listened.

– Nothing, he said, after a moment. Nothing will happen tonight.

– But it's Hallowe'en, Diana whispered, teasing him. She was beginning to relax now with Kernan; in the darkness, waiting. The car smelled like Kernan's cottage: his earthy, dampish lair. It felt strangely intimate, yet also dangerous.

– Don't mock, you of all people, said Kernan, and quickly regretted it. He hadn't intended this indiscretion, but sitting close to Diana all this time had sent him into a brief reverie. Her perfume was intoxicating; *White Musk* it was. She could only have dabbed a little on her neck before going out, but Kernan's sense of smell was so acute that the merest hint of any scent could be overpowering to him. He knew all the perfumes, would pick up the faintest suggestion of one at the scene of a crime. Before he'd become more circumspect, he used to enjoy showing off this knowledge. I think you'll find there are traces of Christian Dior's *Tendre Poison* on that, he would say of a seemingly clean handkerchief, before sending it off to the lab to have his suspicions confirmed. He'd won several bets on the strength of this skill. Now he was feeling like a drunken bee with his woozy head inside a flower; Diana's *White Musk* had that rich a bouquet, especially on her skin.

– Why not me? I'm the scientist, remember.

– But you're still a Hunter, he said, recovering, hoping it would be sufficient to remind her of her family's reputation. Not to have to say anything beyond that.

– Oh, that's just village talk, she said. I thought we left all that behind when we moved to Otteridge. My mother used to say stuff, of course, but she was full of stories. Perhaps that's why I went the other way, into science. Facts. Then police work.

– Police work can be based on suspicion, instinct.

– Which has to be followed up, justified with factual evidence.

Outside, they heard a dog barking in the distance.

– That's not anything is it? said Diana, in a low voice.

– No, said Kernan. Sounds travel on a night like this. I could name the dog but you wouldn't believe me.

– Try me.

– It's Bess, a mongrel bitch. Belongs to Jack Armstrong up at Long Wood Farm, about three miles east from here, too far to be connected with this caper. She barks in vain at the moon.

– You're right, I don't believe you. You're having me on.

– If that's what you want to believe. *Latrantem curatne alta Diana canem?* What does Diana care for the dog that barks at her?

Diana looked at Kernan in the silvery darkness of the car. The lights of the dashboard cast an eerie mixture of colours on his face, red and green where a faint smile nudged his cheek. His expression seemed to tell her he was not deceiving her, or not about the mongrel and the moon, yet nor was he being completely open. He was playing.

– That dream of yours, she said, deciding to run with his mood. How does it end, after you've cut yourself down from the tree?

– Why do you want to know?

– I'm interested.

– Nosey more like. All right then. And don't laugh at this, he said, expecting her to do so. I'm in a field running great circles around a cow, a white cow, tied to her with a rope. I run faster and faster, clocking the circuits using the old sheep-counting words, *yan, tan, tethera*, till I'm almost spinning. Then it turns into a falling dream, and I wake as I'm falling through the air. I'll probably manage more circuits next year. Next year's a seventh year, so I may get past ten. And before you ask: a seventh year is when the spirits from the other world have to turn out to pay their tithe to Hell. All the stories about faery folk dancing round mounds, riding on horses, can be traced to seven-year cycles. Like Tam Linn, the knight who escaped from the Queen of the Faeries. Right back to the Wild Hunt in 1127, and before that too, for centuries.

– You make it sound like historical fact.

– The Anglo-Saxons believed it was. They put it in their Chronicle: *'In this year terrible portents appeared over Northumbria, and miserably frightened the inhabitants: these were exceptional flashes of lightning, and fiery dragons were seen flying in the air.'* That's the weather report for the year 793. Stirring stuff, isn't it?

– There must be a proper explanation for those dragons, a comet perhaps.

– Possibly. But I prefer dragons. I've fought a lot of dragons in my time…

– How about a UFO?

– That's hardly scientific, is it? said Kernan, and then dropped his voice, hushing her. *Do you hear that?*

She listened, but could hear nothing, only a slight rustling in the trees; the dog barking again, and the shriek of some night-bird hunting its prey. There was a small, muted cry. Diana turned to him at that, and touched his arm.

– No, not that, he said. That was just something being taken by an owl; a rabbit by the sound of it. *No, wait.* He pressed a button and the window silently closed, the world outside excluded, muffled.

– You won't hear anything now, she said.

– I will if I tune in the radio…

– But we're meant to be on radio silence.

– That's what I thought. We'll just listen. Kernan turned the dial gingerly, like a safebreaker, intent. They heard a rushing, crackling sound, then burring Loamshire voices:

– Snakecharm, Snakecharm, do you read me, over?

– I read you, Dogbreath. Where is it, over?

– Heading west, through the clearing, towards Hogsback, over.

– Damn, said Kernan, switching off the radio. He pressed the window button again, and looked out into the trees.

– Who is it? asked Diana. Don't we need to hear more?

– Poachers. Probably tracking a deer in the woods. They'll bugger up the whole operation.

– I thought you said no one would show tonight.

– They won't. But we'll get blamed for scaring them off, for letting the poachers through.

– What if it's a diversion, these poachers? Something to do with the murder?

– Not this lot. And they won't get that deer, I'll make sure of that. That's if my friend Herne hasn't already got it sorted.

– Old Herne? Is he still around? He must be a hundred.

– He's one of my ears. My shadow. *No, listen...* He's too far behind. There are some heavy-footed clods up front.

Diana heard the sound of men or beasts crashing through the middle of the woods. She turned to Kernan, but found that he had gone, seemingly vanished into thin air. His car door was slightly open, yet she hadn't heard him go, so intent was she on listening to the sounds coming from the wood.

With her attention distracted, she did not see a light being flashed to the right of Hogsback barn.

She heard a high-pitched whistling sound, from inside the wood. Then commotion, the sound of trampling and shrieks. She looked around her, unsure of how to respond. A few minutes later, her stomach lurched when the car suddenly dipped. It was Kernan, back in his seat, appearing from nowhere it seemed.

– What was that whistling? she said, alarmed.

– Whistling wives, no doubt, said Kernan, grinning. That's what they call witches round here. Because they whistle up a storm. A crooning cow, a crowing hen and a whistling maid boded never good luck to a house. And by the sounds of it, they seem to be doing a good job of whistling through the wood. *Skiddly-idle-daddle-diddle-didle-dadle-dum. I will l'ave you down to rest in the magpie's nest.*

Diana heard a high squealing sound, different from the earlier high-pitched whistle. And men's voices, shouting. Further down the lane, they saw the figures of three men burst out of the bushes, waving their arms, quickly followed by a fourth, more frenetic, bulky figure, also gesticulating, and screaming invective.

– What's happening? Shouldn't we chase them?

– We don't have to. The bats are seeing to that, *tra-la*.

– Bats?

– Those poachers must have disturbed some bats, Kernan said, deliberately, and with some relish.

– But the bats are still after them. Maybe it's the walkie-talkie, the high frequency signal.

– A good scientific explanation, he agreed, smiling.

Just then a shot rang out from the direction of Hogsback Hill Farm, followed by frenzied barking.

Undoing the knot of his tie, Kernan glanced up, seeming to sense someone else's presence in the room. But there was nobody there. He was probably just tired: they hadn't left Hogsback till five o'clock. Outside his window, he heard intermittent chirrups as the birds began assembling for their dawn chorus; next door, Bill Jarman was dragging back the door of the cowshed, his buckets clanking. Others starting their day as his was ending.

An inside-out start to the year, he thought, wondering what this meant. A year beginning, as it always did, with the dream. He paused for an instant, thinking he heard some kind of creaking, and went to the window, almost expecting to see himself hanging from the tree, but it bore no strange fruit in the misty, slowly gathering light of the autumn dawn. In that instant of looking out, he caught a tiny movement out of the corner of his eye, and turned.

He saw a face in the mirror of his old oak dressing-table, which disappeared in the time it took him to blink and stare into the now empty space of the mirror glass. A green-hued face, with leaves for hair, he'd caught that much of it. And there had been more leaves coming out of its mouth and nose, fanning out across the face. Kernan rubbed his eyes, trying to recall if the mouth had been disgorging the leaves, or swallowing them; either way it had seemed caught in that act, frozen in time, as if to move would have meant choking on that foliage filling its throat.

And Augustine's words came into his head, his refutation of the present; that it did not exist because the present was instantly past. The leafy face had seemed to exist in precisely that dimension, its past, present and future all simultaneous. Which was possible on this night: when barriers break down between humans and the otherworld, between the living and the dead. So he took the appearance of the face, in the mirror, as a sign that he should follow it. And since this was the very start of the year, he knew thirteen moons would pass before he would see a resolution to this search.

Kernan knew the face was the Green Man he had last seen in his youth, the night before his departure from Loamfield, the first time the dream had come to him. The following morning, he had set off from the Green as the church struck eleven, his new boots striking sparks on the flints embedded in the dirt road.

A year to the day of his disappearance, at that precise hour.

The hart he loves the high wood,
The hare she loves the hill;
The knight he loves his bright sword,
The lady loves her will.

CHAPTER TWO

We Shall Not Sleep

MARTINMAS: NOVEMBER 11TH

The poppy is sometimes called Blind Buff, for its dazzling scarlet colour can cause temporary blindness. It is also called Head Waak, because its smell can cause headaches. However, poppy heads can be used as poultices to cure earache, toothache and other pains. Poppies, like water-lilies, are a potent remedy against the passion of love.

Diana looked behind her, waiting till Kernan's back was turned; then read the oblong card on the noticeboard to the right of his desk. There was a new one every morning, giving information about some animal or plant, an everyday object or a remedy; or, sometimes disturbingly, a superstition, ritual or other bizarre practice. He claimed to have a vast filing system of these cards, one chosen for each day of the year, and never repeated: each copied out in his spidery hand on an old feint-ruled police filecard.

– We used these record cards for everything at one time, Kernan had told her. Often for logging information about suspects, much of which was probably untrue or unreliable. Now we store our misinformation on the computer.

– So you keep up the tradition, Diana had responded. What irked her most about Kernan's cards – apart from their puerile smugness – was their pretence of authority and the power he exerted through them, for his topics would surface in conversations with people who denied ever reading his cards, or who pretended to ridicule them, often in the middle of a discussion about an important case. On Tuesday she had overheard a complete stranger holding forth on one of Kernan's subjects, giving out the same information as if it were an established fact, even using the same words, as she was telling him now. He wasn't at all embarrassed by this revelation, but grinned like a Cheshire cat.

– Wise men make proverbs and fools repeat them, he beamed.

– There's no fool like an old fool, she retorted.

– He that follows freits, said Kernan, freits will follow him. And he that follows Nature is never out of his way, he added, pointing to his left. The cards were always pinned in the same corner of the cork board.

– Bottom right, under the notice about restrictions on the movement of cattle, he explained. You see, I am a creature of habit, as regular in my ways as the calendar. When I started my cards, you'd find them under a warning about the Colorado Beetle. Then it was Foot and Mouth Disease. Then the Potato Blight and the Millennium Bug. They're all warnings, the posters and the cards.

– Fact or fiction? asked Diana.

– Does it matter? Kernan replied. What's wrong with a mixture of the two? They're all possible explanations. Of nature and our existence, of the matter in hand on any day. We all want to propitiate Fate and invite Fortune, but every week the Lottery says we are *not a winner*; yet still we persevere, just as our superstitions persist as living testaments to ways of thought much older than our own, of beliefs once strongly held but now abandoned or forgotten. Superstitions tell us how our ancestors thought and felt, the elders of our tribe, and who's to say they are not right? If God made the world, man fell, and his only begotten son redeemed our sins, that's all you need to know: our hopes and fears through all the years…

– … are met in Thee tonight, *tra-la*, Diana intoned. Oh yes, I remember singing that…

– But they aren't, Kernan continued. Where they meet is in a false sense of security. For we *aren't* delivered from evil, and we *continue* to wrestle with our hopes and fears. The old religions acknowledge the complexity of our state of flux. Heraclitus said everything flows: no one steps into the same stream twice. The only thing permanent is our anxiety, our restlessness. And it is the same with the police...

– The police?

– Yes, the police, we're just like all the other animals: we look and listen, search and hunt; a case is never closed, not even when we think we have our man – for years later we discover it was someone else – but when we hang up our boots and surrender the notebook, whistle and truncheon, we have finished living. There are never simple answers in any case, only clues. We should never rule out any possibilities, however unlikely they may appear. Nothing is fixed.

– Even when they're contradictions?

– Especially then. Without contraries is no progression, Blake said. Take our good friend Bovine Spongiform Encephalopathy. Did we create this monster by feeding infected sheep's brains to our herbivore cattle, or were organophosphates the instruments of torture and death? Some claim neither. It may be both: either way, we did this thing to ourselves and to our animals, and for money. Perhaps after all the squabbling there will be some hope, some progress. We may actually start *thinking* for a change. Or perhaps not. They're still using OPs. People are still dying from CJD and OPs. They're still denying those deadly initials could be intertwined. So which is it: hope or despair? We usually like to have things both ways, so it's probably a combination of the two.

– Your card's not a warning about BSE.

– That's above it. There are two warnings, two reminders...

– Yours is about poppies...

– *My subject is War, and the pity of War.*

– Bollocks, said Diana, adding, in a catty tone, You think you know everything. What do you know about war?

– More than you know about bollocks. *Sing: Titty-fol-ol, titty-fol-ol, titty-fol-ol-ri-tay.*

A trailer van was parked next to the war memorial on the Green. Inside, two white-coated women were draining blood from the bodies of the villagers, and replacing it with weak tea. Nurse Mary Leech was directing a jet of boiling water into her teapot from a metal urn which looked as if it had previously seen service as a dustbin or mortar launcher. Plates of oatmeal biscuits and custard creams were laid out on a low table beneath a poster of Lord Kitchener exhorting all to GIVE BLOOD.

It's the same finger, Kernan reflected, sipping the execrable tea. In the first war that finger shamed us into giving our lives for King and Country. In the sixties it subverted itself, a signpost to Alternative Reality. But here it was again, back with another message of guilt, this time YOUR COUNTRY NEEDS YOUR BLOOD. Kernan gave his every November when the angels of the Blood Transfusion Service descended on the village, always wanting more blood. That evening Nurse Leech would deliver the blood of his village of Loamfield in plastic bags to a medical store in Otteridge, not far from the police station where he worked, where it would be labelled with a date and refrigerated; much of it would be thrown away, for it couldn't be kept for long. There was a lot of waste. And tomorrow, and the day after, and for years to come, Nurse Leech with her assistant Nurse Snell would call on all the villages of Loamshire, a different one each day, seeking the blood of the willing, as her grandfather, Henry Leech, had done, as Adjutant in the Royal Loamshire Light Infantry, a strutting figure in off-white riding breeches, his cavalry boots highly polished, but not by him; his spurs still attached, unnecessary, like many things.

George Kernan remembered that other accusing poster, the children asking: What did you do in the Great War, Daddy? And thought of those who could not be asked that question, but whose *names* would not be forgotten, according to the statement heading the three cement rolls of honour on the ugly cross on the Green, including one George Kernan under BOER WAR (1899-1902), another under THE GREAT WAR (1914-1918), and a third under SECOND WORLD WAR (1939-1945).

A voice was saying:

– Couldn't I have a cuppa and a biscuit anyway, for taking the trouble to come?

– The tea and biscuits are for the donors, said Nurse Snell haughtily, attempting to prevent a wild-eyed lurching man from entering the van. You know that, Mr Gubbins. I've told you every year. I'm sorry we don't want your blood, but there's nothing I can do about it.

Kernan was staring at the packet of biscuits on the counter, pondering another slogan: ONE NIBBLE AND YOU'RE NOBBLED; as if it were a drug or poison. And *hobnob* meant hit or miss, from *hab nab*, a fit description for a beefburger which might or might not kill you, depending upon when the cow was killed, how the burger came into being, and when you ate it. *Hobnob is his name, give 't or take 't*, said Toby Belch, no doubt when he gave his blood and took the biscuit.

Kernan stood up, showing himself, adding his authority to Nurse Snell's, but saying nothing. The repelled boarder backed down the gangplank, almost tripping: Ernest Gubbins, the unemployed former chimney-sweep, whose father he knew had been judged unfit for service in the last war, by virtue of his state of health, which hadn't prevented him from scaling the walls and roofs of Loamshire for fifty years; by day in pursuit of his calling, the family trade of chimney-sweeping, by night in pursuit of the metals lead and copper.

Outside, a pungent ammoniacal smell lingered over the Green, so repugnant it was almost visible. Even though they couldn't see it, the villagers had learned to recognise a Gubbins cloud, and would leave the footpath to give it a wide berth. At least it was preferable to the other main source of pollution in that part of Loamshire, a snorting chemical factory inexplicably built on the north bank of the River Otter, where the water-meadows had been home in Kernan's youth to many kinds of now rare wildlife. He remembered sultry days by the water's edge when you could pick out the sounds of meadow and river: above the buzzing murmur of bees, the stuttered thin note and burbled squeaks of the reed bunting, the silvery *te-seep* of the grey wagtail, the pipit's rising *peep peep* and then its clicking, whirring twitter of *pe-pe-pe-pe-pe-pe* as it rode the summer thermals. There were otters then too, and the water-voles plopped in and out of the sparkling river; the dragonflies were so lumberingly large they looked like fairy godmothers dangling from the sky. All these had gone not just from Loamfield but from the whole county, while the short-haired bumblebee had joined the growing ranks of extinct species.

In its original sense, Kernan recalled, *pollution* meant the profaning of what is sacred. He stared across the Green at the once imposing tower of St George, dwarfed now by two huge cylindrical fingers giving a V-sign to the surrounding countryside. On days when the wind was from the north, the village was Chernobylled with as much effluent as government regulations permitted Eurochimique UK not to filter from its airborne discharges of waste. This pollution was of the picturesque kind tolerated in rural parts of England, with fluffy white clouds trailing up into the sky like steam from Puffing Billy; and at ground level, an unpleasant all-pervasive odour redolent of a school chemistry lab.

There was a greater incidence of leukaemia amongst children living on the north side of the village than anywhere else in the shire, but the council claimed this was mere coincidence, a denial in no way connected with the voting preferences in local elections of the residents of the Newlands estate. The only person to support them was Ernest Gubbins, who canvassed unsympathetic neighbours in favour of the free provision of a community smell whose aroma was as tingly as bat droppings. But Gubbins was held to be biassed. While the evidence against this one-man threat to the environment was more conclusive than that against his favourite factory, Kernan had been unable to arrest him for contravening the 1993 Clean Air Act because the regulations did not cover his particular kind of pollutant.

The pungent smell had now drifted down Lark Lane, which Kernan correctly surmised meant that Gubbins was heading for Hangman's Wood, where his disreputable friends would be disappointed by his arrival without the promised pocketfuls of Hobnobs and custard creams. But for his gifts of stolen food – and his canary yellow van, useful when transportation for booty was needed, as at Hallowe'en, when it was meant to have carried a deer from Loamfield to the back entrance of the Excelsior Hotel in Otteridge – the cross-eyed Gubbins was not otherwise welcomed with enthusiasm by the band, but was disparaged by the bristling O'Scrapie, especially when he got onto the subject of Mrs Gubbins and her washbasin, although Muffy felt sorry for him, that his livelihood as a sweep had been much diminished by the central heating which most people, unaccountably, seemed to think preferable to a good open fire.

O'Scrapie believed the main reason why the villagers were all going over now to Agas and wood-burning stoves was not economy, or a miraculously conceived regard for an environment they had previously been happy to abuse – and still abused in most other respects – but rather a wish to bar the odious Gubbins from visiting their houses with his long brushes, longer conversations, tedious talk and urinous body odour.

There was also a contradiction in how the sweep was regarded. The women believed it was good luck to meet a chimney-sweep, but only if his face and clothes were begrimed with soot. Now that Gubbins's trade was in decline, he was less likely to be seen looking black as a minstrel; a clean-faced sweep brought no luck at all, and with no soot to hide his features Gubbins now displayed the double-insult of a red-veined drink-wrecked face which most closely resembled the bared backside of a baboon on heat.

In this situation, the men's contrary belief came to dominate: that it was bad luck to encounter a sweep, and that to avert evil you had to spit on the ground as soon as you saw one. The same applied if you came upon a piebald horse, a magpie or a cross-eyed person – though the women said a piebald was *lucky*, unlike a skewbald… However, since Gubbins was both a chimney-sweep *and* cross-eyed, he was doubly offensive to the men. You could always tell which roads and paths Gubbins had taken when walking home through Loamfield because his route would be marked out like a snail's path with a trail of spittle, a mixture of the liquorice-like sputum he himself was prone to hawk forth and the more translucent phlegm his neighbours expectorated in the cause of combating the forces of evil.

It was their last day in the line, a Friday, two days after the full moon on the ninth. The raiding-party had returned exhausted from a messy night-time foray into No Man's Land, empty-handed: no prisoners, nothing to show for their mission. They shouldn't have gone. It had been too light out there, and the Boche had picked off two of them within seconds of them reaching the wire.

Sitting in the dugout, soaked to the skin, they were just starting to clean the thick black mud from their weapons when someone's rifle went off. Sergeant George Kernan turned to see Jack Brock rolling in the slimy trench-bottom, his hands gripping his ankle, face contorted with pain.

While Tomkins held his friend's shoulder, trying to comfort him, Corporal Marshall turned to Kernan, gripping his arm.

– It was an accident, Sarge, I know, I saw it. Jack's gun was that caked with mud, he couldn't see what he was doing.

But it was too late. Captain Nicholas had arrived. The men looked up at him, stunned, not daring to contradict the officer. His red-flushed face.

– Consider yourself under arrest, Private Brock, he said, pointing his service revolver at the wounded soldier. They'll court martial you for this, self-inflicted wound. You're bound to be shot.

Kernan protested, but in vain. He had been looking the other way and had not seen the accident himself, but trusted Jack Brock. He knew him from the village. Brock would not have shot himself, even under pressure. They all knew they were being relieved that evening.

Marshall and Tomkins helped Brock to limp to the Casualty Clearing Station, his arms across both their shoulders, his good leg sticking in the mud as he tried to keep the other raised, all three keeping their heads down at the same time for fear they might be momentarily exposed to a sniper-fire. The last he had seen of Brock was when he had handed him over to an orderly, who inspected his wound and confirmed he would be taken to the Base Hospital. While the man took down Brock's particulars, Kernan assured the young soldier he would speak up for him. The orderly signed the papers, tying a green docket to Brock's muddy uniform on which the letters D.I. were marked in large black capitals.

Kernan tried to stop him, repeating it was an accident, that Brock wasn't a D.I., but the man brushed aside his protest.

– I can't change that, sergeant, he said. Captain said he's a D.I., so a D.I. he has to stay. He's not so bad he needs to go to the D.I. hospital at Havre. So he'll get the chance to clear himself at his Field General.

At ten o'clock, the Loamshires were marched off back across the duckboards, the coarse nasal-voiced Brummies of the Warwickshires taking over from them, still boisterous despite losing five men when a shell landed in the middle of their ranks as they made their way up to the line. Corporal Marshall and Private Tomkins were handed over to their captain, to be left with them until Brock's FGCM, at which they and Captain Nicholas would be the witnesses.

The deer eaten at Nicholas Goodman's table that evening was pronounced most excellent by all but one of the guests.

Mrs Belinda Goodman had assisted her cook in roasting a large piece of the poor animal's leg in her oven, basting the limb with a hot greasy liquid drawn from the bottom of the roasting tin by means of a large pipette, the main ingredients of this gravy being the dead beast's blood and adipose tissue.

Chief Constable Maurice Saveloy, OBE, particularly liked the gameyness of the animal's flesh. He regarded himself as something of a gourmet, attributing his discernment in matters of the palate to his gastronomic ancestry, which he could trace back to the 13th century, when the *Cervelat* family introduced their highly seasoned *saucisson* to the court of King John, based on the Venetian *cervellata*. Each in this distinguished line of sausages was etymologically pure in name, acknowledging its main ingredient as sweetbreads, or animal brains (from the Latin, *cerebellum*).

While the Chief Constable showed great loyalty towards the family banger, which appeared on his recently commissioned coat-of-arms, painted in gules and facing a similarly shaped police truncheon, others said he was come of a blood and so was a pudding, alleging that the salty dog was an apt emblem for such a slippery fellow; and in support of that view they cited – and avoided – his breath, which was said to advertise his excessive consumption of the eponymous sausage.

Ever the thoughtful hostess, Mrs Goodman had seated opposite the Chief Constable the only person able to withstand the effects of his conversation, namely Oliver de Foie, the managing director of Eurochimique UK, in whom only three of the five senses had survived the ravages of his workplace. Now a multinational company, Eurochimique had grown from a small sauerkraut business his great-grandfather had started in Alsace at the end of the Franco-Prussian War, when the Gans family had been amongst the first German incomers to appropriate land from the French. Herr Gans had laid a golden egg, and grew *fett* on his company's success, generating so many jobs for the townspeople in his rapidly expanding plant that the quickly renamed De Foie-Gras family was discreetly assimilated into French society when Alsace reverted to France in 1918. With its prosperity and expertise founded on producing mustard gas and other nerve agents for the German Army during the Great War, the De Foie-Gras company's later move into pesticides was not unexpected, coming as it did when the family firm was renamed Eurochimique and floated on the Bourse.

Bravely chewing his way through what he judged to be 250g approx of rather tough animal flesh, Oliver de Foie was fulsome in his praise of its quality but had derived little pleasure from the excessive mastication required, due to the fact that his tastebuds had long ago ceased to distinguish any flavours, apart from that of the ammonium nitrate he manufactured in his factory, which permeated everything he tasted, including his wife's vagina, into which his tongue was no longer inclined to burrow with much enthusiasm, leading to certain disappointments in their marriage.

His wife Patricia now preferred the Chief Constable's chipolata to Oliver's fat knackwurst, and she thought the deer's flesh awfully good too. Her enjoyment of the wine (Saint-Emilion '61, Château-la-Pelleterie '70 and Château-Canon '62) was heightened by the knowledge that her husband had been forced to foreswear wine long before he ceased being able to taste it, owing to cirrhosis of the liver, which was hereditary in the De Foie family.

Ever resourceful, she had devised a simple expedient to avoid inhaling her lover's sausage-breath during intercourse, namely that of dressing him in a rubber-suit which offered her the facility of half-asphyxiating the Chief Constable by zipping his mouth closed as she rode him like a gymnasium vaulting-horse.

But Mrs de Foie was also a foolhardy and reckless woman. She wore garish fuck-me shoes without irony or embarrassment, and often fell prey to sudden passions she later regretted in the cold light of her bathroom. At this particular supper, she was the only guest infected with Hepatitis B – contracted on a one-night stand with a bisexual vet – but was to pass the virus first to the Chief Constable, and then to the MP for North Loamshire, and via him to two others in the dinner party, before her condition would be treated at the Royal Loamshire Infirmary.

Lady Olivia Prurigeaux devoured the flesh of the deer with undisguised relish. Sipping her Château-Canon '62, she tried not to crush the wine-glass in her jewelled hand, which was so heavily beringed it clinked around her goblet like a milk float. Widow of the late Sir Peter Prurigeaux, leader of the district council until his recent stroke (brought on by a combination of overwork, witchcraft and a surfeit of *pâté de foie gras*), Lady Olivia's liking and capacity for drink was matched by a similarly insatiable appetite for red meat and raw sex.

Mrs Bunty Saveloy had suspected her husband of putting his toad in the hole of her best friend Olivia since finding a pair of pink silk knickers monogrammed with the initials OP stuffed down the back seat of the Chief Constable's Subaru, where they had inadvertently been left when Maurice Saveloy had lent his car to Morton Maw for an assignation with Sir Peter's wife. As she gave the appearance of listening to Patty de Foie holding forth on the subject of social security benefits given to New Age Travellers – who should rather be dealt with by gassing them like badgers in their dens of vice – she chewed on thoughts of her husband's supposed infidelity between mouthfuls of the scrumptious venison.

Councillor Morton Maw, MBE, chairman of the planning committee of Loamshire County Council, greatly enjoyed Nick Goodman's deer, but if pressed might have expressed a preference for the more exquisite pale flesh of Dutch veal. Those

Dutch Johnnies knew how to raise good veal calves; they used crates to stop the little blighters from running around, not like our farmers, who were hidebound with silly regulations.

Councillor Maw was also fond of young fillies, but did not advertise this widely. When he went on trips to the Far East with colleagues, his wife did not accompany him, although her encouragement of these opportunities for healthy male bonding was more to assist her own bonding with Sir Peter Prurigeaux, who would thrash her with a leather tawse, as well as with Patty de Foie, who favoured a horsewhip and double-headed dildo when riding the corpulent Isabella. If you make your wife an ass, she will make you an ox, she told Patty, and both our husbands wear the bull's feather, for all mine thinks himself the town bull.

As carnivorous in his eating as he was in his business dealings, the Rt Hon. Henry Sirloin, MP, much enjoyed his slices of flesh taken from the leg of Nick Goodman's deer. This former junior minister in the Ministry of Agriculture, Fisheries and Food had once commissioned a comprehensive and far-reaching study of pesticides, suppressing it at the same time as another more dangerous report on organophosphate sheep dip on receiving a donation to party funds from a sportswear company with which his good friend Oliver de Foie must in some way be connected or have influence, for the cheque had been sent with his compliments. As a MAFF minister, the Member for North Loamshire had been required to encourage the public to eat the flesh of diseased farm animals even when this was discouraged in reports compiled by the Department of Health but not shown to him at the time, owing to their suppression following a directive issued by a senior civil servant in the Treasury.

The MP's model wife Candida sat beside him, exchanging pleasantries with everyone, and making frequent remarks about how much she too relished the deer's meat; she thought it jolly nice in fact, especially the dark, crispy outer coating which the cooking process had seared to perfection. A much-loved figure throughout the shire, a popular speaker at meetings of women's institutes, townswomen's guilds and Conservative ladies' organisations, Candida Sirloin rode with the Loamshire Hunt – and on some occasions with Patty de Foie after sherry parties at the

Conservative Club, when her husband was at a late-night sitting in the House.

Two incomers completed the Goodman circle that evening, Bruce Tucker, an Australian businessman with few scruples, and his 'significant other', Lizzie Gizzard, a freelance journalist from London who spoke with a media accent. Tucker had recently appropriated a country house from a Loamshire squire who had been bankrupted following a property deal involving a holding company of Gerstmann Holdings Pty Ltd. When Sir Percy Featherwether had accused the Australian of giving him a flap with a foxtail, his response had been philosophical. *Shit happens, mate*, he told the toff. *Shit happens*, he repeated, in case he had been misunderstood. The plain-speaking Bruce much enjoyed the flesh of this English deer, comparing it favourably with the tougher but similarly rich meat of the wild buffalo of the Northern Territory, where he had a mining concession and other interests.

Lizzie's accent was marginally less grating than her consort's. She spoke a media variety of Estuary English, a particular dialect spoken only by inhabitants of the N1 and NW3 postal districts of London, in which vowels are twanged into strange-sounding dipthongs, consonants pecked by a Cockney sparrow, and phrases given stresses in unexpected places in the manner of a television reporter, the voice stretching its white-gloved hands to reach both upper and lower class ends of the musical scale at the same time. She was currently working for several women's magazines as well as *doing some radio*, or so she had said, a little nervously.

Lizzie Gizzard was self-conscious about how she chewed her food, for she was a vegetarian, and as such had been given a nut-roast for her fellow diners to ridicule. They taunted her choice, taking pleasure in praising the venison to her. She did not know what she was missing, they said. *Where the deer is slain, some of her blood will lie*, she wanted to say.

From time to time she touched a small cameo-brooch pinned to the black velvet choker encircling her neck, for the reassurance that it made her feel more English, and like her Barbour with its poacher's pockets helped her pass for "county" in the shire. Sitting beside her, the Honourable Member for North Loamshire found this masquerade extremely arousing, like the pictures he snorted over in pornographic magazines of supposed

English roses undressing from similarly misjudged tweeds and riding boots to display flesh as pink as a piglet's across satin-sheeted, silk-tasselled four-poster beds. It was all so vulgar, and yet so deliciously evocative of the horsey girlfriends of his sister who used to tease him in the school holidays.

Chief Superintendent Nicholas Goodman generally liked his meat less cooked than this venison; his favourite dish was steak tartare. He had shared the deer with Hamish Spermwail, manager of the Excelsior Hotel, to whom he owed certain favours in respect of his use of Mr Spermwail's best suites for masonic and other clandestine meetings as well as for fornication.

Scorning superstition, Goodman had invited eleven guests to dinner, knowing that thirteen would sit around their table. The deer was there in spirit too, but Goodman did not include him in his reckoning, even though the deer's presence made the numbers up to fourteen. As far as the Superintendent was concerned, the deer was only there to be eaten. Apart from Lizzie Gizzard, the others shared that view, and since they could only see the deer as meat, it never occurred to them that the animal had a soul; and in that state of blindness, they did not see the deer's restless spirit as it moved around them in the room, nor could they intuit its existence there by any other sense.

The deer's soul had remained for several days in the kitchens of the Excelsior Hotel, watching much of his corpse being dismembered and consumed upstairs by people he judged unsuitable to eat his once supple and muscular bodyshell, but now that Spermwail's guests had eaten most of his flesh – except for the scraps thrown in the bins for the pigs of Sweeny Farm – and were busy defecating the remnants of his once healthy body via the lavatories of Loamshire into the sewage system and so to the River Otter, the grieving deer followed his antlers to their resting place in the billiard room of the Otteridge Conservative Club, where they were to be affixed to the wall alongside a signed portrait of one Baroness Thatcher of Kesteven, whom he took to be some revered lady of high birth.

The deer later sought out the rest of his body in a garage belonging to Nicholas Goodman, where his hindquarters lay in a locked deep-freeze. His amputated leg had been wrapped in polythene, and laid in a manger of iced metal: it was hard to believe that the leg had once been his, for its sawn-through femur, surrounded by torn, darkened flesh, looked as though it must belong to some other creature. Yet the hair, varying from dun to chestnut in colour, and lighter around the fetlock, was unmistakably his own hair; and the solitary hoof had that small split down one side from when he had slipped on some rocks. It was his leg. It had been his leg. Some person had taken it from him, with his life, and now this one leg was all that remained of his body.

After making several forays around the house of the devilish policeman, he felt impelled to keep vigil in the garage beside the white sarcophagus, which also contained the dead bodies – or parts of their corpses – of several other animals, including a pinkish leg once belonging to a Berkshire White pig, the scapula and shoulder-flesh cut with an electric saw from the body of a young, once perky Suffolk-cross lamb, and some large slices of flesh cut from a dead Devonshire cow. There were also some odd-looking reddish smooth-skinned sausages, and some strange round cakes seemingly comprised of a horrific mixture of flesh from the body of a cow combined with minced parts of its organs, possibly including some of the spongey matter of its brain, no doubt kept as bait for rats or for poisoning unwelcome visitors. Beneath these were two rabbits, not yet skinned, one of whom he recognised. There was no goose.

These creatures had been so reduced by the processes of slaughter and butchery that he could not tell which farms they came from, or even what shires, since the butchers of the supermarket had contrived with their cellophane and packaging to obscure all clues as to the identities of the victims, to the extent that he felt sure that the humans who had placed these remains in their deep freeze must somehow be capable of not accepting the evidence of their eyes that the meat of these animals had once formed the bodies of sheep, cows, pigs, rabbits and other creatures with lives as sacred as their own. The deer was not surprised by these discoveries, which were only too familiar to the whole of the animal community, but having lived in the woods surrounding Loamfield for many years without having much contact with humans, apart from Herne, he could not help but be shocked by the sight of all these once precious bodies crammed so ignominiously into the one frozen grave, revealing as it did the full extent and routine nature of the bestial acts committed by the sarcophagous humans in pursuit of their lust for the flesh of their fellow creatures.

He remembered Herne telling him how Martinmas had been a day of ritual slaughter, and a bull, the Mart, would be killed in memory of the saint who had met his death in the form of a cow; and other animals had their bodies taken, and their flesh salted to provide for the winter ahead. For as every dog had its day, so every hog had its Martinmas, though this was less a cause for celebration for the seared beast, Herne said. And geese would be sacrificed, their migration day being Martin's too, and also the old feast of Bacchus, when men got themselves Martin drunk, reaching that strange state on the other side of drunkenness where they would see apparitions, such as the wandering souls of animals, and on waking from stupor think these the creatures of their inebriate dreams. The fine days of St Martin's Summer would follow, the earth's weather holding a saintly calm in remembrance of the monk who had once given half his cloak to clothe a beggar. But people had forgotten these November Halcyon Days, Herne said. Martinmas had become Armistice Day, marked by the poppy, which wasn't even in flower then. And with death mechanised, their bodies' resting-places were these white sarcophagi, icy as the bottom of Hell, that place of absolute zero where no mercy could reach; here there was only the coldness of absence, more chilling to the soul than the heat of torment.

In the village of Dealchurch, in Goodman's dining-room, the deer now watched the last scraps of his flesh disappear along with uneaten Brussels sprouts and burnt husks of roast potato on the stacked plates of the diners, which Mrs Belinda Goodman was removing to their final resting-place in the kitchen. He noted that all thirteen people were talking nine words at once, many not listening to each other but holding forth aggressively without waiting for the others' responses, as if communication were not the purpose of their discourse. This would never happen amongst deer, who were much more attentive to each other, or even in a flock of sheep. At least sheep emptied their mouths before bleating what they wanted to say.

Able to relax more with the arrival of a lemon mousse dessert, albeit one made with gelatine rendered from a dead cow, the deer found he could pay more attention to the dinner conversation, absorbing much of interest, particularly when the men moved to the next room to smoke and drink port, four of them gathering by the window to discuss the circumstances surrounding his own death on the night of the 31st of October, when he had been shot through the heart by a police marksman.

– So where was old Kernan while all the commotion was going on? Councillor Maw was asking.

– Still parked down by the woods, Goodman cried gleefully. So as you can imagine, I gave him and *Her* a right bollocking afterwards. And that didn't please *Her* one bit, she turned on him for chasing the poachers.

– Blotting her copybook, Saveloy added.

– And the best of it is Kernan's now blaming himself for Brock's death. He's gone into a real sulk, and they're hardly talking, him and *Her*, but snapping at each other all the time like yappy dogs. It's wonderful to watch. His cow has calved, his sow has pigged, and Kernan can't get over the fact that *he* found the evidence that implicated Brock. And then his shenanigans resulted in the deer flying out onto Hogsback Hill.

– And Clegg shot the deer, said Saveloy. In all the chaos he thought it was our suspect making his escape.

– While Brock panics, said Goodman. He hears the shot, runs into the dark barn…

– …impaling himself on the bale-spike of a tractor, whispered the Chief Constable, before roaring with uncontrollable laughter.

– But what I don't understand – interrupted Oliver de Foie – is why Brock went up there if he wasn't the murderer?

– That's the beauty of it, Goodman explained. We don't have to be bothered with that now. Brock was there, so he must have been looking for the gun. Which means he must have killed Tench. He can't say otherwise now, because he's mute as a fish, as silent as our once gabby Tench.

– And are those bale things really sharp enough? Or is it a question of how fast he's going when he runs into it? What did the Coroner say?

– He was persuaded. Death by misadventure. He said it was like a soldier running into a fixed bayonet on a battlefield.

– What's important now is that the Tench case is closed, said the Chief Constable. We know Kernan's evidence against Brock was thin...and why...but Brock's not around to challenge it. And as far as the press is concerned, Brock must have done it because – and here he put on a serious expression – *the police are not looking for anyone else in connection with the murder of Loamfield farmer Bernard Tench.*

– And we've had the delicious deer to eat, said Morton Maw, licking his lips.

The delicious deer in question was eaten up with doubt as well as being puzzled. He had not bolted out onto the field because of Kernan. Herne had led the poachers on a merry dance away from him, and then Kernan had helped, setting the bats after them. It was those other men who had frightened him. He would go and see Herne, and ask him about these things.

Looking round at the animated wine- and meat-flushed faces of the humans sitting slumped in their floral armchairs, the deer observed that most had entered an advanced state of inebriation. Maw was claiming to be drunk as a rat, to the extent that he was referring to his work for Loanshark County Council, while Tucker was speaking of his own condition as that of being pissed as a newt, raising his voice at the end of a non-interrogative sentence in that annoying manner peculiar to Australians. The deer judged this an insult to the humble amphibian.

– You're certainly ape drunk, Lizzie Gizzard told her partner, trying to make it sound like a joke; for when a man begins to drink, she added in a low whisper, he becomes successively like the lion, the ape and the sow.

Tucker grunted in agreement as Mrs Goodman came through with the coats, which she handed to their owners, or usurpers, for some were the skins of animals.

– Good to see you've got your poppy, she said.

– Aussies perished too... But those aren't wild poppies in that vase, are they, Belinda? asked the speculator, whose grandfather and several great-uncles had in fact died at Gallipoli in 1915, mown down by Turkish machine-guns on the beach at Anzac Bay.

– Yes, I collected them from the woods. Aren't they lovely?

– Back home my dad used to say it was bad luck to bring wild poppies into a house... do they say that here? he asked, the rising intonation this time acceptable in a question, albeit one punctuated with a loud belch.

– Bah, useless superstition, said Goodman.

But Lady Olivia Prurigeaux had caught the tail end of the conversation, and interrupted.

– What's that, wild poppies in the house? That can't be true, can it, Belinda, you've not brought poppies in, I hope? That's very bad luck, you know, very bad luck.

– Nonsense, said Goodman, nonsense. But gestured to his wife with a slight nod that she should probably get rid of the scarlet harbingers, all the same. As the limp figure of the Franco-German industrialist's wife was deposited unceremoniously onto the back seat of a taxi, with De Foie urging her, discreetly, not to regurgitate inside the vehicle (a caution she did not hear and which proved prophetic of her later actions), Belinda Goodman took the offending vase outside, throwing the flowers from the edge of her house-lit lawn, one by one, into the darkness beyond.

When she had gone, the deer emerged from the cover of a rhododendron bush to sniff the objects she had thrown out into the night. They smelled and looked like poppies, but poppies didn't flower after September. There was something not quite right about these poppies. They didn't belong there.

– The devil always leaves a stink behind him, said Herne, staring intently up at the house, watching the lights being switched off, the downstairs ones first, as Nicholas Goodman's house was swallowed up by the black shroud of night.

Who killed Cock Robin?
I, said the sparrow,
With my bow and arrow,
I killed Cock Robin.

Who'll make his shroud?
I, said the Beetle,
With my thread and needle,
I'll make his shroud.

CHAPTER THREE

Of My Discontent

WINTER SOLSTICE: DECEMBER 21ST

Never give scissors as a gift to a friend, without receiving a small coin from them in "payment". Otherwise your friendship will be cut.

Kernan sat slumped behind his desk, passing a piece a string through his fingers. Each time he reached a knot, he halted, squeezing it hard; or leant forward, bringing his fist down hard onto a pile of traffic reports, thumping it several times to emphasise his displeasure, the knotted string flailing the papers like a cat. The motion caused a flutter along the line of Christmas cards hanging along a length of cord stretched between the lintel of the door and the top of the window. One card fell from the line, like a bird shot from its perch on a telegraph wire. It was a depiction of a snowy scene with a robin in the foreground. Kernan wondered if this could be an omen, for harming a robin was extremely unlucky. Anyone who robs a robin's nest will not thrive, but will fall into the power of witches or the Devil. He picked up the card, muttering, as he put the robin back on its perch.

– Who's the sparrow, Robin? Point him out... I want that spuggy caught.

Outside, another blizzard. Snow was general all over England. In Loamshire, chaos on the roads. Timid drivers crawling along like beetles aggravating those with too much confidence, too much drink or even greater degrees of stupidity. And he'd be called out, by Mr Plod, to sort out the awkward customers. But sometimes even that was a relief, getting out of this place, out into the fresh air, even if it was cold as monkeys.

He only had himself to blame, Muggins Kernan, agreeing to stand in for Daube, landing himself with Traffic over Christmas. Why had he done it? Gone all meek, a lamb to the slaughter? No, it wasn't meekness, it was self-pity. That and wanting Diana to feel sorry for him, trying to win her round. But that had failed too; rightly failed, he realised: he should have been stronger. Yet all his defences were down. He felt vulnerable, for the first time in more years than he could remember. His powers seemed to be deserting him, and he didn't know where to turn.

Diana wasn't going to help him. She was still angry over the Brock business, whether it was for her own sake or for the injustice, he didn't know.

– But you aren't going to let him get away with it? she had demanded.

– It would appear he has done. And there's nothing we can do about it. *Fal-de-ral, tal-de-ral, fal-ral-lal-day.*

– Nothing you can do about it you mean.

– Or you. Or Brock's widow. Or Tench for that matter.

– And that's how you're going to leave it?

– Goodman's got his murderer. The Chief Constable is satisfied with Goodman's report, based on the evidence I compiled. Now they've closed the case. *Fal-de-ral...*

Diana had stormed out, slamming the door behind her.

That was a month ago, November 20th, St Edmund's Day. Ruefully, Kernan remembered the English king who'd refused to be a puppet for the Vikings. How they'd tied him to a tree at Hellesden and shot him full of arrows, like Sebastian. *So many arrows*, someone had said, *that he looked like a thistle, or a hedgehog.* At least King Edmund didn't have to deal with traffic reports. Unlike St Kernan the Martyr...

Lost in this reverie, he did not notice Diana enter the room, but smelled her immediately, the white musk...

– Since I won't see you till after Christmas, she said, I thought I'd give you your present now. She handed him a small package decorated with holly and robins. Holly for enduring life, protection against the Evil Eye. And of course it was prickly holly; they never put she-holly on cards or wrapping paper, only male holly. As the riddle had it:

> Highty, tighty, paradighty, clothed all in green,
> The king could not read it, no more could the queen;
> They sent for a wise man out of the East,
> Who said it had horns, but was not a beast.

Smiling, he basked in the loveliness of surprise. He hadn't expected her to give him a present. Little fish are sweet, he murmured.

But then he noticed the thin set of her lips, and the shape of the tightly-wrapped package, for she had taken great care and much Sellotape *not* to disguise its shape, but rather to emphasise it in an exaggerated fashion. A pair of scissors.

– For your nails, she said, abruptly.

He reached into his pocket, and dropped a coin into her hand.

– A luck penny for your thoughts. *Fol-the-rol-the-diddle-diddle.*

– I'm not a whore. What are you, man or mouse? She flung the coin on the floor.

Kernan blushed. But looking up into her garnet eyes, felt some of his strength returning. From the office next door, he could hear the muffled voices of a carol concert on the radio; children singing *While shepherds watched their flocks by night.* He indicated the voices beyond the wall with his eyes, trying to draw hers, to thaw their green ice.

– I've been thinking, he began.

– I don't think I'm interested.

– It is Christmas, you know...

– I was aware of that.

He pretended to ignore her frostiness. And plunged in.

– So I wondered if you'd like to call a truce? We could have a drink, before you go off for Christmas. I wouldn't want you to spend the whole time feeling sore and angry. We could talk...

– What about? she glared. Your manners? *Fol-the-diddle-di-do-day-gibberish...*

– Well, for one thing, you know if I wanted, I could ask Goodman to attach you to someone else. He'd see it as me admitting defeat, that I couldn't handle you. And that wouldn't look good for you. I don't want to do that. But you aren't helping things.

Kernan paused, watching her reaction; her face seemed less tense, as though she were softening. He continued, putting his neck out now, taking a risk.

– I want to work with you very much. You may find this hard to believe, but I have enormous respect for you. I also like you very much as a person, and it would please me more than anything for us to be friends. And if you're willing to come some way to meet me, I'll take you into my confidence. I will be – how shall I put it? – indiscreet…more open with you about my working methods, because we can only beat Goodman by working together. Unless we do that, we won't find out who killed Tench. How Brock was killed…

– I thought you'd given up the Brock case?

– Did I say that? I might have needed to give that impression, but it's not just Brock. There's bigger stuff, and Goodman's in it up to his neck…

– If it's that serious, how do you know he's not bugging your office as well as having you watched?

– I just know it. I can tell these things. This office hasn't always been clean, and it has suited me then to act accordingly, until I accidentally damage the bug. But most of my researches don't involve phone work or even interviews. I work in the field, you might say. At the moment this room's clean as a whistle. However – you may as well know this – yours isn't…

– You what? What do you mean?

– I think you'll find there's a listening device inside your phone socket. *Hey diddle dingo. Hey diddle…*

– Why didn't you tell me before? she demanded, showing both shock and incredulity. And then, turning on him:

– And why mine and not yours?

– You weren't getting anywhere on the case, so leaving your phone tapped…

– I think I should feel insulted by that comment…

– Don't, please don't. Don't go back to that.

– But anyway, she said, challenging him. How can you tell?

– All right, here's the first indiscretion. And you'll have to believe me, or we'll never establish any trust between us…

– Come on, I'm waiting. What is it, seaweed or pigs' spleens?

– Those particular devices give off a high-frequency signal. I can hear it. But I can see you're upset, and I'll make sure yours meets with an accident over Christmas, when no one's around.

– Pull the other one. You've been having me on all this time, haven't you? This is all a wind-up. I was almost taken in. You were getting me back for the scissors, weren't you…

Now she was freezing him out again, pulling away, backing off. He was losing her.

– If you don't believe me, go and look. I'd advise against doing anything precipitate though. It would do to let Goodman know you've rumbled him.

Taking the package from his desk, Diana tore off the wrapping-paper; and glaring at Kernan, held the scissors towards him in a threatening gesture, like a knife, before striding out of the room. Kernan sat cursing, tugging the knotted string through his fingers in a vicious parody of a rosary.

Diana returned, flinging onto this desk both the scissors and a small black object with two thin wires attached.

– I'm impressed, said Kernan. That's quite sophisticated. Not standard police issue, not even Special Branch. Possibly military, I'd say. Most probably MI6.

– You should know, cried Diana. You put it there. How else could you know it was there?

– I told you, I could hear it. You have to trust me.

– I don't, said Diana. And picking up Kernan's piece of string, she cut it into two pieces with the scissors.

– I'm afraid I must have bent the points of your scissors on that socket, she said icily. And left.

Taking the two pieces of string, Kernan knotted them together. He sat for a moment, staring at his desk, before sitting bolt upright, swivelling his head from side to side like a great reptile.

– All right, he said to the empty room, you want trouble? I'll give you trouble. He walked out into the empty main office, took a felt-tip pen and wrote 42% on a flip-chart in big red letters. Then underneath the words: NATIONAL AVERAGE OF CRIME SOLVED – WE CAN DO BETTER!

His threat. A declaration of war.

George Kernan had been angry for days. He strode up and down the trench without lowering his head, not even ducking when he walked, not ran, across the sunken road to reach the observation post. The Saxon gunners sitting less than forty yards away couldn't believe their eyes. Each time he appeared in the gap, they opened fire with their machine-gun, but they didn't even graze him. The men said they were probably giving him a chance because it was nearly Christmas, and since both sides were under strict orders not to fraternise this year, they were trying to make up for their damp spirits with a little gamesmanship.

Marshall and Tomkins had brought the news. Brock had just turned sixteen when he was woken half an hour before dawn, and marched out to a piece of ground behind the line. A party of ten men from the Warwickshires had been detailed to shoot him. Their captain had been most apologetic. They blindfolded him with his own gasmask, tied on back to front. After Brock, they shot two other privates, one from the Staffordshires, the other from their own battalion, the Staffs man for running away from a working party after a shell had burst amongst them, killing his best friend. When their man was charged with cowardice, he shouted back *Never!* Then they shot him. Afterwards, one of the firing party had broken ranks to tell the two Loamshire men how sorry they all were.

When Kernan heard, he was speechless with rage. So Jack Brock had been only fifteen when he'd joined up. They had both lied about their ages.

Kernan had changed since their move to the salient. It was an abomination, this place of mud, water and fire – and sometimes gas. It had that effect on many men. At the Somme he had always been watchful, a careful countryman alert to every change in the land around. Now it was as if he didn't care if he lived or died. Nothing he did would alter his fate.

As the battalion had marched out of Ypres down the Menin Road in the dark, shells started landing all around them, almost as if someone had told the Germans artillery exactly when they would be setting off for the line. On both sides of the road were heaps of bodies, mangled corpses piled one on top of the other, dead mules, broken limbers, GS wagons without wheels, bombed-out lorries; and everywhere the stench of death, the smell of burnt and rotting flesh which was to stay with them throughout their tour, not just on that road to hell, but in the trenches where they had to live, and survive, for weeks. Yet what they saw as they marched along, while horrific, seemed as temporary as their own tenuous hold on life, for one moment they would be trying not to take in the sight of yet another mound of silhouetted corpses of mules, horses or men, and the next thing they knew a howling shell had burst into the black heap and turned it into a hellish furnace of burning bodies, parts of which were flying all around them. Those wretches had no peace at all; they'd died once on that road, and now it was as if their deaths were being staged again as a demonstration for the new arrivals.

Kernan marvelled at their discipline. A few men fell out, but were swiftly brought back, reminded that if they ran away, they were deserting, and would be shot there and then. Since there was no escape, they might as well take their chances with their mates.

When they reached the duckboards, they changed to single file, making their slow way along wooden tracks perched precariously on the mudflats, weighed down by all the equipment on their backs, about seventy pounds each by Kernan's reckoning, though every horse thinks his sack heaviest. His own included one precious book, wrapped in a handkerchief, an Everyman Library edition of *Vanity Fair* by William Makepeace Thackeray. It should have been *Pilgrim's Progress*, he thought, in this valley of the shadow of death.

As they picked their way along the slippery boards, a man would lose his grip, and fall into one of the shell-holes around which the track snaked its way. If he managed, despite his exhaustion and the weight on his back, to struggle back to the path, you could be sure that at that moment the sky would be suddenly blazoned with a Verey light, and all would freeze except for the splashing man, whose cries would be lost as the shells started falling on either side of them, or on the duckboards themselves, causing a break they would have to try to cross, with mud up to their waists.

From the numbers of men he heard gasping for breath as they sank into the mud-filled shell-holes, Kernan felt sure that more died on their way to the line by drowning than from bullets, shells or shrapnel. Nothing could be done for those poor unfortunates.

Those spared just had to keep moving along the duckboards, or they would share their fate. At one point a dangling flare had made them visible to a machine-gun post, which opened fire on the line of men, who flattened themselves, grabbing hold of the duckboards as best they could, to try to stop themselves from slipping off into the deadly mud. Bullets whipped into the wood within inches of Kernan's face, sending splinters thudding into his steel helmet, and mud into his eyes. He rolled back, doubling his body round to stay on the board, before another burst of fire tore up the planks in front where his head had been seconds earlier.

On arrival at their dugout, his platoon settled themselves in a mess of mud, boxes and sodden blankets. After the march, it felt like heaven. Kernan had noticed a rope leading out along the support trench. It snaked along the revetting, disappearing at the jutting of the dog-tooth firebay. He lay awake, listening to the artillery blasting their line, and wondered where it led.

The next morning a shell landed in the trench where Kernan had been standing not a minute before. Then a German sniper caught them unawares as they were sorting out their new position, and two men standing on either side of him had both been shot. By now he had become known as Lucky Kernan, and they debated whether it was a good or a bad thing to be with him, for while his luck might protect you from a shell, if a sniper saw you, it was ten to one the bullet would have your name on it, not his. He led a charmed life, they said. Throw him in the Nile and he would come up with a fish in his mouth.

When Sergeant George Kernan went over the top, he didn't flinch or duck when they came under fire. That was the way to death, he felt sure. You had to keep moving forward, keep your nerve. Same as in the trenches. Don't get windy. Don't wince every time you hear a shell, or guns opening up. If they hit you, you're dead. You can't change that. So just carry on normally, imagine you're digging the garden at home. Ignore them.

It was a numbers game, he decided. In every attack over half the men would be killed, wounded or not come back, and the trick was to be always amongst the half who survived. When those men went over in the next assault with a bunch of new recruits, half of that group would be wiped out, and so on. So what were the chances of never being hit, of always coming back? Each time, the sum became more impossible, yet there was nothing he could do to alter those odds. He just had to go along with it. He was powerless.

There were always new men arriving to take the places of the killed and wounded. The same must be true of the Boche. Hundreds of men were dying every day on both sides of the line, and hundreds more men were now being trained to replace them, and be killed themselves. The arithmetic was staggering. The generals must have it all worked out. The question was: how long would the War have to last before they ran out of men? And what would happen then? Who would have won?

Sitting in Nicholas Goodman's office the next morning, Maurice Saveloy gripped his whisky glass hard, his knuckles whitening, the ice-cubes chinking nervously. Although the years had taken their toll, the Chief Constable still took pride in his looks; not quite handsome, he was nevertheless quite dapper-looking with his swept-back pepper-and-salt mane. He thought himself something of a Sean Connery, but what he took to be rakishness others perceived as a manner so misjudged that it was almost seedy. This impression was reinforced by the yellow silk cravat which he felt gave him the air of a dandy, a *roué* like his ancestor, Maurice Cervelat, companion to Philippe, Duke of Orléans, Regent of France.

– I tell you, Nick, he said, Kernan's up to something. This traffic stuff is just a warning.

– I can handle him, said Goodman, firmly, with only a little hesitation. He avoided looking him in the eye, staring at the cravat instead, Saveloy's badge of betrayal; he knew from his surveillance team that when the Chief Constable was wearing this ridiculous canary-coloured paisley cravat, he would be meeting some woman. The yellow cravat meant Saveloy was rutting, his pork sausage was on heat.

– And then there's Hunter's phone-bug: what about that? He must have found out about that and told her.

– I don't know, said Goodman, unable to keep his eyes off the cravat. Who would receive the sausage today? Into whose slippery hot fat would the Saveloy dip himself? De Foie's loony wife again? He imagined the Chief Constable's penis tossed into a pan of hot fat, his sizzling libido finally overreaching itself, setting De Foie's factory on fire, like the beefburger which started that blaze at Heathrow Airport.

– How else could she know about it?

– I've not worked that one out. If he knew it was there, he'd have left it there. He wouldn't have just yanked it out of the socket, and left the wires dangling. That's not his style. Which means he can't have told her; or if he did, they're still working against each other. Or it's a double bluff.

– You're losing me, said Saveloy.

– In some ways, reflected Goodman, Kernan's easier to handle. I know the way his mind works. But Hunter's a loose cannon. It may be more dangerous to have her rushing around like a bull in a china shop while he's lurking in the background, up to something else. If they were together, Kernan would rein her in.

– But now he's the bull, said Saveloy. I didn't much enjoy being arrested last night, and brought back to the station like a criminal. We were with the Maws. It was most embarrassing.

– Good thing I was around to deal with him, said Goodman.

– Yes, he didn't appreciate your intervention. He was quite right of course. I was doing 90 on the bypass.

– But you were on your way to an incident. I called you out.

– Ah yes, an incident. Those sorts of ploys are pretty transparent, Nick, and risky with Kernan sniffing around. This sulky show of his is all a smokescreen. He's got our scent.

Chief Constable Saveloy drained his glass, and started sucking traces of much diluted whisky from pieces of ice-cube.

– I rang you beforehand. But it was a false alarm.

– Alarm's the right word, he *knows* something. Now give me those reports. Let me have a look at them myself.

Watching Maurice Saveloy leaf through Kernan's charge sheets, Superintendent Nicholas Goodman reflected that he now possessed particular information enabling him to control the lives not just of the Chief Constable and his good friend Morton Maw, but also the whole of his own charmed circle, those so-called "friends" who were currently useful to him.

Goodman wondered how they viewed him. Did he frighten them? He thought he must present a magisterial figure, a Chief Superintendent inspiring respect: bullet-headed, large-fisted, dark-eyed, his jaw jutting out like a ship's prow. His great black eyebrows were imposing, unmistakable, like Stalin's moustache. He too was a man who liked lists. Facts set down cleanly as straightforward statements. Problem stated. Solution noted. Decision made. Action requested. People marked with bullet-points.

Example. These were his "friends". He could throw the book at them. Evidence includes:

• Proof of the true nature of Maw's trips to South East Asia, as well as the identity of the other freemasons involved.

• Documentation detailing a business connection between one of Maw's freemason colleagues and Brucellosis Tucker, which if revealed would ruin both; certain records removed from the Factories Inspectorate showing that Eurochimique UK was contravening government regulations on both the handling of chemicals by its workforce and on levels of airborne discharge.

• Yellowing internal council memorandum signed by the late Sir Peter Prurigeaux regarding planning permission for Eurochimique UK's proposed expansion of their a factory unit; plus related correspondence and internal memoranda from both district and county councils concerning subsequent piecemeal additions to the plant, by means of which staggered process Oliver de Foie had been able to build his huge factory in the middle of the Loamshire countryside, which would otherwise not have been possible under both the original and current planning regulations.

• Photocopies of deeds of property in the name of Candida Yeats (later Mrs Sirloin) which the Department of the Environment no longer regarded as land of outstanding natural beauty, along with correspondence from the National Trust containing objections to a sale of this land to Loamshire Country Properties Ltd, a company taken over two years later by a subsidiary of Eurochimique UK (with documentation of that transfer).

• A selection of blurred stills from hidden cameras in the Excelsior Hotel depicting Lady Olivia Prurigeaux, Mrs Isabella

Maw, Mrs Patricia de Foie and Mrs Candida Sirloin, with a variety of partners, male and female, including each other's husbands, as well as other local dignatories, all naked or half clothed, or pictured in compromising positions, including one taken in the bridal suite showing three women, two men and a dog engaged in acts of oral sex, flagellation and bestiality, one of the participants being the Reverend Kevin Devlin, vicar of St George's, Loamfield.

This was just the tip of the iceberg. All this material was sealed in large manilla envelopes inside the locked grey filing-cabinet across the room, behind where the Chief Constable was now sitting. This was his own personal cabinet, with two drawers marked PERSONNEL: CONFIDENTIAL, another COMPANIES, and the fourth, WORK FOR CHARITIES AND TRUSTS. He possessed the only key to this treasure trove of secrets relating not only to Loamshire but also to national and international matters; its contents could affect not only the fortunes of Sirloin's party, but also European trade and the preservation of the environment. That key now rested in his pocket. He pressed his thigh beneath the table, feeling the shape of the metal key. His power.

Superintendent Goodman also possessed documents implicating his Chief Constable in a variety of crimes, but all linked to other members of his dinner party, and he couldn't expose Maurice Saveloy without bringing down some of the others; and with Saveloy removed, the whole lot could easily fall like a house of cards. In those circumstances, he didn't trust any of these imbeciles to keep their filthy mouths shut. While he could extricate himself from such a collapse, he feared that the Assistant Chief Constable, Lawrence Lambert, might discover some means of linking him with one of the miscreants. Since he also suspected ACC Lambert of being in league with Kernan, this was not beyond the bounds of possibility. After all, had not Larry thwarted his attempts to have Kernan "promoted" to another force? He had tried this on several occasions in order to effect the inspector's removal from his beloved Loamshire patch, where he had long been a thorn in his flesh, and had lately become something of a nuisance in delicate matters such as the Tench case.

And he still had nothing on Lambert or Kernan, both were like monks: the skull-headed Lambert with his spectral looks and monastic habits, and the bookish Kernan with his infuriating air of being St Francis to the animals. The inspector was straight as a die. Yet how did he do it? He suspected that one of his own circle must be Kernan's informer.

One of last month's supper-party must have betrayed him. How else could Kernan have known about the phone call to Brock? The message that had brought him up to the farm? Kernan hadn't said anything about it, but he certainly knew, otherwise why had he been going through the station phone records? He was biding his time, looking for more clues. So who was the Judas? And why should they be helping Kernan? Was he looking for someone to turn Queen's Evidence? Immunity from prosecution? Which of those jackals would turn traitor for that?

The Chief Constable would be in a good position to help Kernan, and he wasn't in as deep as some of the others. He was also a devious man, which meant Goodman could usually read him, but not always. When Maurice Saveloy turned on that piercing gaze of his, that appearance of sincerity which made him look so concerned for someone's plight or problem, he convinced the unwary and the foolish that here was someone who *knew* their hurt, someone who understood them and who could be trusted with their confidences. Of course he, Goodman, saw through his deceit, but he still felt there was some vestige of what some might call decency in the man, and that made him unpredictable, and therefore dangerous, a possible liability. He preferred it when Saveloy was clearly so disingenuous that he seemed even to convince himself of his own sincerity; he was capable of a level of deception so subtle that it became self-deception. He swallowed his own porkies: all that nonsense about his French ancestry was clearly bogus, for Saveloy was as English as the pork pies. His family went back for generations in Loamshire, they had always been part of the local squirearchy; there was no French connection, no covert trade in spiced meats as Saveloy was fond of claiming. Kernan could get to him, which might meant going via Larry. He would have to discourage old Sausage-Breath from any possible thoughts of treachery.

Maurice Saveloy looked up.

– I can't see what's wrong with these. Forty motorists charged in one night. A bit excessive, but if they *were* speeding…

– Somewhat higher than our usual haul…

– And he charged fifteen with drink-driving, and got positive results on all of them, both from the bag and from the urine tests. Dangerous driving: six arrests, not bad for a night when the roads were dangerous, black ice and all that…

– You'd know about that, Maurice.

– Quite. And if Kernan keeps this up for the rest of the week, we'll have the best figures in the country. What's the problem?

– You know I threatened Kernan with keeping him on Traffic if he didn't drop the charges against you?

– Yes. What of it?

– He said I wouldn't want to. That he'd clean it up. And I'd have a mutiny on my hands. I've already had Oxter and Clegg in to see me this morning. They're angry as hell. And Johnny Jakes has gone all glum: you know him, always the joker, now he's just snarling. Oxter says they want Kernan out of Traffic or there'll be hell to pay.

– I'm not sure I quite know what you're driving at, Nick. What's wrong with Kernan doing his duty, coming down hard on the drink-drivers, doing what we're supposed to be doing? At least he's not permanently drunk like Daube. Isn't that an embarrassment to Oxter and the rest?

– No. When Daube's stewed, they can do what they like, and I'm quite happy with that, because it keeps them happy. But with Daube drying out in hospital and Kernan running the show, they are – how shall I put it – a little exposed.

– But Kernan's giving them excellent figures.

– Exactly. They don't want their excellent figures on paper. They want figures in their bank accounts. Money in their pockets.

– Are you implying that Loamshire traffic police have been taking bribes from motorists? That's a very serious charge. What are we doing about it? What's been going on?

Was he pretending? thought Goodman. Was it possible that he really didn't know? Or was this another sanctimonious show of innocence by Saveloy, him trying to keep his hands clean? Well he'd show him whose hands were dirty, whose mitts were steeped in the mire.

– It's quite simple, Maurice, said Goodman, with a patronising air of satisfaction. You see our friend Sergeant Oxter knows which drivers have the maximum number of penalty points on their licences, and so he follows them in an unmarked car. Then he pulls them in when they break the speed limit. If they went to court, they'd not only be fined heavily, they'd lose their licences; and many would lose their jobs, or not be able to get around easily if they live in remote parts of the shire. But Oxter wouldn't like that to happen; he cares about the well-being of the local residents. The motorists are also very grateful for this arrangement. It sets the hare's foot against the goose giblets, you might say.

– So in exchange for a small consideration…

– Exactly. And the greater the risk from losing the licence…

– …the bigger the small consideration.

– The motorist benefits. The community benefits, because these people drive more carefully afterwards. The courts don't benefit, of course, but the police do, and their families. We lay the head of the sow to the tail of the grice, the hog's tail in this case being the Police Widows Fund.

– Sounds like highway robbery, said Saveloy, looking self-righteous. And it's damned risky, you must know that.

– But you knew it was going on, Maurice…

– This is the first I've heard about it.

– Your wife's never said anything? asked Goodman, smiling. Those trips to London, shopping at Harrods? She can't possibly afford all those dresses with what you give her.

– What do you mean? She has her allowance. I'm sure that's adequate. But Maurice Saveloy immediately knew otherwise, remembering how he'd questioned her about the clothes and hats he'd found still in their wrappers and boxes, nothing wrong with that, but he had been worried at the defensive tone she took about these purchases, and what this indicated. Oh his foolish, foolish Bunty. But then who could blame her, she was only matching his own subterfuges with this secrecy over shopping.

– I don't think she'd agree with you there, said Goodman, relishing his triumph. But I'm sure you'll find our officers have been most generous to her.

– Oh dear, said Saveloy. How little he knew his wife…but his own meanness had left the silly woman open to temptation. Goodman had no doubt stalked her, knowing from their dinner parties where her weakness lay; and he had used his traffic men to prey on her, until he had only to take her to his emporium and say, *all this you can have*, and Bunty would have succumbed. Beware of Greeks bearing gifts, Saveloy thought, gifts which bound him to the giver.

– All sauce for the goose, Goodman beamed, for don't they say rutting wives make rammish husbands? And you are a bit of an old tup, from what I hear…

– But getting just a bit long in the tooth now, Saveloy managed to whisper.

– An old jade might be that, Goodman laughed, but a ram with dentures is a toothless beast.

– Quite so, said Saveloy, looking down at his glass as he felt the superintendent's eyes almost flensing the skin from his skull. Who has a wolf for his mate needs a dog for his man, he reflected, but his dog was a dachshund.

Goodman smacked his lips, as if responding telepathically to the Chief Constable's distress signal. The wolf knows what the ill beast thinks.

Three floors down, Inspector Kernan was on his way out. Barging through each set of swing-doors, he marched down the corridor, beaming with satisfaction. As he approached the front desk, Sergeant Cobb called to him.

– A good night's work, sir.

– I'm glad someone appreciates it, said Kernan.

– A pity about the cells though. All those drunks. Quite a mess. Poor Meg Merkin's had to go down twice already, like Mrs Partington mopping up the Atlantic.

– You should have left them for longer, said Kernan. Teach them lager and curry don't mix.

– What about O'Scrapie, sir? Do we have to hold him? The others aren't too pleased. We don't usually arrest the little viper, you know…

– Yes, yes, yes, said Kernan, waving his hand peremptorily, attempting a visual parody of an actor playing a policeman.

Release the prisoner! And make sure Hodge fumigates the cell before Mrs Merkin goes in again with her mop and bucket.

– Are we charging him with anything, sir?

– Drunk and disorderly. Grievous bodily odour. Found in possession of body-lice. And harbouring a sheep-tick. On second thoughts, just stick with the D and D. We can let him off the rest. *With-a-D-and-D-and-Di-D-Oh.*

– I can see we enjoyed ourselves, last night, sir. Good to see you back in the saddle…

Kernan waited while the desk sergeant despatched an emissary to the cells. Shortly afterwards, the willowy figure of O'Scrapie slouched through the door, urged forward by a truncheon held at arm's length by a young constable. He glared at Kernan, who stood unmoving as a statue, displaying no expression, as the miscreant was frogmarched through the glass front-doors of the police station.

He had known O'Scrapie's father Jack, a greater villain than this pipsqueak, and Jack's father, Paddy Muttonchops they'd called him, after his sideburns and trade: he'd been village butcher before the war, and implicated in a murder conspiracy when a body had disappeared, though nothing had been proved, Paddy being a thorough cleaner of his block and cleaver, and forensic science not advanced enough then to offer a challenge.

Bad apples, Kernan called them. The villagers had less polite names for the family, and more extravagant stories about their forebears, including one claim that O'Scrapies went back to Biblical times. O'Scrapie played up to this, boasting one night in the Bull how he was related to the Fourth Horseman of the Apocalypse, on his mother's side.

– Which is why we always had black horses, like him.

Kernan had been in the bar, and countered:

– Which is why you've always been liars, more like, he said. The whole lot of you: Jack and Paddy Muttonchops the Butcher, Old Harry and his father before them. Lice-ridden liars, scratchers and snatchers…

– What do you mean? You take that back!

– The Fourth Horseman rode a pale horse, O'Scrapie. The first appeared on a white horse, the second on a red. Red and white for War. Then Famine and Pestilence, the third horseman on a black mount, the fourth on a pale-coloured horse. You should know that. You were there. A snake in the grass, plotting our destruction. But ware the hawk, O'Scrapie, or the bird will have you for breakfast.

O'Scrapie had left the pub with his tail between his legs, his protests shouted down by the other drinkers. Kernan watched him leave, and was not surprised when he looked out the window later and saw O'Scrapie standing in the middle of the Green. He knew what the little schemer would be thinking.

Listening to the sounds from the pub, the raucous laughter he knew to be at his expense, O'Scrapie was vowing he'd get his own back on them. And they would not like it. He'd get that knowall Kernan, Kernans had always been bad news in Loamfield, all the men had been smartarse coppers. Uncanny too. One story had it there were witches in the family, way back; that Kernans had the third eye, eyes in the backs of their heads. This one they called hawk-eyed, his eyes like a lynx. Ears so sharp he could hear the grass grow. But O'Scrapie would get him, get him back for putting him inside, not just once, but thrice. Those spells in Parkhurst, Leicester and Strangeways, all Kernan's doing.

Jack, Jack Joe,
Bent his bow,
Shot at a pigeon
And killed a crow.

CHAPTER FOUR

A Mumble of Moles

ST BRANNOC'S DAY: JANUARY 7TH

To walk or trample on a man's shadow will bring him bad luck. This is because his shadow, like his reflection in a mirror, is a visible manifestation of his soul, or of that mysterious entity, his double. He can be harmed or killed if a malicious person injures his shadow.

Epiphany was yesterday, Herne was saying, when the arrival of a family of magpies stopped him in his tracks. He was just starting a story when the birds appeared in the great oak tree beside the clearing. There were seven perched in the branches overhanging their fire – a tiding of magpies – for Muffy a sign that Hangman's Wood held a secret no one would discover:

> One for sorrow, two for joy,
> Three for a girl, four for a boy,
> Five for silver, six for gold,
> Seven for a secret never to be told.
> Eight for a lover, nine for a kiss,
> Ten for good fortune, a spell, or a wish.

But Herne was fearful. Muffy's rhyme was a woman's spell for a lover, a child or a fortune, he said. For men, seven magpies meant the devil was at hand in the spell he knew:

One sorrow, two mirth,
Three a wedding, four a birth,
Five Heaven, six Hell,
Seven the De'ils ain sel.

He'd first heard this rhyme in the north country, where they call the magpie the Devil's bird. The magpie always has a drop of the Devil's blood under his tongue.

– Sounds disgusting, said O'Scrapie. But to settle the point, I vote we shoot two of the magpies. That leaves five, which gives us silver by Muffy's reckoning, or Heaven in Herne's version. Or we could just kill one, and risk Herne's Hell but go for gold with six of Muffy's birds.

– *But you can't kill a magpie!* cried Herne and Muffy as one.

– Who says so?

– I say so, said Herne. Magpies are our watchbirds. They set up their chattering when wolves are around. They warn us of danger.

– Wolves in Hangman's Wood?

– January is the Wolf-Month, said Herne. That's always been so. You may not see the wolves, but they're there.

– Herne's right, said Muffy. If you don't believe in wolves, they won't let you see them. Until it's too late, and you won't be around then to cry wolf to anyone.

– But a bad dog never sees the wolf, said Herne.

– You won't scare me with all that, said O'Scrapie, darting a glance up into the oak tree when he thought he heard the birds setting up a chatter.

– Someone's coming, said Herne.

It was Gubbins, whose heavy footfalls were soon heard by the others.

– Look what the cat's dragged in, said O'Scrapie, greeting the cross-eyed sweep with a scowl.

Gubbins spat his disgust at being so addressed into the fire, whereupon a bat flew out of the flames, swooping up into the trees, where it sent the magpies scattering in fright.

– *Knuckers,* he said.

– That was impressive, said Flea. Do that again.

– I can't, said Gubbins. That was my disgust. It's gone now. You'll have to wait till I'm disgusted again.

– It takes a lot to disgust you, said Muffy.

– I know, said Gubbins. I'm always disgusting but rarely disgusted. Do you like my new word? It's very disgusting.

– What new word? asked Muffy.

– Knuckers.

– Oh that, said O'Scrapie. It's not much of a word. Where did you find it?

– From a rhyme, said the sweep. *Knackers, knickers, knockers, knuckers*. If all the other words are rude, then *knuckers* must be *really* disgusting, being the fourth word in the rhyme. You can use it instead of *fuckers*. You dirty fuckers, you naughty knuckers.

– I prefer *fuckers*, said O'Scrapie. A word much more to the point.

– Well I think it's a very good word, said Muffy, and I shall certainly use it. It's not often we get a new word, and very rare to have one which sounds as disgusting as *knuckers*. What do you think Herne?

The grizzled woodsman looked unimpressed.

– Herne was telling us a story, she said, when we got distracted by magpies. And knuckers.

– I like stories, said Gubbins, has it got bats in it?

– *Bat, bat, come under my hat*, Muffy squawked.

> Bat, bat, come under my hat
> And I'll give you a slice of bacon;
> And when I bake, I'll give you a cake,
> If I am not mistaken.

– Cows, not bats, said Herne. Flea was wanting to know why today's St Brannoc's Day, and I was saying how Brannoc sailed to England in a stone coffin.

– Sounds unlikely, interrupted O'Scrapie.

– Don't horn in, said Muffy. I like this story. Go on, Herne.

– When he came upon a sow suckling her piglets, he built a church on that spot, and there he cured many sick animals. Two wild deer pulled his plough for him, but not surprisingly his neighbours soon became jealous of his friendship with the animals, which they thought gave him an unfair advantage over them.

– Even though he was a saint? asked Flea.

– Yes. He also had a milch cow, who provided milk for everyone, until one day one of his neighbours stole the cow, slaughtered her and made her into a stew. When Brannoc discovered what had happened, he called to the cow across the fields, and the cow heard him. The beef stew poured itself up from the cauldron like a water-spout, and formed itself back into the milch cow, who walked back to Brannoc's church, where she lived for many more years, giving even more milk than before.

– And no one meddled with Brannoc again after he'd pulled a stunt like that, said Muffy, who was always impressed by animal miracles.

Returning from her Christmas break, Diana Hunter found the police station in turmoil. Inspector Daube had been dragged out of hospital by Oxter and Jakes, still suffering from cold turkey. They carried him back to his office, planted a large bottle of White Horse on his desk, and wished him good health. Sergeant Cobb was told to enter in the station ledger that Daube had reported back to duty. He was fighting fit after his spell in St Nick's, and raring to get back to the important business of running Traffic Division. But first he had to be left to catch up with all the paperwork which Kernan's record-breaking stint in charge had left him to deal with. While he was engaged in that lengthy task, Sergeant Daglock was deputising for him.

– Busy? she asked Cobb, who was trying to sort a mountain of traffic summonses behind the front desk.

– The Inspector's nicked so many people that we've had to bring in two temps to help process the summonses, the desk sergeant told her. He even pulled in the Chief Constable for speeding, and arrested Mr Sirloin, the MP, but had to let him go with a caution. Apparently there were mitigating circumstances. Our laws catch small flies but let wasps and hornets go free.

Diana wondered if Kernan had been trying to impress her. Either that or he was making damn sure that no one ever tried to land him with Traffic again. Yet it was all so different from his usual cautious style, his holding back. It was also childish in its blatant exhibitionism: *look what I can do...* And threatening: *look what you lot haven't been doing.* He'd been exposing himself too, but on Traffic he could just about get away with it. Traffic was black and white, not murky like everything else.

It was all so uncharacteristic, like that charade before Christmas, that stuff about liking her when she'd been giving him so much grief. What was he trying to prove, and to whom? The more he came out into the open, the easier it would be for Goodman to find some way of bringing him down.

Hanging up her coat on a hook by the door, she noted that her phone socket had been repaired. She'd leave it for now, for no one would be stupid enough to bug the same socket again, although they would quite likely try somewhere else. Opening the drawers of her desk, she pictured how she had left the various folders before Christmas; felt sure that someone had been through them in her absence.

She placed a chair in the middle of the room, stood on it and examined the light socket. Then inspected her pot plant, testing the soil for signs of disturbance. Lifting her anglepoise, she checked out the base and the connection at the top of the stem, replacing it quickly when Mrs Merkin came in with her trolley. As she watched her tea being poured, she looked up at the ceiling and spotted the smoke-detector, which she remembered as being dirty and smudged with someone's pawprints. And now it was clean. Should she leave it there, and act accordingly, as Kernan had put it. Or take action?

Standing on the chair again, and unscrewing the cap of the detector, she decided to be consistent. At least they'd know this was her work, not Kernan's. Removing a small device similar to the one from the phone socket, she placed it on the table, took off her shoe and bashed the thing several times with the heel. Then she swept the pieces into a court exhibit pouch, sealed it and walked out into the main office; a pretend cough made sure she was conspicuous. As the others looked up, she wrote TO WHOM IT MAY CONCERN on the label and dropped it into the tray for outgoing post. Then she returned to her office, shutting the door behind her.

Oliver de Foie was not a happy bunny. During the Christmas reduced output period, Eurochimique's security had not been as tight as its security guards. While they were mallemaroking with some females from the village, someone had entered the experimental station and released the mink. Fraser's guards blamed Animal Liberationists, or some person called Gubbins, citing the presence of an ammoniacal smell around the hole in the exterior fence, but Dr Kuru said the plant itself was swathed in ammoniacal vapour when the filters needed renewing, a claim De Foie had to take on trust now his sense of smell was malfunctional.

He had his own suspicions, remembering he'd mentioned to Patricia that the creatures would need to be destroyed after Christmas, and would have to be incinerated. This thought had crossed his mind: that she might have wanted their coats, for herself or one of her friends.

Uncapping his second bottle of Milk of Magnesia, he tipped a quantity into a whisky glass, and sipped at the white liquid which was tasteless but nevertheless possessed a pleasant gritty quality; it was one of his few remaining indulgences. Between sips, he turned the pages of the lab report, not at all pleased by its contents, still less by its recommendations.

Ten of the mink had been fed with the meat and bonemeal of a cow which had died from a disease clinically similar to BSE, and they had all become infected with TME, transmissible mink encephalopathy; some had died or been killed and eaten by their fellows. The other ten animals had been on a neutral control diet, but they too had caught the disease, probably as a result of fighting or cannibalism. No sheep were included in their diet, in contrast with the previous experiment, when food containing scrapie or a BSE infective agent had been given to another batch of mink, and while they too had contracted TME, it was not apparently of the same clinical type.

The latest experiment was complete, and the results were

certainly satisfactory, but the escape of all the remaining TME-infected animals was a matter of some concern to him. Oliver de Foie was aware that it might lead to certain difficulties. The mink could last up to six months in the wild before the disease killed them, but if they were to be caught or eaten by another animal, it was possible that TME might be transmitted to another host, particularly if the predator bit through its spine.

He had seen the report from Alpers' U.S. study relating to chronic wasting disease of deer, a related transmissible spongiform encephalopathy. They had been able to induce spongiform change in the cerebral grey matter, and transmit CWDD to deer and ferrets by means of inoculation.

Turning to another report, he was pleased to note that Eurochimique's work on electrophoretic analysis of body fluids was far in advance of any research by MAFF or BBSRC. While some work was clearly being duplicated, this was no bad thing in itself. Eurochimique had to be in possession of all the facts to protect its commercial interests. On some occasions it had been necessary to make sure that government-sponsored research was discontinued, or held up to give Eurochimique time to develop alternative product lines. When Sirloin had been a junior minister, this had been a simple matter to arrange. Yet the present channels were more expedient, being less direct, and were often quite challenging to execute, like a crossword in which every clue had to be exactly answered to elicit the correct sequence of letters. The right word in the right person's ear would set in a motion a train of events whose outcome was inevitable, like a chemical reaction which always worked in exactly the same way, unless impurities were present.

This latest research charted changes in the chemistry of urine, and was meant to identify diagnostic markers in BSE and scrapie. It could result in earlier identification of transmissible spongiform encephalopathies through the detection of a urinary metabolite. It would be helpful to Eurochimique if the government-sponsored research in this field were inconclusive for the moment. Withdrawal of MAFF funding elsewhere would give his company more time to develop an appropriate product. When he later announced the results of the company's research, Eurochimique would be viewed as a saviour, not just in Europe but around the world, and the commercial success of the new product would be guaranteed.

What should it be called? Some name linking the company with both the diagnostic process and the European market, he felt. It would need to be something that would go down well in Turin. He rather liked the sound of *Eurolagnia*. The Italians would go for that, it sounded like a pasta dish: it could almost be the name of one of their sports cars, or one of those flashy festivals for watersports where they held Olympic trials and film stars went *on the piss*, in his wife's phrase. He couldn't wait to tell Strimmer. What was his expression? He would wet himself. Yes, that was it. Marketing would wet themselves for a brand name as hot as Eurolagnia.

The Germans seemed to be throwing everything at them, as if they were having a clearout. He was happier with bullets. Somehow he seemed able to dodge them, but with mortars, even Lucky Kernan stood no chance. And it was frightening too, the way you could see them coming, some of them quite slow, like the oil cans, which you could run from. These were barmy things, old oil drums filled with explosive and any rubbish that might be lying around, like broken bottles and any old iron. He imagined the Boche having a New Year clean-up, chucking everything in the drum, then lobbing it over. You couldn't believe in them, they were almost comical, like something knocked up in a dodgy scrapyard, but when they landed in a trench, they blew everyone to bits.

When the slow ones came over, time seemed suspended. You stood there for a moment, frozen in disbelief, then ran like hell, keeping your head down all the time. The trench mortar shells were like footballs on sticks; even at night you could spot them hurtling towards you like great Jack-o'-Lanterns, trailing an arc of sparks in their wake. With the smaller whizz-bangs you stood no chance. Hearing the whizz you ducked, and hoped to hear the bang; if it wasn't a dud, you wouldn't be around to hear the bang. That bang was you, your life, gone in a bang, *kaput*.

Waiting to hear what was next on the menu, he heard a distant pop like a bottle being opened, then a loud, sudden whistle ending in a sharp crack and the flash of a "pineapple" bursting just round the bend in the trench. He threw himself into the mud, hearing another pop from along the low ridge, but this one exploded some distance away. These were *Grenatenwerfers*, which the men also called "blue pigeons".

They must be going through their whole arsenal, thought Kernan. Maybe some general was visiting, and they were showing off, giving him some kind of a demonstration. They'd fired everything now except the *Minnenwerfers*. But if they were entertaining their brass, they were unlikely to risk using those.

He was wrong. Hartley yelled a warning, and they all threw themselves face down into the slime. The trench wall opposite blew up, filling the place with filthy black dirt and evil fumes. Kernan waited, his ears sharp as an owl's, tuned to the frequency of shellfire; braced himself as he heard a thud behind them, and looking up was horrified to see that a massive grey-blue shell had smacked into the parados, but by some quirk of fate had not exploded. It just lay there, stuck in the mudbank. Kernan stared at it, never having been this close before to a Minnie. It was over three feet long.

It was hard to comprehend, a thing of this size: what destruction it would wreak, falling on a group of people, on these men who had become his friends. Even the thought of it was devastating: that such a thing existed, that men had created it.

Marshall wrote a single word on a scrap of paper, speared it with a fork, and dropped it down the shaft to the signallers. Whenever the hated Minnies were used, the artillery immediately unleashed an awesome barrage on the Germans in reply. Now they were unpopular even amongst the Boche infantry; he knew this from talking to prisoners in the cages behind the line. Yet they still insisted on using them from time to time, as if to keep the Tommies on their toes.

Something had drawn Kernan out to Loamsley Moor that afternoon. The scrubby pasture sloping up from the River Otter never failed to stir him with its contradictions. The site of an indecisive but bloody Civil War battle in 1647, it was a place over which there still hung a fleeting sense of death, vague as distant smoke, as if the land itself still held its own memory of the men and horses who died there. Like much of the Maw Estate, these fields were waterlogged; bracken covered the upper slopes, and there was sphagnum bogland where these levelled off. Kernan knew that the bodies of the slain would have been trampled into this kind of poor, sodden ground, and left to feed the earth, both man and beast.

The place was also a reminder of Loamshire's depression years, when most of the farms had looked like Loamsley Moor, with its overgrown hedges, its ditches stagnant with slurry-tainted water. Kernan scanned the sedgy field, noticing the darker shades of green where clumps of rushes were taking over, and a recent spread of heather and dwarf gorse, from which rabbits emerged with a proprietorial sniffing of the air. He relished the timeless desolation of the place, but he also knew that it had changed over the past hundred years; that it had gone backwards, for before the Maws had given their name to land appropriated with their industrial wealth, the Estate had been part of the Duchy, which the Loamsleys had taken great pride in managing, not exploiting it in the modern fashion but working with it, preserving the hedgerows, keeping the channels clear.

A curlew swept across his view, then swooped down over the field. He listened for the other birds, picking out the song of an avocet, which pleased him, for they had once been rare. But this made him aware of absences, that he always used to hear corn buntings, tree sparrows and bullfinches in this part of Loamshire, where now there were none, because the farmers had been pulling up the hedgerows and turning over their enlarged fields to cereals.

The lapwings too had gone: they used to raise their broods in grain fields, before moving on to the pasture land. But the mixed farms were becoming a thing of the past. Even the song thrushes were fewer in number; and where were the linnets, where the skylarks? The lark, *oh the lark.*

> Oh the lark is a bonny bird and flies off her nest
> She mounts the morn air with the dew on her breast
> She flies o'er the ploughboy, she whistles and she sings
> And at eve she returns with the dew on her wing.

At least the farmland birds could still find some food on Loamsley Moor. Elsewhere the new pesticides were completely wiping out the weeds. Bernard Tench used to write anonymous letters to the *Chronicle* about this, he recalled, though the villagers could all identify *Name of Writer Supplied* as the strange cove from Hogsback. Remembering him in this place of death, his murder seemed to Kernan to be somehow linked with this wasting, part of this spoilage, just as he himself felt diminished by the decline of land which had nourished him, where he still felt as rooted as an oak despite the ravages of money-mad men like Maw.

Walking up the hill towards Loamsley Wood, he saw a shape like a boulder on the ground ahead, and headed quickly towards it. A bloated ewe was lying on her back, deserted by the rest of the flock. Unable to right herself, she shook her legs helplessly in the air, her eyes wide but blank with uncomprehending terror.

– Come on old girl, said Kernan, heaving the sheep onto her side. He watched her lurch unsteadily to her feet, managing a few yards before toppling over again. She must have been lying there for some hours, for her flat back was sodden and bruised green from the grass, and now her weakened legs could hardly manage to support her swollen bulk. As Kernan approached her again, the ewe made frantic attempts to right herself, to escape from her deliverer, before letting him heave her up again like a great rock.

– Come on sheep, he said, you'll die if I leave you here. You've got to let me help you. She swayed from side to side like a newborn lamb, her bulging eyes seeming to implore his help as she felt herself falling again. Then he knelt in the mud she had churned up, supporting her heaving body with his own, and held her upright.

– Don't give up, he said, get used to that weight. You've got to carry it now. And eased her forward, like someone teaching a child to swim, to let the water take its weight, but once more the sheep managed only a few yards before keeling over. Kernan knelt beside her again, and lifted, gasping as he did so; the sheep rose, stumbled forward, and fell. Five times he repeated his rescue, the two staggering across the field, man and sheep, until the ewe finally managed to stay on her feet, ran forward, and kept running, only stopping when she reached the gorse, when she looked back, still swaying unsteadily, and thanked her saviour.

He picked up a small tuft of wool and put it in his pocket as a keepsake. Driving out to the Moor, he had been going over the events of the past fortnight in his mind, still unsure of himself, excited that he had been drawn out of his sulking, that he had finally taken action, but worried by what this train of events might have set in motion. Looking out over the Otter Valley, he knew this part of England was more precious to him than almost anything; just gazing at the green fields, the woods and the snaking river, was as invigorating to him as the air itself.

He tried to recall the view many years before, blotting out from the picture the roads which scarred their way across the land; adding a copse to one hill, a spinney to another, like a painter dabbing brushloads of colour on a canvas. Above Long Wood Farm, he removed all the forestry plantations, making the six or seven rectangles greyish brown with leafless oak and elm. In the distance, Otteridge shrank from a higgledy-piggledy sprawl of buildings into the old tawny-looking market town, its only landmark the spire of St John's; across the river, the two chimneys of the chemical works erased themselves, along with the metallic plant, and Newlands disappeared. He stripped the railway from beside the river, pulling it from the landscape like a string of stitches, the water-meadows healing themselves back into unbroken stretches of green along its path. Turning finally to Loamfield, he demolished several houses dotted around the village, restoring others in their place, and took out all the box-like houses of the new development along Beech Road; green patches appeared between the buildings everywhere, tiled roofs turned fawn as he thatched them. His keen eyes held the whole of north Loamshire suspended, the land restored to its state of a century before.

Contemplating his handiwork, Kernan could feel the place drawing him into it, as he himself was drawing his own strength from the land. It was like a healing draught pouring into him, a recognition, like *déjà vu*, of a landscape lost in childhood, yet here it was reviving his spent spirit with its own latent energy, a fossil fuel catching fire. This land seemed to hold a promise too that much in him which had been lost, or frozen, might now return. Overcome by this revelation, he lay back on the ground and stared at the sky.

As the landscape spun back into the present, Kernan's worries returned to him, but now he felt more able to deal with them. He knew now he must not let his anger and frustration get the better of him, it wasn't worth the risk. He would have to be more circumspect again, more cautious. Having shaken them with his frenetic purge of the roads, he would settle back into his accustomed slower ways, and let them be troubled instead by what his silence might conceal.

Rising to his feet, he decided to complete a circuit back to the car by going through the woods, rejoining the road at the stile. Ambling along the path, he wondered if it had been the stranded sheep which made him come out this way. His walks were always eventful; there always seemed to be connections between his choice of place and what he found there. Reaching the fence above the road, he found something else which must have drawn him there: a so-called gamekeeper's larder, an affront as great to him as the chemical factory was to the village. Along the barbed wire someone had hung the bodies of five moles and a crow. What this advertised, apart from the person's own barbarity, he was at a loss to understand.

The moles were all young, their tiny pink paws like babies' hands; their eyes screwed up, as if at the light, or worse. And a mole's wee snout was such a lovely thing, Kernan thought, a lump catching at the back of his throat. He stroked the taupe-coloured fur of the smallest with a fingertip. *The little gentleman in black velvet*, he whispered. These mouldwarps had come up for air, and some devil had speared them with the tine of a fork, he could see that from their brutal wounds.

– You should have stayed underground, he told them. Bided your time. Next time you must rise up unseen, like a murmur through a crowd, reclaim the earth from underground. Sleepers in a revolution, you mumble of moles.

Their spectral companion the crow looked like a broken umbrella, its legs askew, reminding him of a photograph he had seen of a man lynched by a mob of brownshirts in Germany, strung up from a lamppost, still wearing his greatcoat; and another more recent image, that of an Iranian hanging from the jib of a builder's crane, his head angled towards his chest.

He had torn this picture from a newspaper and kept it in his copy of Hannah Arendt's book on Eichmann, where it seemed to belong. He had named the man Derek, after Derrick the Tyburn hangman, whose name had first been applied to his trusty gibbet and then, from its similarity, to the contrivance used by the mullahs to carry out the same work, the innocent crane. Derek the Persian, dangling from his derrick, with the people of Tehran still going about their business in the street below. *The banality of evil* was Arendt's phrase. It haunted him. He muttered it like a mantra when liars or their spokesmen appeared on television, to deny or justify their actions. The week before, when Goodman had kept him waiting while he sat behind his desk, pretending to sign some urgent documents, clearing his throat as he did so, he had almost blurted out Arendt's words, as an accusation, but had stopped himself, not wanting to break cover, to be thought deranged.

His mind elsewhere, Kernan took a penknife from his pocket without being aware that he had done so; as he was cutting down the five moles, he came back to earth when the knife-point pricked his finger, drawing blood. Still in a daze, he looked down; his foot was pushing the little bodies of the moles into a rabbit-hole at the foot of a nearby tree, using his shoe to seal the entrance with earth. Then he freed the crow from the wire, intending to carry it home, to bury it in his garden.

But dropped it, startled, when a shot rang out. Something hot sped through his hair, causing him to fall backwards. His head hit a tree trunk, and he passed out.

The next thing he knew, he was lying on a stretcher by the

road. An ambulance was skewed across the grass verge, its doors flung open, and someone else was being lifted inside. He recognised the face of Morton Maw, towering over him.

– Are you all right, Kernan? he was saying. They're going to take you to hospital. Are you hurt?

– The back of my head hurts, he said.

– That was the tree, said Maw. You fell back and hit it. What were you doing up there with that crow anyway? You were all muddy.

– What happened? asked Kernan.

– I'm afraid I was shooting rabbits, said the councillor. I saw a movement up by the woods, thought it was a hare, and shot at it. Missed you, but I hit that other fellow, the old tramp.

– Who?

– Herne, said someone.

– Oh God, said Kernan.

– But he's all right, Maw added quickly. I may have shot at a pigeon to kill a crow, but he's not dead. I got him in the arm, the elbow.

– He needs that arm, said Kernan. And felt suddenly sick.

Goosey, goosey gander,
Whither shall I wander?
Upstairs and downstairs
And in my lady's chamber.

BOOK II

IMBOLC

FEBRUARY – APRIL

The law doth punish man or woman
That steals the goose from off the common,
But lets the greater felon loose
That steals the common from the goose.

CHAPTER FIVE

All Our Swans Are Geese

IMBOLC/CANDLEMAS: JANUARY 31ST–FEBRUARY 2ND

If a candle gutters as it burns, so that the grease collects unevenly, and gradually lengthens into a "winding sheet", this is an omen of death for the person sitting opposite. If it burns with a dim blue flame, a spirit is passing, and this too is a death omen. A bright spark in the wick indicates the coming of strangers.

Quail as well as pheasants had somehow survived the guns of autumn. Now they were scurrying along the edge of Oakwood Copse, making Kernan drive more warily down the long track from the farm, his foot hovering over the brake in case one of the foolish birds should suddenly throw itself under the wheels. The early lambs too were out in the field, scampering around their mothers, looking for mischief as well as milk, but the first one he saw was looking away from him, which did not bode well, especially after the shock of seeing only one magpie that morning in the garden instead of the usual pair.

There was another rabbit on the road outside the cottage. Run over the day before, it was already flat as a flounder.

He had to stop in the lane, waiting for a ewe with two thirsty lambs attached to move out of his path. She stood her ground, not wishing to disrupt their meal. Kernan was in no hurry. He sat watching the spectacle, going over the conversation he had just had with Rachel Brock.

He had wanted to speak to her before, but she had been too distressed. Diana had been to see her after the funeral, and Mrs Brock told her she blamed Kernan for her husband's death, which had greatly inflamed Diana's antipathy towards him. Since the meeting with Herne, when he had learned about the phone call, he had needed to speak to her, and finding an old photograph of Brock's grandfather in a book of Wilfred Owen's poems, had taken this as a sign that he should call on her at Oakwood.

– His family never lived it down, Rachel Brock had said, her hand trembling slightly as she tried to steady her cup of tea, when Kernan handed her the photograph.

– I told them more than once, Jack Brock was innocent.

– I know. Gran told me Mike's Dad wanted to believe you, so did Mike, but the village always said otherwise.

– The village wasn't there. The witnesses were dead, they didn't come back either.

– They even left his name off the war memorial. Mike's Dad never forgave them for that. And he could never stand the shame of it, his father being a...being a coward.

– Jack wasn't a coward. He was a good lad, like Mike was.

– Yes. But Mike was affected by what his Dad did too. Going into the barn and seeing him hanging there. He was only ten. His Mum told me he was never the same after that. He went all quiet. He used to be such a lively little boy, she said. I tried to help him, you know, but he'd never talk about it.

– These things often take years to work their way out, said Kernan. Then he asked her about the phone call, having regained her confidence.

– Mike couldn't understand it. The call was from Bernie. It was Bernard Tench who rang him. Mike's face was white when he put the phone down. He said Bernie hadn't been murdered, it was someone else. He'd been away, and had come home to find the police everywhere, and his family in tears because they thought he'd been killed. But it was someone else who'd been killed, not Bernie. And Bernie was very upset that the police had been thinking Mike had murdered him, so he said Mike should come up to the farm and they'd have a drink.

– Mike was sure it was Bernard Tench? asked Kernan.

– Bernie was his best mate. The two of them used to go off fishing together in Ireland. Mike said Bernie had been to see his father in Kent, and he'd given him some really special salmon flies, a Stoat's Tail and a Silver Doctor. Mike was very eager to see them.

– He didn't think of ringing the police first, to check it out?

– After what they'd been putting him through? You were part of all that, Mr Kernan, you should know.

– I only took his statement. I wasn't part of what followed.

– Anyway, why should he ring them? It was Bernie's voice on the phone.

– Have you told anyone else about this?

– Just John and the family. John's not much help. He's got worse since his father died, just hangs around watching telly all day long. He's not interested in anything.

– And the family?

– They think it's the strain. They don't believe me. I don't know what to think. It was Hallowe'en you know. I know that had something to do with it. I'm frightened, Mr Kernan.

– And it wasn't someone imitating Bernard Tench?

– Imitate Bernie? I suppose that's possible, but his voice was different from anyone else's, it had that huskiness he said was from when he worked in the lab, some chemical had affected his throat. I don't think even those impressionists on the telly could do Bernie, not unless they knew him really well.

– And they'd have to know about Silver Doctors as well, to convince Mike, said Kernan, who realised that Michael Brock had desperately wanted to believe his friend Bernard Tench was still alive. Tench's death must have revived his guilt about his father's suicide. And someone had been able to feed off that guilt, someone who was able to imitate Tench's particular way of speaking, as well as his accent, and to do that and convince his best friend, that person's voice would almost have to take over and become Tench's voice. If there were any uncertainties in that pretence – and he now doubted there would be any – the telephone would have masked them.

Kernan stood up, touching her on the shoulder, trying to reassure her.

– If anyone asks, he said, I came here to drop off the photograph. We talked about the farm, how you were coping now, who was helping with the lambing. The case is meant to be closed. If anyone discovered I was still looking into it, I'd get into trouble, and it would be harder then for me to do anything to help you. But I will try to help you.

The picture showed a boy in uniform, posed by the photographer beside a small vase of cornflowers, his cap with its shiny otter badge resting on the table as if asleep. It had left a rectangular tea-coloured stain on the page, where the poem read:

> What passing-bells for these who die as cattle?
>   Only the monstrous anger of the guns.
>   Only the stuttering rifles' rapid rattle
> Can patter out their hasty orisons.

Nicholas Goodman's bullet-head was flushed dark red like a beetroot. His eyebrows knitted themselves together like head-butting caterpillars. His nostrils flared; his hooves stamped. He was angry, and enjoying himself immensely at Diana Hunter's expense.

– The whole police station could have gone up in flames you know. And for why? Because DC Hunter dismantled the smoke detector in her office.

– I didn't know Hodge would go into my room to smoke when I was out, and set fire to my wastepaper bin.

– He didn't set fire to it, said Goodman. I've accepted his explanation. It was a lapse on his part, and he's assured me it won't happen again. It's *your* behaviour which concerns me. What the hell did you think you were doing? And what was with that envelope, TO WHOM IT MAY CONCERN? Can you tell me that?

– It was a sort of joke, she said, attempting a cover-up as thin as Goodman's pretext for humiliating her. But she had to play along with him. She couldn't tell him why she'd done it. The object could have been a surveillance device, or it might not have been. Kernan hadn't been there to give her his opinion, and in the heat of the moment, she'd just yanked it out and smashed the thing to bits. Kernan had put the idea into her head: he was to blame for that. And she'd believed him, but she wasn't going to tell Goodman that.

– *A joke?* cried Goodman. *A joke?* You think a fire's a joke? Oh yes, let's have a fire. I love fires. I love to see people burning, people going up in flames, choking on the smoke, dying before anyone can rescue them. Let's burn lots of people in a fire, what a great idea.

– I'm sorry, said Diana. She looked at Goodman ranting, or pretending to rant. His red face, his black eyes, dark as a wolf's mouth. That vicious sarcasm. Or was it sarcasm? He almost seemed to be relishing the picture he was painting of the place going up in flames. He was enjoying himself.

He did not calm down, but subsided, his anger spent; and with a wide, satisfied smile, let her go with a wordless gesture of dismissal. Withdrawing like a beaten animal, she felt limp, as if she'd been discarded as of no further use, a lover rejected, licking her wounds.

When Kernan arrived, he tried to hint at the reason for his late arrival, but she only said:

– Goodman called me in. About the smoke-detector.

– You told him you didn't want anyone bugging you? asked Kernan, momentarily amused, before the storm broke, and Diana started screaming abuse at him.

Herne lay propped up in bed, ashen-faced. The weeks spent in the artificial light and air of the hospital were taking their toll of him, draining the earthy colours from his face, leeching his strength. He was a shadow of his former self. Kernan felt distraught, seeing him like this.

– How's the arm? he asked.

– Not good, said Herne. They're now saying I may lose it.

– Well it was never yours in the first place, said Kernan, guying him, trying to bring a smile to his lips. Herne's face did not react, but he said:

– I know, but I've grown rather attached to it.

– Has no one noticed that your hands don't match?

– They look but do not see, said Herne. What they do not expect to see they do not search for. They look only at the bad arm, ignoring the good one. Ever seeing but never perceiving. Just the symptom, not the whole body.

– How are the old wounds? Have they been playing up?

– They wax and wane, and weep the most at the full moon, so today they're bad, but here they're worse of course because they won't give me rosemary or yarrow leaves, just their useless dressings. The doctor was surprised no one had ever tried to remove the shrapnel, but I don't think I'd want that now. I've got used to it. Also, my body's a bit of a hotchpotch, so the monthly seepings are like a clock helping me hold everything together. Mind you, this past Martinmas they were very heavy, I've never known them to weep so much.

– Did they show you the bullet? asked Kernan, changing the subject. I'd like to see it, if that's possible.

– Is that a police question?

– No. They're still saying it was an accident of course. But I'd like to know more.

– There was nothing special about the bullet, if that's what you're thinking. It wasn't silver. It shattered the joint because I was so small when Maw shot me. Remember, I was shadowing you as a hare. I knew you were in danger. My presence distracted him, causing him to miss.

– He didn't miss *you*, said Kernan. And I miss you now, around the place. I have to spend more time out in the field, doing your work, but I'm exposed in my other world without you behind me. You're fading here, Herne, we have to do something. I feel as though my powers are returning, but I need you there to keep me balanced. I must be able to help you.

– You must gather some comfrey for me, said Herne. Cut off and crush the roots, and make half into a syrup, leaving the rest for my arm. Comfrey is a herb of Saturn. The syrup will act upon my inward griefs and hurts. The other will assist the healing of my bones. You know, it's so strong a means of consolidation that if you boil pieces of severed flesh in a pot with comfrey, it will make them whole again. That's how it will help me.

– But where will I find comfrey at this time of year?

– Go to the spring below Cowbound Lane. You'll find some by the ditch there. And you will have to apply it for me. The second time you come, we will need briony, which is very powerful. It is too early for tetter berries, but we can use the root, as with the comfrey. The roots are deep, so take a trowel. There is some near you, under the hedges on the east side of Hoggett's Field.

– And the third time? asked Kernan.

– Eringo, the Sea Holly. You will have to go to Ottermouth for that. Go to the dunes, where the hillocks are clumped with marram grass, where they say the Creek Women used to live in their huts. Again, we will need the roots.

– Eringo for the King's Evil?

– Yes, but you only need to bruise it for that. After you've crushed the roots, boil them in hog's grease, or salted lard, and that concoction will hold long enough to heal my bones as well as renew the flesh where it was consumed. But only you can heal me, with your powers. How are they now?

– The fath-fith is returning, but I can't control it yet. When I woke yesterday morning, I found I had turned into a giant cockroach. I couldn't get off my back. My six legs were waving about in the air, I couldn't work out how to co-ordinate them. It was my Paranoia again.

– You have to learn to control it. I know it's hard when you know someone's trying to kill you. What happened?

– I wrestled with the Paranoia, and eventually fought it off. Later I locked it in a cell at the police station.

– Did anyone see you bring it in?

– Yes, but they weren't bothered, they all bring their Paranoias to work.

– Won't it come after you there?

– I should be safe while it's in the cells. Plenty of people to latch onto, not just prisoners but the guard too.

His old friend managed a small whinny of laughter. Kernan was heartened by this.

– What about Diana? asked Herne. Has she noticed any changes in you?

– I'm sure she knows something's happening, said Kernan.

I will have to talk to her, but I'll need to break it to her slowly.

– The Hunters have their gifts too. How much is she aware of that? Herne asked, with sudden eagerness.

Kernan could see Herne's interest starting to revive; his dark green eyes were brighter now, even showing the occasional flash like a spark of garnet.

– She denies that whole side of herself, he replied. But there's something breaking through, even if she doesn't know it yet.

– Some of your magic may be rubbing off on her, releasing her own powers.

– That's what I'm afraid of. She could be quite destructive if she doesn't know how to handle them.

Here Herne stopped him, looking up to indicate the presence of another visitor. There was no one there, but when Kernan rose to his feet and looked down the aisle, he saw the top of a head through the window of the door to the corridor, and then the diminutive figure of the boy Flea entering the ward.

– You must tell Flea about Werburga, said Herne. I'm beginning to forget things, but anything I tell Flea, he remembers. He's losing his bad streak now he's become disenchanted with O'Scrapie. Muffy has taken him under her wing, and is teaching him everything she knows, her female wisdom. He's learning from both of us.

The boy joined them, his eyes darting from Herne to Kernan and back again, alert as a hare.

– Herne tells me you want to know about Werburga, said Kernan.

– Yes, said Flea, she has the day after tomorrow, and the goose is her bird.

– That's right, said Kernan, though the Church denies it. They don't like animal miracles. She was the daughter of Ermengild, who married King Wulfhere of Mercia, the son of Penda, and converted him. Werburga was an abbess at Weedon when the lands there were plagued by insatiable geese, who ate everything in the fields and orchards. When the people appealed to Werburga for help, she ordered her men to round up the whole gaggle and bring them before her. Not only did the geese apologise to her, they also promised not to eat the people's food, so she freed them on that oath.

– Did these geese talk to her then? asked Flea.

– They didn't communicate with words of course, said Kernan, but she listened to them, and they to her, and they understood each other. But the next day a milk-white gander was back, honking so angrily she could hardly work out what was wrong. It seemed that one of the geese had gone missing, and there were goose bones in a scrap pail in the abbey kitchen.

– Someone's goose was cooked then, said Flea.

– The goose's goose, said Kernan. It was no one else's. But the monk in charge admitted stealing and cooking it, and others said they'd eaten it. So in the presence of the milk-white gander, Werburga ordered that the bones be brought to her. And the gooseflesh instantly returned to clothe the bones, along with the bird's feathers. Then finally she called upon its life spirit. The goose revived, and went off with the gander, and after that the geese stayed away from the fields, no one tried to eat them, and many people were converted to the faith. He that eats their lord's goose will be choked with the feathers.

– That's a fine story, said Flea. Why doesn't the Church like it?

– It doesn't suit them, said Kernan. They want Werburga to be a simple saint, so they say the story was stolen from the life of a Flemish saint called Amelburga, and since no one knows much about her, they can disown the miracle.

– And it couldn't have been Amelburga anyway, Herne added. It's an English story.

– And how do we celebrate St Werburga's Day? asked Flea.

– Why, with a goose feast of course, said Kernan, smiling to humour him.

As he took his leave, Herne reminded him:

– Bring the comfrey on St Werburga's Day, that will be helpful. Then the briony on St Teilo's Day: he is a healing saint, even if he needs three skulls. And the sea holly on Ash Wednesday: I will be shriven by then.

Oliver de Foie studied the note from the Chief Constable, which was headed STRICTLY CONFIDENTIAL. He picked up the empty bottle of Milk of Magnesia, and after swilling a quantity of saliva in his mouth, spat as much fluid as he could produce into the neck of the blue bottle, replaced the cap and shook it vigorously; then sucked the last drops of milky liquid from the bottle before tossing it in the wastepaper basket where it clinked against others already deposited there.

He had not given Maurice Saveloy a full account of the risks posed by the TME-infected mink, since he did not wish to cause alarm or give information which might reach the press and be disadvantageous to Eurochimique's share prices. But he had credited the senior policeman with a degree of intelligence.

Apparently, Saveloy had asked a friend to bring a pack of mink hounds to Loamfield, where they would scour the River Otter, allegedly in response to complaints from landowners about mink causing trouble along the riverbanks. Morton Maw had supplied a pretext for this in a letter published in the *Loamshire Chronicle* in which he had put the blame 'fairly and squarely' on the shoulders of the mink farmers. The paper had also cited reports from Loamfield residents about goldfish being taken from garden ponds.

He could not tell Saveloy about the self-evident risks posed to the dogs from a transmissible spongiform encephalopathy, for it was possible that nothing might happen, that the mink hounds would be unaffected by the TSE, in which case a warning would be counter-productive. But was the man stupid? Surely he realised a risk of that kind must exist?

And what would then happen if one of the dogs were to bite a man? Oliver de Foie would not be responsible for the consequences. It was for the Chief Constable to assess such risks.

The clock behind the main desk in Otteridge police station showed 5.55pm. The place was entering that five-minute period of non-time in which nothing happens. Papers were shuffled, telephones ignored, watches consulted at 30-second intervals. Shopping-lists were surreptitiously torn from notebooks; stomachs rumbled, anticipating food; policemen salivated, imagining themselves already at the bar of the Pig and Whistle. All looked anxiously at the door, awaiting the arrival of the night shift, who were never early. This was the time when sadists called subordinates to their offices for *a short chat before you go home*.

Apart from his lunchtime visit to the hospital, Kernan had been in his room all day, thinking out a plan of action, while pretending to work on a case he had solved two days previously. There were many such cases for him, crimes he understood totally in five minutes; he would then spend several days working his way backwards from the truth to the proof, in order not only to secure a conviction but – more importantly for him – to disguise his methods of deduction.

He had reached a decisive stage in his consideration of the Tench case, and of matters related and events now unstoppable. Taking into account also that people were evidently trying to kill him, he knew he had no alternative but to take Diana into his confidence, now that Herne had been injured. He couldn't do it all on his own, and if he were murdered like Tench and Brock, he'd want someone else to carry on, to track down their killers. Yet this was also dangerous, to Diana as well as to him.

Since All Saints' Day, and then his outing to Loamsley Moor, he had begun to feel more confident of his skills, some of which he knew he had neglected, while there were others he had never used, out of fear or apprehension. Yet now he would have to take risks if he was to find the killer and stop whatever plot Goodman was involved in. The end must justify the means.

He had resisted giving Diana any sense of his true capabilities, but now he needed to reveal something of these to her. He had not only to persuade her but also to regain her trust, particularly after the business of the smoke-detector, and the fact that – judging from the description she'd given him – the device she had destroyed had actually been a smoke-detector. When he'd seen her at lunchtime, he'd heard the real surveillance bug, whistling away (so it seemed to him) inside the plug of her anglepoise lamp, but had decided against appraising her of this.

It was 5.59pm. He pressed the buzzer on the intercom.

– Diana? he said.

– *Yes?* her voice answered, her annoyance only thinly veiled.

– Could you come through please for a moment?

– What is it?

– *Just a short discussion, before you go home, tra-la.* I'd just like to run through a couple of things which have been worrying me.

– What things?

– Come through and find out, he said, and flicked off the switch. And sat back, grinning like the Cheshire Cat, eager now to impress her. It would have to be something foolproof, something she couldn't turn against him like the surveillance devices.

– What is it? Diana said, impatiently. It's six o'clock, I'm sure you're doing this deliberately.

– That's right. I am, said Kernan, smiling. But also trembling, apprehensive of the dangers he was now courting.

– I'd like to show you something which may have a bearing on certain matters we are considering. After that business of the bug...

– If it's more games, I'm not interested.

– Not games. Scientific proof, incontrovertible evidence. We need to join forces, to work together.

– Forces? Us together?

– I'm going to be totally indiscreet. I tried to do this before Christmas, but you resisted.

– Too right I did.

– An example of my working methods, to convince you. No one else has seen me do this before. I don't like party tricks, but you obviously need some kind of demonstration...

– What do you mean, demonstration? she asked, starting to look frightened.

– Go out into the main office, said Kernan. I'll stay here with the door shut. Take any case file, one that includes fingerprints. Copy the prints, cut them out and bring them here. Don't let me see the file, or give me any hint of where it's from.

Diana returned two minutes later, dropping a piece of paper on Kernan's desk. Watching him.

– Well? she asked, seeing him hold the photocopy up to the light. He put it down, and pointed at a thumbprint.

– You could have made it more difficult, he said. You picked an easy one. See that small mark on the left thumbprint?

– Yes? she said, her doubt returning, thinking this was another game of Kernan's after all. But then he delivered his *coup de grâce*, not trying hard to stifle his evident pleasure:

– Glass broken in the kitchen door. 56 Grosvenor Road, Newlands. Tenth of June 1994. The prints belong to Matthew Hardacre. Twelve months for breaking and entering, Otteridge Magistrates Court, ninth of September 1994. *Tra-la.*

– Jesus Christ, Diana gasped. She hadn't expected this, but she was ready for him, for she hadn't just copied one set of prints as he'd asked. Entering into his show-off mood, she dropped another sheet in front of him. He picked it up, looked at it closely, and announced:

– John Openshaw, born 22nd September 1956…

– Ten points, ten points, she cried. And now watching him close as a hawk, dropped a third sheet in front of him.

Kernan did not need to pick it up. His eyes showed immediate recognition.

– You should know I can't read those.

– Why not? What about your powers…

– Those prints were found at Hogsback Hill Farm. They are the other set of prints, not Brock's. I do not recognise them, and as you're fully aware, they aren't held in police files anywhere. They aren't from this area.

– I'm still impressed. Why didn't you tell me all this before? And why have you kept this secret from everyone else? You could be the force's secret weapon…

– That's what I'm afraid of. *Tace* is Latin for candle, and be quiet about it. I've never been able to trust anyone else before, with this knowledge. A candle that lights others may consume itself.

– And that's how you solve all those cases…

– It's not just fingerprints and phone-bugs. There's much more than that.

– I was afraid there might be. You don't have x-ray vision, do you, Batman?

– Come on, that's hardly scientific, is it?

– What is scientific? I'm beginning to doubt a lot of things already. I must know more, you know me, nosier than a cat…

– One thing at a time. It wouldn't do to overwhelm you. Also, I'm not used to revealing anything about myself. *To me rite fol-lol-liddle-lol-le-day.*

– So, where do we go from here?

– I have to pay a few calls on certain associates. I'd like you to see if you can track down some information, *tra-la.*

– What kind of information?

– About Tench and Brock. But you won't be able to use their files. The case is not only closed, their files have been removed from the office.

– And the computer?

– *Access denied for reasons of security.* No way there. Do you know anyone in the RUC?

– There was an Irish girl at Hendon with me, Brigid. She went back there. What do you need to know?

– Start with convictions for salmon poaching in Northern Ireland, probably Co. Fermanagh, between 1992 and 1995. Bernard Tench or Michael Brock. And don't ring her from here.

Kernan dreamed. It was Candlemas, but when was it Candlemas? He saw an altar, a Vickers gun chest covered with a white cloth, two candles standing in tobacco tins, men in khaki kneeling on sandbags. Or was that Easter? Easter to come or Easter past?

Kernan dreamed. A service at St George's, the candles blessed to celebrate the epiphany of the sacred light. When was this? When or where was he now? Leading the singing, the wily Reverend Devlin. The priest had a fox's head.

Kernan dreamed. The soldiers were led by a Roman legionary, they were Herod's conscripts, but he didn't think they'd been recognised, they were looking for babies, for first-born sons. He walked beside the donkey, holding the rein, steadying the beast as the woman held the child inside her cloak, whispering *tace, tace*. Just as the soldiers were almost level with them, a girl ran from a house, a crown of candles on her head, dancing ecstatically. The soldiers stopped to watch her. The donkey plodded purposefully forward, they turned a corner and slipped into the shadows behind a house, waiting there until the soldiers had passed. His mother took him out from her cloak then.

Kernan dreamed. The shepherd was counting as the lamb emerged, head and front feet first: *yan tan tethera, pethera pimp, sethera, lethera, hovera, covera, dik.* As the lamb kicked and coughed, he quickly stripped away its caul as the ewe turned to lick it. Still kicking, he felt himself lifted high up in someone's arms; then sudden warmth as the woman passed him across a fire, three times, a circling deasil movement, before he was plunged into water, warm as the womb. A metal disc pressed into his fur, his wool, his skin, as he lay there. He knew it was a gold sovereign, but that knowledge was without any language to express it.

Kernan dreamed. A young woman dandled him on her lap, singing: *Jack be nimble, Jack be quick, Jack jump over the candlestick.* She's singing because soldiers are coming, he thought. *Here comes a candle to light you to bed. Here comes a chopper to chop off your head.* An older voice chided her: *Must you sing him such songs of Rawhead and Bloody-bones, Brigid? You'll put ideas into the poor child's head.*

Kernan dreamed of warm sunlight filtering through the ash tree in the garden. At Candlemas, if *a hedgehog casts a shadow at noon, winter will return.* It was Groundhog Day, the woodchuck giving its yea or nay to the end of winter. *Candlemas Day, put beans in the clay, put candles and candlesticks all away.* There were blue crocuses in the grass, a month early, an early spring, but their heads had spiky petals, more ultramarine than blue, blue as lapis lazuli. They were cornflowers, but cornflowers flowered in June, or used to, for there were no cornflowers now, they were all dead, dead as winter. Extinct.

Kernan dreamed he had woken with an unfinished song in his head, *he went to court his dear.* But if he was not awake, where was he? When was he now? The moon was a bitten host, two days waxing since the first quarter crescent. The song went round in circles in the dream, like a round. He held a candle, searching, burning one candle to find another. *The moon was shining brightly, the stars were twinkling clear. When he went to his love's window to ease her of her pain.* The moon was Phoebe singing: *Take me in your arms, my love, and blow the candle out.* He wrote his love a letter, he had to go away. The bright moon was a white coin, two days waning since the silver salver. Why had he not taken the full moon on his tongue? The moon was Diana, fearful of her father: *I wouldn't forfeit five guineas now that they should find me out.* Diana singing, *Take me in your arms, my love, and blow the candle out.* And in the dream, Kernan sang.

> O when your baby it is born you may dandle it on your knee
> And if it be a baby boy then name it after me
> For when nine months are over my apprenticeship is out
> I'll return and do my duty and blow the candle out.

Kernan dreamed of Phoebe left behind, taking tea on the terrace at the Rectory with Captain Nicholas, who lied to her about him. He would not, could not return to her, to the child he didn't know about, but he would return to free the sword from the stone, to free the land from the iron grip of his adversary. The coming of Kernan, to the child's child, that was the meaning of the dream, told to him within the dream, how he would be her child too, the son of himself, *when he returned to blow the candle out.*

Kernan did not know when he was dreaming; or if he had only dreamed that he had dreamed, or was still dreaming that he dreamed.

– Do you have another towel? It was Diana's voice, from his bathroom.

Kernan swore at the candle, which he was trying to stop from guttering, but in his nervous state he only made it worse. His clumsy attempts to redirect the wax with a matchstick were ineffective, and he could only watch as a dreaded winding-sheet of melted wax started to form, opposite his chair. He knew he could not change places because the other was where Diana would be sitting. She had been out policing the Loamshire Hunt, and a confrontation with saboteurs had left her splattered with mud. Being near Loamfield, she had stopped off at Kernan's, and he had offered to feed her.

Now he could hear the unfamiliar sound of someone else using his bath, the shifting round of a body in the water, with much splashing, punctuated by shrieks of what he took to be pleasure. He eyed the shape of her muddy coat, slung across the back of a chair, and thought of other clothes discarded on his bathroom floor; that pencil-grey skirt, her pale-blue denim shirt with the buttoned breast-pockets, under which...

– Did you hear? Have you a towel?

Her voice again. The matchstick broke, causing his finger to dive into molten wax. He yelped. The flame of the candle wavered, and a spark started to burn bright in the wick, a tiny yellow jewel.

– Coming, he called. And fetching a towel, replayed in his mind his shameful thought of a moment ago...which he must not encourage, even if instinct said otherwise. He must put all such thoughts from his mind, they were an abomination.

– Here you are, he said, gingerly pushing the door very slightly open, showing by his firm but gentle tone he intended to come no further.

And then, as he was passing the towel through the door, only his hand entering the room where she stood naked, his eyes averted back to the supper table, he saw the candle gutter and go out, as a window was flung open, and a breeze entered the cottage, pushing open the door in front of him.

Diana shrieked as he stood facing her, his mouth open, gazing at her nakedness, her skin glistening with water, her body shining in the aureate light of the bathroom lamp. He only glimpsed her for a moment, but devoured a sight which seemed to him an epiphany of her inner beauty, her body and spirit exposed as one, all she had hidden from the world displayed in this glorious vision of her self and her womanhood. She stood there like a goddess, unbelievably beautiful, yet also, he realised – as their eyes met – unable to speak in that instant, such was the depth of her anger at his violation of her privacy.

He did not even try to start mumbling excuses or apologies, knowing this vision was what he had wanted all along, even while he was denying it. Being forbidden – by himself as well as by her – only made it more exciting to him; even though it would cost him dearly, it was a sight worth any price, this glimpse of the divine in her. In that moment, he understood how those Egyptian men had been willing to die as the cost of one night spent in Cleopatra's bed, the queen both lover and priestess fucking them to exquisite death.

Diana's hands now swept downwards into the bath, and drew a chute of thyme-scented water upwards into his face. What she was saying as she slammed the door shut he did not comprehend. Stepping backwards, he was momentarily blinded by the loss of his sublime vision of her; and staggering under the weight of the change from divine light to doomed blackness, Kernan fell against a table, hitting his head hard on the wood.

He felt his brow where two bumps had formed, on his skull it seemed, and by the time he stood up, he knew they had turned into two protuberant bones, like horns, and that his neck was lengthening, his ears moving up and out into points. His clothes ripped themselves from his body as he started changing shape, growing barrel-chested, upwards and outwards, his skin disappearing under brown hair, his hands and feet hardening into hooves.

Falling onto all fours, he fled to the back door, only just fitting through the space, his body now enlarged to twice its previous size. Diana heard a commotion, but shut it out, as Kernan was struggling through the door, not wanting her to see him, backing himself out, his now resplendent antlers clattering on the door lintel as he ducked his head to complete his exit.

Now a full-sized stag, Kernan tried to control himself, but Diana's rejection of him had set panic fear in his heart, an animal's fear which was not his own. He cared more now about what she would say to him than about his own predicament. He was frightened too at this awakening of her powers, which had wrought such a change in him.

Then he heard barking, and turned to see his own dog Bella looking quizzically towards him; behind her the hounds of the

Loamshire Hunt pouring down the lane like a swarm of black devils. Even though it was now dusk, he could see all their murderous faces from twenty yards away, the evil glare in all their eyes. He turned and ran, leaping to clear the hedge into Hoggett's Field, amazed at the strength of his great deer's body, marvelling at his speed.

He was easily outstripping the dogs as he raced up the hill towards Loamsley Moor, where the full moon now shone like a huge silver salver above the skyline. But entering a clump of trees, he failed to take account of his height, and crashed to the ground when his antlers hit an overhanging branch. The dogs were on him in an instant, holding him down, sinking their teeth into his body, fastening their jaws in so many places till there was nowhere left for tearing.

– Kill him, kill him! cried the familiar silky voice of Mrs Candida Sirloin. Go on my dogs! she yelled. Go to it!

He thought he heard Diana too, shouting his name from the cottage below, and tried to call back, but the note which emerged from the depths of his body was not human speech, it was more like the sounding of a great horn. And hearing this, the dogs immediately fell from his body, and backed away, whimpering. He managed to raise himself up, despite the pain from all his wounds, and stood then facing the dogs, as their leader came forward, its muzzle lowered, sinking to the ground in front of him, submissive and whining.

Looking behind the pack, he saw the huntsmen had gathered by the trees to watch this confrontation. The dogs all came forward then, each submitting in turn, with downcast eyes and indrawn tails. He acknowledged each submission, all the while conscious that the riders were growing restless; there were angry shouts from some, and he saw the red-jacketed Candida move her hand first to her side, then upwards, levelling a black shape he knew to be a gun. Pointing it directly at his head, a target so large she could not miss, even in that crepuscular light.

Imploring help from all around him, deliverance came in the form of an owl, dropping vertically from the trees above. Taking the huntswoman by surprise, it flapped its great wings across her face, causing her to fall from her horse. As the gun flew from her hand, the owl swept towards the prostrate pack of dogs, who panicked, fleeing in all directions, causing the horses also to rear up and bolt. Some of the huntsmen were unsaddled, while others clung desperately to the sides of their mounts as they went flying down the hill.

Seizing his chance, Kernan leapt sideways through some bushes, pursued by the vengeful figure of the angry Candida, who found herself confronting not the strange lordly stag to whom her cowardly dogs had done obeisance but a naked man with blackened face, his body covered in mud and blood, his mad eyes gleaming in the moonlight beneath a thicket of birdnest hair.

The Wild Man of the Woods.

When they arrived at the Royal Loamshire Infirmary, Diana hoisted Kernan from her car, putting his arm around her shoulder, and supported him as he limped through a door called CASUALTY. In his confused state, Kernan read this as CAUSALITY. It seemed appropriate.

The duty doctor helped Diana manoeuvre him into a consulting room, where a nurse assisted the process of lifting him onto a couch.

– Are you a relative? the nurse asked.

Diana looked at Kernan, who gestured that he wanted her to stay with him.

– Yes, she said, I'm his daughter.

– Well, Inspector Kernan, said the doctor, it looks like you've been in the wars. What happened?

– I was attacked by dogs.

– He says they thought he was a deer, said Diana, enjoying the moment.

– Not an easy mistake to make, said the doctor, waiting as Diana assisted the nurse in removing most of Kernan's clothes.

My ravaged body, thought Kernan, is less than divine now. Unlike hers.

– These dogs weren't too bright. It was the Loamshire Hunt,

said Kernan, wincing as his shirt clung to a makeshift dressing.

– They must take after their masters then, said the doctor, who had spent some hours treating victims of disagreements between hunt followers and saboteurs. Now, you're going to need quite a few stitches, and a couple of injections. These wounds will need to be cleaned first.

The doctor followed the nurse into an ante-room. Kernan looked up at Diana, and managed a faint smile. She touched his hand.

– It can only get better, she said.

– I don't think so. This is just the beginning.

They waited, uncertain of what to say in this public room. So she asked, in a low voice:

– What was that stuff you put in my bath? Maybe it was that which gave me the power to change you into a stag? Not that I believe that tale for one minute. I can't see how I could change anyone. If you've started turning into animals, you've only yourself to blame.

– I am both man and beast, said Kernan sheepishly.

– Exactly. But I suppose I must try to forget that business, and my anger, given the state you've ended up in now. But just don't try anything like that again.

– Nor you. I don't fancy ending up on Nick Goodman's dinner table.

– You might do us all a favour, Diana said. If he ate you, your flesh would be poison to him.

– Kill two pigs with one stag, he joked.

– So what was in that bath then, apart from the thyme?

– Ah the bath, said Kernan nervously. Well, there was some rosemary. You steep those two first in boiling water, then strain. Add some powdered orris root, using a sieve, together with some lovage. Stir the mixture, and add to the bath water.

– You did all that, just for a bath? What's it meant to do? Is it a muscle relaxant like clary sage, to soothe the aches and pains?

– Well, not exactly...

– Come on, let's have it. I think I have my suspicions.

– It is meant to invigorate, yes, said Kernan.

– And?

– It is also said to make a woman desirable, irresistible and to ensure that the course of love runs smoothly, in the right direction.

– Well that last part didn't work, did it, moosehead?

– You were desirable...

– But it also means you planned the whole thing.

– The bath potion was a little aberration, but I knew you'd like it. What happened later was not expected, not something I planned. I told you, the window blew open...

– I don't know why I should believe that. And I'm not sure you do either, even though you think you do.

– It also demonstrated that you have powers of your own.

– The power to excite some lecherous middle-aged policeman who's old enough to be my father. I don't want that kind of power, thank you very much.

– You must believe in your own power, said Kernan. It will return to you again, I know it will in this Tench business. You must know how to handle it.

– You're talking cod's-wallop again.

Who caught his blood?
I, said the Fish,
With my little dish,
I caught his blood.

CHAPTER SIX

A Pretty Kettle of Fish

ASH WEDNESDAY

The tench, or doctor-fish, heals other fish with the oils from its skin, and can be used to cure jaundice when slit in two and applied to the soles of a sufferer's feet. Eels can cure warts, sprains and drunkenness. As a remedy for whooping cough, catch a flat fish, such as a dab, and put it on the child's bare chest, keeping it there until the fish dies; or hold the head of a live trout between the patient's teeth, letting it breathe into the mouth of the afflicted child.

February was a time of endless cold. There had been a hint of spring in the air during the past week, but then a raw whining wind had returned.

– *Mackerel sky and mares' tails,* sang Muffy, shivering, *make lofty ships carry low sails. And as the light lengthens, so the cold strengthens.* But look, she said, pointing where the white tips of snowdrops were starting to break through, like fragile promises.

She sat huddled with Flea on a grassy bank beside the River Otter, pointing out and naming a handful of flowers.

– But there won't be many yet, said Flea. It's too cold.

– It's still the Wolf-Month, she said. The Storm-Days when winter hasn't yet released its grip on the land. Since there are so few flowers here, I'll name you the winds which usher in the spring.

– Do the winds have names too?

– Of course. Everything has its name, even if no one knows it. Its name contains its power. There's *Faoilleach*, a ravening wind which lasts for a month. That's been and gone.

– I remember that one, said Flea. It was very sharp all through January.

– Then there are usually nine days of *Gearrain*, a galloping wind. That has passed. Then a week of *Feadaig*, a sharp and piping wind.

– I remember that as well. Then we had that mild spell, but it didn't last long, said Flea.

– That was *Caillich,* a week of stillness. And for the last three days we've felt the soughing blast of *Sguabaig*, which ushers in the spring rain.

– It doesn't feel like spring here. It still feels wintry to me.

They looked down at the reamy lines along the earth of the riverbank.

– It's like the scum-ring round the bath, said Flea.

The froth spread like beer slops out into midstream, where they saw the small fat bodies of several chub bobbing like flotsam.

– This is where we lived, Muffy said. In this bit of Duckwidge Ditch. Our caravan used to be over there. And after Charlie died, that's where Yellowbeard's men left our things. There's nothing left now. I thought I might find some keepsakes, but they've been in with a JCB.

– He died too, didn't he? said Flea. I mean the council man. What was his real name?

– Sir Peter Prurigeaux, and I cursed him by that name, may you rot in Hell I said, but he rotted like a human compost heap once the gangrene took hold. He was a horrible mean man with a mangy tobacco-stained beard which made you itch just to look at it. You know *prurigo* is a blistering of the skin, but one of his warty ancestors tried to disguise their scabby nature by Frenchifying the name. Charlie did a job for him once: felled a whole stand of elms which had the Dutch disease, but could he get him to pay? He would not give his bone to the dog, Charlie said. Yellowbeard's purse was made of a toad's skin. Don't bother me here, he told poor Charlie when he stopped him in Otteridge to ask for his money.

– So did he pay up in the end?

– Charlie had to take the trailer round when the Fat Cat was away, took the logs and sold them. Old Sourpuss was hopping, but he'd have done the same, he'd buy a fox skin for threepence and sell the tail for a shilling. A thief passes for a gentleman when stealing has made him rich. That was how the Prurigeaux brood made their pile, and once they'd made it, old Yellowbeard was going to hang on to every last penny…

– Prurigeaux by name and Prurigo by nature, grinned Flea.

– And he'd not have liked you, Flea, Muffy laughed. Oh no, he'd flay a flea for the hide and tallow, he'd flay a louse and send the skin to market.

– He'd steal a goose and give the giblets in alms. One of my Dad's sayings, that is.

Muffy turned away, still gripped, Flea saw, by the spirit of this ravaged place which had been her home for most of her life, next to the beloved river she was staring at now.

– The water's horrible, he said.

– Full of evil, Muffy replied, turning her back on it now. I took a couple of jars to Mr Tench. He was going to test it, he said. But then he died too.

– He probably drank it, said Flea, poking at a creamy swirl with the toe of his boot.

– Don't touch it, said Muffy. You don't know what's in there. The Otter's stopped being a river. I don't know what it is now. It's neither fish, flesh, fowl nor good red herring, my mother would have said. You know, when she was alive, there were salmon here. She used to live further down, near the coast. She was a Creek Woman.

– What's one of those? Flea asked.

– She guarded the whole river. She wandered the banks, from source to mouth. She knew all the animals.

– Including the otters?

– Yes, there were otters here then, that's right. And they'd catch some of the salmon before they reached their pools, but that was fine, they were part of the life of the river, just as the fishermen had been, many years ago.

Flea tried to imagine the river with fresh water, like in an aquarium, where you could see the stones and weeds beneath the surface, and fish swimming along.

– My grandmother used to say, *if you kill a salmon, you must put its bones back into the sea*. That's because they used to think salmon were people who had put on salmon bodies.

– Well they must be pretty bright, said Flea. Finding their way back to the same river.

– When they die, said Muffy, their spirits can return to human shape, but they need their bones if they're going to come back. The Creek Women had lots of stories about the river and the salmon, and they celebrated different parts of the valley in different stories. When they wanted to remember one of these tales, they looked at the land about them, and the place told them its story. They heard it too in the song the river made in that place. And because the river didn't change, and the valley was always there, the stories were remembered from generation to generation.

– Do you know the stories? Can you tell me one?

– No, I can't. Because everything is different now. They were usually sung. I know only snatches of them. There was one about the river itself, the river's own song, which it made from the valley. The women learned it from the river: how they must protect the river and the valley for its own sake, not for what people wanted to do with it. The river didn't belong to them, it was only in their keeping. A lot of stories are like that: they're already there in the land, and we overhear them. But there's little music now. The salmon are all dead, the women have lost their power.

– And the bones are thrown away, said Flea. Or given to dogs if they're animal bones.

Shortly after Muffy had led Flea away from her former garden, a bevy of four-wheel-drive vehicles pulled up. The back of each was caged off to hold dogs, who were yapping excitedly. The men alighted, pulled down their tweed caps against the cold, and released the dogs, white handsome animals with broad grins like labradors, their tails curved upward like scythes.

The mink hounds milled around, sniffing the grass down over the riverbank, before setting off downstream, the men following behind. Maurice Saveloy did not accompany them, but stood by his Subaru, sipping steaming coffee from a thermos cup, chased with swigs of whisky from a silver hip flask. Surveying the river, he watched several dead carp nosing their way through the water, drawn in a convoy by the current.

– We'll have to talk to Oliver about the state of the Otter, he said.

– What's that dear? said Bunty Saveloy. Otters? You know Oliver doesn't use otters.

Kernan sat on Diana's sofa, making sheep's eyes at her reflected face, as she craned her head forward, putting the finishing touches to her eye make-up. She did not see his admiring gaze, for unlike hers, his face was not reflected in her mirror. Busy at her task, she failed to notice his absence from its reversed image of her room.

– Where shall we go then? she said, stroking her eyelashes with a black-laden stick. I'm so hungry I could eat a horse.

– I wouldn't recommend it. How about the Blue Boar Inn? They do a nice trout.

– You don't fancy a nice juicy steak? she said, her tone both teasing and goading.

– You know I don't eat animals, he said, rather tetchily. Nor should you on Ash Wednesday.

– Ah, do I hear more cod's-wallop coming? Come on then, tell me, why shouldn't I eat meat in Lent? It's not a time for starving, it's a fast, a religious excuse for a diet. Quite handy if you're trying to lose weight.

– Lent is from the old name for March, said Kernan. The fast was called a *carne vale*, a farewell to flesh, though our word carnival has rather lost that meaning. You're meant to give up meat, eggs and cheese for forty days.

– So fishmongers would have done well out of that. It's a wonder Bird's Eye haven't bribed the government to make fish-eating a compulsory religious observance.

– Fish-fingers in the till, said Kernan. It happened under King John. He fixed the market for lampreys: two shillings a gill. Only the rich could afford them.

– No wonder we don't eat many lampreys. Now, how do I look?

– Ravishing.

– No compliments please.

– Beautiful then.

– Enough. And get it into your animal head: I am not beautiful, my chin is too big, my eyes aren't straight, I'm not remotely good looking. I am not lovely to be with, I am not interested in anything apart from the work we're doing, and tonight this meal is supposed to give us a chance to talk, about the case. Nothing else. I give you grief all the time, which I don't particularly like doing but it seems to happen that way with me and men. In your case you deserve it too. Is that understood?

Kernan found her antipathy both delightful and frustrating. The more she insulted him, the more he liked her. And their game of cat and mouse kept them at a distance, which had to be right. Yet their play also acknowledged a chemistry between them; she must be aware of this. There was an attraction there which they both had to resist, however exciting it might feel. If she were ever to respond to his play, he doubted he would be able to hold back, and that would be disastrous.

Her contrary nature mirrored his own. Phoebe was like that, and Cynthia took after her, he'd been told. It ran in the family. They'd kept up that tradition of names: Phoebe, Cynthia, Diana – all versions of Artemis, she who hunts alone. And refused to take any man's name, they were all Hunters, all fiercely independent. Phoebe was one of the first suffragettes, but had ended up marrying that Fabian hypocrite Damian. With her it was self-esteem: her father the Rector, so supportive of her brothers, wanting to nourish their talents, but totally devoid of any interest in her, a mere girl. Her brothers were dreadful too, and when both were killed in the War, the Rector shut himself away, from her as well as from the world. Damian didn't really love her either: he was just another version of her father, the old pattern repeating itself.

Cynthia too had been tied to the sour-apple tree. She'd ended up bitter and resentful of her husband. He looked at Diana doing up her coat, wondering about the effect on her of their rancorous divorce.

– Are you ready? she said. Or are you going to sit there all night, with that hang-dog look?

Would Diana break the pattern? In the brief time he had known her, he felt sure she had a tenderer quality than Phoebe, despite her sharp tongue. She came across as hard, but it was a carapace, self-protection. He suspected she had never been convinced of anyone's love, perhaps not even her mother's, and so she shut out that love. She couldn't accept love from anyone; she didn't want to expose herself to be rejected. Yet there was a part of her which was needy, which badly wanted love, which wanted to share her world with someone else, but her identification of all men with her father prevented that. Even though she despised him, she had to match her father's cruelty with her own selfishness.

– Come on Kernan, she said. You're staring like a sheep.

– A sheep on its way to market, he said. About to get the chop. Would you like to eat me as well as the horse?

– I'll have you for breakfast if you don't watch out. Come on then. *Chop chop.*

He wondered what would happen if her Artemis were ever to admit an Aphrodite. What a powerful creature would emerge from that union. Perhaps this would be the source of the latent power he knew she must possess. He hoped he'd be around to see the result if that power were ever released, but was fearful it might rebound on him, that it might exclude him. After the bath incident, he suspected that it was going to happen quite soon, and that the dénouement might prove catastrophic.

He stopped as they reached the door.

– Do you have to bring that with you? he said, pointing at her shoulder.

– Bring what?

– Your Wound. Can't you give it a rest tonight? It always gets in the way.

– How do you know it's there? Diana responded. What does it look like?

– I can see it perched on your shoulder, it's baring its teeth at me, he said. As he drew attention to it, the Wound started hissing at him. Its tongue uncoiled, writhing, hairy like a centipede.

– That sounds like my Wound, said Diana. But I don't see why I have to leave it at home. You always have your Paranoia with you.

– When was the last time you saw my Paranoia? I'm free of it now. *No-para-noia, no-para-noia, no-para-noia-di-liddle-i-day.*

Diana hesitated. Kernan hoped she might at last be able to shut the Wound out, but it interrupted him:

– I hope you're not thinking of going off to have a good time without me. I can't have you enjoying yourselves. Its tongue shot forward, whipping him across the face, then recoiled so sharply it doubled up and tied itself in a knot. The centipede wriggled all its legs at once.

Kernan had swayed backwards, then seemed to be addressing her shoulder.

– I'm sure she'd be a lot happier if you stayed behind tonight. So would I. I'm sure she'd like just for one night to forget about worries, neuroses, guilt and hang-ups, all that baggage of yours.

– Don't try to speak for me, said Diana. I'm not going unless I can take my Wound.

The Wound unknotted its tongue, then licked its lips with an air of self-satisfaction. Now it could sit back and watch the fun.

– In that case, said Kernan, what about my Shame?

This was a gamble. Would he risk his queen for hers?

– If you bring your Shame, you won't be able to talk about it, said Diana, smiling, as if she had put him in check.

– I know that, said Kernan. My Shame is not to be spoken of, otherwise there wouldn't be any Shame in it. You don't mind then? He returned her smile, his last question posed as a gambit.

– It's no concern of mine. You can do what you want with your Shame, she said, as if it were a pawn to be sacrificed.

– What if it does concern you? said Kernan. He seemed to be saying: do you really want me to move my piece there?

– I can't see how it could, unless it's just lust, and that's normal. All men are lecherous. That's nothing to be ashamed of. It's in your nature. Lust, I can handle.

Lust was exposure, thought Kernan. But there were worse risks.

– But I'm a beast, he said. My Shame is much worse than mere lechery. It's utterly shameful.

Lead us not into temptation, he prayed, despite himself.

– You'd better bring it then. You obviously won't be able to be yourself unless you have it with you.

This was Check, Kernan realised. Checkmate in five moves. Did she realise? He'd have to pull back. *Deliver us from evil...*

– It could maybe talk to your Wound, keep it company, he joked. They'd probably find they have a lot in common.

For thine is the kingdom.

– I'm not sure I like the idea of your Shame sniffing around my Wound, she said.

– You may not be able to stop it.

The power and the glory.

New game. Change round the board. Now let me be white. *For ever and ever.*

Kernan, the Wounded King. The Fisher King.

When Kernan had brought the comfrey, Nurse Mary Faverel had been on duty. She was fond of Herne, whom she remembered from her childhood; she had been about twelve when he had passed through her village, and her mother had invited him to share lunch with them in the kitchen, all the men being out in the fields. It was the first time anyone had told her how her name came from the woolly faverel, a plant not native to Loamshire but which Herne had seen in the north country. She had been fascinated by his description of the faverel with its leafless stalk, and he had shown her how to draw it with her coloured pencils: its slender green stem topped by small star-like pale green flowers with yellow threads in the middle. That evening, as she lay in bed, looking up at the great white disc of the moon riding in the night sky, thinking how it looked like a wafery coin of honesty, or the host at communion, she had felt a vague coursing inside her, and then a trickle of thin blood from between her legs. Happening that same day, she connected this miracle of her body's with Herne's plant, her woolly faverel, which he had said was ruled by the moon.

Now he was in her charge, she wanted to help him. Once the doctor had finished his cursory round of brief examinations and terse questions, leaving the patients to her care, she pulled the curtains around Herne's bed, stripped the bandages from his swollen elbow, and watched as Kernan lay strips of bruised comfrey root around his arm, which now looked as collied as a rotten banana. Half an hour later she returned to find him still sitting beside Herne's bed, his hands gripping the old man's elbow. The following day, it was visibly less swollen, the doctor attributing the change to the unexpected success of antibiotics he had prescribed without really wanting to, having already written off the arm along with the patient.

That week Herne's arm had begun to look less inky, and the swelling was clearly going down, waning with the moon he'd said. Mary Faverel had ministered to him, changing his dressings each day; and then Kernan had returned, this time with roots of briony, which she knew as wild vine. As he laid his hands around Herne's elbow, he told her how this was Teilo's Day, the saint who had been in three places at once, three different churches claiming to hold his remains.

– I have enough trouble looking after one body, Mary had said.

– Two bodies should be enough for anyone, Kernan had joked. Three is greedy. It also complicates his miracle. It was said you could cure whooping cough with water from St Teilo's well, but you had to drink it from his skull. The question is: which of the three skulls do you use?

– None, was Herne's reply. I went to his well at Maenclochog. It dried up many years ago, so he can't help now with the whooping cough. You'd have to use a fish instead. A dab on the chest.

A week later, when Kernan arrived for the third visit, bringing his ointment of eringo root, Herne greeted him with the news that Wednesday was Mary Faverel's day off, and they could expect no help from the relief, Nurse Snell, but rather hindrance, since she was an unsympathetic woman, much concerned with bed tucks, orderliness and something called Ward Routine.

– It sounds like a kind of mind fatigue, said Herne, it must be very numbing. The others call her the Dragon.

Kernan watched her moving like a bee from bed to bed, making small movements at each, chiding the occupants, removing items she considered inappropriate, busying herself with her own importance.

– Do you think we could take time out to do this? asked Kernan. I can't think of any other way. Do you have the strength?

– I hope so. I'm getting stronger. I've not been out since Candlemas. I was very weak then. It took all my strength to enter that owl. I had to struggle with the bird, and in the end it threw me out. The idiot doctor here thought I was dead too, and was about to have my body carted off to the mortuary when I returned. But the trip was certainly exhausting.

– I've not held time for many years. But it's all relative. When the Dragon sees us start, it must be when we've finished. The two moments must be simultaneous, or at least to her eyes.

– Take time when time comes lest time steal away.

Kernan felt suddenly apprehensive, looking around him at all the other people. The minute hand of the ward clock was about to reach its zenith, the hour hand pointing towards 11. He hoped he would be strong enough, and that Herne too would be able to join him for long enough for the sea holly to do its work.

– Are you ready? he asked.

– As much as I'll ever be, said Herne. Allow me to join you…

– At eleven on the dot. Start then. Concentrate. Wait for it, wait for it. *Now!*

As he laid his hands on Herne's arm, Nurse Snell jerked her head towards them, about to rush forward. In that instant everything in the ward seemed to freeze, all its diverse sound held in one single buzzy note. An orderly with a tea trolley holding a cup in mid-air was caught in the motion of passing it to a patient. Behind the trolley, whose plume of steam hung like smoke across her face, the Dragon's staring eyes were held as if in a vice, her nostrils flared, her mouth half-open as if about to breathe forth fire.

The light was caught in a shimmer; it seemed to pulse, but did not move, not for a moment. Keeping hold of Herne, Kernan lay on the bed beside him. As his whole body was reflected in

Herne's, so Herne became as one with him, his shadow, his bodily impression receiving his strength.

Kernan separated, leaving Herne like a departing soul, but in reverse, his body standing above his prostrate shadow. And peeling the white bandages like bark from a tree, he took the small strips of root and laid them around the arm of his own shadow, his other self, and held them there, as the light shimmered without motion, the single note of sound a constant hum.

After what seemed an age, Kernan became aware that the eringo's power was now coursing through the shadow of his arm. He bandaged it then, gave it back its shape, bodied his invisible man, and in that moment, that same instant when they had joined, he released the shadow back into Herne, and the light glared, the note broke, and the Dragon rushed forth saying:

– You mustn't touch his arm like that. It's not yours to do what you like with. Now then Mr Herne, it's eleven o'clock. Time for your pills. You won't get better if you don't take your medication.

– I've just taken it, Herne objected. I feel better already.

But he also felt exhausted, as did Kernan sitting beside the bed, his head slumped forward, as if he were nodding off.

When Nurse Snell had left, Kernan said:

– I didn't think that was going to work at first. It was hard work, very hard.

– Nothing short of a miracle, said Herne. I'm beginning to feel young already. Time works wonders, I must say.

– Not a miracle, said Kernan. The laws of nature are overruled in a miracle, when a god shows his presence. But there's no god here, or he'd stop all the cancers in this place.

He indicated a wasted man opposite, thin and stick-like in his striped pyjamas.

– Cancer is an absence of god, he said. EVIL mutating itself from LIVE. What we did was to work with nature, not against it. No one can claim it as a miracle.

– That's not how they'd see it, said Herne.

– But they *didn't* see it. No one saw us. We did it alone. Did it ourselves.

– With nature's help.

– And this time, with time on our side.

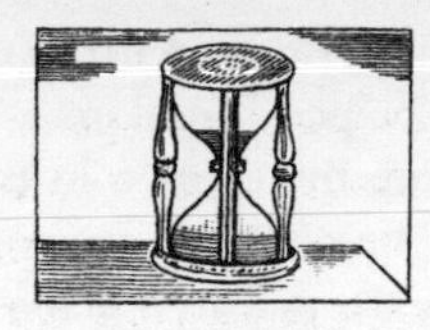

The Boche had been shelling them for at least half an hour, but there were none of the usual big explosions. Something was wrong. They couldn't all be duds. A small shell landed in their trench not five yards away from where Kernan was crouched. It landed with a plop in the mud, between him and Alf Tomkins. Since it hadn't burst, they turned their attention back to the German line, looking out for what might be coming over next, for a shell which would this time explode.

Straining to see what might be on the way, Kernan was suddenly aware that his eyes had started to sting, and that his legs felt hot, as if they were burning. Tomkins was coughing, one hand held to his neck, and using his other arm to wipe a mess of snot from around his nose and mouth.

– *Gas!* he yelled, making a grab for his respirator.

The word was repeated down the trench, and the gas gong was struck. But as the morning wore on, and the masks became stifling, they started to think it might have been a false alarm and they had overreacted, for they could hear nothing now. The shelling had stopped. There was no German attack. They just sat there like mummers with their heads inside the awful masks, staring out at each other through the ridiculous eye discs, until some of the men began indulging in horseplay, pretending to be lions and bears, or animal guisers, batting each other with pantomime paws. When their eye-pieces steamed up they started pulling off their masks, shaking their heads free, and grinning. Kernan did not stop them, but followed suit.

Soon they were all vomiting. Tomkins panicked: he couldn't get his breath, and flailed his arms about, attracting a volley of rifle fire. Hartley tried to calm him, but he had to break away to clutch his stomach, which felt as if shrapnel had burst inside. They started putting their gasmasks back on, but were pushing them away at the same time, struggling to force their heads inside as their guts threatened to choke them with their own vomit.

Kernan felt he had failed them when Captain Nicholas arrived with a relief platoon, all goggle-eyed like phantoms in their masks. Marshall and Hartley helped Tomkins get up, trying to stop him from shouting before the captain intervened; he was screwing his eyes up, saying he couldn't see anything, calling for his mother, when Nicholas slapped him across the face.

In the dressing-station the whole platoon were sat along a couple of planks and told to open wide while an orderly came by and shot something into their mouths. Kernan watched each man recoil in turn, then received his spurt of what must have been spirit of hartshorn, pure ammonia, which seemed to go right through the top of his head, it was that strong.

The next thing he knew he was lying in bed at the base hospital. He was blind. Someone came along and held his eyes open to put droplets in; for a second he prepared himself to feel cold lotion hit his eyes, but it was boiling hot. His legs too were burning, the flesh seemingly soft, incredibly painful, more so when someone started bathing it.

He spoke words into the air, addressed to whoever was on either side of him; to Marshall and Fisher, it turned out. Men were exchanging names and news up and down the ward. Tomkins and Openshaw had died in the night. Hardacre had fared particularly badly, and was being moved; he was stone blind.

Diana was starting to ponder Kernan's miracles. She couldn't get them out of her head; they were fast becoming an obsession, difficult, contradictory, ridiculous as an unsuitable lover, wrong for her but somehow irresistible. On St Werburga's Day (as she found herself calling it), she had dropped Kernan off at the hospital, then went to make her phone call. Standing in the call box outside the Blue Boar, listening to the ringing of a telephone no one was answering, she kept thinking about the milk-white gander and his resurrected mate. What happened to the people who'd eaten the goose? Did they throw it up? Did they *un*eat it? And that ludicrous gander: indignant, honking at the abbess, reminding her of a song she'd long ago forgotten. But had not: *Goosey, goosey gander...Whither shall I wander?*

She must get these geese out of her head.

– Shoo, shoo, she said.

– What's that? said a voice from the telephone, from Ireland. An Irishwoman's voice, Brigid from Donegal.

– Yes, yes, she said. I was just... *Is that you Bridge?* Bridge, I just was shooing away a fly in this phone box...

– Well, don't swallow it, said Brigid's voice. It might be Étaín.

– Étaín?

– The wife of Midir. She became a fly and landed in some soup, which was drunk by Etar's wife, who gave birth to a new Étaín. It's one of the great Irish stories, the wooing of Étaín.

– Oh, don't you start. I get enough tall tales from Inspector K to last me a lifetime... Anyway, have you got anything for me?

– Yes. Quite intriguing too. Your man Brock was picked up by security guards in August 1994 and handed over to Enniskillen police. Trespassing they said. He said he was salmon-fishing on Lough Erne. He wasn't poaching: he had a permit from the visitor centre, but they said he was on private land. The following day, Tuesday 16th August, the same security men brought in Bernard Tench, who they said had been acting suspiciously on the airfield at Ballycassidy. Neither man was charged with anything. You wouldn't have picked this up kind of thing in Britain, but the RUC write everything down. You never know when that kind of information will be helpful. And here's something else which will interest you...

– Yes?

– The person who questioned Brock and Tench was Superintendent N. Goodman. Isn't he with your force? He was here on secondment apparently. So he might be able to tell you more.

– *Ah,* said Diana, as if an arrow had pierced her voice. She stumbled for a moment, then wrenched it out. And continued:

– Who were these security men working for?

– A firm called Straussler. They've had interests in Northern Ireland for some years: they have hotels and leisure complexes, and sponsor golf tournaments. They're stinking rich, those lads.

They were one of the few European companies to make big investments here during the Troubles. The politicians court them like royalty: like flies round a heap of cow dung, as my mother used to say.

– Did the hotels not get bombed?

– No, but that's not uncommon. Probably paid protection money. They wouldn't be short of a few bob.

– And the airfield at Ballycassidy?

– They'd have people using private planes there: businessmen, politicians, celebrities, all those eejits we wouldn't be without.

– Anything else?

– That's all I've come up with so far. It all sounds quite juicy. Do tell me what happens. I'd love to get some dirt on Straussler; I've always thought there was something fishy about them, that they were too good to be true. But what's your Irish connection, apart from Goodman?

– I don't know yet. Kernan knew Tench and Brock went fishing in Ireland. Apparently Brock's grandmother came from a village called Ederny in Co. Fermanagh. Kernan says men always go back to the rivers and lakes they used to fish as children.

– He knows his stuff, your man Kernan, he knew where to look.

As she hung up, Diana turned suddenly in fright, hearing a tapping on the glass of the phone box, but there was no one there. Then the tapping started again, louder. Looking down, she saw a white goose smacking its orange beak against the bottom pane of glass. She held the door open, and the goose walked in under her arm.

– What do you want? she asked.

It honked back at her. She thought she made out the words *dog* and *bone*, but it was probably her imagination.

A man came out of the pub to retrieve the goose.

– She always goes in there for shelter when it's about to rain, he said. She's a good weathercock. But we get complaints when she won't let people use the phone.

Diana paused in the reference section. She had gone to Otteridge Library for information on companies, but found herself looking up Teilo in a dictionary of saints. There was nothing in it about drinking water from his skull. Taking a bulky register of companies to a table, she discovered she had also picked up a book on freshwater fish.

Skimming through the small print of the large book, she stopped to make notes; then to rub her eyes. At that moment, she thought she noticed something move on the table. It was the fish book. She picked it up, slowly opened the cover, and a fish leapt out, wriggling on the table, gasping at the air. The man opposite looked up, staring at her through thick pebble glasses. She put her hand over the fish, stilling its movement. The fish was cold, and after a minute, stopped moving. She swept it into her lap, and started to examine it.

– I've seen people bring in flowers to identify, but fish, never.

It was one of the librarians. He inspected her catch.

– But you don't need a book to find that one, he continued. It's a dace. You used to get lots of them in the Otter, but not so many now. Where did you find it?

– It was given to me, she said.

When the man had gone, Diana looked up *dace* in the index, and turning to *Fig. 9(c),* found a page devoted to the CARP FAMILY, with illustrations of several other fish, including the tench (*Tinca tinca*), but above the caption Fig. 9(c) Dace: *Leuciscus vulgaris*, there was a white space. Placing the fish on the page, she saw that it just fitted the unfilled picture box, and considered closing the book on it, to see what would happen, but didn't want to risk making a fishy mess.

– That's right. It's one of the carp family.

It was the librarian again, pointing at her open book. Looking down, she saw the page was now complete; the dace was back in the picture, snug as a tinned sardine. The book still had a fishy smell. She decided to leave before anything else happened.

Kernan wasn't surprised. She showed him her hand in the car, the glistening scales like skin flakes on her palm.

– Make sure you don't take out any books on snakes, he said. What else did you get, apart from fish on your fingers and the Latin names of carp?

– Straussler is part of a company called Gerstmann Holdings, which is – wait for it – a major shareholder in Eurochimique.

– Ah. I thought there might be something like that. Are there other Gerstmann companies?

– Loads of them. I took a photocopy. Several which might be significant. Like Scheinker, the sportswear people.

– Sirloin's on their board. It was in that declaration of MPs' interests: advisory capacity, unpaid.

– They may not pay him, but don't they make big donations to party funds?

– I don't know. It's certainly possible. Who else?

– An outfit called Alpers Pharmaceuticals (Northern Ireland) Ltd. I'll ask Brigid about them.

– We seem to be getting somewhere at last, said Kernan, *with a fol-de-rol-de-rol-de-rol-de-rigeo.*

– Tench was after some big fish, said Diana, spitting discreetly on her hand, and wiping it with a mansize tissue.

– But there's still more fishing to be done. And we may need to venture another small fish to catch a great one.

– As long as we don't fish for herring but only catch a sprat, Diana warned.

– Little fish slip through the nets, but great fish are taken, Kernan countered.

– Great fish eat up the small.

– That fish will soon be caught that nibbles at every bait, said Kernan. Goodman's shoal has many snappers, and our bait is of their own making.

– You may be right, Diana agreed. He that bites on every weed must needs light on poison.

– *Turdus ipse sibi malum cacat*... The thrush when he pollutes the bough sows for himself the seeds of woe.

On Ash Wednesday, Diana had made a detour to Ottermouth beach, allowing Kernan to collect his sea holly while she made some routine enquiries about the disappearance of some lifebelts from a couple of trawlers. After dropping him at the hospital, she walked through the door of Otteridge police station on the stroke of eleven. At first she thought the place was deserted. The silence was uncanny. But looking over the counter, she saw the bent figure of Sergeant Cobb, about to pick something up from the floor. He was stuck in that posture, like one of the figures she'd seen in the museum at Pompeii. Walking through to her office, she passed other policemen similarly frozen, some staring like waxwork figures, others caught with their eyes closed.

– Kernan, she called out, surrounded by uniformed statues in the main office. Is this your work, or am I doing this? She sat down to gather herself, darting quick glances around the room, breathing heavily. Looking up at the clock, she saw it still said eleven, as if no time had passed since her arrival. The striplights seemed caught in a permanent flicker, a shimmer which glared but seemingly without motion. Suddenly, she stood up, and walked purposefully towards Goodman's office.

The Superintendent was standing in the middle of his room, one foot raised, caught in his tracks. His dark eyes stared into space. Like one of the walking dead, thought Diana, examining his face close-up, looking for clues. *I can't work him out,* she thought, *he's fathomless.* Reaching a hand into his jacket, she withdrew his wallet and took it to his desk, where she went quickly through its contents, replacing everything in the same order. There were cashpoint slips (she made a note of his account details), petrol receipts, several twenty pound notes, and some business cards, whose names she memorised, as well as the prize item, a Polaroid photograph of a naked, rather large woman whom she recognised, despite her dishevelled appearance and red eyes, as Mrs Isabella Maw, wife of the county councillor. The plastic cards slotted down one side of the wallet included his Visa and American Express, his police ID card, membership cards from the Diners Club, Loamshire Lions and Otteridge Golf Club, and a security pass to the Eurochimique plant at Loamfield, and behind that, three Durex Fetherlite condoms in mint-condition white and blue wrappers.

Diana stared at Goodman's three condoms. Without knowing why, but suspecting her motives were not merely malicious, she took a pin from the magnetic paper-clip holder on his desk, and pricked a neat hole in each, in the middle of the British Standards hallmark of quality, at the point where the B met the S, so that the pin-holes would not be easily spotted. Would this single, secret act bring about some change of fate? It seemed irresponsible, not knowing, like a terrorist leaving a bomb which might nor might not explode, which might or might not cause death or maiming; and he would not see the results of his action, for he would be separate from them. But it still felt somehow right; and this action, seemingly guided by some unseen hand, was to save her life, four months later.

Diana stared at Goodman's three condoms lying in the palm of her hand, the seed of a plot growing in her mind. Were these not the means of perpetrating a perfect act of revenge? The hand of fate had given her this once-in-a-lifetime opportunity. How could she refuse such a gift? What would happen, she considered, if she were to prick a neat hole in each condom, a hole so tiny it wouldn't be easily spotted? Could this single, secret act effect some change of fate? If Goodman were to make a woman pregnant, and the woman were to be, say, the wife of the council leader, might this not ruin him, bring about his fall? But no, it might turn out not to be Mrs Maw, but some other poor unfortunate. And what kind of devilish child would Goodman spawn? She would not wish a brat of his on any woman.

Replacing the wallet in Goodman's jacket, she slid her hand into each of his trouser pockets, finding a handkerchief, a toothpick and some coins in one, and in the other, a key.

She held the key in the air, pondering its significance. It was a small flat key, like the key to a drawer or possibly a filing cabinet. But which one? Goodman had a whole bank of grey filing cabinets down one wall, and something told her there wasn't time to try all nine. *Nine*, she thought. *A stitch in time saves nine*, or as Kernan had it, *a fish in brine saves nine*. The fish from the library, the dace she remembered was *Fig. 9(c)*. Ninth drawer, third drawer down was WORK FOR CHARITIES AND TRUSTS. She slid the key into the lock, turned it, and slowly pulled the drawer open; looking quickly behind her, unsure as to how long she could continue. Nothing had changed. Everything around her was still frozen.

The file tags gave a roll call of familiar names. She glanced up and down the tempting labels. There were so many of them. Where should she start? It was like being a child again, standing on tiptoe in Mrs Hartley's sweetshop, trying to decide what to buy with the pound an aunt had slipped her when Dad was out:

ARCHER	AERO	JOHNSON	MILKY WAY
ARMSTRONG	ANIMAL BAR	KERNAN	MINT CREME
BROCK	BAR SIX	KURU	MUNCHIES
BULLEN	BOOST	LAMBERT	OLD JAMAICA
CLEGG	BOUNTY	MARSHALL	PICNIC
COBB	BOURNVILLE	MAW	POPPETS
COOMBES	BUTTONS	MORSE	REVELS
DAUBE	CARAMAC	O'SCRAPIE	RIPPLE
DE FOIE	CARAMEL	OXTER	ROLO
DEVLIN	CURLYWURLY	PRURIGEAUX	SMARTIES
FELCHER	DAIRY CRUNCH	ROUTLEDGE	SPIRA
FISHER	DAIRY MILK	SAVELOY	STAR BAR
GALLSTONE	DOUBLEDECKER	SIRLOIN	TIFFIN
GOODWIN	FLAKE	SPERMWAIL	**TIME OUT**
GREEN	FRUIT 'N' NUT	SLURRY	TOFFEE CRISP
GRENNAN	GALAXY	STENCH	TOPIC
HARTLEY	KIT KAT	STRIMMER	TREETS
HERNE	LION BAR	STRINGER	TRUFFLE BAR
HOCKLE	MALTESERS	TENCH	TWIRL
HODGE	MARATHON	THATCHER	TWIX
HOGG	MARS BAR	TOMKINS	WALNUT WHIP
HUNTER	MEDLEY	TUCKER	WHOLE NUT
JAKES	MILKY BAR	YEATS	WISPA

As she stood back, pondering her next choice, she whistled, and a bird came flying through the doorway, like a sparrow through the hall, in Kernan's story. It looked like a blackbird, but was larger, with bluey-black coloured feathers. A police bird, she thought. But it was a chough.

– *Chee-aw, cheeaw, chee-aw... chuff*, it said.

Sensing it had come to warn her of something, she slammed and locked the filing-cabinet, and rubbing the key with Goodman's handkerchief, dropped it back in his pocket. Finally, she wiped the filing cabinet, and gave his desk a quick dusting. Stuffing the hankie back in the trouser pocket of the bullet-headed dummy, she quickly withdrew, shutting the door behind her. And was half way across the main office when all the statues sprang to life in one instant.

– What was that flash? asked Roger Hodge.

– A power surge, I think, said Diana. Let's hope the computers are all right. She looked around for the chough, but there was no sign of it, apart from a white streak of birdshit on the back of PC Hodge's newly cleaned uniform.

A sign of good luck, she thought; but said nothing. Unlike PC Jakes, who announced:

– Look at old Todge. Some bird's shat on him.

– Shit happens, said Sergeant Oxter.

Little fishes in a brook,
Father caught them on a hook,
Mother fried them in a pan,
Johnnie eats them like a man.

CHAPTER SEVEN

Hitting It Off

SPRING EQUINOX/LADY DAY: MARCH 20TH–25TH

Keys with round shafts can be used as amulets against the Evil Eye, but a flat key has no power. The older the key, the greater its power to ward off evil. Old iron keys are the most powerful and should be kept in the right-hand trouser pocket, or in a handbag. When touching a key to ward off evil, grasp its shaft in your right hand.

Three keys that unlock thoughts: drunkenness, trustfulness, love. And kisses are keys.

George Kernan had not expected to enjoy the Loamshire Farmers Hoedown, to bear the hoots and howdies of outrageous music. He'd grumbled that his subjection to such a travesty of his beloved English folk tradition went way beyond the call of duty, and could well be classed, if not as torture, then surely as inhuman treatment under the European Convention of Human Rights. He was thus surprised to find himself warming to Whitethroat and the Warblers as they went through their hillbilly birdboy act.

They neither whooped nor yodelled. The speciality of these twitcher musicians was bird impressions, which they performed to the accompaniment of twangy guitars and Whitethroat's shrill fiddle. Each member of the group had a birdname. In their final stomping number, *Tennessee Warble Fly*, which had even Kernan stamping his feet, the demonic fiddler's sawing wing-like arms imitated the whitethroat's sudden, excited fluttering, his jerking downward movements the bird's arrowing back into a hedge.

Wood Warbler was Lionel Tench. After his father's death, he'd thrown himself into his music. Neighbours rarely saw him, and he refused to have anything to do with John Brock, who had been his best mate. The two sons no longer mixed with the village lads, but kept themselves to themselves. Kernan knew it would be useless as well as dangerous to try contacting him, aware that someone was still keeping the house under surveillance. Lionel was occasionally seen driving his father's Land Cruiser, his drum-kit crammed in the back, but he'd stopped using the village shops. Once Kernan had tried following a black four-wheel-drive tailing him, but he was fearful of drawing attention to himself, and turned off after a couple of miles.

By the interval, the marquee was heaving, as were many of the hoedowners, who'd been drinking since five o'clock. As two men in check shirts started lurching at each other, yelling and throwing useless punches, Kernan chose this moment of commotion to collar his Warbler by the bar.

While various farmers made feeble attempts to stop the fight, and others joined in, Kernan tried to get Tench to listen to him. Aware of his antipathy, and also of the likelihood that they were being watched, he made several quick conversational thrusts.

– Lionel, I know you don't trust me, but believe me, I do want to help. I want to find out who killed your father.

– I thought you knew. Tench spat out the four monosyllables. It was Mike Brock, wasn't it?

– I don't think it was.

– Well you're the only person who doesn't think it was Mike. I can't help you. Now if you don't mind, I'm having a break.

– Did your father ever mention a firm called Alpers Pharmaceuticals?

– What if he did?

– It might be important, said Kernan, his lynx-sharp eyes darting between Tench's son and the men exchanging blows, who had just overturned a table, sending bottles and glasses crashing to the floor.

– I don't know anything about Alpers.

– In 1994 he was apprehended at Ballycassidy airfield in Northern Ireland by security guards working for a company called Straussler…

– You don't need me to tell you about them. Straussler's part of Gerstmann, which runs Eurochimique. Alpers is part of the same group.

– So Bernard *did* talk about Alpers, Kernan asserted, glancing anxiously to the right again where the two pugilists were now tearing into each other like a pair of Kilkenny cats. A woman whose baby was crying was screaming abuse at the flailing Jack Marshall, who roared like a bull in response.

– Not much, said Tench, which is hardly surprising. He was only attached to them for six months when he worked for Eurochimique. Kuru cancelled his secondment.

– Alpers has a research laboratory not far from Ballycassidy…

– OK Kernan, you've done your homework. But I'm not interested in that stuff any more. I just want to get on with my life. I don't want to end up being bumped off like my Dad. So *leave me alone*, or I might start drawing attention to the fact that you're trying to talk to me. And that might be of interest to a certain copper who's currently watching the fight.

Kernan saw the man, standing apart from the crowd, sweating in a double-breasted fawn-coloured raincoat.

– He's no copper, he said. Or if he is, he's not from our force. From the way he's making himself look conspicuous, you'd think he was one of Oxter's crew, but he's not a Loamshire man.

– I'm not surprised, said Tench. All the more reason for not talking to you. *Now will you go away…*

– If you change your mind… said Kernan, solicitously.

– Just leave me alone.

– I'll be at Ottermouth beach tomorrow night at five o'clock. Under the third breakwater. I won't kiss the hare's foot, and I'll wait… A good place to walk the dog.

– Not if it's pissing down with rain like it is now.

– It won't be.

– How do you know?

– A little bird told me. A warbler.

– What about my tail?

– I'll make sure he's otherwise engaged. And I'll start by giving him something to think about now.

Kernan strode through the tent as if he'd just arrived to deal with the fracas, saying *What's all this then?* in his best *Dixon of Dock Green* voice, confronting the two fighters, who immediately stopped, and stood with downcast eyes, as if he had tamed them.

– *Joe Hartley*, he said, *you should be ashamed of yourself.* (Jack Warner had used the same words.) *Now go on home before I tell your missus what you've been up to.* (George Dixon again.)

– *And you, Jack, how much have you drunk today?* Kernan slapped him on the back just a little too hard, pushing him forward, making him stagger into the crowd, which parted before him. Jack Marshall reined himself back like a horse as he paused in front of the man in the fawn raincoat, who was taken by surprise; and started to edge away.

– *Hang on pal*, said Jack. *I know you. I seen you in...* He did not complete his accusation, for at that moment the remains of two steak pies, two packets of salt 'n' vinegar crisps and some chips spattered with ketchup, swimming in a stomachful of Ould Rodger, decided to carry out a reverse manoeuvre, and flooded forth in a hot yellow torrent from his mouth, forcing the man in the fawn raincoat to run outside, where he stood for a minute in the downpour, the rain offering the only quick means of cleaning his mackintosh.

– Still raining cats and dogs, growled Jack Armstrong, looking up as if to implore some heavenly intervention which would stop the downpour, as the fight had been stopped. It was still chucking it down. No miracles had been forecast.

– *Weather meet to set paddocks abroad in*, Kernan responded, and when this met with sheep-like stares, added, *slimy paddocks, toads and frogs.*

– Should have asked Ken-Toadfaced-Livingstone's fucking newt to kick things off instead of that slimebag Sirloin.

– It rains by planets, said Kernan.

The Right Honourable Henry Sirloin, MP, was not feeling himself, although he felt like doing just that. He heard the sound of a bath being run across the landing, which meant Candida was not going to return to bed after all, even though it was Sunday morning, and according to the man on Radio 4, the first day of spring. After Saturday's torrential drenching, he had not expected any spring sunshine, yet had hoped for some springy delights from his wife. In that he was to be disappointed, but drawing back the curtains, found the sun was indeed out there, the shameless hussy, dazzling as a hotel whore.

He put on his slippers, and stomped downstairs to retrieve the interesting bits of the *Sunday Times* from the mat. He flipped through the magazine bit quickly, hoping to find some pictures of beauties on a Caribbean beach, some fashion editor's excuse for showing off a half-clothed model, but there wasn't even the usual posh cow pictured in her bedroom or with her home-made cakes or dopey relatives. He stood up.

– I want a shag, he said quietly. Then louder: *I want a shag. I haven't had a shagging shag all week, and now I want one. A shag!*

He went to the bathroom, knocked, waited, then said hesitantly through the door, in a low voice:

– Are you coming back to bed, darling? Shall I make you some coffee and toast? Warm you some croissants?

– No, came the reply. I must get up. I'm worried about Shuck. He's still all floppy. He's not been himself since he had that scrap with Maurice's minkhound.

– Yes love, I'm worried too, we'll have to take him to the vet, said Sirloin, slowly, his dismay audible even through the thick oak door, yet his solicitude was not for the dog, but for the listless state of his penis, which he knew would benefit greatly from some good vigorous exercise of the rumpy-pumpy kind.

– You go back to bed, darling, said Candida, moved by her husband's concern for the dog, which she had thought he did not particularly care for. Who knows, I may change my mind.

Diana Hunter had drawn the short straw. Sunday duty was bad enough, but she had been assigned the car boot sale at the Blue Boar Inn. Yet she had not expected the sun to be shining, so it might not be so tedious after all; she might pick up a few Robin Hood's pennyworths, and it was always a good place for gossip as well as to find stolen property, her premise for being there.

She identified several specimens from the horsey set, including young Tom Maw, rusticated from Oxford for over-enthusiastic horseplay at a college Gaudy, the details of which he was elaborating for the benefit of Lucy Saveloy, who clicked her tongue in feigned disapproval. The surly Australian stood to one side of the group, glancing at his watch, making circular movements in the gravel with the toe of his shoe. Some woman was keeping him waiting, Diana knew, smiling at his discomfort.

Then her eye was caught by a messy display of brass and other metal ornaments, some probably quite expensive, but all these objects just scattered across an old blanket with no regard for presentation. Behind them, slumped in a canvas chair, was a scrawny youth with striped tracksuit trousers and a bulging Tommy Hilfiger jacket, hidden behind *The News of the World*, making no attempt to draw in potential customers. He shifted in the chair, rubbed his knees, and started idly scratching his badger-striped thigh. It was John Brock.

He had the exhausted look of someone whose body was weighed down with an oppressive illness. In his case, the weight was supplied by a curious-looking reptilian creature attached to his back, about the size of a dog but segmented like an insect, its great crab-like legs secured to its host's hips, clutching his belly around the front. Brock seemed totally unaware of the creature's presence, but was clearly suffering from the effects of walking around with it hanging onto his back like an overloaded rucksack.

Diana could not see it, but her Wound reacted with a show of aggression. The two creatures took an immediate dislike to each other, adopting threatening postures which caused some pain to their hosts as the sharp points of bestial claws dug into human flesh. The Wound flailed the air between them with its giant centipede tongue, hissing. The other creature responded by grating its mandibles with a sound like chalk on a blackboard, and thrashed the ground with its tail, which was thick and heavy like a crocodile's.

Diana picked up an old key, and felt its weight, gauging it to be iron. There seemed to be a tiny inscription in the handle, and grasping the key by the shaft, she held it up to the light, trying to make out the letters. Through the oval of the handle she noted a disturbance amongst the Barbour crowd, where the big Australian looked as if he was panicking about something. The longer she held the key up, the more frantic he became, until eventually he broke away from the group, and ran down the side of the pub. She heard the sound of a car being started, then saw his Jaguar pulling away, skidding in the gravel as he made a sharp left turn before driving off like a maniac.

– He seems to be in a bit of a hurry, she said.

– You wanna buy that key? Brock asked, ignoring her attempt at conversation.

– How much?

– Dunno. Two quid.

– It's worth more than that.

– I wouldn't know. This isn't my stuff. I'm just minding it for some mates. They're doing the car auction.

– And these mates of yours,

Diana's Wound went on the attack, challenging John Brock's bellicose retainer to a fight, shoulder-beast versus back-beast, but the other demurred, pleading in a whiny, wheedling voice that it needed to stay attached to its host. The Wound thought this a poor excuse, and said so, charging its previously belligerent adversary with cowardice. No demon worth its salt should be so dependent upon its human that it could not break off for a claw-fight, said the Wound, dismissively.

– But I'm not a demon like you, the other replied. You're all emotions. You can survive away from the humans, knowing they'll always seek refuge in your pain. I'm man-made, but completely artificial. A new species entirely.

– I thought I hadn't seen you around before.

– I've no emotional or mental existence, for I'm a completely physical parasite. I'm a cold killer, cold as a key.

– But if that's true, said the Wound doubtfully, why can't they see you then? Eh? Answer that one, you overgrown louse. It grinned its triumph.

– They don't need to see

Diana said, would they be from Otteridge?

– Yeah, what of it?

– But you're from Loamfield, aren't you?

– Yeah, so?

– Why aren't you with the village lads then?

– They don't want to… Hey, what is this? You a copper?

– DC Hunter, Loamshire Police. She showed him her ID. And I think I'd be right in thinking that these antique keys were stolen from a house in Ottermouth two months ago, along with other items. I can't see anything else here from that burglary, but these are definitely the keys. You see the date on that one?

– I don't know nothing about that. They're just a bunch of old keys. I told you, I'm just looking after this stuff for my mates.

– You're in possession of stolen property, and that's an offence. At this point I should caution you, and take you in for questioning. But in view of who you are, I'd like to ask you about some other things first. And if you co-operate, I may forget I saw you with the keys.

– What do you mean, who I am? What's this about? asked Brock, his eyes suddenly alert, as if her carefully enunciated me, they feel me, but they don't believe in my existence. If they could see me, they'd be able to get rid of me.

– Pluck you off like an oversized sheep-ked, drawled the Wound, not without spite.

– Something like that, said the backpacker, who was called Ginger Jake.

It explained that its body was made from a chitinous compound; it fed from the human by means of hollow tubes in its claws through which it drew out enzymes from the host's blood, lymph and tissue. Its chitin would be totally translucent but for presence of its Nine Organophosphates, which gave it a pale sandy appearance, hence the beast's name. The magic nine were all lethal substances, it boasted: Methamidophos the headcase; Leptophos, what a killer that was; the venomous Fenthion; Merphos the Greek; Propetamphos, his war-like relation; Guthion, no need to say any more about old Guthion, nor that sly bastard Diazinon; nor the brothers Chlorfenvinphos and Chlorpyrifos, whose killing sprees were far worse than anything perpetrated by the Krays, not even Quentin Tarantino could keep up with their slaughtering, not in his wildest dreams.

words were drawing him out of his lethargy.

– Your father's death, said Diana, slowly. And Bernard Tench's.

– My Dad didn't kill Bernie, said John. He wouldn't have done that. They was mates. And as for Dad, I think your lot killed him, so I don't know why you're talking to me. What do you want? Can't you let it rest? I thought the case was closed. Can't you leave us in peace? Haven't you done enough already?

– I don't believe he killed Bernard Tench. And as to how your father died, I'd like to know more about that too. Is there anything you didn't tell the police which it might be helpful for me to know?

– Why should I trust you after what happened?

Her green eyes flashed like Athene's. They caught him unawares, like a silent arrow flying through a thicket, coming out of nowhere.

– What have you got to lose? she said, pointing at the blanket. You could get two years for this… And don't you want to get your own back at them? Not just for Bernard and your father, but for yourself?

– *Me?* What have I got to do with all that? He wondered

– What do these nine killers do then? asked the Wound, its tone now curious, placatory, its interest suggesting flattery.

– Two things, said Ginger Jake, warming to the account and to the Wound's attentiveness, for while demons are adept in using flattery and guile on others they are susceptible to it themselves, generally being starved of any kind of love or other nourishing sustenance.

– Firstly, the creature continued, somewhat pompously, they inhibit the neurotransmitter acetyl cholinesterase…

– Who, Colin Esther? Pull the other one… the Wound, started to say, but then stopped itself. If it was to know more, it had to try to gain the other's confidence.

– It's what I live off, hornhead. Cos when my boys start working over this enzyme, my boy Brock's autonomous nervous system is fucked. He gets cramps, nausea and diarrhoea. And because the enzyme's out of action, his central nervous system is all kaput, he doesn't just feel dizzy, he starts trembling, gets anxious and confused. He doesn't know what's hit him, that's the great thing about this lark.

– But how did you get on to him in the first place? the

what her interest was in him.

– Plenty, I'd say. Let me guess. When you're not out with the Ridger lads, you spend most of your time sitting at home watching TV. You don't help much on the farm any more. You're not making life easy for your mother...

– Come on, what's with the guilt trip...? Now she was sounding like his mother.

– Hang on John, let me finish. You're depressed. You get headaches all the time, yes?

– Yeah, how do you know? He glared at her, uneasy, talking about this stuff to a woman ...I went to the doctor about all that, and he said there was nothing wrong with me.

– And *is* there nothing wrong with you? Again, Diana's eyes caught his glance. He tried to look away, but couldn't. His resistance was melting, as if she'd found some weak spot in him, some place where he was exposed, and was stroking it.

– Of course there is, he told her. I can't sleep. I'm always coughing. I get stomach ache, and it's nothing to do with what I eat, it's just always there, hurting. My skin gets itchy too. Doctor said it was normal: everyone gets like that now, environmental pollution he called it.

Wound asked gently, its question phrased like a general enquiry, apparently neutral.

– Oh, shit happens, said the parasite.

– Come on, there must be more to it than that. I take it that he brought it on himself.

– With sheep dip. But now I'm there, he hasn't been able to get rid of me. When his cells start to synthesise more cholinesterase, I infiltrate them with the Dirty Four, that's my undercover MMLF team, they may be slow but they're lethal: Methamidophos and Merphos, Leptophos and Fenthion. They go for an enzyme called neuropathy target esterase, but it's a few weeks before young John feels the effects of their work when he starts getting this tingling sensation all over. They attack the victim with ataxia: that way he can't control his muscles. This is their speciality, delayed neuropathy, which affects the motor and sensory nerves of the legs. I'm now trying to paralyse him completely but I haven't managed that yet.

– And how do these Dirty Four manage to do *all this*? the Wound asked, pretending to be impressed.

– That's the simple part, said Ginger Jake, not realising he

She noticed he was rubbing his arm again.

– Billy Johnson's the same. He was a squaddy, but the army kicked him out; he just hangs around the town now. But I wasn't in the Gulf War, you wouldn't catch me fighting in any army.

– You used to help your dad with the dipping on the farm, didn't you?

– Yeah, I know about all that too. But Dad stopped using that stuff once it wasn't compulsory. Bernie told him all about organophosphates; once he knew, he wouldn't use them any more.

– But the effects can last a long time. And if you weren't wearing the right gear...

It was weird. She seemed to know everything about him, everything that had happened.

– The gear was fine, he said, but sometimes the stuff still got in. You found the insides of your boots had somehow got wet, you might have a leak, they might be split. We gave them a good scouring of course. But anyway, it can't be that, can it? Government says there was no risk, it was safe all along. So I can't be ill from that, can I? I'm just a fucking layabout, that's what they all say in the village.

was being gulled: They hit the distal axons of the nerves, causing them to "die back".

– Sounds painful.

– It is.

– So are you really going to *kill* John Brock? the Wound asked slowly, with an air of friendly complicity, one demon to another.

– I'm trying, but he's a real fighter, said the chitinous beast. Runs in the family I'd say. You should see the amount of cholinesterase he's churning out. If he carries on like that, I'll crack up, disintegrate.

– And how many of you are there, Ginger?

– Just a few thousand in this country, but we've grown to around three million in the Third World. They have a pretty high fall-off rate there, but still managed to kill a good quarter of a million people last year. There aren't the same restrictions on pesticide use. Our target last year was to hit 3% of the agricultural workforce, and we managed that with no problems. But we don't need to bother the African suicide farmers: they still use DDT illegally imported from the States and Europe...

– That's all I need to know, said the Wound, interrupting. Did you get all that, Diana?

– You could get treatment.

– Not here, I can't. Illness not recognised.

Except by her. She knew where he hurt.

– If you don't do anything, you could get cancer, you know.

– They won't believe that either. No one believes anything I say. Like no one believes Mum about that phone call.

– We see not what is in the wallet behind, Diana shrugged, watching John Brock hunch his shoulders. And behind her, she knew, without turning, someone was watching them. A man in a fawn raincoat, standing with his hands in his pockets.

– What are you doing, talking to your host? Ginger Jake asked, suddenly worried.

– Not talking. Just letting her know. And she's taken it all in, I can tell. She'll be able to use it. I may be her Wound, but I've got a lot of respect for her. She's rather special, our Diana. She may not realise it yet, but I think my days as her Wound are numbered. She thinks she's still fighting me, but she's really just shadow-boxing now out of habit. And she's actually kicked the habit I plagued her with.

– I have to go, she said. We must talk more. Give me those keys, I'll take the lot. *The used key is always bright.*

She waved a five-pound note in the air, making sure it was seen, and dropped all the keys into her bag, except the big iron one, which she gripped in her right hand; and as she moved towards the raincoat man, saw him start to look anxious, then back away from her. And just as the Australian had done, he turned on his heels, almost slipping on the gravel. And he ran.

And Ginger Jake shrank inwardly, suddenly aware of his own mortality.

The new moon was four days old, and would reach its first quarter the night before Lady Day. It was time to visit the river again. Uncertain whether it was better to pay her respects to the Otter on the day of the Equinox, when she did obeisance to Eostre, the dawn goddess, or on Lady Day, when she venerated the Great Goddess as well as the Virgin, Muffy always went there on both days, just to be sure.

She took handfuls of vegetation, addressed them as Death, and cast them as far as she could into the river. This rite was meant to show Death the door, and to bring fertility for people as well as for plants. In the old days her mother used to masquerade in leaves and flowers, and dance along the riverbank. In that state she had surprised a fisherman, had his clothes off before he knew what was happening, and made love to him in the guise of Blodeuwedd. She never saw him again, which she claimed was evidence, if any was needed, that he must have come to her from the Other World. Muffy was not so sure, but wished she had been able to meet and know her father, who must have been an exceptional person, whether he was mortal or ethereal.

Her own theory was that her father was a salmon returned to human form, for salmon and sermon have their season in Lent. This also explained her affinity with fish and her liking for all scaly creatures.

She was always especially pained to see the shoals of dead fish floating belly upward in the Otter, particularly at the Vernal Equinox, and on this day decided to incorporate them in her ritual. Using a long stick to draw in as many as she could to the shore, she set about making a Croagh Patrick of fishes on the grass, including bream, perch, roach, carp, dace and chub, around which she made a circle of eels laid head to tail, overlaying them like ropes of pastry round a flan.

– *Well that's that*, she said, *and butter's for fish*.

This was the spectacle which greeted the driver of a black four-wheel-drive who had pulled off the road at Duckwidge Ditch to urinate. He approached the conical hillock of fish suspiciously, and walked around it, trying to establish its significance, and indeed its possible relevance to his current work, for most things in this detestable county of Loamshire seemed somehow to be linked, especially phenomena from the natural world. His shadowing of Inspector Kernan had taught him that much, and he suspected this fish mound indicated something untoward which he must be wary of. Perhaps it was some zodiacal rite, this being the day Pisces gave way to Aries in the heavens?

He was directing a golden stream onto the topmost dace when a naked hag emerged from the bushes and rushed towards him. Guessing that his glazing of the fish represented the source of her fury, he backed away, trying to return his penis to a safe haven before making his escape, but in his confusion, tripped and fell backwards over the bank, and into the river, where he hit his head on a rock, rolled over and then started floating out into the middle of the river, face downwards, his arms outstretched like a bat, joining a convoy of sticks and dead chub.

Muffy walked over to the black Suzuki. The spare wheel fixed above the bulbous tow-bar had a cream plastic cover on which was pictured a black rhinoceros. When someone came upon this shining car, she felt certain they would not report it, but would surely steal it. It was a gift horse, and the person or rhinoceros who claimed it need not look it in the mouth.

A hundred yards downstream, around the Dealchurch bend in the river, Herne had been looking for otters, but of course there were none. Their old haunts had been taken over by the vicious little mink. Sitting on the elm log where once he had watched young otters splashing each other in the shallows, he saw the body of a man drifting out into the current, its fawn raincoat trailing in the water like a stingray's wings. The dead man was a dead fish now. He stared at this apparition, trying to convince himself that it wasn't there, not because he couldn't believe in the corpse-fish but because it didn't belong in his river. The strange sight felt somehow familiar, as if he had seen it before, somewhere else, in another time. A man fish, dead. A fish man. Fish or man. Fishman. Fisherman, angler.

And he, Herne, a fisher of men. Fisher.

Kernan looked down at the water fizzing on the shingle. He heard a wood warbler's sibillant stutter in the bushes behind him.

– The sea is calm tonight, he said, into the dusk, from where he judged the trilling *tee-oo* call had come.

– Matthew Arnold, said a voice, as if in reply.

– No problems with the tail? asked Kernan.

– None at all, he seems to have disappeared, said Lionel Tench, emerging from behind the breakwater.

– Same with me, said Kernan. I don't suppose it will last, so let's make what we can with this brief respite.

– There's not much I can give you, said Tench, except perhaps a few leads. As you must know, the Superintendent took away all Dad's papers, part of the investigation he said.

– I didn't know that. But you can get them back now.

– The material can't be found. It has gone missing, as they say.

– Do you know what was in it, what he was doing?

– Experiments. I'm not a scientist myself, but I used to help Dad, taking down readings, washing flasks and tubes, that kind of thing, while he was working, and he used to talk away about this stuff, though much of it was over my head.

– These experiments, they were about BSE? Kernan asked.

– That's right. Dad didn't think BSE was linked to scrapie. He said the two diseases were both caused by a rogue protein, something devoid of DNA and RNA called a prion, or PrP, which is short for 'proteinaceous infectious particle'. This prion mutated in the brain, and that could happen in any mammal, including man, without it being transferred between species, although transmission was theoretically possible, and had in fact happened with some TSEs.

– TSEs?

– Transmissible spongiform encephalopathies. Scrapie in sheep, BSE in cattle, CJD in humans. The first PrP mutation occurs on its own, probably triggered by some environmental factor. It's called the two-hit theory. They say one poison drives out another, but Dad said this was more a case of one poison kicking off another. One possible catalyst is organophosphates, used in farming, as in sheep dips. And there are OP traces in drinking water. Once the mutation occurs, it can be passed on to other animals of the same species. The whole thing's a chain reaction, from mutation to infection. Dad was always saying that: *it's all to do with chains*. Chains and amplification were the two words he kept worrying over, like a dog that couldn't leave a bone.

– *Chains and amplification*, Kernan repeated. *Chains and amplifications*, as if these concepts from science were somehow vital clues to the Tench case, which he had to decipher, or apply in other ways. As a writer would in plotting a novel.

– Scrapie's been around for over two hundred years, Lionel Tench went on, but there's rarely ever been more than ten sheep affected in a single flock. They have been known to pass it on to goats, and they've also passed it to their young, probably in their milk, but never to cattle.

– And BSE? That can't have been around that long…

– Only since 1986 in Britain. But what caused it to spread, according to Dad, was MRM, mechanically recovered meat, which is like putting a cow through a wringer and turning the whole animal, bone, meat, marrow and brains, into paste. And when you mince up the remains of an infected animal, and feed it to another poor unsuspecting herbivorous cow…

– They get infected.

– Exactly. And because the MRM is *concentrated*, the power of the infection is *amplified*. Although to be fair to the farmers, many of them didn't know what they were giving their stock. They thought it was something called protein mix. But before BSE came along, Dad was involved in developing a method of pasteurising animal concentrates. I remember him being very angry about that. He said the treatment was ready in 1978, but a year later, it was dropped. It would have added a penny to the price of a bag of feed.

– A penny a bag? said Kernan. And since then they've had to fork out millions…

– Yes, it wasn't implemented, and that opened the door to changes in processing. The fat used to be removed with solvents. But with MRM, that wasn't necessary. It was all grist to the mill.

– *Grist and gristle*. But there must be more to it than that, that's just the meat process side. What's the connection with CJD?

– Dad used to say the main connection was money and war. He said pesticide technology grew out of research on nerve gas. VX was developed during the last war by I.G. Farben in Germany for use in the gas chambers as an alternative to Zyklon B, before it was modified into an agricultural pesticide. Military nerve gas used in Iraq contained OPs as well as phthalimid, the basic unit of thalidomide. Sarin was used on the Kurds by Saddam and in that attack on the Tokyo subway. And whether in nerve gas or pesticides, the result is the same. OPs destroy DNA, causing blindness and triggering mutations. It's not a coincidence that research on OP pesticides was carried out at Porton Down...

– All right, I can see the war connection, but where's the link with money? Presumably big business?

– I don't know. Dad was just involved in the scientific side. But he said he knew the real threat now was money, not war.

– But why would anyone want to kill him if he didn't have the full story?

– Maybe they thought he did. Or perhaps he was getting close, I don't know.

– He must have been onto something, even if he didn't know it. It may have been staring him in the face. Something tells me I'm looking at the same clues, even if I can't see them yet. I think I'm following a trail of money, but I don't know where it's leading me.

– Dad said time would tell. We just had to wait, and it would all come out. The whole thing would unravel.

Who'll carry the link?
I, said the Linnet,
I'll fetch it in a minute,
I'll carry the link.

Oliver de Foie was going through some old notebooks of his grandfather's, looking for something he knew Hans Gans had written about admixtures. They weren't easy to follow, scrawled in thick Gothic script with a scratchy pen whose black ink went thick and thin as Hans must have dipped it clumsily in and out of his laboratory inkwell, trying to keep up with his racing thoughts.

He recognised the passage he had been searching for when he spotted a large black inkblot, which Hans's Swiss friend

Hermann Rorschach would have relished deciphering, for it looked like a man on a cross; and there, as if summoned by the image, was his grandfather's account of his work on the two mustard gases, Grünkreuz or *green-cross* and Blaukreuz, *blue-cross*. Blaukreuz was a strong irritant that could partially penetrate gasmasks, whereas Grünkreuz was merely 'typical' in its behaviour, as Hans noted, a poison gas not unlike phosgene. But mix the two together and you had Buntkreuz, and anyone attacked with this *motley-cross* gas would tear off their masks as it penetrated them, exposing themselves to the rest of the cocktail.

The concept was brilliant, a kind of double-hit mixture. One gas did the penetrating, while the other killed the victim. It ought to be possible to do something similar to the warble grub. To do that, you had to penetrate the skin of the cow but without turning the whole animal into a poisonous environment. You had to be careful too about the amount of phthalimid in the mixture. You weren't bothered about that in a nerve gas, but in a systemic pesticide you had to be careful. Apart from anything else, the word itself was emotive to the English, after that thalidomide business in the sixties.

Words were curious things, he thought, they seemed to hold a power for own, like chemical names, or these German coinings in his grandfather's notebook. He said them aloud, to relish their sound:

– *Grünkreuz, Blaukreuz, Buntkreuz. Grünkreuz. Blaukreuz. Buntkreuz.*

He liked *Grünkreuz* especially. Wasn't there a piece of Beethoven, the Grünkreuz sonata, or something like that? He would have to ask Patty. She knew such things. She listened to music.

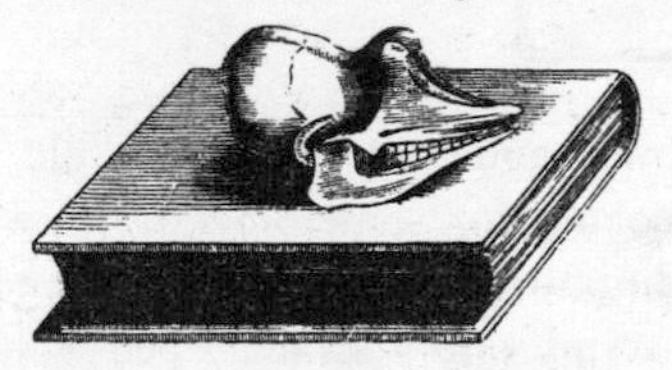

A shot rang out in the woods above Long Wood Farm. A couple of seconds later, there were two more, accompanied by a flurry of indignant rooks above the tree-tops. Diana was always unnerved by these isolated gunshots. They were always shooting something around Loamfield. It was too early for pheasants, unless these were poachers.

There was a dead rabbit on the road, but it had been run over.

She climbed the stile, and headed up the field towards the woods. Halfway up, she caught sight of Jack Armstrong bobbing along on his quad.

– Hello Bess, she called to his dog, who raced ahead of her master to greet her. It was usually a good idea to address a farm dog in Loamshire, otherwise the farmer might ignore you, particularly if you were a woman. Armstrong replied on behalf of the dog, keeping the engine running.

– Evening, he said.

– What's that shooting up there? she asked.

– Rabbits most like, he said, as if the animals themselves were firing the guns.

– Busy day? she asked.

– Could say that, he said. I been putting in spring wheat in the top field. Just finished now.

Above the sound of the puttering engine, Diana could hear a clamour of voices from the layby below where she had parked. There was barking too, not the yappy cries of farm dogs but the discordant bass growling of larger animals.

Gesturing to the noise over the rise, she told Armstrong:

– If those men ask if you've seen a woman around Long Wood, take them to the hedge and tell them you last saw a woman here when you'd just finished sowing your wheat.

She fixed him with her eyes, holding him to her will until he had no choice but to comply.

– That'd be true, he agreed. Only I wouldn't want to lie to their kind. They'd know at once.

– First give me a lift on your quad, said Diana, up to the top gate by the woods.

She clung onto the seat as they lurched up the hill, the dog running alongside excitedly, dancing round the wheels. They heard more shots from the wood.

– You mind them others too, said Armstrong as she left him at the gate. He was watching her disappear into Long Wood when the men from below came over the rise with their sticks and dogs. Their leader, a bullet-headed man, was wearing army surplus camouflage trousers, with a rope-patterned thick green pullover patched at the elbows and shoulders.

– You seen a woman here? he asked gruffly, confronting the farmer, his voice harsh, his manner sharp and unsubtle.

– Last time I seen a woman up here were just after I put in my wheat, he answered, pointing over the hedge to the top field he had sown that afternoon.

The men followed his finger to where the tall stalks waved in the breeze, a whole undulating field of wheat moving as one, rippling like the fur on the back of a vast sleek animal which had slept all through the winter, and was now coming to life.

The narrow lane leading up to Long Wood Farm was lined by high walls, bounding woods on the one side, the Maw Estate on the other, both walled off to keep the deer in and the poachers out. Through the trees the white glow of the waxing moon gave Kernan just enough light to see his way. Sensing a trap with every step, his lynx-sharp eyes scanned the road ahead, as well as the capstones along the two Loamshire sandstone boundary walls.

Diana had not returned. He knew something was wrong. Because he had to move stealthily, he had left his car near the crossroads, where the old drover's track met one of the two bitumen roads. From there he had made his way on foot, aware that taking the road was dangerous, but confident his senses were now so acute that he would see, hear or smell anyone long before they were close enough, giving him enough time to scale either of the walls and make his escape.

The danger, when it came, was not the kind he'd anticipated. He had expected a man, or men, lying in wait, but instead was suddenly aware of the shadowy form of a car in the middle of the road ahead, black and silent, seemingly empty. He saw a movement inside as someone swung up from the seat, turned on the ignition, and accelerated with a flying start, headlights full on, bearing down upon him. He stood still, frozen, like a hare caught in a blinding beam, knowing there was no way he could clamber over either wall in time. Waiting for the car to hit him, he took in its shape, recognising a Suzuki four-wheel-drive.

If Sergeant Oxter was expecting to feel the satisfying thump of a body hitting the murderous bull-bars of the boss's new car, he was to be disappointed, for in the instant when Kernan had stood in the dead centre of the road, his arms outstretched as if crucified, when his right foot was pressed down hard on the accelerator, and he must have been within a car length of bashing him into oblivion, he had found himself hurtling into a white dazzling light. Jamming on the brakes, he skidded to a halt further down the lane, and looked back to where it seemed that a bright blaze of light was disappearing, pooling up through the trees like a white fireball towards the crescent moon.

Diana was waiting in the clearing at the top of Long Wood, gazing up into a white radiance which seemed to descend from the moon itself. She had given the men the slip, and while this manifestation of light was so awesome she should feel frightened, she was not afraid. Whatever it was, she felt sure it was opposed to the posse she had evaded. She could almost bathe in this pure white moonlight.

Then a figure stood before her, golden-robed, with white-feathered wings, like a swan's, stretching out from the shoulders in a great effulgent canopy, and a kindly face, green-eyed; whether a man or a woman she couldn't tell, it didn't seem to matter. Yet while acknowledging the staggering beauty of this fulgent being, she also felt there was something very familiar about this angel.

– Fear not, it announced.

– Don't worry, said Diana. I'm not afraid. You don't have to go into that routine.

If this was one of Kernan's tricks, he was not going to get away with it. She would treat this angel the way she treated its creator.

– Talk of an angel and you'll hear his wings, this one said, as if reading her mind.

– Talk of the devil and he's sure to appear, she countered.

– Diana, thou art highly favoured. The Lord is with thee, blessed art thou among women.

– I've heard that line before, she said. If it's a shag you want, you can forget it.

– Oh woe, said the angel, with a hurt look. Oh where now is purity of thought? Where is beauty of language?

– Get to the point, said Diana. What do you want?

– It's not a question of what I want, said the angel. It's the Boss. He wishes to be reborn through you, to have His Second Coming.

– The first time was too quick was it? It always is.

– Come again?

– Where do I fit into this plan? Do I have any choice? I don't think I want to sleep with your Boss…

The angel flapped its wings in annoyance, making a draught so powerful it almost knocked Diana off her feet. Angels weren't used to being treated with this kind of disrespect, except by demons and heretical theologians.

– Look, you've got this all wrong, the angel said. This is a great honour, you will give birth…

– How am I going to manage that, if I'm not going to sleep with him? Diana protested. I'm not sleeping with someone I've never met, least of all some bloke who can't even come and ask me himself. Where's the romance in that?

– You do not have to sleep with Him, said the angel, pausing to recall the speech he was meant to be delivering. Her impudence had spoiled its oratory flow.

– His Holy Ghost shall come upon thee, the angel continued. That sounded good. What else was in the script?

– Come upon me? What, all over me? *Yum yum…*

– The power of the Highest shall overshadow thee, said the angel, getting into the rhythm of what was really quite a good speech for an annunciation. Therefore that holy thing which shall be born of thee shall be the Son of God, because you are undefiled. And you shall call him Cernunnos, which means Lord of the Forests…

– Ah, said Diana, I thought *he'd* have a hand in this. But was Kernan himself the angel, or had he sent the angel to her? Either way, it was very convincing, this splendid angel, with its dashing looks and great wings, she could almost fancy it. She could imagine how Leda must have felt when Zeus had laid her. If Kernan really had become this creature, she might have some fun with it at his expense.

– You are free from original sin, the angel continued. You can redeem the sins of Eve. Your womb is a garden enclosed, a spring shut up, a fountain sealed…

– Hang on, said Diana, don't get carried away too soon. I'm hardly a virgin, am I, so how am I free from original sin?

– You have not committed the sin of sexual intercourse. The devil has not tempted you to sleep with a man.

– You've got that wrong. I've been tempted a few times, yes, but the foreplay was usually so bad I sent them packing. Men are so clumsy. They don't know how to use their fingers, let alone their tongues. But a woman knows how to satisfy a woman. And if you know all about the state of my womb, you'll know I've slept with many women, so I can't be a virgin.

– That doesn't count, said the angel. You're still a virgin in the eyes of the Lord. Your womb is uncorrupted by man's seed.

– Bollocks.

– And the Saviour must be born of a virgin if he is to be immortal and redeem the sins of the world.

– What about the natural processes of birth? asked Diana. They're good enough for the animals – they're without sin – so why aren't they good enough for you?

– They are links in the chain of original sin, the angel replied. What you call natural is bound to the corruption of sexuality and decay. Death can only be overcome by denying the natural process of entry into life. If you are not born, you cannot die.

– So you're saying spirit is separate from nature? Does it say that in the Bible, the holy book which is the word of God?

– Luke gets close to it. Mary is the inviolate vessel for God's holy word. As he says, *For with God nothing shall be impossible*. And if you read Augustine, or Ambrose, or Jerome…

– Male revisionists, said Diana scornfully. I thought as much. And you've taken on all their claptrap. I thought nature was meant to be sacred. It's the men who have tried to divide us from nature, Augustine and Aquinas, with all their talk about us being tainted from our mother's wombs. They go on about their precious spirituality when what they're really doing is trying to have everything their own way, denying nature, denying women.

– Don't blame me, I'm just the messenger, said the angel, looking uncomfortable. To tell you the truth, I'm not that happy with it myself. Things were different when we didn't have this monotheopoly. There's no competition now. Belief was much more fulfilling when we had a free market. You didn't just do what you were told, you worked things out for yourself. You thought about things more because there were no easy answers.

– And women didn't have to choose between Eve and Mary.

– Precisely. There were many possibilities. I remember when I worked for Artemis: she may have been demanding, but you knew where you were with her, even if she was a bit harsh on poor Actaeon. I served Aphrodite too, as well as Demeter, Persephone, Hera and Hestia. Ares and Zeus didn't get much of a look in then. The women kept them on their toes. Things were more balanced.

– We're agreed then?

– So you really *don't* want to be a vessel for the Lord? asked the angel with sudden surprise, as if not realising that Diana had moved the theological goalposts. That's what came of listening to reason. What *would* the Almighty say when He found out?

– Not at the moment I don't, said Diana. If I change my mind, I'll let you know. And if I do, I won't want any immaculate conception. I can get that from a clinic. If I'm going to give birth, I want everything to be natural, and that includes the sex, which I imagine in this case could be heavenly as well as animal. I'd expect nothing less from the Holy Ghost, no fumbling from that quarter...

– It wouldn't be the Ghost if it was physical. It would have to be the Father or the Son.

– Either would be an improvement on the men I've known, said Diana, smiling broadly, as she realised the infinite possibilities of celestial sensation. She wondered what a beatified orgasm would feel like. Perhaps this wasn't such a bad idea after all.

– God isn't a man. He is neither man nor woman, but both; He is all things.

– So why do you say He, and why is He called the Lord?

– That's just a manner of speaking...

– Very convenient for the men.

– We could hardly call Him *It*, like an animal.

– Aren't animals all God's creatures? The divine immanent in nature? Isn't our nature part of nature? Women have always believed that.

– That's how they got into trouble with the Inquisition, said the angel, ruefully. They said witchcraft comes from carnal lust, which in women is insatiable...

– And they also said nature had to be constrained, said Diana, touching the scatter of leaves and sticks on the ground with her foot. But it's not just the priests, you know. It's the same in science. Francis Bacon said you had to *torture* nature's secrets from her, that nature had to be *hounded in her wandering, bound into service, made a slave to man*.

– I've never been comfortable with that notion. I prefer Blake myself, *everything that lives is holy*.

At the mention of Blake, Diana looked up, and found she was talking to Kernan, who had lost his great white wings and all his shimmering angel's radiance, yet there was still an iridescent aura about him, many colours faintly dancing on his skin, but with green predominant.

She started beating him on the chest with her hands.

– You bastard Kernan, she said. You got me to say all that.

– But it was *in* you, he said, and grabbed her flailing arms, gripping them to still her frantic attack. And I could see you were starting to get interested, I could see it in your eyes. *With a fol-de-rol-de-rol-de-rol-de-rigeo, in-your-eyes-ee-oh*.

– No way, she protested. No way.

– You wouldn't like to be taken by the Angel of the Lord?

– Not on your life.

Simple Simon went a-hunting,
For to catch a hare;
He rode a goat about the streets,
But couldn't catch one there.

CHAPTER EIGHT

The Dead Spit

EASTER: APRIL 4TH–8TH

Spittle, like blood, is a centre of soul-power, and a potent agent of magic and protection. To avert evil, you must spit on meeting a piebald horse or a magpie, a cross-eyed person or a chimney sweep, or when seeing the new moon for the first time. To be safe from spells, spit into your right shoe before putting it on, or into your own piss. Always spit before going into any dangerous place.

Composing herself in preparation, Muffy looked up at the Great Hare on the moon's bright face, which men not surprisingly called the Man in the Moon, just as they'd made everyone believe that 13 was unlucky. She knew otherwise. The Hare was a picture of Eostre, whose movable feast followed the goddess's first appearance in the spring. While the men had turned Easter into their Christian festival, they still followed the Hare, celebrating their own god's resurrection on the first Sunday after the first full moon after the spring equinox. And was it not the custom once to welcome Green George, the witches' god and spirit of spring on that same day, the moonday following the sunday when the Christ was resurrected? This then was a lucky day, one of the year's 13 full moons, when Muffy refreshed the earth with her magical blood. A day of miracles.

She stood where the shore jutted out at Duckwidge Ditch, where the man in the rhinoceros car had tripped backwards and fallen into the River Otter. The only sign he had been here was a small strip of red and white police incident tape attached to a tree. But no one had come after her, accusing her of complicity in his fate. His death had not even been reported in the *Loamshire Chronicle*, which was strange. It was as if he had never existed, and so could not have died. And if he did not die, she could not be blamed for his death. The Otter had taken his body, and someone had taken his black car. Apart from her, only the river gods seemed to know of his death. They said he was not a good man but a spook. The water was always pleased to carry off a man of bad intent, especially one without a name or identity.

Standing naked like a wraith on the riverbank, Muffy watched the play of moonlight on the water. This was always a magical time of night. It was too dark to see the shoals of the fish dead which must be clustered around the long black branches making their steady progress downstream. There was only this silver light, and the sound of the water. She began to chant:

> I shall go intill a hare
> With sorrow and sych and meickle care;
> And I shall go in the Devil's name
> Ay while I come home again.

Ernest Gubbins was perplexed. Much as he disliked the thought and act, he needed to wash. If he wanted to spend time with his new friends Wild Bill Fraser and the other security men, his body odour had to be less pervasive than the greater smell, that of the white ammoniacal plumes joining the two colossal chimneys of the Eurochimique plant to the low cloud cover, droplets from which hung over the village like invisible mist, but unfortunately, as the saying goes, *reek comes aye down again*

however high it flees. The lovely hartshorn smell was ever omnipresent, pungent as smelling salts, it never went away. The other waste gases, those leaking from the side-vents, he found less pleasing – their aroma rather too understated for his taste – unaware that this particular cocktail was actually more potently carcinogenic than the more visible main cause of public concern. If an ecological action group had gained access to Gubbins' nose and powers of discrimination in matters of pollution, his data would have enabled them to have the factory shut down.

In order to wash, you needed water, but his wife believed that water might harm her six-week-old washbasin, which she had produced after a painful labour. She said the basin, a white Tudor Ambassador from the *Gloriana* range, with gold taps and a white plug on a gold chain, was so large it had needed to be delivered by Caesarian section. He was pleased he had not been present to witness this spectacle. She also claimed that the set of matching yellow and orange hand-towels and flannels which had come with the basin had been rolled up inside the placenta.

Gubbins was dubious, but what lent credence to his wife's tale was the fact that when you turned the cold tap, it did not spout cold water but a stream of curses. He tried it again, just to make sure, hoping this time that water would issue forth instead, but what trickled over his hands was a curse on his drunkenness:

Piss a Bed,
Piss a Bed,
Barley Butt,
Your Bum is so heavy
You can't get up.

The same curse kept repeating itself, so he turned off the tap. When he tried again, it was a different curse:

Who with thy leaves shall wipe, at need,
The place, where swelling Piles do breed:
May every ill, that bites, or smarts,
Perplex thee in thy hinder-parts.

– *Knuckers*, he said, hoping the magic of his own word would have some effect on the obstreperous basin, but was disappointed. It gurgled briefly, then belched.

He decided against trying the hot tap, which he knew delivered blessings – C for *Curses*, H for *Hot Air*. He'd rather be cursed than blessed any day, but at that moment he was more interested in carrying out this unfamiliar act of washing himself. He would have to speak to the Coot.

Sitting in her television bower, Mrs Gubbins tut-tutted a favourite soap opera, tossing back her black hair, which was streaked from the brow with white, like the plumage of a coot. Now spring had arrived, she was starting to moult like a dog.

– That shouldn't be allowed, she was saying. It's not right that they should make us watch this kind of thing in our own homes.

– You could always switch it off if you don't like it, suggested Gubbins, spitting his disgust into the fire.

– What's the use of having TV if you can't watch it, she replied, frowning as she watched her husband hawk forth another gobbet of phlegm.

– I wish you wouldn't do that, she said. His yellowish sputum sizzled on the coals, turned black, then sprouted wings, flying blindly around the room, knocking against the lightshade so that the light swung crazily about. She looked up as her husband's latest bat flapped against the ceiling above her, making threatening squeals, before taking a run at the window and smashing through the glass like a high velocity projectile.

– Do what? asked Gubbins.

– Make bats in the fire, she replied, running her fingers through her hair and shaking out a tuft onto the floor.

– I'm only spitting. A man's gotta spit or he ain't a man.

– But your spit turns into bats which break my windows.

– So what's new? My wife gives birth to a washbasin. I wanted a son and my wife gives me a basin that curses me every time I touch it.

– Who said the basin was yours? she said, darting an evil-looking glance at him.

– So it's not my basin?

– How could it be? You've seen those towels. It wouldn't have got yellow and orange flannels from you. I think the father was that Bird's-Foot Trefoil I met in the woods. Eggs and Bacon, it called itself. She shook her head sagely, and hair flew out like airborne down. Gubbins sneezed.

– But I let you keep it in the house, he said.

– Would you turn it out on the streets? I suppose you'd throw it in some skip for anyone to find. You're a hard man, Ernest Gubbins. You don't just stink, you're rotten to the core.

– Not as rotten as you, Gubbins retorted.

– You stink like a skunk.

– And you look like one.

– You stink like a goat, worse than a polecat. You're a pain in the arse, a ked in the bed.

– *Coot, coot, get under my boot…*

> Bat, bat, come under the tap,
> And I'll give you her eggs and bacon.
> And when I fart, I'll give you a tart
> To lick out in her basin.

The Coot did not respond. Her eyes were glued to a woman cursing her husband on the television.

– You've no more wit than a coot, he sallied, turning the knife.

– You are a very codshead, she spat back, glancing from her husband to the television ogre. You'd seek a hare in a hen's nest, she added, addressing his double on the screen.

– The wit of you and the wool of a blue dog would make a good medley, he snarled, firing the channel zapper at the TV as if to kill it. The fuzzy picture shrank into black silence.

– You're not worth a tinker's turd, and you smell like one, Ernest Gubbins, his wife cried, snatching the remote back from him. I should have listened to my mother. All that man's fancy talk is nothing but tripe, she used to say of you.

– Tripe's good meat if it be well wiped.

Henry Sirloin looked at his wife. She had just rejected his sexual advances, pushing his hand from her usually eager breast, with a string of negatives:

– No, no Henry. I can't. I don't think I can bear to have my breasts touched. Not now.

– I'm sorry, he said. And for once his apology was genuine. He did not know how to cope with this situation, having to think about Candida's feelings. He had been confronted too with his own feelings. Where once they had both flitted between different lovers, yet still enjoyed each other's company and love-making, now he only wanted her.

– I love you, he said, squeezing her hand. You know that, don't you, old girl?

Henry Sirloin couldn't remember when he had last told his wife that he loved her. He hadn't thought himself capable of caring, and used to say she cared more about the dog than him. But now Shuck was dead. And Candida had breast cancer. He didn't know how, but the two blows seemed somehow connected.

Later that day, sitting in his study, he found himself going through some old fileboxes. He wasn't sure what he was looking for, but knew it related in some way to Candida. There was something he remembered from some Ministry report about cancer. He hadn't given it much thought at the time, it had just seemed like one of many scares he had to deal with every day. While much of this information was suppressed, he had kept his own copies of many of the documents; if there was any truth in them, it had seemed wrong to destroy them totally. Although the lure of power, money and a good lifestyle had put paid to most of his convictions, his sense of fair play had always held back his advancement in the party. He knew he needed to be economical with the truth, but to do that convincingly he had to fully know for himself the nature of the truth he was required to hold back.

Here it was: a report warning of the dangers of oestrogenic chemicals in detergents and plastics, which had caused sex reversal in fish. According to the lab reports, they were also present in packaging materials, and the scientists believed they could leach from containers into food. He hadn't given this much credence at the time, being scornful of findings based on sex changes in dace and roach. Yet since then there had been that business of chemicals in baby milk affecting sperm counts. He ploughed through more statistics about fish until he came across the item he had been seeking: that oestrogen mimics made breast cancer cells multiply and spread. It also stated that another cause of breast cancer was DDT.

Candida's father must have used DDT products on their farm. When he died, they had sold the place in that scam, which had ended up with Oliver getting the land he needed for expanding his factory, while they had been able to buy Hackerton Manor. At the time he remembered thinking it appropriate that land which had thrived using Oliver's fertilisers should now be taken over by Oliver's plant. However, Oliver must have changed over from DDT as soon as the dangers were known; the changeover had been quite sudden, as such things went. He decided to give Oliver a ring, to reassure himself.

Once connected by an officious operator, he found his friend in a jovial mood.

– Just a general enquiry, Oliver, he said. One of my constituents has some worries which I'd like to allay for her, about DDT.

– Oh yes, said Oliver, laughing. We haven't made DDT for years, not for use in this country. You can tell her that. But best not mention that DDT's still around of course.

– What do you mean?

– Well, it doesn't just go away once you stop using it. It stays around in the environment, probably for up to fifty years. Organochlorines were very strong. Good product. Did the job well.

– But it had unfortunate side effects...

– Everything has side effects, Henry. Nothing's pure. Nothing's safe. The least unsafe, that's what we go for, isn't it, like in politics. What is that phrase of yours, *political expediency*? Same as in your love life, from what I hear, he giggled. You hope you won't get caught. And you hope you won't catch anything.

– But you managed to find something to use instead, didn't you? Sirloin persisted, ignoring the goad. You made a quick switchover?

– Quick? I wouldn't say it was quick, my friend. The public thought it was, that's true. One minute it was DDT, the next it was OPs. But we couldn't market our own product for some time. Foreign companies had the patents, and we couldn't have our farmers buying from them, could we? So everyone carried on using DDT, and no one was the wiser till we changed. But Henry, don't tell your woman that. It's no joke, I can tell you. We lost a lot of money over that business.

– Thank you, Oliver. That's all I need to know.

Putting down the phone, he felt a lump at the back of his throat. And started to cry.

Kernan sat on the stile, waiting for his informer, whom he trusted he would recognise. He was pleased that Diana had not asked him how the rendezvous had been fixed, for she might not believe him even now. A grey crow had brought him word from the magpies in Hangman's Wood that they'd been told by a chough that someone important wished to talk with him. Magpies were generally fickle, inclined to embroider stories to suit their own fancies, but if the original source were a chough they might not have dared change anything in the message. Many of the birds believed that King Arthur lived on in the form of a chough, and since you could never be sure which chough it was, it was advisable to honour the word of all choughs. The villagers must once have held a similar belief, for they thought it was not only unlucky to kill a chough, but somehow sacrilegious, as if it held some sacred power, like the raven, which they feared as well as respected. Kernan's regular informers included two ravens, whom he named Hugin and Munin, after Odin's messenger birds, who were as reliable as the crows. As the saying went, *The raven told it, the grey crow told it:* anything they said had to be true. He that takes the raven for his guide will light on carrion.

A murder of crows, an unkindness of ravens, though ravens were kind enough to assist in his policing of Loamshire; not for nothing were choughs called a chattering, and starlings a murmuration. He wondered if Goodman had any inkling as to the nature of his network. His feathered friends certainly thought so, pointing to the relish with which the superintendent blasted any passing bird out of the sky when supposedly engaged in killing just pheasant or grouse.

– *Don't you want to talk then?* said a voice.

He looked down. Lost in his bird thoughts, he had not seen the hare arrive.

– I'm sorry, he said. I didn't see you.

– What you cannot see you will not find, said the hare mysteriously. You must not forget these are the Borrowed Days. What does that mean to you?

– The first nine days of April are borrowed by March: *three to fleece the blackbird, three to punish the stone-chat, three days for the grey cow.*

– Good, said the hare, you have it. Remember that. Now tell me the prophecy of Finneces, teacher of your Fionn Mac Cumhaill.

– That he'd catch the Salmon of Knowledge? Kernan tried.

– Yes, but what happened when he caught it?

– He set Fionn to cook it, but as the fire grew hotter, the fish-juice spat out onto Fionn's thumb, which he thrust into his mouth to cool, so receiving all knowledge. The youth gained the knowledge the old man had sought, by an accident.

– That's right, said the hare, you have it. Now tell it the Welsh way. Why do they remember the 30th of April?

– That was when the poet Taliesin was washed into Gwyddno's weir, where Elphin found him. As the boy Gwion, he tended Ceridwen's cauldron of knowledge until, again, he accidently splashed his finger and received all knowledge.

– And what did Ceridwen do when she saw this?

– Taliesin turned himself into a hare, and Ceridwen chased him as a greyhound; then he became a bird and a grain of wheat, and she an otter and a hawk. As a hen, she ate him as a wheat-grain, and he was reborn of her womb.

– You have it all, the whole story, said the hare. Now you have to put it together.

– How will I know when I've done that? asked Kernan.

– You will know when it happens, said the hare.

– But how may I change shape? I cannot do it at will.

– How it does it happen then?

– Often by accident, said Kernan, and paused, realising he had stumbled on something of significance. Or it happens when I'm in danger, or when someone else's life is threatened.

– So you must not be afraid of danger. You will only receive knowledge by seeking danger. That is why it has taken you this long. When you were not sulking like Achilles in his tent, you were avoiding danger...

– ...and involvement?

– You will have to die many more deaths before you find yourself through someone's death and someone's love…

If maidens could sing like blackbirds and thrushes
If maidens could sing like blackbirds and thrushes
How soon the young men would go beating the bushes
Sing: Fal-de-ral, tal-de-ral, fal-ral-lal-day.

If maidens were hares and raced round the mountain
If maidens were hares and raced round the mountain
Young men would take guns and soon go a-hunting
Sing: Fal-de-ral, tal-de-ral, fal-ral-lal-day.

If maidens could swim like ducks in the water
If maidens could swim like ducks in the water
Young men would turn drakes and soon dive in after
Sing: Fal-de-ral, tal-de-ral, fal-ral-lal-day.

If maidens could sleep like sheep on the mountain
If maidens could sleep like sheep on the mountain
How many young men would lie down beside them
Sing: Fal-de-ral, tal-de-ral, fal-ral-lal-day.

And if all the maidens were trees in the valleys
If all the maidens were trees in the valleys
Then all the young men would creep up on their bellies
Sing: Fal-de-ral, tal-de-ral, fal-ral-lal-day.

He was about to ask another question, but with its last *fal-de-ral-lal day* the hare had gone. Just then he heard behind him in the lane the footsteps of Jack Armstrong with his dog Bess. The farmer had spotted the policeman sitting at the edge of his field. He was apparently talking to the ground, but nothing surprised him where Kernan was concerned. His dad used to say Kernan's father was a strange cove too, the dead spit of his grandfather.

George Kernan had not slept at all that night, anticipating the morning attack, his first in daylight. He had crouched on the fire-step, watching the snow falling from above into the trench, opening his mouth like a chameleon to catch the cold wet flakes on his long tongue. Water had been napoo for days, and he had even accepted the rum ration, which he'd usually spurned as the officers' poison sop to the men, a means to despatch them half-fuddled to their deaths. But snow was better; it was cleaner. He would rather die clear-headed, to know the exact moment of his own death. For hours he had counted the minutes till zero, unable to grasp the slowness of their passing. When the others woke, they were all glancing at their watches, their heads jerking down like obsessive birds pecking at seed. As they neared zero, their wide eyes as well as their watches seemed synchronised. They had five minutes left.

This was the maddest of times. A clear blue sky on Sunday, no wind; then a foot of snow overnight, everyone wet through, the first wave now dashing towards the barbed wire in broad daylight, into a blizzard. He looked at his watch again: the Irish Fusiliers had been first over, followed by the York and Lancs. The Loamshires were next, *four minutes*. He heard the chatter of machine-guns, the mechanical rattle of death's production line, then the clamorous shouts and cries of the men, who could almost be urging on their team from the touchline at home. *Three minutes.*

Waiting for the whistle, he felt relieved that this longest of Easters was about to end, possibly with his death, certainly with the deaths of many of the new intake, these Loamshire farm-hands, straight-talking but windy youths who embraced their "duty" as a fact of life, however unfortunate, something they never thought to question, like their oft-stated belief in God. Yet their loyalty was less to King and Country than to village and home; they enlisted out of family pride, and stayed the course because they were all in it together. They weren't afraid to die, they said, but he had seen their hands shaking when they took communion. They were like frightened rabbits. *Two minutes.*

There had been three Easter services, and Kernan had attended all of them, hoping the rituals might offer some distraction, if not solace. They were makeshift affairs, the first an evening service on Good Friday at 5.30; then on Saturday morning, communion at 10.30. A young lieutenant had been so moved that he had stood up after the sermon, and asked if he could add a few thoughts of his own. He said he was placing his body in God's keeping, and would be going into battle with His name on his lips, full of confidence and trusting implicitly in Him. Kernan looked around as he spoke. The others looked at him blankly, nodding their assent.

– Not all of us here will survive this attack, announced the lieutenant, whose name was Coombes. You know what the men say: if a bullet has your number on it, there's nothing you can do about it. I don't go along with that idea of fate. But if it's God's holy will to call me away, I am quite prepared to go. I could not pray for a finer death. Any man here who does not come back will have died doing his duty to our God, our Country and our King. There could be no greater honour than for us to give up our lives for the sake of King and Country. We have no choice but to do our duty, for this sacrifice we've been asked to make is a necessary one.

As the others muttered agreement, only the Colonel looked away from the fresh-faced lieutenant. He knew, thought Kernan. Those rumours about Haig and Lloyd George. They were true, he knew that now; just the downward set of the Colonel's shoulders told him that. Theirs would be a totally worthless sacrifice. Captain Nicholas had hinted at the battle plan: once the infantry had broken through, the cavalry would charge in after them and wreak havoc behind the German lines. Against machine-guns. Against artillery shells. Thousands of men would be slaughtered needlessly on both sides, just because Haig was obsessed with his campaign of attrition, because he had to be pushing forward all the time, because he had to stay in command at all costs. This was no sacrifice. It was bloody murder.

Despite the sick feeling that was growing inside him, Kernan had gone to the Easter Sunday gathering as well. Was it really too late for the madness to stop? On this day, of all days, couldn't something happen to end it? A miracle, a change of heart, or simply divine intervention? This service had been at 8.30. All the services had started exactly on time, just as the attack had, at 7.30 on Easter Monday morning. And in one minute precisely, he would go over the top.

There had been about twenty communicants kneeling in three rows on sandbags, officers and men together, facing an altar consisting of two candles perched on a Vickers gun chest with a white cloth in front. Kernan had stopped singing *Nearer my God to Thee* when the words struck home: was this indoctrination or willing sacrifice? Then the chaplain preached what seemed impossible in that place: *Love your enemies, do well to them that do spitefully to you.* Afterwards, the Colonel had chipped in with a short sermon on bayonets, and their usefulness. German prisoners needed to be fed and were no use unless they had information. The Church would lose them the War if given too much rope.

Kernan heard no whistle in all the commotion, but everyone was now mounting the parapet, so he spat at his feet and followed suit, urging on others to his left. As he went over, he knew not to stop, but strode forward, and kept striding, until the machine-gun fire was so thick that everyone ahead of him was falling, some knocked sideways, some just slumping to the ground like dummies, others cut into pieces. Suddenly all were throwing themselves to the deck, as if by a signal, and they lay there on the open ground for some minutes, waiting for reinforcements, or for the artillery to take out the guns or smash a hole through the wire. Or for a some kind of miracle. But nothing happened to save them. The Boche gunners started picking them off one by one where they lay, standing out like blackbirds in the snow. Bill Armstrong cried out when he was shot in the chest. Then Wilf Hartley, his leg blown off. In thirty seconds, Lieutenant Coombes disavowed the notion of sacrifice; propped up one elbow, he was trying to stop his intestines from spilling out of his belly. He called across to the others for someone to shoot him, but none of his platoon could obey him. They were all dead.

Watching from the trench through his field-glasses, Captain Nicholas saw his latest batch of Loamshire lads being wiped out in front of his eyes. This time Kernan would not survive. But then he picked out the figure of the sergeant in the middle of No Man's Land standing like a March hare bolt upright in a field. He seemed to be darting from side to side, weaving a kind of dance like a bee, all the time firing off rounds at the German line, whose gunners followed him with a hail of bullets which somehow he evaded. As he drew their fire, the other men began picking themselves up, and moving forward, till within minutes they had all reached the other side. The next division soon caught up with them, and they too went down into the German trenches. The machine-guns had stopped.

His last sight of Kernan had been of him whirling like a

dervish in the middle of the blizzard, all the Boche seeming to train their guns on this one extraordinary figure, as if mesmerised into having to kill this one man instead of the hundreds of others converging upon them. Rushing through the snow towards the spot he had memorised, he saw the sergeant standing there, out in the open, waiting at attention as if for orders from above, as if he had expected to die that the others might live, but having survived, against all odds, needed some new purpose. He looked shell-shocked.

As he came near, their eyes met, and Kernan must have known at once what was in his mind, for he moved sideways like a crab, as suddenly as a rabbit from the hooves of a horse, dropping down into some kind of bolt-hole, a dugout or shell-hole.

Until Kernan's reaction, the Captain had not been fully aware of his own intentions, but now they were clear: that he would make sure the only decoration his sergeant would receive for his mad bravery would be a posthumous one, for in the chaos of the battlefield it would be an easy matter for him to shoot him here. He knew he must be exhausted, and was probably cowering like a cornered animal, shivering in the snow.

When Captain Nicholas reached the dugout, he found it empty. Its only inhabitant was a large grey rat, which he chased away in order to retrieve Kernan's Lee-Enfield. But of Kernan himself, there was no sign. The Captain picked up the rifle, and examined it, as if looking for an explanation. He saw immediately that the gun had not been fired, and yet he had seen him with his own eyes firing and reloading, again and again, firing, stooping and reloading, those jerky movements in Kernan's frenzied dance of death.

Captain Nicholas swore as the rat ran across his boot. He turned his gun on it in anger, but stopped himself, saying:

– Don't sink to that, shooting a bloated trench-rat, when it could have been Kernan. No use wasting good bullets on a rat.

Although it was now dark outside, Superintendent Goodman ignored his anglepoise, preferring to work in shadows. In the flickering half-light cast by his computer screen, his vulpine features were exaggerated to ghostliness, his dark brow furrowed as if about to strike, like the tensed back of a cobra.

Kernan's files were like a labyrinth, drawing him down hopeful paths only to confront him with one dead-end after another. Clicking the mouse to retrace his steps, he returned to the main menu, then started off down another track. He hadn't expect to find anything specific, but what he *didn't* find might in itself be a clue. For example, which files had Kernan *not* accessed? He was also likely to have started a hare, to have lodged a few red herrings in the system. Recognise those, and he would know to follow opposite directions. Or might Kernan anticipate that, and the hare be to follow a contrary trail?

He started fishing through Kernan's file menus, and finding a folder called FISH, pounced on it with the mouse. Inside was another folder called FISH. And inside that another FISH. He kept clicking, going from folder to folder, as if through a series of Chinese fish boxes. This was a game of Kernan's, but he couldn't resist playing it. Even if it was meaningless, the contents of the last folder might be significant simply by virtue of what it said about Kernan's state of mind. Of course he might just find another empty folder, but he credited the Inspector with more wit than that. He'd have to put something inside it.

If he achieved nothing else, Kernan was certainly winding him up. There seemed to be hundreds of folders to click through. And yet they must end. There had to be a last folder. By the time he reached it, his mouse finger was starting to ache.

Inside the folder was a document. He clicked on it, and the file opened to reveal a single sentence in large letters:

THERE'S NOTHING A VULTURE HATES SO MUCH AS A GLASS EYE

He looked blankly at the white screen. What does *that* mean? he asked it. What's he saying? *Is that it?* He spat the words at the computer, his spittle hissing on the hot machine.

The tomb was empty.

BOOK III

BELTANE

MAY – JULY

I saw a fishpond all on fire
I saw a house bow to a squire
I saw a parson twelve feet high
I saw a cottage near the sky
I saw a balloon made of lead
I saw a coffin drop down dead
I saw two sparrows run a race
I saw two horses making lace
I saw a girl just like a cat
I saw a kitten wear a hat
I saw a man who saw these too
And said though strange they all were true.

CHAPTER NINE

May Day, May Day

BELTANE: APRIL 30TH – MAY 1ST

On Beltane Eve, nine men must take nine sticks from nine different trees and make a fire drill. Two separate bonfires are lit from this new flame, and all animals and people driven between them, to purge all life of winter diseases, plague, famine and other misfortunes from the dark or Samhain half of the year. This ordeal is remembered in the Scots Gaelic expression 'hotter than the fires of Beul'. Brands kindled at Beltane fires are borne to each household to rekindle household lights and fires previously extinguished in preparation for the coming of this new light. In different places Bel fire is also called Bale fire, Need or Neat fire, Wild or Will fire, Forced, Forlorn or Running fire.

N*eed fire*, Kernan wrote. He was writing a lecture for the Loamshire Antiquarian Society. His paper on May lore wouldn't frighten any horses, but it had his own thoughts racing as he picked out gobbets from his notes, between mouthfuls of a festive breakfast of scrambled egg and smoked salmon:

> Beltane fires were condemned by the Church as a pagan practice in 742, but in 1834 a public kindling took place in Carlisle during an outbreak of Foot and Mouth Disease, and "need fire" was made at Troutbeck in 1851 as a remedy for cattle plague.

Pushing his plate to one side, he sucked his reddening thumb. Distracted by the implications of *need fire*, he hadn't given enough attention to the cooking, and hot fish-juice had spat from the pan and burned his hand. Was this a sign? Was he fiddling with his folklore while England was burning? He'd been preoccupied with the question of the Church's ambivalence towards Beltane, how it stood for everything they held in low esteem, like dancing, singing, and…

– *As I roved out one bright May morning, one May morning early*, he started to sing, his voice trembling at first, then lifting with excitement and expectation.

As I roved out one bright May morning
One May morning early
As I roved out one bright May morning
One May morning early
I met a maid upon the way
She was her mama's darling.
With me roo-rum-ra
Fal-the-diddle-a
Star-vee-upple-al-the-di-dee-do.

Unmarried sweethearts went to the woods on Beltane Eve. He would put that in the paper.

At times of self-doubt he'd often wondered if his energies might not be better directed elsewhere, yet he knew his work, his real work, was what sustained him. His knowledge illuminated everything else in his world. Even when wrestling with the most difficult of problems – and the Tench case was more thorny than most – he felt sure that any answers or possible solutions lay partly within himself. He had to look inside as well as outside. He had to make connections between the two.

He remembered how when Patrick lit his Paschal Fire before the druids had kindled the fires of Beltane, this was an open challenge to the custodians of the old religion, an acknowledgement that this age-old celebration of love and renewal was also traditionally a time for conflict, for warfare, feuding and raiding.

At Beltane, cattle weren't just driven through the fires to kill disease or ward off evil, they were also driven away by reivers, just as people were stolen away then into the other world. May Day was when Orfeo's queen Heurodis was kidnapped by the King of the Faeries; and after Gwythyr ap Greidawl's beloved

Creiddylad was carried off like Persephone to the Underworld by Gwyn ap Nudd, King Arthur made the two meet in combat for her for every May Day until Doomsday.

The roving troops of the Fianna led by Fionn Mac Cumhaill were billeted upon and maintained by the people from Samhain until Beltane, when they went forth, living off the land, but he might leave this out, for the phantom armies of the slain still fought it out each May Day at Loch Ashie in Scotland, where Fionn won his great battle. Every year, they hacked each other to pieces with their great swords. He had seen them do it. It was a sickening sight.

O'Scrapie was not at all comfortable with his latest guest, but Acarus wasn't going anywhere else now. He wasn't about to sprout wings and fly off, even though his new host offered him less sustenance than a sheep.

Dr Gallstone, however, was delighted with the little mite. This was the first case he had come across of *Psoroptes communis ovis* causing psoroptic mange, or sheep scab, in humans. As he described in salacious detail the effects of the disease to his patient, he ordered him to stop scratching his skin.

– It will make the inflammation much worse, he said, making notes not just for O'Scrapie's bulging medical file but also for an article he intended to write for *The Lancet*.

– What can you give me for it then? asked O'Scrapie.

– If you were sheep, said the doctor, I might prescribe diazinon or propetamphos. They'd kill off the wee mite, but they'd probably kill you as well.

– I'll chance it, said O'Scrapie, furiously scratching his arm. I have to get rid of this infernal itch. Give me a prescription for them.

– I can't. Those are organophosphate pesticides. They don't sell OPs at the chemist's.

– I must have a fix, where can I get it? said O'Scrapie, with a frantic look in his eyes, like an addict in cold turkey.

– Complete immersion in a bath of sheep dip, the doctor suggested. Try asking for that at the hospital.

– Hospital? asked O'Scrapie, suddenly alarmed.

– Yes, you're going to have to be quarantined. This form of mange is highly contagious in sheep, and we can't run the risk of you spreading it to humans. So I'm afraid I'm going to have to request that you be held for compulsory treatment under the provisions of the Sheep Scab Order of 1976.

He that will not endure to itch must endure to smart.

Unknown to Acarus or his host, another infection was taking place at that moment. After weeks of abstinence, Henry Sirloin was no longer able to restrain his lustful inclinations, and had accepted a thinly-veiled invitation to 'lunch' with Lady Olivia Prurigeaux.

– On *Mayday, Mayday*, she had said on the phone. You know, Henry, a distress call has nothing to do with May Day. It is French, and it means *M'aider, m'aider*. Help me, help me.

– What would you want me to help you with? he had asked, in a teasing tone.

– That depends, she had said. We can start with a joint of beef.

– Do you think you can manage a big piece of beef-on-the-bone at lunchtime?

They were now onto dessert, or more precisely, the widow of the Leader of Otteridge District Council was sitting astride the Member for North Loamshire, sliding her hands under her buttocks to playfully scratch his penis as it entered her for the ninth time.

Olivia Prurigeaux liked to maintain the tradition of having uninterrupted sex for several hours on May Day, and as a result was now quite sore. As her fingernails drew more blood from his maypole-like shaft, he gave her a final shot of his best semen along with an unwanted present from Patty de Foie, the virus Hepatitis B.

Goodman was in his element. Fire. *Two fires.* The red cock was crowing in stereo, two roaring crackle-voiced firebirds. He stood next to the larger of the bonfires, feeling its wall of heat, mindful of the village youths running at breakneck pace through the narrow gap between them, a local custom, so he was told, yet it seemed more like a red rag to the rowdiest elements of the Bull. They spilled from the pub onto the Green, excited like puppies, merry as soused grigs, goading each other in the afternoon sunshine to greater feats of bravado as they emptied rows of tankards down their throats.

Now they were cheering a squad of Morrismen, who were cracking swords together in a stick dance, bells jangling from their legs, resplendent in the red and white costume which advertised their allegiance – the drinkers claimed – to the local football team.

– *Otter, Otter, Otter!* one called out.

– *Ridge, Ridge, Ridge!* the others responded, as the Morrismen romped towards each other, with a *clack, clack, clack* of their wooden weapons. Finally the dancers encircled the tall bobbing figure of the Jack-in-the-Green, a man covered from head to foot in dense foliage, topped with a white floral crown. Like an unsteady hedge, he swayed from side to side, trying to avoid the wooden swords being thrust towards him. Each time a Morrisman lunged forward in an exaggerated gesture, sinking his weapon into the greenery, the men outside the Bull jeered, their enthusiasm heightened not just by ale but by the knowledge that this year's Jack was their old adversary, Sergeant Malcolm Oxter, who had "volunteered" as his contribution to Inspector Kernan's community policing initiative.

Kernan himself was the Jack's attendant Green Man, his face begrimed with burnt cork like a combat soldier beneath a bushy headpiece. He jogged along beside the dancers, his leafy costume rustling as he swept his wooden sword above his head in pantomime fashion, preparing for the final blow. Once all the Morris-men had delivered their blows, and the Jack-in-the-Green fell over dead, it was his task as Green Man to strike off his floral crown, before the crowd would be invited to each take a leaf or flower from the Jack for luck.

As he was about to topple over, it seemed to Kernan that the Jack was changing shape, that he was no longer the jaunty half-comical human hedge but a huge Green Man, a real Green Man with green skin and grassy hair floating like a green silky fan around his shoulders, his beard a nest of leaves tumbling over the fur-trimmed hood of a green cloak. His clothes were all green, and embroidered with brightly-coloured birds and butterflies. Behind him there now waited a green steed, its mane and tail plaited with twists of shining gold and green gossamer, its saddle and accoutrements studded with garnets and emeralds. In one hand he held a holly cluster; in the other, a giant axe of greenish steel, its great haft wound with iron, hung with green tassels.

When Kernan started to back away, the Green Knight moved towards him submissively, proffering the green axe.

– You are the Hawk of May, he said. Gwalchmai ap Gwyar, you cannot refuse my challenge. You must strike my head from my shoulders, and in a year's time submit yourself to the same trial.

Kernan looked about him. The crowd was silent, waiting. Then he took the axe, and bowed. The Knight knelt before him, pulling back his hair to expose a bare green neck like a young tree stripped of its bark. Sunlight glinted on the green blade as he swung it in the air, bringing it down upon the Knight's neck, severing his head with a single blow.

As the head rolled to one side, and blood gushed forth from the neck stump, the Knight did not fall or falter, but sprang forward on legs still sturdy. Kernan stood motionless, frozen with fear, knowing, unlike the crowd, that the Green Knight would collect his head, and ride off.

– Meet me in a year's time, said the headless man, bending down to pick up his head. Kernan was unsure whether the voice came from within the body or from the head now held under one arm. With his free hand, the Green Knight pulled himself up into his saddle.

– At the Green Chapel, said Kernan, looking up. And was momentarily disconcerted to see the tall Jack-in-the-Green overbalancing, falling towards him.

– Get out the way, Kernan, said a rasping voice from inside the hedge.

Kernan obeyed, and as the Jack-in-the-Green toppled like a tree to the ground, the crowd yelled *Timber!* He stood over the fallen figure, as if unsure of his next move.

– Don't just stand there! called someone.

– Crown him! another shouted.

– Knucker him! cried Ernest Gubbins.

– Clobber him! ordered Superintendent Goodman.

He did so, bringing down the wooden sword with a swagger and shout to please the crowd, with none of the dignity of his ceremonious despatching of the Green Knight. The floral crown came off in a flurry of white petals.

– *Ouch*, said Oxter. *That was a bit close.*

Shell after shell whined over their heads, some exploding along the line of barbed wire, some hitting the barely visible concrete pillboxes, others landing behind, sending up massive exclamations of earth. In the dull half-light of dawn, with the half moon still giving some illumination, Kernan strained his eyes, trying but not wanting to see the shapes or parts of men thrown up in these explosions.

Kernan watched Lieutenant Lambert, waiting for the young officer's hand to grasp the whistle hanging from a khaki lanyard round his neck; as when an umpire's hand moves inexorably from his side, to raise a finger in the air, so he dreaded that moment which would end all waiting.

Touching the bulky, unfamiliar revolver at his side, as if to check it was still there, he exchanged glances with Marshall, Fisher, Johnson and Gingell. Their faces were tensed. They looked like bandits from the Wild West, criss-crossed with khaki bandoliers of cartridges, and with a sack of Mills bombs hanging from one shoulder. They gripped their trusty Lee-Enfields.

Nicholas was not going on this raid, only a select team of a dozen men was needed, which meant it must be dangerous... *or had been devised to be so*, thought Kernan. They would be in good hands with Lieutenant Lambert, the Captain had told them. Kernan doubted it. Lambert was a decent enough fellow, but he was raw. This week was his first action in the lines, he was straight out of OTC. At this moment, he was staring into space, as if he'd just seen a ghost. His pale spotty face was visibly twitching. The officer was scared shitless, but trying not to show it.

The plan was that once through the wire, which a patrol would have cut during the night, they would split into two groups, one under Lambert including himself, the other under CSM Fraser, and each would tackle a pillbox. Two men would throw their grenades inside, while the others would dash round the back to grab at least one startled prisoner. Captain Nicholas did not seem to think it worth mentioning that these were the same invincible machine-gun posts which had repelled all their previous attacks, and that the Boche gunners would be firing bursts at them through the very slats through which the bombs had to be hurled. But the men knew this. Kernan wondered if Lambert did.

The bombardment stopped. Seconds later, the lieutenant blew his whistle, and climbing the steps, urged them all to follow, his fluty Public School voice half-strangled into a barely coherent squeak. Kernan was next over the top, with Marshall, Johnson, Gingell and the new lad Davis scrambling after him, Fraser's six hot on their heels. They spread out in a straggly line, stumbling towards the places where the wire was meant to have been breached. Getting himself and two of the others through the rusty entanglement of spiky wires, Kernan did not realise at first that Lambert was not with them, but looking back as they started moving towards the pillboxes, he saw the lieutenant wriggling in a dense bush of wire, crying out in a thin, pleading voice, becoming more snared the more he struggled.

As the machine-guns opened up all around them, he signalled to the others to keep their heads down and, ducking, half ran, half crawled back to the line of barbed wire. Pushing Lambert's frantic head and shoulders downwards, he lifted the wire up, pulling the ripped material of his clothes from the hateful spikes. As he did so, a bullet burned through his left hand. He thrust it down in a sudden reaction, causing the wire to spring back onto the officer's back.

– *Shit!* he said, looking at his red pulpy palm, disbelieving what his eyes saw, as if the hand were someone else's. He winced at the pain, then returned to help Lambert, who hadn't noticed his sergeant had been hit. He looked up with frightened eyes, as if he thought that in letting go of the wire, Kernan had decided to leave him there.

– *Now keep flat on your belly, sir*, he said. *Crawl like a fucking snake.* He was surprised at himself, swearing at an officer, but he had to be firm. And his hand was burning like hell.

– Thank you, thank you, Lambert squealed.

– *Keep down!* said Kernan, as across to their left he saw Fraser's group being cut to pieces by machine-gun fire as they struggled to get through the wire. He shielded Lambert from the sight, pulling at him with his good hand every time he stopped.

One of the men seemed to be pinned to the wire. In the next instant a burst of machine-gun fire caught him in the neck, severing his head. As the head flew off like a coconut, blood gushed forth from the man's neck stump. He did not fall but stayed standing, his arms stretched out like a scarecrow's, holding him there. Headless. Kernan turned away.

– You have to go forward, he said to Lambert. We'll be killed out here.

– Yes, yes.

Amid the staccato cacophony of the machine-guns and the bonfire crackling of rifles, with bullets flying so near he could feel their draught in his hair, Kernan had not realised that despite their slow progress they were almost beneath one of the pillboxes. His hand reached out and touched what he knew immediately was a body. It was Jimmy Gingell. Both his legs had been blown off in a hail of bullets which must have disembowelled him. Slumped against Gingell's corpse, Lambert was moaning. Kernan lay on his back, staring at the concrete monster spitting fire above him.

Then he saw a rapid movement to the right of the pillbox, and the figure of Marshall dancing quickly to lob a Mills bomb through a gunslot, jumping backwards in almost the same movement to avoid the blast. But he was too late, and the débris from the explosion knocked him down the slope.

– You wait here now, he said to Lambert. Just lie there, and *don't move*. He stressed the last two words, knowing the officer wouldn't be going anywhere, but wanting him simply not to do anything. Right now he needed to help Johnson, Fisher and Davis, if they hadn't been killed.

Ducking from machine-gun fire directed at him from the other pillboxes, he ran forward, crouching as he did so, one burning hand hanging useless, his other clutching the revolver as he rushed the side of the concrete blockhouse, and caught up with Fisher, who was firing at the Germans inside.

– You can't do that, said Kernan.

– That was for Bill and Jimmy, he said. And the other lads.

– All right, all right, said Kernan. Now that's enough. And pointing his revolver into the smoky blackness, he yelled inside in German that anyone still alive should come out with their hands up, and they would not be shot.

Two grey-uniformed men from a Saxon regiment stumbled forward, a private and an unteroffizier.

– Search them, he told Fisher. And *don't* shoot them.

– You there, he said sharply. You speak English?

The officer shook his head, pursing his lips to show he would tell them nothing. The private, however, began babbling in a twangy Saxon dialect which Kernan found hard to follow. He seemed to be a simple lad.

– His name is Ernst, he told Fisher. He comes from near Dresden. His father is a dairyman. I can't make out much of the rest. His accent's very thick. He's in a state of shock, all his talk is about the farm. I'll see what I can find out in there.

He lowered his head, and went slowly inside, holding out his revolver like a divining rod. Dismembered bodies were thrown across each other; which limbs belonged to which men he could not tell. How the others had survived he was at a loss to know. Everything was burnt or mixed with earth, rubble or human flesh. There were no documents. Nothing was left. Nothing.

Returning to Fisher and the two prisoners, he stopped at the entrance to be sick.

– We'll have to cross further up, Kernan said. They have a clear line of fire where Fraser's group got stuck.

– You look after that hand. I'll get these Boche back.

They set off back down the slope, Kernan stopping for Lambert, who was still lying on his belly, shaking. Fisher went ahead, his rifle prodding the two Germans through the tangle of wire. As they ran across No Man's Land, another pillbox opened fire, killing the prisoners in the first burst. Kernan tugged at Lambert:

– *Come on run! There's a trench over there, we have to reach it.*

The hail of bullets reached them just as they fell down into an outpost trench, Kernan pulling the officer in after him. The lieutenant was gibbering in a high-pitched voice like a monkey, gabbling something incomprehensible. Kernan slapped his face, and grabbing his shoulders, spat at him.

– We've made it! Now don't let Nicholas catch you like this.

– Like what? barked the Captain, suddenly upon them. Like what, sergeant?

– It's nothing, said Lambert quickly. And look, the sergeant's wounded, he added, noticing Kernan's hand for the first time.

– The bullet seems to have gone straight through, Kernan said. It's hard to tell with the swelling, but it seems to have gone straight between the bones. I'm lucky.

– Davis could have done with your luck, said a familiar voice. Kernan recognised Jack Hart, the gamekeeper from the Estate, a different man in his corporal's uniform.

– But a St Joseph's child... stammered Kernan.

– No, he's not dead. They took him to base hospital, what's left of him, his body that is. He was quite untouched, looks fit as a fiddle, but Joe himself has fled the fort. He's a ghost...

– What happened to you? Nicholas interrupted, glaring at Kernan.

The luck of the man.

Almost out of eyesight, a lemon-coloured speck seemed to be dancing in the black mud. Kernan lay still, listening to its thin staccato song in the eerie silence. It was a long time since he had last heard a yellow bunting, and now to hear one, on this day, of all days! It repeated its familiar song, which sounded like *A-little-bit-of-bread-and-no-cheese! A-little-bit-of-bread-and-no-cheese!* If he had some bread with him now, he would willingly feed it to the little finch.

He remembered that belief of the Scots, that the yellowhammer, as they called it, was a bird from hell, its colours, a wasp's yellow and black, the Devil's livery. They heard its song as *Wheitil te, wheitil te, whae, harry my nest and the de'il take ye*, ending in a shriek; and on May Day the yellowhammer drinks a drop of Satan's blood. Some said the little vampire-finch sucked blood all year round, which was why the yellow bunting was almost hunted to extinction in some parts. He tried to hear the *Wheitil te, wheitil te, whae* phrasing in its song, but all he could hear was *A-little-bit-of-bread-and-no-cheese! A little-bit-of-bread-and-no-cheese!* Then a shot rang out, and the yellow bunting soared skywards in response, but cleanly, for it hadn't been hit.

– Damned bird, said a voice not far behind him, probably less than ten yards away.

He kept his head down. He dared not move an inch.

So Maw was on the prowl again, Kernan reflected. And was not shooting game good cover? *Jack, Jack Joe bent his bow, shot at a pigeon and killed a crow…*

Bruce Tucker had fled back to London, following a series of frantic calls on his mobile. He couldn't believe what was happening. He was supposed to be the most predatory operator in Aussie real estate, yet someone else had the gall to speculate with shares in one of *his* companies; and that same someone was probably behind the recent poaching on his territory. But where were they getting their information? Bluey and Slim Jim had been no help at all.

– Thatshowitis sometimes, said the fat Queenslander. Shit happens.

– Slimsright, agreed Bluey. Thing is notta lit it gitchadown, she'll be orright mate.

– Shit happens, said Slim Jim again, as if his repetition of a phrase Tucker liked using himself might be helpful to him.

As she watched his black Jaguar disappear down the drive, Lizzie fingered her honeysuckle, noting with satisfaction that it was starting to take over. Soon it would display its lovely yellow flowers, whose scent inspired erotic dreams in young girls. Idiot farmers used to drape their cowsheds with honeysuckle and rowan to protect their beasts from the malign influence of witches, unaware this only kept warlocks away, not witches, who loved all rich-scented flowers, honeysuckle especially. Perhaps it was true. Tucker was no warlock, but nor was he easy about the honeysuckle, joking how he was a man who thought plants belonged in the garden not in the house; still, he let her have her way in matters of furnishing and decoration.

He never lingered in the porch. She couldn't trust anyone who wasn't easy with plants and animals. Yet for all his untrustworthiness, Tucker was still trusting where she was concerned, mainly because he had never actually taken much interest either in her or in her work. Like many men, he did not actually know or understand the woman he lived with; instead, he had an idea of who she was, and he would try to slot the woman herself into this idea, just as he would try to slot his cock into the woman when she seemed disposed to accept it without protestations of tiredness or shows of indifference to his needs. Most of the time, he spoke and she listened. She was a good listener, and she actually seemed to follow his accounts of his business dealings, or certainly those involving people she knew. She'd helped him through some sticky patches.

But when Lizzie tried to discuss her magazine work, she never got far, because he would switch off and start to talk over her about his business associates and their dealings with him, waving his mobile phone in the air like a prop. Which was fortunate for her. His moby often chose that moment to ring, providing a further distraction and a cause or excuse for their conversation to take off in other directions afterwards.

Lizzie also possessed a mobile phone. Now she took it from her bag, tapped out a sequence of numbers, and waited.

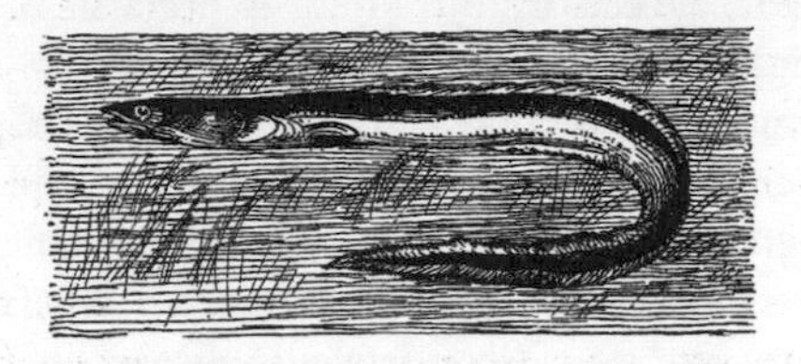

Checking his booking with Flitch, the red-faced proprietor of The One-Eyed Eel, Assistant Chief Constable Lambert included his first name, Lawrence, with emphasis.

– *Lawrence* Lambert, he said, Table for two for eight o'clock. My friend is meeting me here.

It was something ingrained in him after years of trying to expunge the nickname which had followed him from school. *Always Lawrence, never Larry*, he would tell anyone on first meeting them. In consequence of this habit of overemphasis, the dreaded nickname had inevitably resurfaced in every new work-place, as in Otteridge, where he was known to all in the Loam-shire Police – but never to his face – as Larry the Lamb or Never Larry, or sometimes as the Bald-Headed Lamb, a play on the name of a pub in the town. He was never happy as Larry.

Never Larry never called himself a bachelor. He had become one not by choice but simply because the right woman had never come along, or so he liked to think, because he was a workaholic, and had neither time to socialise nor opportunities to meet anyone outside the police. He ate his cock alone and saddled his horse alone, yet it was his unacknowledged hard graft which kept his Loamshire team together, whatever his junior officers might think, for the canteen view, he'd heard, was that Never Larry never went anywhere, never got much done, and never took the initiative. Saveloy's absences weren't a problem – the golf-course was the best place for him – he got more work done when the Chief Constable wasn't around. But when Saveloy was at the station he was usually closeted with Goodman, and Never Larry never felt comfortable about that, although taking part in meetings with the two of them could be even more unsettling.

He would hover at the door, repelled by Goodman's dark threatening eyes inside the room as well as by Saveloy's pungent breath, which hung around the doorway like the stale smell of old fat drifting from the air vent of a fish and chip shop.

Now the young DC, Diana Hunter, greeted him, rising from their table as he approached. She at least seemed pleased to see him.

He wasn't used to a liaison of this kind. It seemed somehow wrong, as if he were married and they were having an affair. The waiter's attitude certainly seemed to register that interpretation. They had each driven twenty miles beyond Ottermouth to this restaurant, as if acknowledging a mutual clandestine purpose. While he had many misgivings – an ACC having dinner with a young woman constable in the same force – that possible misinterpretation of their meeting had at least served to cloak its real purpose when he had agreed to it, not just from others but for himself. He recognised that a confrontation with Goodman and Saveloy was inevitable now, but he was still wanting to avoid it, to drag things out as long as he could. Yet while his instinct was to prevaricate, he had not hesitated to agree to this meeting. It was as though he had recognised that events were now moving so surely that they must be unstoppable, and where once he had feared any intervention on his part would have ended in a bungle, and in his fall, now there was a strong chance of a different outcome.

He filled the awkward preliminaries with talk of starters, what was the soup of the day, whether they should have red or white wine. Preferring white himself, he sensed in her hesitation that she would like red, and so asked for a good red. When the main course was being set out, and he had still not moved beyond pleasantries, Diana stabbed a potato and deposited it on her plate, naming their *bête noire* as she did so, as if she were piercing the superintendent with her fork.

– Goodman has… she began, I mean Super*intendent* Goodman has – so I believe – his own "archive" of material not recorded in the files, on the computer. This is what I've been told.

– Yes, I've heard something similar, said Lambert.

– And should you not have access to this, as Assistant Chief Constable?

– In theory, yes. But in practice, I cannot interfere. This material is not meant to exist. I am not meant to know about it. If I were to raise the matter, I would need the Chief Constable's permission to pursue it. I am – you might say – caught between a rock and a hard place.

– You're caught between the devil and the deep blue sea, Mr Lambert.

– Yes, yes, he replied, adding: *Lawrence*, you can call me Lawrence.

– Lawrence, she repeated, making him look up. For the first time he noticed her eyes, how green they were.

– The only way of getting at that stuff would be with a proper search of his office and house, he continued. And since Goodman has, apparently, done nothing wrong, there's no way I could justify seeking such a warrant. It would put me in an impossible position. I'd need a reason to act. I'd need to be sure that I'd find something which would be incriminating, incontrovertibly so.

– But you can't know what's there unless you look for it. If you want to find answers, you have to ask questions.

– It's not just a question of asking questions, I have to be *able* to ask questions, said Lambert, trimming a piece of fat from his roast lamb and pushing it to the side of his plate. At the moment, I can't go that far.

– What would change your mind? What would you need to persuade you? asked Diana, fixing him with a penetrating gaze, from which he turned away, to attend to the slicing of his meat.

– Information that is 100% accurate, he said. Which I *know* and have *proof* is 100% accurate. And support. I would need support from others because any move against Goodman would be hostile to Saveloy. I would have to go over his head.

– And you can't do that yet? Not with all the doubts which must exist in certain people's minds?

– No, said the ACC, struggling to keep some peas balanced on his fork. Because they both know too many other people. They're in a strong position. And they're partly there – they can stay there – because I'm perceived in certain quarters as a check on them. There are some things they won't do, actions they won't take, because I'm around, and most people want to keep things that way.

The peas fell off his fork. One splashed gravy on the white table-cloth, and rolled across the table. Lambert watched its progress, making no attempt to stop it from dropping onto the floor.

– There's nothing I can do, he said. *Not yet*. He was in retreat. He wanted to move forward, but couldn't.

– So dun is in the mire, said Diana, wiping some food from the corner of her mouth with the thick starched napkin.

He saw the brown stain on the white cloth, and thought for a moment of her underclothes, what they must look like. Just a faint trace of soiling, that was rather an attractive thought. He looked at her hands gripping the cutlery, her long fingers, the tiny crescent moon at the base of her thumbnail, wanting to reach out and touch that hand, to feel its warmth and softness through his fingertips, to reassure her and himself. But he couldn't. He knew he couldn't do such a thing, even that kind of casual gesture many men practised, the touching of an arm, a hand laid across a shoulder. That was why he had remained a bachelor. He was scared. It went back to when he'd lost most of his hair while still at college. His premature baldness was like a stigma: he only had to touch his smooth bony head, or glance at other men's flowing manes, and he would take himself down another notch. Recently he had taken to shaving at night, to cultivate a daytime stubble where the hair still grew, making a fashionable virtue out of his disfigurement, but this affectation only made his skin look rougher than a dogfish's, and increased the resemblance of this lanky man to a skeleton with a pig's head.

Lawrence Lambert was on a losing ticket. The more he tried to improve his looks, the worse they became. As in his work, so in his personal life, he usually ended up doing nothing, for he didn't want to risk being attacked or rejected. He wanted to be sure that if he touched a woman, that she would respond to him, that if he proffered even a kiss in parting, that she would want him to kiss her, not on the cheek but on the lips. A cheek was non-committal, passive. But when you kissed a woman on the lips, you knew from the way she kissed, the way she moved her lips, whether or not she wanted you. The phrase went round and round his head: *not on the cheek but on the lips.*

Diana Hunter's lips were moving now. They were saying *Goodman, Goodman*. He tried to separate her words into *Good man, Good man, Good man.*

Their two heads, facing each other, clearly animated, could be seen through the window of The One-Eyed Eel. Outside in the car park, a man followed their conversation, relayed to his car by a directional microphone planted on the window-ledge.

What was he doing here, spying on his own side? Kernan asked himself. Why had he followed them? Didn't he trust Diana to carry out this assignment without his involvement?

The sky was clear. The moon had been full the night before, and Muffy looked up at the nearly round moon, huge over Loamsley Moor, and above where the land rose towards Otteridge, the resplendent pilgrimage route of the Milky Way, the Walsingham Way, that great spattering of sperm across the night sky. In Hoggett's Field, the Friesians tore at the grass, their white and black dewsilky flanks shining in the moonlight. Muffy stood amongst them, protective, resting her hand on the back of one silvery cow who gazed up at the stars as she chewed her way through mouthfuls of wet grass, as if following the story Muffy was telling her about the Milky Way and the reiving of animals.

– You know the Welsh name for the Milky Way is Caer Gwydion, after Gwydion who stole the swine of Annwn?

The cow nodded, and carried on chewing.

– But we know it's the Road of the White Cow, don't we, *Bothar na Bo Finne*. And cows are special, cows have always been adored.

The cow liked this, and stopped eating, nudging Muffy with the side of her great cow's head, her big cow eyes staring at the old woman. She gave a deep low:

– We cows are your second mothers. When your mothers take you from the breast, we give you our milk. You humans forget that when you want to eat us. Would you kill and eat your own mothers?

The cow gave a deep bass sigh, and went back to cropping the grass. Her long back was as flat as a table. Muffy ran her hand along it, and started singing an old Irish song about Queen Medb, who wanted to seize the Brown Bull of Cuailnge. In the fight that followed, thousands were slaughtered. Thousands of warriors were slain, because of that one woman and her obsession with the cow.

When Herne lifted the chain from the gate, letting himself into the field, he saw a cow standing apart from the rest of the herd. Beneath its udder sat a doe hare, her head stretched upwards, her mouth pulling on the end of a teat. She did not move away when he approached, but kept supping, giving the cow an occasional gentle tug. A messy drinker, she had milk smeared down her brown fur like a white bib. Herne watched her, entranced, and from somewhere in the field, thought he could hear singing:

Cushy cow, bonny, let down thy milk,
And I will give thee a gown of silk;
A gown of silk and a silver tee,
If thou wilt let down thy milk to me.

CHAPTER TEN

The Living Daylights

JUNE 7TH

The Gaulish month of June-July was called Equos or Horse-Time, the season when you could ride out freely in good weather, and a time for horse-fairs and races. If you see a white horse, you must spit and make a wish, or make a cross on the ground with your foot, or cross your fingers and keep them crossed until you see a dog. The same ritual should be observed on seeing a piebald, which is lucky, though a skewbald frequently is not.

It had seemed like a good idea at the time, but now she was desperately trying to scissor her knees around the horse's belly, Lizzie Gizzard wasn't so sure. She hadn't expected to be so high off the ground, seeing the world from the dangerous height of a small tree. However, when Tom Maw had suggested he show her how to ride, she knew this was too good an opportunity to miss, even if it meant putting up with his braying. Horses would help her strike up closer friendships with the women, whom she knew to be indiscreet. When you're on horseback, you don't just know all things, you hear all the stable talk. Tom might be an airhead, but he blethered on about Mummy this and Daddy that, to the extent that she'd already picked up enough hints to confirm the liaison – of which he seemed unaware – between his mother and Superintendent Goodman.

She had to keep herself free of Brucellosis long enough to pursue these liaisons. The wild goose chase she had set in motion had kept Bruce busy in London for the past few weeks, but she doubted she could keep him running for much longer. There was no flying without wings; sooner or later the bubble would burst, and if he flew with Jackson's hens, she'd lose Featherwether Grange and her foothold in Loamshire. She had to keep him up in the air, which probably meant a change of tactics soon.

The main problem with the horse was staying on, as it jogged along, trying to give her as uncomfortable a ride as possible, though Tom had assured her that her mount, Charlie, was docile, and wouldn't take off because she had thrush in the frog of one hoof. Unlike a man, you couldn't fool a horse. It had known immediately that she was inexperienced, and seemed determined to take full advantage of that, weaving whichever way it pleased, sometimes to put an overhanging branch in front of her, under which she had to duck to avoid being knocked off, sometimes to effect a sudden, steep descent to a stream, from which it would drink, while she looked down from the unaccustomed height of its back, wondering what would happen if the horse turned quickly and she toppled forward into the rock-strewn water. *Trust not a horse's heel nor a dog's tooth.* If this was what horses were like, she'd hate to ride on the top deck of a camel.

The horse gave a sudden lurch, and she felt a jolt go through her pelvic bone. She was starting to feel sore, and would have to stop soon. She needed to stay in good condition.

Tom wasn't being very helpful. As usual, her estuary accent was prompting that familiar English county habit of patronising one's social inferiors. He spoke slowly and loudly when giving instructions, as if she were the horse. But she was grateful for the hybrid accent, while still surprised that men were so easily gulled by the invented voice. The disguise was certainly helping her work, as were her large breasts, even if they felt somewhat uncomfortable when made to swing up and down by this over-jaunty horse.

When men assumed she was stupid, they didn't ask many questions. Henry Sirloin had made that mistake. It had lulled him into a false sense of security; he hadn't even noticed her plying him with more and more drink. He'd been so desperate to get her into bed that he'd blabbed away like a boastful schoolboy, all those slips of the tongue when playing her game of Cash-for-Questions, Sex-for-Answers. That had yielded the name of the friend in the Department of Health who had seen that Tench's milk production licence was removed on spurious hygiene grounds. From the way he grabbed her after blurting out the name, Chawdron, his eyes foolish with drunken lust, she felt sure he wouldn't even recall that indiscretion when he tried to remember the events of that night. He'd been so far gone he'd fallen asleep on top of her, and she'd had to wrestle his leaden body off before she could slip away.

No one had mentioned this case, and there had been no note about it in the Tench file. He was sure he would have remembered it, even though the hearing was ten years ago, according to the newspaper microfiche. Kernan knew he should have read the story in the *Loamshire Chronicle*, which meant it must have been withheld by the editor, despite its local relevance.

Apparently Bernard Tench had refused to have his cattle treated for warble fly with organophosphate pesticide, and had taken the Ministry to the High Court to defend his right as an organic farmer not to have his animals subjected to that particular treatment. Happening long before the BSE scare, the story had only merited a couple of paragraphs in the *Telegraph*.

Tench had stated that the OP chemical was poured along the backs of cattle, whether infected or not, and was designed to penetrate the skin, 'turning the whole internal environment of the cow into a poisonous medium'. The purpose was to kill off the warble grub that could be found even inside the central nervous system itself, but Tench had argued that the chemical could permanently damage proteins inside the nervous systems of both the treated cows and the farmers carrying out the treatment.

The first recorded case of BSE had been two years later, Kernan realised. Lionel Tench had mentioned his father's theory about spongiform encephalopathies being triggered by protein mutation. There must be a connection here, he thought. There was also that later newspaper report, how no case of BSE had occurred in home-reared cattle on organic farms.

But if Bernard Tench had been so successful, even winning his court action, it seemed – with costs awarded against the Ministry – how had he come to stop dairy farming? Why had he switched to arable when cattle were his particular interest? And what had made him start going back to the market years later, just to find and buy infected cattle? More to the point: since this was almost a public service – keeping BSE cattle out of the human food chain – why would anyone want to stop him? The compensation payments only covered his losses, so there was no money in it for him.

Or had Tench been rocking the boat deliberately, trying to draw attention to himself, or to something that was going on? And perhaps he had thought that by doing everything so publicly, he could not be harmed, because whoever he was trying to expose could not risk a court case or investigation. Whatever powder-keg he was sitting on would be blown sky-high.

According to the Geordie sapper, the tunnel under their trench was stuffed with a hundred tons of ammonal, enough to blow a thousand men to pieces. Jackie Laidlaw was proud of his work. A pitman from the Durham coalfields, he'd been transferred from the Durham Light Infantry to a Tunnelling Company of the Royal Engineers. Unknown to most of their troops – and they hoped to the Boche – his team had dug a network of over twenty tunnels. It had been back-breaking work, not just tunnelling with their heavy broad-bladed picks, but putting in the timber supports, then humping back the sandbags of earth, some of it blue clay, which had to be hidden from sight of the German balloons, planes and OPs, and so taken out at night, sometimes thirty or forty bags in a shift. Finally, they set the charge, lugging fifty-pound bags of ammonal down the tunnels, which were hundreds of yards in length.

The Germans had discovered and blown some of tunnels, but most were intact and now nineteen were ready to blow. This was the curtain-raiser to the morning attack. They were sitting on a time-bomb which would go off at dawn, at 3.10 am precisely, exploding the whole skyline from Hill 60 to the Messines Ridge.

As Jackie talked about the state of his hands, after all that digging, Kernan looked down at the reddish star-shaped scar in his left palm, like one of Christ's stigmata, he thought, his own memento of the May Day attack. The wound had healed faster than anyone thought possible. But he still felt a throbbing there, a dull pain around the bones, like that wrenched feeling that survives after a tooth has been pulled.

He remembered how Lambert had visited him in the field hospital, clearly nervous as he sat down by the bed, embarrassed, but also excited like a little boy. Kernan knew at once that the lieutenant had his own news to give, which he was having to delay sharing, to listen first to his medical report.

– They've given me the Military Cross.

– That'll be good for you, said Kernan simply.

Lambert had expected him to ask what he had been given, but Kernan had not said anything more. He knew he had to tell him, but found it hard, and started spluttering.

– I told them you should get one too, or at least a DCM, after all you did, but Captain… I mean they said… They said you're to be offered a Military Medal, or a hundred francs. I wasn't sure which you'd want, neither's exactly appropriate is it? Can't put a price on bravery and all that. But many chaps don't like medals either. It feels a bit like you're showing off, even if you don't mean it that way.

– What about Fisher? Kernan asked.

– He took the francs.

– I don't want anything, said Kernan. Tell them… No don't tell them. Just let them know, please, that I don't want to be given anything. Medals aren't what this war's about. Not that it's not good for you. Officers seem to need them, don't they? They come with the job.

He knew he sounded as though he were playing the martyr. It was hard to avoid the role, because it probably fitted him, but looking up at Lambert, he realised the man was too naive to realise the fault.

– Don't you want a commission? he was asking. I could recommend you.

– I wouldn't get one, so why bother? I don't want one anyway. But thanks for telling me. I'm glad it was you who told me.

That was a month ago, and now he was back in the line. He realised that Jackie had started whispering, for their heavy guns had stopped; the German batteries, as if thankful for the respite, had gone silent too. It was still half an hour before the dawn fireworks, and the night was warm, the moon full and high in a clear, starry sky. It didn't seem possible that this massive explosion, probably the biggest bang in human history, would happen in just thirty minutes, and take the enemy completely by surprise.

And then they heard them, the nightingales. Despite all the shell-fire of the past days, the birds were still there, and singing. He used to hear them often, during lulls in the firing, from somewhere out towards Wytschaete, but thought they must have gone, been killed, when all the trees there were blasted to stumps, the fields pulverised into mud, the farms reduced to rubble. It seemed like a miracle. They were still alive.

Looking around him, he saw the wide-eyed faces of the men. They were all waiting for the imminent attack. A minute ago they'd been checking their watches, looking out at the dark skyline of the ridge, which they'd just been told was about to be blown to Kingdom Come. But now every face was filled with wonder at the song of the nightingales. Every man seemed to be holding his breath.

He wondered who would die today, out of these men listening to the nightingales. Young Lieutenant Lambert perhaps? He'd conquered his fear. His family would be proud of him now: he looked almost dashing, eager to prove himself worthy of his MC; and so youthful.

And Fisher?… Foul-mouthed Ken Fisher, who'd drunk his hundred franc reward in an estaminet in Péronne? Was this his last day on earth? And himself, George Kernan? Could it finally be his turn today, after so many escapes?

Who'll bear the pall?
We, said the Wren,
Both the cock and the hen,
We'll bear the pall.

Who'll sing a psalm?
I, said the Thrush,
As she sat on a bush,
I'll sing a psalm.

Diana's Wound was inflamed. It had plagued her throughout the dinner at the Twa Corbies, stopping her from concentrating on Lawrence's conversation, or from following much of its relevance. When he started talking in a quiet, tentative way about how men found it hard to express their feelings, the Wound delivered an offensive whispered commentary from its perch on her shoulder into her left ear, attributing base motives to this latest invitation from the man it called Old Skullhead.

Until Kernan came along, she thought she'd been able to shut out the Wound, put it behind her. For a long time it hadn't been able to make itself heard. But Kernan had not only heard it, he claimed to have seen it too, and once she acknowledged the Wound, it started making her feel ill at ease, uncomfortable, on edge again; she would become tetchy or even angry at the least provocation, and hurt those she loved, like Mum and – she supposed – Kernan himself, not that she loved him, or could love him, that would be impossible, but she did feel close to him, and knew how to hurt him. She blamed him for the Wound, for bringing it back.

He didn't like her seeing Lawrence, she could tell that from the way he offered her his 'fatherly' advice about not getting too involved. But nothing would happen between her and Lawrence, Kernan should know that. It was an alliance and a friendship, nothing more; it was also useful to Kernan, she had to remind him.

The Wound was as sore now as when she'd lived at home, when she'd had to watch Mum being hit. She recalled that phrase of Dad's, his threat to beat the living daylights out of her, how she'd rushed to Mum afterwards asking if her daylights were all right, and she'd laughed through her tears, and said yes her daylights were fine; if Diana looked after hers when she grew up she was sure to be all right.

Now Lawrence was talking about his mother's disappointment that he hadn't wanted to follow his father into the Army, the Wound was replaying one of Dad's virulent attacks on her; on her ideas, her behaviour, even her clothes. It was his Lady Di routine, the one in which he pretended to puff her up, citing her school results, her place at college, then pricked the bubble, brought her down to earth, how she knew *nothing* about the *real world*, how he was sick of her *la-di-dah* ways. And went for her.

The mental abuse, the Wound reminded her, lasted longer than the violence. It wouldn't still be there to remind her of that if it weren't true. She thought she was so clever, but she hadn't been able to cope with the Wound. She was nothing, it said. She'd never have a successful relationship with anyone because she wasn't capable. She didn't matter. She was a mistake, conceived when Dad had forced himself on Mum when drunk; then the cause, he said, of his later banishment, his estrangement from the woman he called *his* wife, with an emphasis on the possessive, as if he owned her.

But he never owned her daylights, Diana responded: she kept them alive herself, on her own. It wasn't true, what the Wound kept telling her. She *could* love someone else, but only someone she respected and who respected her. It was just that...

– ...*I just didn't meet many people*, Lawrence was saying. *The right person never*...

Diana half rose from her chair, one hand clutching at her shoulder, holding the Wound, trying to throttle it.

– I'm sorry, she said, turning to him, I don't feel very well, I don't know what it is.

Lawrence Lambert looked up at her, solicitous but also fearful. Had he failed again? Had he gone too far in telling her about his feelings of inferiority? Was it anything else he had said? That stuff about being needy maybe? This had surprised him as much as her: he'd felt as if he were making it up on the hoof, he'd never talked about himself like that to anyone before, it was she who had drawn it out of him, her careful questions. Or perhaps she really was just ill, all the colour seemed to have drained from her lovely face, she'd gone white as a sheet, as if she'd seen a ghost.

– *Go on*, said the Wound, *tell him.*

– *Tell him what?* Diana hissed, turning her head to one side to address the squat little demon.

– Tell him your Wound's been playing up. He'd like that. Tell Old Skullhead about your Old Wound and watch him run a mile.

– I've told you before, she whispered. *Don't call him that.* His name is Lawrence, never Skullhead. And never Larry.

– Never Larry never left the starting-post, snarled the Wound. The bald nag's still waiting for starter's orders.

Bill Jarman was talking about his grandfather, Albert. They sat drinking tea in the farm kitchen. His boots stood to attention by the door, reminding Kernan of something he couldn't place.

– He was in the Loamshires. I've still got his medals.

– Military Cross, said Kernan. Passchendaele.

– That's right. You sure knows your stuff. *History of the King's Own Loamshire Hussars,* it's all in there, isn't it?

– I wouldn't know, I was... Kernan began. The cavalry was never my field. It's the infantry I know something about...but they were always meant to link up, weren't they?

– That's right. Grandad said they'd all been told it was sandy up on that ridge, ideal country for horses, but it wasn't of course. It was just mud like the rest. Not that they got there with the horses. Most had been killed in the bombardment, and if they'd tried sending in the cavalry, they'd have been slaughtered too. Horses against machine-guns, I could never understand that, doesn't make no sense.

– Haig thought it would work. That was his theory. Break through the line then have the cavalry charge through the gap to rout them from behind.

– No, but for all he didn't used them in attacks, he as good as killed all them horses on the Western Front, they all died because of him. Shouldn't have been there in the first place.

– Yes, said Kernan. Fourteen million men were killed in the Great War, and twenty-five million horses.

– And after the War, there weren't any horses for the farmers. They packed 'em all off to France then never got 'em back. That's why they went for tractors, so quickly, I think. But Albert's horse came back, my Grandma saw to that.

– Yes, said Kernan, you used to see him in Hoggett's Field, not that he was fit for any work by then.

– That's right, said Jarman. What was his name now, that horse? My Dad told me once.

– Bertie, said Kernan, before he could stop himself.

– Bertie, you're right, said Jarman, not noticing anything odd in Kernan's reply, caught up in his memory of his father's story of the horse who came back. And you know how we got him here? Dad told me that. Grandad had to leave Bertie behind, but he was told if he wanted to buy him afterwards, he'd to clip his initials on the horse's rump, give in his name, and they'd let him know if Bertie was ever being sold. Grandad never saw him again, he was killed when they shelled the troop train at the station. Don't seem fair that, surviving all that time with the horse at the front only to die that way. But anyway, Grandma gets this letter addressed to Albert Jarman, brown envelope marked *On His Majesty's Service*, and she thought this was bad of them, that the Army was still writing to him, but when she opened it, she was overjoyed, Dad said. It was a notice saying that Bertie was being sold at Tattersalls.

– And she got someone to buy him for her? asked Kernan.

– No, said Jarman. She went herself. Everyone else said she was mad, the horse would be next to useless, and she couldn't afford to buy it on her widow's pension. But people chipped in all the same. They could see it was important for her. And Bertie cost her fifty guineas, which was a lot for them days. She said she'd have paid a hundred pound for him. She brought him back in the guard's van of the train, saddled him up outside Otteridge Station, and rode him back to Loamfield.

– She must have loved that horse, said Kernan.

– Dad said she was devoted to Bertie, said Jarman, laughing. When she was much older, she got mixed up and called him Albert. No wonder, Dad used to say, she spent every daylight hour with Bertie, saw more of the horse than she did of him.

– He had one white foot I believe, said Kernan, risking this.

– A white foot. That's right, I remember, Dad used to tell me a rhyme. He said Grandma used to sing it to him. It went:

> One white foot, buy him,
> Two white feet, try him,
> Three white feet, look well about him.
> Four white feet, do without him.

I'd forgotten that. It's years since I knew that. Dad said she used to sing it to the horse.

The fat cat was away with the fairies, shutting its eyes while stealing cream. *Weel kens the mouse when the cat's out of the house*, Izzie had teased. But Nicholas Goodman was no mouse, even if he had been itching to play.

He felt that he was being drawn into a trap, caught in a pincer movement. Lambert's questions had become more pointed. Saveloy wasn't helping, only confirming what he knew himself, that his answers had to be consistent. Oliver had been getting frantic about that leak, blaming him for not stopping the turncoat Tomkins from selling the story to the nationals. And Sirloin had been onto him, questioning him about emergency procedures in the event of an accident at Eurochimique. He'd never been bothered about this before, so why did he want to know now? He didn't believe that line about concern from his constituents. Then there'd been those scrambled phone calls from that woman who said she knew about his affair with Izzie. He'd offered her money, but she'd turned it down; wouldn't say what she wanted. Who was she and what did she know? And Kernan: what was he up to? He couldn't have been inactive while all this was going on. He suspected Kernan's hand lay behind all these plots, but couldn't link him directly with any of them.

He would have to finish with Izzie. It was too risky. There was too much at stake. He'd have to go without for a while. He wouldn't tell her, but this would be the last time they'd share a bed. It was a shame, giving her up, for he adored women with luxuriously corpulent bodies, and she was one of the few who made no demands upon him; she let him enjoy her fleecy flesh without having to discuss *feelings.* He loved fat women with huge, wobbly breasts in which he'd bury his great bullet-head. He loved their wrinkly bellies, their great folds of blubber, the way you could swim on top of their flesh, grabbing handfuls from anywhere as you thrust down into softness. They were always sweaty, and when you stuck your tongue inside their belly-buttons, they'd be yeasty and rancid in there. It was so, so delicious, being with a fat cow, and Izzie was the best and hairiest. He told her this now, and she looked at him in surprise at the rare compliment, her momentary look of puzzlement showing perhaps that she suspected some change had occurred in him.

– Have you got the protection? she asked, pulling at the handcuffs to feign helplessness.

That was one of their awful jokes, their police version of baby-talk in bed, he'd miss all that: his whistle, dick, helmet, Old Bill, truncheon, knob of butter; her bobbies, posse, panda, siren, jam sandwich. Izzie the superintendent, demoting him to inspector, his bullet-head inspecting the scene of the crime between her legs, when he'd have to say *Hello, Hello, Hello* – slowly, the sweep of his tongue enacting the L. And condoms were always 'the protection racket'.

His long arm stretched out from the duvet, clapping a broad hairy paw on the shoulder of the jacket draped across the chair, before fumbling inside for his wallet.

The Fetherlite condom which Goodman extracted was one of three that Diana Hunter had held in her hand some five months before in his office.

He did not look at the blue and white wrapper, but bit at it, tearing it open with his teeth without examining the sheath, which was perforated with a neat pin-hole, hidden when he

He did not look at the blue and white wrapper, but bit at it, tearing it open with his teeth without examining the sheath, *which Diana had wanted to prick* with a neat pin-hole that would

pinched the bulb at the end, his penis standing smartly to attention to be fitted with its translucent rubber riot-gear.

Precisely five minutes from commencement of penetration, Isabella Maw was screaming at the ceiling. Nicholas Goodman was delighted, snorting like a horse, and coming in short, quick bursts, like a pump-action gun, as he slapped her fleshy flanks like a champion jockey reaching the finishing-line. Because they'd always used protection, Isabella had never experienced the sensation of feeling Goodman's semen stinging the doughnut ring of her cervix. It was excruciatingly painful, burning her flesh like napalm, which was not surprising, for Goodman's testes, amongst other substances, manufactured a dilute form of sulphuric acid as well as a scouring agent, introducing varying levels of each into his seed according to degree of arousal. His left testicle produced acids, while the right

have been hidden when he pinched the bulb at the end, his penis standing to attention to be fitted with its translucent rubber riot-gear. But Diana had held back from that act of revenge, not wishing to inflict a brat of his making on any woman, even though this might have provided the means to prompt his fall from grace.

Precisely five minutes from commencement of penetration, Isabella Maw was screaming at the ceiling. Nicholas Goodman was delighted, snorting like a horse, and coming in short, quick bursts, like a pump-action gun. Because they always used protection, Isabella Maw had never experienced the sensation of feeling his semen stinging the doughnut ring of her cervix. It would have been excruciatingly painful, burning her flesh like napalm, which was not surprising, for Goodman's testicles manufactured a dilute form of sulphuric acid as well as a scouring agent, introducing varying levels of

made various alkalis, such as potassium, sodium and caesium hydroxide, but when a state of equilibrium existed throughout the labyrinthine tubes of his epididymis, the pH value of his semen could be maintained at 4, the logarithm to base 10 of the reciprocal concentration of hydrogen ions in the policeman's ejaculate.

Isabella did not blame him for shooting these chemicals inside her, thinking her pain had been caused by inflammation from her thrush. But nor did she conceive when Goodman's black whip-tailed spermatozoa stormed her womb like an SAS snatch-squad. They did not bury their tiny bullet-heads in the walls of her eggs, but blasted them into microbe-sized shreds too tiny to be seen even with a x2000 magnification electron microscope. Her little ova were, quite simply, obliterated.

But her thrush had returned fire, Goodman discovered that evening in his bathroom, while examining a sore spot on the underside of his truncheon. There was definitely something wrong there. Had he caught something? He examined the beast carefully, noting patches

of red where thick blue snakes of veins bulged under the skin. each into his seed according to degree of arousal.

Isabella would never have cause to blame him for shooting these chemicals inside her, or for thinking her pain might be caused by inflammation from her thrush. Nor would she ever conceive by him, for Goodman's black whip-tailed spermatozoa never poured like storm troopers into her womb. She might later regret that they had never buried their tiny bullet heads in the walls of her eggs, but little ova never had that pleasure. She had loved those daylight hours in bed with the lustful policeman, loved being wanted by him, even though she knew he'd never really wanted *her*, Isabella; he only lusted after her corpulent body. They'd never spent a night together, and she wondered what he would have looked like then, his bullethead butting the darkness, those eyebrows shading his black pools of eyes, a long black bush beneath his spiky hair.

That evening, running the tap in his bathroom, Goodman heard the telephone ringing in the hall, and ran to answer it. His car was ready to collect from the garage.

Later, driving home, he spotted Diana Hunter in the

Wincing as he dabbed on evil-smelling witch hazel, he heard the phone in the hall, but let it ring, thinking the machine was on. Had he taken the call from the garage, he would have been told his car was ready to collect. And would have driven back along the walled lane by Long Wood, in case anything was happening up that way.

walled lane by Long Wood. No one else was around. If he ran her down, nobody would ever know it was him, he had ways of making sure of that. He pressed his foot down hard on the accelerator.

Mrs Bunty Saveloy was arranging a spray of mauve and blue wild flowers in her hall, having gathered larkspur and forget-me-nots on her walk. During her absence, a bulky man had scaled the outside wall, sending two flower-pots crashing from a window-ledge to the gravel path as he ducked inside a first floor window which Bunty had left open to air the rooms.

Standing in the bedroom, fingering a pair of pink silk panties he'd just found in a drawer, he looked up when he heard her shut the back door, and stuffed the knickers into his pocket. They must be valuable, he thought, for they'd been hidden in a black velvet jewel-case. He'd keep that as well, as evidence. In one corner he'd noticed the monogrammed initials OP, and wondered what this stood for. It should be someone's name, but the only OP he could think of was organophosphate sheep dip, which some of the farmers had been complaining about.

Bunty looked up, hearing some kind of sound from upstairs. Was someone up there? It couldn't be Maurice, he wasn't due back for hours. Nor the dog: *Wurst* was asleep in the kitchen. Listening for further tell-tale creaks from the floorboards, she resolved to take decisive action, first running into the hall and making a great deal of noise, then rushing the stairs, stamping her feet as she did so. When he heard her go into the next room, Ernest Gubbins climbed back out the window, shuffling along the wide ledge, where the plant pots had stood, until he reached the drainpipe.

As the former chimney sweep clambered back down the outside wall, Bunty Saveloy stood in her bedroom, staring at the gold and mother-of-pearl handled drawers hanging from her white dressing-chest, their contents half spilled onto the floor. She rushed forward to check whether the jewellery had been taken, but found her diamond necklaces, the bracelets and family heirlooms still safe in their various hiding-places. She must have come home just in time and disturbed the intruder.

The only thing which seemed to have been taken was the black velvet jewel-case in which she had hidden that pair of Olivia's knickers, the pink ones she'd found in the car. She would not be able to report those missing, and decided to say nothing about the burglary to Maurice. He would be annoyed with her for leaving the window open when she went out. But the intruder, whoever he was, would get a surprise when he opened the case, if he expected it to be filled with gold or pearls.

She noticed a strange smell in a room, like ammonia, not unlike that nasty chemical whiff you sometimes caught when driving past Oliver's factory at Loamfield. But at least the porky smell of her husband's sausages had gone.

Standing back from the vase to admire her work, Muffy turned to her host.

– Don't believe what anyone else tells you, she told Lady Olivia Prurigeaux. I say hawthorn is lucky. Bring it in the house in daylight, that's what I say, though I know Herne disagrees.

– What does he say? asked Lady Olivia, still unsure about the wisdom of Muffy's action, remembering her mother's warnings.

– That it's unlucky, because hawthorn comes out at Beltane when the faery folk encourage all kinds of rumpy-pumpy. And you know what they say about May animals, that they're nothing but trouble. He says you're bringing the chaotic outside world into the house with the hawthorn, that its smell is too strong and will lead to disorder inside. But that's the men's version. They want to keep the women under their control. They don't want to risk having anyone else calling on their wives with hawthorn in the house.

– But the may's rarely out on May Day itself, so that couldn't be true.

– No, said Muffy. Herne's right about Beltane: remember they stole eleven days from us when they changed from the Old Calendar. The hawthorn's always out by May the twelfth, which is my birthday, Old May Day. And you know May colts are their own bosses, try making them cross water and they'll lie down in it. May-farrowing sows will eat their own litters unless you give them plenty of bread and butter to eat instead. And May chickens come cheeping.

– We had a May cat once, Olivia recalled, born on the last day of the month. I called her Petronilla, not for Peter, as he thought, but for her saint's day. She never once killed a mouse or a rat, but you should have seen the other creatures she brought in and laid on the bed as presents for us. Adders, slowworms, frogs, toads and grass-snakes. And then she'd look up at you as if butter wouldn't melt in her mouth, as if to say, you know I must love you both so much, I've just brought you this tasty snake.

– May cats are like that, little schemers. People always used to drown kittens born in May. Throw them in the Otter in a sack with some bricks.

Hey diddle diddle,
The cat and the fiddle,
The cow jumped over the moon;
The little thrush sang
Inside the frog
Of the horse in the middle of June,
Of June,
Of the horse in the middle of June.

Hey diddle diddle,
The cat and the fiddle,
The Beast came out in the day;
The daylights stayed
Inside the maid
And Beauty ran away with the May,
The May,
And Beauty ran away with the May.

CHAPTER ELEVEN

The Plot Thickens

SUMMER SOLSTICE – MIDSUMMER DAY: JUNE 21ST – 24TH

Three smiles that are worse than grief: the smile of melting snow, the smile of your partner after sleeping with another, the smile of a leaping dog. Three things that are not to be trusted: a cow's horn, a dog's tooth and a horse's hoof.

Lunchtime drinks in the Bull had stretched into late afternoon, with none of the gang eager to venture outside in the June heat. The phrase *Mad dogs and Englishmen* prompted a string of anecdotes featuring both, to which Thomas Maw now added his own tale of a roasted horse.

It was just before Easter. He'd been riding out near Hackerton Manor when he came upon Candida walking her dog. Roger had shied when they met unexpectedly, around the dog-leg turn in a footpath. He'd landed in a bush, so no damage there, but blow me, he said, if the damned mutt didn't go apeshit with the horse running around, afraid of its hooves, Candida said, and it bit him on the leg, had to go to the doctor's for a rotten jab, rabies, tetanus and all that. But what riled him most was that Candida had been more concerned about the dog, and the dog hadn't been bitten, had it? A chap needed a bit of female sympathy when something like that happened, and all she was saying was *Shuck, Shuck, are you all right?*

– Good thing that damned dog's dead now, serves it damned well right, he said. You know that blasted dog was grinning like a maniac, grinning from ear to ear it was. Never mind Shuck, it was more like bloody Mutley, the way it was sniggering.

– It must have known who it was biting then, Tom, said Lucy brightly.

– What kind of dog was it? Lizzie asked.

– Oh I don't know. Labrador or something. Yes, that's it, a black lab, fierce-looking creature.

Lucy Saveloy patted his knee in mock reassurance, squeezing his leg a little too far up his thigh. Watching the two together, Lizzie noted an ease of play between them, like two young cubs, and wondered if this showed they were sleeping together. Lucy had said it was just a friendship – Tom saw lots of girls – but she'd surprised her in the Ladies.

– Isn't it a bit hot for a scarf? she asked, indicating the small green gold-glittered headscarf which Lucy was refolding.

– Well, yes it is, I suppose, said Lucy, flustered by Lizzie's appearance behind her, but I like this one, it's Indian, Tom's Daddy brought it back from Thailand, it goes with the top, don't you think?

But Lizzie's interest lay more in the round strawberry bruise on her friend's neck, which Lucy had been trying to hide.

– Oh dear, said Lucy, it is a bit embarrassing, isn't it?

– I hope it's gone by the time James gets back, said Lizzie. He's due back on leave next week, isn't he?

– Yes, unless there are further problems over the ceasefire.

– Does he know about you seeing Tom?

– Of course, Tom's one of his best friends, but I'm not *seeing* him. We're just knocking around a bit, it can be awfully boring when James is away, you know, and Tom's gots loads of dosh at the moment, so much he doesn't know what to do with it all. I'm helping him spend some of it. It's just a bit of fun.

– You be careful though, Lizzie warned. You know what they say about Tom Maw: he's a buck of the first head and woos for cake and pudding.

– He's certainly living at the rack and manger, Lucy agreed.

Morton Maw had been pleased to be back. Bangkok had been damned good fun, but hellish hot. Out on Loamsley Moor with the old shooter, he'd been blasting away at the few rabbits that seemed to be left, when he spotted what he immediately seized upon as the cause of their decimation. A weasel, jerking about in a most unweasel-like manner. Usually they dashed for cover as soon as they heard you. But they were curious blighters, always wanted to see what they'd run away from. You'd see them pop up their heads and long bodies like periscopes to look around them, and that was your moment. *Pop goes the weasel* if you were quick enough.

One less weasel meant more rabbits to shoot. People thought weasels lived off rats, mice, voles and game chicks, but it was rabbits they really went for. Stood to reason: rabbits gave them a bit of sport. He'd seen one stun a rabbit by jumping on its back, then hanging on, biting its neck until it got through the backbone and bunny dropped down dead.

Relaying this information to Dr Gallstone, he turned again to the manner of the weasel's attack.

– It'd been dashing around the field like a madman, so I took a few potshots at it. Weasel stops dead in its tracks. I thought great, must have got it, but then it rushes at me. I was that surprised, nearly dropped the gun. Bit me on the ankle.

– Yes, I know, you've said all that before, said Dr Gallstone. I believe you, of course, but it still doesn't match with the lab findings.

– Which are?

– I'm sorry to have to tell you this, Mr Maw. And I wouldn't like to speculate about how this might have occurred. I'm sure there must be a perfectly innocent explanation…

– Come on then, what have I got? Don't beat around the bush man.

– First of all, you've got NSU.

– NSU? Isn't that a car? You're having me on, Gallstone.

– Non-Specific Urethritis. And you didn't get that from a weasel, did you? Which means you're going to have to tell your wife...

– Oh I don't think I'd want to do that...

– But if you're...

The councillor stopped him.

– No danger of that, man. You don't think I sleep with my wife, do you? Good God, what a thought. Have you *seen* the woman?

– Yes, Mrs Maw is one of my patients, as you should know, said Dr Gallstone, who had just written out a repeat prescription for her thrush.

– Tied by the tooth, that's my trouble. Damned good cook, Izzie is. You've never married, have you, Gallstone?

– *Who would keep a cow of his own when he may have a quart of milk for a penny?*

– You're right, said Maw. They come with a price. If you buy the cow, take the tail into the bargain. What I hadn't bargained for – you didn't *see* each other then, not till the knot was tied – was my wife's *hairyness*, her flesh being dressed lamb fashion. She has a twat like a toison. It was like sleeping with a sheep.

– But while your wife's fleeciness may protect her from the wolf, said Gallstone, the same is not true of other more skinny creatures he preys upon. So you'll need to talk to whoever you have been with recently, to let them know.

– Yes, of course, said Maw, who had no intention of doing so.

– *Beware of after claps*, as the saying goes. He that has one foot in the straw has another in the spittle. But if you don't want your name called out in Ward 9 of the RLI, I will recommend a private clinic. I also need further samples from you of blood, urine and stool for the follow-up tests.

– Tests?

– Just routine, said the doctor, we always do them. This assertion was not strictly true. The lab had requested further samples, querying irregularities in the first batch. There was no question about the NSU. They had a positive ID on that. But Dr Doddypoll had certain worries about other matters.

– And what else do I have then?

– I'd say you're sick of the silver dropsy, Dr Gallstone replied. When you're not tumbling with Winchester geese, you're forever sniffing round Tom Tiddler's ground, worshipping the golden calf despite the recent restrictions on the movement of bulls and bullion. Is that not right?

Morton Maw still thought the weasel was the culprit, not the Winchester goose or the golden calf, but since the weasel in question was now marinating in a drainage ditch on the Maw Estate, nobody could prove a link with any of these creatures.

No one would subject this particular weasel's decomposing body to a forensic examination in which the tiny round holes in its skull might be discovered. These were made by the parasitic worm *Skryabingylus nasicola*, and would have proliferated and caused death within two weeks had it not been for the intervention of a mink, which had bitten the weasel's head in a fight, its sharp canines penetrating the skull through an area of bone weakened by the tunnelling of the parasite.

He was feeling much better now, more alert, as if a great weight had been lifted from his shoulders along with the sports jacket he had discarded and given to Oxfam. He did not witness the act, but Ginger Jake had left in Transylvanian style, disintegrating into a smoking handful of dust, turned into chitinous powder by a blazing dawn sun.

The white stripes had disappeared from his arms and legs, and the names of other men from his clothes. All signs of his earlier branding had gone, including even the embarrassing rash of logos. Having made this complete recovery from Hilfiger's Disease, his self-confidence was returning as he found himself able for the first time in years to identify with his own name, JOHN BROCK. Now he was back in the saddle at Oakwood Farm.

He'd spent the day hoisting sheep up onto the trailer for the shearers, watching them unzip the fleeces with a few buzzing sweeps of the electric clippers, each ewe bucking itself free with a back flip as it scampered away. The whole flock was stripped in a steady production line to the rhythm of the shearers' ghetto-blaster, which belted out the Animals' *Greatest Hits* above the frantic baas and bleats of two hundred sheep and lambs.

Kernan had called by as they were milling round in the kitchen, demolishing the beer. In his day, he said, the shearers had made their own music:

> Come all my jolly boys, and we'll together go
> Together with our masters, to shear the lambs and yowes
> All in the month of June, of all times in the year
> It always comes in season, the lambs and yowes to shear
> And then we will work hard, my boys, until our backs do break
> Our master he will bring us beer, whenever we do lack

Sitting at the table, listening to the policeman singing *Shear them close, my boys* and *Bend your backs and shear them well* in his old-fashioned tenor voice, John winced, trying to stretch his aching back.

And he remembered an earlier gathering, whose significance began to dawn on him as Kernan was demonstrating how he could recall all ten verses of *The Black Ram*, before starting on a rant about the cattle at Hogsback Hill Farm. He'd not given it much thought before, but it was Kernan's phrase which brought it all back, for that was what Bernie had said, *it's a numbers game*.

When John started to explain then, Kernan went quiet, turning to him with his sharp eyes staring, his ears almost visibly pricked. Joe Davis had dropped by to borrow some tools when his Dad had been talking fish with Bernie in the kitchen, John said, and the three of them started on about the state of the Otter, the pollution and all that; then the neglect of the Maw Estate, how that affected the wildlife. That had got Joe onto the subject of young Tom Maw.

– And he had a lot to say about him, said John. Joe detests the little runt.

– He's the son of a white hen, said one of the shearers.

– And now he has Adidasitis, he thinks he's really cool, said John contemptuously. At least I had the excuse that I *was* one of the lads, whereas he's just scumming it.

– What, you mean he's branded? asked Kernan with surprise. That's rich, isn't it, for a man who smirks like Jeffrey Archer.

– A pig in clover can still put skunk stripes on his arm, John replied. Tom follows the herd at the same time as he milks it.

– He farts through a 24 carat ring, said the shearer.

– Scummers used to wear donkey-jackets, said Kernan. That was bad enough, but at least they didn't pay for the privilege of being someone else's walking billboard.

– And some of those sportswear companies give money to the *Tories,* said the shearer, spitting the last word out in disgust as if it had been distasteful to have it pass through his lips.

– It's probably meant as a provocation, mused Kernan. He's a man of three letters like his father, though NIKE has four and is a stolen name. But it's kindly that the poke savour of the herring.

– It's certainly a fishy business, John continued, for apparently Tom had been round the week before offering Joe around over £600 a head for his steers, depending on weight. He'd get them collected, he said. He'd got himself this job as agent for the Otteridge Meat Company, and Joe said we all knew how he got that. Since all the farmers were desperate to get rid of their cattle, and there was this big backlog, he thought he'd do Joe a special favour by offering to take these steers off his hands.

– For some kind of cut, presumably? asked Kernan.

– No, said John, it wouldn't cost Joe anything. He said he'd get his slice from the abbatoir. He'd pay Joe the going rate for live cattle. Joe's herd was free of BSE, they'd been certified healthy, but he couldn't sell them for beef, so he was fast running out of money. The Government had banned the sale for food of all cattle over thirty months old, and that included prime young cattle. Remember, they were wanting to slaughter 25,000 cows a week to try to get the Europeans to lift their ban.

– And thousands of perfectly healthy cattle were killed, said Kernan, just because Hogg and the rest had cocked things up.

– Including Joe's whole herd, said John. It was very neat the way they did it, you couldn't help admiring them, even if Joe wasn't that impressed. First, the rate for old cows was 86 pence a kilo, live weight, which meant you'd get about £500 a beast, but prime beef cattle were bought up for destruction at 111p, because they were more valuable. Originally you were meant to take your cattle to market in the normal way and hand them over at what they called "collection centres", where they'd weigh them before taking them off to the abattoir. So the farmers said they'd take them direct to the slaughterers. But because many of the slaughterhouses didn't have any way of weighing live animals, they agreed on a new price of 222p per kilo deadweight.

– That sounds like a fair deal, said Kernan, eager to show off his knowledge of cattle. A cow's carcass normally weighs about half the live weight, doesn't it?

– Ah, said John. You made the same mistake. That's what the Ministry thought too. With a worn-out old beast, half the live weight would be fine. But a young steer bred for meat will have a much heavier carcass, and some of the continental breeds can yield 65 per cent of their live weight.

– So Joe would have got a lot more for the young, healthy steers?

– He would have done, yes, but the slaughterhouses also saw a chance of making a fast buck. Only a few of them were licensed to handle the young, mature cattle, and they decided they wouldn't accept cattle direct from the farms, it wasn't practical they said. Otteridge was one of those. The farmers had to sell to middle men, and these middle men could decide which cattle they wanted.

– And this was what Tom was doing?

– Right. Tom paid Joe at the rate for live cattle, so he might get somewhere around £650 a head, but he could sell the carcass of a live heavy steer for £850. The agent makes a profit of about £200 per steer. And it was all perfectly legal.

– But he got away with taking all that? asked Kernan.

– Oh no, said John, that's all part of the deal. He goes snacks with the slaughterhouse. That's his commission, half the profit.

– And the Ministry allowed this to go on?

– Their mistake. They changed things later of course, but for a good while Tom Maw and the rest were coining it in. Eventually the story got into the papers, but the media didn't say much. It was just figures to them. They were too busy slagging off the Germans. But from the way Bernie talked about all this, you could tell it was just the tip of the iceberg. He reckoned that Tom must have been making around 25 grand a week, and with Otteridge killing about a thousand cattle a week, the slaughterhouse would have been making a hundred grand a week clear profit.

– All money which could have gone to the farmers.

– And which needn't have been paid out in the first place, if the Ministry hadn't made the same mistake as you about the dead weight of cattle.

– We all make mistakes, said Kernan.

And every mistake, he thought, every false move, theft or error of judgement, has its consequence:

> The robin and the redbreast,
> The robin and the wren:
> If you take them from their nest
> You'll never thrive again.

Captain Nicholas had taken tea at the Rectory with Phoebe. He had not needed to hint at any intimacies. The simple fact of their meeting again was enough for Kernan. He could not go back to Loamfield, not yet, not in his present state of mind. There was too much he couldn't say to her. When it was his turn for leave, he headed for Paris.

He never got there. For two days and nights, he sat on the wooden seats of trains – no discomfort after the Front – some marooned in the middle of nowhere, others actually reaching stations where passengers were told to alight, because of a derailment, a bombing, or – so rumour had it – the strikes. He waited on bare, heat-baked platforms, trying not to think about Phoebe.

As another train took him through the countryside of northern France, he looked out the carriage window and imagined he saw her there, especially as the day wore on into evening. In the fading midsummer light, as the thin crescent of the waning moon appeared like a quartz fingernail in the dark blue sky, he kept seeing Phoebe's face reflected in the glass, more radiant than a full moon. When they stopped by a river, he heard her in the sound of the water, the painful music of her bright summer laughter. He sat bolt upright for hours, wide awake, listening to the rushing of the river in the dark, the muffled thuds of distant shelling, as the two Frenchmen opposite chattered about the riots, the derailed trains.

– You did not know about this? one of them asked him.

– No, said Kernan. We're told nothing at the Front. Except of course that your General Mangin's Sixth Army had nearly broken through the Hindenburg Line.

– They were slaughtered, the man said with obvious bitterness. They never had a chance. That is why our soldiers refused to go back to the Front. My brother's regiment was forced to go back, but on the way the men started baaing like sheep to show they were lambs being driven to slaughter. When their commanding officer told them off, they simply turned round and marched back to their rest billets. Henri told me this. But he is dead now.

– Like sheep, that is right, said the other man.

– Henri told me the Boche knew all about General Nivelle's plan weeks before, that is why they withdrew. He and the other officers warned him not to go ahead with his advance, but he refused to listen. That is why not just the soldiers but the people here are angry, not only with the generals but the government. Painlevé knew. He should have stopped Nivelle.

– What happened? asked Kernan. Were there units prepared to mutiny?

– Of course. You did not know this? But perhaps it is not so surprising. The week after he was killed, Henri's division, the 21st Colonial Infantry, refused duty. Nivelle had the ringleaders arrested, and two days later ordered the men back into action, against the most heavily defended section, of course. Virtually the whole division was wiped out. Not the Senegalese, they'd already gone: they disappeared one night, every last one of them, just upped and left. Then my regiment refused to go up the line, the 120th Infantry. Most of the other corps followed within days. Some trenches were virtually unmanned along the Champagne front.

– If the Germans had known this, said Kernan, they could have broken through the line.

– If it had continued for much longer, they would have done. For a while everyone went wild. One regiment even tried to blow up the Schneider-Creusot munitions works. But then Pétain took over. According to the official figures, only 23 mutineers were shot. But I know that 250 were marched off to a quiet sector and annihilated by our own artillery. Some of the ringleaders were banished to the colonies, but Pétain followed Nivelle's lead with the rest, making sure they were sent to the most dangerous parts of the line.

– Like David and Bathsheba, said Kernan. You remember, he sent her husband Uriah the Hittite to fight the Ammonites, put him at the head of his vanguard troops to make sure he was killed.

Once the tough-sounding north country man on the radio had glamorised it as 'roots', Flea had started listening to folk music, at first just those songs given a thumping, rollicking beat by new bands like Ploughmen Electric, the Twa Corbies and Rankin Mr Lankin. When he got in with Herne and Muffy, the penny dropped, the English one. He realised those songs were just the tip of the iceberg, the latest versions of a tradition that went back for centuries; never mind all that American music on the radio, that had little to do with him, it was another culture's city music. Flea had discovered his own tradition, recognising songs from his shire, his land. His current favourite was 'The Red Herring' by the False Brides, who sang:

What have I made of my old herring's guts?
Forty bright women and fifty bright sluts.
Wantons and sluts and everything.
Do you think I've done well with my jolly herring?
 2ND BRIDE: Why didn't you tell me so?
 1ST BRIDE: So I did, long ago.
 2ND BRIDE (*spoken*): Thou lie!
 1ST BRIDE (*spoken*): Thou lie!
Well, well, everything.
Do you think I've done well with my jolly herring?

Going to meet Herne to catch pheasants in Hangman's Wood, he worked his way through all the verses, clicking his fingers to the rhythm, but each time he reached the chorus, just as he was about to say, not sing, the spoken reply, it seemed that the words *Thou lie! Thou lie!* were whispered by the soughing highest leaves of the trees above him. On reaching the end, he started again, but paused after the second verse:

What have I made with my old herring's eyes?
Forty jackdaws and fifty magpies,
Linnets and larks and everything.
Do you think I've done well with my jolly herring?

Someone else was singing, he was sure. *Why didn't you tell me so?* he heard, followed by a harsh chattering cry, and looking up into the great oak tree by the clearing, saw the magpies jiggling the branches. Then from the elm he heard *So I did, long ago!* – the first bride's line punctuated with the jackdaws' raucous cawing.

– *Thou lie! Thou lie!* came the rustling reply from Herne, standing behind him. The boy nearly leapt out of his skin.

– You know that song then? asked Flea, recovering.

– I first heard that one many years ago, said Herne. In the West Country, where they say *Of all the fish in the sea, herring is the king.* They thought it was just a bit of tomfoolery, the singers, but the tune is quite primitive. I think it went with some kind of magic ritual to do with a sacred beast. I wish I knew its origins. That's the thing with these songs, sometimes you know the rhyme but not the reason.

– You must know plenty about poaching, said Flea, fishing. Any about pheasants?

– Oh dear yes. 'The Poacher's Fate' is a good one. It starts:

Me and five more a poaching went,
To kill some game was our intent,
Our money being gone and spent,
We'd nothing left to try.

But that's quite a new song.

– How new? asked Flea.

– From Napoleon's time.

– I don't call that new.

– But it's still just as relevant. It's about five soldiers who came back from fighting Boney. You know there were riots here then. It was a time of depression, and half a million men returned from the wars to find there was no work for them at home.

– So they went poaching...

– They were desperate. There were fights between the demobbed soldiers and the gamekeepers; some were clubbed to death by men who'd only wanted a rabbit to eat. The centre of the unrest was Cambridgeshire. They hanged five men from Mill Pond in Ely for poaching pheasants. On the 28th of June 1816.

– Hanged them? said Flea, incredulous.

– Yes, the people blamed their deaths on the landowners. Not only that, within days the butcher whose cart had been used to take the men to the gallows was found drowned in his own cesspit, and the coffinmaker ended up dead in a pipe that took water to the brewery.

– And all that's preserved in the song, said Flea, with a sense of wonder.

– Remembered, not preserved, said Herne. Songs are living things. But to keep them alive, you have to keep singing them, pass them on from one generation to the next.

– And that one's not old?

– A century is a short time in song.

Though he was tired, and could not follow the plot of his novel, Kernan put off sleep. He kept reading and re-reading the same pages, seeing the words but not focusing on their meaning: having to go back to the previous page, again and again, as if his pain were mirrored in the book. While he knew he would stay awake for hours, as he had done for many nights, fretting, unable to free himself from his turmoil, he did not want to slip his tether, to drift into the dream world he could not control. He could only face his enemies by knowing where they were, keeping them at a distance, separate from him.

In his mind he pictured a search map for a manhunt, with markers that were moved with each new sighting. He had them all pinned there, in their places, even Lambert who was on his side, whom he distrusted because of Diana, who had rightly said she could see or be with whom she wanted; she was not tied to anyone, least of all him. But in a dream, as in the past, they would not remain where he had fixed them but would creep up on him from behind. He would have no choice then but to meet them – on their terms, not his.

And those enemies in himself, how might they be controlled? Useless, unworthy emotions: his love now tarnished with lust, anger and misplaced jealousy. Yet he could not think of Diana now without desiring her; he loved her more than any woman he'd ever known in his life, yet they had not even kissed, and nor should they. And Lambert, who only wanted someone to talk to, she claimed, a friend who understood him, he hated with a vehemence which would have given Goodman the greatest satisfaction. But he felt powerless against the force of these feelings, and everything he witnessed only served to reinforce them. The more he brooded on them, the more they swallowed him up. While Lambert dithered like a donkey between two bundles of hay.

Larry the Lambert was such a pathetic clueless scraggy creature, lean as a shotten herring: even his baldness was appalling to look upon, like a ewe's shorn skin. *And he that makes himself a sheep shall be eaten by the wolf.* He couldn't imagine any woman wanting to touch such a man whose head was so obscenely bare, like the skin of a slug: his bristly hogface with its bull's pizzle of a nose, those little piggy eyes screwed up like a mole's behind owlish glasses, as ridiculous as that stupid hat of his...

> I have a cock in my father's yard
> That never trod on hens, sir.
> I have a cock in my father's yard
> That never trod on hens, sir.
> Well he claps his wings and he never flies
> Don't you think you're just like him, sir?
> *Aye-fal-the-dal-aye-day*
> *Well he claps his wings and he never flies*
> *Don't you think you're just like him, sir?*

He must stop this. He had to free himself from thinking like this, or it would take him over.

It seemed a pity to suffocate the pretty white flowers, but this was something her mother had once told her to try. You also had to jump through a midsummer bonfire to rid yourself of illness, but she'd give that a miss. The farmers used to drive the animals through the fire as well, like at Beltane, to banish the evil spirits.

Diana sniffed at the yarrow before placing it under her pillow. Latterly her dreams had become quite worrying, like premonitions of danger. In one dream she was being chased by rabid dogs, like a fox pursued by the hunt. She hoped the yarrow would ward off the dogs, that she really would dream of her future beloved, whoever that might be. As she drifted off into sleep, she seemed to glimpse many fleeting faces, none of them known to her; their voices drifted in and out like static, phrases repeated themselves, words rhymed and chimed: *fades, shades, blades... kill, ill, bill... hook, look, shook... shock, knock, brock... bark, hark, dark...*

Hark, hark,
The dogs do bark,
The beggars are coming to town;
Some in rags,
And some in jags,
And one in a velvet gown.

Hark, hark
The dogs do bark
My wife is coming in
With rogues and jades,
And roaring blades,
They make a devilish din.

Diana cried out. And sat bolt upright in bed. If that was what yarrow did, she wanted nothing to do with it. Grabbing her pillow, she seized the flowers and hurled them away. That was no dream of her beloved but the dogs again. And Kernan was there, dragging her up into a tree, away from the dogs.

I'll sing you a song,
The days are long,
The woodcock and the sparrow;
The little dog has burned his tail,
And he must be hanged tomorrow.

CHAPTER TWELVE

Worse Than a Dog

3RD–11TH JULY

A thief can be exposed by taking a sieve and a pair of sheep-shears, and invoking the help of Saints Peter and Paul. First dig the points of the shears into the sieve's wooden rim, so that the handles stand upright and the sieve is suspended. Then recite the charm of the Sieve and Shears (also known as Turning the Riddle), naming your suspects in turn. When the thief's name is spoken, the sieve will turn or fall to the ground. The sieve's power comes from its ancient status as a sacred and magical instrument, symbolising the clouds through which life-giving rain falls upon the earth. Witches are said to sail through the air or over water in sieves, but this is a later, unconnected belief, probably erroneous.

Bunty Saveloy was lost for words. *Pink as a piglet was not quite right*, she was explaining, it was more the pink of a sugar mouse, the kind that have a piece of string for a tail; and there was a sort of gusset underneath with a white frilly hem; not so much a gusset as an opening. So it was all rather embarrassing, she told Muffy, for this was not an *ordinary* pair of panties but one of *great sentimental value*, a gift from her husband. She didn't want Maurice to know about their loss, nor to bother the police with something so trivial at a time when they were investigating all those burglaries in which thousands of pounds had been stolen. But a woman understands these things, and she really did appreciate her help.

– And those monogrammed initials, you mentioned, asked Muffy, what do they mean?

– Maurice bought them in a *very* expensive lingerie shop in Paris, she said. The letters stand for *Ordure de Poisson.* That's not what it sounds like, it doesn't mean Poison Order, it's what they call a false friend, words which sound like something else in another language. But what it actually means I can't remember. Maurice did tell me, it's something exotic and fragrant.

– Sounds rather fishy to me, said Muffy. The hartshorn smell mentioned by Mrs Saveloy pointed the finger at Ernest Gubbins, but she had to be sure.

– Now, she continued, you put the middle finger of your right hand through one handle of the shears, and I'll do the same with the other. And let's see if I'm right...

Bless St Peter, bless St Paul,
Bless the God that made us all.
If Gubbins 's nicked Bunty's knickers,
Turn about riddle and shears and all.

The sieve swung sharply round, pulling itself free from the points of the shears, and as if catapulted, shot across the floor of Mrs Saveloy's kitchen, hitting her sleeping dog Wurst on the muzzle. The dachshund yelped.

– Our cat burglar is well named, said Muffy.

Slamming down another three-month bale of *Loamshire Chronicles,* Diana Hunter resigned herself to another tedious hour of dog-work. Where was Kernan? She was worried about him. He was meant to have met her in the library after seeing Herne.

She reached Saturday 11th July 1987. She was still at school then. What did she remember about that summer? The Tories got back in. But Martina Navratilova had been magnificent, her sixth successive Wimbledon win. Then there was the death of Rudolf Hess, unless he was someone pretending to be Hess, in which case it was probably the impostor who killed himself; whereupon the Russians immediately demolished his prison, whose one remaining inmate Hess had, or hadn't, been. But whoever he was, he had become the only reason for Spandau's existence.

And Kernan, what was he doing then? How old would he have been? Indeed, how old was he now? According to Sergeant Cobb, Kernan had always been a legend in the force, he'd been around for donkeys. All he ever said was he went back a long way – many a dog was dead since he was a whelp – and yet he couldn't be *that* old. Going through the old *Chronicles*, she'd come across occasional references to him giving evidence in court reports, but she was confused, never sure whether it was her Kernan or his father, they were all called George; his grandfather was another George, he'd not come back from the war, missing presumed dead but named among the fallen on the war memorial at Loamfield, unlike Jack Brock. Only last week she'd stood looking at the ugly cross on the Green, hoping he would not drive past and see her there; she'd wanted to read his name, George Kernan, on different sides of the pillar, and imagined for a moment that it was some kind of trick – and the same man had died twice, three times even, that he'd been in both wars – like that game she had played at school, when they took the long photograph with the panning camera, and she'd run along behind the chairs on which the back row stood, and ended up appearing at both ends of the same picture, two Diana Hunters, the left one smiling innocently, the right with mischief, but which of the two had been sent home with a letter from the head she could not remember.

From Spandau Jail to Loamshire School: what connected them? The *Chronicle* gave her one answer: a full moon seen from both on 11th July 1987. What other delights did that day bring, on the home front? Ah, Loamshire Otter Hunt disbanded: District Council leader Sir Peter Prurigeaux regrets decision. The otters, presumably, would not have agreed? But no, there were none left, only the single otter on the town arms and the school badge. Play abandoned due to lack of otters. *See also letters page.*

Otteridge otters

Your article last week 'No pollution link with otters' included several statements by Eurochimique UK's chief research scientist which cannot be left unchallenged. According to Dr Kuru, the level of polychlorinated biphenyls in the River Otter is so low that they cannot even be measured using standard water testing procedures, but PCBs concentrate in the tissue of water creatures and accumulate exponentially as they move from animal to animal up the food chain. Through this process of biomagnification, concentrates of persistent chemicals which resist breakdown and accumulate in body fat can be 25 million times greater in a top predator such as an otter than in the surrounding water.

To demonstrate this in layman's terms, I would offer this analysis of the food web of Loamshire river fauna. First, microscopic organisms pick up PCBs from river sediment. They in turn are eaten in vast numbers by tiny filter-feeding animals on the river-bed, in whose bodies the persistent pollutant becomes concentrated by a magnitude of several hundred. These creatures are then eaten by larger species such as river shrimps (PCB concentration now x50,000); these crustacea are eaten by minnows (PCB x800,000); the minnows are eaten by trout (PCB x3,000,000); and finally, the trout are eaten by the larger otters, whose body fat can contain up to eight times the concentration of PCBs as the fish in their diet. The original pollutant may be weak in the water, but its effects are *amplified* right up the food chain as the great fish eat up the small. This is not dissimilar to the so-called butterfly effect in Chaos Theory (discussed in last week's letters): a butterfly flapping its wings in Loamfield can be the cause of a storm in the middle of France.

If our otters have disappeared, as they have from many English rivers, I would point the finger at the Eurochimique's plant at Loamfield, the only significant source of industrial pollution in North Loamshire. Some conservationists have blamed the pesticide dieldrin, but the more likely culprit is PCBs, synthetic chemicals used to insulate electrical equipment. Eurochimique used to manufacture both these products, which are persistent pollutants likely to remain in the environment for many years.

Dr Kuru is dismissive of 'ill-informed comment from pseudo-scientific amateurs and woolly-headed green lobbyists', and cites habitat destruction resulting from Otteridge's urban spread along the river as the main cause of otter decline. I would refer him then to the work of two highly respected British scientists, Drs Chris Mason and Sheila Macdonald, whose book *Otters: Ecology and Conservation* was published last year by Cambridge University

Press. Their studies show that an equally if not more important factor is local and wind-borne pollution.

In Western Europe, otters now thrive only in countries such as Norway, Scotland and Ireland, and in south-west France and western Spain, where the prevailing winds blow off the Atlantic. Otters are disappearing in highly industrialised countries and in places downwind from major industrial regions. Residents of Loamfield affected by aerial pollution from the Eurochimique plant would confirm that the prevailing wind in North Loamshire is from the south-west. The former otter haunts along the river follow a south-west to north-east path.

Many scientists now believe that PCBs, either on their own or coupled with other contaminants such as mercury, are the main cause of the disappearance of otters. Before Dr Kuru dismisses these as maverick views, I would suggest he consults the authoritative article on the subject by Drs C. Mason, T. Ford and N. Last, 'Organochlorine Residues in British Otters', published last year in the *Bulletin of Environmental Contamination and Toxicology* (issue 36, pages 656–61).

(Name and address supplied)

Lieutenant James Prurigeaux was not overjoyed with his homecoming. He had been looking forward to his much delayed two weeks' leave, but what happens when he gets home? No one there. No welcome. Empty house.

Sitting at the bar of the Black Bull, English pint in hand, he patted his black cap like an animal. Like a mole, the rolled Royal Loamshires beret pushed its brass snout out from his shoulder strap, as if to sniff the air, the otter on the cap-badge scanning different parts of the room each time he twisted awkwardly around, swaying on his stool, berating McDonald the landlord, and casting an exaggerated look at the ceiling every time loud barking was heard from upstairs.

– Where did she shay they'd gone, Jockey? he said.

– I told you before, the Bahamas. But it's none of my business, Mr Prurigeaux, said Jock McDonald.

– The Bahamash, thatsh right, said the soldier. A fortnight, you said. And Tom is her 'escort', thatsh the word, innit, *escort*. That was our job, the Loamshires, U.N. escort. But she knew I was coming back, Jockey, I wrote and told her, didn't I?

– I wouldn't know, said the landlord. All I know is Miss Saveloy was telling her friends your leave had been postponed again, and she couldn't wait any longer. She'd been under a lot of pressure, she needed a break. And now, if you don't mind, sir, I have other customers to serve...

– *Pressure?* What kind of *pressure*? James Prurigeaux played with the word, framing it in a series of interrogatives: *Pressure*? *She* was under *pressure*? What kind of *pressure* did she think *I* was under, being shot at by both sides? We're meant to be protecting them, you know Jockey, both lotsh. We're the peacekeeping force. Blessht are the peacemakers? So what do the blighters do? I'll tell you what they do, *their snipers shoot our men*, and we're meant to be protecting *them* from *each other.* Sometimes I think we should just pull out, let them get on with it.

– Yes sir, said the white-haired Scot, who had been a major's batman in the last war, so that humouring the English officer breed was ingrained in him, useful training for a pub landlord.

– Tom Maw, said Prurigeaux. Never trusted him. Mealy Mouth Maw we called him at school, you know. Gift of the gab, a sly dog like his father. There went but a pair of shears between them. *Thomas Maw, A Man for All Reasons,* we wrote on his locker. So don't think I believed that escort line for one minute... He stopped, his angry head jerking up at the ceiling as the barking upstairs started up again, louder than before, this time accompanied by yelps and howling. And boots: no longer just crashing on the floor but stamping in unison.

– Country's going to the dogs, he said, laughing at his own joke, and cast a hard look around the bar to see who responded. The drinkers peered down at their glasses, avoiding him. Cowards, they were all yellow-bellies like Mealy Mouth Maw.

– *Noisy aren't they!* he shouted.

– They're not doing any harm, said McDonald, in spite of his own disquiet. They pay for the room. They drink enough beer. *That's all I ask*, the landlord added, with overemphasis, as if to emphasise his unspoken worries. He hoped there wouldn't be trouble. When the meeting finished, and the Anubians came downstairs, Prurigeaux was bound to say something to them, an untactful comment or even a blatant insult, thinking his army status gave him immunity from assault. And yet it hadn't, by his account, on the latest peace mission. It was almost as if he wanted to be attacked.

The door opened, and half a dozen dogheaded men moved towards the bar, a German shepherd doghead in the vanguard, asking the others what they wanted. The talk in the bar became more subdued. Prurigeaux held his pint up, gripping the glass like a brandished weapon, his forearm forceful, erect, at attention. One of the dogheads brushed against him, and he swung round, hackles raised, staring into the hazel and black eyes like nutty marbles. He was still drunk, but suddenly alert, as if he had switched himself in an instant into military readiness, the soldier caught relaxing, carousing, when the enemy arrived in a village meant to be under his protection. Slowly, he began to sing, almost through gritted teeth, in a low, intimidating voice:

> Old McDonald had a pub, *ee-aye-ee-aye-oh.*
> And in that pub he had some dogs, *ee-aye-ee-aye-oh,*
> With a *woof woof* here, and a *woof woof* there,
> Here a *woof,* there a *woof,* everywhere a *woof woof.*
> Old McDonald had a pub, *ee-aye-ee-aye-oh.*

And he pretended to sneeze, adding:

– Sorry, must be the hair, not used to it, you know. Don't have dogs at home.

As the German shepherd doghead was handing a ten pound note to the landlord, Prurigeaux snatched it from his hand, tossing it to the floor.

– *Go fetch*, he called out, clenching his fist to emphasise the instruction.

The doghead straightened himself, baring a jagged line of teeth and pink gums, and looked about to strike, like a snake, when a voice called from across the room:

– *No you don't! Enough of that!* Outside you lot. *All* of you.

– It was just a joke, said Prurigeaux.

– I know, said Kernan. You should be going home now, Lady Olivia will be wondering what's happened to you.

– We weren't doing anything, snarled the German shepherd doghead. I was just getting in some drinks.

– Well you can do that somewhere else, said Kernan. You've had your meeting. Now get off home. I'm not having any trouble round here from your sort.

– We've done *nothing* wrong, the doghead barked, his tail sweeping back and forth, only just missing a pint of beer on a nearby table. You can't blame us. It was him who started it.

– You've not had your drinks yet, there's your money, said Kernan, picking up the ten pound note which Prurigeaux had thrown on the floor. You've still time to catch last orders in Otteridge.

– But we were... whined one of the other dogheads.

– You were just going, Kernan interrupted, starting to usher them backwards, towards the door.

– I won't stand for this, said the German shepherd doghead.

– Do you want me to arrest you? said Kernan. Do you? Do you? Now get off out of it, go on. He urged them back more forcefully. Two of the dogheads protested, but the policeman's will prevailed, and as he slammed the bar door shut behind them, he added, for the benefit of the bar:

– Clear off before I set the dogs on you.

Unlike James Prurigeaux's earlier insult, this remark was greeted with a murmur of approval from the villagers. He turned to the soldier.

– And you should be off, young James. Wait till those pups are out of the way. I don't think you should be drinking any more now.

– No, said Prurigeaux, and slapped the policeman on the shoulder. You're a good man, Inspector Kernan. I like you. My father might not have agreed, but I say you're a good fellow.

Kernan gestured to Jock McDonald:

– I'm sorry about that, he said. Didn't mean to be so heavy with them, but they really get my goat, those dogheads. I've seen what they get up to in town. I know they're customers of yours, but they get out of hand. Very quickly. If I hadn't stepped in, unjustly I know, you'd have had a real dogfight happening here, and other people would have been drawn in, not just soldier boy here.

– Don't worry, George, said McDonald. That's the last time I hire out that room to the Sons of Anubis. That stamping on the floor was the last straw. I'd have banned them for that, even if the trouble hadn't started here.

– Riley banned them from the Blue Boar, said Kernan. The only Otteridge pub that still lets them in is the Pig and Whistle, and that's only because of pressure from certain friends of theirs. But the Pig doesn't have a meetings room. That's how they ended up coming all the way out here.

Kernan had been criticised at the station for his hardness towards the Anubians. *Not correct*, he was told. They had their rights. But he wasn't being racist, though he knew some people's antipathy towards the dogheaded men took that form. He had seen enough of their work to know that any intolerance came from their side. He was sure that dogheads had been involved in those attacks on Asian holidaymakers, that they had torched the caravans at Ottermouth; but there was no evidence implicating them, apart from the doghead urine he'd smelled at the leisure park. His worrying at the carcase of a dead case was said to be spoiling Goodman's plan to establish a police doghead team to carry out security duties, and he'd been told to bury it. It hadn't helped that in a playful canteen scrap with Clegg on the subject, he'd referred to Goodman's Force K9 as 'the Hitler Woof Movement', a morsel which the fawning constable had quickly taken back to his master, not mentioning of course that Kernan's discomfort was shared by several other officers, including Johnny Jakes, who'd quipped that he'd think twice before opening his door to anyone from the Dog Squad, especially a whole bunch of dog collars, because many dogs may easily worry one hare. And he was a man who'd worked with animals all his life, who was used to their ways, Jakes had said, yet these dogheads unnerved him, especially when they had to keep them under control when rival supporters taunted them at the match. It was frightening then, to hear them barking back in unison; and you almost didn't want Otteridge to score, because when the ball was fired into the other side's net, they set up that blood-curdling howl that was even worse when we let one in, so chilling it was that sometimes the rest of the crowd fell completely silent.

The dogheads always looked tensed, Kernan thought, and he sensed that there was a kind of inhuman brutality simmering in them, a dangerous mixture of human anger and blind animal fury, as if they had somehow inherited the worst traits of man and beast. Yet they weren't angry because they'd been born with dogs' heads, they loved it. They exulted in their outcast status. And because they were all male, theirs was a prison culture. He'd heard one boasting to a young secretary in the Pig and Whistle about the length and hairyness of his tail, inviting her to stroke it, and when she professed indifference to his canine charms, he snapped at her, and would have bitten her wrist if Riley hadn't been there and given him a sharp smack across the muzzle.

The men at the station said the dogheads' penises were not just long and slender but pointed as well. Rumour had it they fellated themselves. Could this be true? pondered Kernan. Were they not meant to be totally divided, with dogs' heads and men's bodies? Yet they did have tails. Where did one part end and the other begin? Was it just at the neck and coccyx? And were dogs capable of evil, or only men? What of the combination?

Later, walking home across the green, Kernan stared at the war memorial, shocked, but not surprised at the sight of the black dogleg cross sprayed across the names of the dead. His own name, and those from other Loamshire families, obliterated by a slash of black. But on the other side, from another war, George Kernan survived.

The Right Honourable Henry Sirloin knew the consequences: guilt and dishonour. Yet whom did he dishonour? Candida certainly, now in hospital for her mastectomy. He shivered at that thought, as if from the knife itself, as Lizzie rubbed her own, much larger breasts through the forest of his chest-hair. She was moving slowly down his body, working her way towards the place of non-refusal; then her questions would start, and he would tell her anything she wanted to know. But it did not seem to matter now. He no longer believed his own side. *Scratch a Tory and you'll find a thief,* Lizzie said, that was the meaning of the name; and they were all liars, like him. What they had done, what he had colluded with, had brought down a plague upon his Loamshire as on all the shires of England. This man-made devil, this angel of death was taking men as well as animals. He had been its servant, as culpable as Oliver de Foie. And now its shadow lay over Candida, his wife, who would return to him scarred, betrayed, without a breast.

Lizzie had started, her quick tongue exquisite. She was eating him alive, swallowing his soul. He was beyond redemption now.

– Don't stop, he said, when she took him from her mouth, as he knew she would. Those were their rules. Now she would ask him something outrageously ordinary, about business or politics, which he would have to answer quickly, very quickly, or the rising inside him would be lost, like him. He wanted her tongue.

– The Otteridge Meat Company, she said, her hand still holding him, squeezing.

Oh no, make the question quick, his eyes urged her. An abattoir was the last thing he wanted to think of now.

– What of it? he said quickly.

– Shareholders.

– There would be lots of them…

– Come on, Henry, significant people. *Names.* Do you want me to start kissing you again? Name the names.

– Oh yes, please, *please*. Well Morton Maw's the obvious one. Peter had a smaller stake, that's now Olivia's. I don't think there's anyone else whom you'd think important, relevant. Yes that's all. So I've told you the names, you can…

– De Foie? Isn't he involved?

– No, he's not a shareholder. He doesn't need to be.

– Why not? Lizzie asked, digging in her fingernail, playfully, but with a hint of malice.

– Ouch, that hurts.

– Come on then, tell me, said Lizzie, or I shall bite it off.

– Gerstmann is the parent company.

– Of course, I should have realised. Thank you, Henry, that was very good of you. Now for your reward, she said, sweeping her long mane across his belly.

My God, what a vixen she was, he thought. He stroked her hair where it fell across her shoulder, his fingers skirting the tattoo, as they always did. It shocked him, the grinning animal with the words LONE WOLF, those bluish lines on her smooth skin like the mould-veins of a Rocquefort or Danish blue cheese. He supposed he was old-fashioned, but he'd never liked tattoos on women, especially girls as beautiful as Lizzie; he thought them common, sluttish. It was probably a class thing. Yet he wondered if her wolf was a clue, staring him in the face. He still didn't know why she wanted this information.

A freelance journalist, that was what she'd said that night at Nick Goodman's, when he'd first feasted upon her, that black choker around her smooth neck with the phoney cameo brooch. He'd thought her simple then, another London media tart of Bruce Tucker's wanting to be part of the county set. Yet now he realised her pretence of being a tittle-*Tatler* was itself a disguise. He wondered if Tucker had cottoned on. He might be a high flier in business, and a ruthless operator, but Tucker was unintelligent in some matters of the world, and could be manipulated by a woman. Was she a reporter then, or some other kind of investigator? Government or opposition; intelligence, or some underground group? Or was he seeking in a sheep five feet where there were but four? An agent of a foreign power, perhaps, but that was less likely, for the estuary accent, while it might be invented, would be fiendishly difficult for a foreigner to imitate. Anyone could do Australian or South African, but to do Estuary English, you had to have lived here, to know how to bastardise your own voice, to add your English upper crust to Cockney's eel pie gabbiness. Or was he barking up the wrong tree again?

And was it just information he was giving her, facts and connections, or was he setting up his own fall as well as those of others?

– Oh no, he said. It was question-time again, just as his thighs were starting to sing. But of course, she could tell that from the way he moved. She was bound to stop now.

– Denis Thatcher, she said.

– Oh no, he repeated.

– His businesses. What do you know about them? Start with Atlas. And his grandfather? What was all that about?

– Oh Lizzie, all that would take ages to tell. Even a *summary* would, you know, spoil things... Couldn't you, um, finish first, I'm almost there, just a little more, please, and then I'll tell you everything I know. I will, I promise. Please, is that a deal?

Afterwards, while Henry Sirloin was washing himself in the bathroom, Lizzie scribbled quickly in a small, blue-marbled notebook. Denis Thatcher, born 1915, the child of prosperous farming stock, made wealthy by a sheep-dip cocktail: his grandfather Thomas Thatcher had discovered that sodium arsenite was an effective killer of sheep parasites and also weeds. To market the cocktail he founded a company, Atlas Preservatives, with a man called Owen. The firm, which was eventually passed on to his grandson, later diversified into wallpaper and paint. His sale of the family firm to Castrol in 1965 for half a million pounds had assured the Thatchers' financial security. Then just a small-time businessman, Denis nevertheless gained a seat on the board of Castrol and – following a later takeover – on that of Burmah Oil. Another company was Chipmans of Shoreham, whose spray trains were used to treat railway embankments, but using banned pesticides. The Mafia link was with Atwoods, the toxic waste disposal company. Insurance losses on their dumps in the States had contributed to the Lloyds Names débâcle.

Hearing the water stop, Lizzie slipped her notebook back into her bag. Henry emerged, rubbing his face with a towel.

– If things were different, he said, would you leave Tucker? Live with me?

– No way, I'm much too old for you, Lizzie joked. And anyway, I wouldn't want us to get into any kind of domestic routine. What we have is good because it's forbidden.

– You make me want to break all the rules.

– I don't make you do anything.

– When you've milked me of all the information you want, will we still see each other? he asked, plaintively.

– Probably not, she said, smiling. I won't have any use for you then, will I?

– Isn't that a bit brutal? Unchivalrous.

– That's what men do, isn't it? Take a women, then chuck her away. *Who wats may keep sheep another day.*

– But I'm not like that, he said.

– Liar.

– I've changed, he protested. You've helped change me.

– That's Hackerton's cow, said Lizzie, looking at him as a cow on a bastard calf. The wolf may lose his teeth but never his nature.

– I see a wolf, he stammered.

– The fox may grow grey but never good.

– I'd like to set my saddle on the right horse.

– You just want to save your bacon, she said coldly.

– And aren't you selling yours? he asked, his smile both winning and cruel. A wool-seller knows a wool-buyer, Lizzie.

– It's not my bacon, she replied. I'm only borrowing it. If you take away the salt, you can throw the flesh to the dogs.

Kernan stared at Phoebe's inscription beneath the promise the book alone had kept: *Everyman, I will go with thee & be thy guide, in thy most need to go by thy side*. She seemed now like a creature from another world, where all was vanity, as the book said. Yet *Vanity Fair* had been his talisman throughout his time in Flanders, its saga of an earlier other world, where another war in this same place, a hundred years before, had seen Osborne instead of Dobbin marry Amelia Sedley, only to be killed by a stray bullet at Waterloo.

He pondered the name, *Waterloo,* which seemed like another of the soldiers' jokey translations, like Wipers for Ypres. For him one of the few joys of this ravaged land had been the names of its places, long beautiful words he spoke aloud to relish their sound, names which often survived the villages themselves. When the war was over, those same names would return the land to its people, he was sure, names which described their origins, and what was special about each of these places. So that he had hated hearing the men talk of Ploegsteert as Plug Street, or worse, Godwaersveldt as Gert-Wears-Velvet, as if it weren't enough that the Germans had razed these strange clusters of red-roofed houses to the ground, the English had tried to kill their names, the keepers of their souls. Some they changed completely, like Battersea Farm, where the platoon had rested up, not that even *farm* described that place, it was just a heap of rubble, surrounded by makeshift dugouts, only the cellar still intact, where the officers had their mess.

Soon, if the Boche were pushed back, he might see Shrewsbury Forest and Surbiton Villas. They hadn't even reached them yet, but already these places had their English names. It was almost if to take them, they had to give them their own names. If the savage Highlanders headed the advance along the Menin Road, their prize might be Inverness Copse, Stirling Castle and Glencorse Wood, while the London Scottish could take Dumbarton Lakes on their way to Tower Hamlets.

While none of these false names would survive, he thought, what of their coinings for all those obscure places without names or importance in peacetime, a crossroads, a turn in the road, a small brow or an insignificant junction, like Shrapnel Corner south of Ypres? At Crucifix Corner near Pezières, where the green fields were pitted brown by shells, he had seen the Christ figure first wounded in the heart by shrapnel, then obliterated at Easter by a direct hit. Would Crucifix Corner or Hellfire Corner be resurrected? Or Dead Horse Corner? He could imagine a name like that in Loamfield, which had its Brockhole Wood, Dog Leap Bottom, Duckwidge Ditch, and the old drovers' road, Cowbound Lane. Englishmen had to fight and die for some of these places which were no places, to hold them at all cost, because some general had decided that this name or that name on the map had to be 'taken'.

It was Ken Fisher's turn to read the book next. He couldn't imagine the rascally Ridger reading any kind of book, yet he had witnessed the others' enjoyment of it, how they had shared their views on Becky, Amelia, Jos, Dobbin, Rawdon and the rest, how *Vanity Fair* had become almost another life for Kernan's platoon, a select club to which anyone who read the green, gold-tooled book belonged, so that as each new reader progressed from chapter to chapter, he was questioned by the others on what he thought of Becky's latest slyness, what he would say to Mrs Bute Crawley if he were in her care at the dressing-station, how he would deal with the servants, the duns or Lady Southdown with her religious tracts. In this unreal place, where they slept in holes in the ground, the inhabitants of Queen's Crawley, Russell Square and Curzon Street, even the pompous Collector of Boggley Wallah, became more real to them than the Belgian peasants they saw behind the lines, who spoke a kind of gibberish, or the Boche soldiers they tried to kill like targets at a fairground, people they couldn't believe in. Sometimes *Vanity Fair* seemed more credible than 'home', the villages of Loamshire where their families waited for news of their sons, the mothers and fathers, wives and sweethearts, who had no idea at all of the numbing agony of their lives at the Front, who could never know or reach them in their nightmare. Fed by the fictions of the press, by self-deluded liars like Horatio Bottomley, how could they believe in anything other than their heroism, their victories?

With Kernan claiming his right to read the book again each time someone finished it, *Vanity Fair* also became a test and a measure for their lives. Matt Hardacre had only reached the death of the first Sir Pitt Crawley when he'd been blinded in the gas attack; and according to Hartley, he'd wanted the nurses, or other wounded, to read him more, but they hadn't been willing to carry on, it didn't have the same reality for them as it had for Kernan's men. Jack Brock was still in Miss Pinkerton's academy for young ladies on Chiswick Mall when his gun had gone off. Wilf Hartley had got as far as the Duchess of Richmond's ball, and had been planning to visit the Hôtel de Terrasse in the real Brussels, even expecting to see Becky there when the Allies advanced further into Belgium, but he had died at Arras, at Easter, with Bill Armstrong, who'd been eager to meet 'that little minx' after Hartley had followed her fall from grace. Even Johnson's card school, hearing the others' accounts, wanted to gamble at *écarté* as a change from Slippery Ann, but no one knew the rules. They all yearned to reach the promised land of Germany in Chapter LXII, when they would visit the little town of Pumpernickel during the carnival, where a masked Mrs Rawdon Crawley, her breasts displayed like pink globes of fruit from a temptingly low-cut dress, would welcome them to the card-tables in the Stadthaus with an invitation to try their luck with her at *trente-et-quarante*. Yet apart from Kernan, only four men, Marshall, Tomkins, Openshaw and Armstrong, had reached Ostend, and finished the book, and they were all dead now.

Handing the book to Fisher, Kernan turned away, not wanting to see him poring over Phoebe's inscription. He sat watching the hundreds of swaying poppies lining the lip of the trench, their scarlet heads ruffled by the light summer breeze. Further back, he knew, there were clumps of blue larkspur along the parapet of the travel trench, those vital parts of his Loamshire clock, but at home the larkspur would flower a few weeks later, after the mauve forget-me-nots, which grew here round the latrines. At the cottage, the sweet-scented honeysuckle would be trailing into the air, above where his faithful foxgloves would be standing to attention by the door, presenting arms, awaiting his return.

And now the bluebottle which had plagued them earlier had returned, and was buzzing around their heads. Fisher made to hit it with the book. Kernan intervened, moving his hand to catch it with a swipe, but as he swept at the fly, he raised his head just slightly too high, and at that moment, a bullet spun him round, keeling him over. He was more surprised than hurt.

Wounded more by the sudden end to his reverie, Kernan looked around in indignation, his initial shock giving way to puzzlement over the source and direction of the bullet, which had not seemed to impact anywhere after grazing him. There had been no sound afterwards, and the revetted parados behind where his head had been was seemingly undamaged.

– Where's it gone? he said.

– Does it matter? said Fisher, smiling. Can't have had your name on it.

– Yes, but someone was trying to kill me. I don't like that.

Maurice Saveloy always marked the third day of July, the first of the Dog Days, when the dog-star Sirius rises with the sun, by eating seven hot dogs, and continued for forty days to feast on further specimens of the skinless sausage lubricated with tomato catsup and slippery fried onions. His belief that this would bring him good luck was derived from an age-old confusion between the Dog Days and the period of July and August known to the Romans as *caniculares dies*, 'the hottest days'.

Had he been versed in the beliefs of the haggis-eating Gaels, the Chief Constable would have understood why the more likely consequence of an overindulgence in reheated sausages at this time of year was not good but ill luck, in the person of Private Diarrhoea and his squad of Cramps, for in Scotland the Dog Days are known as the Worm Month.

In Loamfield, the exiled landlord of the Black Bull celebrated this Gaelic time of readiness by offering his customers a drink called the McDonald's Surprise, a urine-hued American lager with a worm wriggling drunkenly at the bottom of the glass which was said to advertise the ebullient Scotsman's dislike of the fast food chain which had usurped his good name and his distaste for its dead cow burgers.

O'Scrapie had that morning drunk six of these concoctions, inviting a sextet of jazzy chaetopods to dance a rumba around the cilia-waving tubes of his alimentary canal, while Maurice Saveloy had eaten the same number of hot dogs containing a larger contingent of worms. Superintendent Nicholas Goodman sat at some distance from the malodorous pair, avoiding their flatulent duet, but also experiencing some discomfort himself, not from the consumption of beer, worms or sausages, but from his harbouring a contingent of six penile warts.

– So we're agreed then, said Goodman, it's the only way to stop the rot.

– I still think *wasting* Kernan, as you call it, may be risky, said the Chief Constable. And while we're talking about *waste*, what about the squad car? Oxter has written off three cars already this year. We can't afford to lose another one. We've nothing left in the budget. Not a sausage.

– We'll use the van then, said Goodman impatiently, that's due for replacement in the autumn. We can get an earlier write-off.

– Yes, and then get a new one. One of those big flashy jobs like Kent have got, with a siren like a banshee...

– As far as *risk* is concerned, Goodman added, while it will *look* like an accident, none of Kernan's lot will see it that way. And with him out of the way, the whole conspiracy will fall apart.

– But won't they see that his brakes have been tampered with?

– Who's *they*, Maurice? *We're* they. Internal police investigation. No mechanical fault discovered on the vehicle. Pour some Sheep Dip down the throat of the corpse, Kernan's favourite whisky. Post-mortem shows the inspector had been drinking. Judgement impaired. Swerved the wrong way when the police van pulled out. No further questions.

– Yes, I'm sure you're right, said Saveloy, wincing as his boisterous guests began carrying out serious demolition work in his duodenum. Now, if you don't mind gentlemen, I think I need to go upstairs. Something I've eaten seems to have disagreed with me. Thank you, Mr O'Scrapie, for your help in this damage limitation exercise. We won't forget your contribution.

– You'd better not, hissed O'Scrapie, getting up to leave. And I still think I should have something up front. Cheese and money should always sleep together one night.

– What would you do with it? Goodman snapped back. Spend it. People would know in no time that you'd come into money. Cheat and the cheese will show. Kernan would smell a rat.

When O'Scrapie had departed, Maurice Saveloy clutched at his stomach in attempting to rise from his chair.

– One more thing, he said, gritting his teeth. I know we're playing a dog's trick, but I still don't understand why we need this O'Scrapie fellow. We'll have to watch him carefully. The dog that fetches will carry.

– We have to make a cat's paw of him, said Goodman. It's safer that way.

– But he's a most unsavoury character, hardly trustworthy. A snake in the grass.

– And he hates Kernan's guts. He wanted money up front, but he still agreed to do it when I refused.

– Couldn't we have done it ourselves? Have Oxter fix the car?

– I don't want to lose Oxter. He's a useful man.

– What do you mean *lose*?

– You don't think I'm going to have O'Scrapie running round afterwards, flushed with his triumph as well as with cash, do you?

– So O'Scrapie gets the chop as well?

– We give our dog roast meat and beat him with the spit. He meets with an accident. They converge, the accident and him. Afterwards there is no afterwards. Shit happens.

Superintendent Goodman shifted uneasily in his chair, conscious of an unpleasant sensation in the member's enclosure of his Y-fronts. During the meeting one of his warts had started to suppurate, and the purulent discharge had dried, the scab attaching the outer skin of his penis to the cotton material of his underpants. When he attempted to move, the front panel rubbed against the spot in question.

The Chief Constable clenched his buttocks. It seemed to him that some demon of the Inquisition was searing the insides of his rectum with a heated metal utensil. The portals of his fundament had been breached by Beelzebub's trident. Edward II could not have felt worse, he thought – attempting to distract himself with the historical reference – for all that the assassin's poker had killed him.

In the Apocalypse, the angel swears there will be no more time, while Dostoyevsky's Kirillov held that time wasn't a thing, it was an idea which would die out in the mind. For Maurice Saveloy too, the idea of time had ceased to exist in a relative dimension. Time had died out in his mind. It had become an eternity of anal pain. Time had been transformed in the interval between starting to run and reaching the cubicle of the gents toilet on the top floor of Otteridge Police Station. The moment of contact between his lowered buttocks and the welcome coldness of the lavatory seat was simultaneous with the instant of his first impulse for flight. Likewise, there was no time present in the flames of his personal Hell. Unlike the salamander, alchemical emblem of purifying sulphur and fire, he would not survive the all-consuming inferno.

When the Chief Constable farted, all Hell broke loose. In the next cubicle, PC Roger Hodge had been leaning back to draw the last blissful drags from his cigarette, relishing a moment away from the world. Now he left it entirely.

The explosion was heard in Loamfield.

At the Eurochimique plant, Oliver de Foie ran to look out the window, fearing to see what he had dreaded since the revelations of the previous November. But the unstable no.9 tank was still intact. He was safe after all. Looking across towards Otteridge, he saw black smoke rising from the west end of the town, somewhere near the police station. That will keep Goodman busy, he thought, returning to his desk, where he had been entering the results of a chemical reaction in a blue marble-patterned notebook.

I'm a little blue-arsed fly
Born in a cow pat,
Flutterby taught me to fly,
Run round the cow pat
Till I drop the day I die,
That's now and now that

I'm a little blue-arsed fly
Born in a cow pat,
Flutterby taught me to fly,
Run round the cow pat
Till I drop the day I die,
That's now and now that

I'm a little blue-arsed fly
Born in a cow pat,
Flutterby taught me to fly,
Run round the cow pat
Till I drop the day I die,
That's now and now that

CHAPTER THIRTEEN

The Dance of the Blue-Arsed Fly

ST CATHERINE'S DAY: 20TH JULY

If a thief always carries a dried toad's heart, he will not be caught. A toad, killed and dried in March, worn in a silk bag next to the skin, will discourage nosebleeds; dried toad's heart beaten to a powder and swallowed in a drink will prevent epilepsy. Witches have familiar spirits in the form of toads, and occasionally take that shape themselves.

Unbuttoning her collar, Diana jerked back her head, tilting it upwards like a heron. She poured a third glass of water down her throat, but still she could feel it – or was it just her sense of it – that it had been there? She almost thought she could taste it.

– You did swallow it then? asked Lambert.

– Yes, said Diana, it went right down. She coughed, but that didn't help. The sensation was still there, like a guilty secret that would not go away. The moment the fly had entered her mouth, she'd thought of Kernan, that he had sent the creature to spy on them; and remembered Brigid's story of Étaín, whom Etar's wife had swallowed as a fly; how she later gave birth to a new Étaín.

– You were saying? she said softly, her composure returning.

– Goodman has put a permanent tail on me, said Lambert.

– A tail suits you… she started, but noting Lambert's pallid, expressionless face, stopped…

– He probably thinks it's only a matter of time. But we don't actually have very much.

– Time? Diana asked, her gaze fixed on the Hogarthian image presented by his skullish face. *Memento mori.*

– No, evidence.

– What about Tench and Eurochimique? she persisted.

– Nothing concrete.

– Gerstmann and the slaughter scam?

– Legal in itself, said Lambert, ever cautious.

– And the land deals: all above board, as far as we know, said Diana, thinking: this torpid man will be dead before he does anything. His will is frozen, like his emotional life. She looked at him again, the vein on his forehead captured by his taut hairless flesh. The skull beneath the skin.

– It's probably all linked, but nothing connects, Lambert was saying. Nothing we can pin on Maw, let alone Goodman.

– But *he* doesn't know that, Diana protested. He's desperate now, running around like a blue-arsed fly, trying to work out what to do next. He's completely paranoid, remember. He'll think we know more than we do, and that you being made Chief Constable, despite opposition from his cronies on the police authority, shows you must have friends in higher places.

– Which I don't, Lambert said simply. I don't know the story, but it certainly wasn't a conspiracy. A cock-up or compromise is the more likely explanation. Anyone who backed me against Goodman would be cutting their own throats.

– What if they think the game's up? Diana demanded. They've never been able to touch him themselves. They must resent him. This way they can make sure that if they go down when the shit hits the fan, he goes with them. *A hog that's bemired will try to bemire others.*

– But we still have nothing on our hog. No real dirt to mire him with.

– What about those files?

– I'd need a good reason to search them. I could only do that if he was under suspension. And anyway… He paused, looking down at the floor, trying not to meet her green eyes.

– What? she cried, staring at him.

– They've gone. I was in his office yesterday, and they're not there now. He's been having his room decorated. Said he needed a clearout...

– Oh great, she said. You're Chief Constable now, Lawrence. You have authority over the whole of Loamshire, but you can't even stop someone removing a filing-cabinet from your own police station which probably contains enough evidence to convict Goodman and the rest for murder, corruption, theft and goodness knows what else. He'll always be one step ahead of you, Lawrence. You *have* to take risks, beat him at his own game.

– I can't afford to take such risks. We don't actually *know* those files contain anything incriminating. Without something to back up my actions, I'd be out on my ear as soon as I moved against him. He'd set his dogs on me.

– But you've got half the Police Authority on your side now.

– Not enough to stop him from having me hauled over the coals. He'd have my guts for garters.

– Even Sirloin's backing you now, Diana protested. And there are others who want to see the force cleaned up. They're full of admiration for you, for what you're trying to do.

– Full of courtesy, full of craft. *Gentle puttocks have long toes.*

– So despite everything, Diana interrupted, you're still between hawk and buzzard.

– Nothing is certain yet, Lambert said dully. But I don't want to jump the gun. To fright a bird is not the best way to catch it.

– One does not catch rabbits with a dead ferret, Diana retorted, making no attempt to disguise her disdain.

– A man must plough with such oxen as he has, said Lambert. He that has patience has fat thrushes for a farthing. The hindmost dog may catch the hare.

– You may gape long ere a fly fall in *your* mouth, said Diana, throwing her head back again. You have to get out there and *hunt* your prey. Larks won't land in your mouth ready-roasted.

– But my position remains precarious, said Lambert with a resigned air, sensing that he had lost her respect; yet she was *so* precipitate. You must know I have no special powers in these circumstances, he added quickly.

– Well *I* have, she cried. And it's about time I used them.

– But what about... Lambert stammered.

Her soup not drunk: not eaten but left to cool. In the theme restaurant called the Three Bears, with its gingham-aproned Goldilocks waitresses, a stuffed bear's head above the fireplace watched her rush out.

Afterwards, sitting in her car, trying to calm herself while only half-hearing the coded chitchat on the police wavelength, Diana regretted her outburst, yet she had been so angry with him. Impossible man! She needed to think now, but reaching down to kill the inane police banter, to cocoon herself, found the radio was not switched on.

She could not have been listening to it after all, and yet she knew she had. There had been a break-in at Threshers off licence, someone had looted the till and had been seen riding off on a bicycle with a yellow box of Famous Grouse balanced on the crossbar. She radioed in for confirmation, and Sergeant Daglock corroborated the story, though not the brand of whisky. If the booty had been Irish Powers, she would not have been surprised. But she knew that when she went to question the owner, he would check his stock and tell her the missing box was indeed Famous Grouse. So Kernan's magic was starting to rub off. Or was it her own in the first place, which he was releasing, renewing in her? She was not sure. This kind of thing must happen all the time in his domain.

And if Kernan had been in Lambert's position, he'd have had the whole place turned upside down by now. Goodman and Oxter would be under arrest. He might not have enough evidence, but by the time they appeared in court he'd have the complete story, chapter and verse. He'd done that many times, taken his opportunity, made an early arrest. Even last week, with Goodman about to demand the release of the suspects in the Grennan case, Kernan waltzed in with a pile of papers, objects, photographs, tapes, the whole caboodle. How he had managed to amass such evidence in so short a space of time, Goodman never knew, but Diana had her suspicions.

– If I know they're guilty, Kernan had told her, if I know they did it, because my sources have told me, all I need to do is get them out of the way, and then I go into action. With a little help from certain quarters...

– These unpaid informers of yours?

– Unpaid? I wouldn't say that. They're paid, but in the right way. Sometimes I only need to share my food with them. A bannock and a blessing.

– What does that mean?

– When you make your oatcake, shape it on the palm of your hand, but you mustn't put the loose-meal back in the meal-chest or the Cailleach will sit there and eat the luck of the house.

– You're bonkers...

– Lay the bannock on your left palm while turning your right thumb deasil through the centre. You know Loamshire people never throw away food, for fear that want will come upon them later. Especially now in July, when people used to face weeks of famine before the harvest. It's ingrained in them, their memory of the hungry month of July.

– Where does the blessing come in? she'd asked, marvelling that where once she'd scorned these tales of his, now she listened eagerly, wanting to learn, wanting to know him also through his telling of the stories. Her protests had become milder, but remained part of the ritual, like a child's pretending.

– It's the mother's blessing, said Kernan. When children set off to seek their fortune, she asks them if they will have a large bannock and no blessing from her, or a small bannock and a blessing. Those who choose wisely will achieve their quest, sharing their bannock with hungry strangers they meet on their way, or with animals, who later help them in their turn.

– What did you choose?

– Small bannock, with blessing. But I was too eager. I shared it with everyone, till there wasn't a crumb left for me. And I've been hungry ever since, but never without my helpers.

– I'd give you a big piece of my cake, if I had one, said Diana, surprising herself that she had made no smart rejoinder, her usual wit dissolved by Kernan's story.

– I'd like that, he said, and sang:

> Some like the lassies that's gay weel dressed
> And some like the lassies that's techt above the waist
> But it's in amang the blankets that I like best
> To get a jolly rattle at the cuckoo's nest.

Skiddly-idle-daddle-diddle-didle-dadle-dum
Di-didle-dadle-dum-daddle-diddle-didle-dum
Skiddly-idle-daddle-diddle-dadle-diddle-didle-dum
To get a jolly rattle at the cuckoo's nest…

His voice tailed off at the second cuckoo's nest. Touching her hand, he moved quickly away, returning to the papers he'd been checking.

Remembering that conversation and his song, as well as her threat to Lambert, Diana Hunter knew that something had changed inside her, that some part of herself which had been hers and hers alone, she now wanted to share. And Kernan, she was sure, knew more about those powers of hers than he was letting on. Despite his resistance, whatever that meant, she must pursue him now if she was to fully know herself. If she did not take that risk, she knew that she would die inside, become a mouse like Lambert.

That it would end in pain was certain, but if she didn't allow herself to be hurt, she would never know what it was to love, and be loved. Kernan loved her, she was sure, but he had been holding back, for her sake, because he didn't want to wreck their friendship and their work.

But hadn't she hurt him enough already, by seeing Lambert? Wasn't that a sign that she should resist this madness, that she would only hurt him more, and herself, when it ended?

No. She knew she loved him now, and wanted to feel his love inside her, filling her, fulfilling her. She wanted to be with him now, fully with him, to surrender herself to him. It had to be worth it, to feel, to know and be all that, whatever was lost in the end. And it had happened now. She had acknowledged it, was moving with it. It was unstoppable.

The bluebottle was dive-bombing the food which Muffy was trying to pass around.

– *Pesky fly*, said O'Scrapie, trying to swat it, quoting his favourite line from the *Beano*.

– *Fiddlers, flies and dogs come to feasts uncalled*, warned Herne.

– *Knuckers!* Gubbins cried, launching a bat from his coat in pursuit of the winged invader.

– Don't deride the fly, said Muffy, it may be someone's soul.

– Arsehole more like, said O'Scrapie. Are they yours Gubbins, these flies?

– None of mine, the sweep replied, there are no flies on me.

Gubbins grinned, aware that despite appearances and smells to the contrary, he was actually sharper than his chief tormentor, who after all had been caught and jailed three times by the lynx-eyed Inspector Kernan, whereas he, Ernest Gubbins, had never been detained at Her Majesty's Pleasure. He had never been caught. He had even half-inched a valuable pair of ladies' under-whatsits with the 3-in-1 smell in a black velvet case belonging to the widow Saveloy; no one knew about that, not even the Coot. He always carried a dried toad's heart in his jacket to protect him from policemen and other devils.

Another blue-arsed fly shot across the gathering, twanging a metal foil takeaway container which had contained stolen egg-fried rice.

But this high-speed invader was not another pesky bluebottle. It was a bullet from a Webley service revolver. Since it made no impact with them, they failed to spot the difference.

– Where's the whisky? said O'Scrapie. Come on Gubbins, don't hog the Grouse, pass round the Poacher's Piss. Give some to old Muff too.

– Now, said Muffy, silence in the pig market and let the old sow have her grunt.

– We're all ears and curly tails, said Flea.

– Now where was I? Muffy asked.

– July? Flea suggested.

– *July*, repeated Muffy, as well as being the hungry month, July is *Elembiuos* in the old calendar, Claim Time. These are the weeks leading up to Lughnasadh when unfulfilled obligations are claimed, unfinished business concluded amongst neighbours, sealed with the two parties spitting, with recourse to the judge if friendly agreement isn't made. So I want you all to think about your claims, and if there's anything to sort out with each other, let's do that now. Herne will be our judge.

– Why not me? demanded O'Scrapie, I'm leader. And no spitting from Gubbins, we've had a plague of bats already.

– It has to be a *brehon*, someone who's unbiassed, said Muffy.

– In that case, I make the first claim, O'Scrapie insisted. His first thought was he wanted Kernan turned into a spit-roast, but that was going to happen anyway, thanks to the slippery bullet-headed superintendent, whom he would have to watch all the same.

– Come on then, who do you want to wrangle with? said Gubbins, half afraid it might be him.

– Becky Sharp, said O'Scrapie, before he knew what he was saying. The others roared.

He didn't want to wrangle with her, he said, he wanted her for himself. He'd always wanted her, ever since he was a child when he'd seen Becky the Minx played by Susan Hampshire on the box, before she was Fleur, with her turned-up nose like Rose his scheming sister, all innocence and devilment. This was his claim. If his days were numbered, this would be his last wish, before his execution.

Herne was not surprised. He knew about the spell the green-eyed adventuress had cast over him. That time when O'Scrapie had been banged up in the cells, he had lent him his precious bullet-scarred, mouldy-covered Everyman *Vanity Fair* which always went with him in his canvas bag, Kernan's from the war. The man hadn't stopped talking about her for months afterwards, his ideal woman, such a manipulator, what a partnership they'd have made, never mind that useless Rawdon, she'd been wasted on him. What schemes he and his Becky would dream up; they'd be unstoppable. The Crown Jewels themselves wouldn't be safe from such a team.

If O'Scrapie was, as he said, a doomed man, then he must have his Becky Sharp, Herne decided, for a dying man's wish in Claim Time could not be disregarded, particularly if it was in his powers to grant. It didn't go against the laws of nature, only those of authorship, and who was to say Mrs Rawdon Crawley was not now a free agent, a self-made woman capable of acting against the whims and wishes of Mr William Makepeace Thackeray, a jilted lover who faulted and begrudged the independent spirit of a creature who enthralled him?

– When do you want her then? he asked.

– Now, now, said O'Scrapie, eagerly, ignoring the incredulous looks of the others.

– No, I mean when in the book? asked Herne.

– It's got to be Vauxhall Gardens, when Jos gets pissed and doesn't propose. She's just out of school then, ripe and ready to be plucked, without a friend in the world. I'd love to have her then, when she's really young and fresh.

– But she'd not want you, said Herne. She'd know she could do better. You're not exactly good-looking…

– Nor was Jos Sedley, the fat git.

– But he had money and prospects, said Herne. He was the Collector of Boggley Wallah, and stood to inherit from his father. You need to try her when she's seen her hopes dashed, when – I hate to say it – she's a bit desperate.

– All right then. After Steyne and Rawdon have dumped her, and she's running round like a blue-arsed fly, trying to speak to that shithead Pitt Crawley, who won't see her, the fuckwit. I'll have her then.

– Still wouldn't work, said Herne firmly. She'd take one look at you and run a mile. Remember, she's only just lost her nice little love-nest in Curzon Street. You'll have to cross the water…

– What, go to Boulogne? Me in Frogland?

– No, Germany. Pumpernickel's the place, before Amelia gets there on her tour with Jos and Dobbin. Catch her when she hasn't got a penny to her name, and she's yours for as long as she can use you.

– And I'll use her too, said O'Scrapie, the spittle starting to glisten on his lips.

The fly was considerably larger than the small spider which had trapped it on its filmy web, and when it started buzzing furiously, trying to free itself with its powerful wings, Kernan expected to see the spider leap on its back like a lioness downing a struggling wildebeest, but the predator allowed itself to be shaken with the movement of its prey on its taut line of gossamer. It hung on as the fly went berserk, and every so often hightailed up and down the tether to make technical adjustments, it seemed, or to draw in the web, to cocoon its meal more securely. When the fly was finally still, the spider mounted it briefly, then walked nonchalantly away.

Such scenes of life and death struggle in the animal world never failed to absorb his attention. He did not take sides, like some people he knew, or intervene as others would, freeing the fly or killing the spider, seeing themselves in the underdog. *He who would wish to thrive must let spiders run alive.*

But eating the fly was different, especially if the fly were a bullet or a soul. You bit the bullet, you caught the soul.

> I know an old woman who swallowed a fly.
> I don't know why she swallowed the fly.
> Perhaps she'll die.
>
> I know an old woman who swallowed a spider
> That wriggled and jiggled and tickled inside her.
> She swallowed the spider to catch the fly
> But I don't know why she swallowed the fly.
> Perhaps she'll die.

And the bird swallows the spider, Kernan considered, but she still doesn't die. She swallows all the animals in turn without dying, even the cow, which may have BSE if it's been fed on MRM. It's only when she swallows the horse that she comes a cropper, which can't be because of its size because she's already managed the cow with no apparent ill effects, but if the horse is badly glanderous, the farcy could be transmitted across the species barrier to the old woman who swallowed the fly. Glanders was fatal in horses, asses and humans.

Kernan's spider would grow fat on a few more flies before his good friend Arthur Hugh Chough, waiting on the kitchen window-ledge, would despatch it with one expert stab of his curved scarlet beak, with a cry of *chee-aw, chee-aw, chee-aw*, punctuated with a final end-stopping *chuff*. That was Arthur's vocal comment on anything: *chee-aw, chee-aw, chee-aw...chuff*. The rest was unsaid, or unsayable.

So that when O'Scrapie had offered to wash his filthy car for five pounds, because he needed to raise some cash, Kernan had not hesitated to agree, knowing that Arthur would keep a watchful eye on the miscreant, and afterwards, his green Clio transfigured, sparkling like a bright sword of jade in the sunlight, Arthur had pronounced:

– *Chee-aw, chee-aw, chee-aw... chuff. Chee-aw, chee-aw, chee-aw... chuff.* The kingly bird looked up at him, his small beady eyes fixing him with a true chough's stare, dipping his bill courteously, ruffling slightly his glossy regal-black plumage.

And Kernan had understood.

Diana's alarm was therefore disturbing, not in the matter of her concern but rather in its breathless manner.

– Oh Kernan, she said, I've just seen that O'Scrapie slinking round the back. God knows what he was up to.

– I'm deuced if I know, said Kernan, I thought he was washing my car in the lane. But our fidging mare is well guarded.

Taking her jacket, he stood at arm's length from the red-polled head he found so adorable. Moving round her, he watched her eager, vivacious face, the cheeks flushed like fruit, her green coruscant eyes gleaming like Athene's, thrilled to see her gaze absorbing him just as he was drawing life from hers. He remembered her first visit, her thirst to know tempered then by a wounded woman's caution, attacking to defend her untouchable, impregnable soul. Now she was wide-eyed and hungry, touching his arm, meeting his look. She seemed to drink him in. He was scared and exhilarated by the change.

– Now since it is St Margaret's Day, he said, seeking the distraction of facts, I have made us Heg-Peg Dumps, or my version of them.

– Your version? she asked, seating herself at his table like an eager pupil.

– With fish, not meat. They should be meat dumplings made with suet, but as you know, I will not eat sentient creatures...

– And fish aren't sentient? Diana asked, a mischievous glint in her eye, signalling play.

– Cows, sheep and pigs are sentient, where I'm concerned, he explained. Like cats and dogs, they have souls. The beasts in the field and the fowls in the air all speak to me, but not the fishes in the flood. Fish *exist*. I respect them...

– But you eat them...

– I know it's inconsistent, but at least I spare the birds and beasts. Although it may be true, as my grandmother used to say, that we were descended from the Creek Women...

– Oh, don't start on them again. But tell me, she said, eyeing the dumplings swimming in their sea of fish chowder with some apprehension. Tell me about Margaret. Why do you celebrate her day, but not the others?

– I mark many days, replied Kernan. But usually those of suppressed saints, those thrown out by the church, declared apocryphal, because they're often the most powerful. Mythical outcasts like Margaret, and George of course. Werburga and so on. Legends for the French as well as the English. Margaret appeared to St Joan you know, and both Margaret and George slew their dragons.

– I didn't know about Margaret's dragon, said Diana, stabbing the pink armour of a prawn with her fork. But I thought they were an extinct species. Didn't the zealots wipe them out?

– Dragons are still around but few can see them, said Kernan. When people believed in the Devil, they would see his dragons. At least they could be slain then. Invisible evil is harder to fight, that's why demons have such a hold over our modern world.

– You believe in demons then? Diana asked, not surprised, but seeking confirmation.

– I know their ways, said Kernan. Goodman is a demon. I know his sort. Or if he isn't a devil himself, he is possessed by one.

– How can you say that? In these times...

– Exactly *because* of these times.

Could he tell her now? How else could he hold her back, make sure she wouldn't fall for him, stop her from being hurt? He knew he could not, should not love her, except as a child. Yet he had to keep his secret safe, even from her, whom he knew he did love with a fierceness he'd never felt before, not in a hundred years. Yet if Diana Hunter really was his match, might his destiny not lie with her?

– I recognise their work, he said. I saw it first in the war. In many wars.

– What do you mean, *many* wars? she asked, suddenly alarmed.

– I am not who you think I am, he said simply. Or should I say rather: I am not just George Kernan. I am all Kernans, all Georges.

And he began then to tell her his story, beginning with the fly and Arthur.

Who saw him die?
I, said the Fly,
With my little eye,
I saw him die.

Reaching the top floor of the Elephant inn, O'Scrapie paused to get his breath back. He hadn't realised the stairs would be so steep, or that these buildings would have such low ceilings. When he'd told the surly landlord to get a lift installed, the fool just looked at him blankly, repeating his word *leeft*.

– Oh forget it, said O'Scrapie. Just tell me how I find Mrs Rawdon Crawley.

– Ah, Madame de Raudon, said the man, then started gibbering away in German. O'Scrapie shrugged his shoulders in the manner recommended by the guidebook, whereupon the host wrote the figure 92 with his finger on the bar counter and pointed upwards. He obviously took him for one of the English riffraff of the place instead of – as he'd tried to convey – an eminent visitor from the Serene Court of His Transparency the Duke of Pumpernickel. Reaching the door of her garret, he announced himself as such with a light tap of his cane on the middle panel.

– I am an associate of my lord Tapeworm, the Chargé d'Affaires, whom I gather you know, he added, as she opened the door. And stood staring at her almost mythical green eyes, her sandy hair, mumbling how she might note the similarity of their names…

She was just as he had imagined her from the book. By way

of morning robe, she had a pink domino, a trifle faded and soiled, and marked here and there with pomatum; but her arms shone out from the loose sleeves of the dress very white and fair, her tawny hair tumbling shamelessly around her bare neck. She was no spring chicken, he could see, but her figure was still trim. He noticed traces of rouge on her cheeks, and as she took his gold-tipped French cane, eyeing it, gauging its value (which was high, for he had stolen it from the Pariser Hof that morning from no less a personage than M. de Macabau), he smelled her brandy-tainted breath. Oh, delicious fallen woman!

The room too was exactly as the novelist had described it, so precisely correct in every detail that he felt sure that Thackeray himself must have visited his Galatea – as Herne had called her – in this place. As Becky sat down opposite him, on the bed, he knew the clanking sound behind her neat bottom betrayed the presence under the bedclothes of the secreted sausage on its plate, the hidden rouge-pot and brandy bottle, because that character assassin had put them there. Thackeray – or Titmarsh, to use his earlier pen-name, which seemed preferable – had wanted to besmirch his divine creature by introducing that tawdry hoard.

She looked up at him, her large eyes trying to work him out. One of her gowns hung over the bed, another from a door-hook; her bonnet half-obscured the mirror. Beside a cheap-looking candle on her bedside table lay a book, a French novel; tilting his head just slightly to read the title over her shoulder, he saw it was *Bout de Ressources*.

– My friend Tapeworm thought we should be acquainted, Mrs Crawley, he said, for we have interests in common. I invariably meet with luck at the play-tables. Indeed, my facility is such that I am no longer welcome at certain houses in London, Paris and Rome.

– Rome, you have been to Rome? she asked, her quavering voice the sweetest music he had ever heard. And was this recently, Mr O'Scrapie?

– Indeed, and I had the good fortune to relieve someone whom I believe you know of several hundred pounds at écarté, a Mr Wenham…

– I did not know he played.

– He did so when I was there, which I believe was shortly after your own visit was curtailed, for he gave me such an interesting account of your brief sojourn that I vowed if ever I found myself in the same town as Mrs Rawdon Crawley, I would have to make her acquaintance.

– Mr Wenham's depiction of my character did not discourage you from doing so? I cannot think that he would feel any kindness towards me, not that I ever wronged him or his master, for that was all such a dreadful misunderstanding, and yet I have only ever heard that he spoke ill of me, Lord Steyne having been so false and cruel to me.

– Mr Wenham was by no means kind, Mrs Crawley, said O'Scrapie, yet I was inclined to overlook his vulgar discourse the more careless he became in his playing.

– And you are a good player, Mr O'Scrapie?

– I am not unwelcome in those places I mentioned because I play badly.

– It was not for cheating then? Becky asked, her green eyes sparkling.

– If I ever did so, that has only been when fortune became fickle, so favouring others that they became foolish with their successes. I never left such a table with less than a thousand pounds in my pocket.

O'Scrapie wondered how long he could keep this up. Herne had rehearsed him well, but he was unused to this manner of intercourse, being more inclined to the other. He was desperate to get her into bed, for all that there was that sausage, and the rouge-pot and brandy nestling under the coverlet.

Oh Becky, Becky, he thought, you've not had a fuck for over a hundred years, don't you want one now? What must I do to make that happen? I must be able to work something, *in loco autoris*, or whatever it was Herne said. But no, I'm probably wrong; she'll never be without her admirers, even here. She won't have gone without, and she'll always be here, in this book, in this other time.

Suddenly, there was a tapping at the door, and a voice at key-hole level, pleading.

– Angel Englanderinn! Do take compassion upon us. Make an appointment. Dine with me and Fritz at the inn in the park.

We will have roast pheasants and porter, plum-pudding and French wine. We'll die if you don't.

– *Knuckers*, said O'Scrapie, *I'll make you die all right, go on, be off with you!* There was a scampering on the landing. That was encouraging. He acted, and those German no-goods ran for it. He tried addressing Becky in that same mode:

– *You didn't hear that, Mrs Crawley. That didn't happen.*

– I beg your pardon, Mr O'Scrapie? I was distracted for a moment. You were speaking of your winnings, I believe.

Good, she had not heard. It worked. He could be the puppet-master, as Titmarsh called himself. He was running the show now. He wasn't only pulling the strings, he was in the play himself.

– I would like you to remove your clothes, and get into the bed, Becky.

– Mr O'Scrapie, what is the meaning of this? You are most improper...

– Sorry, wrong mode. Should have remembered the slanty type, so try this, in italics. *Remove the plates and bottles first. This is an authorial instruction. It does not form part of the charade you've been playing till now. It is just, how shall we say, a little diversion. When we've finished, you can return to your Chapter LXIII and await the arrival of your old friends. I just have to think what I want, and it happens. If I want you to undo your domino, you do so. I don't even have to say it. I just think it and it happens.*

O'Scrapie sat back in his chair, and watched his very own Becky Sharp start to undress in front of him, affecting an air of modesty while exposed to this new, much more rapacious Pygmalion who had come into her life at a time when Mr Thackeray's thoughts were with Amelia and her entourage in Cologne. Her green eyes were cast down, but when they looked up, they were very large, strange and immensely attractive to her admirer.

– *Come into my parlour, said the Spider to the Fly...*

He wondered how many times she had fluttered her eyelashes at old Titmarsh, outside the pages of his book. He hauled her towards him on the thread of a thin smile. She would give him anything he wanted, even her life.

Nicholas Goodman tapped his sulphur-yellow nicotined fingers on his desk with a rhythm so insistent and repetitive that Malcolm Oxter thought at first it was a drum-roll summoning him to judgement, and that the superintendent would reach into his desk and remove either his Webley revolver or a judge's black hanging cap. The effect of the interview was no less frightening. Goodman's black eyes looked like burning coals. The stubbly hairs on his bullethead bristled like the coat of a hedgehog. The sergeant had never seen him so hopping mad. He was as angry as an ass with a squib in his breach. After a tirade of curses and expletives spat into his face, his boss was now talking slowly, deliberately, with a low audible hiss lubricating and then punctuating many of his words.

– And what happened then, *ssss*sergeant (*hiss*), when Kernan braked as you pulled out, and his car *ssss*stopped (*hiss*) in the road instead of colliding with your van? he asked, the snakey sibilance tailing off after his last word had been enunciated.

– Well by then of course the van was nosedown in the river, and Inspector Kernan, um, as it were, was good enough to... er, rescue me, sir. He pulled me free from the van.

– I *sssss*ee, said Goodman, elongating the *S* sound to allow spittle to play through his clenched teeth.

The big sergeant tried to avoid Goodman's black stare. The hissing seemed now to be continuing independent of his speech, as if from the floor or walls. Oxter even imagined for a moment that he saw thin smoke trailing from the policeman's ears.

– And what did Kernan *sssss*say (*hiss*) to you, *sssss*sergeant?

– He made a joke, sir. A derogatory comment about the van.

– What *kind* of comment? he snapped.

– Well, it was to do with the front of the van being under the water, so that you could only see the last four letters of the word POLICE along the side. There was no PO, you see, all you could read was...

– I get the picture, *ssssss*ergeant. You don't need to *ssssss*pell it out. I don't think anyone el*ssssss*e would find it funny.

– Oh you'd be surprised, sir. Inspector Kernan took a photograph and stuck it on the board downstairs, and everyone...

– *Enough!* Goodman bellowed. Then lowering his voice: Do we know what's happened to O'Scrapie?

– Word is he's gone to Germany, sir, after some woman.

– And how did he afford that? I wasn't aware that his giro would cover the cost of foreign travel, or that he was as yet in receipt of any other payments? Goodman asked. His voice had become peremptory and dismissive, the sigmatism less pronounced.

– Inspector Kernan said he'd been washing cars. Doing jobs for people. Stuff like that.

– *Pulling jobs more like!* Goodman sneered. I'll give him *stuff like that...*

– Oh and someone's looking for him. Some old geezer was in the station this morning, very eager to find him he was.

– Who was this?

– Don't know. Inspector Daube spoke to him, but he didn't seem to remember much. He's off the old Paddy waggon again. Said this bloke was a big man, with a broken nose and funny-looking glasses. Lots of shiny buttons on his coat.

– *Buttons?* Goodman demanded. What was his name, this *Buttons*?

– Said first his name was Wagstaffe, then Thatcher or Thacker or something.

– *Thatcher...?* Goodman jumped on the name. *Thatcher...?* he repeated. And grabbing his right hand with his left, began cracking his knuckles. When he started doodling in a spiral-bound notebook, Oxter noticed for the first time that Superintendent Goodman was a southpaw. Why had he never twigged this before? He'd never seen him writing, he supposed. Goodman was usually on his high horse, delivering his sermon from the mount. And when the Almighty blethered away, it was his job to listen, to try to follow his long sentences and fancy phrases. Now the Boss was silent for once, just looking down at his desk, distracted, no longer seeing the stout sergeant occupying the space in front of him. Given this chance of non-existence, Malcolm Oxter backed out of the room.

'O bide, lady, bide,
And aye he bade her bide
The rusty smith your leman shall be
For a' your muckle pride.'

Then she became a turtle dow,
To fly up in the air,
And he became another dow,
And they flew pair and pair.
'O bide, lady, bide,' &c.

She turned herself into an eel,
To swim into yon burn,
And he became a speckled trout,
To gie the eel a turn.
'O bide, lady, bide,' &c.

Then she became a duck, a duck,
To puddle in a peel.
And he became a rose-kaimd drake,
To gie the duck a dreel.
'O bide, lady, bide,' &c.

She turned hersell into a hare,
To rin upon yon hill,
And he became a gude grey-hound,
And boldly he did fill.
'O bide, lady, bide,' &c.

Then she became a grey gay mare,
And stood in yonder slack,
And he became a gilt saddle,
And sat upon her back.

'Was she wae, she held her sae,
And still he bade her bide,
The rusty smith her leman was,
For a' her muckle pride.'

BOOK IV

LUGHNASADH

AUGUST – OCTOBER

As Johnny walk-ed out
One midsummer's morn
He soon became quite weary
And sat down beneath a thorn.
And there he spied a pretty fair maid,
As she was passing by
And Johnny followed after
With his long and wishing eye.
With his long and wishing eye, brave boys,
With his long and wishing eye.
And young Johnny followed after
With his long and wishing eye.

Good morning, gentle shepherd,
Have you seen my flock of lambs?
Strayed away from their fold,
Strayed away from their dams.
O have you seen the ewe-lamb,
As she was passing by?
Has she strayed in yonder meadow
Where the grass grows very high?
Where the grass grows very high, brave boys,
Where the grass grows very high.
Has she strayed in yonder meadow
Where the grass grows very high?

CHAPTER FOURTEEN

The Passion of Kernan: I

LUGHNASADH: AUGUST 1ST–4TH

If an owl enters or flies around your house, or perches on the roof, this is a death omen; so too if it tries to come down the chimney. If it perches on the church roof, there will soon be a death in the parish. Similarly, constant hooting near a house means death is near; and if an owl hoots for three nights running, death will certainly pay a visit to this house within seven days. If an owl cries by day, the omen is doubly unfortunate. Killing the owl does not avert these omens.

Hoggetts Field had swayed as one in the wind, the flowing beard of John Barleycorn golden in the sunlight, but now the hired Deutz-Fahr combine with its blades so sharp had cut him off at the knee. Where once he had been rolled and tied by the waist, he was still served most barbarously, but mechanically, sliced through by the machine's deadly-toothed rake and sucked up its chute. The corn god was no longer pricked to the heart by the hired men with the sharp pitchforks, he was scythed in seconds, flattened like Shredded Wheat. Had the resurrected Osiris appeared for his harvest supper, wanting his corn soaked in honey and covered with chopped nuts, Herne would not have been surprised. But the god would have been disappointed. For this wasn't corn for bread or barley for ale but rye grass for silage, and soon each giant roulade would be spun on a wheel and wrapped with its winter coat of black plastic.

As the combine made its final turn in the early evening light, the old countryman moved in to drive retreating animals out of their last refuge, away from the path of the great red juggernaut with its terrible whirling-bladed mouth. In the old days, he remembered, no mower would want to scythe the fabled last sheaf, so they all threw their sickles at once, sometimes with their eyes closed or with their backs to the Neck of the Mare, as the fateful sheaf was called, as though to lift the blame for its death from any one man. In other parts he'd heard the last sheaf called Plaiky, the Old Sow, Cripple Goat, the Maiden and the Hare. In the north country men set it alight, and cooked peas in the ashes after their rite of Burning the Old Witch, while in Loamshire the custom was to make hare and rabbit pies from animals caught during the harvest.

Suddenly a young woman appeared beside him, as if from nowhere, as was his own manner, and without speaking, joined him in his task of animal scaring. Together they sent rabbits, hares, fieldmice, voles, stoats and weasels flying across the stubble towards Kernan's cottage, where he was dismayed to see a white police van parked, and standing at its open rear doors, the bulky figure of Sergeant Oxter, reaching inside to unfasten the dog cages. Soon, the animals fleeing to the bottom end of the field were facing the jaws of more agile attackers, the three police dogs which their handlers had brought out for scent training, but none was caught. To Herne's amazement, the girl waved her arms to and fro like Isadora Duncan, the animals seeming to follow her movements, filtering off left and right down ditches, through gaps in hedges, all escaping, down to the last tiny shrew.

While the dogs ran around yelping in frantic circles, unable to frustrate this orchestrated mass breakout, Oxter seemed to ignore the dance of the woman and the animals, but looked across the field blankly, as if nothing untoward were happening there.

On a warm evening such as this, he found it pleasant to watch the two shirtsleeved constables labouring under his direction, driving wooden stakes into the ground to simulate an invisible house in which an imaginary burglary had taken place, then moving further afield to drop small objects which the dogs had to find by smell alone. The inspector not being at home, and the place unlocked (as was his inexplicable practice), the sergeant had taken the liberty of entering the cottage like Goldilocks; he'd borrowed several items from the kitchen, each of which would carry traces of human scent, including a doll thing which someone had evidently made out of corn cut from some other field. Any dog which could pick that out in all the stubble would earn full marks and an extra helping of Lassie Meatie Chunks.

Their work complete, the two animal-scarers sat down at the opposite end of Hoggetts Field, curious to see how the police alsatians would perform, but there was not much they could see from that distance, apart from the dogs moving nosedown between the wooden posts; then following the track of some scent out to the objects hidden by their handlers in the stubble.

They sat silently for some time, absorbed by the spectacle, Herne wondering why he didn't feel embarrassed, sitting beside this young woman, whose white muslin blouse, he had noticed, was partly unbuttoned, revealing the sun-freckled skin of her breasts, which were so large they might almost be filled with milk. Yet he felt totally at ease, as if he had known this girl all his life.

– I thought you needed some help, she said, in a strange accent. Especially with those police dogs turning up.

– You were very good, said Herne, I took you for a townee.

– You should know better, said Lizzie Gizzard. Appearances can be deceptive.

As they talked, Herne related harvest stories, including those of the Last Sheaf, and what he knew of St Sidwell, whose day it had been on Monday, and whose name given to a healing well which sprang up on the site of her beheading with a scythe suggested that this martyr's life postdated her death.

– So it's probably pagan, said Lizzie, an early harvest-sacrifice story which the Christians stole. And she gave Herne such a dazzling smile as nearly knocked him over, before picking up the straying thread of his harvest reminiscences with an account of a later death on St Sidwell's Day, that of the Conqueror's son William Rufus in the year 1100, shot by his fellow huntsmen in the New Forest, supposedly an accident, but had not his blood been spilled on the ground, as required, she said, for a kingly harvest sacrifice, and when his body was carted back to Winchester, it was buried there without last rites and with little ceremony.

– But the assassination, if such it was, said Herne, resulted in the accession of England's first King Henry. Was that not also a reason?

– Frazer's *Golden Bough* was founded on such a death, said Lizzie, that of the slaying of the King of the Wood who guarded Diana's sacred lake at Nemi, a king sacrificed to appease the gods.

– You should talk to my friend Muffy, said Herne. She could tell you a lot about Diana.

Kernan knew they were too far forward. On their right flank, from the ground which the northerners of the 30th Division of II Corps had been meant to take, enfilade fire poured across them, hot lead in the midst of cold driving rain. As they slid around in the mud, trying to lie low but not sink into the stinking black slime, Fisher revived the old joke about the Germans making it rain to order. This time no one laughed.

When the rains had started, after their artillery had spent a week pounding the ground in front of them, they had waited a day before going over the top into No Man's Land. By that time the ceaseless barrage and unrelenting rain had turned the ground into black porridgy ooze, like the sludgy mudflats of Ottermouth Creek at low tide, but churned up, pitted with shellholes in which men drowned, crying out for help which couldn't come. And this was the big advance which they'd been preparing for. Such madness, Kernan thought.

As the hours passed, and they lay there exposed, he saw this flower of Loamshire's youth worn down and reduced to black rags of men, pitiful creatures floundering in this swamp, each dying, inevitably, in his own dreadful way, as the machine-guns, mortars and 77s took their toll of them.

When, six hours later, the order came from Captain Nicholas to retreat, because their position could not be held, he was the only man in the platoon still able to slither back on his belly towards their former position. Even that old survivor, his black sheep Ken Fisher, hadn't been able to save himself. For an agonising minute he had watched him slip beyond anyone's reach, into a shellhole, into whose black water the wounded farmhand had sunk exhausted, almost relieved; and afterwards floated there, a ghastly swamp creature, his khaki coat trailing out into the water like the wings of a ray.

It took Kernan three hours to crawl back a hundred yards. The shape of a tank loomed out of the foggy rain, a mass of ripped metal, with the black mud-sodden bodies of men dumped around it. One of its articulated tracks had been blasted from its side, and reared up on its own, in a great jagged loop, like some giant phantasmal insect. Beneath its leering jaws lay a young soldier, his body broken like a match, his hands and face a mass of blue phosphorus flame, a victim, Kernan guessed, of the new Boche gas they'd been warned about.

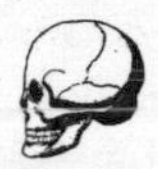

The evidence was mounting. That it had taken nearly fifty years was testament to the utter stupidity of the human race, in the view of Oliver de Foie. And if people were so stupid, and chose to ignore all the warnings, why should he not benefit from their ignorance? Even today's trendy scientists, spouting their stuff for the BBC, didn't know half the picture. And the public only understood the toxic approach, being obsessed with cancer and AIDS, and not with the threat to future generations from oestrogenic chemicals. Falling sperm counts and congenital abnormalities were just the tip of the iceberg.

Oliver had known all along, but no one would have listened to him, even if he'd been interested in making a name instead of a fortune. When Lindeman and Burlington published their research on feminised roosters, no one had followed it up. His father had shown him the paper a few years later, when he was still a student: 'Effect of DDT on Testes and Secondary Sex Characters of White Leghorn Cockerels', published in the *Proceedings of the Society for Experimental Biology and Medicine.*

– Look at this Oliver, he'd said. This came out in 1950 and

no one's done anything about it of course. No funding for the research. But when someone does look into it, the whole DDT market will go up in smoke, and that must happen soon. We will have to develop alternative pesticide products for introduction when that happens. You must think about that now, so you can help us when you join the firm. Make sure you keep up with all the latest research, read all the American journals. I want you to pay particular attention to anything you see on organophosphates. Once the penny drops, we will have to change our product lines very quickly. The days of OCs are numbered.

His father had been right about the change, but wrong on the timing. Eurochimique had continued to market its DDT pesticides in Europe right up to 1972, when President Nixon declared his vote-seeking War on Cancer in the States, and even then, the foetal risks were hardly touched upon, while in the Third World, the export market had remained healthy right up to the present, with DDT products being sold to customers in India and Africa even now.

But the politicians were such jokers, thought Oliver. Who could take such people seriously? Fools like Maw, Prurigeaux and Sirloin with power over life and death. What did they do? Like everyone, they looked after number one. Take Nixon, whom Prurigeaux had boasted of meeting. What was that devil doing before he banned DDT? Answer: giving it to his troops to spray across Vietnam, who dropped 19 million gallons of herbicide over forests the Viet Cong had in many cases already abandoned. Their so-called Agent Orange pesticide contained 2,4-D and 2,4,5-T, and a schoolboy would know 2,4,5-T was easily contaminated with dioxin during manufacture. And what happened then? Obvious. The soldiers got cancers – soft-tissue sarcoma, non-Hodgkin's lymphoma and Hodgkin's disease – and the politicians denied for years that Agent Orange had anything to do with it. Meanwhile 2,4,5-T was used as a domestic lawn spray for another ten years, and Eurochimique (Pty) Ltd was free even now to market it in Australia. This was how he had come to know the odious Tucker, who'd told him that if an Aussie farmer's been killing off fucking bugs with your shit for years without killing himself, he won't switch to some other shit just because some fucking Pom or Yank says your shit's shit. Tucker respected his countrymen for their plain speaking and their straightforward approach in such matters.

In Oliver's view, none of these people was straightforward. They were not scientists after all. They ran around chasing their own tails. Was not Sirloin himself infected? Some busybody constituent had been pestering him about DDT. He should look in the mirror, thought Oliver, smiling. That so-called skin complaint of his was obviously chloracne, from exposure to dioxin. And where did that come from, my foxy friend? It is right in front of your nose but you cannot see it. It was like that rhyme,

> The fox was sick,
> and he knew not where.
> He clapped his hand on his tail,
> and swore it was there.

Now Oliver had the PVC business to worry about that, but there again, it had taken years for the public to find out, and they were still barking up the wrong tree. It was the usual pattern, as ever. Eurochimique had been adding nonylphenols to polystyrene and PVC as an antioxidant to make the plastics more stable and less breakable. This was an optional improvement to the product which made it more marketable. Alkylphenols had been thought to be inert. They had, after all, been in other products, with nonylphenol used to synthesise nonoxynol-9 in contraceptive creams. But now some bright spark discovers not just that chemical breakdown in detergents and pesticides gives rise to nonylphenol, but it happens also in their "personal care" products, and that makes them wake up, because of personal care! The vanity of these people, thought Oliver. *Personal care: personal hogwash!* Draff is good enough for swine.

The world market for alkylphenol polyethoxylates amounted to £600 million, of which the Eurochimique companies had a good share. The twist was that while the products such as detergents were not themselves oestrogenic, it turned out that bacteria in animals' bodies, in the environment and in sewage plants will degrade the alkylphenol polyethoxylates, creating nonylphenol and other chemicals which do mimic oestrogens. The PVC studies had not proceeded far, Oliver knew, because of lack of funding, and such was the comical state of research that some evidence had been uncovered by scientists working in other fields, such as John Sumpter, a biologist whose interest was in sex changes in fish.

Oliver had a photocopy of a paper by Sumpter and Jobling, 'Detergent Components in Sewage Effluent Are Weakly Oestrogenic to Fish: An *In Vitro* Study Using Rainbow Trout (*Oncorhynchus mykiss*) Heptacytes', from an issue of *Aquatic Toxology* published as late as 1993. He was amazed they had taken that long. Bernard Tench, being an angler, had known about intersex fish even in 1987, when he'd started blotting his copybook by writing those letters to the *Chronicle*, and Oliver had blocked his proposal for a study of 'sexually ambivalent dace (*Leuciscus vulgaris*) in the River Otter'. Kuru's nickname for Tench was *Tinker-Tinker*, after his fish's Latin tag, and true to type he had gone ahead with the project in secret (or so he supposed), but working outside a team had inevitably been led astray by his own obsessions, focussing on effluent from Eurochimique instead of on discharges from Harold Hockle's sewage treatment plant.

So now the recipe would be changed, Oliver thought, but that was part of the game. You bear with the stink while it brings in the clink. There were thousands of synthetic chemicals, and new products coming on line all the time. It was impossible to know which of these might later be seen to have unexpected side-effects. Such results were inevitable. As Tucker would say, *shit happens.* When shit happened, as with the detergents, the product was withdrawn. The trick was not to be caught out when the shit hit the fan. You had to gamble on keeping enough of the market for each product for as long as possible, and to keep ahead of the game, make sure you knew what might fall under suspicion next. For one thing was certain: next year something else would be found to be poisonous.

Helping PC Jakes to force the three idiot dogs back into their separate cages in the white transit, Sergeant Malcolm Oxter looked up to see Kernan's green Renault Clio pull into Jarman's farmyard. How had Kernan known to choose exactly that moment to return, catching him red-handed? He was meant to be with the incident team in the Forest of Otter.

Caught in the act of returning the dog bait to Kernan's kitchen, the sergeant affected an air of bonhomie.

– How's the dig, sir? Have they found any more bones?

– No, just the one skeleton, said Kernan. But it's very old. Probably been there since the last century.

– Finished then have we?

– No, they're taking a break. I came back to look for some cuttings. The place reminds me of something which happened a long time ago. I wanted to follow up the hunch.

– A hunch?

– Looks like I was just in time to stop you from disposing of the evidence, Kernan joked, quickly putting the sergeant on the defensive, already interrogating him with a searching look which put him in the wrong while giving the appearance of not minding.

– I'm sorry about this thing, said Oxter nervously, indicating the savaged corpse of Kernan's corn dolly. As you know, the dogs are trained just to find the objects by scent. They aren't meant to tear them to pieces.

– Don't worry about that, said Kernan, it was just something I was making in an idle moment. But what about the other things?

– Other things? Oxter queried. I've brought everything back. Jakes made a list, didn't you Johnny?

– Well you can't have been very thorough. There was also a cotton-reel...

– Oh yes, the cotton-reel, said Oxter, I remember that now.

– A dish and a wooden spoon, Kernan added.

– Yes, yes, you're right, said the sergeant, but how did you know about those?

– You don't think I'd leave this place unwatched?

– You've cameras, of course, said Oxter, but afterwards, walking up the field, holding the wooden spoon and thinking how Kernan must have enjoyed making him look silly in front of the two constables, he wondered how the inspector had been able to replay his security video when he had only just arrived. And how also, standing in his yard, he had been able to point out the exact locations of the dish, the spoon and the reel which all three dogs had been unable to locate? Above him a noisy black bird like a jackdaw was making a *chee-awing* sound which was quite unsettling. It wouldn't let up.

– *Chee-aw, chee-aw, chee-aw... chuff*, the bird went. *Chee-aw, chee-aw, chee-aw... chuff.* Again and again.

It seemed to be following him.

Who'll be the parson?
I, said the Rook,
With my little book,
I'll be the parson.

Henry Sirloin looked at himself in the mirror, at the red spots which diminished his desirability. It seemed churlish to even mention his annoyance with the rash to Candida, when she had just returned from having the second breast removed, and was starting to lose her hair as well from the chemotherapy.

But the rash was definitely getting worse. He thought of making another appointment with Dr Gallstone, but decided against it, not wanting another prescription for a useless smelly cream which he suspected the rash rather enjoyed being smeared with. He didn't want to be told again it was normal.

– Shit happens, Gallstone had said. This kind of acne is nothing special, Henry. You have to expect these things at your age. You're no longer young, and nor is your skin. You're no spring chicken now, my friend.

– It wouldn't by any chance have anything to do with that stench from Eurochimique, would it?

– Of course not, Gallstone insisted. You should know that. Their discharges are within the legal limits. If there was anything harmful in their effluent, the government inspectors would have put a stop to it. You try this antiseptic cream, it may not clear up the rash entirely, but it should alleviate the inflammation.

As Dr Gallstone tapped his instructions into Henry Sirloin's file on the surgery computer, its whining printer spat out a prescription for an unguent whose ingredients included the supposedly inert nonylphenol. The ointment was manufactured by the Eurochimique subsidiary Alpers Pharmaceuticals, which provided the good doctor with free samples, personalised stationery and an annual holiday in a Mediterranean resort of his choice, in return for his prescribing its product range.

That rascal Devlin had gloated over Henry's misfortune at the harvest festival, when he'd asked after Candida.

– She's not well enough to come to church. She missed a good sermon, Sirloin lied.

– My harvest message, said the vicar: *They have sown the wind, and they shall reap the whirlwind.* Hosea 7.

– She might not have appreciated that in her current condition.

– But what of yours, Henry? I see the Red Sea still encroacheth on your skin. I hope it is not a judgement. In the words of Paul: *Be not deceived; God is not mocked: for whatsoever a man soweth, that shall he also reap.* Ephesians 3.

– Wasps 14, Sirloin parried: *The itch of disputing is the scab of the church.*

Who'll dig his grave?
I, said the Owl,
With my pick and shovel,
I'll dig his grave.

Sergeant Cobb was suddenly aware of the presence on the other side of what looked like a huge black dog, scrambling up the bank at the far end of Devil's Bridge. He accelerated down the clattering ramp, and began to whistle the theme tune from *One Man and His Dog* to distract Diana, knowing she would turn to berate him, so that as the car sped past the phantom creature, they were both looking the other way. In this way the sergeant made sure that no evil would befall them as it had the good people of Blythburgh on that day over four centuries years ago, as he had just read in the *Loamshire Chronicle*'s ON THIS DAY column, which related how on the 4th of August 1577 the church steeple in that Suffolk village had been toppled by Black Shuck the Demon Dog, killing three parishioners. After leaving still visible claw-marks on the church door, the slavering apparition with eyes like flaming coals had killed three more villagers in nearby Bungay before departing in a whirlwind.

The paper stated that all known sightings of mysterious lone pumas, fiendish panthers and black devil dogs in remote parts of England had postdated this manifestation, and that Black Shuck, along with all these creatures he had clearly sired, should be acknowledged in all the English shires, as he was throughout East Anglia, as an infallible portent of death. At Stowmarket the lost treasure of Clopton Hall was guarded by a monk with the head of a dog claimed by locals to be that of Black Shuck. Next Wednesday was the total eclipse of the sun, when Black Shuck was likely to slip back under cover of the daylight darkness.

– And the dogmen, said Cobb, what of them?

– You've not discovered any more than we know already, that many of them work for Eurochimique. The company claim that Anubians don't object to the heated, cramped working conditions in some parts of the factory, and as long as no health and safety laws are contravened, no one can have any objection.

– But why do so many of these houndmen work for De Foie?

– They don't only work for him, said Diana, and this was true, for while the first bus to Loamfield was always raucous with barking packs of Anubians, which other early morning passengers found unnerving, many other inhabitants of what was known locally as the Dog End of town worked in Otteridge itself. There were those lugubrious black setterheads employed by Cerberus, Cerberus & Cerberus, the funeral directors, while the Excelsior Hotel had its perky dalmatian waiters, whose white heads with black patches gave them a sporty look in keeping with their magpie livery of white shirts with black-tailed, gold-frogged jackets, white kid-gloves and spotted bow ties. Hamish Spermwail told guests that his canine harlequins added to the general rakish ambience of the former coaching inn, which was also the favourite watering-place of the Loamshire Hunt. As the dalmatians darted between tables delighting his diners, who tipped them extravagantly, Spermwail beamed, proud as a dog in a doublet.

– Who else do they work for? Cobb persisted. From what I overheard, that's what's significant. And Oxter wasn't at all happy with what's been going on. Nor Jakes. Jakes was very worried, you could tell from his tone.

Diana was worried too. But what possible connection could there be between the hotel, the funeral directors and the factory? She would ask Kernan when he caught up with her.

– You were going to drop me off at the forest.

– Ah yes, another meeting with the bones, said Cobb. I hope it's true, as they say, that this man has been dead for a century.

– We don't know that he's a man. I don't know what he is.

With the windows open to clear the musty smell, the net curtains ghosted into the room. Lady Olivia Prurigeaux sat in her late husband's study, sliding her long fingernails down the wooden slatted rolltop of his writing bureau, rattling his bones. She had left his things untouched for several months, but now, feeling alone again, after a painful parting with her son, she was growing restless to bring about some changes in the house, to make some kind of new start. They'd talked about it before James flew back to his peacekeeping unit, and he'd encouraged her to make even just a few tentative incursions into his father's territory.

She had to do something, though quite what, she wasn't yet sure. Emboldened with her third G&T, she cast her eyes about his lair, finally deciding to unlock the cabinet, scared to open what could be a Pandora's box if it contained private letters. She had known about his fling with Patty. That she could bear. But she hoped she would discover nothing else of that kind. The picture of Peter she cherished was that he was always so overworked he never had time for anyone else; she hadn't really minded taking second place to his work, it gave her more time to pursue her own interests. That these included extra-marital relationships was not something she found inconsistent with her insistence on her husband's fidelity, for had he indicated any interest in devoting more of his precious time to sexual intercourse, she would have gladly done away with the whole messy business of using outside suppliers and instituted a new policy of in-house fornication, which would have been safer on health as well as moral grounds. However, as long as his only other mistress was Lady Alcohol, she had been content. In the end, Lord Gullet had done for him, but Peter's gluttony was another story.

Taking care not to damage her nails, she turned the small black key in the bureau lock, and pushed back the roll-shutter, releasing a cloud of dust. Most of the contents seemed to be council papers. Having just heard James's account of the episode in the Black Bull, she registered the word ANUBIANS on one of the documents, and noting also the warning STRICTLY CONFIDENTIAL, her curiosity was aroused. It was evidently an internal report from Eurochimique (not for circulation) by Dr Jabez Kuru: 'Anubianism in Loamshire Dogs: Interactive Effects after Exposure to Low Concentrations of Oestrogenic Compounds from Environmental and Industrial Sources, with Particular Reference to the Otteridge Cluster'. Written in dense scientific language studded with acronyms, and including incomprehensible lists snaked with polysyllabic chemical names, Olivia found it hard to follow, but her interest was whetted by recognisable phrases such as 'enchorial predilection of Loamshire males to engage in sexual intercourse with animals, especially dogs and sheep'.

Turning to the back of the document, she found a more comprehensible summary:

In conclusion, my "three-hit" theory is based on the following premises:

(1) The diet of the animals included plants containing oestrogen mimics, whose concentration is greater in the spring, when young shoots will respond to grazing by producing even more oestrogen at the site of the injury to the plant tissue. Famous examples of such plants include the pomegranate, whose fleshy seeds were used as contraceptives by the Greeks and feature in the myth of Persephone, who ate the forbidden fruit in the Underworld when the Earth was made barren during the winter, and the weed Queen Anne's Lace, cited by Hippocrates as having the power to prevent pregnancies and precipitate abortions, whose seeds have been shown by recent studies to contain chemicals that block progesterone, a hormone necessary for the establishing and maintenance of pregnancy.

Hormone mimics are found in a variety of common sources: in herbs (e.g. parsley and sage), cereals (wheat, barley, rye and oats), vegetables (potatoes, peas, carrots, beans and alfalfa sprouts) and fruit (apples, cherries and plums), as well as in foodstuffs not consumed by animals, such as coffee and bourbon whisky. This phenomenon was first documented in relation to "clover disease" causing infertility in Australian sheep, but more recent studies, such as those by Claude Hughes, have stressed an evolutionary perspective: that these plants are manufacturing hormonally active substances in order to disrupt the fertility of animals which feed on them, thus improving their chances of survival and increasing their spread. In Patricia Whitten's experiments, mother rats given low doses of coumestrol, a plant oestrogen found in sunflower seeds and alfalfa sprouts, transmitted this to their pups in milk, altering sexual differentiation in the brains of the young rats.

Further research should focus on analysing the diet of the mother animals in the Loamshire cluster to establish which of these plants is responsible.

See: H. Bennetts, E. Underwood & F. Shier, 'A Specific Breeding Problem of Sheep on Subterranean Clover Pastures in Western Australia', *Australian Veterinary Journal*, 22, 2-12 (1946); C. Hughes, 'Phytochemical Mimicry of Reproductive Hormones and Modulation of Herbivore Fertility by Phytoestrogens', *Environmental Health Perspectives*, 78, 171-75 (1988); P. Whitten, C. Lewis & F. Naftolin, 'A Phytoestrogen Diet Induces the Premature Anovulatory Syndrome in Lactationally Exposed Female Rats', *Biology of Reproduction*, 49, 1117-21 (1993); J.M. Riddle, *Contraception and Abortion from the Ancient World to the Renaissance* (Harvard University Press, 1994).

(2) The sheep and dogs with Anubian offspring were themselves affected by endrocrine disruptors present in man-made chemicals released into the environment from industrial and agricultural sources including, in particular, persistent bioaccumulative organohalogen compounds, such as pesticides, as well as industrial chemicals and some metals.

Such chemicals known to disrupt the endrocrine system include: DDT and its degradation products, di(2-ethylhexyl)phthalate, dicofol, hexachlorobenzene, kelthane, kepone, lindane and other hexachlorocyclohexane congeners, methoxychlor, octachlorostyrene, synthetic pyrethroids, triazine herbicides, EBDC fungicides. certain PCB congeners, 2,3,7,8-TCDD and other dioxins, 2,3,7,8-TCDF and other furans, cadmium, lead, mercury, tributyltin and other organo-tin compounds, alkyl phenols (non-biodegradable detergents and anti-oxidants present in modified polystyrene and PVCs), styrene dimers and trimers, soy products, and laboratory animal and pet food products. The company should note that this list includes many chemicals manufactured or synthesised by Eurochimique both at the main Loamfield plant near Otteridge as well as at smaller plants in other locations where less concentrated clusters have occurred.

Recent studies have documented the effects of these chemicals on animals, including: thyroid dysfunction in birds and fish; compromised immune systems and decreased fertility in birds, fish, shellfish and mammals; decreased hatching success and gross birth deformities in birds, fish and turtles; metabolic and behaviourial abnormalities in birds, fish and mammals; demasculinization and feminization of female fish and birds. The number of studies relating to these phenomena are too numerous to cite here, but convenient summaries are given by Theo Colborn, John Peterson Myers and Dianne Dumanoski in *Our Stolen Future* (Little, Brown and Company, 1996), which while marred by a partisan anti-corporate approach does neverthless include thorough accounts of many important areas of research, as well as the full text of the Wingspread Consensus Statement published by 21 leading American and Canadian scientists in 1991.

(3) Cross-species fertilisation has also been widely documented. Originally scientists believed that successful hybridization was only possible between plants, where it is a well-known phenomenon. However, infertile animal hybrids have always existed, such as mules (ass and horse, usually he-ass and mare); and amongst birds, there have been canary and finch hybrids (also called mules). More recently, geneticists have achieved other animal hybrids in laboratory conditions, such as sheep-goat crosses, but this work has been deemed sensitive, owing to public concern fuelled by alarmist and ill-informed media reports, and results have often not been published, even in scientific journals, although some information is available on the internet.

Dosage and timing of exposure to oestrogenic mimics and OP compounds have influenced DNA interference in Anubian mothers. The Porton Down research has shown how OPs in nerve gas and sheep dip can not only destroy DNA in humans but also cause mutations. In the case of sheep, conception of hybrids has usually occurred in October, after the arrival of new rams from the September tup sales, so that normal intraspecies hormonal activity in the ewes has produced conditions favourable to hybridization with human males, but the hybrid foetuses have usually not survived the sheep's six-month gestation period, with a high incidence of contagious abortion; all remaining sheep-human hybrids surviving the full term have been stillborn.

In dogs, however, bitches are in heat for longer periods, and at different times of the year, and are often denied frequent intraspecies mating opportunities. Conception of hybrids has usually coincided with a full moon, when a large proportion of human females are menstruating, causing the human males to seek alternative outlets for sexual activity. The shorter gestation period of the dog has been more conducive to successful hybrid *in utero* development. All surviving Anubian offspring of the *homo canis* variety have been male; female offspring have always gone missing after a few weeks and are presumed to have all perished in the wild. Numbers of live births in the Otteridge cluster have increased from 3 in 1966, the first year when the phenomenon was recorded, to 26 in 1969, 58 in 1975, and around 100 a year from 1990 onwards. Infant mortality has been high, but has levelled off in the past ten years at around 25%, partly due to more sympathetic medical care instituted by the Anubis Trust. The number of dog breeds involved has so far been limited to alsatians, labradors, setters, dalmatians, lurchers, collies, wolfhounds and large mongrels of various kinds, with only one known occurrence amongst St Bernards.

Socio-behavioural factors have also made Otteridge a fertile breeding-ground for Anubians. Loamshire men have long been noted for a lack of discrimination in their choice of sexual partners, which has made them the butt of proverbial jokes at agricultural fairs and markets in neighbouring counties. The standard insult directed against farmers from the locality has always been 'Go home Loamy and fuck your dog', first recorded in 1696, by John Aubrey in his *Miscellanies*; while James Boswell, in his 1791 *Life of Samuel Johnson*, noted the lexicographer's amusement on hearing a similar expression levelled against a Loamshire man during a brawl outside an inn in Banbury in August 1774 ('Get back to Loamshire, dog, and tup your ewe').

Diana was still reeling. It had been hot inside the unmarked car, and Cobb had driven strangely, his hands clasped tight to the wheel, returning again and again to the subject of the dogmen.

She set off down the forest track, shaking her head to try to lift the feeling of tiredness which had come over her while cooped up in the car. Then she stopped, realising she had been walking for at least five minutes without really taking in her surroundings. Her wits were at a wool-gathering: this was not the right track, but one further down the hill from the incident tent in the clearing, where Kernan would be waiting for her at the grave.

This was a different clearing she was entering now, the August sun beating down through the wide gap in the trees, making her feel even wearier. She kept remembering the way Lambert had looked at her, dog-eyed but uncomprehending; a parody of her own feelings for Kernan, which he wanted to reciprocate, but couldn't and wouldn't say why, the one thing he had held back from her in his story. She knew he loved her, and desired her: what did it matter if he was old, centuries old even? Age didn't seem important to her now. The problem, the impediment, was to do with his uncertain powers, as well as – he had implied – with her latent ones, and they had to wait until the Tench business and Goodman had been dealt with before they would know what was possible for them. Or was that all a false trail, another red herring? Was there something else she hadn't yet grasped?

This heat was too much. She needed to rest for a few minutes. She would have to take her jacket off, lay it on the grass and lie down. There was no one around, so she peeled off her skirt as well, it was much too thick and heavy for this weather. She rolled it up and fashioned a pillow from it. If anyone came near, she would hear them approaching.

The place reminded her of another woodland scene, the make-believe one they'd created for their *Midsummer Night's Dream* at school. She'd been Hermia, and remembered the inept Lysander, how he had fumbled over *Fair love, you faint with wand'ring in the wood.* She laughed, recalling the next line, how she had needed to whisper it to him when he dried: *I have forgot our way.*

– *Be it so, Lysander: find you out a bed, for upon this bank I will rest my head*, she continued, reciting the words now as she acted them out.

– *One turf shall serve as pillow for us both*, the youth had replied, leering at her, *One heart, one bed, two bosoms, and one troth.*

Two bosoms. As in both their bosoms, or was it just her bosoms, plural? Her breasts? Kernan would know. But would he ever know her breasts? Would she ever know how it would feel to have him touch her there? She looked down her blouse, trying to imagine this, and summoned up his mellow tenor voice; and then that song he'd been singing snatches from all week: *As Johnny walk-ed out one midsummer's morn he soon became quite weary*...as she was now... *And there he spied a pretty fair maid*...

Closing her eyes, she undid the buttons one by one, pretending her fingers were Kernan's; then slipped her hand under her bra, and squeezed each breast, slowly, gently, trying to imagine Kernan's touch, how he would stroke her, teasing her nipples between his fingers; take them into his mouth.

The sun beat down on her. A single bead of sweat ran down her cheek. Thinking she was alone, she darted out her tongue to catch its saltiness.

With his long and wishing eye, brave boys,
With his long and wishing eye.
And old Kernan followed after
With his long and wishing eye.

Turning on her side, she slipped off the blouse and bra, before raising her bottom to strip away her knickers. Picturing his face as she began to masturbate, she felt herself slipping away into a delicious midsummer daydream of Kernan.

Coming on her asleep in the forest
clearing, stripped naked as a winter tree,
he quick-changed into goggling wolf, to feast

on breasts while gobbling her, tugged her free
of clinging tree limbs, not before she stopped
his jaws, flexing firm her boa'd body

to pike his throat, and then erupting, wrapped
his neck round, her coil of muscled snake
wring-pulling his swelling head, till he slipped

himself free, leaped rearwards to attack
her as a hellish civet, wiry-haired,
demon-eyed devouring her with a look

of pure devilment, speckly-pink gums bared
to eat her whole, his tongue low-lolling, forked
to divine her well, his pounce she countered

with her fastest switch, sloughing off a rucked
and concertina'd snake-sleeve to emerge
a Bengal tiger, mounted and fucked

him like damnation, their horny frottage
boned him, barking mad, rocked into tree
she clove him trunk to root, her hoofed discharge

of lightning shuddering him out of his tree,
quenching him headlong in river
plunge through Eden's azure which she,

the redhead sun, showered with light of a
kindness he'd never known, crystal-raining
down, drinking each other's fire-water

torrenting, her tongues of flame delighting
his tensed skin, an insect water-skater
licking water-lily lips, extinguishing

their long burn in light-play on water,
misting together, his hot spring sprinkling
into gentle spray, they rolled over

their river-bed, heads and tails lunging
in and out, each chasing the other,
paws and hooves a-fly, sinning tongues singing

till they lay on the far side together,
rakehelly, no more damned changes to ring,
ram-wolf with civet cradled by tiger,

her jasper-yellow 'n' black stripes snaking
furred limbs around him, demon lover
addressing hell-mate in the slaking

tongue of our coke 'n' sulphur-sniffer
down El Diablo's way, in Belial's ling-ling:
That was trooly delish, one hell of a

fook, my black shepe, no need woolly's clothing
to fleece my fancie, you tasty geyser,
lingo'd the lewd tyger, as snout snuffling

he wolfed down her strawberry-velvet oyster:
Paradise, the catte quoth, wet-whiskering,
Let's out wi' a bang for ould Lucifer.

CHAPTER FIFTEEN

Picking a Bone

ST MAELRUBHA'S DAY: AUGUST 27TH

When a woman's period is late, she must piss on a newly-made molehill. If she is not with child, her bleeding will start immediately she does this. Sir Thomas Browne records this in his Pseudodoxia Epidemica (1646).

Removing his hat, the bespectacled stranger stood for a moment where the buddleia straggled over the doorway of the cottage, waiting. A large man, he had to stoop to enter the kitchen, awkward as a hog in armour.

– Yes, do come in, said Kernan. I've been expecting you for a while. You're almost exactly as I imagined you, right down to those pretty buttons. May I take your coat?

– You've taken everything else, sir.

Kernan hung up the man's white upper-coat, which was ornamented with cheese-plate buttons, on each of which was engraved some stirring incident of the road or chase. Underneath his visitor was wearing a green cut-away coat with basket buttons.

– I see you've put on a bit of weight, if I may be so bold...

– My later years were somewhat aggravated by extreme dietary indiscretions, said the big man wearily. As the late Mr Milnes observed: *My exit is the result of too many entrées*. I still remember that last dinner: the 23rd of December 1863. And I would have had such a feast that Christmas, but I couldn't wait. It was after midnight when I arrived home. I'd guttled and gorged myself so freely that I started retching. Burst a vein in the head. Died instantly, two days short of a most excellent plum pudding.

– Not a nice way to go, said Kernan, ushering his guest into his book-lined lair.

– I don't know about that, said the man, fitting himself into Kernan's favourite armchair; and eyeing the walls of books around him just as Diana had done, he began to recite a litany of his last supper.

– Green pea-soup. Boiled salmon. Mussels, crimped skate. Melon entre-course. Carp, stewed with mushrooms. Roast turkey with cauliflower and butter. Fillets of venison piques, with asa-foetida sauce. Stewed calf's ear. Stewed cherries, rice-pudding, some gruyère cheese and twenty-four different kinds of cakes.

– You ate all that?

– I'd been to an opening first, the man told him. I was never one to separate art and food, the two always went together for me. I swear I ate everything I've just named, along with three rolls of bread and a score of potatoes. I could have had roast turkey and a rack of lamb as well you know.

– Maybe, said Kernan, but not on the 23rd of December 1863. The dinner you've just described to me took place after you'd been to the Musée des Beaux Arts. You wrote about it in *A Pictorial Rhapsody.* You've just moved it from Brussels to London.

– Did I? But then I always was a fiction-maker, turning life into art.

– Or life into life.

– Is there a difference? the man asked, stroking his grey fleecy side-whiskers.

– Can I offer you a drink? Kernan asked, adding, with a mischievous glint in his eyes: I could make you a *mezzo-caldo* perhaps? Rum, sliced lemon, pounded sugar and boiling water…

– Spare me the recipe, sir, something else you stole from me.

– But you'll have one with me all the same?

– If you make it as good as the Café de Paris.

– You mean the Café Greco, said Kernan, smiling.

– The deuce you say. In Rome, was it?

– You should know. It was you who made Clive Newcome drink *mezzo-caldo* at the Café Greco. In Paris, I believe, it was the *huitres de Marenne* which most delighted his palate.

– And mine. But my memory was never that good. When something occurred to me, I'd draw it into whatever I was writing, but afterwards I might forget it entirely, or use it again in another book without realising. I had to ask my publisher to return the first part of *Vanity Fair* because the thing had gone clean out of my head. I'd completely lost the thread of it.

– Which is why you're here, said Kernan, and looked at him expectantly. You have a bone to pick with me.

– You have it, sir. For I have a cuckoo in my nest. Your man O'Scrapie has interposed himself into Becky's life, and I believe he will remove her from Pumpernickel before Amelia's party arrives, unless we do something about it.

– Can't you stop him? asked Kernan.

– He's not one of my characters. I have no control over him. If Becky doesn't stay there, she will not be able to confront Amelia with George's letter. Mrs Osborne must become Mrs Dobbin. Becky must be allowed to milk Jos Sedley. That is how my threads are tied. And quite apart from that, the thought of that scoundrel making love with my Becky is more than I can bear.

– But you married her to Rawdon. You allowed Lord Steyne to buy her. Not that you were ever explicit, but that diamond necklace, and those gold saucepans in the kitchen at Gaunt House…

– Spare me the details, sir. Right now I need your help.

– Why should I help you? After what you did to Becky? And after the way you threw away your talent after *Vanity Fair*. You treated them both the same, your greatest gift and your greatest creation. You turned your back on them.

– What do you mean by that?

– You never allowed Becky any happiness. You hounded her through England and Europe. You wanted to possess her yourself through the book, to own her completely, as you'd never owned Mademoiselle Pauline in Paris. But then you had to be vengeful too. You weren't content to make her totally untrustworthy, you even made her hate her own child. And as for your art, once you were successful, you became exactly the kind of toad-eater and tuft-hunter you ridiculed in *Vanity Fair.*

– Look here Kernan, I'm not one of your fictional characters. Don't expect me to be consistent. Becky was never allowed to be a child herself, just as I wasn't, when my mother sent me away to England at the age of five. I lost my whole world then, and I lost it again at the gaming-tables. When my wife lost her reason and had to be locked up, I started writing *Vanity Fair*. There's a lot of me in Becky you know; she was what I might have been. In many ways, Becky *is* me.

– And you are Becky, said Kernan, which is why you don't want anyone else interfering with your nice little set-up.

– Doesn't every writer feel that way? It's bad enough that one has to admit readers into one's own world. But they pay the bills.

– You need readers for your books to stay alive. Otherwise they die. Like *The Virginians* and *The Newcombes*... *Pendennis* and *Henry Esmond*. Who reads them now? But they were never alive in the first place, they were dead at birth.

– *Pendennis* isn't a bad book, said its author.

– It's not the book you could have written, if you'd believed in it as you believed in *Vanity Fair*.

– Once I was successful, I suppose wrote for money, to keep my place in Vanity Fair, the man observed, with some sadness.

– And to fill your belly, Kernan retorted.

– And to *live*, Kernan, as *you* want to live, which is why you've sent that fellow O'Scrapie after Becky.

– That wasn't my doing, said Kernan. It was Herne's idea.

– Amounts to the same thing. Gets him out of the way.

– But it won't stop Goodman in his plot to undo me.

– Yet it undoes *my* plot, and that's hardly fair to a fellow author. Given you're such an admirer of my work, despite its flaws, can you be happy with that?

– This isn't just a book we're talking about. If O'Scrapie comes back here, Goodman will have him killed. Would you want a man's blood on your hands? A scabby man, I know, but real flesh and blood.

Kernan's visitor buried his face in his hands, sighing deeply, then looked up suddenly, as if a breath of inspiration had caught hold of him.

– What if he were to stay in 18— but well away from Becky? he suggested.

– Becky's the only reason he's there, said Kernan.

– What if he had a job?

– Who'd give O'Scrapie a job?

– Horrocks might need a hand at the Crawley Arms, said the novelist. He'd be getting on now, and would want to pass on the place to Betsy if she only could find a husband to run it with her. No one from Mudbury would go for such a creature, in her cap and with those splendid but now faded ribbons...

– What, marry off Ribbons to O'Scrapie? said Kernan. What a stroke of genius...

– And it can all happen offstage, out of the main action, just as Mrs Wenham was prevented by one of her headaches from even appearing in the book.

– A person made a pretext, said Kernan approvingly. And their son could go to find work in Loamshire. Later, the son's son Paddy becomes the butcher in Loamfield. O'Scrapie is simultaneously grandson and grandfather to Paddy Muttonchops the murderer. A family circle of crime, the snake eating its own tail. I like it...

– Might we scotch this snake between us then, Mr Kernan?

– This is the right time for it to work.

– I beg your pardon?

– This is *Edrinios,* what the Gauls called Arbitration Time, said Kernan. In the month after Claim Time and Harvest, when disputes should be settled. *With me room-rum-ra fal-the-diddle-a star-vee-upple-al-the-di-dee-do*.

Diana was lost. The forest was a labyrinth. She thought she was heading towards the grave, but then found herself back in the same clearing where...

Chee-aw, chee-aw, chee-aw... chuff. It was that bird again. So she was not alone. From the way it swung on a thin hazel branch, bending it down like a divining rod, the chough seemed to be beckoning her. When it flew to a hornbeam fifty yards away, Diana followed, even though it seemed to be the wrong direction. Reaching the bird's new tree, it called her, *chee-aw, chee-aw, chee-aw... chuff,* and flew off. Again, she followed, and when she caught up with the chough, it called her a third time before heading off down a long avenue of gnarled, diseased elms, which looked vaguely familiar. At the end of this desolate stretch, she saw a fallen elm, and behind it, the original track to the grave.

She had been distracted by that strange face looking at her, a face which had seemed to float in front of an oak. When she reached this tree she found it was simply a misshapen bole which had looked from a distance like a man's head. It was a very agèd tree, two or three hundred years old.

Having found her bearings, she could relax. Now she would answer the call of nature; and squatting in the undergrowth over a small black mound of fresh earth, looked up to see the chough high above her.

– I don't know what you're looking at, she told the bird, releasing a thin golden stream which foamed on the fresh earth of the molehill. It was beautiful, that feeling of release.

Chee-aw, chee-aw, chee-aw... chuff, the bird agreed.

Yet the full moon was due the next day, on the Saturday night, and there was still no sign of her period. Diana had always followed the moon, and had never been late before. She checked the molehill for blood, but there was none.

Today was St Maelrubha's Day, Kernan had told her. *He who had suffered the white martyrdom of exile in England,* he had said, with some force, as if drawing some particular significance from the tale of this Irish saint, a descendant of King Niall of the Nine Hostages who had a Pictish mother. He still kept a lot to himself. There was also a limit to the number of questions you could ask him. If you queried everything he said, you'd be forever lost in a maze of myth and lore.

Because Maelrubha's name sounded like Mourie, Kernan said, the two became fused. At his saint's chapel on Eilean Maree, he was known to the Scots as God Mourie. Bulls were sacrificed to him as recently as the 18th century. Other practices survived even later, including tree-worshipping, and pouring milk into the ground to protect cattle from disease.

Diana wondered if the god had led her to the Forest of Otter that she should worship its trees. She certainly felt at one with them, with the sunlight filtering through the top branches, dappling the ground through the soughing leaves. She almost felt at home in the forest. It was a sensation something like *déjà vu*, a sense that she had been in this place before, spent some time amongst the trees. In another life perhaps?

And Kernan would be a bull today, he had told her, in honour of the Irish saint Maelrubha and the pagan god Mourie, as well as the Persian god Mithra who had slain a great bull, thereby immortalising man's victory over his animal nature. Initiates into the cult of Mithraism were baptised in the blood of a bull, but Kernan preferred to drink a red wine from Hungary which his victuallers had christened Bull's Blood. If he came upon her as a bull in the forest, would he eat her like the Minotaur, or slay the bull in himself and turn into Theseus her saviour?

All the time she had been in the forest, something had been nagging at her. She felt sure that something connected this grave with Tench. It was nothing rational she could put her finger on, more of a hunch, and the more she dwelt upon it, the more certain she became that the skeleton they had found in this shallow grave had something in common with Tench, that there was some thread between the man murdered and buried here, probably a hundred years ago, and Bernard Tench, found dead last year, as if something in the distant past were now echoed in the present. Not echoed, but echoing.

Chee-aw, chee-aw, chee-aw... chuff. The bird again, perched on a low branch, dipping it up and down. It was calling to her. She looked down and realised she was holding the leather-cased tape measure. Not knowing quite why, but taking the chough's lead, she walked towards its tree still holding the tape; and then, when the bird flew off between the branches, followed it to that oak which had seemed to hold a man's face. *If you go into a labyrinth, take a clew with you*, she remembered. The clew was a clue: a ball of thread. Attaching the end of the tape to a new shoot growing from the nose of the head-like bole, she started playing it out from its leather case, this time taking the right track for the clearing. When she reached the grave, the tape went taut. The distance from the grave to the tree was exactly the length of her measure. What could that mean?

She tugged sharply at the tape, intending it free it, but the tree held it fast. She would have to go back to unhook it. As she walked, turning the handle like a fisherman reeling in a catch, she noticed that the tape never went slack, but remained as taut as if she were pulling in a fish of some weight. She also seemed to be going further into the forest, and there was still no sign of the tree with the face, even though the tape was still attached to it, and she was playing herself towards it. It was leading her in a straight line through the forest, so straight that she had to clamber over logs and push herself between bushes to keep with it.

She could see more sky between the trees now. It was getting lighter, as if this Ariadne's thread really was leading her out of her father's labyrinth. Whatever this fish was, she thought (a tench crossed her mind), she was no longer in control of her catch; her prey was leading her, and she had let herself go with it. Yet she did not feel she was being drawn into a trap, for the end of the line kept itself at some distance from her.

Clack-clack, clackety-clack, clack-clack. What was that? The sound was familiar, but she could not place it. There it was again. *Clack-clack, clackety-clack, clack-clack.* A sound like the metal stuttering of pawl and ratchet as a rack or hawser is tightened; not like something in the forest, but a noise from outside. It was like the magazine of a gun being snapped on, followed by a pulling back of the bolt, and then the final *clack* as the first bullet was rammed home into the breech. *Clack-clack, clackety-clack, clack-clack.* She heard it again. Then it came to her. This was the old road crossing at Devil's Bridge, just below the Forest of Otter. Cobb had taken that route the other time. The bridge was a long plated structure, the road a single carriageway, and he'd had to wait for someone to cross from the other side before he could drive onto the bridge. So she was coming to the edge of the forest, which meant she had been led by the tape, in a direct line, as the crow flies, from the grave to Dealchurch, where Goodman lived. She hoped the force drawing her with the taut line was nothing to do with him. She did not think it was.

The tape was definitely shorter now. She was reeling herself closer to the end, and soon she saw it, the tree with the mis-shapen bole looking like a face, yet not where she had first seen it. Now it was next to a wooden fence at the edge of the forest, but rooted there as solidly as any tree, as if it had always stood there. Reaching it, and unhooking the tape, she ran her hands over its bark. She was sure it was the same oak. She could feel it. It was a real tree. Yet if this one was real, what was the other tree? Had that tree been real, or had she imagined it?

Looking up, she saw the small squat tower of St Belial's above the roofs of Dealchurch. Black birds were circling it, probably crows. Beyond that, to the right of Loamsley Moor, was Loamfield, where she could see the ruins of Loamfield Abbey; and behind that, as if framed by the twin chimneys of the Eurochimique plant which dwarfed it, the church of St George's, which looked even tinier from this distance.

A straight line would connect all three with her, she saw. And with the grave behind her in the forest. They were all in one line. She held her breath, trying to measure the significance of this discovery.

Then she saw something else. An imaginary line, from east to west, would connect Otteridge on the one side with Hogsback Hill Farm on the other, passing across Loamsley Moor, where she could just make out the brown shape of Maw House, with Loamfield in the middle. But not only was Loamfield in the middle, it was at the intersection of the two lines. The exact point where they crossed, she guessed, would be behind the church. Her line would pass through the Black Bull, across the Green and towards Hoggetts Field.

She did not need to make any more calculations. The answer was obvious. The two lines would cross at the cottage, the place where Kernan lived.

Kernan was the key to his own mystery.

The stench made me want to retch. All around us there seemed to be a dark-green swamp, but as the sun started to disperse the early morning mist we realised that we had been marching past an almost solid sea of mud-caked corpses and monstrously bloated dead horses, with wheels and pieces of wood from waggons jutting out like bones from this putrid slough of blackened meat. Between there were crumbling shell-craters filled with liquid mud, merging with streams broken by the continuous shelling. The surface of the water was filmed with scarlet, streaking like rainbowed oil in a puddle, but only one colour, red. As we passed one pool we saw a bubble belling upwards which seemed to burst slowly, with a deep sigh, as air was expelled from some man's submerged body. We had all been down the Menin Road, but this was far worse, no one had seen carnage on this scale before. By the time we reached the crossroads, where the column had to negotiate a disembowelled mule, the men were no longer staring wildly but looked blankly ahead, only seeing the backs of those in front of them. Nobody spoke a word, and when Lambert finally gave the order to halt, a long gasp seemed to precede his choked command. We crouched and waited at the long line of white tape stretching like a tether holding us there. When we heard the sound of a whistle, we would spring forward, released from life into death.

I thought how each charred piece of flesh had once been a man with a wife or sweetheart and a family who loved him, and that he had laughed, sang and chattered with them. That each had his own special life in that lost world called England; had gone to school there, grown up, and then been taken to this other place. And for what? As my legs carried me along that road, I felt so utterly wretched inside that the physical sickness clutching at my whole body seemed unimportant. My very existence had ceased to matter, my own self had become as meaningless as the lives of those pitiful men whose bodies had been blasted into nothing by weapons devised by other men, weapons fired by men like us. For we had done this thing and now were part of it.

I wanted the shells we knew we would soon hear from over the ridge to rain down on us, to cleanse those fields where wheat and corn had once been grown, to consume the bodies of the dead and the living in a fire which nothing would survive. For nothing mattered now. There was nothing left.

I looked at my watch. It was 4.45. At that moment the whole earth around us burst into flame in a single, deafening roar as hundreds of guns behind us hurled Death into the Flanders sky. Then far off we saw the yellow and red crackling line of fire where our shells were falling, where German soldiers, young men whose ancestors we shared, were meeting Death from England. As the heavies crashed and pounded, the jagged air was alive with shells screaming all kinds of different cries. A line of coloured lights went up from the Boche, like an expression of surprise. When the whistle shrieked, there had still been no retaliation from their batteries.

After some minutes, we came upon a sleeper track, and were ordered to follow it. It was then that we made out the sound of a different kind of crack, and looking up saw the sooty curls of heavy shrapnel. These were frightening to see, like omens of someone's death, but they stayed at a distance, taking other lives. We kept going, heading towards the barrage the other side of the ridge, the road gone now, so that we were marching through shell-holes, across a black churned wasteland which gave under our boots. We tried not to look to either side, or at what we were walking upon, but fixed our eyes straight ahead, into what we now realised was a curtain of fire. Thirty yards short of this wall of flame, someone shouted, and I dived into a slime-filled shell-hole, from where I lay staring into what seemed like the shrieking, crashing mouth of Hell. I did not want to run away, like the windy soldier I heard shouting in the next shell-hole. I wanted to pass into that fiery hail and be obliterated.

I was too close then to be killed, except by a direct hit, and one gun was firing into a place just a few yards in front, just far enough away not to bother me. We waited for a brief respite from the machine-gun bullets now sweeping over us, and when it came, Lambert gave the order to advance. As I lifted my body out of the mud, I saw everyone else rising like wraiths from a grave and stepping forward without faltering into the shell-torn air. We walked calmly forward into the fire-spitting inferno, amid bursting shells and keening shrapnel, a stream of bullets whining above us. Nobody ran or flinched or ducked, we just walked forward as if it were the most natural thing in the world. I felt proud to be with those men.

Those blown over by shells blasting almost at their feet either stayed on the ground, dead or wounded, or got up again, and rejoined their troop. As fragments of shrapnel flew around, some men staggered and fell, or lurched forward and died in one movement, or simply dropped like limp dummies. Others received direct hits and disappeared in a burst of flame and flying flesh. But the rest of us kept walking, until we realised we had somehow passed through the thickest part of the barrage, and by some miracle were alive.

We stayed in that morass of mud, metal and corpses for three days and nights, crawling around like the rats which followed us from shell-hole to shell-hole, sometimes finding a low concrete pillbox in which to shelter, before moving forward again, finally reaching a nondescript place where we crouched for several hours in the dark amongst rubble which had once been a farm, until another regiment caught up with us. It may have been the Ox and Bucks, I'm not sure now, but those men relieved us, and we were ordered to fall back.

This was just one chapter. Three days in August 1917 when a hundred and fifty men from our battalion walked to their deaths. And there was more to follow. For much of the time of course, we just sat around, resting in some village which had ceased to be a village. Being drilled, cleaning weapons, playing endless games of cards (always Slippery Ann), and eating foul slops from dixies which somehow sustained us. Breakfast was a biscuit, a piece of bread and jam, with half a mug of sweet tea; lunch, Maconochie stew, half a biscuit and half a mug of tea; then at teatime, more bread and jam, with half a mug of tea. Always half a mug of tea, when there was tea; sweet tea, when there was sugar. Sometimes there was porridge. Or cheese. Chocolate in parcels from home. Yet this resting-up time was unreal, a kind of limbo which only existed in relation to what we knew would follow, when we went up the line, when rum was issued before action, and we moved off with its fiery taste in the backs of our gagging throats.

That whole time in the Salient seems like a dream to me now. In the middle of all that, I went to Paris on leave. I never got there, but I was away from the Front for days, in what seemed like a different world. I heard about the French soldiers who'd gone over the top baaing like sheep, they knew they were going like lambs to the slaughter. They protested but we did nothing. We were Englishmen, so took it all on the chin. We said we were laying down our lives but it wasn't that kind of sacrifice. The old sacrificed the young on the altars of their pride. It wasn't for God and country. When Abraham led Isaac out, God stayed his hand, but our generals weren't listening. Our officers murdered us by telling us to walk into a hail of bullets. We did as we were told, and all of us were killed, officers included. It was slaughter, not sacrifice. We were all betrayed.

I've never spoken of this to anyone. I couldn't speak of it. I buried it inside me, whoever I was. I could not recognise myself after the war. When people said, How are you? I said fine, very well thank you. And they said nothing further. It wasn't that they didn't want to know me, I knew they couldn't know me because they hadn't been there. And what was there to know? I had survived, but who had survived, and how? I was not a man, I was a husk. I hardly slept for years: I'd lie awake in a state of nothingness, terrified of what might happen if I allowed myself to dream.

I had stopped living, stopped thinking. Everything inside me had stopped growing. My frozen spirit was marooned in time. I went by the name George Kernan but Kernan had been destroyed. He lived in Loamshire, in England, but his England was no more. It was just a place which somehow existed, which happened around him. Its soul had died.

Yet somehow a vague sense of that English spirit has remained with me, like a blurred memory from childhood; sometimes it returns as a kind of presence, as when I stood on Loamsley Moor where the battle was fought; or a song or story can set it off, but then I recall our betrayal, how we are still being betrayed by our leaders, and the spirit shrinks into nothing. All we ever seem to hear from their lips is lies. BSE is just the latest betrayal.

As a policeman, you spend your time tracking lies, hunting those who prey on others. Then you make them swear to tell the truth, the whole truth and nothing but the truth. And you think: if only England could do the same for itself.

That day, by the time Lizzie Gizzard arrived to interview Colin Coombes, his slaughtermen had stunned and cut the throats of 150 pigs, a tally amounting to .0001% of the fifteen million pigs killed in Britain in a year, as he was pleased to tell her. He was a man who dealt in facts. There was no time for beating about the bush in a high-throughput slaughterhouse like Otteridge, which had earned that status with an annual target always in excess of 20,000 cattle units per annum. Time was profit. Time had to be reduced in all areas, not only to maximise throughput but to maintain product quality.

– Am I allowed to be technical? he asked.

– For this particular piece, yes, but not too much, said Lizzie. *Farming Today* listeners want to know the latest thinking. Remember too that farmers care about their animals, they want to know they're being treated well, humanely killed. Any reassurances you can give along those lines go down well.

– Yes, of course, said Colin Coombes, who tended to forget that the people who raised the animals he slaughtered would be bothered at all about their welfare once they had sent them to be killed. Yet handling the beasts with care was also good business.

– The nearer the farm, the shorter the journey, the better the meat, he explained. That's why Loamshire Lamb is such a good product, if I can be allowed a plug there, ha ha. We try to keep as few animals as possible in lairage overnight. It's important to reduce stress on the animals, particularly pigs.

– It's good to know you do that, said Lizzie automatically, staring about her as Coombes talked, taking in the cold light, the strange steamy atmosphere of the place. The smell of blood, disinfectant and ammonia.

– Stress in the run-up period to slaughter can affect the rate and extent of post-mortem acidity – the pH value – of the meat, said Coombes. It can have such adverse effects as PSE meat in pigs or dark cutting meat in cattle, which is inferior not only because of lower keeping quality but also because of less desirable colour and flavour.

– BSE? she asked. Above their voices she heard the clanging and clatter of metal gates, the rattle of shackles, the loud continuous din of the conveyor-belts, the shouts of slaughtermen trying to make themselves heard. The shrieks of pigs squealing like babies.

– No, P-S-E. Pale, soft and exudative. In pigs you have a complex of properties including meat colour, water-binding capacity and final pH. These are combined to describe the PSE-DFD complex: pale, soft, exudative or dark, firm, dry. You get the best product from intensively raised, fast growing, young animals. And having reduced stress on your pigs, you need a quick kill and chill. While rapid chilling doesn't prevent the formation of PSE-meat, delayed evisceration and delayed chilling will cause the product to be pale and watery. And the customer won't buy that kind of product.

– Colin, tell us how you look after the animals, once they arrive here? asked Lizzie, trying to shut out the background hubbub she had said she needed to record for the programme.

– First they're housed in lairage, where we give them a settling down period to overcome the stress of transportation. Horned and fractious animals are kept separate if they're here for any length of time, and different social groups of pigs are also kept apart, to avoid the risk of them fighting for ascendency, but otherwise the animals are kept together, which reassures them.

– And then...? she asked, queasily.

– They pass through the approach races, which have a slight rising gradient to encourage forward movement.

– Don't they panic, finding themselves in this strange place?

– Pigs will often crowd and clamber over each other in the approach race, but we keep these areas well lit. Cattle will hesitate if they're moved into a darker area. They don't like shadows, patches of light or even puddles. And sheep and pigs don't like moving downhill. Our design takes all those factors into account. I'll take you past the race now to the stunning pen.

– The stunning pen...

– Don't worry, said Coombes. The men are on their break. So you won't see any killing, he added in a patronising tone.

The slaughterhouse manager opened a door, ushering her into a high echoing room through which a conveyor-belt passed, from which lengths of metal chain swung at intervals in jangling bunches. Each chain a noose, Lizzie thought. In half an hour, each would hold the shackled body of one of the pigs whose cries she could hear now above the noise of the machinery. No longer a living creature.

– You may think those pigs are noisy, said Coombes, seeing her expression, but they're like that, Lizzie, for whatever reason they're being handled. They're no noisier when they see their fellows being stunned in here. Sheep aren't so vocal, they usually bunch together in the stunning pen, but their main concern seems to be with the prospect of being caught and handled. They don't show any obvious fear of being stunned, even when seeing their fellows being stunned, shackled and hoisted. It's much the same on a farm when you have to carry out a mass slaughter, such as when there's a Foot and Mouth outbreak. They show no apparent alarm even when their fellows are being shot.

In front of their eyes, thought Lizzie. She remembered then what this place reminded her of. It was a scene from a film, when women had been jostled into a place like this and ordered to line up naked. A nattily dressed SS officer had feasted on their bodies, staring each up and down, and then in the face, before tapping one on the shoulder with a swagger-stick. That one woman had been spared, and would recall the scene years later, trying to come to terms with the ignominy of her survival. Its cost in other lives, in her degradation.

– Sheep separated will always be uneasy, Coombes was saying. They follow each other quite placidly up the approach races when they're together, but when isolated, they're immediately worried. So when we settle them in the restrainer, they find a fleece placed in front of them. They think it's another sheep.

– How about the blood? asked Lizzie, unconvinced. Doesn't that upset them, the smell of it?

– The whole place is unsettling to them, he said, gesturing at the jangling conveyor-belt with an expansive sweep of his arm. We don't deny that. But we try to allay their fears as much as possible. We don't know if they're aware of their fellows being bled, but the amount of blood in evidence after bolt-stunning is negligible compared with that gushing out after sticking.

– How do you stun them? Lizzie asked, afraid of her own question, but needing to know.

– There are different methods for different beasts, often chosen in accordance with the kind of product we want, said Coombes. For pigs, sheep and calves, we use electrical stunning. A current is passed through part of the animal's brain causing instant unconsciousnessness. Smaller animals are killed with low voltage tongs. Not less than 75 volts and not less than seven seconds.

– How do you make sure they're properly stunned?

– The tongs should be on a line between the eye and the base of the ear, to ensure that the brain is directly between the two electrodes.

– Not behind their ears then?

– No, nor on each side of the neck, otherwise the animal may be paralysed without being rendered unconscious and may suffer severe pain. Only a small current traverses the brain – about 95 per cent of the current flows into the body – but this is enough to set off an electroplectic fit and insensibility.

Insensibility. That was the word for how she felt, thought Lizzie, stunned. There was a poem called *Insensibility*, she remembered; and immediately the opening came into her head: *Happy are men who yet before they are killed can let their veins run cold.*

– We've stopped using low voltage on sheep, said Coombes. It was inefficient. We often had to stun them twice, which reduces product quality. The wool on their faces prevents good electrical contact. Horns create a similar problem. With sheep you have to pay a lot of attention to ensuring that the correct voltage, current and time application are used. You need a minimum of 90 volts to stun a sheep. High voltage costs more, but done correctly results in a better product more acceptable to the housewife...or should I say the *consumer*? he added.

What a patronising shit, thought Lizzie. And I hate *that* word as well. *Consume*. Even on the carton of her favourite orange juice you were told to *consume the product within seven days of opening*. You didn't *drink* or *eat* anything now, you *consumed* it. A nation of consumers. And when you died, your body was itself consumed, by fire.

– Some people believe high voltage produces unacceptably high levels of blood splashing and bone shattering in the meat, but those result from incorrect application of the tongs. Both are problems resulting from the contractions and convulsions of the stunned animal and can be minimised if the beast is stunned correctly, preferably in a restrainer.

– Doesn't an animal suffer when that happens? Lizzie asked, her eyes wide and staring like a calf's.

– There's no evidence of that, said Coombes, anxious to reassure her. He felt uneasy now, talking about the slaughtering of animals to this attractive woman. It seemed somehow wrong that she should be the person asking him these questions. He would be happier talking to a man. She looked like one of those clever, glamorous women you saw interviewing politicians on television, not someone you'd expect to see in an abattoir. She was clearly quite upset by what he was telling her, but he admired her professionalism, that while fearful she was also unafraid. Women were like that now. He wondered if she was a vegetarian, but knew he couldn't ask such a question here. It would be somehow indelicate as well as a criticism of himself. He heard himself saying: But it emphasises the importance of making sure that high voltage stunning is quickly followed by sticking.

– And how do you stun the larger animals? Lizzie asked, matter-of-factly. She had come to this place of death to ask this one question. It took all her powers to disguise it as just one of many questions Colin Coombes might expect her to ask. After she had teased out as much detail from him as she could elicit without arousing his suspicions, she would have to ask other questions, about life after stunning, which would be more unpleasant. He must not think this was the last, the most important question.

– For cattle, calves and goats, said Coombes, and also for some pigs and sheep, we use captive-bolt pistols...

– *How do they work?* asked Lizzie, almost biting her tongue. She need not have asked, shown such readiness. Coombes would have told her without prompting. She would have to let him talk on. Only when he seemed to have finished his train of thought should she interpose further questions seeking more detail. But he seemed not to have noticed her special interest in the captive-bolt pistol.

– The bolt penetrates the skull and destroys part of the brain, he said. You want to render the animal insensible without stopping the operation of the heart. Coombes stopped. He did not think she would want to know more than that. But from her expression he saw that she did. She was urging him to continue.

– Do you use cartridges or compressed air? Lizzie asked. This was a neutral question, not related to her interest in the pistol itself. She knew Otteridge favoured cartridges. Her apparent ignorance would throw him off the scent.

– Ah, you know more than I thought, he said, to her dismay; she could have kicked herself.

– We've carried out trials with compressed air pistols, Coombes went on, but the men were very resistant to them. I suppose no one likes change in the workplace. I was keen to try them out because they're quieter and throughput is quicker without the need for reloading time. But Jack Marshall our foreman was very vocal in his dislike for the system, as were all the men. They said the equipment was too heavy – it's about twelve pounds in weight – and you always end up having to hold it with one hand, which meant it was rather unwieldy. Their stunning was less accurate.

– So you still use cartridges, said Lizzie.

– That's right. Again, correct positioning is important, but our slaughtermen find this easier with a freely held pistol. With cattle the muzzle should be pressed exactly in the middle of the forehead. If you imagine two lines drawn from the back of the ear on one side to the corner of the eye on the other, their intersection is your point of penetration. This is the thinnest part of the skull, the brain is directly beneath the bone here. For sheep the stunning position is a little higher up. With pigs you choose a spot about two centimetres up from a line between the eyes.

Lizzie did not need to ask about people. Coombes had already told her the salient facts. Transpose his instructions about cattle, sheep and pigs to the human head, and the imaginary lines would cross in the exact place where Bernard Tench's skull had been pierced. So whoever killed Tench had known how to use a captive-bolt pistol. Yet what was significant was not that they had minimised Tench's suffering by stunning him humanely, it was that by choosing to use the correct method the killer had shown professional expertise. It was also efficient to stun him correctly; the killing would be neater. It meant that only one cartridge had been necessary. The fact that Coombes took such pains to emphasise correct positioning indicated to Lizzie that many animals killed at Otteridge must need double shots. They didn't have to re-stun Bernard Tench.

– And you can tell when the stun has worked? asked Lizzie, noticing how the beads of sweat were gathering on Colin Coombes' dome-like pate before running down his forehead to settle on his eyebrows.

– The beast collapses, usually with all four legs flexed under the body. There will be muscle contractions for up to five seconds and sometimes the body and neck will quiver before the head finally rests on the deck with the ears drooping.

– And you really do know it's unconscious then? People tend to be alarmed if the animal is still moving in some way...

– It's only natural for people to react that way, Lizzie. Even after successful stunning, erratic uncoordinated reflex movements can occur – they can even happen after decapitation – but that doesn't necessarily indicate consciousness or sensibility.

Sensibility, thought Lizzie. And insensibility. Clinging to life on the one hand, preparing for death on the other.

– The stun is fully effective, Coombes continued, if an electroplectic fit takes place in which the hind legs stretch full out, and the head jerks backwards. Then the beast stops breathing.

Bernard Tench would have done that, jerked his head back, his eyes rolling. Before he died.

– If you need a final check, said Coombes, you touch the eye, on the cornea. There will be no blink reflex. Not that we need to do this but if you shine a bright light into the animal's eye, the pupil will not contract if it's totally unconscious. So you can tell.

– What happens next? asked Lizzie. I've heard about a two-stage kill. How does this work?

– Stun and stick, said Coombes. Once unconscious, the beast

is immediately shackled, hung and bled. It is insensible to pain and does not suffer. Death is caused by what we call exsanguination, when there's not enough blood circulating to feed the body and brain with oxygen. About 70 per cent of the total blood loss occurs within two minutes of sticking. The amount left afterwards is about 40 per cent of the animal's blood, with 20 to 25 per cent remaining in the viscera and 15 to 20 per cent in the muscle and bone. For optimum keeping-quality of the meat and for the product to have the right appearance, the heart should remain beating as long as possible after sticking to ensure that the maximum amount of blood is removed from the flesh and blood vessels.

– How do you make sure the *product* is tender? asked Lizzie, emphasising Coombes' word, *product*: in what they now called the *beef industry*, a living animal became a *product*. She measured the meat by the man, making sure he registered her distaste, strengthening both his belief in her – that she was who she said she was – as well as his feeling of superiority over this woman professional who was allowing her feelings to interfere with her work. For he knew her type. She was hoping her factual account of his slaughterhouse would upset some of her Radio 4 listeners, not the farmers but others who tuned in, make them think twice about eating the meat he produced. But if she wanted to squeeze the last drop of blood from this opportunity, he would give her blood. She would see it in her dreams.

Lizzie saw Jack Marshall enter through a side door, followed by three other men wearing grubby white caps, all exchanging banter, and looking across at her, staring. Their rolled sleeves revealed unstained forearms which they must have scrubbed clean before lunch, she thought, noticing how their dark green overalls and aprons were splattered red with pig's blood. Joe Hartley was raising his voice above the clangour of the machinery to make a joke to Pete Gingell which included a reference to her and the word *meat*. Frank Fisher brayed like a horse in response. These men did not know her, but she knew them all right. The wiry Pete Gingell loved his lurcher more than his wife, and he'd kill anyone who as much as threatened his dog. When Jack Armstrong had spotted him once out at Long Wood in the early hours with dog and lamp, the farmer had peppered Ginger with his shotgun. Pete Gingell had gone for him then, knocked him unconscious with one blow. Yet while he could have one chosen animal as his blood brother at home, he spent the daylight hours taking the lives of other beasts.

– There are two methods of making it tender, Coombes was saying, electrical stimulation and enzymes. The first is still called stimulation whether it's low voltage to a live, stunned beast or high voltage to a carcass. Electrical stimulation speeds up the onset of rigor mortis to enable early chilling or freezing without "cold shortening" – which would otherwise toughen the meat.

– So you electrocute the animal when it's still alive? asked Lizzie. I didn't realise that.

– But it's unconscious, Coombes added quickly, it doesn't feel anything. We attach heavy duty clips to the lip or nose of the hoisted animal after it has been stunned and shackled, and pass a current through it at approximately 90 volts for 30 to 60 seconds. I'm sure you wouldn't like to see this happening, Lizzie, because the muscles tremble quite vigorously, but that's only the effect of the current. But I can assure you the beast doesn't feel any pain. Some producers prefer to treat their animals after they have been stuck, but it makes no difference to the beast, and we believe the product is best improved with post-stun stimulation. There's also high voltage stimulation of carcasses, but that's more costly and not necessary if you can apply stimulation after stunning.

– Or use enzymes?

– On cattle yes. This happens immediately before stunning. We give them an intravenous injection of a preparation containing oxidised papain. This is something we do with prime beef animals. By the time death occurs, the preparation has been allowed to circulate throughout the cow's bloodstream. Papain is a vegetable enzyme, and the effect of introducing it in solution into the circulatory system of the animal is to accelerate the breakdown of protein molecules in the meat, thereby tenderising it. The preparation remains inactive until the meat is subjected to temperatures of 40 to 50 degrees centigrade, which happens during normal cooking.

– But doesn't injecting the cattle upset them at that stage, just when you want them to be relatively calm?

– By then, there's not enough time left for that to matter. The cow is driven into a crush. Its head is tied and pulled up, and its neck extended to present a vein for injection. Our men are well trained in this, in assessing the dosage, based on the weight of the beast. Afterwards, the cow is released immediately from the crush and moved forward into the approach race and stunning box for normal captive-bolt stunning. You're talking about five minutes from injection to slaughter, it's very quick.

– What happens if they get the dosage wrong? Lizzie asked. Surely that can happen sometimes? Her tone had become plaintive now. Coombes was pleased to note the change in her voice, which she had introduced to reinforce the impression that while she might appear to be a high-powered journalist, she could not help but be affected by his expert account of animal slaughter.

– Very rarely. If an animal becomes violent, we abandon the injection, and if because of what has happened it can't be killed immediately, we put it back in lairage where it's observed overnight before being slaughtered the next day without re-injection.

Unluckiest of beasts, thought Lizzie. *As good luck as had the cow that stuck herself with her own horn.*

– Adverse reaction to the dosage itself is minimal. We lose about one cow a year, and our throughput is over 20,000, so that's pretty good. In any case, the enzyme is inactive, and the live animal soon excretes it through its kidneys.

Lizzie looked down at the floor, the red film like a glaze on the concrete. Noticing what he took to be emotional withdrawal, he touched her shoulder.

– Come on Lizzie, you must have seen enough now. I can see it must have affected you. Coombes felt a small sense of triumph in saying this to her, that this attractive power-bitch had shown herself vulnerable.

Sensing he had taken her bait, that she had thrown him off the scent, Lizzie turned to him with grateful eyes.

– It's good to see the animals still get some natural light in here, Colin. She gestured towards a high window through which a bright beam of August light poured into the hellish room. The sun's mercy held a play of sparkling dust and dancing insects.

– That's part of the building design, I'm afraid, said Coombes, relishing this moment, as proud as a pig with two tails.

– What do you mean?

– When the animals enter the stunning box, their natural inclination is to look for a light source. As a means of escape. If there's a window above the box in line with where the slaughterman stands, the animal looks up to the light, so presenting its head in the best position for stunning.

As Lizzie looked up at the window again, Coombes stared at the single silver pendant attached to one of her ears, and behind her, the light from a gathering of shackle chains flashing, it seemed, in response to her glinting earring. On her long tanned neck, he could see her bluish jugular vein rising from a white jumper which hugged her breasts.

She was unaware of his predatory gaze. For around the high window she saw that the souls of many pigs had gathered. These were the pigs which Jack Marshall and his team had killed that morning. Having followed their carcasses into the cold store, they had returned to hold the usual ritual of observing their killers, trying to understand them. There was a soul-gatherer answering their questions, which mainly expressed their incredulity that the humans who had fed and looked after them had given them to these other men, who had taken their lives. What right had they to do this? Did they not realise that all animals had souls, and every living creature had the right to live? Why should the humans eat the flesh of their fellow creatures? Could they not eat plants and berries, fruit and vegetables, which were very tasty? The gatherer was very patient, Lizzie thought, answering each question in turn, slowly and sympathetically.

Soon all the pigs were calm and quiet, as they had never been in life. But that did not excuse the crime. Their betrayal.

This choogey pig went to market,
This choogey pig stayed at home,
This choogey pig had roast beef,
And this choogey pig went *wee-wee-wee*
All the way home.

CHAPTER SIXTEEN

Holding Fire

MABSANT / HOLY ROOD DAY: SEPTEMBER 14TH

The Devil, as the common people say,
Doth go a-nutting on Holy Rood Day.
And sure such lechery in some doth lurk,
Going a-nutting do the Devil's work.
[1709]

While she might not be called upon to satisfy many of his appetites, the one lust of Morton Maw's which his wife was both able and willing to sate was his hankering for wholesome, traditional English food, especially the more exotic Loamshire specialities, such as devilled kidneys, powsoudie and jugged hare; but his favourite dish – which he would kill for – was Squirrel Nutkin Pie. She would serve the pie when they wished to honour friends, *they* meaning *he* when the occasion involved toad-eating. Such was the case on Holy Rood Day, which might be too late for grouse (all killed a month past) but not for grey squirrels, when the Maws were entertaining Bruce Tucker and Lizzie Gizzard.

Sitting in the kitchen with her guest, Isabella Maw was puzzled by the turns their conversation had taken, for between the stages of her commentary on her particular method of making suet crust pastry for a Squirrel Nutkin Pie, the young magazine journalist had been telling her the meaning of Nutting.

– A plentiful crop of nuts in a parish at Mabsant means there will be many births there in the coming year, Lizzie explained. The more hazelnuts, the more bastard children... You know that song, *The Nutting Girl*...

> It's of a fair young damsel, she lived down in Kent
> Arose one summer's morning, she a-nutting went
> *With my fal-lal, to my ral-tal-lal*
> *Whack-fol-the-dear-ol-day*
> *And what few nuts that poor girl had*
> *She threw them all away.*

Anything Isabella queried, her tone suggesting such rural English lore was oddly esoteric for a girl from the smoke, Lizzie would check with a passing reference to a programme or article she had once researched.

Outside the shooting continued in the rain. Isabella's pie only accommodated four squirrels, each of which – after skinning, gutting and quartering – would contribute about half a pound of flesh, but her husband had been so keen to show off his gamekeeper's expertise in drey-poking that twenty tree-top squirrel homes had now been shaken, stirred and ethnically cleansed in the past hour, and Maw and Tucker had despatched almost twice that number of bright and bushy-tailed rodents into the next world, many dreys having housed families of two or three animals. Between attacks, the two men sheltered under the trees to finalise the details of a property development involving land compulsorily purchased by Loamshire County Council and later sold to Gerstmann Holdings out of which they both stood to make a killing.

Morton Maw knew better than to bring the sodden corpses of three dozen squirrels into his kitchen. He retained only the four animals required by his wife, instructing Phil Hart to dispose of the rest. His gamekeeper later amputated thirty grey tails and consigned the sleek bodies of their unfortunate owners to the compost heap.

As the two killers closed their deal in the next room, the squirrels were drawn and quartered by Isabella (while Lizzie looked the other way), and cooked in a pressure cooker for half an hour, so that the flesh became tender and separated from the bone and shot. On this particular occasion, however, with the kitchen conversation loosened by several gin and tonics, Isabella failed to remove every piece of shot, leaving in one piece of squirrel muscle two lead balls fired earlier from the shooter borrowed by Bruce Tucker, now destined to return to the gunman, caught like numbered balls in the pool-table pocket of his waiting appendix.

She showed her vegetarian friend how the stock needed to be of a rich, jellied kind, such as might be made by immersing a pig's trotter in three-quarters of a pint of rich guinea-fowl stock, and to that adding half a pound of fatty, home-cured belly bacon, a tablespoonful of brown sugar, a glass of Loamshire cider, some nutmeg and a handful of pearl barley to give the pie some body. Six plump pink-gilled mushrooms picked that morning by Lizzie and a handful of blanched hazelnuts were then deposited in the pastry case before the glutinous porcine squirrel hash was slopped into the pie dish, and the mixture of animal, vegetable and metal consigned to the oven. Lizzie's own nut-roast, while delicious, would not compare with the squirrel pie the others would eat.

During these culinary proceedings, the grey souls of the four squirrels gathered between Isabella Maw's Magimix food processor and a white fluted dish in which slender asparagus nestled like severed green fingers, amazed to witness their flesh being cooked with the trotter of a pig and part of the belly (previously salted) of a completely different pig from another country, namely Denmark. The woman seemed to be taking a lot of trouble in devising her dish of death, so much so that they almost felt honoured to be so treated, not just with the company in death of two pigs but of the guinea fowl as well, the latter, unlike the supernumerary pig, being native to the shire.

As the four lately disembodied grey souls drifted into the next room, the first-killed squirrel noted an inconsistency in the men's discussion: that the decimation of the squirrel population was justified not for the making of the Squirrel Nutkin Pie but because squirrels caused damage to trees. The third squirrel quickly interposed his own view that far greater damage was caused by the humans felling the trees, and the fourth that the humans were culpable of damage on a massive scale to the whole environment of Loamshire, a habitat shared with millions of other animals.

– I cannot understand this man, ventured the first squirrel. From the way he is talking, anyone would think he owned those trees, that they are his possessions to treat as he wishes.

– Like our lives, the second squirrel added, brushing the bulbous, rubicund nose of the councillor, causing him to sneeze and spill amontillado sherry on his previously spotless fleecy carpet, which looked like a coat skinned from a long-haired white dog, only larger. But such a dog would have measured thirty feet from nose to tail. Its fleas, scaled up to the same size, would be fatter and more deadly than the bats of Mictlantecuhtli, the Aztec lord of the underworld, which carried severed human heads in their claws.

O'Scrapie was taking chunks of bacon-rind upstairs to set them out on the rain-damp window-ledge for the friendly chough to eat. He paused on the landing, knitting his brows. For the first time in his life, it seemed, he had almost been content, but for the Dan business. Finally married, and to a woman who only ever stopped him drinking to drag him off to bed; a bit of an old slag, it must be said, but Betsy laughed at his jokes, filled him up with rabbit pie and mutton stew, and together they ran this place, the Crawley Arms, where they could eat, drink and fleece the drunken labourers of Mudbury.

He didn't like having to bow and scrape to Sir Rawdon, but they didn't see him that often. He wasn't a bad sort either, not like that old rascal his grandfather. From all accounts old Sir Pitt had taken poor Betsy for a ride when she'd been a young housemaid at Queen's Crawley, and after that she'd never felt easy about the Family, as she called them. He'd only ever known Sir Rawdon of the Queen's crew, having landed in Mudbury somehow, almost by accident it had seemed, pretending to be looking for work after leaving the King's colours, and finding a welcome from Horrocks at the inn. By then he'd been desperate, after months on the run. The captain's uniform he'd stolen from a corpse in Germany was in tatters. Not that he'd hit the gamekeeper, it was one of his mates who struck the blow, but he'd swing for it if ever they caught up with him. Dan hadn't meant to kill him, they only wanted to make their escape with the two rabbits. They hadn't eaten for three days.

Anyone who's really known hunger will tell you how it changes a man. Once you get to a place where you can always eat, you make sure you keep things that way. You never want to be hungry again.

– *Chee-aw, chee-aw, chee-aw,* went the bird again, tapping the window with its scarlet beak. *Chee-aw, chee-aw, chee-aw... chuff.*

– All right, Arthur, said O'Scrapie, opening the casement. Here's your dinner. Don't eat it all at once.

But now those men had turned up, friends of Dan's. He owed them a favour, Dan had said. Meaning that if he was caught, he would sing. It was only a small favour they wanted, and it wouldn't cost him anything. O'Scrapie wasn't so sure.

Dan had let it be known that Betsy's new man was a learned fellow. What a joke that was. And because the landlord was under an obligation of some kind to their friend, he would not be able to refuse giving them his help. They only wanted him to write a few letters for them. What kind of letters? he wanted to know. They growled like dogs in reply as they tossed their dice into the air and let them clatter on the table, howling as they barked out the name of the winner, whom they paid with nuts, not coins, for this was a mabsant game, they laughed, and he was none the wiser.

He tried showing them his handwriting, to put them off. No one's writing could be more offputting, a messy illiterate scrawl with *nuffink spelt rite*, he emphasised. But the men looked pleased, nodding their heads. They shook him by the hand, and made approving guttural noises in their impenetrable dialect.

The pistol swinging from its hook. That's how Joe saw it. But it'd be more than his bloody job was worth to say anything now. Someone had just put it back, it was just settling to a rest. The movement was more than would be caused by a draught from the door. Then he'd heard a car start up, and saw a flash-looking Subaru four-wheel job hightailing through the yard gate. Old Maw sometimes had a car like that – someone said it had been the Chief Constable's – but it couldn't have been Maw, not at eight o'clock on a Sunday morning. The man wasn't alive at that time.

There had also been the business of the break-in. It didn't add up. If Maw had needed to borrow the gun, to put down some sick beast on one of the Estate farms maybe, he could of just walked in and asked for the lend of one. It wouldn't of been needed on the Saturday. Fucking power was still off.

The lights had gone out on the Friday afternoon, dead on three o'clock. It all went dark, like at last month's eclipse. He remembered the time because Jack Marshall made a joke. Must be the bleeding Crucifixion, he'd said. The usual hum of the slaughterhouse had died a death, so all you heard was men's shouts, and a hollow clatter as they went round shutting gates to stop the flow of cows up the approach races. The conveyors had stopped, leaving all the carcasses dangling there, and he and Pete was told to take the fuckers down, and hoist the bastard beef onto the metal trolleys normally used to take the frozen carcasses out to the lorries. The power from the emergency generator was enough to keep the cold store working, and he and Pete had to push trolleyloads of fucking beef down a long dark corridor to the fridge section while Jack and Frank rounded up other men to help them get the live beasts back into lairage.

Later, he heard about the break-in, how the alarm system had been fucked by the power cut, so nothing was caught on film. Someone had smashed the window of the jakes in the admin block, and got in through there. But as far as they could tell, nothing had been lifted.

He hadn't connected this at the time with Tench's murder, because there'd been nothing in the paper about a captive-bolt pistol being used. They'd only mentioned a knife. And when it all came out, how Brock had killed his mate over cash, something to do with BSE compensation, and had gone back to the farm for his machete, he put it from his mind.

It was only when he got talking to Lionel Tench that things started to click. And he didn't like the sound of *that* kind of click, not one involving his job. That night in the Pig, when he'd gone out with his old mates again for the first time since the murder, Lionel had got rat-arsed and maudlin. The lads had tried to put him right with more fucking drink, but he just kept going on about how he'd walked into the barn and found his dad swinging from a beam. As soon as he caught a butchers, he knew he hadn't fucking topped himself, not like Mike Brock's old man.

Tench had been stripped and strung up by his feet with a length of rope. His jugular vein had been cut, and there was a round hole in his skull.

Joe Hartley knew his gun had been fired. He'd used that same fucking gun for years, and he could tell if someone else had been handling it. A different kind of cartridge had been used. Not the high velocity type he'd drawn on the Friday for cattle, but something less powerful. The kind of cartridge you'd use for a sheep.

He guessed that if they'd checked the stores after the break-in, they might have found the door had been forced. But that fucking door was always faulty anyway. You'd only have spotted something if you knew what you was looking for. And if one or two cartridges had gone missing, no bugger would of known.

He'd not said nowt at the time, so why should he say owt to anyone now? They might even think he'd done it, and had smashed the window himself, as a cover-up, to make out some villain had half-inched his cow-pow.

Yet the gun had been put back. That was what didn't make no sense to him. But if something had gone wrong, he thought, and the gun hadn't been put back afterwards, then the break-in would have a purpose, to make out that someone outside the company had nicked the gun to carry out the murder.

But what he couldn't twig was why the rozzers hadn't been interested in the break-in. Oxter and Hodge had looked at the bog window, asked a few questions, "established" there was nothing missing, and that was the last they heard from the boys in blue. No follow-up. No fucking CID. Nothing.

Yet those fuckers knew about weapons. Their ballistics bods could work out what calibre gun had been used on Tench, and that it must have been a captive-bolt pistol. The Otteridge Meat Company was the only outfit in North Loamshire where that kind of hardware was used, and there had been a break-in at the chop-shop on the day of the murder.

The copper in charge of the murder investigation, as they all knew, was Kernan. Why hadn't he made the connection? He was a smart fucker, old Kernan. Wasn't born yesterday, not like most of that lot.

In the dimly-lit outer office of Cerberus, Cerberus & Cerberus, funeral directors, the company's two black settermen were commiserating with the young policewoman.

– We are so very sorry, madam, but that simply won't be possible, said the senior dogman. He was most apologetic, and regretful that she had been caused such inconvenience.

– We could've told you that on the telephone, said his assistant.

– Yes, we could, we could, but you were insistent on coming to see us. I did try to explain then that an interview with any one of the three heads of CC&C would be totally impossible, out of the question.

– Out of the question, the younger hound repeated, nodding his head dolefully. He was so sorry they could not accede to her request. They really would like to help her, but she should understand that the heads of the company had not received visitors for many, many years.

– Not in all the time I have had the pleasure of working for CC&C, said the elder setter. That is why my colleague and I are employed here. We see to the public side of the business.

– We console the loved ones of the departed, added his colleague. We relieve them of all their worries about the practical aspects. The relatives know they can leave all that to us.

Diana saw she was getting nowhere with these two. They had been most unforthcoming in not agreeing to cooperate with her enquiries about Bernard Tench's funeral, managing to sidestep even the most direct question on the grounds that it was not appropriate for them to offer a response on such matters. And yet they were so concerned not to inconvenience her, not to mention regretful of the trouble she was being caused, and, moreover, mindful of the burden of her disappointment, that the last thing she wished was to respond to their courtesy with anything so crude as a warrant.

It was also by no means certain that one would be granted, given Lawrence's current indecisive state of mind. The Chief Constable had been finding it impossible to persuade Superintendent Goodman to rein in junior officers under his control. Unless they agreed to restrict their "freelance work", he would be obliged to consider implementing certain disciplinary measures, he would say no more than that.

Goodman had snorted in response to this threat. He simply walked out of Lambert's office, turned his back on him, daring him to act, sure in the knowledge that Lambert was cornered, and that the longer he floundered, the less secure he became, and the more likely it was that he could soon be blamed for presiding over the very activities he was tentatively seeking to bring under some kind of limited control, for he would be culpable in not having taken any decisive action. Keep him dangling was Goodman's tactic, as advocated to Sergeant Oxter and others: give the impression of co-operating, keep giving him more rope but on unimportant matters, and finally, when he's taken the bait, he'll have hung on for so long that he'll have hung himself.

Lambert's memorandum to Kernan was therefore a surprise. Copied to Goodman, it authorised the inspector to follow up certain irregularities regarding property belonging to the late Bernard Tench which had been taken from Hogsback Hill Farm during the period of the police search of the property, while emphasising that the murder case itself was closed, and he should confine his investigations to the missing items and not seek to widen his lines of enquiry. While Goodman was confident that Kernan would find any attempt at the latter frustrated, and likewise his search for the objects of his quest, he nevertheless acknowledged that Lambert's unexpected move had put him under pressure, not least from Maw, who was becoming impatient over his inability to discredit the new Chief Constable.

Diana decided on a gamble. Without saying a word, she reached into her bag and withdrew a plastic *Gateway* bag containing two bulky objects and held it over the desk. The elder setter-head looked at her quizzically, his nose twitching.

– Gateway, you've been *there*?

Then she pinched a corner of the bag, shook it with a theatrical flourish, and two large bones clattered onto the doghead's ink-blotter. They were sheep's scapulas, a matching pair, left and right.

– You really don't think we would be persuaded by such a... began the lugubrious undertaker, and stopped, letting his jaw drop and his tongue descend, watching as Diana took a small polythene bag from her pocket containing a rusty substance which looked like cayenne pepper or curry powder.

It was aniseed.

She sprinkled the red dust liberally over each bone, without taking much care to stop it from falling not just across the blotter, but onto the funereal antique leather-topped desk itself. The two dogheads still said nothing, but followed her actions. When she sat back, licking her fingers, they continued to stare at her, with worried downward glances at the two paprika'ed shoulder-blades on the desk. Finally, not wishing to leave anything to chance, Diana leant forward and blew gently on the bones, so that some of the aniseed powder was wafted in a warm liquorice breeze onto the noses and lolling tongues of the two setters. When she stood and walked to the inner door, she knew they would not even protest, but their training and sense of decorum would dictate that they wait until she had left the room before falling upon her unrefusable gifts.

At the top of the stairs were three glass-panelled doors, each bearing the name CERBERUS. She paused for a moment, before knocking hesitantly on the first. Immediately she heard loud barking, angry and flesh-chilling. She decided to ignore that one, and tried tapping lightly on the glass of the second door. More barking, this time deeper-throated, threatening. She would not go in there. At the third door, she decided to be more forthright, knocking the glass with several hard knuckle-knocks; as the barking started, she called out *Police!* and marched in, discovering as she did so, that all three doors led into the one room, and that sitting behind a desk, facing her, was a three-headed dog. The far right head, that of a German shepherd – which had answered the third door – carried on barking, while its two companions, an Irish wolfhound on the left and a black labrador in the middle, regarded it disdainfully.

– Will ye shut that racket up, said the wolfhound. *Yap yap yap*. You German shepherds are all the same. A knock on the door, and off you go, *yelp yelp yelp*.

– You barked when she knocked on your door, snapped the German shepherd.

– Sure I barked, said the wolfhound. I told the woman to come in, that's what I did.

– But she didn't, said the black labrador, because she knocked on my door then.

– And you barked too, said the German shepherd.

– Sure he barked, said the wolfhound impatiently. He was telling the woman to come in. But what does old Rin-Tin-Tin on the right do? Does she say, come in, please, come in? Oh no, our German shepherd mutt starts up yelping and howling like she was auditioning for the part of the Hound of the Baskervilles. No wonder they call you the Devil's Bitch…

– Excuse me, Diana interrupted.

The three disengaged from their argument, and swinging their heads forward, looked directly at her. The effect was disconcerting, like lying on a therapist's couch, thought Diana, and being asked by three analysts speaking in unison: *And what shall we talk about today?*

– You have our undivided attention, said the wolfhound. Diana noticed that his gums were black, but flecked with pink like old rubber.

– How can we help? asked the labrador.

– How may we be of Cerberus to you? added the German shepherd, her prickly tone parodying the middle dog's servile manner.

– Take no notice of her, said the wolfhound.

– She likes getting her own way, the labrador complained, his eyes checking either side, with the trapped look of someone frequently caught in the middle. But sometimes, the black dog added, she gets overruled.

– Silence dog, growled the German shepherd, snapping at the labrador's ear. Diana noticed that the black dog's right ear was nipped like a old-style train ticket with several bite-marks.

– You must forgive our little tête-à-tête, said the wolfhound. We are not used to receiving visitors. It sometimes brings out the worst in us, or should I say the worst of us, he added, gesturing to the far-right dog.

– Our setters usually deal with all our clients, said the labrador. They see to the living, they see off the dead. They are our long suffering dogsbodies.

– They make all our arrangements, said German shepherd explained, her manner dictatorial, brooking no contradiction.

– They arrange, said the wolfhound.

– They set, said the labrador.

– Our setters and arrangers, said the German shepherd.

– Bone setters.

– Body arrangers.

– They make all our arrangements, the German shepherd repeated, emphatically.

– I am from the police, Diana began.

– We heard, said the labrador.

– We all heard, said the German shepherd. And what has that to do with us?

– The setters deal with the living, the wolfhound repeated.

– Though once the dead are dead, the labrador went on, they are our concern.

– But the dead cannot be interviewed, said the German shepherd, not by you. They are beyond the jurisdiction of the earthly police.

Moving suddenly, Diana banged her fist on the table. The three dog heads reared back. No one had ever dared confront them in such a manner before. They stared at her, dumbstruck.

– But I have special powers, Diana said firmly. If I cannot talk to the dead, you must give me the information, or there will be hell to pay. This was a bluff – or so she thought – but it succeeded in forcing the canine trio onto the defensive.

– A moment please, said the wolfhound. We have to consult amongst ourselves.

There followed a three-way altercation, much of it incomprehensible, punctuated by harsh barks and yelps from the German shepherd, who ended the dispute by shaking her head and growling, casting reproachful glances at the two heads to her left.

The black labrador nodded affirmatively. The black-gummed wolfhound spoke.

– What do you need to know? he said. Is it about the cattle disease?

Waking, or so he thought, Kernan found himself in an almost dark room. He lay under a crinose blanket on a bed as hard as those in the cells. Reaching out, he ran his hands down the sides of the bed and confirmed what his back ached to tell him: that he had been sleeping on a stone ledge like a fire-step, which was lined with straw. Next he checked out his body, and was reassured to find it was not hairy but human in form. He was wearing a long garment made of a rough material, which chafed his skin like an army tunic. His chin felt stubbly, but that was normal.

He appeared to be himself, but could not tell in what mode of existence. When he slept he entered that timeless limbo which Australian Aboriginals call the Dreaming, the parallel dimension in which souls wait to be called for birth or ascent, and which dreamers forget when morning dissolves all but a wisp of their time in that place. Now that his powers were returning, Kernan would sometimes wake to find himself in an animal's body, as if his transference were some kind of trial, an imperfect experiment in which mistakes still occurred; while such mishaps corrected themselves, their temporary effects could be alarming as well as inconvenient.

Another side effect of his change was that he sometimes woke from the Dreaming in the wrong time, and had to remain displaced if he could not immediately get back to sleep. But the discomfort and cold he now felt made further sleep impossible. Standing up, he explored the small room which the thin light of an autumn dawn was starting to illuminate, and located a heavy door with a wooden boss at waist level. He gripped it, and gingerly pulled the door open.

Outside he followed a flagged passageway through an arch into a cloister open on one side to the elements, where light rain was falling in a walled garden, and found himself one of a procession of monks. Some were murmuring in Latin, others in a strange vernacular tongue he recognised as an old Germanic form of English. He knew that when he reached the corner of the garden, a dark-cowled figure would descend a steep flight of steps, and move towards him, his arms outstretched. Calling for St Helen's blessing on all present, and quoting the poet Cynewulf's paeon venerating the Holy Rood and its finder, the fellow would address him by name, introducing him to the others as Kernan of Loamfield. It had happened before, this false welcome from the devious Henry of Poitou, who had gained the abbacy of Peterborough by some intrigue. Kernan remembered Wulfhere's description of the abbot's arrival in the *Chronicle*, how he *took up his abode just as drones do in a hive.*

> Everything bees gather, drones devour and carry off, and so too did he. Everything that he could take, from within the monastery or outside it, from ecclesiastics and laymen, he sent oversea. He did nothing for the monastery's welfare and left nothing of value untouched. Let no one be surprised at the truth of what we are about to relate, for it was general knowledge throughout the whole country that immediately after his arrival – it was the Sunday when they sing *Exurge Quare obdormis domine* – many people both saw and heard a full pack of huntsmen in full cry. The huntsmen were huge, black and hideous, and straddled black horses and black he-goats, and their eyes were jet-black with horrible, flaming saucer eyes. This was seen in the very deer park of the town of Peterborough, and in all the woods that stretch from that same town to Stamford, and through the night the monks heard them sounding and winding their horns. Reliable witnesses who kept watch stated there might well have been twenty or thirty of them in this wild tantivy.

And four years later, on the 11th of January, *all the northern sky appeared like a blazing fire, so that all who saw it were more terrified than ever before.*

> In this same year, over the whole of England, murrain among cattle and pigs was worse than any within living memory; so that in a village where ten or twelve ploughs were in use, not a single one was left working; and a man who had owned two or three hundred pigs found himself with none. After that the hens died, and then meat and cheese and butter were in short supply.

Kernan had always known these stories: the great cattle pestilence which had first come to England in 986, after King Aethelred had laid waste the diocese of Rochester, as well as the Wild Hunt in 1127, for he had been at Peterborough himself that Sexagesima. He had kept watch in the woods and reported back. The bullet-headed Burgundian knew this, that he had been one of Wulfhere's witnesses.

History repeated itself, and if Kernan was not to fall into Henry's clutches again, and be forced to repeat his mistakes, he must leave the garden before he was spotted. He had to turn on his heels, return to his cell and sink back into sleep.

If dry be the buck's horn
On Holyrood morn,
'Tis worth a kist of gold;
But if wet it be seen
Ere Holyrood E'en
Bad harvest is foretold.

CHAPTER SEVENTEEN

The Last Job

AUTUMN EQUINOX: SEPTEMBER 21ST – 22ND

Worshippers of Diana the huntress revered cats because they were under her special protection, and because she once assumed the form of a cat. In England, black cats are lucky, but in America and parts of Europe they are thought to be unlucky creatures. A kitten born just after Michaelmas, when the blackberry season has ended, is called a blackberry-cat, and will be full of mischief. If a cat jumps over a coffin, this bodes ill for the soul being mourned, unless the animal is immediately killed. A cat's body, fur and all, if boiled in olive oil, will make an excellent dressing for wounds.

Just a moment before, the wind had been buffeting Diana's car so much she'd had to grip the steering-wheel tightly with both hands, like a pilot taking a ship through rough seas, but turning left towards Dealchurch, she found herself on the tree-lined bottom road, in the lee of Loamsley Moor, where there was not a breath of wind. Here the early morning mist from the Otter was undisturbed. It was like another world, shadowy and sepulchral. The overhanging branches arched to make a tunnel for the road, but there was no light at the other end, only a greyish blur of fog.

Beyond the woods, the road emerged into farmland still veiled with river-mist, passing between the stubbly lower fields now stripped of hay, and the undulating higher pastures, where ghostly sheep and cattle grazed. Looking out for the dangerous junction with the Ottermouth road, where no one had right of way, she slowed down on seeing the black cross warning-sign, staring at a spectral figure in the road ahead. There seemed to be a wraith-like man standing in the middle of the crossroads, stretching out his hands for her to stop, like a scarecrow. Approaching cautiously, she was nervously checking her mirror when she recognised the phantom.

– You had me scared there for a moment, she said, winding down the window.

– I'm sorry, said Herne. I knew you were heading this way. There's something here I think you should see.

He was pointing across the junction to a five-barred gate, behind which the ground rose to a low grassy knoll like a tumulus. A herd of black and white Holsteins stood around it, lowering their heads to take bites from the ground, but none of the cattle stood near or on the barrow itself, though the grass grew long there. A breeze not strong enough to lift the mist was ruffling its green hair, in which she saw red dots like wounds in the skullcap mound, the last poppies of the year.

She'd passed this way many times before without noticing it, but supposed she wouldn't have seen it through the hedge unless it had been pointed out. At first glance she thought it fairly unremarkable, but the longer she looked at, the more she became aware of what she could only think was a presence, like that presaging of past and future death she'd felt on first seeing the megalithic tomb-mound at Newgrange. On that chilly visit to Bru na Boinne she'd had to go right inside the largest of the three passage graves before feeling the latent energy of the site, the awe of death locked into the great stone slabs which closed over her, standing in the inner chamber where some other's crossing of that threshold had been marked by ancient ritual.

Here she stood at some distance, half-leaning on her car, yet already it seemed to be looming towards her from across the field, its darkness drawing her towards it like a precipice or void, tempting her to join it, to jump over the edge. And that freedom was exhilarating, she felt, it would release her from herself, from her body. She need not be tethered to the earth, she could fly.

Now Herne was shaking her.

– I don't need to ask if you can feel anything, said Herne.

You nearly let it take you then. You had me really worried.

– I wouldn't have done that, said Diana. I wanted to see how long I could hold on. I wanted to see over the edge.

– You're wide open, said Herne. I've never seen anyone tune into it so strongly, although it's always at its most powerful today. But you resisted it. You're very strong.

– I didn't use to be, not when I had the Wound. But tell me, she said, turning her back on the field, what is this place?

– It has three different names, he said, explaining how the oldest, the Devil's Night-Cap, related to a legend so black that it had been deliberately forgotten, not passed on. Somehow it had gone from the collective memory, almost by an effort of will equal to the power of the place.

The second name, the Devil's Nut Bag, linked it with Devil's Nutting Day, when only the Prince of Darkness or his relatives and followers could gather the fruits of the earth. If anyone else went a-nutting, they would find the Devil holding their bough for them, and be driven mad or be gathered by him and taken down to Hell. Once when the Devil was out nutting, he met the Virgin Mary, dropped his nut bag and fled. This was where he left it, on this day, hundreds of years ago.

The third name was Alcock's Arbour, named after a thief who buried his booty inside the mound by the crossroads, in an iron-bound thrice-locked chest, leaving a giant cockerel to guard the site. The only person the bird would allow past was Alcock himself, yet while it was also said you could fool him by producing one of Alcock's bones, no one knew where the robber had gone, or where he was buried, whether in a graveyard or in the mound itself. One night someone had gone out to dig up the chest. The next morning the fellow was found lying in the field, a spade by his side, his face and body ripped so badly that his wife claimed he couldn't be her husband. The wounds were made by claws larger than an eagle's, and tufts of feathery white down were said to have been found at the scene of the crime.

– But they are all one, those three, said Diana, to Herne's amazement. They are all connected, I can feel it telling me that. I can't put it into words, but I know it's true.

– What else can you feel? the woodsman asked.

– The link will come to me. And it will help us.

When Kernan woke that morning, at dawn, he felt vaguely uncomfortable. This was the autumn equinox, when night equals day, the halfway house between summer and the coming winter solstice. Looking out he saw the ash tree being thrashed in a merciless wind. With the sun over the equator, there were always gales at the equinox, and at this festival of fruit harvest, he felt particularly exposed, midway through the final season, between Lughnasadh, when the earth's grain filled him, and Samhain, his time of birth and death. This was Alban Elued, the Light of the Water, when the sun begins its descent into the sea; and as if to heighten his sense of unease, this was also not only St Matthew's Day, honouring the taxman-turned-apostle martyred in one or all of three places – Ethiopia, Persia or Tarsuana – it was Devil's Nutting Day too, when you had to be careful what fruits you gathered, and be wary of offers of help from strangers.

On this morning his disquiet was so unsettling that he knew he must have been displaced. At such times his powers could be weakened from the strain of being in more than two places at once. To tether himself to this present, he would drink several cups of strong coffee, and check out his diaries, calendars and chronicles. In *Poor Robin's Almanack*, an entry for September 1670 told him: *Let not thy son go a-nutting on Holie-Rood day, for fear he meet a tall man in black with cloven feet, which may scare him worse than a rosted shoulder of mutton will do a hungrie man.* That was erroneous of course, but he knew many people believed the Devil manifested himself at Mabsant, as in Lincolnshire, where the yellowbellies feared to gather nuts on what they called Hally Loo Day. But Kernan knew the Devil went nutting a week later; and how on this day in 1327, Edward II had been murdered at Berkeley Castle, his assailants buggering him with a hot poker which left no obvious wounds on the outside of his body. When he had visited that part of Gloucestershire, he found the king's shrieks still mingled with the cawing of crows in the high elms, although his companions heard nothing, their ears and minds being as closed and hard as nutshells.

Something made him pick out the *Anglo-Saxon Chronicle*, which fell open at the year 1127. He'd known the story of the Wild Hunt all his life, yet now it had a strange immediacy, a sudden presence like *déjà vu*. The *Chronicle*'s account seemed as familiar as something he might read in the *Loamshire Chronicle*.

When Diana knocked lightly at the door and entered, she found him sitting at the kitchen-table, staring into space.

– I'm always like this on Devil's Nutting Day, he told her.

– Old Nick doesn't always have it his own way, Diana purred. He came a cropper, remember. *The best laid schemes o' mice an' men gang aft a-gley.* But I hope the same doesn't happen to our *wee, sleekit, cow'rin', tim'rous beastie*, for Lambert's trap is sprung.

– What, is the mouse roaring? asked Kernan bitterly.

– You should be pleased, not scornful.

– Nothing about that man pleases me, said Kernan. He's a worm is your Larry the Lamb.

– His heart's in the right place, Diana interrupted.

– I didn't like where he put it in the summer. *With his long-fol-the-riddle-i-do right down to his knee.*

– I've told you before, Diana protested, nothing happened between me and Lawrence; adding in a catty tone: Not that I have to defend myself, I can do what I like, you know.

– And you didn't? You'd swear it on the Blood of the Lamb?

– It was all in your imagination.

– It was real for me.

– You imagined the whole thing.

– It hurt.

– You have to bear that kind of hurt if you want to love, open yourself to that possibility or you'll always be closed, an empty husk. Sometimes it goes wrong. You should know that. Shit happens.

Dr Jabez Kuru was adding up the income from the latest trials of the new product Eurolagnia. This made possible much earlier identification of transmissible spongiform encephalopathies in cattle and sheep through the detection of a urinary metabolite. The work had not gone as well as he'd hoped, so that he'd had to employ what cynics called the Texas sharpshooter method of analysis: drawing circles on your target after firing to indicate the areas you'd been aiming at. This had necessitated the inclusion of data from a number of animals not part of the original sample, using retrospective methodology, though this would not be apparent to readers of the published results. The company received a government subsidy of £700 per head payable to the owners of all animals sampled, but since those supplementary trials had used urine from some cattle which did not exist, except on paper, there was a net gain of 80 x 700 = 56K from tests which had incurred none of the high costs of the earlier, less satisfactory trials in which the beasts had been real.

Writing the sum in full, as on a cheque, Dr Kuru underlined it, *fifty-six thousand pounds*. That would buy a lot of equipment for the lab if Oliver didn't get his hands on it. He was just starting to make an inventory of what he might buy with these funds when there was a knock at the door. This was most irregular. It was after hours, and no one else should be in this part of the building.

– Yes, who is it? he called, a querulous note in this voice. A woman opened the door. She had a shock of red hair, and when she spoke he recognised an Irish accent.

– The name's Morrigan, she said, and I've come for the £700 you owe me for treatin' the piss of the brown bull.

– I don't know how you got in here, he began, but...

– But nothing. I'm not moving till I get me money. I've got nothing else in the world to me name, so I need it. In cash.

This woman was not to be trifled with, Kuru realised. He remembered the name Morrigan, but running his finger down the list of owners was surprised to find it among those he thought he had invented. It must be a copying mistake, he thought; he must have transposed hers with a fictional name when combining the two lists, and so she had not received her cheque in the post as the others had. Sensing she would not let matters rest, and the error would best be rectified with the payment she had requested, he asked her to wait in reception while he collected the cash from a safe in another part of the building. Five minutes later, it was with some relief that he handed her a bulky brown envelope stuffed with twenty pound notes, like one of those packages Oliver used to give Sirloin, not for asking questions like those other MPs, but for not asking them. Then he watched the woman disappear through the swing doors.

But Kate Morrigan no longer had a bull to supply her benefactor with samples of piss. She'd last seen the bull by the Midluachair road to Cuib, where it had stayed with the milkless cow of Dáire, before it tore up the ground of Gort mBúraig, the Field of the Trench. It later fell down dead at Druim Tairb, the Ridge of the Bull.

Until Dr Kuru had summoned her back to life through the act of naming, her own existence had been similarly insubstantial, her previous appearances long forgotten. Now she walked across the bridge over the Otter into the village of Loamfield, with the stranger's money stuffed into her coat pocket, but no other possessions, no friends or relatives, no childhood or youth to look back upon, and no recent memory, apart from the collective one in which she had once been active, centuries earlier.

Where should she go? This was a strange place, this English village, for the likes of a Morrigan. All she had was the money the shifty-looking fellow in the white coat had given her for the golden piss of the great Brown Bull of Cuailnge. What kind of country was this, where they would pay you a fortune for a bottle of animal's piss you had not even given them? The piss of a strange beast that has neither head nor tail nor pizzle nor anything inbetween.

Looking up, she saw the sign of a bull, a black bull, and from the look of the building saw it must be a hostelry where she might be given drink and food. Immediately that thought occurred to her, she began to feel ravenously hungry.

She only had to think something, she realised, and it became real, as she had done, her word becoming flesh. But she would have to learn the ways of this place where piss was liquid gold, and the ale, she discovered, was thin and watery, perhaps through the landlord's trickery but more likely by intention, for these dough-faced eejits might prefer it like that, they were strange fellows. The bread and cheese they gave her was the ploughman's lunch, so what would he be given to eat instead? If she upset the ploughman, she might not gain acceptance here.

The men were playing a game with darts, but not very well. They kept missing the bull. This might be a way to gain knowledge of the place, she thought, and asked them why they did not hit the bull when they aimed their darts at it. They looked at each other, and one called Jack gestured to her that she should show them if she thought she could do better, so she did; and repeated this simple feat on being urged to do so. When they said she had to split the outer ring instead sometimes, she did that also, firing all three darts into the same strip marked by whatever number they called out, her successes earning her not compliments but jeering. Her face flushed red, she felt like a child here, unable to understand what these men wanted, why what she did was wrong. And so returned the three darts to the fat angry man, cursing him under her breath.

The only fellow who had been pleasant to her was the one who stood her a pint of ale. He was called Bill Jarman of Hoggetts Farm. She was a fine player he said, and he was only sorry the others wouldn't have a woman in their team. She saw he was a good man, so when he returned to play against the other fellows, she made sure that each of his darts hit their targets, which annoyed his companions. He looked across at her on winning a third game in succession.

– I seem to have hit a lucky streak. You must have brought me luck, Kate.

This would be their last job. Goodman had made that clear. After tonight, they could no longer count on his protection. It was too risky now, with Lambert poking his nose in everywhere, and Kernan popping up when and where he was least expected. But this job was irresistible. Prurigeaux's house was a thief's dream, and the burglars wouldn't have been able to clear out much in their small van. A yellow vehicle had been spotted in the vicinity, which pointed the finger at Gubbins. His crew of amateurs wouldn't have known what to take anyway. They were bound to have left some ripe pickings for the police lads to take and blame them for.

Immediately they got the call, Sergeant Oxter radioed for assistance. When he swung the Transit round to the side door, Jakes leaping out to help him back up past a garden statue, the weasel-faced Clegg was waiting.

– Back door forced, dirty footprints, he reported. Can't see what's been taken, sergeant. Word is the foxy lady's on her way back now. Time for one load only, but if you'd care to take a look in the hall, you'll find a little something I prepared earlier. Just pop it all in the van, drive for 30 minutes at gas mark 80 miles an hour, and hey presto, you have a tasty treat big enough to serve four people, a veritable Aladdin's Cave on wheels.

– Good work, said Oxter. But cut the crap and get the stuff loaded before the fat cat sings. Come on, we haven't got all night, *chop chop*.

As they began passing their trove in a human chain through the house to the van, the sergeant was suddenly aware that one of the line was not one of their number. A tall, dark-coated man was handing a Chinese vase to Jakes. He was most obliged to be of some help, he was telling Clegg over this shoulder.

– I was just taking a shortcut through the grounds, he said, when I saw you fellows. I'm always keen to assist the police in their work.

– Thank you kindly, said Clegg. But we could have managed on our own. These are things taken in a burglary which we are removing for valuation, part of a follow-up process, a time-consuming but necessary task. We have to cross all the tees and dot the eyes these days you know, it is the new way, the pen-pusher mightier than the sword. And while the police are filling in their forms, there are villains and varmints out there committing murder and mayhem, cow theft and crop trashing.

Oxter regarded the man suspiciously. He'd never seen him before. He clearly wasn't part of the household, and claimed to be a stranger to Loamshire, so when Clegg offered to give him a lift to the station – where he had apparently been heading – that seemed like a good idea. With luck, they might just send him on his way, with no one the wiser, especially if Clegg kept up his usual rate of talking bollocks. If so, there would be no need to acquaint Goodman with this unexpected complication.

But there were no trains at this time, he realised, as he watched the unmarked car disappearing down the drive, the weaselly constable at the wheel. Its tail-lights were soon swallowed up in the darkness.

A heavy knock on the hut door made Wild Bill Fraser look up.

– Come in, he called, straightening his snakeskin tie and stetson, not to honour his visitor but because he'd been sound asleep and wanted to signal his alertness to the unprepossessing Ernest Gubbins, whose alarming greatcoated figure now filled the doorway. Like many security guards, the third-generation Scot was a former active member of the criminal fraternity, a group with whom he still maintained some contact over business matters, chiefly to dispose of second-hand items to supplement his otherwise inadequate income. Since the disappearance of O'Scrapie, the cross-eyed sweep had become main supplier.

Gubbins was mad as a March hare, he knew that, but everyone was mad, in Fraser's opinion, it was all a question of degree: how much your barking measured on the Rictus Scale. Most folk were mildly whimpering idiots who lived as slaves to suspicion and prejudice in the small world of their work-place and home, obsessed with pet-hates and pot-plants, while others were completely off their trolley. Those who frightened him most were people who claimed to be normal, they had a narrowness of mind that was tighter than a gnat's arse; he had a terror of being trapped in a lift with a group of normal people, who would argue and shout, blether and blubber, and use up all the oxygen. But the most dangerous of all were fanatics like De Foie and that wee shite Kuru, beside whom the wild cannibal Sawney Beane would have seemed a decent wee chappie. He recognised the contrast when Dr Death had blamed him for releasing the mink, after the wee beasties had been liberated by De Foie's black-stockinged Valkyrie, live on CCTV, whom he witnessed rabbit-chopping those she wished to retain for skinning. He was replaying the vid when the mad cow burst into the hut, forcing him to erase the evidence, the point of her brown-ridged bull-whip pressed into his face to enforce his compliance.

– I've spoken to Dogbreath about Yellowbeard's place, Gubbins announced. But I want to wait till next month, when the clocks go back. We'll do it in the extra hour. That way I'll have an alibi.

– You know the auld shitehawk fancied himself as a collector, said Fraser. Must have stacks of valuables stashed away. The widow's a walking advert for Ratners, with gold pouring out of her ears. There should be jimmies galore, Jimmy.

– Jimmy? queried the sweep.

– Jimmy Jewels.

– I'll want to keep one for my shrine. I'm looking for a ram-stone, said Gubbins.

– A ransom? asked Wild Bill, tilting his hat to peer out at him. You're not kidnapping the black widow? He flicked one eyebrow upwards, nudging the hat brim.

– No, a *ram stone*, he repeated. It's a *ramstone* I want. No one has ever seen a ramstone and lived, but I'm destined to find and keep one, because I've been chosen by the Great Ram.

– If no one's ever seen one, how will you know it?

– By its smell, which will be ammoniacal. And I know what it's supposed to look like: it is written in *The Book of Ammon*.

His latest obsession with rams was worrying. You didn't hang on to loot, you passed it on, but Gubbins had embarked on his quest for this mythical stone, coiled in form like the chambered shell of an ammonite, the fossil cephalopod he said was named for its resemblance to the horn of his ram-headed god Ammon.

Wild Bill suspected the old woman Muffy had fed this tale to the sweep, who was passionate about anything connected with hartshorn, his name for ammonia, which he sanctified as if it were his lifeblood. According to Gubbins, this Egyptian god had his temple and oracle in a Libyan oasis, and he'd written to Colonel Ghaddafi for more information about this place, offering his own help in Ammon's cause to a fellow enthusiast. Ammonia, said Gubbins, was a holy compound of nitrogen and hydrogen, designated by the sacred code NH_3, and first obtained in gaseous form from sal-ammoniac, a discovery of the ammoniac people living in the vicinity of Ammon's temple, who had made this liquor from camel dung. Its solution in water, which others might know as ammonium hydroxide, Gubbins asserted had been called spirits of hartshorn long before scientists had imposed their Latin name on it. They were like colonialists, he said, a bunch of filthy knuckers, staking claim to the earth's fruits, annexing them for their evil purposes by this imperialist act of misnaming. For hartshorn was the antler of the red deer, and its spirit a decoction of its shavings.

This last advance would take the ridge, they'd been told. Kernan doubted it. Their first objective, Eagle Trench, was one of the most highly fortified positions in the salient. The Rifle Brigade had taken part of it a month before, only to be beaten back with heavy losses. It was only 700 yards beyond the village of Langemarck.

The sky ahead was screaming, the 75s raging hysterically. Hidden batteries started up from behind them. In the distance a small spinney like Duckwidge Copse was caught in the fire as all the shelling seemed to descend upon that one spot. Uprooted trees flew through the air like a clutch of celery, and as the smoke cleared, Kernan saw that the little wood had completely disappeared. The ground there was as flat and featureless as the rest of No Man's Land.

Through all this clamour, they continued their march alongside other supporting battalions. Troops swarmed everywhere, their apparent chaos somehow ordered, so that one column headed one way, another moving purposefully in a sideways direction. Teams of farm donkeys hauled at wagons stuck in mud; tethered to great guns, the poor sad-eyed creatures seemed to know they belonged elsewhere, lifting their hooves almost quizzically as they teetered in the black slime, like uncomprehending ballet dancers. At Vancouver crossroads they had to stop for a ragged group of men with walking wounded who'd come from Pheasant Trench. A soldier with one half of his face bandaged called across to them in a broken voice.

– There go the cemetery reinforcements, he said, almost jeering.

– Watch out you lot, cried the man supporting him. There's a shortage of coffins up there!

Kernan always felt uneasy at crossroads. This was where the devil lay in wait for anyone cocky or proud, greedy or ambitious: which road would they take afterwards? He remembered another march, along the old Red Mill Road to Pigeon Ravine, when they'd stopped for a breather at Épehy crossroads. A dead German lay by the road, with a cat squatting on his chest, eating his face. When they approached, the creature sprang snarling at them. Fisher swung at the cat with a rifle butt and sent it fleeing into the ruins of some houses; then someone covered the Boche soldier with a piece of sacking. They passed back through Épehy later that day, heading for Longavesnes. The body covered by its sack was still in the same place, and a few yards away was the cat, lying on its back. A runner resting at the crossroads told him the cat had returned to feast on the corpse, and an officer from the Warwickshires had seen it moving under the sack and shot it.

That act had seemed cruel, to kill a farm cat deprived by war of its home, and eating the only food available. The soldier was already dead. What was one dead Boche amongst so many slaughtered on both sides? But he recalled an incident from Loamfield, how when a black cat had leapt from the church wall over a coffin being passed through the lych-gate, the mourners in the funeral procession had refused to move an inch further until the cat had been enticed down into the lane, taken behind the Bull and strangled.

Hours later Kernan found himself remembering the two cats, how similar they had looked, as they waited at the tape for the Verey light. The bombing parties had gone ahead under cover of the barrage, and the moment the trench mortars stopped, he knew they would be bombing their way along Eagle Trench from either side, with Lambert urging them on, his shrill voice like a lost bird piping on the battlefield. The white flare went up, and Captain Nicholas loomed over them, a mad-eyed demon screaming *Now! Now! Now!*

The Rifle Brigade were ahead of them, attacking with bayonets – their swords, they called them. He saw the flashing of their blades. Within minutes they had caught up with the advance troop, and stood over a trench through which a line of complaining Germans was being ordered along, their hands in the air. Others had crowded into two block-houses, and they were starting to herd them out, with curses which must have been incomprehensible to the benighted creatures, when one of their number slipped. As the man was recovering his balance, Captain Nicholas caught the sudden movement out of the corner of his eye, swung round with his revolver and shot him in the chest, as nonchalantly as a squire might bag a clumsy pheasant just driven from cover. The Boche slumped forward, his companions falling back to either side, staring up at the dark-eyed bullet-headed officer, frozen with fear. One man moved forward of the others accusingly, but with a pleading look. As Nicholas raised his arm to shoot again, Kernan grabbed him, saying:

– Haven't we had enough killing for one day, sir?

Snarling, Nicholas pushed him away, but when he turned back to the group of Germans, he found them all shuffling forward as one gormless group, stepping over the man he had killed, all now meek as lambs, no single soldier offering the least provocation.

– You watch yourself, sergeant! cried Nicholas, his words a spluttering staccato. The next bullet may have *your* name on it.

– He didn't have a gun, said Kernan, simply.

– I don't take risks! Nicholas yelled at him. Your Lieutenant Lambert is already *dead.* Did you not know that?

The sharply scored fricatives of the captain's announcement tore through him like hail of bullets, each *d* and *t* sound spat out as if the words themselves were contemptible.

When Henry returned from France, he learned of the latest twist in the plot. This time the man had gone too far. Yet his adversary would not know he no longer had his support.

– Who will free me from this turbulent priest? he stormed.

– You can't pull that one again, his mistress mocked. And he's no priest is he?

– He is a priest of darkness. They're all devils, him and his henchmen. I blame them for all that has happened, all the deaths and maiming. Not content to strip this land of all its fruits, killing all the cattle, now they rob the dead, they steal from their own friends. They're all in it together. Even Gallstone, him and his ointments. You know I went to see the old witch…

– Homeopath you mean, said Lizzie, poking him playfully with her finger, scratching her nail down through the forest of his chest until she reached his cock. Then grinning broadly, she leaped on top, miaowing like a cat, before sitting up and pulling him into her.

– Look, I'm Muffy now, she said, riding my broomstick. Gee up Henry, harder, harder. Take me higher. I want to fly across the sky on your cock. Then sucking her lips into her mouth, Lizzie mimicked an old witch's toothless grin. Rolling her eyes like a madwoman, she pretended to cackle, and sang from the ballad:

> Some meat, some meat, ye King Henry,
> Some meat ye gie to me!

And when I land, we will rest. And then you must dive into Muffy, give me your long, lying politician's tongue.

– Now you really are the witch, he cried, feeling his whole body lifting, a potion bubbling within him, rising to the boil.

And Lizzie sang:

> Her teeth was a' like tether stakes,
> Her nose like club or mell;
> And I ken nae thing she appeared to be
> But the fiend that wons in hell!
>
> Mair meat, mair meat, ye King Henry,
> Mair meat ye gie to me.

And Lizzie asked, slapping his stinging thigh a third time:

– What did she *say*, Henry? What did the old witch say?

– Oh not now, not now, he pleaded. This isn't politics…

– I want to know the dirt, Henry, tell me, tell me. Or I'll jump off. I'll leave you there. Talk dirty. Give me the politics of skin.

– *Chloracne*, he gasped. That's what she said.

– Cause? she asked, what was the cause? Grabbing his nut-bag from underneath and squeezing.

– No don't!

– What was the *cause,* Henry? she repeated, leaning forward, encouraging him to hold and manhandle her breasts.

– Exposure to dioxin, from the plant. *Now please…*

– And who helped *build* that plant Henry? said Lizzie. Who was it? *Say* it, I want to hear you *say* it. Now she was moving up and down, slowly, beguilingly, like a snake-charmer drawing him up then down, up then down.

– It was *me*! he cried. I did it. I helped them do it.

– And now you're going to help me, *aren't you Henry*? It was not a question but a statement he could not refute, not now.

– Yes, yes, yes, he said, feeling himself being drawn up into her, like one of those high-speed lifts, he thought, the ones which pull your body skywards faster than your innards.

– Control yourself, she said. You're mine now. You belong to me. So wait now, wait…

– Yes, yes, he said, I'm putty in your hands…

And raising her arms, she held her hands high above her head, and cried out like a banshee. She came. He saw. She conquered.

Afterwards, as they lay side by side, he stroked her lone wolf tattoo with his fingers, no longer repelled by it. He moved his lips across the creature, kissing it, his tongue-tip licking salt from the animal's blue fur.

And then he howled at the moon.

Jack Marshall oiled his gun, then squirted the special lubricant down the barrel which acted as a blood repellent. How many cattle had he killed that week? He'd lost count after 50. He hated counting, but couldn't stop now. It measured his disgust, like the number of pints he downed in the Pig and Whistle after work.

He was damned. He remembered that Irishwoman's muttered curse in the Bull. She thought he hadn't heard, but a cold shiver had gone through him like a knife. An ice knife. Now he could only kill the animals by despising them, not caring for his victims. What kind of job was this for a man anyway, to spend five days a week, 48 weeks a year, shooting cows, pigs and sheep in the head with a pistol at point-blank range, then stringing them up and slitting their throats. So that when each batch arrived, he lay about them with the electric goad, using it like a weapon to urge them on, not just on the rump, but in the head and shoulders, up the arse and in the belly, only showing restraint when Coombes was on his rounds. And since he was foreman, the others followed his example, Joe, Pete and Frank, especially with the pigs, all of them whacking the squealing porkers up the race, so that they clambered over each other in their panic. The noisier they were, the more they used the goads on the fuckers. Never mind Coombes with his claptrap about pre-kill stress, they were all going to die so what did it matter? Afterwards, they were just meat.

There was usually chaos when it came to pig stunning. If they did them one at a time, as Coombes wanted, they'd never get out of there. No matter if that meant dragging stunned animals over others waiting their turn, or seeing some creatures trampled. This was no place for being nice, for pretending you were doing the animals any favours. There was no dignity in this business, no point in namby-pamby notions like Coombes's *stun-and-stick, stun-and-stick, stun-and-stick*. You couldn't mess about like that, even if this meant you sometimes had to go back and stun a second time, because you'd been rushing them through. It was like that song from *Rawhide*,

> Don't try to understand them,
> Just round them up and brand them.

Rolling, rolling, rolling, keep them doggies rolling, they'd shout as the beasts crashed about.

It was usually quickest to do half a dozen together, *then haul them up and stick them*. That way they gave Coombes the throughput he wanted. For all his talk about safeguards and careful handling, what he demanded at the end of the day was chilled carcasses lined up in the store. That's what he asked for. That's what they gave him, what he paid them for at piece rates, with bonuses for hitting their targets for their weekly number of cattle units. And what he didn't see, he didn't mind. Coombes was a three monkeys man: see no evil, hear no evil, speak no evil. That was him all over. All he cared about was profit. He didn't have to do the killing himself. And with the BSE cull, he'd really cleaned up, him and Maw and the others, they'd made a packet out of the whole fiasco.

When he stripped off his overalls at 4.45, and cleaned up, Jack Marshall didn't want to hear another bleating sheep or squealing pig. He just wanted to go home for his tea, wolf it down, and be through the doors of the Pig by half-six to start horsing back the pints. His wife knew that. She knew not to complain to him about anything, and the kids too, they didn't want to feel the back of his hand. They let him eat in silence.

She looked up with relief when he pushed back his chair, hovering, ready to go. When he walked down the hall, taking his coat from the hook, he belched because she hated that; he burped as noisily as he could, so that it carried to the kitchen, where she sat with the kids waiting to hear the front door slam behind him. He recognised that pained victim look, her painted smile wishing him a good time. She betrayed herself, saying nothing. She only wanted him for his pay packet, no matter that every pound of it was blood money, his sweat and labour.

She wanted him to go out every night. She wanted rid of him, for him to obliterate himself, and he didn't care because he knew she hated him. His own children were frightened of him, his own flesh and blood. They hated him too.

As a toad emits a poison to repel, to make predators spit it out, so Ernest Gubbins had always discouraged the police from arresting him, and thus evaded capture and imprisonment.

The gasmasks Oxter and Jakes had worn in arresting the sweep would not be appropriate apparel for an interview, Kernan felt. Gubbins was therefore put in the room on his own, the inspector interrogating him via microphone and video-link.

– Where am I? he asked, removing the gag. That was my snot-green hankie, you know, and it wasn't very pleasant to have that cloth stuffed in my mouth, apart from the bogeys, which were quite tasty, to tell the truth, as all bogeys are...

– *Shut up*, the intercom crackled. *It is a foul clout a man will not wipe his nose on.* This interview is taking place at Otteridge police station on the 22nd of September at 10 a.m. I'm the interviewing officer, Inspector Kernan and with me is DC Hunter.

– You might be a constable for your wit.

– Give me your name.

– I can't, said Gubbins, it's my name. If I give you my name, I won't know who I am. I'll have lost my identity and I don't mean to lose it. I will see your nose cheese first and the dogs eating it.

– We'll put you in an identity parade with the usual suspects then. If you're the culprit, your victim will point you out.

– I don't have a victim.

– We are all victims, said Kernan. State your name please.

– Ernest Gubbins.

– Your occupation?

– Chimney sweep, retired, said Gubbins. And before you ask, my special subject is the ram-headed god Ammon.

– I want you to tell me what you were doing on the night of the 21st of September, between the hours of 11 p.m. and 2 a.m.

– As I've already told you, I was drinking with Wild Bill.

– A yellow van resembling your Vauxhall Astra vehicle was seen in the vicinity of Lady Prurigeaux's house at around 11.

– I stopped near there for a piss in the bushes, said Gubbins.

– And shortly afterwards, someone broke into her house and removed various items of her property...

– None of which you found in my house.

– But we did find one item of Lady Olivia's, namely a pair of rather smelly pink silk open-crotch panties monogrammed with her initials, OP, inside a black velvet jewel-case.

– *Knuckers*, said Gubbins. But those are *hers*, are they? I was wondering what the OP stood for, and why there was the hole.

– Do you deny you stole them from her?

– Yes, I do. I got them somewhere else.

– Mr Gubbins, we have information from a reliable source that you were planning to break into Lady Olivia's house.

– That's right, said the sweep. I was planning that job, but it wasn't going to happen until next month. Someone else got there first. It's not a crime to think about doing something, is it?

– Conspiracy is a crime.

– The only spirits I conspire with are Scottish malt. You've got the wrong man, Inspector. This is someone else's conspiracy.

– What about the panties? How do you explain them?

– *How can a cat help it if the maid be a fool?* Gubbins replied.

How does anyone *explain* such a pair of knickers? Pink silk open-crotch panties with that potent cocktail of smells. Sweat and sausages, 1881 and 3-in-1 oil? Plus some fancy woman's perfume.

– Thank you, Mr Gubbins, said Kernan. This interview has been terminated at 10.15 a.m. Please make your own way out.

– You're letting him go? Diana asked, clicking off the intercom.

– I believe him, said Kernan. Someone else was the real burglar, but most of the stuff disappeared afterwards. Lambert's homing device is still in the jewel-box at Jakes's place. We'll be able to track it from there, so now we play a waiting-game.

– Shouldn't we have held him on suspicion? Make them think we've caught the culprit, lull them into a false sense of security?

– Oh no. Let's make them sweat, put the cat among the pigeons. Then they'll make more mistakes. Like with the panties. I'm sure they're significant, especially if they didn't come from Lady Olivia's house. I can believe that. It adds up. And Gubbins' sharp sense of smell has just given us an important clue.

– His smell?

– His description of the panties. What he called some fancy woman's perfume is *Escape* by Calvin Klein.

– You've sniffed them then?

– Of course. Not just *Escape*, sweat and sausages, but Cerruti's *1881* and...

– 3-in-1.

Tak aff your claiths now, King Henry,
And lye down by my side!
O God forbid, says King Henry,
That ever the like betide:
That ever the fiend that wons in hell
Should stretch down by my side.

Whan night was gane and day was come,
And the sun shone through the hall,
The fairest lady that ever was seen
Lay atween him and the wall.

CHAPTER EIGHTEEN

All Change

MICHAELMAS: SEPTEMBER 28–29TH

It is unlucky to gather or eat blackberries after Old Michaelmas Day. When Satan was cast out of Hell by Michael on the first Michaelmas Day, he fell into a bramble bush, cursing its fruit, and has since cursed the berries on every anniversary of his fall by scorching them with his breath, or stamping or spitting on them, throwing his cloak or club over them, or wiping his tail upon them. Blackberries were never eaten at all in some parts of England because people believed they bore the Trail of the Serpent.

The ammunition wagon had six horses harnessed to it, and when the shell exploded, the animals went berserk, pulling in all different directions, so that the whole team veered off the supply road into the mud-filled shell crater as one flailing body. Corporal Hart and his platoon formed themselves into a human chain, managing to drag the drivers out, but the wild-eyed horses struggled as they sank. There was no way they could cut them free; they went down that quickly, wagon and all. The men looked desolate; they'd struggled for days to get the guns up the planks onto Westhoek Ridge, and now, in just a couple of minutes, they'd seen their sturdy animal companions swallowed up by the black slough which surrounded them.

Kernan watched the ostlers opening their mouths like fish, but no words came out. Could there be no mercy in this place? They must feel so alone and bereft, after those horses had seen them through hell and high water, it had to end like this. His acute sense of pity overwhelmed him, until he realised that the men were speaking, but he could not hear them. The shell-blast had deafened him. He knew now why the whole episode had seemed like that flickering moving picture he'd seen in the church hall; it almost had the same slapstick quality, a jerky drama of frantic men and animals played out in monochrome before his disbelieving eyes.

He shouted to them, but knew there could be no help for him here. The shelling had pinned them all down. It would soon be dark, and they were still stuck in the same place, not quite at the top of the ridge. As everything became murky in the deepening dusk, Kernan looked more intently around the landscape, staring at its shadowy features, as if the night might take his vision too, but soon he could neither see nor hear anything. Beneath him he felt the ground shudder; I can still feel, he thought, but felt himself stripped by the loss of sound, then sight; reduced, isolated, exposed to the bombardment lighting up the sky, its flashes, streaks of flame and firestorm his only illumination. It was like a firework display, but silent, as if seen from a distance. He sat there, a light drizzle falling on his face, watching the lights, denying sleep despite his exhaustion, refusing to descend into total blackness. Eventually, the rain stopped.

The night before, there had been a full moon, and now he watched it ride out like a billow-sailed galleon, a great white circle sailing through charcoal smudges of cloud. He had never been so pleased to see the moon. It made him think of home, the moon seen from his bedroom window, ghosting the glass. And now, from the ridge, he saw the ugly line of the front in a different light, no longer the brown appalling swathe of wasteland, its torn earth and stumps of trees stretching into the distance, but a living, pulsing creature of orange and yellow, with white flares rising and falling from a long body snaking through the night, searchlights spiking out into the darkness.

The Line was an awesome fire dragon, the whole landscape at its mercy, demanding the sacrifice of thousands of young lives.

The only sheep to survive the past week of slaughter was now being offered a cheese and pickle sandwich by Gubbins' cousin Gus, who shared his employer's three-monkeys philosophy of life, and so had kept his job of nightwatchman at Otteridge Meat Company by *not being watchful, not hearing nothing,* and *not telling no one about nothing*. No one, that is, except Mickey the Judas Sheep, with whom he held long one-sided conversations in the dimly-lit lairage, well into the night.

Gus Gubbins was fond of poor Mickey, the biggest mug he knew in a mug's game. Each day Mickey was joined by a new flock of sheep, and as soon as he'd had time to make friends, he led them up the approach race to where he knew there was food, in the stunning-pens he was never allowed to reach himself. Mickey had been trained to be their leader. The flock follow the bell-wether, and he had led thousands of his fellows up the race to the promised land. One day, Gus knew, Mickey would either wise up or wind down, and Coombes would give orders then for him to go through with the others, but he would offer to buy him, and would keep him on the wasteground behind the caravan.

No one else liked Mickey. He served as scapegoat for everyone in the abbatoir. Jack Marshall was particularly unkind to the beast, kicking him as he passed and calling him Tricky Mickey and Judas the Betrayer. Coombes too disliked the ram, but thought him a necessary evil; his good work of calming the others ensured minimum disruption and stress, so ensuring optimum product quality. Even the meat inspectors were iffy about his employment. He'd heard one telling Coombes that Judas sheep were frowned upon by the Ministry, because their secondment to the workforce contravened Section 22 of the Slaughterhouses (Hygiene) Regulations 1977, which required all animals delivered into a lairage to be slaughtered within 48 hours. When he passed this titbit on to Mickey, the sheep nodded his head, seeming to understand, and gave him a low baa in response.

– The rule is 72 hours in Scotland, Mickey had replied,

having picked up this fact from an Aberdeen Angus, but not understanding the sheep's language, Gus Gubbins was unaware that the animal had followed his account with interest; indeed, that fondness which Mickey reciprocated was due not only to Gus's freely offered friendship but to the fact that the garrulous watchman was his main source of information about the world outside the slaughterhouse.

He was particularly interested in the gobbets of news Gus fed him from his daily newspaper, while wishing his human friend would show more interest in the Northern Ireland talks, the financial affairs of Charles Haughey, and the fortunes of Fianna Fail, the party the sheep had founded. For in a previous life, Mickey the Judas Sheep had been Éamon de Valéra, Taoiseach of the Republic of Ireland for sixteen years. While the sheep knew he had betrayed his former comrade Michael Collins, making him sign his own death warrant by sending him to Lloyd George in the full knowledge that Collins would return to Dublin discredited as a traitor, having signed the Treaty faced with the British threat of all-out war, yet he had not killed him. Indeed, the fatal bullet was probably a ricochet from Emmet Dalton's gun, just as Walter Tirel's arrow had glanced off a deer on the 2nd of August 1100, felling the sheep's former brother William Rufus, enabling him to become England's first King Henry in an even earlier life. Both their hands had been clean when their respective adversaries had fallen.

With his soul promoted to this higher, animal state of being, the sheep knew he should not worry about his human record in the preliminaries, but one thing which still got his goat, almost as if to poke him with a nagging sense of regret, was that the humans of this time insisted on calling him Mickey, which was Collins' name. He knew he could not expect them to know this, for humans were so limited, but the sheep couldn't help wishing that someone with insight might pick up on this reversal of their names, and address him as Dev instead.

He had since made it up with Collins many times over, for every time the big fellow arrived at the slaughterhouse, usually in the form of a great Suffolk cross lamb with a sturdy back flat as an ironing-board, he would thank him once again for springing him from Lincoln Jail on the 3rd of February 1919; and despite all that had happened between them in the four years leading up to the ambush between Macroom and Bandon on the 22nd of August 1922, he hoped Collins might forgive him now if he showed him a place where there was food aplenty, just a short distance up the ramp.

As early morning light filtered through the curtains, Henry rolled over sleepily, throwing one arm over his lover's hips, pressing himself up against her warm buttocks. He heard her sigh gently, and fell back to sleep, snug as a bug in a rug. When the grandmother clock downstairs struck eight, he woke again, still nestled against her, and sensing that she now was also stirring, started to kiss the blue wolf tattoo on her shoulder. Her skin had that saltiness he loved, but there was also a hint of woodsmoke; and while still drowsy, he felt it was somehow different, her skin, it seemed less soft, there was a puzzling roughness to it which made him catch his breath in the moment she turned over to kiss him.

He screamed.

– What is it, Henry? she asked.

– *What...*

– Don't you still want me when I look like this? I'm still the same person.

He gaped, starting to pull back from her. Her wild white hair and raddled face.

– No, he said, this can't be happening. I don't believe it.

– You're old yourself, said Muffy, with Lizzie's voice. So why can't I have tough old skin like yours? Must I always be young to satisfy you? Or would you throw me away like your wife when I get too old? But look, she said, lifting the duvet for him to see, I still have my paps. Wouldn't you like to suck on them now?

– You're a witch, he said, I always knew there was something odd about you.

– You never complained before, said Muffy. You wouldn't have known the difference sometimes, in the dark, or when you were pissed. Do you think I liked it when you couldn't get a hard on, or when you fell asleep when I hadn't come? Are you really such a stallion?

– I'm going, said Henry, pushing her away. I'm getting out of here. I'll tell Tucker what he's got living in his house.

– That would be despicable, said Muffy, unworthy of you. He wouldn't believe you anyway? You know what he's like.

– Then I'll…

– You'll tell everyone that while Candida's been in hospital, with the mastectomy and then chemotherapy, when you should have been standing by her, you've been knocking off an old witch from the woods. But worse than that, when your wife became bed-ridden, you still carried on with your affair, pretending you had to stay in London for late-night sittings in the House. That won't do much for your chances of re-election, will it, especially with the constituency association being almost run by her family, which is how you got the job in the first place?

– Oh God, said Henry.

– Don't bring Him into it. This is between us.

– There is no more *Us*.

– Do you want me to blow the whistle on you? she asked, fixing him with her piercing green eyes.

Was the game really over? he wondered; and thinking there was no escape, that he was cornered, fought back hissing:

– *You know what happens to whistle-blowers round here.*

– I could whistle up such a storm first, she threatened, before anyone could do anything. But before that happens, I want to make sure the guilty pay for what they've done, just as you do, *don't* you Henry?

– Yes yes, he said, turning away from her to lie on his back. From where he spoke to the ceiling.

– I'm sorry about what I said then. I didn't mean it, what I said about whistle-blowers. That was unworthy of me. It's the shock, Lizz*ieee*… Her name tailed off, he didn't know what to call her now. He snatched a sideways glance, hoping to see her transformed back to her old self, not that he would do anything with her now, but the sight of the shrivelled old hag lying beside him in the bed was so awful. What had he done to deserve this? What would Candida say if she could see him now…

– She'd say you'd got your just desserts, said Muffy helpfully.

– What, you're telepathic too? What hope is there for me now? he lamented.

– Not always, said Muffy. But sometimes your real thoughts are so badly hidden I don't need to ask questions. The answers are written across your face. I can read between the lines on your furrowed brow, Henry. What you were thinking back then was uglier than I'll ever be.

– What will we do now? he asked, surprising himself. He couldn't still be in her thrall?

– How about fucking me? she suggested playfully. You could close your eyes. I sound like Lizzie, don't I? I *am* Lizzie...

– No no no, he said. I'm sorry Lizzie, Muffy, whoever you are. I can't. I don't know you any more...

– Oh come on, Henry, you never really knew me before. You had your idea of me, and you shut out everything else. You knew I was pumping you for information as well as sex, but still you carried on. You were excited by it. It made you feel powerful, at the centre of things, instead of pushed out, no longer good enough to be a minister.

– It wasn't like that. I couldn't carry on lying. That's why they didn't want me any more.

– But you missed the headlines, the ratpack outside the house, photographers snapping you everywhere you went. I was the secret they wanted, which you kept from all of them. I was your Christine Keeler, wasn't I? You wanted to think I was someone else's mistress too, the Russian attaché and all that?

– No, no, said Henry. It wasn't like that.

– What was it like then?

– I don't know. I don't know anything now.

– Well here's something to chew on, Muffy said. *Snakes!*

– Not more snakes, I hope you've not got snakes in here, he cried, pulling his feet up in the bed, but still lying on his back, staring at the white plaster ceiling-rose, not looking at her.

– You know what Pliny said about the sex-life of snakes?

– No. And I don't think I want to know.

– The male snake fertilises the female snake by putting his head in her mouth and letting her eat him.

– Are you going to eat me? he asked. He almost welcomed the thought.

– Not with my mouth, she said. You look like a man who misses his mother's womb, Henry. Wouldn't you like to get back there now? Let me feel the dome of your head between my legs?

Clack-clack, clackety-clack, clack-clack. It was unnerving, that sound, walking upriver towards Dealchurch, and now, standing beneath Devil's Bridge itself, Kernan looked up each time the clacking started at the far end, watching the cantilevered underbelly as a car lumbered slowly above him, each *clack-clack* like a crash of thunder. Standing in the bridge's shadow, he felt as if a metal-armoured Angel of Death were passing overhead. Those couldn't be cars he heard; they were like tanks returning from wreaking death on a battlefield. *Clack-clack*, they went. *Clack-clack, clackety-clack, clack-clack.*

It was raining again. It wouldn't stop raining, as at Ypres. Something was going on here. Something was wrong. The rain told him that, dancing on the river. Where he stood, sheltered by the bridge, it was dry. He waited.

He considered the story of this place: how an old woman's cow had strayed across the Otter here on another day of unceasing rain, but by the time she was missed the water was in spate. The Devil appeared on the bank and offered to build a bridge across the river overnight, but on one condition. He was to have the first living thing to cross it.

But the woman wasn't to be tricked. When the bridge was ready, she threw a bone across for her dog to fetch. According to the legend, the dog, having no soul, was no use to the Devil, who rushed away in a temper, leaving behind his collar (which he'd taken off while working), his fingermarks (imprinted on the coping-stones of the bridge), and some spare stones strewn up the bank. Before the old bridge was destroyed in the great flood of 1763, you could still see his marks. The iron bridge was later built in the same place, alongside the Devil's Marbles, as the stray stones were called.

The tale was wrong in one respect: the dog did have a soul, of course, but being an animal soul, higher on the scale than a human's, it was untainted by treachery, and therefore of no use to the Devil, who wanted souls he could inveigle into manipulating others. The pure soul of a faithful dog was as useless as an angel's. The Devil's frustration and spite would remain in this place where his trick had rebounded upon him; where he had built a bridge through the night with no reward.

As he stood listening to a *clack-clack, clackety-clack, clack-clack* so loud it must be a truck, he felt something grab his ankle, and pull at him. Losing his balance, he topped headlong into the river. A huge eel had wound three coils about his foot, and was trying to pull him under the water, to drown him.

He felt his strength was weak here, in the shadow of the Devil's bridge, and fought the water like Cúchulainn, banging his foot against a rock to try to dislodge the water-snake. Finally, after gulping down mouthfuls of foul water, he dragged himself up the bank, the eel still pulling at his ankle like a tether, and flung his body down on the grass. Beside him a flame-haired woman lay naked, wet as a fish. He panted, trying to get his breath back.

– You fought well, Cernunnos, she said. I almost had you there. Almost dragged you down. But you have the gallows in your face. He that is born to be hanged shall never be drowned.

– Morrigan, he said. I knew it was you as soon as I felt your grip. I saw you in Hoggett's Field with Bill Jarman. I thought I recognised you then, but I wasn't sure. You've changed. What are you doing with Bill? He's a good man, not your sort.

– I help with the milking, she said, smiling, her green eyes flashing through watery lashes. I drink the cows drier than stones.

– You leave him alone, Kernan warned her. He's a good man.

– Don't worry about him. It's you I want. And I'll have you whether you like it or not. I can change into anything, you know. I can be a wolf one minute, a heifer the next.

– But you didn't stay an eel for long. You hadn't the strength. Your powers are weak here, you aren't used to this place. I've been here a long time. I'm rooted here, as fast as a tree.

– I'll pull you free. I'll untether you, and I'll ride you myself.

– You can't do that on your own. You know you need the others, the scald-crow Badbh, who haunts the battlefields, and Nemain, goddess of panic.

– But you are wrong there, Cernunnos. They are near here in time. Soon I will contain them all, Morrigan the Great Queen of the Demons. All three wives of Nét will be one in me.

– Why should I believe that?

– You have seen Badh. She haunts the battlefields, feasting on the bodies of the slain. Sometimes as a crow, sometimes as a cat. You will know her again when we take you, when you panic, when you lose your head.

– You can't take me, I belong to another now.

– Cernunnos, belong to a mortal woman? she cried scornfully. *Who has a woman has an eel by the tail*, and you cannot hide an eel in a sack. Who is this creature? I must meet her. I will destroy her, and then you will be mine.

– What if she isn't mortal? he asked, testing her.

– I have no rivals in this place, she said, haughtily. They are all worms here. Even the river is rotten with their shit.

– Shit happens here. Who knows, it may happen to you.

– I will have none of their shit.

– You may not be able to avoid it. Their shit is everywhere, he said, gesturing towards the two-fingered chimney salute of the distant chemical plant.

– I was summoned to that place, she said. I will not let it take me back. I will destroy it too.

– How will you do that?

– I will make the place destroy itself.

Their weapons clattered on the table: axes and hatchets, and a long jagged-toothed saw. If the display was calculated to intimidate him, the plan had worked. He was searching a drawer for some ink powder, trying not to look flustered. He didn't like the look of their gap-toothed leader, who had stabbed the table with his huge cross-handled knife. It stood there, upright: an accusation or a threat, he wasn't sure which, but the rust-tinged blade said this was no Excalibur. The man's face was blackened with burnt cork, and O'Scrapie had to lean back to avoid his tobacco-laced spittle and his rancid breath with its reek of old meat, onions and shit.

– Write it down, said Bogbreath, go on, but make it sound clever, as like an officer has wrote it.

O'Scrapie tried to dress it up as best he could: *Sir*, he said, and began reading out the words as he scratched them on the parchment with the feather thing, *Sir, Your name is down amongst the Black Hearts in the Black Book* (he liked that bit, that was Bogbreath's phrase), *and this is to advise you and the like of you, who are Parson Justasses* (he almost wrote jack-asses), *to make your Wills.*

– That's good, said the smell, that'll show the blackguards.

– *Ye have been*, he continued, *the Blackguard Enemies of the People on all occasions. Ye have not yet done as ye ought. If your threshing machines are not destroyed by you directly we shall commence our labours. Signed...*

– How do I sign it? he asked.

– You must sign on behalf of the whole, the smell said. But we need a name, Captain.

– I've told you before, I'm not a real captain. It was just an old uniform they gave me when some bastard took my clothes while I was bathing in the river.

– Very well then, but sign it Captain. They won't know it's you because you was never in no regiment. But they have to think you was.

– If they find out, I'll *swing* for this, said O'Scrapie, certain that if he were brought up before the magistrates they would know about the Dan's killing of the gamekeeper. He would be an accessory.

– That's it, said the man, sign it now: on behalf of the whole, *Captain Swing*. And he choked on the name, hawking up a wad of green-slimed tobacco. (O'Scrapie hoped it was tobacco.)

– But there is no Captain Swing, he protested.

– We'll tell all the others to sign theirs the same way. Then no one man will be held to account, and they'll think this here Captain Swing's behind all the attacks and go looking for someone who don't exist.

– Attacks? O'Scrapie asked, now more worried than before.

– Nobody's been killed, not yet. All over Kent they've been burning the ricks and barns of anyone who wouldn't pull down their machines, and it's spread into Sussex and Hampshire. The Justices is calling it a contagion. But now they've got the message, some of the farmers is breaking their machines before we get to them: not that they're theirs, most of 'em's hired.

– And you leave them alone then?

– After they've given us a couple of sovereigns for the relief of the Poor.

– The Poor? said O'Scrapie, thinking the farmers were paying for air. He imagined a mob of four hundred putrid-breathed men. They only needed to belch and the ricks would go up in flames. They'd scorch a swathe through the county just by breathing.

– That's what it's about. The farmers here is on our side, that's why they don't act against us. We wants two shilling a day for each married man in the winter, and two and six after Lady Day. Sixpence a day for a single man.

– That doesn't seem much, said O'Scrapie, trying to work out what sixpence would buy at the Crawley Arms.

– But the farmers can't afford to pay, the smell said, because the rents is so high, and because of the tithes. So they're telling the parsons they've to cut their tithes by half. Mr Cobbold in Selbourne agreed that three hundred pound a year was enough for a parson to live on. That's five pound a week. They was living off the fat of the land before, our fat, and we was starving.

– Yeah, I can see you've got a case there, said O'Scrapie, trying to distort the normal shapes of his letters in signing his name, *Captain Swing*.

When he'd said history stank at school, they shouldn't have cuffed him, giving him the line that if anyone stank it was him. Now he knew he'd been right all along. The past was a smelly place. Gubbins would have been at home here, he thought, and almost wished he was back in Hangman's Wood talking to the pongy old sweep. Here everything was humming, and there were more pesky flies than he'd known existed. But what was he thinking? The wood wasn't *back*, it was so far forward that it was out of reach.

The three women sat at their usual table in the Bald-Headed Ram. Lady Olivia Prurigeaux tapped her long fingernails on her jingling saucer to summon the waitress.

– Another pot of Earl Grey here please, she said. And turning to her companions: We will need more tea if we're to sort this one out. This time, I'm sorry to say, those men have gone too far, and Nick is to blame for letting them get away with it. We'll have to talk to Belinda, get her on our side.

– I'm sorry about that panties business, said Bunty Saveloy. I jumped to conclusions. You know what Maurice was like.

– That's past now, said Olivia. Don't worry about it.

– That's no comfort to Isabella though, said Bunty.

– I don't mind, said the corpulent Mrs Maw. Morton will get his comeuppance one of these days, and I don't think I'll be sorry, as long as he doesn't drag me down with him into the mire. That's why we have to be united.

– Perhaps you could talk to her after the funeral, Bunty, Olivia suggested. You two are close. She's bound to get very drunk. And with poor Candida gone, she'll be feeling especially angry with the men, after what they've been doing.

– We haven't been so close lately, said Bunty, not since Maurice's death. I put that down to Nick's difficulties, but I have felt she was avoiding me. Some people are like that after a death. They don't know how to talk to you.

– How about you Isabella? You could talk to her, said Olivia.

– I don't think so. You know I was having an affair with Nick.

– Really! the other two cried in unison.

– What was he like? Tell us, said Olivia.

– I didn't think he was interested in sex, only power, said Bunty.

– The town bull is as much a bachelor as he, said Isabella.

– What a devil, cried Bunty. And what a dark horse you are, Isabella, you never gave a hint of this before.

– It was between us, Isabella continued, releasing a sugar lump into her steaming tea-cup. I thought he loved me. But he gave me turnips, just dropped me without saying anything. I sat round for days, waiting for the phone to ring, for his car to pull up outside. But he never came near me. It was as if I'd never existed in his life, once he'd decided he didn't want me any more. I still don't know why. Then I thought...what did I think?

– The bastard? suggested Bunty.

– Exactly.

– We'll get him, said Olivia. Don't you worry, Izzie, we'll get our own back.

– And your jewellery and paintings as well? said Isabella.

– But we'll need help, said Bunty. Belinda won't be able to do much.

– But Kernan will, said Lady Olivia, with a smile of triumph.

– If we give him a few leads to follow, said Mrs Bunty Saveloy.

– Just as far as Nick, said Lady Olivia Prurigeaux.

– Nick the devil, said Mrs Isabella Maw.

– Put him in the nick, said all three. Scratch Old Scratch.

It would happen now, they knew it. Now they were working together.

In the nick of time.

Cobbler, cobbler, mend my shoe,
Get it done by half-past two;
Half-past two is much too late,
Get it done by half-past eight.

Sandman, sandman, mend my sow,
Make her quick and make her now.
Two o'clock will shut the door,
Get it done the hour before.

Sandman, save my Wessex sow,
Bring her back if you know how.
When your minutes are all taken
Give me pig instead of bacon.

Sandman, save my bonny bull,
He is mad and masterful.
If Jack Marshall interferes
Knock him down and box his ears.

CHAPTER NINETEEN

Twice the Speed of Time

ST LUKE'S EVE – GIG FAIR NIGHT: OCTOBER 17TH – 30TH

If a clock's ticking suddenly changes rhythm, this is a death omen, especially if the ticking becomes faster. If a clock left unwound suddenly chimes or strikes of itself, that also foretells a death. If a clock strikes thirteen, some say a man will die; but not a woman, for thirteen is the moon's number, which men have slandered to counter the power of women.

DESCRIPTION of TWO MEN detected in the act of SETTING FIRE to a STACK of OATS in the Parish of LOAMFIELD, in the County of Loamshire, about Eight O'Clock in the Evening of St Luke's Eve, MONDAY the 17th of *October*, 1830.

One a tall Man, about 6 feet high, large black full whiskers extending under the chin, apparently between 30 and 40 years of age. Wore at the time a snuff-coloured straight coat, with light-coloured pantaloons, and low shoes. The other Man was apparently about 5 feet 2 inches, with large red nose, and apparently between 40 and 50 years of age; had large sandy muttonchop whiskers. He wore a blue frogged coat military in style, light coloured breeches, and boots with cloth overall-tops. Both men were seen at Loamfield at half-past twelve at noon on Monday, coming from Dealchurch, and probably by the low road under Loamsley Moor.

£50 REWARD.

The TRUSTEES of the CHARITIES in LOAMFIELD, having received Information that a most scandalous and disgusting Letter has been sent to the Rev. A.S. PRURIGO, Lecturer of that Parish, THREATENING him, and the Premises in his Occupation, with

DESTRUCTION,

DO HEREBY OFFER A REWARD OF

Fifty Pounds

TO ANY PERSON

who will give such Information as shall ensure the CONVICTION of the WRITER of this Letter, purporting to be a "CAPTAIN SWING".

OCT. 18TH, 1830.

PRINTED BY LOAMSHIRE CHRONICLE, OTTERIDGE.

Loamshire to wit} To the Constable of *Loamfield* and all other Peace Officers in the said *County* of *Loamshire*.

Forasmuch as the *Hon. Martin Maw* of *Dealchurch, a Gentleman residing* in the said *County*, hath this Day made Information and Complaint upon Oath before me, *George Kernan*, One of His Majesty's Justices of the Peace in and for the said *County* that *"Captain" O'Scrapie, also known as "Muttonchops", said to be from Mudbury in the County of Hants., on the 17th Day of October instant at Loamfield in the said County of Loamshire, together with divers other persons to the number of one hundred and more unlawfully and maliciously did break damage and destroy a certain Machine or Engine called a Thrashing Machine at Long Wood Farm in the Estate of Maw Hall.*

These are, therefore, to command you, in His Majesty's Name, forthwith to apprehend and bring before me, or some other of His Majesty's Justices of the Peace in and for the said *County* the Body of the said *"Captain" O'Scrapie* to answer unto the said Complaint, and to be further dealt withal according to Law. Herein fail not.

Given under my Hand and Seal, the *19th* Day of *October* in the Year of our Lord One Thousand Eight Hundred and *thirty*.

Geo. Kernan

Warrant, 2.-C. Sold by SHAW & SONS, 137 Fetter Lane, London.

PUBLIC
NOTICE.

THE *Magistrates* in the Hundreds of *Loamfield* and *Dealchurch*, in the County of Loamshire, having taken into account the disturbed state of the said Hundreds and the Country in general, wish to make it publicly known that *it is their opinion* that such disturbances principally arise from the use of Threshing Machines, and to the insufficient wages of the Labourers. The Magistrates therefore beg to *recommend* to the Owners and Occupiers of Land in these Hundreds, to *discontinue the use of Threshing Machines, and to increase of Wages of Labour* to Ten Shillings a week for able bodied men, and that when task work is preferred, that it should be put out at such a rate as to enable an industrious man to earn Two Shillings per day.

The Magistrates are determined to enforce the Laws against all tumultuous Rioters and Incendiaries, and they look for support to all the respectable and well disposed part of the Community; at the same time they feel a full Conviction, that *no severe measures will be necessary* if the proprietors of Land will give proper employment to the Poor on their own Occupations, and encourage their Tenants to do the same.

SIGNED,

WILLIAM CERVELOIS.
BENJAMIN COOMBES.
P.M. GRENNAN.
GEO. KERNAN.
J. LAMBERT.
D.J. TAYLOR.
S.R.F. THIRSK.
T.M. TOMKINS.

Otteridge,
20th October 1830.

PRINTED BY LOAMSHIRE CHRONICLE, OTTERIDGE.

"Captain" O'Scrapie, of no fixed address, said to be an Innkeeper of Mudbury, Hants, and Daniel John Alcock, of Horsham, Sussex, a shoemaker, escaped yesterday from the custody of the Peace Officers at Loamfield, who were conveying them to the gaol at Otteridge, under a commitment for feloniously breaking a thrashing machine at Long Wood Farm, near Maw Hall. The two felons were last seen crossing the Devil's Bridge at Dealchurch, heading up the hill road towards the Forest of Otter. A reward of £50 each has been offered by the Rector of Dealchurch, the Rev. E. Nicholas, for information leading to the capture of either of these two persons. Both men are the subject of warrants for offences of violence committed in other shires, and armed help from as many hands as possible should be sought in any attempts to apprehend either or both of these fellows.

Loamshire Chronicle, 22nd October 1830.

It was a twelvemonth since Flea had first seen her, the bonny policeman's daughter, Lucy with the sloe-black eyes and her cheeks like roses. She had been with her soldier boy, who left to fight for the Queen.

She was a rum one
Fol-the-diddle-di-do-day
But a bonny one
Fol-the-diddle-di-do

But his pretty maid had not waited for her sweetheart, she'd been courted by the false deceiver Tom, who left her full of woe, his head turned by the yellow glint of gold. Gold worth nothing now to cruel Tom, except to pay the nursing home where he lay wracked in his bed, shaking like a leaf and cursing both dogs and cattle.

When her father had exploded, she'd flown back with her tail between her legs. And she changed then, left bad company behind. Now a sadness flickered in her coal-black eyes. Yesterday she'd spoken to him, standing at the bar of the Black Bull, asking for crisps and a drink. Hallo, she'd said, seeing him there, just one word, but to him, Flea, and he'd been speechless, like some clumsy village chawbacon. All his bold boy to bonny lass lines lost in that instant when his eyes blazed a frightened hare response to her smouldering look; at which she'd smiled, and returned to sit with others. He confessed his burning love to Muffy, who told him to bide his time.

– But she is as rare as a black swan or a white raven, Flea protested. How can I wait?

– You must eat a yard of pudding first, Muffy replied, adding mysteriously that he would hold his true love's lilywhite hand and kiss her milkwhite breast when two black fingers disappeared from a blue sky, not today or tomorrow but a six-month from tomorrow. She would be true to her name then, Lucy the lightbringer, and as true as a turtle to her mate.

– Tomorrow, she added, the world was created. So men say.

– How can you know that? asked Flea.

– I don't. I don't actually believe it, any more than I believe the Millennium is Christ's 2000th birthday, so why all the hoo-ha. They should have had their party in the 90s when Thatcher and those other devils were thrown out of Cloudcuckooland. Even the scholars say the calendar is wrong, that Jesus Christ was born not in the year zero but several years earlier, some time around 4 to 8 BC.

– So he was born before he was born, said Flea.

– That would figure. What's our time to an immortal?

– And he died some years after he really died.

– A lot of people are like that. The Early Fathers say the world was created on the 22nd of October 4004 BC, so if Christ was born four years before he was born, he hit the manger at the mid-point of time.

– Four thousand years from the year dot to the year zero, said Flea. Is that why the clocks go back on Gig Fair Night?

– It's probably to do with that, though I think the world's much older anyway. But whatever the reason, we get our hour back which we lost in the spring. I didn't like to think of it being missing all that time, a whole hour.

– An extra hour in bed, said Flea.

– No, said Muffy, a repeating hour. At two o'clock on Sunday morning, you go back to one o'clock, and have the same hour again. A second chance hour, time in which to put things right which weren't right first time round.

– A kind of Groundhog Hour? Flea suggested.

– Which most people sleep through. But I shan't. I'll be using that hour. It's a time of dormition like Mary's, like the three days before the new moon, like Christ's three days in the tomb.

– When he disappeared?

– Exactly.

– Where did he go?

– He went out.

– Like Captain Oates, said Flea. Herne told me about him. I'm just going out, he said, and I may be some time.

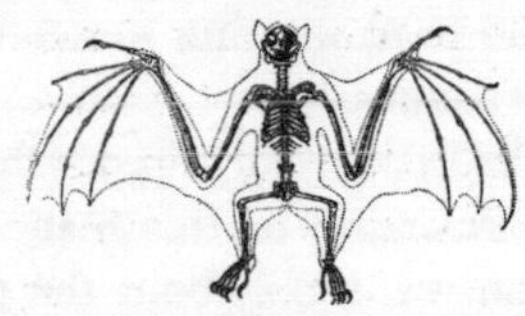

Dr Polly Kettle formed an attachment to the bodies in her charge. This skeleton from the shallow grave was particularly intriguing. She had pondered it for hours. The less she had to go on, the more she could flesh it out in her imagination. But for the purposes of the report, she had to confine herself to facts.

– I'd put him in his early thirties, about six feet in height. The bone is about two hundred years old, which means he'd have been born around the turn of the 18th century, and was killed between 1825 and 1835.

– Killed? asked Diana.

– Most definitely. The skull has been broken by a small projectile, but there are incisions in the vertebrae of the neck, suggesting a heavy knife was also used in the murder.

– Any idea who he was?

– From the remnants of clothing, a soldier. Or someone wearing a military-type coat if I must be precise. Possibly a local man: there's a flaky badge embossed with an otter, the symbol of the RLI. I checked with the V&A and the brass buttons are of a kind favoured by Wellington's officers at Waterloo.

– Officers?

– Yes, that surprised me. I thought our man was a demobbed soldier, returning after the war. Many came back from fighting Napoleon expecting a hero's welcome, only to end up on the parish, because there was no work; or they took to poaching, or emigrated. With no money, they'd have had to keep their soldiers' uniforms till they were in shreds, like this man's.

– Anything else? Diana asked.

– Yes, the clothes are too small for a man this size. He was six feet tall, as I said, which was very tall indeed two hundred years ago. The clothes belong to a shorter man.

Dr Polly Kettle found this annoying: such an inconsistency would have been seized upon by the investigating team had the man been killed two instead of two hundred years ago. But no one would follow this up. She would never know why Charlie, as she called him, had been wearing someone else's clothes.

– What about the panties?

– The panties? asked Polly, surprised. Oh yes, the other case. I thought you were referring to this man. They're interesting too. Inspector Kernan was right about the perfumes, *Escape* by Calvin Klein and Cerruti's *1881* aftershave. But the *1881* is interesting. It's very weak...

– It would be if it's been around that long...

– It's been diluted, either because the user mixed it with water, but more likely because it was sold that way.

– Sold watered down?

– Yes, perfume sold in markets overseas is often either an imitation, or else it's diluted to make it go further. The packaging is often stolen. Perfume piracy is very big in the Far East.

– Gullible businessmen wanting cheap sex and bargains to take home.

– Exactly. But the 3-in-1 is even more interesting. It's been adulterated with a lubricant called Biethylenetripropethyl-6.

– What does that do?

– It repels organic substances. It was developed initially for use in abbatoirs, to stop equipment getting clogged up with animal blood and faeces.

– So how would Lady Olivia Prurigeaux get this Biethylwhat-everitis-6 on her panties? And the oil?

– Obviously her panties have been used to wipe some piece of equipment. But not the usual kind, she added, smiling mischievously. If I didn't think I'd be ruled out of court, I would say a captive-bolt pistol used for stunning animals. But no one wants to know about those round here.

– What do you mean?

– You remember the Tench case?...Well, I gave my opinion that the hole in his skull was consistent with the use of a captive-bolt. The hole stopped dead. It didn't go right through as a bullet would. But Goodman wasn't happy with that, and called in some expert from the Home Office who said some kind of spike had been used, but there would have been more bone shattering with a spike, it would have been much more messy.

– And didn't you challenge his report?

– What, challenge Goodman? You must be joking. Anyway, once they had their proof that Brock had been the murderer – but Brock was dead – the case went no further. It was shelved, so there was no point in making a fuss.

– Can I see your report? said Diana.

– You can, but only because I kept my own copy.

– But don't mention this to Goodman. And if I may make a suggestion, don't explain the uses of Biethylwhatsit in the report. Just list the findings. Then Goodman won't ask questions. He's already embarrassed about the panties. He thinks Ernie Gubbins was some pervert who stole them from a washing-line. He doesn't want to pursue him for the burglary now. Apart from the panties, there's no evidence. It's all disappeared.

– And he wants to keep it disappeared? asked Polly.

– Yes, said Diana, he almost seems to be scared that someone will find it.

– Is that everything?

– Oh no, I almost forgot. Kernan wants you to run a DNA test on the body. Then put it through the computer for a match. Don't tell Goodman, he'd think we were barmy.

– Run a match with Charlie? He's over a hundred years old...

– Yes, I know, said Diana. It's one of Kernan's theories. We should humour him.

The field was lined with hedges, and in one corner the ground rose to a bank like a tumulus or fairy mound. It shone like an old man's bonce in the moonlight, the grass turned to fine silvery hair. Kernan had been thinking about this place all day, the Devil's Nut Bag, also known as the Devil's Night-Cap and Alcock's Arbour, said to be guarded by a giant cockerel. Diana had felt the power here on Devil's Nutting Day.

Then on Friday, turning from Polly's report on the body in the forest to the *Chronicle*, Kernan had read its account of *This Day In...* Here they were: "Captain" O'Scrapie and Daniel Alcock, a shoemaker. Alcock's Arbour mentioned too. The ringleaders in the Captain Swing riots were often shoemakers, subscribers to Cobbett's *Political Register*; who spread the 'contagion' of subversion from village to village. That was the word they used then, *contagion*, Kernan remembered. Nothing had changed.

And tomorrow was St Crispin and St Crispinian's Day: patron saints of shoemakers, the two martyred brothers from the 3rd century invoked by King Henry for England and St George against the French on this day in 1415 at Agincourt:

> And gentlemen in England now a-bed
> Shall think themselves acurs'd they were not here,
> And hold their manhoods cheap whiles any speaks
> That fought with us upon Saint Crispin's Day.

...Crispin and Crispinian weren't even English but French; and Shakespeare had Henry's vastly outnumbered army kill ten thousand French in their name, with only four English nobles killed '*and of all other men but five-and-twenty*'. England were but a fling then but for the crooked stick and the greygoose wing. Hoggie could have used the Swan of Avon for telling porkies about BSE.

As Kernan reviewed his troop of clues, trying not to lose his train of thought, his chain of missed connections, he caught sight of a slight movement behind the mound, or was it inside? He knew at once it was the watchers again. He'd not been this close before, but with his eyesight now as lynx-like as it had been before the crimes of Crimea, he was able to take in their low stature, and with his reawakened sixth sense absorbed the knowledge that behind the blackthorn bushes their skins were giving off a green sheen in the moonlight. They thought themselves invisible.

– Come forth, he challenged them, gently.

Now he heard them too, felt their indignation, but just as quickly knew their mood had changed from suspicion to one of decisiveness. These were instinctive beings, who knew what they wanted before they'd thought of it; their perceptions more refined and immediate than any he'd known in the animal world. They were otherworldly, he knew, and where before they had been tracking him, now they were giving him some kind of warning.

They had not moved towards him, as he'd asked, but did not need to do so, for they had become almost obeisant to him. He realised that somehow they had recognised him not as the hunter they thought they had been hunting but as one related to themselves, though what they were he was still unsure. He considered a possible connection with the little green men of science fantasy, not a fiction, he knew, or a wishful figment of folklore, but a way of describing visitations by ancestral spirits or future souls who lived in the parallel world, who were sometimes too eager to be called over to this one, because their love for certain animals, plants or people was so overwhelming. He wondered if his love for Diana would become like that if he were taken back.

These particular spirits addressed him now. Their manifestations could be dangerously beneficent, he now realised, which was why government agencies were employed to suppress all information about sightings and so-called close encounters, to make them seem far-fetched, make witnesses the objects of ridicule by interpreting their experiences in terms of abductions to craft or other planets. For earth angels took their chosen friends not away from but *back* to the earth, to their own and Kernan's domain, this was what they were telling him; they still wanted to share the earth, despite all the humans' attempts to destroy it, if not by world war then now by environmental catastrophe.

They were alien, they let him know, not in being from other worlds but in the sense of being *other*, for their other worlds were all part of the one world: the earth, in which souls had their physical lives; the earth with its complex interdependence of animals and plants, of land and sea and air, in which the life of every species was related to another, and all creatures were affected by each others' actions as well as by minute changes in land or water; the earth which was almost a creature in itself, which they called Gaia (though even that name admittedly held a whole set of misapplied contradictions), a creature composed of all creatures, all systems and substances. The earth's climates and the balance between all the lives it held guaranteed both Gaia's health and the well-being of its creatures, while its cycles ensured their continuity and renewal.

They knew Kernan loved this creature he and they were part of, and his earthly love for animals and plants, for the land, for Loamshire and England, for his village, its people and most of all, his love for Diana, these were all a part of an all-embracing love which had nothing to do with any God, though some might call it that, except that Gaia demanded not just respect but self-respect, for humility if wrongly directed verged on denial of the self, of the physical, of sensation, of the fullest love of others and the world; it meant denial of Gaia's whole being, Gaia's gift of life to all; it was a social imposition, an artificial construct always emanating from the power base of one individual or group or country or gender or church who wanted dominance over others.

For Kernan, stories were living things, they could not be fixed in tablets of stone, frozen as dogma, they had to be told and retold to remain part of the earth's living testament; the gods figured in church, temple and mosque were no longer gods of the earth but decadent man's own rival gods, testaments to some half-remembered, stagnant relationship that condensed in them when those gods were uprooted from the earth and their worship became more important than the relationships they originally sanctified.

If Kernan was the earth's policeman, they were saying now, his brief covered not only murder and manslaughter but the murder and needless killing of animals, as well as evil, corruption and conspiracy. All these came together, they were trying to tell him, in the murder of Bernard Tench. That one case, when amplified, stood for everything that was wrong in the chain of being; that child's mantra of Loamfield, Loamshire, England, the Earth, the Universe.

It was all getting out of hand. One life stood for all life, whether man or animal. A threat to one put all at risk, and Goodman was the agent of destruction. Goodman's plot to kill not only Tench and Brock but also Kernan and Diana was part of the greater plot, which Kernan must frustrate.

He wanted to ask more questions, but realised he must hold nearly all the clues now. If the answers were within his grasp, he only had to connect the threads to compete his quest, to deny Goodman his evil end.

What else was there? What else could he ask?

He had to think quickly, before they dissolved or dispersed. Or disappeared.

They sensed his impatience, his earthbound frustration.

– *What is it, Kernan?* they seemed to be asking. What else do you need to know?

– I'm trying to think, hang on! he said. I'm *sure* there's something else, something vital.

– What is it? What is it? they seemed to whisper.

– Don't go, there *is* something else, I *know* there is. Something I *have* to know to solve the case. Oh god, I know it's something *really* important.

– Is it about the cattle disease?

STAR CHARTS FOR LOST SHEEP

Scorpio (*23rd October – 21st November*)

CAREER: This month sees major career developments and you'll make stunning progress. Your career path is opening up, but don't let doubts creep in. Stop dreaming and make it happen. For the first half of the month, they'll keep you from the ewes, but you'll have been in their pens, if only briefly. If you're lucky you'll have touched them through the hurdles. The ram effect starts then. They know you're not far away. The ewes will have a silent heat for the next few days of the month, and some will come on heat again after a short period before settling down to their 17 day oestrus cycle. Your perfect opportunity comes on the 14th when you'll be one of three rams with 100 ewes to tup. Do well, and they'll keep you on for another four seasons before culling you. Beat the average score of 63 lambs sired, and your job will be protected.

HEALTH: This month you should aim to be at peak fitness. Your hooves should be in good shape if you've been following the Footvax system. Remember how those other tups were culled back in August when their feet were trimmed and footrot discovered? If you've been short of silenium and vitamin E, you should have been taking Vitenium for the past ten weeks to enhance your semen quality. After worming and the Heptovac P booster, try to eat a kilo a day of 18% protein Dalgety concentrate: you need to reach CS4 (fit and firm) by tupping time. You have to be reliable: sickness at this time is fatal because you won't get a second chance. Illness affects semen fertility. A high index stock ram needs testicles as big as a shopping bag: scrotum at least 36 cm in circumference.

LOVE: With this week's tricky aspects involving both the unreliable Neptune and Uranus, planet of the unexpected, you'll be able to mate freely with any ewes on heat for the first nine days, but Sunday's pivotal Full Moon in your opposite sign of Taurus heralds the fitting of the raddle harness. You were most frenetic before harnessing, which should ensure you won't get harness sores on the brisket, but those leather straps and buckles mean you're now entering a highly erotic phase. Inhibitions are dropping away as all the ewes make themselves available, sending you round in circles of tail-sniffing. A red raddle crayon will mark the ample bottoms of all the white woolly ladies you tup for the next ten days. When Neptune (representing illusion and idealism) moves into Aquarius (kindness and gentleness), the crayon changes to blue, your mood for the last twenty days of mating. Your love life takes a dive when the harness comes off, but this is also a period of recovery, a time to take stock, for healthy rams like you take six to eight weeks to produce the love juice. Once you're back to winter grazing, content yourself with kicking and butting the other rams. You'll also need to build yourself up with hay and concentrates.

CRIME: Mercury's meeting with your ruler, the planet of truth, Pluto, brings harmony to your investigations. Next week's extraordinary aspects to Jupiter usher in a series of clues involving milk or scabs...

• The entrails of an animal made a fish's milk run dry (*8 letters*).
• The company which eats the company which kills the cow is itself a transmissible spongiform encephalopathy (*9 letters*).
• His grandfather invented an arsenic-based sheep dip which cost a pound a drum in 1881 (*3,5,8*).

– *Chawdron, 8 letters*, answered Kernan, a beast's entrails. Chawdron's in the Department of Health. I thought he was mixed up in this. But how can I be sure?

– I have it from the horse's mouth, said Muffy.

– And the second answer must be Gerstmann, I knew that one already, which links De Foie with the Otteridge Meat Company. Who told you that?

– My sources are my secret, said Muffy. I must protect them, as you protect yours, especially since I'm still alive myself...

– I'm not dead, Kernan interrupted.

– Not dead but sleeping, said Muffy. Like Arthur.

– No, not like him. Arthur's in me, a part of me, as I am in the world. The police are always watching. My ways are mysterious.

– What is the third answer then?

– The third must relate to Owen's Sheep Dip, which replaced the old tobacco wash as a treatment for sheep scab. Made by the Atlas Preservative Company of Wanganui, New Zealand. Proprietors: W.T. Owen and Thomas someone, grandfather of...

– Someone with his name, said Muffy. And Tench was going to name names.

– Names aren't names unless you name them, said Kernan, who needed names to find the key. When you named someone, you gave them a life, just as words gave them their voices; and when you knew their names, you had power over them. They revealed themselves through their names. Or they set up a false trail like Goodman. And Gizzard, of course. Why had he not made that connection? Because he had not met her in the flesh perhaps, though Herne had told him Lizzie Gizzard was no devouring Maw: her name then was a disguise, a mask to let her move among the Maws and Sirloins, she was more mole than maw. Who or what had blinded him, that he had not absorbed what his shadow revealed? Was this Muffy's work or Diana's spell? Were all three of them in it together? In it, but with him, on his side: Diana, Muffy and Lizzie?

– One of the three names is always a red herring, Muffy went on.

– There are always three rams used for tupping, said Kernan. Two mature rams and one ram lamb per hundred ewes. Two old head-butting tups with their apprentice. A trinity of rams.

– High Index Suffolks are best.

– Aries the Ram, said Kernan. Another clue.

– A birthday clue, not mine, for I am a May cat born under the sign of the Bull.

– The cat is sacred to Diana the Hunter, who could take on the form of a cat.

Lizzie Gizzard had taken some time to recover from her interview with Colin Coombes. Her thoughts kept returning to the pig souls in the rafters. Nine thousand pigs had met their deaths at the hands of the slaughtermen of the Otteridge Meat Company since her visit to the abbatoir on St Maelrubha's Day. The information gained had been helpful to the plot she was hatching, but that didn't help those hapless porkers. Was one man's life worth the life of nine thousand pigs? How did you measure these things? Couldn't she do *something*, even just to save one poor beast from being stun-'n'-sticked, or better still, bring one back like Werburga's goose? Had she the power? Could she do it in the extra hour? No, not unless…

As she stood in the darkened kitchen searching the hydrator for a lettuce, the glow of white light from the fridge made her usually green aura appear albescent, as if she were some ethereal visitor. Touching a small foil-wrapped package at the back of the vegetable compartment, testing its softness with a finger, this shimmering apparition became incandescent, its fluid skin pulsating with argent verdigris.

A ham sandwich! What was *that* doing there? Dead pig in *her* refrigerator! No doubt Bruce's tucker, left there on his last visit, whether out of thoughtlessness, or to goad her, she couldn't tell.

What emerged then from the icy light, clutching its grisly find, was a long bony ashen-skinned hand with blackened, bitten nails.

– This poor creature must be helped, cried Muffy, rushing out of the room, into a night lit by a moon like the great white effulgent eye of a cyclops in the firmament.

Otteridge High Street was empty but for two raincoated figures flitting from the thin drizzle into the sheltered foyer of the Bank of the Black Horse.

– I like milking the wall, Gubbins was saying, though she's dry tonight. This is my milking parlour, all these stainless steel piggy banks with their buttons to press. But that's not why we're here. Come on, you've got to stand here as well.

– But I use the mattress, said Dogbreath, I don't have no bank account with no pig or black 'orse. And the mattress is stuffed with *chestnut* 'orsehair. Not *black*. Black 'orse's unlucky. Always a dark brown 'orse in the races.

– Captain Swing was black but they called him dark brown when he won the Frog Derby at Chantilly Lace.

– Celtic Swing, not Captain.

– Chief Singer too, said Gubbins, dark brown thoroughbred, but he was black too, and he took the July Cup at Newmarket.

– Never mind splittin' hares, Dogbreath insisted, no good'll come of a black'orse, you mark my words. It has to be dark brown.

– This is the Great Dispenser, the Great Money Sow.

– But the 'orse won't have nuffin to give yer, Gubbins, yer said yer was skinned, stony-broke.

– That's not why we're here, remember. Now, timecheck.

Dogbreath lifted a heavy paw, then sighed, remembering his stolen Puma watch only gave the right time twice a day; pumas were unreliable creatures. The belly was the truest clock. He pointed to the tower of St John's. As if on cue, the church clock tolled, not just once, as they'd expected, but thirteen times.

– Must be playing up with the time change, said Gubbins. Thinks it's thirteen o'clock instead of just one. You stand next to me, where it can see you, and I'll press these here buttons.

– What, roight next to yer? said Dogbreath with evident alarm. Yer won't fart or nuffin, will yer? That hartshorn pong o'yers is worse than the stink from the Bog of Haughey when they're corruptin' the peat.

Gubbins ignored the insult. A blunt-muzzled pipistrelle clinging to his coat hem crept up his trousers, nipping his shin.

– *Knuckers!* Yeah, right in front. When I press the last button, it'll ask me what I want. And its hidden camera takes a picture of us in case we try anything on.

Gubbins shook his leg, and the bat dropped onto the ground, as if from a chute.

– That don't look like one of mine, he said. The bat flew off, eager to transmit its rabies virus to someone else as accommodating as its erstwhile host. In the past twenty years, virus variants from insectivorous bats have been associated with sixteen out of the twenty-nine cases of rabies diagnosed in humans, although bites were reported in only eight cases. Ernest Gubbins was the last of these.

– What, like threaten it wi' a shooter, make it 'and over all the dosh it's got in there? Dogbreath asked.

– No, we might have stolen someone else's card, and if we've got their pin number, we can milk their sow till they've got no pin money left in the ould Black Horse. No, this is what I want.

A chit of paper curled from a slit in the machine.

– See that, said Gubbins, *nil pwan*, a balance of fuck-all, dry as an ould ewe's pap. But it tells me the time too, 1.01 a.m. on the 30th of October. And it gives us our alibi. For it's photographed us here at 1.01 a.m.

– So we can't be at the Grange, robbin' the widow Prurigeaux.

– No, not there. Someone else has already cleaned her out.

– But we've only just started the extra hour. They can't have done her already, unless this isn't the extra hour, but the hour after the extra hour…

– I was thinking of something a bit more adventurous, take a leaf out of O'Scrapie's book. What Herne'd call a lit'ry theft. We'll play the devil in the horologe.

– What if we don't come back? I don't want to be stuck in the Land of Loggin the Log. You won't get me checkin' the ould stool every time I has a dump. I'm no turd inspector.

– We'll steal the bicycle from *The Third Policeman*. I've got the book here. No one will know it's missing till the second one a.m.

– But where will we hide it?

– In another book of course. I was think of *A Brief History of Time*. Every book about time needs a displaced bicycle if it's to answer the big question, Nine what?

– Nine what? asked Dogbreath.

– Stitches in time, a beaming Gubbins replied.

– As in, a stitch in time saves nine?

– Nine what? Gubbins fired back.

– Nine what? his foul-breathed friend repeated.

– Exactly, said Gubbins. If a stitch in time saves nine there must be nine stitches in time. Three is a trinity, and nine is a trinity of trinities. Time is a healer but time itself is a wound with nine stitches, and because there are always nine stitches to be saved, time will never be staunched.

– *In my end is my beginning*, said Dogbreath, remembering Father Sheeder's pronouncement on the same subject.

– Exactly, said Gubbins, for just as a man's back end is his arse, so the universe must have an arse where its end is in its beginning, which is why God is dead, for God made the Big Bang when he farted and imploded on himself, just as Elvis did after eating too many beefburgers. Now God has gone to join Elvis in Graceland, but his arse broke into an infinity of celestial recta in the great explosion. So there are many Black

Holes, but each Black Hole is in effect the same Black Hole, which is the Almighty's dark sphincter, for if you were to enter one Black Hole you would be simultaneously entering all Black Holes. All are one, and the One True Hole is the Ring of the Lord of the Rings, just as all the Elvises seen in different places around the world are all aspects of the one true Elvis who danced with a wooden chair and a hound dog. Elvis is Lord of the Lucan.

– That sounds pretty heretical to me, especially the hound, said Dogbreath. Though not as schismatic as Kernanism. But the idea of God farting...why should God fart if he doesn't eat?

– Everyone likes the smell of their own farts, said Gubbins.

– But you won't get far, said Dogbreath, if yer talk like that. Yer have to sound Irish to get inside *The Third Policeman*, or *Oirish to be sure*, for it's the Cod Irish you have to talk, like the Irish in England, who sound more Irish out of Ireland than the Irish in it. The longer we're away, the stranger we sound.

– A good idea, said Gubbins, if I speak Cod Irish I can pass myself off as a tinker or a cursing fish, for a fish's speech bubbles are written in Cod Irish, and if exiles speak it, so too must the dead novelist, for the dead are longer away than any. That is why their speech is so strange, for it never changes.

– A ghost talks like a fellow in an old film, a ghost's tongue is stuck in 'is own time. That's why a ghost is so scary.

The silver moon looked down over Otteridge. Not since the Year Dot had Muffy seen it as refulgent. As a veil of rain drifted down the valley, she saw a great curving bow in the sky above Loamfield, a moonbow with all the colours of a daytime rainbow, but muted, transparent like gauze, with blackness showing through its night palette of sombre shades, from dull scarlet, through chocolate orange and mustard yellow, to olive green, ultramarine and an indigo so pale that it seemed more like a smear; then last the merest hint of parma violet. She would chase this rainbow not to a pot of gold but to a pool of blood.

The clock in the town had just struck thirteen, making Gus

Gubbins look up to check the digital thing which Coombes had installed, being a man of numbers, not hands. The red figures clicked every minute, like the snapping teeth of a terrier. Now they said 1:01. That was right, room 101 this was, and Gubbins was Muggins, the cat's paw pulling chestnuts from the paper to entertain the sheep.

He was at a loss to know how it was that he had changed from buying *The Sun* to *The Times*, but change he had, and Mickey seemed to like the sounds of the longer words he was reading in the big broadsheet paper; either that or it amused him to see the nightwatchman struggling with the huge paper which flapped around his flailing arms like an albatross when he tried to turn the page. He had just read out a whole article stretching down three or four columns, all about the Northern Ireland talks, and every time he'd paused, or made to leave the piece for something more interesting, the sheep had nudged at his hand with its muzzle, as if to urge him not to stop reading at that point.

– Well, you may think otherwise, Mickey, but that's a load of ould bollocks. Wouldn't trust any of them. They're all in it for what they can get, those politishens.

He poured himself a last glass of Famous Grouse, and horsed it back like medicine.

– *Buurrrp!* Pardon me, Mickey.

– *The two sides have to be brought together. And it's Dev, I keep telling you.* But the Judas sheep's advocacy of a pragmatic strategy involving compromise was lost on Gus, who only heard his woolly friend bleating in an agitated fashion, and wondered if he wanted something to eat.

– Do you want a sandwich, Mickey? Is that what it is? A *roll?* He emphasised the word, rolling the *r* in *roll*, as if trying to make the beast understand he was talking about food, as he would address a foreigner with a limited command of English.

– It's all about common ground. Each side has to make concessions, starting off with the decommissioning of weapons...

– Oh, no. I've only got ham. Can't feed pig to a sheep, can I, Mickey? Ha ha. Never mind what Maw and his chums get up to, feeding cattle to cattle and all that. Never seemed right to me, that.

– Nor me, said Muffy, whom Gus Gubbins found suddenly

materialised in front of him like an avenging angel when he lowered the wings of his paper; and snatching the roll from the surprised nightwatchman's hand, she whipped out the succulent ham and threw the bread to the sheep. Then reaching into her pocket, she withdrew a tin-foil package, and opening this revealed another sandwich; again, she stripped out the pinky meat, and threw that bread to the sheep also.

– Your ham, she said, and this ham – waving both pieces in the air like a magician – are both Old Oak Ham, and from the same pig. And I'm going to unham the ham sandwich, give this succulent flesh back to the pig it came from…

– Bloody hell, said Gus. Even Mickey was surprised, but started urging Muffy to carry out her recreative trick.

– You'll have to call the soul back too, said Mickey. It may not want to come, not back to this place.

An Aberdeen Angus leant across from the lairage stalls, and gave a deep *moo*. It stamped its hooves in the straw, and shook its head, as if to draw attention to its woolly chestnut hair, which looked recently permed.

– That beast kicked Jack Marshall in the head, Gus told Muffy.

– The wee baaastard deserrrved it. He was marked by the curse of the Morrigan.

– He was giving him the injecshun when the bull gave him whatfor with his hoof, and broke out of the crush. They had to put him back in lairage overnight. He'll be for the chop in the morning, but this time without the injecshun.

– They're not gi'in me any more o' that *papain* shite. *Tenderise the meat*, is what they say. What anthropocentric arrogance!

– My, aren't we an angry beast, said Muffy, still waving the two pieces of Old Oak Ham like a red rag to the bull, but troubled by the beast's mention of the Irish demon.

– Too *reet*. Ah want some tenderrrness in passing between worrrlds. Not some oaf sticking that stuff in yerrr neck wi' a great spike like a knittin' needle. Knocks yer heed off, it fairrr does. Yerrr last five minutes o' life, and they have yerrr staggerrrin' rrroond like ye've just had am*mo*nia shot oop yerrr neb. It's inhooman, that's worrit is, inhoomane, but what do they caairrr? It gans rrreet through yerrr, makes ye want tae piss rrreetaway.

– Most undignified, Muffy agreed, staring at her fist of ham.

– Then it's outae the crrrush and intae the box. Out wi' the gun, and *pop!* Ye'rrre parrralysed, pal.

– Not unconscious then?

– Nae way, said the brown bull. That's what *they* think, or what they *want* tae think, or want *ye* tae think. Naw, we feel it aal. Hind legs tied wi' chains, then hoisted oop afore they pooll the knife on ye and…

– Slit your throat? said Muffy, drawing her ham-filled hand across her neck, much to the alarm of Gus, who had only heard the human side of this dialogue.

– And therrre's me, an Aberrrdeen Angus wi' a line gannin' back tae Aberrrdeenshire humlies 'n' Angus doddies. A rrreal bovine arrristocrat, Ah am, and Ah put up wi' this bootcherrry everrry time, just tae get it ower quick. Aalmost like some foockerrr's tellin' me Ah should gan back tae hooman, and sparrre meself this each time, but nae way pal. Ah've seen what ye folk dae tae each other. Ah'll stay a bull, me, higher form of life, that's what they say, isn't it?

– A short life but a happy one…

– …till the only hoomans ye've kenned tell ye it's slochter-time agin. They're aal the same. They turn their backs, then pack yer off to hell in a cattlefoockintruck…

– *An angry beast?* queried Gus, with a quiver in his voice. *Undignified, unconscious?* he added, looking frantically about him. *Slit my throat? Short life but a happy one? What are you saying?*

– Not you, the sheep assured him. She's talking to Angus, Gus.

– What have I done? asked Gus, looking at the stupid ram, baaing like it had something to say. What had he been doing, reading the paper to a fucken sheep, and now the dopey creature would watch him have his throat cut by this madwoman. And just carry on munching hay like nothing had happened.

– It's all right, Gus, the sheep added. Nothing to do with you.

– It's all to do wi' rationality, the bull continued. Ah learned aal that when Ah did my human stint. Gans back tae that Immanuel Kant. Aal foockin' heed an' nae heart he was. His granfaither was Scots, Ah helped oot in his saddlery when ah was a wee bairn, that's how Ah kenned the foocker.

– Every event has a cause, said the sheep, who remembered

wrangling about the teachings of Kant with Father Sheehy at Charleville Christian Brothers' School in 1898.

– A cause? Muffy repeated. The clammy ham was making her hand smelly now.

– What cause? Why? cried Gus. Still seated, he started edging to one side of his chair, looking to the sheep with goggling eyes.

– And Kant says animals are nae ends in theirselves because – wait for it – *we are nae rational beins!* So man has nae duties to the beasts, but can treat the whole foockin' animal world as a means to his ain foockin' ends? An' we end up in this place, to be slochtered.

– A means to an end, said Muffy. You're right, it all ends in slaughter. And she raised the ham in the air again as if to demonstrate the point.

– Means to end! What end? Slaughter? Why me? pleaded Gus.

– But *they* can't be cruel, oh no, said the bull. So Jack Marshall needs a wee lesson in Kantian ethics, that's what Ah say.

– That's right, said the sheep. Cruelty to animals debases man's nature, John d'Alton taught me that at Blackrock, and he was later Cardinal of All Ireland.

– Never mind about *them* being debased! the bull exclaimed. What about us! What about *our* debasement at *their* hands! What's he got to say about that?

– He wasn't a cow, though, was he? the sheep offered. Though he might be now.

– Or a sheep, said Muffy. He could be a sheep.

– What do you mean, a sheep? asked Gus. What are you *saying* now? You aren't going to stick me like a sheep... He looked from face to face, from hag to bull to sheep, they were all off their heads, all mooing and baaing, yakking and yabbering. And now Mickey was off again.

– But like all men, Kant was inconsistent, the sheep was saying. How can cruelty to animals be any different in purely ethical terms from cruelty to people?

– Least he dinnae gan alang wi' *Rennie Day Cart,* said the bull.

– That's right, the sheep agreed. He thought animals were actually *unconscious*, though from what I've heard tonight, this lot still believe that when it comes to stun and stick time.

– Or *Spin Oozer*, the bull added.

– Not sure about that one, said the sheep. He thought animals *were* conscious beings, but they were still entirely at man's disposal, to be used for whatever he likes, even when that involves inflicting great pain on the poor beasts. How does Kant differ in that? And there's nothing in either Spinoza *or* Kant which says man can't *enjoy* giving pain to animals.

– They certainly seem to enjoy gi'ein' pain to each other, the bull added. So nae surprise there pal.

It was almost like a duet, thought Gus. *Baa, moo, baa, moo, baa, moo*, with the old witch throwing in the odd weird word, like she was conducting the two animals. He'd never witnessed the like in his life.

– The creek women saw all forms of life on earth as intelligent kin. Man was just another creature sharing the same place.

But perhaps she's not about to stab me after all, thought Gus. Yet what was this cock and bull story she was giving him now?

– All creatures were spiritual beings who occupied body masks which could be borrowed for food, and plants and animals would give of themselves for food as long as you respected them. But then the men started wanting to put up fences to keep the animals where they wanted them, even tethering the beasts...storing seeds to be planted at particular times, all of which put them in contest with nature instead of working with nature, as a part of nature.

She was certainly getting those two beasts worked up about something. It was almost like they were following this claptrap she was coming out with, agreeing with it even, judging from the way they were nodding their heads.

– Too many foockin' folk for that to work now, said the bull. Before the world managed its ain natural resources. Now Man's ta'en ower the whole foockin' show. Before ye had plagues, drochts 'n' famines to keep the wee foockers doon, if they hadn't already wiped each other oot wi' killin' 'n' wars, but now they're so foockin' clever they control the diseases which used to keep their numbers doon. An' they breed like foockin' rabbits, build their foockin' roads and cities wi' mile on mile o' bricks 'n' concrete across the whole foockin' land till there's nae trees, nae fields, nae room for any other beast but *homofoockinsapiens*.

Muffy remembered her fistful of ham. Well if Man's done so much against nature, she said, do either of you two have any philosophical objection to my doing a little something against nature in this borrowed hour? Something to *correct* Man's excesses, and save the life of one poor creature?

Oh no, thought Gus. Now she's remembered me. Watch out Gubbins, or this hour will be your last.

– I'm all for it, said the sheep.

– Me too, said the bull. That ham's from a Wessex Saddleback, is that nae reet? I wouldnae ken the pig in question, but Wessexes are usually pretty guid sorts, unlike their keeperrrs...

No, this was more madness. The beasts were off again. But the old crone mightn't be dangerous, as Gus had feared. She was just doolally tap, and the sooner he made a move and showed them who was boss, the sooner he'd clear her out and get some sleep before the Sunday morning shift arrived. It was nearly 2 a.m. Couldn't have her still hanging around then. What would Coombes say? He'd be in here first thing to make sure the Angus bull was first in the queue for the stunning box. And Jack would be hot on his heels, wanting to be the man with the stun gun.

He stood up suddenly, and spat his contempt at a pool of pig's blood on the floor. The gobbet made pink foam in the little lake of vermilion.

But Muffy raised her hand, pointed to the Puma watch on her wrist, and spun her finger round the face, anti-clockwise. Gus Gubbins backed away.

– *Widdershins, widdershins, widdershins,* she cried. *Let* EVIL *be turned into* LIVE. And the watch hands started to spin backwards, so fast they became a blur. The digital clock on the wall set up a high-pitched whine as the flashing numbers turned into a two red holes like hot ingots; they stared down like cat's eyes.

– *Now take, take, take from me. I give you my undying love. Undie, undie, undie. In this time of no time, your death shall be undone.*

The pink phlegm swirled around on the surface of the pig's blood, losing its redness as it swooped like a skylark off the ground and up into the air, back into Gus's mouth, his own spittle shooting back through through his pursed lips.

No longer resolute, Gus had a pained, surprised expression on his face.

– How did you do that? he gulped.

– I call it suspension of disbelief, said Muffy. Now watch the rest, she added, throwing the two pieces of ham up in the air. The meat hovered there for a moment, and Gus looked up hearing the sound of a trolley clanking towards them down the corridor. It burst through the swing doors with a clatter into the room. A pig's carcass chained to the rack swung like a ship's rigging from side to side as the trolley veered off up the approach race towards the stunning pens.

With one kick, the Aberdeen Angus broke through the lairage barrier, only to trot meekly to Muffy's side; and they all set off in pursuit of the trolley, a motley crew, Muffy and Gus, together with the brown woolly bull who had known Immanuel Kant's granfaither and the ram who had been Éamon de Valéra, like Dorothy and her ragged entourage, the Judas sheep trailing behind, taking his first hesitant steps up the ramp, hoping the approach race was the yellow brick road to Oz and not the winding one to Béal na mBláth. The ham flew ahead of them, and they were in time to see the two pieces of Old Oak slap against and disappear inside a now airborne pig's carcass.

After sucking up a torrent of blood from the concrete floor, the carcass burst its chains like Houdini and shot backwards into the stunning pens, where it leapt off its back and onto all four trotters. Giving a final squeal, the pig came running towards them, stopping at Muffy's feet and giving her the most impudent of oinks.

When Gus Gubbins woke from his short nap just after 3 a.m., after the strangest of dreams, he discovered a scene of chaos. Animal rights activists must have broken in and smashed through the lairage pen. The Aberdeen Angus had gone, and they had taken poor Mickey as well. The door to the cold store was broken too, but nothing was taken from there, except that an empty trolley had been wheeled up the race and toppled on its side in the stunning pens. He wondered how he could possibly have slept through all that commotion, and put it down to the bottle of Famous Grouse his cousin had given him. He would have to feign an attack on himself or lose his job.

Seeing what looked like pig's blood on the floor, he smeared it across his temple and rubbed some in his scalp and hair. Then Gus Gubbins took a stunning mallet from the cupboard, and hit himself on the skull, but slipped on the blood as he did so.

When Jack Marshall arrived for work at 6.25 a.m., the first of his holy day shift, he made immediately for the lairage. It was a tradition in the abbatoir that anyone injured by a rogue animal should be given the honour of killing the beast, if it hadn't already been despatched by his workmates. Now Jack was eager to eyeball the Aberdeen Angus bull, wanting to taunt it before it was led through for him to *stun* (the muzzle angled away from the skull, to make sure it was still half-conscious) and *stick* (hard, with a jagged bastard of a cut). He was going to *enjoy* this killing, he was sure of that.

Rushing through the swing doors, Jack Marshall was so buoyed up with murderous anger that he failed to notice the prostrate body of Gus Gubbins, and tripping over the unconscious night-watchman, went flying forward, head over heels; struggling to regain his balance, he slipped in a pool of pig's blood, fell backwards and split his bandaged head open on the bent-back bars of the empty lairage pen.

He never saw that the Aberdeen Angus had disappeared.

Who'll toll the bell?
I, said the Bull,
Because I can pull,
So Cock Robin, farewell.

BOOK V

SAMHAIN

NOVEMBER – JANUARY

I know an old woman who swallowed a cow.
I don't know how she swallowed the cow.
She swallowed the cow to catch the goat.
Just opened her throat, and swallowed the goat!
She swallowed the goat to catch the dog.
What a hog, to swallow a dog!
She swallowed the dog to catch the cat.
Now fancy that, to swallow a cat!
She swallowed the cat to catch the bird.
Now, how absurd to swallow a bird!
She swallowed the bird to catch the spider
That wriggled and jiggled and tickled inside her.
She swallowed the spider to catch the fly,
But I don't know why she swallowed the fly.
Perhaps she'll die!

CHAPTER TWENTY

The Passion of Kernan: II

SAMHAIN: OCTOBER 31ST – NOVEMBER 1ST

If a cow lows after midnight, this is a death omen for someone in the district. If a cow lows three times in a man's face, he has not long to live.

Peering into the darkness of the garden, Kernan saw that the man was still hanging there, the rope creaking as the wind swung him back and forth. But he wasn't hanging by his neck. He was upside down, strung up from his feet.

The rope keened like an aching tree.

The hammering in his head grew more unbearable. *Clack-clack, clackety-clack, clack-clack*, it went. This was a different sound. He could hear chains as well, the whine of pulleys. The hollow thud from a bolt-action pistol fired at point-blank range into an animal's skull.

Taking the bread-knife from the cutlery drawer, he went outside. When he reached the ash tree, the hanging man pointed not to his side but to a round wound in his forehead, as if he were to blame for this.

– You have not found my killer, the man said. He is not free that draws his chain.

– Everything has an end, and a sausage has two, Kernan replied. The end makes all equal. I'm getting close.

– I offered myself to the earth. I danced the Tyburn jig for you. I preached at Tyburn Cross.

– Thereby hangs a tale.

– They've taken my horse and left me the tether, the man whispered, pulling at the noose. And look, the end is still loose.

– A year has two ends, Kernan responded, but when we make ends meet at the end of the year our slate is clean as a whistle or a new penny.

– I did it for you, the man insisted.

– Let every herring hang by its own head and every sheep by its own shank. A fish in brine saves nine.

– I did it nine times nine.

– A cat has nine lives, but a lie has ninety-nine.

– I scourged myself.

– A cat of rope has nine tails.

– The end is nigh, the man warned, his voice breaking.

– *In my end is my beginning*, said Kernan.

– Cut me down. It's time we started again.

As Kernan started sawing, he felt the rope tighten round his own neck. For an instant he was hanging within an inch of his life, his own body about to kill him with its weight, until the bough above him broke instead, and he fell.

And kept falling. Down, down.

His guts were going the other way, heading for his head.

He thought at first it was the same dream again, but this time was different. Someone else was there. He felt a terror like the war, clutching at the pit of his stomach.

When he hit the ground, Kernan found he was lying in a different field from the usual one. He recognised the mound in one corner, the Devil's Nut Bag; and saw across towards the boundary hedge a gigantic bird the size of a horse, whose great spectral figure was stalking the shadows along the hedgerow, its great bulbous wattle glistening silver in the moonlight. Like a pawnbroker's sign, he thought, in an empty street at night.

The giant bird rushed at him, then withdrew; and again,

shaking his huge claws like skis. And a third time, his beak darting forward, showing him the way. At first Kernan denied the cockerel any ground, standing firm, not allowing himself to be intimidated, but finally had to relent and be forced backwards. The cockerel was not barring his way, as in the Alcock story. It was saying he should walk up the mound. His manner was dismissive, almost arrogant, like that of an executioner who has overseen the building of his scaffold, and then takes pleasure in urging a condemned man to mount its steps.

On top of the mound, which he knew the animals always avoided, there was a white heifer tearing at the long wet grass, which had never been cropped. A cow in a fremit loaning. The thin grass seemed to float, making green silky fans around her hooves, like the flowing hair of the Green Knight.

The heifer had red ears, like a fairy cow. She was tethered to the mound, separate from the rest of the herd. But the tether was not a rope. It was a length of white tape.

He stood in front of her then, feeling her breath in his face, warm it was, sweet and carroty. She gave a dullish low, almost a rumble, like distant thunder. Then another, louder. And a third, more threatening. Kernan counted, as if waiting for the flash of a Verey light, or a whistle.

– *Yan... tan... tethera,* he began; and at the third low, untied the tape from its wooden stake. Taking the end of the tether, he walked slowly away from the cow, until the tape swayed almost taut between them. Then he passed it round his waist, but pulling at the tape, to secure himself, found he was tying a knot of hempen rope, a knot like a figure eight.

It was then he saw Diana standing by her car at the edge of the field, next to the crossroads, mouthing something he could not hear. Motioning to her not to alarm the cow, he was suddenly gripped by a sense of panic which was new. Panic, he thought. It was Nemain, she was here, with the Morrigan. As if on cue, a crow alighted on the mound, with a raucous cry. Badbh the Scald Crow.

Diana must not be hurt. He could see her struggling, trying to resist the Devil's Night-Cap, but also drawn to it. Wanting to save him. He would not let her come near. He knew there were others too, waiting. The Morrigan and her followers.

He started running away from Diana, around the heifer. The cow stood still as he circled, tied to the end of her tether, like the hand of a clock, but going backwards. Anti-clockwise. *Withershins*. The wrong way. He cursed himself for not realising before, remembering how the Morrigan had pursued Cúchulainn as a water-snake, a she-wolf and a red heifer. This was a white heifer, with red ears, as it had to be.

Each time he passed the stake, he counted.

– *Yan*, for the first.

– *Tan*, for two circuits.

– *Tethera*, for three.

With each circuit running faster. Towards the Morrigan, for she was the heifer, and he would enter her.

– *Methera*, he gasped.

– *Pimp*, she said with him. *Pimp for me, Cernunnos, you are mine now.*

– *Sethera*, he said. *Six*, the heifer lowed.

– *Lethera*, after the seventh, always the toughest circuit, but not now, for he wasn't fighting, he was letting himself go, to save Diana. The cow stood still like the dark bulk of a standing stone.

– *Hovera*, he cried. And still the Morrigan took the strain while Kernan ran his circle, his tether pulling like the sleek body of the eel, pulling him towards her.

– *Dovera*. Soon he would be hers, the Queen of Demons.

– *Dik!* Tied to the Great Queen, instead of consort to the Great Mother, as should have been his fate.

– *Yan dik! Yan dik!* Undone by his love. And now the Morrigan was pulling him down, as she had at Devil's Bridge.

– *Tan dik!* Twelve. *Tan dik, tan dik*, he chanted at the milk-white cow shining in the dark field like the moon above them. The heifer that was drawing him towards her, even as he ran his orbit at the end of his tether.

– *Tethera dik!* Lucky thirteen, the number of the lunar months, the number of times a woman is fertile, or bleeds from her womb.

Some massive centrifugal force was tearing him limb from limb, violently but without pain. He was separating, spirit from body, leaving the dream yet not waking, but being hauled backwards, as if the rope were his umbilical cord reclaiming him, and the Morrigan his mother.

He heard Diana, calling as if from a long way off:

– *Kernan, where are you? What's happening?*

But he was being swallowed, and she was growing fainter by the second.

– Kernan, where have you gone? *Please, oh love, please say where…* Her voice died away.

Now he was inside the cow. He had left his body, but had stopped falling.

Nor was he dreaming now.

– I thought you'd never get here, said the Morrigan.

– Where am I? he said. Is this some kind of hell? He tried to shift his body, but swayed on his feet, unused to his great weight. The Morrigan held him firm, stopped him from toppling over. She seemed able to control the movements of his body. Their body.

For it wasn't his own body. Looking across the field, he saw a blue flashing light coming down the low road from Otteridge. His human body lay on the grass in front of him, his hand clutching a length of white tape. Diana was running towards it.

He was inside the cow. The cow's body was his body now. It was also the Morrigan's.

– That felt good, she said, when you came inside me. Our bodies became one.

– One? he said. But mine's down there.

At the foot of the mound Diana was cradling his body in her arms, her hair falling across his face. Her grief was radiant, like Mary Magdalene's. And now he couldn't feel her holding him. She looked up at the heifer, like Mary at Calvary, trying to understand what had happened to her son. She was powerless. There was nothing she could do to help him now. He saw her weeping, the first time he'd ever seen her cry.

– You've left that body behind, she said. Mine also has gone. It was a temporary thing, the word become flesh. We don't need our human bodies now, Cernunnos, not now we have each other.

– But what about the cow? Doesn't the cow have a say?

– I changed into the heifer. There was no cow before. Now we are the cow, a much higher form of life than the humans, as you know. And we are one now, female and male together in the one being.

– But we're still separate, said Kernan, even though we're joined in this cow. And this may be fine for most souls – living as a cow in a state of almost permanent meditation, with none of the distractions of human life – but don't we have work to do? My powers of good are now totally absorbed by your powers of evil, and vice versa. Neither of us can act, for good or evil. You can't change into anything else now, and nor can I. We are powerless.

– You're right, said the Morrigan. In my eagerness to have you, that hadn't occurred to me. You were undone by the purity of your love, and I by the all-consuming power of my lust.

– So we're both stuck here then? In this cow? For all eternity?

– No, she has a mortal coil, this heifer. But we will have plenty of time to get to know each other. There's no escaping me now, Kernan. No escape.

– I hope you like grass then, said Kernan. There's nothing else to eat. And when I want to eat, you have to eat.

– We have no wills of our own. What I want is what you want.

– And you have to do what I want to do. We do everything together. Even shitting.

– Shit happens.

There was a little man and he had a little cow,
And he had no fodder to give her,
So he took up his fiddle and played her this tune,
'Consider, good cow, consider,
This isn't the time for the grass to grow,
Consider, good cow, consider.'
So the poor cow lay down on her side,
And considered, and considered, and considered, till she died.

CHAPTER TWENTY-ONE

Nothing Left

GUY FAWKES – ST LEONARD'S DAY: NOVEMBER 5TH–6TH

The newly dead need the help and protection of the living during the uncertain period between the death and the funeral, to help the soul on its perilous journey to the next world, and to stop demons from bearing it off to Hell. Mirrors should be veiled or turned to the wall, lest the spirit become entangled in the reflection and remain to haunt its place of death. This veiling should be done with love and kindliness. The living should avoid mirrors lest they see the dead looking back at them from the glass: a sign of another imminent death, showing that the soul was waiting to take someone else with it (usually, though not always, the person who sees it in the mirror).

Very soon, the much hated figure of Superintendent Nicholas Goodman would go up in smoke. The crowd was calling for his death. At Herne's instigation, Muffy and Gubbins had fashioned his effigy for burning on Guy Fawkes Night. Two Hallowe'en pumpkins bound tightly in a sack formed his bullethead, into which they had scorched hollows to hold the coals of his black eyes. A police uniform had been procured with the willing help of Malcolm Oxter, who had himself been burned as a scarecrow plod on a previous occasion, although his limited choice of cast-offs had involved their victim being demoted to sergeant for his pyre. At first their choice was popular, but local tradition demanded that the straw Goodman be perched on top of the bonfire on St Crispin's Day, since when his baleful figure had presided over the Green, more threatening than comic, for ten days and ten nights. Even the crows kept their distance from this Worzel Goodman.

Jock McDonald grumbled that he was losing trade because his customers felt they were under police surveillance, and couldn't enjoy themselves with Goodman around. Kernan too had sensed he was being watched all the time. But now he was dead.

The level of resentment and ill-feeling towards the towering Goodmanikin was now so intense that all Loamfield's presence at its immolation on Bonfire Night was virtually guaranteed, particularly since many of the villagers thought Goodman was responsible in some way for Kernan's death, and the more superstitious felt that burning him at the stake might work as an act of ritual revenge, and perhaps even be helpful to Kernan's troubled soul, which must still be lingering around the village.

As the crowd gathered on the Green around the war memorial, they exchanged nervous mutters, wary of the presence of the bullet-headed guy, but almost imperceptibly, their nervous mood changed as they began to chatter like birds, snatching at titbits of gossip about Kernan; growing bolder, they went out into the open to stab at the Goodman's character, playing off the good of the late inspector against the evil of the soon to be ignited superintendent.

Waiting for St George to strike the hour, when the pyre would be lit, a knot of older men stood around Herne, whom previously they had always avoided like the Plague, because of his khaki bag. They nodded at his explanation of the Loamfield custom of stringing up the most unpopular person in effigy on St Crispin's Day and having him deputise for Guy Fawkes on Bonfire Night; that festivity had itself been displaced in Jacobean times when the traditional Samhain fire festival marking the new year had been moved five days back in the calendar and transformed into a grisly affair celebrating the failure of the Gunpowder Plot.

Although the effigies had only been torched in Loamfield for about 150 years, Herne said, the practice was centuries old in the other shires, repeated every year in remembrance of the

English archers at Agincourt, who had attributed their success in routing the French not just to superior skill but also to finer weaponry, their long bows being made from the best English yew. Since much of this wood had come from the Forest of Otter, it was right that they should celebrate their own contribution to the great victory in the time-honoured style of the radical shire celebrated by the likes of William Cobbett and Henry Hunt. After all, many of the soldiers who fought in the Hundred Years War had come from Loamshire as well as from Kent and Sussex, counties which maintained proud anti-French traditions well into the nineteenth-century, with bonfires lit on St Crispin's Day in the Sussex villages of Slaugham, Cuckfield and Hurstpierpoint.

The first of Loamfield's spitting images was made in 1830 at the instigation of an incomer called Dan, a cobbler who brought the custom with him from Horsham. The Sussex man was said to have disappeared immediately after making his effigy, and when he had not returned by Guy Fawkes Night, the villagers had burned Lord Melbourne, the Home Secretary in the new Whig Government, who masterminded the suppression of unrest in the English shires. Remember, Herne told them, the country felt ill at ease after losing many fine young men in the fight against Napoleon, but not seeing much changed at home when peace returned, they were coming to despise their out-of-touch rulers with a fury greater than their hatred of the French.

– They were fired up by their roasting of the hated Willie Lamb, Herne said, and they resolved to burn other figures of authority in future years. But the idea of burning someone out of office, that's more recent.

The men lamented how four straw Thatchers had gone up in smoke before the evil cow was toppled, while it had needed a hat-trick of burnings to do the trick for Douglas Hogg.

– Wee Dougie Hogg with his ready-made Guy Fawkes hat, said Jock McDonald. He looked the part all right.

From his place of concealment behind a yew tree in the churchyard of St George's, Nicholas Goodman heard the loud banter of the villagers and their even louder squeals of delight as they set him on fire, marking the faces he saw illuminated by the flames licking his ankles. The unsavoury oaf they'd pulled in for the burglary was there, that Gubbins person, and he was cavorting like a jumping jack, leaping about like a parched pea on a griddle, probably got too near the fire and singed his arse, serve the fucker right. Then he noted the presence not only of Constable Jakes and Sergeants Oxter and Daglock amongst those dancing round the pyre but also of the Right Honourable Henry Sirloin, MP, who seemed to be egging on a line of cat-calling women at the back: to the left, the widows Prurigeaux and Saveloy; to the right, Mesdames de Foie and Maw, the former holding a whip, the latter a small jerrycan of petrol.

He felt a burning sensation at the back of his throat, such as he experienced when ostentatiously puffing his favourite Havana cigars, the kind he used for emptying rooms of silly, chattering women. He was not smoking now, yet tiny curls of smoke drifted from either nostril. And from his ears.

Two stabs of red heat in the dark beneath the yew answered the burning coals of the pumpkin-headed joker on the fire.

The flames from the Loamfield bonfire leaped into the air, higher and higher, making the sky above the village glow as if from a great beacon, illuminating swirls of cloud which would otherwise have remained invisible in the moonless night.

Henry Sirloin watched the firelit rooftops recede in his rear-view mirror as he drew up at a kiosk window labelled SECURITY. He wound his window down, calling his name to the guard, who was unaccountably dressed like a cowboy complete with stetson, but waved him through, muttering something incomprehensible in what sounded like a drunken dialect of Scots. He caught the phrase *what the fuck's* – or was it *the fox*? – followed by a burble of garbled epithets in which only *bare breasts* or *bear's vests* were recognisable.* Oliver seemed to employ all sorts at the plant. But at least he didn't put the dogmen on the gate. That would really be too much. It showed the man possessed some sense after all, even if he did have few senses and no sensibility.

As the MP's black sedan slipped under the raised barber's pole of the security gate and hiccupped over a sleeping policeman,

* *The fox fares best when he is cursed.*

two smouldering bats dropped onto the road from the spout of its exhaust. These had detached themselves from Ernest Gubbins's burning coat, and sought immediate refuge up a pipe protruding from beneath a car.

They spluttered for breath, recoiling from their dose of carbon monoxide, before propelling themselves briefly into the sky like the Wright brothers leaving the terra firma of Kitty Hawk beneath them on Thursday the seventeenth of December 1903. The two creatures crashed into the side of a huge metal structure bearing a giant number 9, and plummeted groundwards, pulling back at the last second to shoot through a vent their radar located along the bottom of the structure. Inside, they found they had landed in a tank containing some kind of chemical, which reacted with the carbon monoxide inside their lungs as they drowned. Their fur began to burn like a fuse.

In Oliver de Foie's office, Henry Sirloin was wagging a finger at the industrialist. Hearing a screech, the two men turned to the window, breaking off from their argument to watch the bursting rockets fired from the village green light up the whole sky over Loamfield, crackling diamond showers sparking like sapphire, ruby, topaz, emerald and amethyst.

At zero hour on the sixth of November, the final attack on Passchendaele began. When Kernan reached the village crossroads at noon, his platoon supporting the Canadian advance, he realised for the first time that the place called Passchendaele no longer existed, except in the memory of the villagers who had fled from the two armies. The name which had drawn him forward all these months was a muddy maze of German Army trails. Even the old cobbled street and dirt lanes had gone. There was only rubble, heaps of stone and brick, pillboxes and shell-holes, all shrouded with mud and sand. One larger pile was recognisable as the feeble remnant of the church. He sat on his own, resting against what looked like part of an altar.

The place was hardly a ridge. They couldn't have been more than fifty feet above the Flanders plain. Below him he saw thousands of Tommies moving like ants. On the other side, to the east, were the Boche, spread out across the lowland near Moorslede. The artillery still pounded the ridge from both sides, each army's field guns flashing in turn, their smoke merging above him. Listening to their futile interchange, he almost wished his hearing hadn't returned.

Now he heard a whizzing sound, and looked up, hoping to hear a bang somewhere else. In front of him stood Captain Nicholas, his revolver raised towards him.

– *Slacking are we, sergeant*? he hissed.

– There's a whizz-bang coming over, Kernan said quickly, trying to ignore the captain's gun.

Nicholas fired, and threw himself backwards, landing behind the altar slab against which the sergeant had been leaning a minute before. In the same instant, it seemed, before the bullet could meet its target, the shell hit the church, the explosion sending rubble flying in all directions.

Kernan disappeared.

And his shadow fled from him, across Passchendaele, down the western slope towards Gravenstafel, where the remnants of the Royal Loamshires lay scattered, their bodies strewn one over the other, some with legs and arms flung many yards away, or missing. Kernan's shadow dissolved into the bodies of the men he'd led and inspired, filling them with his pity.

On one body stood a great black crow, pecking at a man's face.

On the kitchen window-ledge, a large black bird stood, pecking at a piece of fat she had put there.

Chee-aw, chee-aw, chee-aw, chuff, went the bird. It sounded like the one which had led her through the Forest of Otter. The chough, Kernan had said, which could be King Arthur himself. Or could it be Kernan now? Whichever it was, himself or his messenger, she would allow herself to be guided by it this time. Its presence made her feel he was watching over her.

Lawrence had been surprised that she'd wanted to move into Kernan's cottage rightaway, but she felt restless anywhere else. Here it was painful, living with Kernan's things, but it also felt somehow healing, being where he had lived. Even with his body lying in the other room, awaiting its long delayed interment.

The cottage also seemed to hold many possible leads, in Kernan's books and papers; in the place itself, next to Hoggetts Field, surrounded by animals, which kept congregating in the yard. There were all kinds of birds, from sparrows and thrushes to ducks and geese. There were rabbits too, sitting motionless on the grass, as if waiting for something, undisturbed by the weasels, who sat not far away, their heads raised like periscopes, looking up at the window, watching her. The two horses in Hoggetts Field seemed to stand on permanent guard at the hedge bordering the garden. It was as if they had come to the house, not just to mourn, but to offer her their support, and to urge her not to give up, to continue Kernan's work. That morning, there were two new arrivals in the field, a huge Aberdeen Angus bull and a ram which appeared to be muttering. Bill Jarman said they were probably strays from the Maw Estate, where the fencing was never well maintained.

Goodman had wanted to suspend her, claiming she was somehow involved in Kernan's death, but Lawrence had given her compassionate leave instead. The post mortem had been inconclusive, but with all possible tests done, all of them negative, Goodman had no alternative but to agree to the body's release for the funeral. If Kernan had outwitted him in not dying at his hands, he might as well be pleased with the consequences, however inexplicable. Kernan couldn't touch him now, and nor could any of the others without his help.

Dr Kettle's report had simply stated: 'Despite his age, Inspector Kernan was in perfect health – surprisingly so. There were no marks on his body indicating an attack. There were no clots suggesting a coronary, and his heart was as supple as a young man's, without any sign of disease or even wear. The large feather found near the body seemed to be that of a Rhode Island Red cockerel, but is much too large for that. I do not know what significance to attach to it, nor can I offer any theory as to any possible cause of Inspector Kernan's death.'

His solicitor said Kernan had no known living relatives, but his will had always stated that one Diana Hunter would be his sole beneficiary. He had never altered it. His house and all his effects and property were hers. A notice to that effect would be placed in the *Chronicle*, but he didn't expect anyone to contest it, and would not object to her taking immediate possession of the cottage.

She looked at the cards she had brought from his office, remembering how she had once found them infuriating. Now she knew they were his calendar, his means of plotting a way through the modern world by drawing on the wisdom of the ancients. Turning up the card for the 6th of November, her face went white. *'The newly dead need the help and protection of the living during the uncertain period between the death and the funeral, to help the soul on its perilous journey to the next world, and to stop demons from bearing it off to Hell...'* She read on, taking in the strange details as if they were facts she had to learn, and act upon. Moving through the box, she found he had prepared cards for six months ahead, right up till May. Some of them were extraordinary, some objectionable, but she knew she would use them. His wisdom would become hers.

Then she stood up and walked into every room, looking for mirrors to veil, but there were only two, a small round shaving-mirror in the bathroom with a reticulated stalk, which looked like the eye of a large metallic insect, and an oak-framed mirror set into an old dressing-table in his bedroom. She moved towards it with a green silk scarf she had brought from her bag, knowing she must not look into it, but whether because she was still weak with loss, or because she wanted his spirit to stay entangled with its house, she could not avoid looking into the glass.

What she saw, or glimpsed rather, for it was that fleeting, did not surprise her. She had almost expected to see it there, standing by the window, reversed, a face like Kernan's but green in hue, like the skin of the children in the picture book her mother had once read from, a story of the Green Children of Woolpit, who had appeared one harvest at the side of one of the village's old wolf-pits. Their speech was strange, and they would eat nothing but green beans. She remembered how the boy had died, pining for the place he had come from, but the girl had thrived, learned to speak the language of Suffolk, and lived to an old age.

The man's hair seemed to be made from leaves, and there were leaves coming out of his mouth, like a green cry. She turned from the mirror to look behind her, to see him, but he had gone.

And all the birds of the air
Fell a-sighing and a-sobbing
When they heard the bell toll
For poor Cock Robin.

Matt Hardacre was pleased. He tightened the last screw, and patted his handiwork, signalling to Pete Gingell that they could bring in the truck. Those animal rights nutters had been giving him a lot of work. And his mates had been putting the jobs his way. That morning he'd fixed the perimeter fence at Eurochimique. He was still meant to be over there, and Wild Bill would log him out at five o'clock so that he got paid for a whole day's work. It was Jack Marshall who'd got him odd jobs at the slaughterhouse. The lairage pen should have been fixed over a week ago, but it had taken that long for the new gate to arrive. He expected the work would continue even now Jack was dead; his acceptance of the gaffer's methods of payment should ensure that.

The lamb they were just now loading into the back of his van would see the kids right for Christmas, and earn him a bit extra from a few pub managers. Not *quite* fit for human consumption – but only just – was how Coombes had described the carcass, nothing more than a technicality really, one day past its sell-by date sort-of-thing. But who'd know the difference when it's on the plate, Matt thought, as long as it tasted like lamb and didn't give you the shits.

It had been hard to keep his hands clean, but he was managing it now. After that last stretch when Dawn had left him, he hadn't wanted to go down again: she'd fenced the stuff, got herself a new fur, but he got twelve months for breaking and entering, nicked by that Kernan copper who was dead now. It was four years now since he'd been inside.

The beasts were already being led into the lairage, making a real fuss they were, snorting and bellowing. One cow was really making a meal of it, funny looking thing it was, white with red ears, and it was kicking out and stamping the ground, its hooves sparking like flints. Three times it crashed into the gate he'd just secured, frantic in its efforts to escape.

– Better get that'un through first, cried Pete Gingell, before she sets the straw alight!

– You watch it when you stun 'er, said Joe Hartley. Don't want you ending up like Jack.

– Strange beast, that'un, shouted Gingell above the commotion. She's got a real bee in her bonnet.

– Good lean meat though, said Coombes, who had come to watch the unloading. Look at that rump, pretty good eh? You get all sort of beasts in here, he told Hardacre. Brown cows, black cows, black and white cows, or white like this'un, but they're all the same inside, good English beef if the rump's as bulky as that beast's. I wouldn't mind a cut of that haunch myself.

Stepping into Kernan's shoes had not been easy, but Inspector Emma Gimmer was beginning to find her feet. Transferred to Otteridge from Pigglingford at Lambert's request, she was quick to sort the sheep from the goats in her new station, and dividing the latter into nannies and billies, was soon able to assign the right people to the right tasks. She might need to snap at their heels like a collie to keep them in order, but when the black sheep was not with the flock, the rogue rams did not stray so far, and she could separate the older, more recalcitrant sheep from the impressionable younger tups, and make the more woolly-headed constables behave better with the ewes and hoggs.

Coming from a farming background herself, Inspector Gimmer was quick to adjust to her new Loamshire patch, and setting aside objections from the rogue rams, announced a new plan for managing it. She would head a new operational unit reporting direct to the Chief Constable, and including DCs Hunter, Twinter and Theave, Sergeant Cobb and DS Daglock. Cora Theave had worked with her at Pigglingford, where their match of hair to name had amused Sergeant Sheeder: the unshorn Gimmer with her long, shoulder-length brown hair penned in a room with the close-cropped Theave, who – as a shearling – should have been the older ewe.

In the light of new evidence, the Bernard Tench case would be reopened, and she wanted immediate reports on the deaths of Michael Brock and Inspector Kernan and on the disappearance of PC Clegg along with the unmarked car whose insurance and road tax had now expired.

When news of the second body had been brought to Inspector Gimmer, she was unimpressed.

– This body, she said, you say these workmen found it buried behind St Belial's?

– That's right, said DC Cora Theave. They were laying a new drain through the churchyard.

– I don't mean to sound dim, but isn't that where people normally bury their dead in Loamshire? Legitimately, I mean?

– Not on the north side of a church, said Theave.

– Come again?

– North is the devil's side, Theave explained. That may sound like some arcane superstition, but it's a belief which has affected the boundaries of churches, and not just in Loamshire. Usually the north wall goes right up to the church so that there's no burial ground at all on the north side. But Belial's was built over a much earlier Pre-Christian site which folk say had satanic associations, and while the land north of the church has never been used for burials, it's enclosed by the boundary wall.

– So who uses it?

– Dogs, mostly.

– Sounds like a load of hogwash to me, said Gimmer. You really believe all that stuff about satanic rites?

– Dealchurch does have its dark past. The name is supposed to link it with Devil's Bridge, which is nearby. Records from the Middle Ages have it spelled Deilchurch...from devil's church. Herne filled me in on the background.

– Herne?

– Friend of Kernan's, said Theave. Bit of an amateur detective if you ask me, but the locals swear by his knowledge. Vicar didn't say much, must have been buried on the wrong side by mistake, was all he said. Don't think he liked us being there, kept muttering about how we ought to be out catching criminals instead of investigating 200-year-old skeletons buried where they should be, in graveyards. Wasn't very helpful.

– He does have a point, which I'm sure the superintendent would be keen to affirm.

– But he said he didn't know who it could be – there was no headstone – yet he knew its age.

– Another double centurion?

– Yes, Polly's confirmed it. She's very excited. And she says from the age of the bone this man was murdered around the same time as the chap in the forest.

– Murdered?

– There's a round hole in the middle of his temple. Polly says he's shorter and older than the other man. But what's getting her really excited is that the forest man was wearing clothes which were much too short for him, whereas the church man's are too big. She's laid them out together in the morgue, and their clothes would be a nigh on perfect fit for each other.

– So the two corpses somehow swapped clothes underground?

The cows were pressed up against each other in the stunning pen, channelled towards the crush where Frank Fisher was brandishing a syringe as ugly-looking as his red-flushed porcine face. The white cow was in front, the stray which the farmer hadn't known what to do with, and which had been acting strangely ever since. Sweeny's black herd with the one white cow in Alcock's Field had mirrored the flock of mule ewes in the lower pasture, that bunch of white gimmers with the one black theave. The slaughtermen watched the red-eared heifer as she was urged through the gate.

– This is the bit I always dread, said one of the cows. The anticipation is almost as bad as the slaughter itself. I used to think the dentist was bad, but at least the injection cut out the pain. You never had pain like this as humans.

– Not unless you were killed on the electric chair, said a cow with a crumpled horn.*

– This is the price you pay for staying a cow, the first cow said. You have to put up with this barbarity at the end. Still, it's nothing when you're used to it, as the eels said when they were being skinned alive. At least we get our years of passive meditation. They think we're stupid, but most of the time our minds are off elsewhere.

– Until they do this to you, said a third cow. They're like a bunch of Nazis, the way they go on, so self-righteous about it all. If they didn't *breed* us, there wouldn't be any cows, that's what they say. Just because they've got the upper hand now.

– Who does not kill hogs will not get black puddings, said the cow with the crumpled horn, though he that never ate flesh thinks a pudding a dainty.

– When the devil is a hog, the first cow responded, you shall eat bacon.

– When the devil's a cow you shall eat beef, and then we shall as good eat the devil as the broth he is boiled in.

The white heifer lurched forward, Frank Fisher smacking her rump to urge her out of the crush. Her flailing hoof caught the side of the gate, the metal singing. The slaughterman jumped back, screwing up his little piggy eyes. He gave vent to a colourful oath, imploring help from the son of God.

– But they can't help being stupid, offered the first cow, thinking themselves so superior when it's the animals they kill who have kept their spirituality while they've lost theirs, or most of them have. And some of those who haven't will become cows.

– But then they'll get treated like this, said the cow with the crumpled horn, indicating the white heifer, who was about to be stunned. And they get eaten by the next generation of humans.

– So a human could eat his own grandmother and not realise? asked the third cow.

* *This is the cow with the crumpled horn, that tossed the dog, that worried the cat, that killed the rat, that ate the malt that lay in the house that Jack built.*

– That's right, the first answered. How many times have you died then?

– How am I supposed to know?

– That means only once as a cow then, either that or you're just out of limbo, said the first cow, who had been to all the seven circles. You don't know the score when you're born, but unlike humans, cows can remember their past lives. This is my twentieth cow life. I go back a long way. But I've never ceased to wonder at the stupidity of the humans.

The white heifer looked up from the stall at the man holding the stun gun over her head. So this was the end then. There was no escape now. Kernan recognised Joe Hartley, whose grandfather he had seen butchered.

– Do you know these men? asked the Morrigan.

– Yes, said Kernan, and their families. This man's grandfather was at Arras, he died in No Man's Land, his leg blown off. And Gingell over there, his grandad and most of his mates were slaughtered in another raid, he lost both his legs and died within minutes.

Joe Hartley pressed down and pulled the trigger. *Zzzzzzzzzzt.* The heifer dropped to the deck, like a great sack of potatoes, a red round stigma in the white hair above her eyes. Then she was hoisted up in a sling, and the upside-down body lifted over to have its throat cut by Pete Gingell.

– Can you *feel* that? cried the Morrigan indignantly. This is barbaric!

– Of *course* I can, said Kernan, trying to stifle his anger.

– They never killed the cattle like this in Ireland. I will make them suffer for this!

– But you must forgive these men, they don't know what they're doing. They think we're unconscious, not just paralysed.

– How do they work that one out? Whose devilish invention was this gun of theirs?

Pete Gingell raised his knife, and sank it into the heifer's jugular vein. He stood back to let the beast's blood spout forth.

– This is even *worse*! And we can do nothing about it, we just have to let them do it to us. Oh I wish I'd never come back, I've never felt such *pain*. That I, the Morrigan, should be subjected to this!

– Not very nice is it, chipped in the first of the black cows, who was next to be sticked. Still, I wouldn't like to be a chicken, even though they get to die more quickly. Not only do they have their throats cut while fully conscious, but many are still alive when they're plunged into the scalding tanks. You know, humans often start off as the beasts they later kill. That's what makes them such perverse creatures.

– They torture each other too, said the next cow. Can you beat that? The voltage they've just used to stun us is the same as they use on fellow humans in their torture chambers.

– How do you know? asked the cow with the crumpled horn.

– One of their boffins figured it out.

– That's right, Kernan explained. It was a scientist called Harold Hillman from the Unity laboratory of Applied Neurobiology in Guildford. He studied torture, resuscitation and death for thirty-five years, and exposed the lie that electric stunning always caused unconsciousness. Survivors of torture from South America, the Middle East and China all told him that the pain increases with the voltage, and they did not immediately fall unconscious.

– But because stunned animals don't react to light – that's the test they use – they think we're unconscious when we're only paralysed, the second cow added.

– So if they know all this, why do they still slaughter animals in such a brutal way? asked the Morrigan.

– They don't believe the evidence, said Kernan.

– Or maybe they enjoy it, said the first cow. And died.

– They're just brutes, said the cow with the crumpled horn. And died.

– Worse than any animals, said the third cow. And died.

Released from the their carcasses, the three cow souls could not suppress their curiosity when Kernan and the Morrigan came up to join them.

– We thought there was something odd about your white heifer, said the first cow soul.

– So you had two souls in there, said the second. How did you manage that? Who are you?

– And who was *that*? enquired the third cow soul, as the Morrigan was gone in a black flash of darkness.

– But you're not really dead are you? said the first cow. I can tell. That wasn't your body. You're still in limbo.

– I'm Inspector Kernan of Loamshire Police, and if you don't mind, I'd like to ask you a few questions.

– Is it about the cattle disease?

Who'll be chief mourner?
I, said the Dove,
I mourn for my love,
I'll be chief mourner.

Herne held them back, the two slaughtermen, Pete Gingell and Joe Hartley, both drunk and pungent as skunks. The more they tried to barge past him, pressing their bull-like shoulders against his frail, stick-like figure, the more immovable he became in the small doorway, resolute as Horatio holding the bridge.

– It doesn't matter that it's Kernan's dog, Gingell was saying. You should know the form, Herne, you of all people.

Diana sat in the corner of the curtained room, behind the coffin, her arms wrapped around the whimpering animal, saying its name, *Bella, Bella*, while Herne held the door.

– That's right, said Hartley, who had come with his workmate without knowing why to pay his respects to the policeman who had arrested him several times for drunkenness, and now found himself pissed as a newt in the inspector's house, laying down the lore.

– *If a dog or cat jumps onto or over the body*, cried Gingell for the third time, *it must be killed at once to avert even worse luck to come.*

– And you'd kill a defenceless dog, would you? said Herne. Like you kill all those other helpless beasts, for money, most of which you spend on your own dog, that wiry lurcher. And would you kill Ginger then, and eat him, like you eat the pigs, cows and sheep you slaughter? What's the difference? They're all animals with souls as bright as your dog's and this dog's, brighter than yours. They all have as much right to life as this Newfoundland bitch, and as much right to life as your lurcher...

Pete Gingell dropped to the floor, like a sack of potatoes, as if he'd been felled by a blow from behind. Joe Hartley sank down and turned to help him, crouching as if avoiding danger from the same direction, ducking his head instinctively.

Herne looked down at the two stocky men, one lying on the carpet blubbering, the other looking about him in bewilderment.

– Something's happened, he said. Bella wouldn't have jumped on the coffin without Kernan's permission. *Come on, get up you two, give me a hand.* Look, try lifting this. It's as light as a feather.

Pete Gingell stood up, swaying slightly, pushing Hartley to one side. Then he was suddenly upright, clear-headed. He looked at Herne, his heavy stupor lifting in a moment of understanding, as if the cold light of day had come into the dark room, visited him like that bird he could hear going *chee-aw chee-aw chuff* on the window-ledge outside.

– If there's no body in there, he said slowly, the dog's in the clear.

– And the luck is on *our* side, said Herne.

Diana looked blankly at the coffin, thinking, no, that was right, he wouldn't be there. Not even his body. That would have gone too. And Bella knew that, she was telling us. They didn't even need to look inside. It had to be empty. It had been All Souls' Day on the 2nd. She'd read his card then, warning that animals had to be kept out of the presence of the dead; and she had kept the door to the room shut, but Bella had slipped past her when she went to open the front door to the two slaughtermen. It was all unfolding now. All would become clear. She just had to read the clues, to listen, to watch; to see and hear with Kernan's eyes and ears; to be aware, and wary.

– You're pretty sure about this then, said Hartley, who had also stood up. And was no longer drunk. But knew then why they had come.

Herne was speaking to Cobb on the phone. That's right, Sergeant, he was saying, the body has disappeared.

Joe Hartley motioned Diana to follow him to the hall, where he had hung up his greatcoat on arrival like a dead beast waiting to be sticked.

– I think you've been looking for this, he said, pulling a large cloth-wrapped object from his pocket, and handing it to her.

Who'll carry the coffin?
I, said the Kite,
If it's not through the night,
I'll carry the coffin.

Goodman had pissed on a nettle. He glared through his smoke-palled office at a trembling Malcolm Oxter.

– At least she's dropped the body in the forest, said the sergeant, only to be contradicted by a memorandum Goodman screwed into a tight ball and threw at him across the room, hitting him in the face.

– Read that! Goodman hissed. They've found another body. Case re-opened.

The paper projectile was flung with such force that it split his cheek open. When the sergeant was later treated for the injury in the Royal Loamshire Infirmary, he needed nine stitches to close the wound.

On the first of March
The crows begin to search;
By the first of April,
They are sitting still;
By the first of May
They've flown away;
Crowping greedy back again
With October's wind and rain.

CHAPTER TWENTY-TWO

At the Going Down of the Sun

MARTINMAS: NOVEMBER 11TH

A single crow is unlucky, yet two foretell a wedding and three a birth. If several crows flutter around a man's head, he is marked for death; and if all the crows suddenly forsake a wood, disaster will follow.

At the eleventh hour of the eleventh day of the eleventh month, Captain Nicholas sat in his dugout, sipping tea from an enamel mug, aware that in exactly one year, his task would be finished. But left unfinished. Yet successful all the same, especially now Kernan was dead. He hadn't even needed to shoot him. The whizz-bang had done for him.

This was an inbetween time. Now he had no men left, he awaited orders for a transfer.

Then a shadow fell across his desk. A haggard man stood in front of him. He hadn't heard him appear.

– *Don't you know to knock first, soldier*? he demanded.

– There was nothing to knock, sir. Just the tarpaulin.

The fellow was a sight for sore eyes, obviously been in the wars. He looked as though he'd make a crow a pudding. His skin was so weathered it was sallow, almost green, his hair straggly like a ravaged bird's nest. His face and hands were scarred and blistered. He thought he'd seen him somewhere before. There was something about this strange cove which was strangely familiar, but he couldn't put his finger on it. The soldier's appearance worried him, like guilt, or how he thought guilt must feel. His deep eyes, his cheekbones, his wingnut ears all reminded him of someone, but no one person. The man had a chopped-up look to him, almost as though someone had invented him, made him up like one of those identikit pictures the police would be using in a few years. He had that kind of impossible appearance, as if he shouldn't exist.

– What is it then, man? he snapped.

– Reporting for duty, sir.

– Who the hell are you? I have no men now.

– You do sir. I'm Herne. The last of the 4th Loamshires. I'm all that's left of them.

This was the same crossroads where Herne had appeared from the fog like a ghost, and there, across the hedge, was the mound where Kernan had died. Or been taken, something told her. There must be some clues here, Diana thought. Kernan wouldn't just have gone like that, he'd have left some lead for her to follow.

The investigation had come to a dead end. Ballistics had confirmed that the small hole in Tench's skull had been made by Joe Hartley's stun gun, but they could throw no light on who might have pulled the trigger, except that the killer had used Lady Olivia Prurigeaux's panties to wipe the handle afterwards, and had also used 1881 aftershave on the day of the murder. That was as far as they'd got. Gimmer was impatient for results; she wanted more signs of progress to keep Goodman at bay. Lambert wanted some link established between all the murders and disappearances. Diana was sure there *was* a link. There must be. What *did* they have in common?

– I don't know why she swallowed the fly. Perhaps she'll die.

What was that? A voice, but no, there was no one there, there was no voice.

– She swallowed the cow to catch the goat...just opened her throat, and swallowed the goat...

– I don't believe I'm hearing this, she said aloud, to no one.

She looked down then, hearing a rustle in the leaves strewn along the grass verge. A tiny grey fieldmouse was standing at her feet, looking up at her. It wasn't talking, not even squeaking as she felt a mouse should, but she took in what it was telling her.

– *I know an old woman who swallowed a horse. She's dead, of course!*

She remembered her mother singing that song to her as a child, and began singing it herself, trying to remember all the verses, the succession of different animals swallowed, from the fly to the horse. She counted out the animals on her fingers, saying their names in turn: fly, spider, bird, cat, dog, goat, cow, horse. One animal eating another animal. But the chain began with the human, the woman swallowing the fly by mistake, but the other swallowing was intentional, to correct the earlier mistake. Eating the chain of animals hadn't worked, it had backfired on her. The cat had eaten her count. There was that other story too, the Irish one which Brigid had told her, about Étain the wife of Midir who became a fly and was swallowed by Etar's wife, who gave birth to a new Étain.

And hadn't *she* swallowed a fly too, when had that happened? She began to feel there was a connection with her own fly. But this was all getting a bit far-fetched. *All* this couldn't be relevant, could it? Unless, *unless*... She remembered what Kernan had said about the earth, how everything connected. But why couldn't she see the whole picture? What was she missing?

The mouse didn't appear to be saying anything else, it just peered up at her, listening as she ran through the ditty herself, as if to give her time for its meaning to sink in. She remembered Kernan's stories of mice in fairytales and spiders in African stories, who were often spirit helpers, creatures of the threshold; how kindness done to an animal would not go unrewarded. Remember Androcles and the lion, he had said.

> Beware of the dog. Beware of Shuck.
> Beware the black dog who brings ill luck.

What was that? The mouse was trying to tell her something about dogs now. Dogs were in the song too, so where did they fit into the picture? She found herself remembering another song her mother used to sing.

The little black dog ran round the house,
And set the bull a-roaring,
And drove the monkey in the boat,
Who set the oars a-rowing,
And scared the cock upon the rock,
Who cracked his throat with crowing.

Another chain of animals, she realised, another chain of cause and effect, one thing leading to something else.

She sang the song again, emphasising the names of the animals, *dog, bull, monkey, cock*, but could make no sense of the sequence. Perhaps there was none, perhaps she was deluded. Who would believe it, what would Gimmer think if she could hear her now, warbling these silly songs, trying to emulate Kernan's methods of free association with animals in some way, in her futile attempt either to find him if he wasn't really dead or to find out what his death meant? *Warble.* Strange word. She'd never usually use that word, *warble,* so was that significant too? *Warble warble warble*, she burbled. Ah, she thought, warble fly. The chain led back to Bernard Tench, his treatment of cattle for warble fly.

Looking to the mouse for further hints, she realised that the creature had gone. Another voice was beckoning her now, from a black car parked beside the road. She had not heard it pull up.

– *Get inside*, it barked, flourishing an open door for her to enter. She stood still, frozen to the spot, paralysed, as if she had entered some kind of limbo in which she could no longer move or make decisions of her own. She had to obey this voice and shuffled forward, staring into the dark depths of the car, where she saw a gun glinting in the paw of the thick-set person who had called to her.

– *Get inside*, the creature snapped at her.

In the fading light of the November afternoon, Long Wood seemed a timeless place, the English countryside wearing its autumn coat of reds, golds and browns which hadn't changed for centuries. Phil Hart remembered his grandad saying how he'd stood in this same clearing at Martinmas, breathing in the smells of Long Wood, when he'd decided to volunteer in 1916. Within a month he was hitching up supply wagons in knee-deep mud on the Somme, seeing his horses and mates blown into chunks of meat, wishing he was back here; still managed to set traps with his one good arm when he came back, but couldn't fire a gun. Never understood all that killing, his grandad, the Tommies and Jerries bombing and shooting each other across this patch called No Man's Land, which seemed to sum it all up, the English who was all related to the Saxon lads across the way, so Herne said, fighting for a King who was German against the army of his cousin Kaiser Bill; but it was nothing to do with them personally, war was all politics and generals, he used to say. Still the same now. Politicians fuck everything up for everyone else.

The gamekeeper's contempt had been reinforced by the bigwigs he'd met on the shoots. He was never really part of these conversations, he was just there in the background, reloading guns, fetching and carrying, and Maw's fat cat mates rabbited on as if he didn't exist or have opinions of his own; when they did acknowledge his presence, it was to ask him to agree with some shit they were coming out with (which he'd say he hadn't been following), or for reassurance that when he nodded as if in agreement, this meant that what they were doing had the support of those they called The People. It was all bollocks, he thought, but what those bastards did still ended up hurting people, it affected their lives, like with BSE, the way that ruined folk round here.

Plodging through the mud he mulled over the changes which had transformed his daily rounds. The diseased Dutch elms had finally all been felled, creating new clearings where the bracken was taking over, giving more cover for the birds. But he viewed the oaks with a sense of foreboding, following the spread of the stipply brown fungus on their jigsaw leaves. He had his work cut out now, and even had to go out nights as well, lamping for foxes, who were on the increase and killing too many pheasants. Yet although his heart would miss a beat when he found a break in the fence a fox had scrabbled through, he still couldn't help but admire Reynard for a cunning he'd call deviousness in humans. It was the lack of any evil intent on the part of the foxes that made him want to track and shoot the animals himself, not leave them to provide sport for Maw and his crew. It was unpleasant, but it had to be done, or there'd be no birds left for those arseholes to shoot, and he'd be out of a job.

He looked up at the high branches. Their silence was unsettling. For the first time in living memory the crows hadn't returned to Long Wood in October. He used to curse their din, but now he missed them; it was something else that had changed, which wasn't right. The frenzied cawing had often continued for days, encouraging the locals' belief that the birds were either witches' familiars or witches themselves. There were said to be a hundred crows in the hundred acre upper wood.

It was so quiet now he could hear a deer foraging in the brushwood in the lower clearing. He waited, stood still, following its progress till he spotted a movement, branches turning into antlers which jerked suddenly away, startled by some danger, the sound of undergrowth being trampled by heavier feet. Glancing up, Hart saw two figures approaching, about two hundred yards away. He recognised the high-stepping gait of the shorter of the two men, and decided to avoid an awkward meeting with his employer, slipping away as soundlessly as the roe buck.

Morton Maw was lamenting the loss of his crows. The bickering denizens of the elms and high oaks had been renowned throughout all Loamshire for the almost permanent cackle they set up in Long Wood, a cacophony that would be picked up by the occupants of one tree to sample and rework into their own scratch birdsong before being tossed like a gobbet to their neighbours, who'd treat it as grossly as they would a rabbit's corpse.

– Hart says it's a sign of disaster, the crows all gone, Morton Maw reflected, but disaster for who, us or them?

– Kernan's gone, said Goodman, with an air of forced cheerfulness. Tench and Brock are out of the way, so it could be them.

– Unless it's a war of attrition, when both sides cop it just as bad, said Maw. Like the first war, if the old man was right. Rain undid them. Double the average rainfall in one month. Bad planning, never underestimate the power of the old weather. The English should have known that, but then Lloyd George put that Frog in charge. Didn't support our own man. Should have given Haig his head.

– Yes, said Goodman ruefully, you wear each other down till there's no one left on either side. First Prurigeaux dead, then Saveloy and Candida. Tucker out of the game now. All in a year.

– Own goals though, said Maw. Maurice was his own worst enemy. Too many sausages.

– And Peter certainly bit off more than he could chew.

– Candida had cancer: self-inflicted wound.

– But Tucker's bankruptcy, that's a clear hit. He may have had it coming, but someone did something to push him over.

– Could still be helpful though? said Morton Maw quizzically. Contacts and all that. Must have his fingers in a few pies still.

– That was his trouble, said Goodman, too many pies, overreached himself and swallowed a spider. Apparently his appendix burst, it was full of lead shot.

– He ate the calf in the cow's belly, observed Maw. Swallowed a fly too, always driving his turkeys to market, any hour of the day. You can't have a clear head for figures if it's full of bees. Bees and business don't mix.

– He's nothing without his money, said Goodman scornfully, and wasn't worth a sheep's brain with it.

– He brought haddock to paddock, till the codshead wasn't worth a haddock.

– Not worth three skips of a louse, Goodman gloated. He doesn't exist now, he's nothing. No one wants to know the cunt. That Gizzard girl has dumped him too, somehow ended up with Featherwether Grange, which he put in her name as a tax dodge.

– The redhead with the tits? Smart filly, she knows a cat from a coney. Underestimated her. Bit like that Gimmer creature, too clever for her own good, but a tough old bird, a wolf in sheep's clothing. You haven't managed to get shot of her yet...

– Can't, said Goodman. Lambert's standing by her. Bloody women. They've got him now he's Hunter's poodle.

– And her up the duff too.

– It's a sorry flock where the ewe bears the bell, said Goodman morosely. They have me running round in circles, these mad cows.

– Can't talk to them, Maw growled. Swine, women and bees cannot be turned. Women are queer cattle, a law unto themselves. *Where there are women and geese, there wants no noise.*

– A woman's tongue wags like a lamb's tail, Goodman agreed.

Quietness is best, as the fox said when he bit the cock's head off.

– She's as quiet as a wasp in one's nose, that Gimmer woman. But what about the body count? Can't look good. Kernan disappears into thin air… Morton Maw waved his arms as if to demonstrate the mode of the inspector's spiriting away, causing Phil Hart to duck behind a clump of bushes, as if Maw's wild hands were his own. He had been tracking this brace of dodgy game from a parallel path.

– I know, Goodman was saying, I went to Lambert about that. She had the labs tied up for a week going over two skeletons that had been dead for nigh on two hundred years. Thought I'd get her then. Kettle even did a DNA match on them both, unauthorised of course.

– Are they all going barmy? She wouldn't get a match… Maw's face reddened, not so much with indignation as from indigestion and a failure to grasp what was outside his knowledge.

– But she *did*. Claims the one found in the churchyard was none other than our old friend O'Scrapie…

– I thought you said he went to *Germany*, said Maw, his tone emphasising his distaste for the place.

– But he came back, Goodman growled. Kettle says there's no doubt of that. Positive ID from prison records. Dental set identical. Exact match of DNA, the lot. The bones are two hundred years old, and decomposition is consistent with death taking place in 1830. But the two men are one and the same. So it's no longer just something for the historians to chew over, it's a murder enquiry. They're calling it a scientific breakthrough. We've made history in Loamshire. If they're not the same man, O'Scrapie was descended from himself.

– How do they make that out? Maw's face was flushed, as if he'd already had his afternoon tipple.

– Incontrovertible evidence. O'Scrapie was alive here now but also in 1830. This "Captain" O'Scrapie had children in Hampshire, who came looking for him after he disappeared. He had an inn, but someone torched it, so they settled in Loamfield. Their father was known as "Muttonchops", and the sons and grandsons sported the same kind of tash.

– I remember the old man telling me about a murder in Loamfield in his youth, offered Maw. Chief suspect was the village butcher, Paddy Muttonchops I think they called him. Never pinned anything on him.

– O'Scrapie's grandfather, or grandson, it turns out. All villains in that family, Goodman spat.

– And what about the other chappie, the one in the forest?

– Gimmer has an ID on him too. Daniel Alcock, a cobbler from Sussex. Bit of a trouble-maker, sort of rural Luddite, broke machines and so on.

– Commie eh?

– There are accounts in the *Chronicle* which show he disappeared around the same time, after wrecking machinery on your estate, at Long Wood Farm.

– I didn't know about this! Where was Jack Armstrong? cried Maw indignantly. He's a bit too trigger-happy with the old shotgun, you know. Blasts away at anyone he finds on the land. He peppered that Gingell chappie from the abbatoir when he caught him lamping with his lurcher, but blow me if the fellow didn't go after him and give him a jolly good hiding.

– This was 1830, Goodman pointed out. Jack Armstrong wasn't around then. But your lot were. The Honourable Martin Maw applied for the warrant.

– Old Martin, eh? There's a painting of him in the North Wing, you know, flanked by two of the fiercest looking hunting dogs you ever saw. We call them the Hounds of the Baskervilles in the family, you know. Poxy looking cove. Not sure I'd like to know him. So he shopped your man Alcock then?

– Then there's that superstition about the Devil's Nut-Bag, Goodman added, which they started calling Alcock's Arbour some time in the last century. Odd how Kernan copped it there...

– What's Gimmer saying about all this? asked Maw. Does she have a story on Alcock?

– Says they must have fallen out. They're on the run and they have some disagreement. O'Scrapie bumps off Alcock. He's been demobbed but he's still wearing his uniform from the war...

– The war?

– Against Napoleon, Goodman explained. You know, Battle of Waterloo, 1815...

– Yes of course. One of the Maws lost a leg in that caper.

– So he strips the body, and puts on Alcock's clothes. Wraps

Alcock in his own clothes, so when someone finds the grave they'll think it's O'Scrapie who's dead, not Alcock. Only someone catches up with him and he gets killed as well. Buries him in the churchyard, where no one will think of looking.

– Sounds plausible. Any suspects?

– Chief suspect is the Rector, the Reverend Nicholas, who put out a reward on the two men.

– Still, he's pretty safe. They won't be trying to arrest him, will they?

– I wouldn't put it anything past those two. Gimmer's trying to prove herself, while Larry the Lamb's on HRT these days. Throwing his puny weight around, and with Sirloin apparently egging him on, giving him support, he's got the bit between his teeth, he has the Police Authority eating out of his hand.

– He's like a bantam strutting round the farmyard, a crowing cock with no comb.

– And he thinks he's spiked our guns.

– Wants bringing down a peg or two, eh? Maw suggested, his voice darker for an instant. He touched Goodman's arm, as if hoping he would take a bait he could always deny offering, for he had said nothing of substance. Hearing a faint cracking sound, he looked to his right. Hart became a shadow.

– It's not so easy now, said Goodman, affecting a sigh of resignation. He had to do something soon, he thought. Something decisive, to turn the tables. Maw wasn't much help now, the pressure was getting to him; not only had he started to walk in that odd jerky fashion, disguising his high-stepping gait now as a way of negotiating the long wet grass, but he was tilting his head to one side, talking out of the side of his mouth like a gangster from the Cloudcuckooland he seemed to inhabit now. Maw's influence had weakened with Saveloy gone, and with Sirloin unpredictable, playing some kind of rogue game of his own.

– And whatever Sirloin's up to, he can't be trusted, said Maw in a low growl, as if reading his mind.

– He's as cunning as a dead pig but not half so honest, Goodman sneered.

– No, said Maw quickly, you underestimate him. His poacher turned gamekeeper act is a dangerous game.

– You may be right, Goodman sighed. It's an ill thing to see a fox lick a lamb.

– You don't like confrontation, do you Nick? Maw said, his low rasp not unlike James Cagney's, the resemblance to the Hollywood hood ending where the councillor's head almost touched his shoulders. I almost think you preferred it when Kernan was around. More your style, all that cat and mouse business.

– With Kernan you were never sure who was the cat and who the mouse, Goodman said with an air of weariness, but bristling like a cornered cat. It often changed from day to day. He even robbed me of the satisfaction of beating him at his own game. Dying in that field for no reason. No explanation of the death, open verdict. Then his body disappears like Jesus-Fucking-Christ…

Seemingly lost in his tale of frustration, Goodman looked blankly ahead, not registering Maw's evident unease at this blasphemy, as if the policeman were tempting fate like a crow in the gutter. The councillor shot an anxious glance down the empty avenue of spectral trees, silhouetted in the mist, making as if to cross himself. Hart melted into a tree.

– It's almost as if the wily fox is still out there, Goodman went on, pondering a slowly hatching plan of revenge. You know, trying to outsmart me. But you're right, sometimes I do wish the old dog was still here.

Inverness Corpse had changed hands eighteen times. They all went down to the wood, but few returned, the English, Irish, French, Welsh, Scots, Australians, New Zealanders, Canadians, all crawled through the mud and died with Saxons, Austrians, Bavarians, Rhinelanders and Prussians amongst the blackened sticks of trees. Now it was behind the line; and some of the mud-caked stumps nudging the shellholes of foul water, the bilge-filled ditches, inky wheeltracks and shattered duckboards, had never been wood, but had been left as detritus by either army, whether from man or mule not even the crows could tell. As friend and foe had turned into the same slime-black creatures slithering on their bellies, mudskippers grasping at cloth and metal, with only their cries, English or German, to tell them apart till their tongues were stilled, so the wood they had bombarded from east and west, north and south, became the one pulverised wasteland, flat and featureless but for the same repeated heaps and craters, the tar-black channels leading nowhere, all punctuated by rough makeshift posts which had once been trees.

Into this bleak black landscape, the birds came to feed, scavenging for shreds of any kind of putrid carrion, a hundred or more black-winged harbingers starved of food or means of prophecy, for there was no one there alive to witness their behaviour, to draw meaning from anything or any creature in that place, and if the largest of the hooded crows had been Badbh herself, she would have gone unrecognised, for all that she feasted on death and misfortune. Some of the dead of both sides would have called these the Devil's birds, or hags and monsters, who came in place of the promised reinforcements, or were the new troops themselves posted from another front; others would have said their coming foretold even more rain, or even that three of the crows seen together foretold good luck to come. But these exhausted birds were unaware of any point to their task, apart from survival, and were almost subdued in their cawing and croaking. As it grew dark, their almost invisible hopping and pecking was the only movement in that cold bitumen-black place, which seemed to draw them into itself, as if its shroud of night and earth were their chosen disguise.

One bird only amongst the hundred did not eat. It wandered as if without hope, seemingly lost, listless, dragging its blue-black wings, trying the ground with its red legs before taking off again; then landing a few yards off, its head swivelling, eyes looking, searching, hunting, the only bird whose call might be an attempt at song. It tried its voice, faintly at first. *Chee-aw,* it managed. *Chee-aw, chee-aw.* No more, for now then. The rest was silence.

CHAPTER TWENTY-THREE

A Cat's Chance in Hell

MIDWINTER NIGHT, ARTHUR'S BIRTHDAY: DECEMBER 21ST

Stepping in dogshit will bring you luck, but only if you do it by accident, and with your left foot. If you do it on purpose to attract good luck, you are very stupid because luck doesn't work that way, and you will just end up with a foul mess of dog poo on your shoe, or worse, between your toes if you've done this with bare feet.

Yawning as she straightened her arms out, Diana felt like a lobster with heavy outstretched claws. She must have been standing for hours, yet the queue never seemed to grow any shorter. The faces of the other shoppers became more fretful as the waiting continued. Hadn't it been eleven the last time she'd looked at the clock? It must have stopped then.

These Gateway checkout girls were all Anubians, she noticed. One terrierhead was yapping at the man ahead of her in a rather peremptory fashion. It still felt strange to her, being served in a shop by someone with a dog's head. Usually it was the males you came across, like the ruffians who worked at the plant, and the lugubrious setters at CC&C; these were the first doghead bitches she'd seen. There were more Anubians behind the glass of the supervisor's office, an Irish wolfhound, a black labrador and a German shepherd, who looked vaguely familiar. The whole place seemed to be run by the dogfolk.

Diana was starting to feel hungry, and decided to break into a packet of biscuits. She still felt guilty when she did this, remembering how as a child she would eat some fruit or a packet of crisps from the trolley as she went round the supermarket with her mother, who never noticed, and by the time they reached the checkout she'd screwed up and thrown away the packet. Her fingers pulled at the end of the *Hobnobs* wrapper now, and catching sight of the slogan down the side, ONE NIBBLE AND YOU'RE NOBBLED, she leapt backwards in shock.

– What was that? she exclaimed.

– You must be new here, said the man behind her. You can't eat the food you know, not till you've been through the checkout. If you try anything, you get an electric shock. It's the same with the forms; if you do them wrong, you get an even bigger shock.

– The forms? Diana asked.

– You don't know? You can't have been in the queue for long then. Haven't you filled one in yet?

– I've not been given a form.

– They'll give you one at the checkout then and send you to the back of the queue.

– But why can't I have one now?

– Because you're still in the queue.

– How long will it take before I get one?

– There is no how long here. You just wait.

– And what's this form then?

– It's your inventory of course. The list of your sins.

– My sins? What about the food I've bought?

– Oh, you won't be given that. Not the first time, not that it would do you any good. We're all hungry here. We're starving.

– But that's awful, said Diana.

– That's why we go along with it all. We're all too weak to argue.

– You know, I might be able to help you, if you help me…

– There's nothing you can do about it. You just have to wait in the queue.

– But if you told me how to answer the form, I'd be able to

get through more quickly, and then I could come back and give you some of my food.

– You won't get back, not across the chain.

– You can't cross the chain, said the woman in front. Oh no, you'd never get past the chain.

– And even when you get outside, the man added, and you put your shopping in the back of your car...

– So there's an *outside*, is there? asked Diana, suddenly alert.

– But it's a car park, said the woman. The whole outside is a car park. You drive up and down the lines of cars, following the exit signs, but there is no way out; you just keep ending up where you started.

– And then you decide to stay in your car, said the hungry man, and eat some of the food you've put in the boot. But when you get out and open it...

– The boot's empty, said the woman. And the shopping's all gone.

– So you have to come back here to buy some more.

– And they give you another form to fill out.

– And you never quite remember how you completed the last one.

Ahead of her she saw a dapper-looking old gent with a tossed-back mane of grey hair. His yellow cravat was like Maurice Saveloy's. Raising her head slightly to get a better view, she saw that his trolley was filled with packets of sausages. Plucking up courage, she called out.

– Sir, sir! she said. He didn't turn round. She tried again. *Sir, sir*, Chief Constable! Then more loudly: *Is that you, sir?*

This time he did turn.

– No one's called me that in ages, he said, his eyes alight, changing from a dulled glaze to the familiar boyish glint of old. Who is that? DC Hunter isn't it, oh yes. It *is* you. Don't you realise we're all the same here, no one's meant to have precedence over anyone else? We're all in the queue. His demeanour had been resigned, but now his hunched shoulders seemed to shake themselves free; he was the young steed again, stamping the ground with impatient hooves. You're a bit young to be here, he said. What happened to you?

– I'm not sure. I just found myself here.

– Did that *raassscal* Goodman have you bumped off then? Is that it?

Diana was surprised, registering the flip he gave to the word, the trilled *r*, the extended *aasss* in the middle, suggesting both disapproval and ridicule of the fearful superintendent's sibilant anger. She said nothing, but showed by her open gaze that he should continue.

– I never should have gone along with him, you know. A gradual decline, that's what it was. He took advantage of me, you know, abused his position. I should have put a stop to it, but I was as devious as him in many ways. He knew the mind of his prey, so he knew how to exploit me. You get a lot of time to think out your mistakes here.

There was a difference in him, she could tell. On first acquaintance, Maurice Saveloy would come across as sincere and trustworthy. He must have been handsome in his youth too, not quite Sean Connery exactly, more Leslie Phillips perhaps; and he might have swept many women off their feet were it not for his malodorous breath, which tended to make them back away, as she herself had done when cornered by him. But now the reeking breath had gone, she realised; in fact, there were no smells at all in this supermarket, even the floors were so clean there wasn't even a hint of flower-scented disinfectant.

– What is this place? she asked.

– It's the Gateway of course. Haven't you filled in the form?

– No, I've not been given one.

– Not given a form. That's rather odd. I should ask for one if I were you.

– But that man says I can't leave the queue.

– That's right, said Saveloy, if you leave the queue, you get an electric shock. The floor's wired up. I tried bunging a few sausages on it one time, to see if I could get them to fry, but they wouldn't cook. It was me who got fried. Didn't try that again...

– How does this form work then? If you could tell me that, it might help me.

– Easy really, Saveloy explained, there's a list of a hundred sins, divided up into mortal and venal, and you have to tick in the boxes against all those you committed.

– What happens if you miss one out?

– The checkout bitch feeds in your identity dogtag and then runs her barcode gun over your list. If you've missed out any sins, the red light flashes and you get an electric shock and have to go the back of the queue. And you can't take out any food until all your sins have been checked through.

– So why not tick the lot? Diana asked.

– Same happens if you lie in any way, he told her. Eventually you remember exactly which sins you committed and which you didn't out of the hundred. Then you have to complete a box marked OTHER SINS. You have to think about what else you've done which doesn't fit into the main categories. It's like being charged with an offence: what else should the court take into account in deciding your sentence?

– And there's enough room in this box is there?

– No, but the form says: *You may continue overleaf.* And they key in these extra sins, and say *Is there anything else*? Then if you've still missed out any other sins they know you've committed, the red light flashes, you get zapped and have to take another form and go to the back of the queue again. It's a bit hard for me, I tended to believe my own lies, so sometimes I can't remember if I really did commit a particular sin, or I just thought I had; or thought I ought to have done, so started believing I had done it when I hadn't. I'm still filling in the bit over the page. Soon I'll be onto the next stage, which is called *You may continue on a second sheet.*

– What about that queue over there? asked Diana. How is it they're going through so quickly?

– Oh, they're the Catholics, said Saveloy. They have this express queue called SEVEN SINS OR LESS for Catholics who've been recently absolved. They just have to confess to more recent sins, plus those they kept from the priest. So it's quicker for them.

– It seems like a long queue, even though it's quicker.

– There are lots of Catholics here. It's because they all believe in Gateway, whereas the rest of us are sceptical. We know we're here, but we still have ambiguous feelings about the place. We may be wrong, but some of us think we'll get out eventually, once our sins have been wiped from our slates, so to speak, whereas Catholics believe they'll be here for all eternity, because they think they deserve it. We feel a bit hard done by, especially the English.

– I can see why you must think that. Who's that man over there, going into the supervisor's office where the three dogs are?

– That's the Regulator, he's the boss. And those aren't three dogs but one, a three-headed dog called Cerberus...

So that was it, thought Diana. That was how she'd been brought here.

– Cerberus is the manager, you might say. He keeps the Anubians in order. Makes sure they don't get lenient with anyone. They all have to be Jobsworths, the dogs. You try to say, oh why don't you correct that box for me, it was just a slip of the pen, and what you get is *Sorry, more than my job's worth...* But it's very clever, the way they've always kept the doghead males and females apart; that way they can control them, keep the bitches servile and the dogs vicious.

– Didn't Goodman try to set up a doghead security squad? asked Diana, remembering Kernan's opposition to Force K9.

– That's right, said Saveloy, but I had it disbanded. Put my foot down for once. Goodman made sure they were taught proper discipline, but you could see they were straining at the leash in the training, and he seemed to be encouraging that. Said people needed to be afraid of them, even though they wouldn't bite, it was the threat that counted. I wasn't so sure. The dogheads seemed to view Goodman as their employer, not the police; and they were most brusque with me. They say he who sleeps with dogs must rise up with fleas, but it seemed to me that the fleas were jumping the other way. What's that other saying? *The dog that is idle barks at his fleas, but he that is hunting feels them not*. That's Goodman all over... Maurice Saveloy was starting to ramble.

Diana stared at the man behind the glass. He was tall, dressed in a smart business suit with sleeked-back black hair, reminding her of Michael Douglas's Gordon Gecko in *Wall Street*. In Gecko's world greed was a virtue, not a sin. It was an essential part of the modern capitalist economy. But he created a hell for others which became his own hell. She wondered if the people here created this Gateway place themselves. Once they had fire and brimstone, and demons with forked tails prodding the damned with red-hot pitchforks, a hell invented by the church to raise money for the priests. You prayed and paid for the souls in Purgatory. This new purgatory probably existed in a kind of cyberspace powered by the collective guilt of all the damned. An endless supermarket where you queued for all eternity was probably something modern man would conceive of as the worst kind of hell.

The slogans seemed to confirm this intepretation. BETTER THE DEVIL YOU KNOW declared one banner. Another – directed no doubt at the English in particular – said THANK YOU FOR NOT WAILING.

But unlike the rest, she wasn't dead. She hadn't been given a form, after all, but was still being held in their place of limbo. Unless that was all part of it: that she really was dead, which meant she had an even longer wait than the others.

The queue hadn't moved, and it was still eleven o'clock. The man at the front was now arguing back, and the terrier had pressed a bell for assistance.

– This man wanted cashback, she growled.

A security officer had come to her assistance, a weasel-faced man wearing a blue outfit obviously designed to resemble a police constable's uniform.

How long had she been in this place? It seemed like weeks now. That day she'd met the mouse, when was that? The day after Guy Fawkes. She remembered Kernan's card for St Leonard's Day, something about ghostly black dogs haunting burial mounds whose appearance was ominous of death or disaster. A dog that howled on Christmas Eve had rabies and should be killed. Anyone the dog had nipped must eat some of the dog's hairs or a piece of its cooked liver.

Kernan would use that kind of knowledge, somehow, to escape. Black dogs haunting burial mounds. Where did that lead her?

Inspector Gimmer faced her accusers, straining to read their names on the long yellow and red triangular box-things in front of them. But each name-plate seemed just to say TOBLERONE.

Was that a kind of Swiss chocolate judge? she wondered. If so, why were the two men on either side of the hairy tobler in the middle not called TOBLERTWO and TOBLERTHREE? And if she bit one of their arms, would she find it was made of chocolate, with little chewy honeycomb granules inside their flesh?

The serious-looking yellow-bearded tobler coughed, announcing himself as Sir Peter Prurigeaux, chairman of the bench. His fellow magistrates were, on the left, Sir Harold Hockle, to whom he waved off-handedly, and on the right – to whom he crossed himself, left-handedly, as if to ward off evil – the Reverend Ebenezer Nicholas.

– Now if you're all sitting comfortably, said Sir Peter, we will begin. Inspector Gimmer, you are accused of neglect of duty, wasting police time and failure to solve some easy murder cases. Added to that, there is the more serious charge, one which may have to be taken up in a higher court, that of... your turn, Reverend...

– The heresy of Kernanism, said the bullet-headed Vicar of Dealchurch, touching his dog collar for emphasis. You have not only stepped into Kernan's shoes, you have become one of his followers. You espouse his ideals, you have no respect for the rule of law, you communicate with villains, you commune with animals, and you think you can investigate cases from different time periods...

– Objection, your honour! A horse had interrupted, banging its hoof like a gavel on the wooden table. It was a compact bay colt with a white splash from forehead to muzzle.

– Yes, Mr Shergar?

– The Reverend Nicholas himself is from a different time period...

– Objection overruled, all the bench are dead, so the matter of the Reverend being dead for over a century can be of no importance.

– But the late Reverend Nicholas is suspected of involvement in the murder of Daniel John Alcock in October 1830...

– So? What's your problem, Mr Shergar.

– My client is investigating that murder...

– How can she be? roared Sir Peter. That case is outside her jurisdiction...

– I'm also objecting to the presence on the bench of yourself and Sir Harold Hockle...

– This is really too much, said the Rector of St Belial's.

– As Chairman of Loamshire Water Board, the horse asserted, the late Sir Harold Hockle was in charge of a sewage treatment plant whose bacteria degraded alkylphenol polyethoxylates in household products originally manufactured by the Eurochimique company and released the effluent from this process into the River Otter, causing grievous bodily changes of sex in the dace population, this in turn resulting in the deaths of all the otters in the Otter.

– But there are no otters in the Otter, Mr Shergar. Objection overruled.

– Other poisonous substances released into the river resulted in the death of Muffy's husband Charlie. And if I may refresh your memory, your Honour, you as leader of Otteridge District Council signed the papers enforcing the eviction from his lawful home at Duckwidge Ditch of the same Charlie, and your employees enforced that order on his widow while she was attending his funeral...

– *Shame! shame!* bleated a flock of sheep in the public gallery.

– Order in the court! bellowed Sir Peter Prurigeaux. Clear all sheep from the court...No, not the prosecution, PC Hodge. Mr Merino is allowed to stay.

– Thank you, your Honour, said Mr Paul Merino, attorney-at-law in the State of New York, ducking his fine-woolled head in feigned obeisance.

– We also object to the participation in this case of my learned counsel, Mr Merino...

– ...who is representing the interests of the Crown, said Sir Peter Prurigeaux, clearly growing impatient. You should know, Mr Shergar, that following its recent privatisation, the work of the Crown Prosecution Service was put out to tender, and the contract awarded to Mr Merino's chambers.

– But Mr Merino also acts for several persons implicated in the cases being investigated by my client, Inspector Emma Gimmer.

– Objection overruled. Mr Merino acts for those others in a private capacity only. His private caseload has nothing to do with the business of this court.

– Members of the jury, you will ignore all of Mr Shergar's objections. He turned to the twelve dogs in the jury seats, who all nodded their heads gravely in agreement.

– Ignore ev'ryfing said by the 'orse, barked the dalmatian foreman, turning round to make sure the hounds in the back row had understood the direction.

– The Clerk will strike from the record everything back to the Reverend's bit about Kernanism. None of the rest was said.

– Objection, your honour! A horse had interrupted, banging its hoof like a gavel on the wooden table. It was a compact bay colt with a white splash from forehead to muzzle.

– Yes, Mr Shergar?

– This is a magistrate's court, and yet a jury has been sworn in…

– You're right, Mr Shergar. Objection sustained. I should have spotted that. Who put those dogs in there? The jury is dismissed.

The dogs set up a frenzied chorus of snarling and growling.

– But we was called 'ere, your Honour, pleaded the dalmatian. We thought we'd get a week off work for this… The six basset hounds forming the back row yelped their agreement.

– Order in the court! bellowed Sir Peter Prurigeaux. Clear all dogs from the court…No, not the Clerk, PC Hodge, Mr Cerberus is allowed to stay.

– Thank you, thank you, thank you, your Honour, said the three-headed Clerk to the Court, the wolfhound, labrador and German shepherd all bowing their heads in turn.

– Now, can we please get on with the business of the court? said Prurigeaux. Mr Merino, would you please begin your cross examination of the defendant.

– How cross am I allowed to be? asked the sheep.

– Objection, your Honour!

– Yes, Mr Shergar…

– The merino is a cross-bred Spanish breed of sheep. Since it is already a cross, it cannot be cross in the court, nor can it carry out a cross examination when it is itself a cross.

– You're splitting hares, Mr Shergar. We have dogs for that.

– But your Honour, the horse protested, I would submit that scrapie derives from the merino, who has had the disease for centuries. Indeed, many would regard it almost as a familial trait in this particular breed of sheep. The merino was interbred with other strains and the resulting sheep severely inbred to produce strains which were genetically reliable, not just for soft wool, but also for scrapie. But what the defence would like to know is: how is it possible that this apparently genetic trait in sheep could not be bred out of an inbred group?

– That is hardly the business of this court, Mr Shergar...

– But the Crown Prosecution Service is meant to be impartial, your Honour. How can that be maintained in the light of possible interspecies links between transmissible spongiform encephalopathies?

– Mr Shergar, as you are well aware, the Government published the findings of Professor Southwood's working party on Spongiform Encephalopathy, and I would refer you to its ruling of 3rd February 1989 that Bovine Spongiform Encephalopathy cannot be transmitted to any other species, including man... *Or pigs*, he added, elbowing awake Sir Harold Hockle, who had been snoring while sitting upright.

– But within four months, your Honour, the Tyrrell Committee was wanting offal banned from human food, which the Ministry at first refused to countenance, but then backed down, although insisting that liver and kidney should be excluded from the ban. And yet liver and kidney had been shown to be infective in other transmissible spongiform encephalopathies. The only possible interpretation to be drawn from that exception was those offals had a specific price, and abbatoir income would suffer badly if beef liver and kidney were banned.

– If you are suggesting that the Ministry of Agriculture, Fisheries and Food acted improperly, Mr Shergar, I must ask you withdraw that imputation.

– I withdraw it unreservedly your Honour, said the horse, backing down. But the defence still objects to the prosecuting counsel. As well as harbouring scrapie, the merino has round curled horns like the Swaledale and Herdwick breeds. My client would prefer to be questioned by an English sheep. If not a Swaledale then perhaps a long-headed Leicester, a chunky Cheviot or a cuddly Suffolk.

– Objection overruled. The Swaledales didn't get the CPS

contract, nor did any of the other sheep chambers you mention. Make sure you write all that down Mr Cerberus. The defence is making an ass of this court, but the law is an ass already. *And a hog too!* he cried, shaking the snoring Hockle, whose head had been lolling uselessly forward while the magistrate drove the grunting pigs in his throat over Swarston Bridge.

– Objection, your Honour!

– What is it this time Mr Shergar? I'm warning you…

– Mr Cerberus has three heads. If two heads are better than one, even if one's a sheep, then three heads should better than two, even if two are sheep's heads, but none of Mr Cerberus's heads is that of a sheep.

– A good thing for him that it's not, said Prurigeaux, for the lone sheep is in danger of the wolf. If one of his heads were a sheep's, it might be worried by the two dog heads…

– But three heads should have three tails, the horse insisted, and Mr Cerberus only has one. This suggests he has been attacked by the farmer's wife, who cut off his tails with a carving knife, and as we know Dame Dob the farmer's wife is a witness in the case of the Crown *versus* Little Johnny Green, who put the pussy in the well.

– Who pulled her out?

– Little Johnny Stout.

> What a naughty boy was that
> To try to drown a poor pussy cat,
> Who never did him any harm,
> And killed the mice in his father's barn.

There is therefore a chain of connections, the horse continued, and these link Mr Cerberus not only with this case but with several others, which means he cannot be counted upon to keep an accurate and unbiassed record of these proceedings. For Little Johnny Green's cat killed the three blind mice, which meant Dame Dob had to seek her tails elsewhere. And Old Mother Hubbard, having failed to fetch her poor dog a bone, went to the hatter's to buy him a hat, but when she came back, he was feeding the cat, which suggests collusion between the Hubbard Dog and the Green Cat. And not only that, but when the Black Sheep was stopped by the police and asked, *Baa, baa, black sheep, have you any wool?,* the sheep is alleged to have replied that it had three bags, but when the sheep's premises were searched it was found to be in possession of no wool at all. When questioned, it claimed it had been fleeced by a three-headed dog, but did not think anyone would believe a black sheep, and so attempted to keep up the pretence that it still had three bags full, one for the master, one for the dame and one for the little boy who lives down the lane, not least for the purpose of keeping its song, for if it was known that the three bags of wool had been stolen, people would stop singing the song because it wouldn't rhyme if the sheep's response had to be that the wool had been stolen by a three-headed dog, and without the song the black sheep would not only be out of a job, it would cease to exist, for the song confirmed its existence in the same way that a name does.

– I remember that case, said Prurigeaux, staring into space. The sheep pleaded not guilty because many go out for wool and come home shorn, and the wool was its own wool in any case, but Judge Sludge ruled that the wool belonged to Farmer Palmer, and since no three-headed dog was ever found or charged, the sheep was found guilty and sold to Mahatma Gander, who turned him into Lamb Pasanda.

– And the police treatment of the sheep was later the subject of a full judicial enquiry. For when the sheep was interviewed, it kept replying *Yes, sir, yes, sir, three bags full sir*, to all their questions. The officers who were disciplined claimed they had beaten up the sheep for being cheeky, but the enquiry ruled that they had also shown unintentional prejudice towards the sheep because it was black.

– It was also claimed that the police knew the identity of the three-headed dog, Prurigeaux commented, but they ensured that he couldn't be charged by making a dog's breakfast of the investigation. The police evidence was as flimsy as a piece of tripe.

– My point exactly. For as we know, R is the dog's letter, and there are two Rs in Cerberus. When there are two Rs in the mutt, the sleeping dog will lie, shit and talk through its Rs. *Thank you, your honour*, the horse said finally, I arrest my case, and I will use this pair of police handcuffs to hoofcuff myself to a briefcase bearing the gold-tooled initials O.P.

– Mr Cerberus, began Prurigeaux, you have heard Mr

Shergar's story. Is there any truth in his allegations? Is it true that you stole the black sheep's wool?

The three-headed dog cleared its three throats, waking Sir Harold Hockle:

– *Yes, sir, yes, sir, three bags full sir.*

– Mr Cerberus, I will have to ask Inspector Gimmer to place you under arrest. We will also need to appoint a new Clerk to the court. At this point we would normally adjourn, but since the magistrates are all dead – or fast asleep – we have no need to clear off for lunch. I say, *wake up Harold!*

Sir Harold Hockle slumped forward, drooling strands of spit from his lower lip, whereupon Prurigeaux thumped him hard on the back, inadvertently banging his ejector button. The knight's false teeth shot out of his mouth at the speed of a dung missile from the arse of a coughing cow. But instead of smacking into the dung-line which marks all byre walls at cow arse height, the teeth were intercepted by the horse acting for the defence with an effortless one-hoofed catch that earned him a round of clucking, snorts and cat-calls from the poultry, pigs and pussycats in the public gallery.

– *Thank you for that*, Mr Shergar, said Prurigeaux. And my *apologies* for the uncourtly behaviour of my colleague from Hogs Norton, where pigs play on the organ.

– Not from Lincolnshire, where hogs shit soap and cows shit fire then? the horse queried, prompting a further round of boisterous farmyard applause.

– Order in the court! cried Prurigeaux. Enough! Now, if you have no *objection*, Mr Shergar, I will ask the Lark to take over as Clerk to the Court, for you sang so sweetly in the Cock Robin case, Mr Lark. Will you be the clerk?

– Aye, said the Lark. If it's not in the dark, I'll be the clerk.

– And can you say, *The court will rise*?

– The court will rise, said the Lark ascending, and everyone stood, pretending they were back at school saying their prayers.

– Very good, said Prurigeaux. Sit down all of you. The Lark will strike out everything Mr Cerberus has written, which will all be three-headed two-tongued one-eyed Wee-Willie-winking pork pied lies, right back to the Reverend Nicholas's bit about Kernanism. None of the rest was said.

– Objection, your honour! A horse had interrupted, banging its hoof like a gavel on the wooden table. It was a compact bay colt with a white splash from forehead to muzzle.

– Yes, Mr Shergar?

– When Wee Willie Winkie ran through the town, upstairs and downstairs in his night-gown, rapping at the window, crying through the lock, *Are the children all in bed, for now it's eight o'clock?...*

– Yes?

– Why wasn't he arrested?

– Because, said Prurigeaux irritably, at six o'clock their mummies and daddies had taken them home to bed. By the time Winkie committed his public order offence, the children were all long asleep with their tired little teddy bears. Isn't that right, Mr Merino?

– *If you say so, your Honour*, said the ovine advocate wearily.

– I do say so, said Prurigeaux.

– *Yes, sir, yes, sir.*

– Well, don't just stand there bleating, ram. Why aren't you questioning the defendant? Carry on, Mr Merino.

– *Yes, sir, thank you, sir, your Honour, sir*, the sheep spluttered. Now, Inspector Gimmer, before there are any further interruptions from bench, barn or byre, I would like to question you about events on the night of September the 22nd.

– The autumn equinox? Emma Gimmer replied. But I wasn't appointed to the force until November...

– But you have been investigating a break-in at the house of Lady Olivia Prurigeaux...

– Objection, your Honour! the horse called out. The burglary in question was that of your own house. With respect, I must suggest that you have a vested interest in this case and must...

– Objection overruled, said Prurigeaux. The house belongs to my widow now, and being dead I can have no influence in the case. I also want to find out who did it. Continue, Mr Merino.

– Inspector Gimmer, the sheep began again. Am I right in thinking that you have been carrying out covert surveillance on members of your own police force in connection with this burglary?

– Is that true? Prurigeaux demanded. Speak up woman, who are they? *Name the culprits...*

– Yes, that is true, said Gimmer. We have been following the movements of PC Jakes, Sergeant Oxter and Inspector Daube.

– All good men, according to our man Goodman, said Sir Harold Hockle, who had been woken by the word *culprits*.

– Quite, quite, said the sheep. And what led you to suspect your own colleagues of involvement in this crime?

– Ridiculous idea, said Hockle.

– This was before I took over the case, said Gimmer. This was Inspector Kernan's idea...

– *Heresy!* cried the Reverend Nicholas, rolling his eyes in the manner of Dr Ian Paisley. This woman is a closet Kernanist...

– Hold on, said Prurigeaux, let her continue.

– Inspector Kernan...

– *Heresss...*

– *Shoosh* Nicholas! said Prurigeaux. You be quiet or I'll have you dismissed from the bench.

– The, er, Inspector, had prior knowledge that the burglary...

– *Heresy!* cried Ebenezer Nicholas. The defendant is suggesting that Kernan had foreknowledge of what was going to occur, whereas only the Almighty has...

– I've had enough of this! cried Prurigeaux, standing up.

– *...whereas only the Almighty has the divine right to...* the Reverend Ebenezer Nicholas managed, before being wrestled to the floor by the chairman of the bench.

– Order in the court! bellowed Sir Peter Prurigeaux from the floor. Clear all vicars from the court...No, not the witness, PC Hodge. The Reverend Devlin is allowed to stay.

– Thank you, your Honour, said the Reverend Kevin Devlin, Vicar of St George's, Loamfield, ducking his bald head in feigned obeisance.

– Objection, your Honour! roared the sheep. The witness is not dead. We cannot have live witnesses in this case.

– Mr Merino is right, announced Prurigeaux. Mr Devlin must either be ejected from the court or killed on the spot. Objection sustained. Which would you prefer, vicar?

– The former, if you please, although I was hoping to give evidence on behalf of...

– Not allowed! thundered Prurigeaux. Evidence from live

witnesses is inadmissable. Out, brief canon, out! The defendant will continue her answer...

– Where was I? Oh yes. Inspector Kernan had heard from his informants...

– Names? asked the sheep.

– I do not know their names, nor would I be able to disclose them in any case.

– Mr Lark, said Prurigeaux, turning to the sweet-voiced bird. Note that down: the defendant refused to disclose the names of her informants.

– Not mine, said Gimmer, but Kernan's. Oh what does it matter? Anyway, because he had received this tip-off, he arranged with Lady Prurigeaux...

– Olivia, my wife...

– Yes, he arranged with Lady Prurigeaux that she would leave a jewel-box of pearls out on her dressing-table and a homing device was hidden in the velvet lining, so that if the burglary did take place, the thieves would be sure to take this box...

– Objection, said the sheep. This is entrapment...

– Objection overruled, said Prurigeaux. Sounds like a good idea to me. And who are you meant to be acting for, Merino, anyway, the policemen suspected of the crime or the prosecution?

– I withdraw my objection, your Honour, said Merino. I was forgetting...

– You can't withdraw it, it's already been overruled, which means it's noted in the proceedings, isn't that right, Mr Lark?

– Aye, said the Lark, three bags full sir.

– Three bags full of objections? asked Prurigeaux.

– No, the Lark replied, they're full of lawyers' tongues and policemen's fingers for the Devil's Christmas-pie. The four and twenty blackbirds got away.

– Please continue, Inspector, said Prurigeaux, ignoring the bird's larking. If this jewel-box containing the homing device was taken in the burglary, how have you not nailed the culprits? No charges have been made against the three policemen.

– No, not yet, said Gimmer. The homing device apparently showed that the stolen goods were being kept at PC Jakes's house, but my special operational unit decided to mount a raid when the signal started to move around Benny Hill Farm. The pattern of movement was short-range, as if the jewel-box were in someone's pocket, and they were walking around the place.

– So you planned to arrest whoever had the jewel-box in his pocket?

– That's right. But when we arrived at the farm, there was no one there, although the homing device was still active. Eventually we traced it to the corner of a barn, where we found a rat...

– A rat? exclaimed Prurigeaux. What has a rat to do with the case?

– With the jewel-case, more's to the point, said Gimmer. The homing device was inside the rat...

– Where is this rat?

– We have the rat here, said the horse. In this cage...

– And what explanation did the rat give of itself?

– The rat? queried Gimmer.

– Of course, said Prurigeaux, did you not interrogate the creature?

– Well, no...

– You didn't interrogate the rat? exclaimed Prurigeaux. I don't know, it seems you must be guilty of neglecting your duty, Inspector. Let's see if we can't do your job for you...PC Hodge, put the cage on the witness stand. Get the rat to swear an oath; if it won't use the Bible, any kind of oath will do...

– Yes sir, said the late PC Roger Hodge, who lifted the heavy cage with ease, having given up smoking after his demise.

– You, rat, said Prurigeaux.

– Who are you calling a rat? Mr Rat, if you don't mind...

– Objection, your Honour, said Merino. This is another live witness and...

– Objection overruled. Rats are not rational beings...

– Who says I'm not rational?

– Immanuel Kant, I think it was, said the horse.

– But that's where the word came from, *rat*-ional, said the indignant rodent. Rats not rational, my rat-arse!

– I smell a rat here, said the sheep. The rat has just demonstrated its rationality, your Honour, so...

– *Leave it,* Mr Merino, Prurigeaux ordered. Let's just hear what the rat has to say. Mr Rat, would you please tell the court how you came to be in possession of a police homing device, previously secreted by the late Inspector Kernan in the lining of a jewel-case belonging to my wife, Lady Olivia Prurigeaux, which, if I am not mistaken, I gave her with the pearls inside on the occasion of our silver wedding anniversary in nineteen…

– All right, all right, said the rat. Spare me the details. It's me who has to put up with the gut-hake.

– So rats get tummy upsets? Isn't that the inevitable result of eating excrement and genetically modified potatoes?

– Shit happens, said the rat, lashing the bench-top with its tail. A diet of hordure is not without its disadvantages, your Honour. But in this hinstance, I found myself looking at this black box with red lining, and that particular velvet's just the kind I likes to chew through. Good roughage, you know. So there I was, gnawing away, when I swallowed this hobject…

– Which you now know to be a police homing device, said Prurigeaux, trying to be helpful.

– Of course I know what it is now, snapped the rat. I'm not stupid, you know. I know a cat from a coney.

– And can you tell the court anything else about this box? asked Prurigeaux. Where it was, for example? Who put it there? Whether you witnessed anything suspicious which might be of relevance to this case?

– What, about them rozzers you mean? asked the rat.

– Good bunch of lads them, said PC Hodge, always good for a laugh, especially Johnny Jakes, a real card, that one…

– Did you hear them say anything? demanded Prurigeaux, ignoring the interruption.

– Only that now things had died down, they were going to move the widow's jimmies.

– Her jimmies? asked Prurigeaux. Her jimmy jewels? Where to? Tell us where.

– Objection, your Honour, said the sheep. This rat is hardly a reliable witness. It is well-known that a rat would rat on…

– Objection overruled. Shut up Merino. Carry on, Mr Rat.

– They didn't name the place, your Honour. But it was somewhere no one would dare to look.

– Not *dare* to look? Now where would that be? Inspector Gimmer, this is meant to be your case. What are you doing about it? It would appear that my wife has cast her pearls before swine.

Steam was rising from the metal bucket. Moving closer to investigate, Lambert saw that the handle had been bound to the spit across the fireplace with wire. Several halves of potatoes were bobbing in a swirl of boiling foam. They looked soft and about to disintegrate. On an upturned box beside the hearth there were two blue-lipped white enamel mugs half-filled with a thin brown liquid which looked like well-stewed tea. Whoever had rigged up this makeshift arrangement had clearly left in a hurry.

The cottage looked less lived in than camped in. There were family pictures on one wall, rain-stained smudged images of strangers behind shattered glass, but mostly the house showed signs of rougher occupation, obviously more recent to judge from the discarded cans at the back of the hearth.

– Untidy fellows, these gunners, said a flutey voice.

Lambert looked up. He thought the room had been deserted, but in the far corner sat a man in a mud-splattered officer's uniform which for some reason he recognised as a lieutenant's.

– Where are they? Lambert asked, peering into his pallid face, which was blotched, a young man's face pitted from the ravages of an adolescent skin complaint. The rigours of army life seemed to have aged the youth's appearance, changing a reddish complexion into a raw mask like a side of beef. But it was not just the army, he realised, it was war. He heard the distant crackle of rifle fire before the room shook as a shell boomed not far away.

– You're asking me that, Lawrence? You should be able to work out what's happening here. You're the policeman, aren't you?

Who was this man? He was sure he'd met him somewhere before, but something stopped him from asking. There were some questions he couldn't ask here, like how the man knew his name. He had to deduce his answers from what he saw and from what the man did tell him in response to questions he could put to him.

– Where are *we* then? he said. Can I ask that?

– You can, but what will it mean to you? You don't know anything, he said, with a resigned air. You can't change what's already happened. Ten days ago this lot were resting at St Quentin. Now they've almost been pushed back to Amiens. The Germans have broken through, in case you didn't know. They're advancing on the village now. These poor buggers here are hightailing it up to the woods...

Lawrence Lambert stared at this bedraggled English officer, and for a moment thought he saw himself in his hurt, defeated eyes. The man's hand hovered over a deep scarlet hole in his tunic, a brownish patch which had spread across the breast pocket of his tunic, almost reaching a single torn white medal ribbon, white with a block of blue in the middle.

– The Military Cross? said Lambert, not so much as a question but to show he knew. I know what your medal is, he added, because my grandfather was given the MC. I have it at home, my father gave it to me...

– At home, is that right?

– In Otteridge.

– Should have been Kernan's, said the lieutenant. He took the pillbox, not me. Saved my life.

– He saved your life? Kernan? asked Lambert, his head suddenly reeling. There was something he wasn't getting, something just out of reach. But then this was a dream, wasn't it, and when the German soldiers arrived to mop up the stragglers, he would wake up. They might haul this wounded officer off with them, but not him. He would be back home, in Otteridge.

– I know what you're thinking, the soldier said.

Lambert's felt his heart miss a beat. Maybe somehow he wasn't going to wake up.

– I can read you like a book...

The firing was getting closer, and he would be shot in the chest by the Germans just as this officer had been shot by them.

– Not by *them*, the man said, by *him*. The lieutenant was answering his thoughts.

– I was shot in the back, he continued. In the assault on Eagle Trench. In all the confusion, no one saw him do it. He wanted to get me out of the way. I was protecting Kernan.

– Who did? asked Lambert, automatically.

– And I wasn't just wounded, Lawrence.

– You're dead, aren't you? You're already dead…

– You have to stop him before it's too late. You have to *do* something…

– But I can't, Lambert protested. I have no evidence on which to…

– The evidence is there. Arrest him and you'll find it.

– You know my position is weak…

– If you leave it much longer, you won't have a position left to hold. There will be nothing there for anyone to find. You'll overrun his house and find your bird has flown.

– But the bird has friends, Lambert pleaded. He realised he was sweating, his whole body was shaking.

– And they're on the run, Lawrence. Or else they're dead. Arrest him for the murders of Oxter and Jakes.

– But they're not dead, Lambert cried, almost pleased to find that everything wasn't slipping away from him after all. He knew more than the lieutenant about some things, and that meant he didn't have to obey him.

– Arrest him for *their* murders first, the lieutenant insisted. And then you can get him for all the rest.

– But… Lambert began, but stopped, the two men lapsing into silence as frantic voices shouted in German outside the window.

The door swung open, and a thick-set soldier appeared in the low doorway, ducking his grey tortoise helmet to enter the room, but looking straight through him, as if he didn't exist.

Looking up from her mattress on the floor, Muffy heard a small noise outside, like a branch rapping in the wind against the wood of the boarded-up window. But it was her bird, she knew, for every year on Midwinter Night it came to her, and tapped out its message. At Duckwidge Ditch it had sat on the roof of the caravan, and she had fallen asleep to the sound of the chough's beak tapping away, and its familiar *chee-aw, chee-aw, chee-aw chuff* would follow her into her dream, like a protective chant. It was always the same dream. Now in this cold room in the derelict Newlands house, she heard the chough again, going *top-top-top, taap-taap-taap, top-top-top*.

The man appeared by the river, cowled, wearing a grey cloak, not saying anything. Behind him on the bank would be a pair of otters, who slipped into the water when he gave the creatures a gentle wave. She waited to see one of the otters break the surface of the water, a silvery fish in its mouth, the fork of its caudal fin flicking a spray of water around the otter like a halo in the moonlight, at which point the man would throw back his hood and speak:

– Twelve battles did I win against the Saxons, and I will come again when my people need me. I will rise from the earth like that otter from the water.

But this time the otter did not appear. She stood watching the place in the middle of the river where it always rose up with its fish. And the man remained silent, his head hidden in the black depths of the cowl.

He was taller too, Herne decided, a fellow of Kernan's build. Why had he usurped his dream, this dream of the otters which the chough had brought him every Midwinter Night for the past eighty years?

The bird was still sitting on the window-sill when he drew back the curtains, calling to him.

– *Chee-aw, chee-aw, chee-aw... chuff.*

It held a small silver key in its beak. When he tried to coax it into dropping it, the bird swallowed the key. Then flew off. He rubbed his eyes, wondering if the creature had really been there. With the key.

Morton Maw was pleased at his choice of restaurant. There was no shilly-shallying about 'catering for vegetarians' at this new place: the Happy Heifer had PRIME ENGLISH BEEF blazoned across its menu blackboard in large red letters. Below this proclamation was the chalked shape of a sheep, like a murder victim outlined on a road, marked BEST LOAMSHIRE LAMB, and next to this, a cartoon hen sitting astride three yellow eggs, labelled FARM-FRESH CHICKEN.

– Look, Nick, he said. They've even got meat on the bone: oxtail soup, T-bone steak, rack of lamb. I'd like to give Larry the Lamb his comeuppance with mint sauce and gravy…

– You go for Larry, said Superintendent Goodman. I rather like the look of the chicken.

In one corner of the restaurant, a palm court combo had returned to their instruments. The pianist, a well-clipped ewe, gave a short lady-like cough to introduce the next set.

– And now a medley of popular Hungarian tunes, said the sheep, starting with the Goulash Polka, then Reynard's Foxtrot – here she gestured to the smartly dressed fox, who flicked his viola bow in response – and finishing with the Creutzfeld Waltz, in which Percy our fiddler will give us a bravura display of pizzicato playing. Here she nodded to the pig violinist, who bowed, a trifle superciliously Maw thought, before turning to bring in the cellist, a black cow resplendent in black suit and tails, like a negro minstrel, her fore-hooves fingering the fretboard with the dexterity facilitated by a pair of dandyish white gloves of the kind worn by Mickey Mouse. Launched by a deep groan from the cow's cello, they began playing their polka.

– Waiter, said Maw, I think I'll have the lamb.

The music stopped. With a clattering of cutlery, all the diners on the other tables were suddenly silent, except for one tut-tutting woman whose husband snarled at her to be quiet. Maw looked around the room, registering the stares, the whispered reproaches of *Lamb!* and *He wants the lamb*; and tucking a napkin into his collar, seized a fork to emphasise his intention.

– The lamb, if you please, he said firmly.

– In that case, said the waiter, if you'd like to follow me, sir… This flunkey's exaggerated deference amounted to impudence, Maw decided. He had about him an impertinent air, not unlike that manner of feigned obeisance Kernan had always adopted towards him.

Above the kitchen serving-hatch was a large signboard reading THUD-U-LIKE, and below it a row of guns hanging from pan-hooks. The chef came forward, leading a diminutive looking lamb, who looked plaintively up from the floor and bleated at the kitchen staff, some of whom came across to give her reassuring pats on the head.

– Best Loamshire lamb, Mr Maw, said the chef. You will see for yourself how this lamb will be freshly killed in our own kitchen. You'll be able to choose your own captive-bolt pistol, and my staff will be happy to show you first how to stun the animal…

– I think I know how to use one of these, Maw began, nervously.

– And then how to stick it, so that the meat you eat will be the freshest, most delicious lamb you've ever tasted. Tender lamb roasted with sprigs of rosemary freshly picked from our own kitchen garden, which will lend the succulent flesh its resinous but subtle flavour which will become richer through the cooking process. But hold on…

The chef bent down to the lamb, which made whimpering noises into her ear.

– Oh I'm sorry to hold you up, Mr Maw. You'll be getting hungry. Little Lambkins here wanted to say goodbye to its mother before you kill it, but we can't be having that kind of behaviour at the Happy Heifer, can we? Everyone is happy here, and the happiest of all is our happy customer who wants his lambmeat fresh as a daisy. No time to say ta-tas to Mummy when our good friend Mr Maw wants his din-dins darling.

The waiter interrupted.

– The gun, sir, he said. Would you like me to restrain the animal while you stun it?

Maw had the sense that this entire conversation was being overheard in the restaurant, which was still as hushed as a morgue. The palm court musicians had evidently downed their instruments, for the pianist had entered the kitchen, and was ripping open her blouse, baring her fleecy chest to him Isabella-fashion, offering herself for his dinner in place of the young lamb.

– I mean no offence, madam, but I like to sink my teeth into young flesh. And you must be the twinter side of a gimmer, or even a good year older.

– But this lamb is my daughter, Mr Maw. Would you want some great beast to eat your son Tom? I'm sure you would rather give yourself in his place...

Morton Maw thought this something of a presumption, and was about to protest when the chef broke in.

– Oh no, he said, don't shoot the pianist. We do not eat our musicians here, Mr Maw. Their skills have saved them from the ovens. If you want to eat lamb, then this little darling will delight your palate with her rich juices and soft flesh.

The lamb had moved across to him, and was nuzzling his leg, bleating for him to feed her.

– On second thoughts, he said at last, that nut roast did look quite appetising.

A cheer went up from the diners as he returned to his table.

– They seem to like me, Maw mused. A bit like the elections, eh Nick? All that applause. What'll you have? Will you join me in the nut roast?

– As I said before, I will have the chicken, Goodman replied. Farm-fresh chicken, that's what it says, and that's what I'll eat. And if they want me to wring the little bastard's neck, just let those lily-livered idiots bring it over here, and watch the feathers fly. For this place must be Lubberland, where the pigs run about ready roasted and cry, *Come eat me!*

After all their fellow diners had walked out, the waiter brought their meals. Maw admitted to enjoying his nut roast, and attempted to convey his compliments to the chef, but was unable to rouse Goodman to much conversation, mainly because – as the superintendent's glowering indicated – the kitchen staff and musicians were sitting around them at the adjacent tables, pretending to sip coffee and following their every word. Not discouraged by this display, the policeman made a point of stripping every last piece of white chicken flesh from the bone, holding each leg ostentatiously in the air while he gnawed at it, finally wiping his greasy fingers in the white linen napkin before flinging it on the floor like a pair of soiled, discarded underpants. And he belched, loudly.

– Excellent! he roared, thumping the table. Best chicken I've eaten in ages.

The belch had hardly left his mouth than it seemed almost to implode, to race back into the jaw of the surprised superintendent, causing him to gulp and clutch his stomach.

– Nick, what is it? asked Maw, anxiously.

– *Cur...*

– What's that?

– *Kernan.* Look, behind you! Goodman pointed, to where the Inspector stood beside the kitchen hatch, his hand raised high as if in anticipation of some imminent action.

– I see nobody, said Maw, looking round. Just the chef and the others. There's no one else here, Nick.

– But it's him, said Goodman, starting to lift himself, scraping his chair backwards until he almost fell over.

– What is it? asked Kernan. Did you think you'd seen a ghost?

Goodman yelped, and Maw touched his arm, attempting to restrain him.

– Come on Nick, he said. You've been overdoing it. And that business with the lamb in the kitchen. It's all been a bit of a strain.

– You should have had the Werburger, said Kernan, laughing. Not that you'd have seen it on the menu, but you'll taste it now, in the name of St Werburga...

As Goodman started to choke, Maw stopped offering reassurances, but looked about him for assistance. No one moved. The superintendent bent over the table, and his whole body started to shake. His chest heaved, his throat gave a loud gasp as if he were being strangled by invisible hands. And then, his teeth grinding so hard it looked to Maw that his whole head was being crushed, Goodman lurched forward and projected a brown stream of lumps and liquid onto his plate, which quickly became a mound of food and then reassembled itself into the roast chicken he had eaten, the chicken's legs and wings clicking back into the body. With a small leap in the air, like a sheep bucking after shearing, the chicken jumped off the plate, its feathers sprouting as it did so, and its severed head shot into the room from the kitchen, planting itself back on its neck. Allowing itself one final peck at the policeman's arm, the chicken hopped from the table, and was clapped back to the kitchen by the chef and waiter.

Maw stared, open-mouthed.

Goodman sat back in his chair, and looking to see where Kernan had gone, found that the wily inspector had disappeared again.

Entering the Regulator's office, the visitor crossed himself, spun three times widdershins, and threw a sprinkling of white powder over his left shoulder with his right hand. His adversary snorted contemptuously.

– You must have done your homework in the Middle Ages, he said. Those tricks were never enough, my friend.

But the man spat on the floor, and smiled, before looking up at the dark-browed Regulator.

– That's better. I am impressed. Not everyone knows the bit about spitting. Now tell me who you are before I send you back to stoke the boilers. I should *know* who you are, but...

– Inspector Kernan of Loamshire Police, said his visitor, holding forth a plastic-coated identity card like a crucifix. And if you don't mind, I'd like to ask you some questions, Mr...

– Let's drop the formalities, just call me Nick, said the bullet-headed executive, indicating the nameplate on his desk: NICHOLAS SATAN, REGULATOR AND CHIEF EXECUTIVE. But while I'm not obliged to say anything, Inspector, I would suggest that it is you, if I may be so bold, who should be answering questions, for you have no jurisdiction over me here.

– Nor you over me. For being neither dead nor alive, you cannot touch me. I hope my theology is correct on that point...

– Not you, yes, but I can of course *touch* anyone else. And you might not approve of my choice...

Without being aware of what he was doing, Kernan stared hard into the Regulator's eyes, trying to fathom the depths of their blackness, causing him to stagger slightly, but being intent on his probing, he failed to notice the effect this had on the businessman.

– My, we are touchy, said the Regulator. You needn't worry about her, she is only being held here. Not being dead she cannot be harmed either, but nor can she leave without my permission.

Over his shoulder, Kernan saw his adversary's reflection in the mirror, not the back view of the well-dressed Armani-suited character he was questioning, but the traditional fork-tailed fiend with a beast's horns and pointed ears. Noticing him freeze, Nicholas Satan stepped forward.

– If you've seen that, he said, you're more than a displaced policeman, Inspector Kernan. But looking at your expression of surprise, I think I'm right in thinking that you don't *quite* know the measure of your special powers. That being so, you won't be able to prevent *this*…

Swinging round, he walked directly into the mirror and melted through the glass. As he did so, the sign on his desk crackled like a log in a fire, sending up a plume of smoke. When it cleared, Kernan saw that the nameplate now just read PRINCE OF DARKNESS, in which guise the demon immediately reappeared from within the mirror, his great scaly paw shooting out to grab him by the collar and haul him through the glass. As when someone falls from a bridge or a ship to hit the water below, so Kernan felt himself plunge downwards and smash into another element.

– I call this Virtual Unreality, said the Devil. It allows me to show you how we treat our customers.

– Your *customers*? Kernan queried, his hands flailing for something to hold. They were falling down some kind of shaft.

– Don't resist it, Inspector. This is a black hole we're passing through, one of my own devising. If you look out now you'll see we're over the Gateway.

– It looks like some kind of supermarket. But there must be millions of people…

– But this is just Level 1, cried the Devil, laughing viciously. Those are the damned, Inspector Kernan, they're all our customers, he went on, grinning wildly. They're happier thinking that. It gives them the illusion of choice, when of course they have none at all. That's a laugh, isn't it? We find it easier to manage them if they think they have some free will. Ha ha. Mr Cerberus there is in charge of our threshold. It's a kind of purgatory from which we draw our unredeemed souls.

– You seem to relish all this, said Kernan, but shouldn't you have sympathy with those who've followed your path in life?

– Not at all, said the Devil. Our evil is the total opposite of your good. We *are* evil, that is our nature. But these sinners had free will, and they *chose* evil. On Level 1 we deal with volition, separating the sheep from the goats, those who led from those who were led. We have seven Levels, as you probably know, and each has its own level devil...I mean its own *manager*.

They had left the brightly-lit Gateway and continued their downward plunge. The Devil's explanations became more animated as he warmed to his account. Kernan wondered what he was preparing him for; and how and where he was going to hold him at one of these levels.

– Mr Moloch here runs Level 2, the arch fiend continued, indicating another sleek-haired executive wearing a pastel shirt and red braces. In less enlightened times, he demanded human sacrifices from the Ammonites. His victims had to *pass through the fire*, as it says in Kings. Since he has always demanded what people hold most dear, he's in charge of Customer Relations.

– Good morning, Inspector, said the vengeful god of Rabba and Argob, once worshipped to the stream of utmost Arnon, his realm now a thickly carpeted reception area furnished with black leather armchairs and Scandinavian couches. I believe we're soon to have the pleasure of receiving a friend of yours on Level 2.

Kernan flinched.

– A Miss Hunter, isn't that right, sir? he added, nodding to Satan for corroboration. Someone whom I believe you have a great deal of time for, and we shall certainly have a great deal of time to offer her here...

Before Kernan could protest, they had dropped suddenly down again, this time stopping in what appeared to be a gigantic black marble-walled bank.

– Level 3, Investments, Satan announced. Looked after of course by our good friend Doctor Mammon, indicating a man in a pin-striped suit tapping at a computer keyboard.

– Good morning sir, he said automatically, and how may we help you? He did not wait for a response, but quickly returned to whatever urgent matter was set out on his screen, all his thoughts and looks engaged in following the flashing scrolls of green figures.

– Not very interesting, except to him, said the Devil, although he is of course the backbone of the enterprise. And next – here he pretended to push a lift button – we enter Level 4.

They seemed to be at the hub of a huge dome. It looked like a cross between a health farm and a shopping mall. Seven long corridors led off like a rainbow of spokes from the centre, each painted a different colour.

– Meet our Operations Manager, Mr Beelzebub. Lord of the Flies to some, though he'd prefer Lord of the Lofty Dwelling.

– But not so lofty here, said Beelzebub, though I am, as the poet Milton said, *one next himself in power...*

– ... *and next in crime*, said Satan, completing the line. Matthew, Mark and Luke all called our Beelzebub *prince of the devils*, and he it is who offers our customers a choice of different treatments.

– A *tranch* of treatments, Inspector, Beelzebub insisted, handing him a sheet. These are today's multiple choice options...

beelzebubble

THE RAINBOW DOME

Today we offer our customers a choice of seven different treatments, each located in the sector designated by its colour. Our staff will be pleased to help you choose the treatment best suited to your needs. The seven colours of the rainbow stand for important service values:

RED: Working together as a team.
ORANGE: Being professional.
YELLOW: Making customers welcome.
GREEN: Building customer relationships.
BLUE: Ensuring customers feel positive.
INDIGO: Helping customers with problems.
VIOLET: Ensuring customers' peace of mind.

Please tick box to indicate your choice of treatment for today:

☐ **RED:** ***Acupuncture.*** Heated needles, plus acid bath.
☐ **ORANGE:** ***Hot water enema.*** And it ain't half hot, mum!
☐ **YELLOW:** ***Sulphur baths.*** Pumice or traditional brimstone.
☐ **GREEN:** ***Aromatherapy.*** With bile or excrement.
☐ **BLUE:** ***Turkish.*** Fight the flab. Nothing like a spot of hacking to get those muscles trimmed.
☐ **INDIGO:** ***Chinese.*** Not for the faint-hearted...
☐ **VIOLET:** ***Pit of serpents.***

– I'm spoilt for choice, said Kernan. They all look quite invigorating. However, I don't think I'm quite up to the health farm routine today. I'm really not sure which I'd want to choose.

– It wouldn't matter, said Beelzebub, grinning. All the treatment rooms connect with the violet sector.

– He means they all end up in the pit of serpents, Satan explained. But our customer choices turn out to be rather different than they imagine on Level 5, where Mr Belial administers what we like to call our Stakeholder Society: here our customers are able to drive stakes into each other in the belief that increasing the pain they inflict on someone else will decrease the level of pain they feel themselves, but the opposite is true of course. The essence of Level 5 is that no one learns anything here. Mr Belial calls it his Vicious Circle. We try not to use such phrases in front of the customers, but you know what Belial's like, *a spirit more lewd fell not from heaven, or more gross to love vice for itself*. He is not inclined to moderation. Which brings us of course to Level 6, the Cardboard Room, our newest attraction, where – as you see there – anyone who voted for Sin is put in a cardboard box soaked in her urine and smeared with the excrement of *she who sprang from my head, woman to the waist, and fair but ending foul in many a scaly fold voluminous and vast, a serpent armed with mortal sting,* where they can shiver uncontrollably under this railway arch while listening to loop-tape recordings of the She-Devil's most excruciating speeches and interviews.

– You *cannot* look after the hard-up people in society unless you are accruing *enough wealth to do so*, the voice boomed. Good intentions are *not enough*. You need *hard cash*. We should not expect the state to appear in the guise of an extravagant good fairy at every christening, a loquacious companion at every stage of life's journey, the unknown mourner at every funeral. My job is to let the country begin to exist within sensible and realistic economic disciplines.

There was no stopping this onslaught. Satan smiled, seeing the immediate effect on his visitor of what he called his Kestevil treatment. There was no devil so bad as a she-devil.

– Deep in their instincts people find what I am saying and doing *right*, the voice continued. And I *know* it is, because that is the way I was brought up. I'm *eternally* grateful for the way

I was brought up in a small town. We knew everyone, we knew what people thought. I sort of regard myself as a *very normal, ordinary person*, with all the right instinctive antennae. I *really* am trying to bring into British life everything I *deeply* believe about democracy...If I give up, we will lose. If I give that up, I just think we will lose all that faith in the future. We'd lose the justification. I hope that doesn't sound too arrogant.

– No stop! cried Kernan. Stop, stop! Stop it, please!

– There are legitimate fears among white Britons that they are being swamped by people with *a different culture*...Four million blacks by the end of the century...We are not in politics to *ignore* people's worries, we are in politics to *deal* with them.

– *Oh please, no more...*

– In those anxious months the spectacle of bold young Britons, fighting for great principles and a just cause, lifted the nation. Doubts and hesitation were replaced by *confidence* and *pride* that our younger generation too could write a *glorious* chapter in the history of liberty.

Kernan tried to block his ears, but found he couldn't. The harder he pressed his hands against the side of his face, the louder the voice became inside his head...

– *I'll* win the war for these buggers, and then I shall go... But it was *not* sailing away from the Falklands. *U*-turn if *you* like. The *lady's* not for turning...The two great problems of the British economy are the monopoly nationalised industries and the monopoly trade unions. We had to fight an enemy without in the Falklands. We always have to be aware of the *enemy within*, which is *more* difficult to fight and *more* dangerous to liberty...There is no week, nor day, nor hour when tyranny may not enter upon this country, if the people lose their supreme confidence in themselves, and lose their roughness and spirit of defiance. Tyranny may always enter – there is no charm or bar against it.

He tried shouting out, singing, barking, bellowing like a bull, anything to stop the unrelenting attack, but instead of his own voice, what emerged from his throat was a haughty echo of the She-Devil's words. He had become her ventriloquist's dummy, a pantomime dame with a false voice schooled by a cloth-eared elocution teacher, one moment shrill and tyrannical, the next syrupy and condescending. He wasn't sure which tone was worse.

– *I'll* win the war for these buggers, and then I shall go, he heard himself saying, his head swivelling round like the little girl in *The Exorcist*. Then I shall go. *I'll* win the war, he said in a higher-pitched, even more strident voice, like Vera Lynn doing a Joyce Grenfell impression on the *Goon Show*. It was agonising and demeaning, losing his own voice, his ability to choose his own words, and to have these awful phrases coming out of his mouth. Indignant, he threw himself down, and started pounding the floor with his fists. Still the voice continued to ring out like a banshee.

– But it was *not* sailing away from the Falklands. It was *not* sailing away from the Falklands. *Not* sailing away...

The She-Devil's words penetrated his whole being. They boomed out, echoing around the curved, dripping walls of the railway arch, as from a tannoy, until snatches of lines started to return, intertwining, contradicting. It was unbearable, a merciless torture for the vicious modern age.

– *U*-turn if *you* like. *Not* sailing away from the Falklands. The *lady's* not for turning. Good intentions are *not enough*. The two great problems of the British economy are the *enemy within*, an enemy without four million blacks by the end of the century, bold young Britons fighting for great principles and four million blacks. The *lady's* not for, not for *glorious* chapter in the history of liberty, the history of the *enemy within*, enemy without *confidence* and *pride*, *confidence* and *pride* are *not enough*. Swamped by people with *a different culture*. My job is to win the war for these buggers, my job is to fight an enemy without legitimate fears, legitimate tyranny may always enter *a very normal, ordinary person*, with all the right instinctive antennae, *a very normal, ordinary person* with *a different culture*. I hope that doesn't sound too arrogant. *Not* sailing, *not* sailing away...

– Very impressive, don't you think? said Satan, flicking back a switch, whereupon the Kestevil voice shrank immediately to a low burbling sound emitted from beneath a metal drain cover beside the cardboard boxes of the damned.

– But we have a special arrangement with Himself, he continued. He allows the dead souls to receive visits from people whose deaths the She-Devil caused, not only in the devastated hospitals of your country, but in the prisons and old people's homes, and on the streets, as well as the suicides, who tell them how their lives and hopes were blighted, and how they eventually died. Those who voted against Major-Ballcock in 1997 get early remission, but the rest will remain in their smelly boxes until we have the men who killed Stephen Lawrence.

– You know you're getting them then? asked Kernan.

– Himself has their names, said Satan. Apparently they're all due to be despatched here at the same time.

– He must know something we don't...

– Allegedly, replied Satan sharply. They're to get our Special Treatment when the rest switch to Mr Smiley's lockjaw régime. Belial wanted to use the She-Devil, but she's getting out of control.

They came to a halt at what felt like the bottom of a deep lift-shaft, a colder, even danker place where they had to squeeze between great reticulated oily cables dangling down from a height which felt so cold their ringed surfaces burned into him as he tried to heave them aside. These were the work of the Serpent of Envy, the Devil told him.

– This is the Basement of the Animals, he said, where the Seven Deadly Sins are present in the person of the Level Seven Beasts. Those who could not resist the Serpent of Envy in life are here embraced by her cables, made from whatever metal or substance the person most coveted; if that was flesh, then the cable is of course a snake. So too the Bear of Sloth smothers the indolent with his rancid fur, but here his fetor is bitingly cold. Those voluptuaries who lolled around sating themselves on warm musky smells, soft fruits, liquor and languor, discover their opposite in the icy grip of the Ursuric. Their lassitude will ensure that these rigours cannot be shaken off.

– And you will have the Lion of Pride, said Kernan, if I am not mistaken, along with the Unicorn of Wrath, the Scorpion of Lechery, the Fox of Covetousness, the Swine of Gluttony. All personifications which are insults to the animals themselves...

– Ah but that is the beauty of it, Satan interrupted. The Basement is where Man is reduced to the level of the beasts, in his own terms not theirs. Man debases the beasts all his life, projecting onto them the most unsavoury aspects of his own nature. Here he gets it all back.

– From the Devil's Dog.

– When the shit hits the fan, said Satan.

– Or the floor, said Kernan, pointing. Shit happens, he added with a laugh, a trick to catch the old one.

But his warning came too late. Distracted by his showing off, the fiend had stepped on the smooth chocolatey coils of slippery poo deposited by Black Shuck, as deadly a substance as the venom of the Serpent of Envy or the rank yeasty sweat of the Bear of Sloth.

And with his left hoof. Such are the reversals of fortune between heaven, hell and earth that such a slip could only be lucky for his companion, for whom shitten luck was good luck, while he himself plummeted immediately downwards in a free-fall more precipitous than any he had managed since the first St Michael's Day. As he tried to arrest his descent, the Devil felt a pang of regret, remembering that first headlong plunge when he and his team of smooth-talkers had been ejected from the top floor. This latest twist of fate would never have happened but for Kernan. The police were always trouble. Now his whole master-plan was in jeopardy again. Kernan had turned the tables on him. He had probably thrown away the game, all because of pride and dogshit. All Kernan had to do now was keep his head, keep his wicket intact, and press home his advantage. Not be tempted outside the offstump. If Kernan's team bowled a good line and length when the Other Side was batting, he would see his side home, as long as they didn't put down too many catches.

On Level 1, Diana was remembering more details from Kernan's card about the canine apparitions whose appearance was ominous of death or disaster. You had to beware of Padfoot, Black Shuck, Trash or Skriker, who appeared in dog form, while the Barguest could be a calf, goat, pig or dog, but could always be distinguished from mortal animals by its great size, its saucer eyes, its paws which left no tracks and its terrible howling.

There was no mention of its poo, yet if a Barguest decided to dump its load on one of its nocturnal outings, the results might be none too appetising: not unlike that black smoking mound of what looked like dogshit outside the Regulator's office. The flames playing over the clarty glob made it look like a huge Christmas pudding which had been soaked in brandy and set alight, but the resemblance did not extend to its smell, which was unimaginably foul. It reminded her of the septic tank in her mother's garden, how that had smelt when it had overflowed, yet even that was possibly preferable to the Barguest's fuming black excrement.

Behind the door, she could hear voices raised in an argument, one abrasive with a sibilant edge like Goodman's, the other more mellow, not unlike Kernan's in his most combative form.

Suddenly the door was flung open, and the Regulator stepped forward, not noticing the Barguest's gift on the threshold. As one highly polished black leather shoe shot forward, its owner performing a double somersault, Kernan himself emerged from the office, laughing.

– Shit happens, he said.

– Quick! she cried. Follow me, in the name of St Margaret. But watch out for the Barguest. And whatever you do, don't look back.

– A Barguest, where? asked Kernan, turning.

A dark cave. In the middle, a river boiling. Thunder.

ISABELLA: Thrice my fat cat husband mewed,
  Time for slime his scabs exude.
BUNTY: Thrice the bullet-head hath whined
  Demon's semen makes you blind.
OLIVIA: Kernan cries; 'tis time, 'tis time.
ISABELLA: Round about the river go
  Bats to make the chimneys blow;
  In the poisoned Otter throw
  Sarin gas in H_2O.
BUNTY: Dead fish in the water falls –
  Poisoned by the chemicals.
ISABELLA: Pubic louse from Goodman's balls,
  Tench's blood-stained overalls.
OLIVIA: Penile warts that weep and seep…
BUNTY: Scrapie from a Loamshire sheep.
ISABELLA: Moo-moo cow from down the lane…
BUNTY: Spongey matter from her brain.
OLIVIA: Hoof thrush caught by Johnny Jakes
  In the river boils and bakes.
BUNTY: Muffy's rags of Old Oak Ham.
ISABELLA: Shitty dags from Suffolk ram.

OLIVIA: Ernest Gubbins' hartshorn phlegm,
Offal paste of MRM.
BUNTY: Larvae laid by warble flies,
Factory gases stinging eyes.
BUNTY: Pour them in to spread disease –
DDT and PCBs,
Nonylphenols mixed with faeces,
Recipe for extinct species.
ISABELLA: Sheep scab mites and ovine ticks,
Biethylenetripopethyl-6.

ALL: Double, double-hit is trouble;
OPs burn in sheep-dip bubble.
OLIVIA: Cool it with a mad cow's blood,
Then the curse is firm and good.

ISABELLA: Mix them all up, mix and mash,
Turn this poison into cash,
Do it quickly, dash for cash.
Kill some men with sheep-dip rash.
BUNTY: Throw their bodies in as well.
OLIVIA: We all saw you, and we'll tell...
ISABELLA: And we'll curse you as you sell
England's soul with yours to hell.

ALL: Double, double-hit is trouble;
OPs burn in sheep-dip bubble.
OLIVIA: Cool it with a mad cow's blood,
Then the curse is firm and good.

KERNAN: (*That's enough curses...*)
ISABELLA: He was cursed in his mother's belly that was killed by a cannon.
BUNTY: As wholesome for a man is a woman's curse...
OLIVIA: As a shoulder of mutton for a sick horse.
ISABELLA: Curses, like chickens, come home to roost.

BOOK VI

IMBOLC

FEBRUARY – APRIL

I saw a black cow eat a sheep.
I saw a weasel's headwound weep.
I saw a black horse – no, dark brown –
I saw it canter round the town.
I saw a toad's heart help a thief.
I saw a demon felled by beef.
I saw a Suffolk ram a road.
I saw a Barguest drop its load.
I saw three rams begin to mount
a hundred ewes who couldn't count.
I saw three gimmers, tethera yowes.
I saw a green man tether the cows.
I saw a man who saw these too.
The cow ate him. The cow ate ewe.
The crow told it. It must be true.

CHAPTER TWENTY-FOUR

With One Stone

IMBOLC/CANDLEMAS: JANUARY 31ST–FEBRUARY 2ND

A sparrow means you will marry a poor man but be happy; a robin denotes a sailor; a dove symbolises money and happiness; and a goldfinch promises happiness and boundless wealth.

Muffy stopped in her tracks, hearing distant footsteps on the pavement, followed by a strange scraping sound, a screeching like blackboard chalk but heavier. She did not need to look round, knowing the identity of her pursuer from the noise, by now a harsh metallic rattle, grating like the chain hoists in the slaughterhouse.

At last he came abreast of her. It was Kernan. They didn't look at each other or say a single word. He fell into step beside her and they marched into the police station, the Inspector's spectre dragging his clattering metal burden along the wooden floor.

They saw, standing with his back to them, an enormous policeman with a bullet-shaped head, looking as if he'd eaten bull beef. His back appearance was unusual. He was standing behind the reception desk; his mouth was open as he chomped noisily, diving a paw into a rustly bag of potato crisps, and he was looking into a mirror which hung upon the wall. Drawing back and pointing, the ghost said with bitterness:

– A symbol of English art. A packet of potato crisps, roast beef or salt 'n' vinegar. The potato, staple food of a nation, processed into bite-sized pieces, with artificial flavouring. Our spud-bite culture.

– I shall tell that to Gubbins, said Muffy.

– It's the rabbits, they heard the policeman say abstractedly and half aloud. The rabbits have all been squashed into doormats. They are all that's left. A squashed rabbit butters no parsnips.

His face, when he turned, surprised them. They noticed that his eyebrows almost met in the middle, and that his eyes were so dark they seemed like bottomless pits of blackness. His bullet-head was thinner than Muffy remembered, sleek as a cartridge instead of bulging like a mortar shell. He has a worm in his brain, Muffy thought, seeing him look up anxiously, then return to his rummaging, breathing heavily as he stooped down to pick up a notebook. She pretended to cough. He came to the counter.

– Is it about a bicycle? he asked.

– It is, said Kernan. But it is not you who should be asking...

– I always wanted to have that line, said Goodman.

– Where is Sergeant Cobb? asked Muffy. He should have had it. It's a desk sergeant's line.

– Can't remember where Cobb keeps the notebook, Goodman started muttering. And why have they put me on the front desk? Why have I put me on the front *deshk*, that's what I'd like to know. I should be upstairs giving orders. There was a notebook here five minutes ago. It had a blue marbled cover, the kind you used to be able to buy from the stationers in the High Street. They don't make them any more, you know. Another thing you can't get now, like rabbits which haven't been squashed on the road. Why are there so many rabbits squashed on the road?

Muffy coughed again, pointing to the notebook in his hand.

– No, that wasn't a line from a joke, he chuckled, but it could be, couldn't it, he said, not a very good joke though; adding a nervous, whinnying laugh almost as an afterthought.

– Here's a good one though, he wheezed, grinning like an ass. Listen, he said. Do you know the one about the goose?

– About Werburga's goose? asked Muffy. Wednesday's her day, the third of February. How unusual for you to remember...

– No, nothing to do with burgers, Goodman interrupted. Not burgers but geese.

– What about geese?

– Geese, said Goodman, who said anything about geese? What do *I* know about geese?

– You were going to tell us a joke about geese.

– Was I? said Goodman, looking puzzled. But I don't know any jokes, and certainly none about geese. Do you?

– I know one, said Kernan, impatiently. It may be the one you're looking for. It's a good one to tell on St Werburga's Day. It goes like this. What does a duck *try* to do, a goose *manages* to do, and a lawyer *ought* to do?…

Goodman stared blankly.

– I don't know, he said, what does a goose try to do, a lawyer manages to do and a duck ought to do?…

– No, that's not it. But I'll tell you all the same…A duck *tries* to, a goose *manages* to, and a lawyer *ought* to…

– Yes?

– *Stick its bill up its arse!*

– Oh that's a good one, said Goodman. I'll tell that to Merino. But hang on. That's the joke *I* was going to tell. You stole my joke. Saveloy told me that one, old Sausage-Breath.

– A good tale is none the worse for being twice told, said Muffy.

– But a tale ill told is marred in the telling.

– A tale never loses in the telling, said Kernan.

– Like your risen Christ, said Goodman. Long may he live, long may he die, long may his story be told. Or was that Wyatt Earp? You revenants confuse me with all your resurrections.

Goodman was trying to fix them with his vulpine stare, and their first instinct was to turn away, but the expression started going wrong, it turned back in on itself so that the stare was directed at the starer, who quailed and cowered behind his reflection in the mirror.

– No government watchdog, that's what's wrong, isn't it? Goodman suddenly said, trying to distract them from the temporary problems he was having with his countenance.

– They get away with murder when there's no watchdog, said Muffy.

– Like with the cattle disease, said Kernan.

– Oh no you're wrong there, Goodman insisted, starting to sway from side to side. Problem with the beef was the watchdog had no teeth. Whoever heard of a watchdog with no teeth?

You can't have a bite without any teeth
You can't have a sniff without your nose
You can't have burgers without any beef
You can't get undressed without your clothes

– A watchdog with no teeth? he repeated. That's a good one. It was that Dr Beeching, he's the man behind it all. Didn't like the English cunt, the English countryside. Stamped out the branch lines, closed down half the alsatians and replaced our English shepherds with German shepherds which were only obeying orders. Got rid of the lovely old steam trains and introduced the spanking new diesels. And a diseasel can't be infected by a trainspotter if he's wearing an anorak. Now if you want to buy a train ticket from an alsatian, you have to put on a Johnny Morris or a Peter Parka, or the bitch won't let you have one. It has to be fluorescent if you need a return or if you need to come in by the back entry.

To bite an arse you need your teeth
To kick a butt you need your toes
To stick it up you need a sheath
To swill it out you need a hose

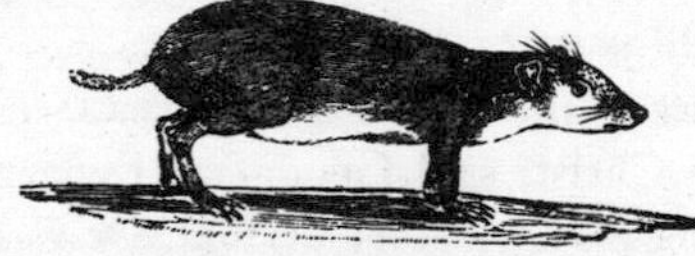

Paddy Muttonchops was sharpening his cleaver. He ran his finger along the blade, but being dead, couldn't feel if it was sharp enough. He pressed the corner until a bead of crimson appeared on his fingertip. Seeing is believing. Now he knew he had blood on his hands. That meant the cleaver must be ready for what. While ghouls can't feel, they must be able to see to have a ghost of a chance. The proverbial butcher had to manifest himself and his badness to the living and be manifested and manifestly bad. He had to make their blood run cold. Blood was a language they had understood, and it had always been his language. It was the black pudding of life. It was in his veins.

Paddy Muttonchops had lived in tubercular times. Everyone coughed up blood then and his blood was bad blood. They had always been bad, the O'Scrapies, it ran in the blood. Bad blood ran in the family. Bad blood was good blood. Good blood made bad puddings without groats or suet, and they never had many groats, except the groats they stole. Where bad's the best, bad must be the choice. And they were good at being bad, by Jove they were good, good by any definition, bad by any other. They were all filthy liars, but bad liars, as bad as their words. Vulgarity without duplicity is like a pudding wanting suet, he always maintained, and the suet had to be best beef suet, nothing less, nothing more.

Now that he was dead, he only had his words to go back on, his turns of speech. Words had a life of their own. He turned them in his grave, turned them over. Words would keep his memory alive, words like his name, Paddy Muttonchops. As long as people spoke of Paddy Muttonchops, he would continue to have an existence for them and for himself.

But now his grandfather was telling him he was not his grandfather but his grandson. Then his grandson claimed that he, Paddy Muttonchops, was not his grandfather but his grandson. He didn't know which to believe. They both sounded the same. Both were O'Scrapies, which meant both were liars, but if both were lying then neither was right. If neither was right then neither was wrong. But the dead are always wrong. If both were wrong, then both were claiming the opposite of what each other said, which meant neither was right and neither was wrong.

And if that was the case, and both were the same, then he could not exist. Moreover, he could not be dead, because that implied he had been alive once to be dead now, and if he had not existed in the first place, then how could he *know* that he could not exist, since to *know* that he had not existed must imply that he once had an existence, unless that was a lie. If it was a lie, did that mean his life had been a lie too?

He should know if anyone knew, but he was not just anyone. He was the last person to see himself alive.

And was his death a lie? His life had been defined by death, his own death which ended it and the death by which he made his name, the death of the man he was said to have butchered. Nobody had proved that he committed that murder, but nobody listened, and if nobody listens nobody knows anything. If nothing was proved, because nobody had proved anything, perhaps that meant it never happened? What if the reason it had never happened was because he had never himself existed? Kernan had tried to point the finger of suspicion at him, but Kernan only imagined it was him. Was it all in Kernan's imagination?

The only thing anyone remembered about him now was that Paddy Muttonchops was the village butcher who was supposed to have killed a man, and who was said to have destroyed the evidence afterwards by chopping up the fellow's body before feeding him to the pigs. No one remembered the name of the man he killed, only that he was the man killed by Paddy Muttonchops. After he chopped up the pigs, they say he sold their flesh in his shop, but that meant he had fed the man to the villagers. The people of Loamfield had eaten the man they have now forgotten, which made them accomplices in the crimes of murder and collective amnesia.

In one version of his story, the man he killed was a stranger, a man passing through, a cobbler from Sussex, it was said. In another it was a rival, a man who was courting Paddy's sweetheart, or the man had himself been jilted by her for Paddy. The two men had met in Hangman's Wood. Paddy had killed him, he hadn't meant to. The man had left Paddy for dead, and went on the run. He was a soldier home on leave. They'd got into a fight. The next morning the man left for France, he didn't come back. He never caught the train from Otteridge, Paddy had killed him and hidden the body.

He liked contradictions. Two many cooks spoiled the broth, but many hands made light work. Both and either could be right. Neither or both were wrong: honour might be virtue's reward, but honour buys no beef in the market. You might think there were more ways to kill a dog than hanging it, yet scabby donkeys scent each other over nine hills. The flesh is aye fairest that is farthest from the bone, but nearer the bone the sweeter the flesh. When he had the finger of suspicion jabbing at him, he encouraged the differences, planting inconsistencies for others to discover and consider later. The black cat and the cross-eyed sweep, the magpie and piebald horse: lucky in one place, unlucky in another. They were like different versions of myths and superstitions, the more contradictory, the longer they survived. With different beliefs, nothing fitted, you took from each what you wanted to take. This was the Gospel According to

Muttonchops: one man's meat is another man's poison. Every man as he loves quoth the good man when he kissed his cow. Believe in what you will and no man need kill or be killed. Truth made no one free, truth breeds hatred.

The more lines he spun, the bigger his web of deceit, his homespun wisdom, the fabric of truth. So they would continue to talk of him as long as O'Scrapie and his descendants were there to remind them of Paddy Muttonchops, there were so many strands to catch at. That house was where he'd lived. That's where the fight happened. But if O'Scrapie's existence was now in question, he was in danger of being wiped out himself. He had to retain a foothold in living memory, and if words were no longer sufficient, deeds might be necessary.

– You wouldn't be lying to me about all this? Paddy Muttonchops asked O'Scrapie.

– Me, lying, your own grandfather? O'Scrapie exclaimed.

– *Knuckers!* said Paddy. No use asking you that, is there?

– Me, lie to you, your own flesh and blood, your own grandson? May the Lord strike me dead if I dishonour the family name.

– This is getting us nowhere. It's the story of my life.

– Story of your death.

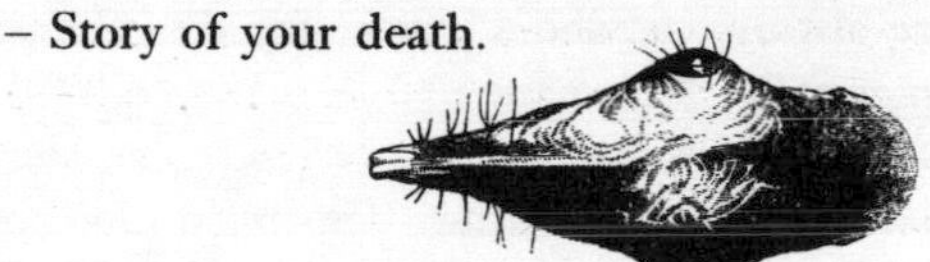

Goodman was barking. He was mad as a mullah. Muffy almost wished he was the raging bull of old, the giant policeman who snorted and pawed the ground. This shambling creature with its swinging moods was harder to deal with. Now it was trying to appear aggressive, assuming what it thought was its predatory look. She wanted to respond in a reassuring fashion, to let him think he was still able to inspire fear in others, but she could only smile weakly, avoiding his eyes yet showing in her uneasy response that it didn't matter that he had ceased to be attractive; he was still untrustworthy. Goodman snorted gleefully, pleased that she had not ducked the leer he had tried to make as commanding as possible in the circumstances. Then he turned from her to the writer, fixing him this time with *his best quizzical look*.

– Is it about a bicycle? he asked again.

– You can't say that, said Kernan. That's not your line.

– What should I have said?

– *Is it about the cattle disease?*

– Why should I ask that? said Goodman.

– You're responsible for it, said Muffy.

– I asked about the bicycle, said Goodman, ignoring her, because Mr Bones here is holding an old boneshaker of some description. A bicycle without wheels, if there can be such a thing…

– A vehicle with two wheels, one before the other, driven by pedals or a motor, said the dictionary. From the Latin *bi-*, twice, and the Greek *kyklos*, a circle or wheel.

– Your vehicle has no *kyklos*, Goodman asserted. Your wheel forks are holding nothing but air. Therefore it cannot be a bicycle. It is a biforkle, not a bicycle.

– It *was* a bicycle, said Kernan. And your men stole it from *The Third Policeman*, just as they stole the widow's jewels.

– What do you know about that? Goodman thundered. And what were you doing in *The Third Policeman* without a warrant? You're not even meant to be in this book now, you're exceeding your powers. You're history, you should have stayed in the past.

– I heard it from a police informant.

– A rat, no less, said Muffy.

– And why should anyone believe a rat? demanded Goodman. What credibility does a sneaky rat have as a witness?

– A lot, said Kernan, although I don't usually disclose the species of my sources. And I've decided to give him a job. I need an undercover rodent in my new book, just a small part, you understand, for he's inclined to be ratty, though no more rat-arsed than your Inspector Daube. He starts work for me when this book's finished.

– Don't give me that, said Goodman. You're dead, so you can't be writing another book.

– It's a posthumous book, said Kernan. I started writing it on St Agnes' Eve, three full moons after I died. I needed the winter to get over my death. But writing isn't so easy when you're dead, because there's no time like the present. I'm calling the new book *The End of My Wether*, the wether being…

– A castrated male sheep, said Muffy.

– And *The End*...

– Is what you have at the end of a book or a sheep.

– Except in my book the wether is a policeman. My agent, Mr Caradoc King, has already discovered the opening chapters of the manuscript in my papers, and I need to finish the rest of the book before he finds it.

– Before he finds out you're talking hogwash, more like, said Goodman.

– Sheepwash, you mean, said Muffy. Or should it be sweep-wash?

– Sweeps don't wash, said Kernan indignantly. Gubbins will tell you that. Nor do the dead. The dead are the great unwashed.

Paddy Muttonchops was waving his cleaver. The cleaver defined him, but could he use it now? No way. O'Scrapie ducked as he swung it round his head.

– The dead don't eat, said the butcher, so you can't use it for chopping meat with. The dead can't be killed, so you can't chop them up with it.

– Except metaphorically.

– What use is a metaphorical cleaver?

– What use is a metaphorical anything?

– Who needs metaphors? Paddy sighed, fingering his woolly muttonchops.

– If we didn't have metaphors, said O'Scrapie, we'd have to invent them. Otherwise there would be no metaphors. And if we didn't know what a metaphor was, you wouldn't be able to say you were only speaking metaphorically when you weren't and wanted to lie about what it was that you weren't being metaphorical about.

– You're right there, said Paddy, unless you're lying. So how do we get out of this metaphorical conundrum?

– Do someone a good turn, said O'Scrapie.

– That might give me a bad turn, giving someone a good turn, said Paddy Muttonchops. Unless the fellow has been skewered on a spit and I'm giving him a good turn on the old fire, making sure he's properly cooked all over, all crispy. Then I can give him another turn because one good turn deserves another, and everyone likes a good piece of crackling.

– So you'll do this turn then? asked O'Scrapie.

– Why don't *you* do it? *You* turn if *you* like...

– O'Scrapie's not for turning. It has to be *your* turn, Paddy, and a good turn, because you're the best and worst butcher of words as well as a bad apple, a bad penny even.

– The rotten apple injures its neighbours.

– Which are we, Cox or pence?

– The unrighteous penny corrupts the righteous pound, said the dead shopkeeper. You don't get as many bad pennies to the pound now, a hundred instead of two hundred and forty. Bad apples used to be ten a penny. But there is good land where there is foul way. We can at least take the foul way in doing this good turn.

– The good turn is for a foul man, said O'Scrapie, a man who lived up to his name, Prurigeaux.

– He lived and died by it, said Muttonchops, more an eruption than a man, he was half dead before he died. The gangrene took his foot before his leg and then the rest of his cursed body.

– He wants a good turn.

– He wants throwing in the fire. Turn and burn. Burn and turn.

– He wants his widow's loss made good.

– She's well rid of him. Turn him out. Turn him over. Make sure he's cooked right through.

– She misses her jewels, her gold rings and ornaments. Goodman's men stole them and put them where no one would dare look, which means the earthly police have no earthly chance of finding them.

– Who told him that? Paddy asked.

– A rat.

– I see. I must act upon the word of a rat.

– Rats won't lie to liars. The jewels are hidden at Alcock's Arbour. But no one will go there because the place is cursed and guarded by the giant progeny of Chanticleer. Being dead, the big bird shouldn't bother you, but if it does, you'll have your cleaver, which should be mythical enough to see off a cockerel whose renown is legendary, but only in these parts, whereas your story will be told as long as there are men to hear it.

– Given that only half of what you say is likely to be true, I'm only half convinced, said Paddy Muttonchops.

– People will talk of this for years, said O'Scrapie. How Paddy Muttonchops slew Alcock's monster rooster and restored the widow's wealth.

Muffy was trying to sleep on the slippery padded bench in the police station. Goodman was being more obstructive than Cerberus on a bad hare day. The longer he argued, the less demented he appeared, until he reached a state of cold rationality, like a Broadmoor killer trying to prove his fitness to stand trial for a murder he believes he didn't commit. The supposed novelist was going round and round like a fly in ever decreasing circles, flicked off by the spokes whenever he got near the hub of the bicycle.

– What's all this to do with me? asked Goodman.

– You stole the bicycle from *The Third Policeman*, along with the widow's jewels. I've restored the bicycle to its rightful author, but the wheels are still missing. We all need wheels to write. The wheels turn on the plot and the plot turns on the wheels.

– I've never been near *The Third Policeman*, said Goodman. I've never read it, so how could I have got inside the book and made off with the bicycle?

– But you know who the first and second policemen were?

– Everyone knows that, said Goodman. Burgess fled the novel after tipping off Maclean, who wrote himself out of the book three pages before the arrest scene. When the police arrived to take him into custody, they found a blank page.

– And I think you know the identity of the fourth man?

– But Sir Peter's dead.

– That doesn't matter, said the ghostwriter. As part of the action of my posthumous novel, Sir Peter Prurigeaux wants me to find the man who betrayed him.

– Which one? Goodman asked. There were many betrayals.

– The man who slept with his wife.

– Which one? There were many. Lady Olivia is an attractive lady, her fingernails are sharp as talons. She wears fuck-me shoes.

– The one who gave her the infection.

– But why should I want to help a dead man? Goodman said, glaring. That might mean betraying the living.

– Because Sir Peter was your friend, as he asked me to remind you. He also says you owe him one. And if you don't assist me with my enquiries, with my research for my book, he has furnished me with certain information which he says you would find not only embarrassing but detrimental to any hopes you might still have of escaping unscathed from Otteridge.

– That's not enough, said Goodman. I'll need a fast plane and two suitcases, one stuffed with half a million pounds in used banknotes, the other filled with bars of Cadbury's Dairy Milk if I'm going to a country where you can't buy decent chocolate.

– No deal. All I can offer you myself – and you can make your own way after that – is a cameo appearance in chapter 27 of *The End of My Wether*. That will get you away from here. Once you've done my scene, you'll be free to go.

– All right, said Goodman, you win. But I can't help you with the bicycle. My men didn't steal that. You'll need to go after Gubbins and Dogbreath for your wheels.

– Mr Gubbins? You're not telling me Mr Gubbins is a thief? Well, *knock me down with a feather.* So he stole the wheels, did he?

– I swear it.

– And the fifth man?

– The man's name is on the captain's bullet. Tell Sir Peter that. He'll know what it means.

– I'll take your word for that. But one more thing...

– Yes?

– This man, does he use *1881* aftershave?

Goodman nodded.

– Thank you, said Kernan, that will be all.

Where had that line come from? Listening to himself, Kernan felt like a man impersonating a police officer, or a member of the West Midlands Fictitious Crimes Squad. But you had to ham it up a bit when you were dead, otherwise no one would believe you were who you said you were, particularly now when so many policemen look and talk like thugs. Like it says in the Police and Criminal Evidence Act, unless you can show the court the holes in your hands, they won't believe you've suffered crucifixion in police custody.

The interview room at Otteridge police station. A single bare light-bulb hangs above the table, casting...

No, none of that Gestapo stuff. Make it a strip-light, please, with a slight flicker, the kind that obsessive people find irritating.

The white plastic light-casing is lined with dead flies.

All right, you can have some flies.

On the left side of the table are SUPERINTENDENT NICHOLAS GOODMAN, *who is cloven-hoofed like a goat, a fact unknown to his colleagues in the police force, and his attorney*, PAUL MERINO, *a sheep.*

His solicitor you mean.

No, attorney: Goodman's attorney. That's what they always say in films. I want to speak to my attorney. Get my attorney on the phone.

But this isn't a film, and it's England. We have solicitors here. Get my legal eagle on the blower, on the dog and bone.

Merino is an attorney-at-law in the State of New York, but he works in England. He's famous for representing Butch Cassidy and the Sundance Pig, the Tamworth Two, as well as the Collybirds Four, the Proud Walkers Six, the Lilywhite Boys, the Seven Swans a-suing, Six Geese appealing and the Partridge Family in their pear tree.

All right, you win. Attorney it is.

...and his attorney, PAUL MERINO, *a sheep. In the middle of the table is a water-jug with five glasses, and a tape-recorder, from whose recording this transcript is taken. Facing the man and the sheep, on the right side of the table, are a lamb, a hogg and a gimmer.*

Come again?

Facing them: Chief Constable LARRY THE LAMB; *former Agriculture Minister* HOGG, *a male sheep; and the* GIMMER, *a female sheep.*

Why sheep?

Hogg, hoggerel, hogget. A sheep between its weaning and first shearing. Not to be confused with the GIMMER, *a female sheep of the same age, the* WETHER HOGG *being a castrated male between weaning and shearing, its days numbered like the* DOUGLAS HOGG'*s While gimmers become ewes and wander, hoggs become stews and pasanda.*

But what's the hogg doing here?

The cattle disease…

Nevertheless, he doesn't belong in this scene. Get rid of him.

Suddenly, a distant sound is heard, coming as if out of the sky, like the sound of a string snapping, slowly and sadly dying away. Silence ensues, broken only by the sound of an axe striking a tree in the orchard far away. In the garden, a rope creaks as the wind swings the body of a man back and forth.

What was that?

DOUGLAS HOGG *being deselected, as you asked.*

You can't do that, he's not one of our characters. He's a "real life" person like O'Scrapie.

Don't worry about it. I got Chekhov to kill him off. He said he always wanted to add another line to the end of The Cherry Orchard. *The axe blow was too muted. He wanted to see someone else dance our Tyburn jig, and who better than Douglas Hogg…*

Gimmer's not a sheep though, is she?

Gimmer. The female sheep until shorn: also gimmer hogg, ewe hogg, sheeder ewe and ewe tegg: the female sheep until shorn.

And from first to second shearing…

Shearing ewe, shearling gimmer, theave, double-toothed ewe or gimmer.

Second to third shearing…

Two-shear ewe.

Twinter…

Two-year-old ewe.

Very good. But our GIMMER, THEAVE and TWINTER are female police officers, not ewes.

That's for ewe to decide. The police as sheep. The sheep as police. The sheep police. Whichever.

We need a bird as well, to do this scene. You know what kind.

On the outside window-ledge, a blue-black bird with red legs is perched, a CHOUGH, *or possibly* KING ARTHUR *taking the form of a chough, if the Cornish legend is "correct".*

GIMMER: This interview is taking place on the first of February at the crack of sparrow fart, I mean at 6.30 a.m…

GOODMAN: White rabbits! It's before twelve o'clock.

GIMMER: …in interview room 3 at Otteridge police station, and on page 486 of *The End of My Tether*, a novel by Neil Astley.

LAMBERT (*striking* GOODMAN): A pinch and a punch, first day of the month...and no returns.

MERINO: The Chief Constable is striking my client. It may be the first day of the month but this is police brutality on any day.

GOODMAN (*kicking* LAMBERT *under the table*): A thump and a kick, for being so quick...and no returns.

GIMMER: Children! If I may continue...Present are the two interviewing officers, that is myself, Inspector Emma Gimmer, and Chief Constable Lawrence Lambert, both of Loamshire Police. We are interviewing Superintendent Nicholas Goodman of the Same Force, who has been cautioned and arrested on two charges of murder. Also present is his solicitor, Mr Paul Merino, and the author.

GOODMAN: I don't recognise this author. Everyone has free will to act as they wish, or as I tell them...

MERINO: My client withdraws that statement. The author is of course omnificent and omnipresent. Nothing happens without his knowledge. Or if it does, he may re-write it afterwards without that affecting the validity of the interview transcript, as happens with stage instructions, court records and *Hansard*.

GIMMER: Superintendent Goodman, you have been charged with the murders of two police officers from this force: PC Johnny Jakes and Sergeant Malcolm Oxter. What have you to say in response to these charges?

MERINO: Careful...

GOODMAN (*looking anxiously around him*): I've not killed anyone. If they've been murdered, where are their bodies? When were they killed and how? You don't know, Gimmer. You've got nothing on me...

MERINO: Not so fast...

GOODMAN (*staring into space*): You think you can work like Kernan, but you're trying to pull a fast one, too fast. Without any bodies you have no evidence. You can't work back from truth to proof, you don't have any *ssss*special powerssss, do you...

MERINO: Hold it...

GOODMAN (*angrily*): You can't hold me here. You need evidence or a confession, and you won't have either by the time you have to let me go. And when you do, there'll be hell to pay. I'll have your guts for garters, Gimmer, and as for *you*, Larry...

LAMBERT: Lawrence. Always *Lawrence,* never Larry. I've told you before…

MERINO: You don't have to say any…

GOODMAN (*standing up and swaying on his feet*): As for you, meek little Larry the Lamb running round after that bird of Kernan's, you'll be roasted by the time I've finished with you, you'll have ewe-nuts for balls and mint sauce for glazing, with nothing but your own dags for dinner. You'll be out on your ear-tag. Out of the force, out of the flock. You pathetic, clueless, useless, skull-faced, orf-lipped bald git with *pigshit* for brains!

MERINO: Careful, Nick, careful. Better the foot slip than the tongue. Birds are entangled by their feet, and men by their tongues.

GOODMAN (*shouting*): The *bird* is known by his *note*, the *man* by his *words!*

GIMMER: A bleating sheep loses her bit.

GOODMAN (*thumping the table*): Let every sheep hang by his own shank!

LAMBERT: The ass that brays most eats least.

GOODMAN (*with a nervous laugh*): Every ass likes to hear himself bray.

GIMMER: Every bird loves to hear himself sing.

MERINO: Careful, Nick. If you sing before breakfast, you'll cry before night.

GOODMAN (*grinning to himself*): Better a night of cries than a breakfast of flies.

MERINO: A closed mouth catches no flies.

GIMMER: The fly that plays too long in the candle singes his wings at last.

GOODMAN (*puzzled*): What do you mean?

GIMMER: I mean *Candlemas*, Superintendent. Tomorrow is the Purification of the Virgin, when candles are blessed to celebrate the epiphany of the sacred light.

GOODMAN (*indignant*): So? What's sacred light to do with this case?

GIMMER: Plenty. Remember how St Brigid helped the Holy Family to escape from Herod's soldiers…

GOODMAN (*nonchalant*): I know nothing about those stories of Kernan's. They're nothing but myths.

MERINO: My client didn't mean to imply…

LAMBERT: Brigid the patron saint of poetry and domestic animals.

GIMMER: How she made a crown of candles and capered around to distract the soldiers from their pursuit of the Holy Family? She threw out a tub to the whale, didn't she?

GOODMAN (*nervously*): I don't know what you're getting at.

GIMMER: Are you afraid of the sacred light of truth?

GOODMAN (*angry*): Don't give me that. You're playing for time, Gimmer. You don't know anything.

GIMMER: Your soldiers have been distracted.

GOODMAN (*with an air of triumph*): I have no soldiers...

GIMMER: No, not now you don't, Superintendent Goodman, because you killed them! You killed Oxter and Jakes because they knew too much. Like you killed Bernard Tench. And then you framed Brock and had him killed as well, *didn't* you?

MERINO: You've gone too far now, Inspector. My client doesn't have to answer that ridiculous accusation, and no imputation of guilt must be attached to his not saying anything. He has the right to remain silent...

GOODMAN (*staring at the floor*): He that is silent, gathers stones...

LAMBERT: Dumb dogs are dangerous.

GOODMAN (*storming*): Beware of a silent man and still water. Still waters run deep.

MERINO: A closed mouth catches no flies.

GIMMER: You've already used that one, Mr Merino.

MERINO: So?

LAMBERT: You miss a turn... Silence catches a mouse.

GIMMER: The mouse that has but one hole is quickly taken.

LAMBERT: The hole calls the thief.

GIMMER: At open doors dogs come in.

LAMBERT (*whispered to* GIMMER): It's not working, he may be off his head, out of his tree, but he's not taking the bait...

GIMMER (*to* LAMBERT): The bait hides the hook.

LAMBERT (*frantic, to* GIMMER): Bees that have honey in their mouths have stings in their tails.

GIMMER (*to* LAMBERT): The rough net isn't the best catcher of birds. The higher the ape goes, the more he shows his tail. (*Giving a meaningful nod.*) There's more than one way to skin a cat.

LAMBERT (*to* GIMMER): When the cat goes bonkers, you need more conkers...

GIMMER (*to* LAMBERT): You can take a horse to water, but you cannot wipe its arse.

LAMBERT (*turning to face* GOODMAN): I said, *silence catches a mouse*, Superintendent Goodman...

MERINO: Silence never makes mistakes.

GIMMER: Superintendent Goodman, when I asked Oxter and Jakes to take the digging equipment to Alcock's Arbour, why did you ask them to stop off at Dealchurch?

GOODMAN (*meekly*): To pick up the tranquilliser gun. The police marksman needed it in case the giant cockerel decided to put in an appearance.

GIMMER (*firmly*): Why did you have this equipment at your house?

GOODMAN (*apparently reasonable*): There'd been sightings of a Barguest in the vicinity of the village. We needed to have the tranquillisers ready in case of an attack.

MERINO: My client's right, Inspector. I live near Dealchurch, and St Belial's has been attacked three times in the past week by a giant dog with fire-filled saucer eyes.

LAMBERT (*worried*): Are you sure about this? Did it try to break down the church door?

MERINO: Yes, it did. And its blood-curdling howls could be heard as far away as Otteridge.

GIMMER: Don't let him distract us, Lawrence. The sightings are in the reports, a huge black dog whose paws left no tracks, nothing new in that. It was either Padfoot or Black Shuck the Devil Dog. (*To* GOODMAN.) We accept you had good reason to need the tranquilliser darts, but I would like to suggest to you that when the two policemen arrived to collect the equipment, you... (*searching for words*) ...you...

CHOUGH (*from window-sill*): Chee-aw, chee-aw, chee-aw... *chuff!*

GIMMER: ...When they arrived, you shot them with the tranquilliser gun. Like animals...

MERINO (*whispered to* GOODMAN): What's this Nick? Where did she get that from? (*Turns to face* GIMMER *and* LAMBERT.) My client of course completely denies that accusation. He also wishes to point out again that you have not produced the bodies of the dead policemen...

GIMMER: So you admit they're dead...

MERINO: I didn't mean that...

LAMBERT (*in a low voice to* GIMMER): I said this was a bad idea, that they wouldn't admit anything, but you...

GIMMER: Superintendent Goodman, I put it to you that after you had stunned the two policemen who were your former helpers, you...um...you...

CHOUGH (*from window-sill*): Chee-aw, chee-aw, chee-aw... *chuff!*

GIMMER: ...You shot each man in the centre of the forehead with your Webley service revolver...

GOODMAN (*frantic*): No, no, you *can't* know that...There's no evidence, no gun, no bodies, so how can you...

CHOUGH: Chee-aw, chee-aw, chee-aw... *chuff! Fol-the-rol-day.*

GIMMER: ...You dumped the bodies in the back of your car, and drove them to the abbatoir...

GOODMAN (*desperate*): No, you can't...

CHOUGH: Chee-aw, chee-aw, *fol-the-diddle-di-do-day.*

GIMMER: ...Where you disposed of them in the incinerator used for BSE cattle carcasses.

GOODMAN (*standing up*): You can't know that! You can't know *any* of that! You have no proof, you *can't* have...

MERINO: Nick, *whoa, whoa.* Slow now. Haste is from the devil.

GOODMAN (*shouting*): Come on, where's your proof, Gimmer!

CHOUGH: *Chee-aw-de-ral, chee-aw-de-ral, chuff-luff-the-day.*

GIMMER: ...Every bullet has its billet. The proof of the killing is in the eating.

It was St Catherine's Day, Diana said. Their third meal, in the Three Bears at Ottermouth. She remembered how she had tilted her head upwards like a stork. Was this when it had happened? When she had poured three glasses of water down her throat, trying to get rid of it?

– But I could still feel it, she added. Or was that just my sense of it, that it had been there? I almost thought I could taste it.

– What could you taste?

– What do you think? she said, starting to blush. A single bead of sweat ran down her cheek. Thinking she was alone, she darted out her tongue to catch its saltiness.

– Lambert asked you if you swallowed it?

– Yes, said Diana, the moment I felt it in my mouth, I thought of Kernan, that he had sent the fly to spy on us. I remembered Brigid's story of Étaín, whom Etar's wife had swallowed as a fly; how she later gave birth to a new Étaín.

– Where were you? It wasn't in the restaurant then...

– No.

– You had gone back to Lambert's house?

– That's right. I sat there, looking at him. He has this bulging vein on his forehead. I remember staring at it as he was talking, wishing all the time that I was spending the evening with Kernan instead of with him. The week before, when Kernan was talking about sparrows and bannocks and blessings, I told him I'd give him a big piece of my cake, if I had one, and he said he'd like that. And he sang that song about the cuckoo's nest. I still didn't get it then...

– He didn't sing the rest: *I said it wasnae true but I left her with the makings of a young cuckoo.*

– ... I felt a shiver go through me.

– You said nothing happened with Lambert...

– Lambert was a dry run for Kernan. I knew it would end in pain, but if I didn't allow myself to be hurt, I would never know what it was to love, and be loved. Lambert loved me, but through what happened with him I discovered that the man I loved was Kernan. Lambert had been holding back until then, because he was scared. Kernan was scared too, but of something else.

– So something *did* happen with him?

– With...

– Lambert.

– I told Kernan it was in his imagination.

– Was that true?

– It was real for him.

– You haven't answered my question.

– You believe what you want to believe, she said.

– What does that mean?

– You should know, you're the writer here. You make all this happen, don't you, in your imagination? I need your help...

– I didn't invent the fly. The fly came in the window. Like the sparrow through the hall.

– You sound like Kernan. Was Kernan the fly?

– Perhaps.

– It wasn't Étain…

– I didn't say that.

– And the snake? she asked.

– You were the snake. And the wet-whiskered tiger.

– So he wasn't the tiger? It was me… But the wolf then, who was the wolf? Was that him? And the civet, the wiry-haired civet. Who was that? And the ram…? So was it the fly or the ram?

– The father of your child?

– Yes.

– Not the lamb then?

– I never wanted immaculate conception, not with the lamb.

– *Son los pasariellos del mal pelo exidos.*

– Bunting?

– Sparrow. *Libro de Alexandre.* Which he translates: *The spuggies are fledged.* Remember, *spud*, a potato; *spigot,* a peg for a vent or faucet; *sprog,* a child; and *spuggy,* a sparrow.

The Jolly Bullethead

This little bullet from a captain,
This little bullet burns and sears,
This little bullet went for a spin,
This little bullet flew for years
And this little bullet cried, *Wee-wee-wee-wee-wee,*
I can't find my way home.

This little bullet missed a German,
This little bullet nicked a Hun,
This little bullet missed a Kernan,
This little bullet hit none
And this little bullet cried, *Wee-wee-wee-wee-wee,*
I can't find my way home.

This little bullet went over the top,
This little bullet went west,
This little bullet went, *How do I stop?*
This little bullet knew best
And this little bullet cried, *Wee-wee-wee-wee-wee,*
I can't find my way home.

This little bullet wasn't yellow,
This little bullet wasn't green,
This little bullet missed the big fellow
This little bullet hadn't seen
And this little bullet cried, *Wee-wee-wee-wee-wee,*
I can't find my way home.

This little bullet went down to the wood,
This little bullet was a fly,
This little bullet liked takeaway food,
This little bullet shot by
And this little bullet cried, *Wee-wee-wee-wee-wee,*
I can't find my way home.

This little bullet liked bread and butter,
This little bullet *a wee dram,*
This little bullet liked brain to splatter,
This little bullet liked jam
This little bullet liked jam
And this little bullet cried, *Wee-wee-wee-wee-wee,*
For I've found my way home.

This little bullet hit Morton's jaw,
This little bullet wanted Maw,
This little bullet cried Maw no more
This little bullet floored old Maw,
And this little bullet cried, *Wee-wee-wee-wee-wee*
I've found my way home,
And this little bullet cried, *Tee-hee-hee-hee-hee*
I've found Morton's bone, his bone,
I've found old Maw's bone.

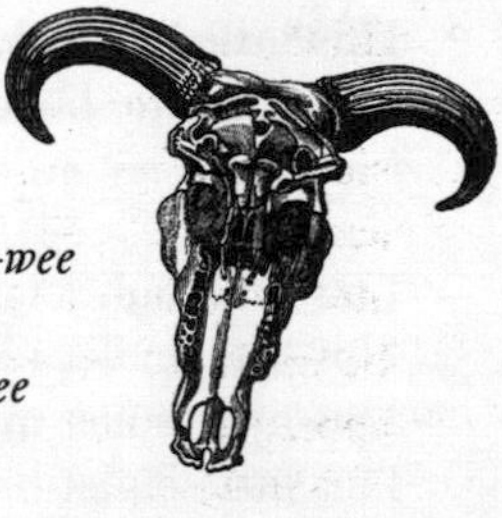

CHAPTER TWENTY-FIVE

The Whole Hog

LADY DAY: MARCH 25TH (LUPERCALIA: FEBRUARY 15TH)

Do not throw away dirty socks, but wash them first, for if you throw out a sweaty sock, you are discarding your own vital force present in the sweat, and with it your power to take luck on the wing.

This inquest has heard evidence from many people during the past two weeks concerning the demise of Councillor Morton Maw, who met his death on the night of Monday the 15th of February, as we have heard, in circumstances which were unusual, to say the least, following events which took place in the car park outside the Buffs Hall in Otteridge. It now falls to me as Coroner of the County of Loamshire to attempt to summarise the events of the night in question which have a bearing upon this case.

The purpose of this inquest is to determine the likely cause of death; or in this case, rather, the *most* likely cause. It is not for this court to pursue questions of guilt regarding *either* the possible involvement of other parties in Mr Maw's death *or* other acts of an alleged criminal nature which have been brought to our attention during the course of these proceedings. If charges are to be made in respect of any of these matters, that will be for the appropriate authorities to consider after we have given our verdict.

Mr Maw, who was chairman of Loamshire County Council's planning committee, was taken ill at a lodge meeting of the Royal Antediluvian Order of Buffaloes at which he was the main speaker, after he had eaten a large dinner, which we have heard included roast beef and Yorkshire pudding. As dessert, he ate a concoction apparently called *Death by Chocolate*, but I think we may safely assume that the chocolate mousse, however rich, was the *least* likely cause of death on this occasion, even if it was topped with thick chocolate cream and a sprinkling of Cadbury's Milk Flake. The starter, however, was a freshwater trout from the River Otter, which we must not rule out as a suspect in the light of evidence presented at this hearing. Nor should the glass of water be excluded from our enquiries. But the beef, while potentially lethal to other diners, is unlikely to have caused Mr Maw's seizure, if the scientific evidence is to be believed.

The main complication involved in this inquest concerns what happened after Mr Maw was helped outside to his car. It has been established that Mr Maw was left sitting in the passenger seat of his Subaru four-wheel-drive vehicle for approximately ten minutes while waiting for his wife Isabel to arrive to take him home. He had attempted to drive the vehicle himself at first, but was dissuaded from doing so by several concerned Lodge members who believed Mr Maw's alcohol level to be over the legal limit. The lab reports have since established that Mr Maw was indeed over the limit for driving, *considerably* so, having 350 milligrams of alcohol in 100 millilitres of his blood, the legal limit in this country being 35 milligrams. Moreover, Mr Maw's consumption of alcohol on the night of February 15th, which several witnesses have attested was 'normal' for him, has been called 'so excessive as to be positively dangerous' by one doctor called upon for a medical opinion. This being so, alcoholic poisoning cannot be ruled out as a contributory factor in relation to Mr Maw's death, particularly in view of statements made by some witnesses to the effect that they believed a person or persons unknown had "spiked" his whisky with quantities of the veterinary drug Mansonil, which is more usually associated with the treatment of tapeworm in sheep.

During the course of the altercation which followed Mr Maw's refusal to be dissuaded by his associates from attempting to drive, one of the Buffaloes, the Right Honourable Henry Sirloin, MP for North Loamshire, is then said to have struck Mr Maw a sudden blow in the face, breaking his nose, this action at first being attributed to personal matters relating to the recent demise of his late wife, Mrs Candida Sirloin.

However, the court has heard that Mr Sirloin proceeded to make other accusations against Mr Maw which were overheard by other Buffaloes, and these statements by Mr Sirloin further inflamed the situation.

As I understand it, Mr Maw was accused of having had sexual relations with Lady Olivia Prurigeaux, and of infecting her with the virus Hepatitis B, which she proceeded to pass on not only to Mr Sirloin and to her late husband, but also – strange to report – to Mrs Patricia de Foie, who in turn infected the former Chief Constable, Mr Maurice Saveloy – while he was still alive, I hasten to add, although the cause of his death was not, as we have heard, this infection but the botulist conflagration at Otteridge Police Station – as well as to Mr Maw's own wife, Mrs Isabel Maw, whom we have heard could *not* have been infected directly by her husband since they never slept together, she believing him to be homosexual; and she in turn passed on the Hepatitis B virus to Superintendent Nicholas Goodman of Loamshire Police, of whom more later, as well as a thrush infection contracted from Mrs de Foie, who had already given this same thrush infection to Lady Prurigeaux.

Mr Sirloin also confessed to the gathered company that he had infected his wife Candida with Hepatitis B. He said he was told this in confidence by her doctor, Dr Vercingetorix Gallstone, when she was dying of cancer, responsibility for which he laid jointly at the door of Mr Oliver de Foie, managing director of Eurochimique UK Ltd, and of Mr Maw, in respect of their involvement in a land deal in which property belonging to his late wife's family passed to a company called Loamshire Country Properties Limited, which firm owned by Mr Maw was subsequently taken over by a subsidiary of Eurochimique UK, the international chemicals company based at Loamfield. Since we have heard a whole day of evidence concerning the possible bearing of the activities of Eurochimique and other companies on the circumstances surrounding Mr Maw's death, much of this information, as I understand, not previously in the public domain, or not in this form, I will attempt a short summary of the chain of corporate connections which appears to me to be relevant. Bearing in mind that several possibly erroneous statements have already been printed in the press concerning allegations made about these companies during the course of this lengthy inquest, I feel that an unambiguous listing of the relevant corporate connections should be included in my report of these proceedings.

The company I have just mentioned, Loamshire Country Properties Ltd, had a board consisting of three directors: Mr Maw; the late Sir Peter Prurigeaux, formerly leader of Otteridge District Council; and the late Sir Harold Hockle, formerly chairman of Loamshire Water Board. Mr Maw had the majority holding of shares. As I understand it, this company was used to effect the transfer of agricultural land owned by Miss Candida Yeats (later Mrs Sirloin) to a company later acquired by Eurochimique UK with a view to its later exploitation for industrial purposes, in contravention both of county planning regulations and of a National Trust protection order which two of its directors, Mr Maw and Sir Peter Prurigeaux should have been upholding as county and district council leaders. This short-lived company was acquired two years later by Braxy UK, a holding company of Gerstmann Holdings Pty Ltd, the Australian associate company of Gerstmann Holdings UK Ltd, which has as its managing director Mr Oliver de Foie, who holds the same directorial position with Eurochimique UK.

Braxy UK, we have heard, had three directors, Mr de Foie, Mr Maw and the late Mr Brucellosis Tucker, and acquired Featherwether Grange near Loamfield two years ago from Sir Percy Featherwether, but went into voluntary liquidation in January of this year following the death by lead poisoning of Mr Tucker. As well as Eurochimique, Gerstmann Holdings is the parent company of four other companies mentioned during this inquest, namely: Scheinker, the sportswear manufacturers, which had Mr Sirloin on its board in an unpaid capacity until his recent resignation; Alpers Pharmaceuticals (Northern Ireland) Ltd, which carries out research on new products for Eurochimique; the hotels group Straussler, which we now know owns the company which owns Mr Spermwail's Excelsior Hotel in Otteridge; and the Otteridge Meat Company, which has or had two directors, namely Mr Maw and Lady Olivia Prurigeaux, a sleeping partner since the death of the chairman, the late Sir Peter Prurigeaux. Mr Maw, we now know, was a serving director of all these companies.

It was alleged by Mr Sirloin on the night of Mr Maw's death – and it has been further alleged by him in the course of this inquest – that in his capacity as a Member of Parliament and one-time Minister he was *'used'* (I use his own word) by Mr Maw and Mr de Foie to secure political favours. Large donations were made to Mr Sirloin's party by Gerstmann Holdings through Scheinker in the guise of funding to assist the promotion of sport and public health, but the intention was that this assistance to Mr Sirloin's party should be reciprocated in the form of certain actions or non-actions and adjustments or lack of adjustments to legislation which have had the effect not of benefiting public health but rather of being positively detrimental to public health, the main people benefiting from this situation being the directors and shareholders of Eurochimique UK and the Otteridge Meat Company. Mr Sirloin has claimed a chains of events was set in motion by these two companies, the main results of which have been the pollution of our environment, both locally and nationally, and the consequent damage to public health and to wildlife (locally to the fish and fauna of the River Otter). He has also alleged that the two companies played a significant contributory role in the growth and spread of the Bovine Spongiform Encephalopathy epidemic, the scientific research and product promotion of Eurochimique being linked both with the causes as well as with the development and slowness of eradication of BSE, while the activities of the Otteridge Meat Company have been – it has been alleged – detrimental to the eradication of the disease, to the livelihoods of the farmers affected by it, and to the health of the company's own employees. Indeed, witnesses have confirmed that immediately before his assault on Mr Maw, the MP made what one person called 'a soapbox style speech', and another, 'an impassioned address', to those gathered in the car park in which he accused Mr Maw and Mr de Foie of having 'run with the hare and hunted with the hounds'; and furthermore, his elaboration of this charge of duplicity, punctuated by the repeated phrases 'snouts in the trough' and 'feathering his own nest', had the effect of changing the attitude of the Buffaloes towards Mr Maw from one of solicitude for an old friend who had drunk too much to one of antagonism expressed in an alarmingly aggressive fashion to one they now regarded as a traitor and an enemy.

Mr Sirloin has made two specific charges with regard to health problems allegedly caused by Eurochimique, either by its products or by airborne and river pollution from its plant at Loamfield, namely the cancer which killed his late wife, the cause of which he now believes to be DDT, and the chloracne which has resulted in his own unfortunate facial disfigurement, caused, he says, by dioxin pollutants emitted from the plant.

Press coverage of this inquest has also focussed upon the possible links between Bovine Spongiform Encephalopathy and new variant Creutzfeldt-Jakob Disease, this being related to other evidence presented both by Mr Sirloin and by the police in respect of the activities of Eurochimique UK and the Otteridge Meat Company, and the extent to which Mr Maw and Mr de Foie, along with two Eurochimique employees, Dr Jabez Kuru and Mr James Strimmer, may or may not have been personally responsible.

One name which has cropped up numerous times over the past two weeks has been that of the late Dr Bernard Tench. The investigating officer, Superintendent Emma Gimmer, has recently recovered a set of papers belonging to Dr Tench, in which he made allegations regarding illegal actions by Eurochimique and other Gerstmann companies and by their directors which appear to support statements made by Mr Sirloin. I have decided that these are not admissable as evidence in this inquest, but they clearly have a bearing on other matters raised during the past fortnight, upon which the police will no doubt be issuing a separate statement at the end of these proceedings.

In this connection I must remind this court that the late Dr Tench was previously thought to have been murdered by his friend and neighbour, the late Mr Michael Brock, and that he in turn met his death by misadventure by running into the bale-spike of a tractor. The papers supplied by Superintendent Gimmer relating to Mr Maw and other matters clearly cast considerable doubt upon that conclusion, as well as on earlier verdicts recorded by myself as Coroner in the County of Loamshire regarding the deaths of these two men. It is now my intention to reopen the inquests into the deaths of both men, which I shall do in the light of having seen this new evidence. I originally likened Mr Brock's injuries to those of a soldier running into a fixed bayonet on a battlefield, but now I shall be asking if his collision with the bale-spike was perhaps not the accident we were led to believe at the time. Forensic evidence produced at the time by Dr Kettle but not submitted to me as Coroner also suggests that the round hole in Dr Tench's forehead was inflicted by a captive-bolt stunning gun of the kind used on sheep in slaughterhouses, and the new evidence alluded to by Superintendent Gimmer in her submission, including the discovery of the weapon itself and the particular article of women's clothing used to wipe it, clearly implicates Mr Maw in the death of Dr Tench.

Two other names which have been on the tongues of our witnesses almost as frequently as that of the late Dr Tench have been those of former Superintendent Nicholas Goodman and the late Inspector George Kernan, the inquest into whose death would have been conducted before that of Mr Maw had it not been for his disappearance, or rather the spiriting away of his body. I would like to make special mention here of the key role of Inspector Kernan in the police investigations carried out prior to his death, the implications of which are only now coming to light, and I would wish to extend that commendation to inspired policing done subsequently under the guidance of Superintendent Gimmer over which Inspector Kernan's legacy appears to have had such an influence.

I wish I could be as generous to another long-serving officer who goes back almost as far as Inspector Kernan, but the evidence presented to this inquest would discourage me from that. It was my hope that Superintendent Goodman would give evidence in this inquest, but we have been told that he cannot do so due to ill health, these same reasons precipitating his early retirement from the Loamshire force. It has been suggested by several people during the past fortnight that Superintendent Goodman's illness may not prevent his arrest on charges relating to matters raised in this court. I could see how it might be possible to come to such a conclusion, but this is a matter on which I couldn't possibly comment.

We now need to return to the particular circumstances of Mr Maw's death on the night of February 15th, before considering the extensive medical evidence. We have heard how there was a confrontation between Mr Sirloin and Mr Maw in the car park of the Buffs Hall, and how other Lodge members reacted to allegations made by Mr Sirloin in a manner antagonistic to Mr Maw. Furthermore, the substance of Mr Sirloin's allegations was also quickly communicated to other friends and associates of Mr Maw in the Bald-Headed Ram public house in Otteridge High Street, as well as to some of Mr Maw's employees who been drinking with several off-duty police officers in the Pig and Whistle across the road.

The next stage in the chain of events which resulted in the death of Mr Maw occurred when the group in the Pig and Whistle, having been acquainted both with the matters already described in respect of the Otteridge Meat Company and of Eurochimique UK, as well as with the alleged involvement of Mr Maw and former Superintendent Goodman in the deaths of Dr Tench, Mr Brock, Sergeant Oxter and PC Jakes, decided to take the law into their own hands, one might have said, except that on this occasions their actions were supported and abetted by at least two Loamshire police officers. This group of men, consisting of Otteridge Meat Company employees Mr Frank Fisher, Mr Peter Gingell and Mr Joe Hartley, Mr Maw's gamekeeper Mr Phil Hart, Mr Billy Johnson (formerly a corporal in the Royal Loamshires, and a Gulf War veteran) and Mr Matthew Hardacre (a jobbing builder), accompanied by Inspector Daube and DS Daglock, proceeded to set about Mr Maw's Subaru with baseball bats and police truncheons, with Mr Maw still sitting inside the vehicle, albeit in a semi-comatose state. The attackers broke all the windows of the vehicle, showering Mr Maw with pieces of glass, several pieces of which caused severe cuts to his face and hands. Two large slivers of this glass became embedded in his neck, the loss of blood resulting from these injuries, along with the bleeding from the broken nose, being another of the possible causes of Mr Maw's death which we have had to consider.

We have also heard how Mr Maw tried to take evasive action in response to this attack, first reversing the vehicle at high speed through the car park, which action caused the death by crushing of Inspector Daube as well as the injuries to Mr Hardacre and Mr Johnson. Pursued by the group of angry men, Mr Maw then attempted to drive the Subaru even faster around the back of the Buffs Hall and through the adjacent children's playground, but instead of rejoining the High Street at a point where he might have made his escape, he skidded into a low wall, bounced the Subaru across the soft play area, demolishing the roundabout and a group of swings, and overturned the vehicle at the top of the bank where the land slopes down to the river. The Subaru rolled over several times before ending up in the River Otter, where Mr Maw may or may not have drowned, one's definition being dependent upon whether or not he was dead before he went under the water, which action was instantaneous in this case due to the fact that the vehicle was by this stage flying through the air at high speed, upside-down and with all its windows smashed in.

The next possible cause of death relates to the fact that the Subaru's brakes had been tampered with, not on the night of the attack, but some time before, possibly up to six months ago, the vehicle having been little used since the death of its previous owner, Mr Maurice Saveloy, in July of last year. Although the Subaru was submerged in the river for some time, the forensic investigation yielded several sets of fingerprints perfectly preserved in the hardened oil around the brakes and camshaft. These have been since been identified by police as belonging to Mr Patrick O'Scrapie, whose body was discovered buried in a shallow grave at St Belial's in Dealchurch last November. His death was the subject of a previous inquest over which I presided as Coroner, the verdict of which was that Mr O'Scrapie had been murdered in 1830 by a person or persons unknown. At that inquest the difficulties of linking Mr O'Scrapie's murder over a hundred and fifty years ago with his alleged criminal activities in Loamshire during the past eighteen months were the subject of much speculation, and I have similar difficulties now in relating Mr O'Scrapie's possible role in causing the death of Mr Maw on the night of February 15th of this year.

It should also be noted that even if Mr O'Scrapie did somehow contrive to cause deliberate damage to the brakes of the Subaru, managing this feat despite already being dead for well over a century, his intended victim may have been not Mr Maw but Mr Saveloy, the owner of the vehicle at the time when the brakes were tampered with.

We now turn to what some have called the most spectacular of the possible causes of Mr Maw's death. As the Subaru was flying through the air, having left the riverbank but before it hit the surface of the water, a single bullet hit Mr Maw in the jaw. The autopsy established that this bullet passed through the roof of Mr Maw's mouth into the lower part of the brain before exiting from the skull via a hole in the middle of his forehead, finally embedding itself in a NO FISHING sign nailed to a tree by the side of the river. The ballistics report indicates that the bullet was travelling along the river from the direction of Ottermouth, that its trajectory was horizontal at a height of approximately ten feet above sea level, and that it could not possibly have been fired from anywhere in the vicinity of the Buffs Hall or other places in the centre of Otteridge involved in disturbances connected with the attack on Mr Maw or with the later riot which resulted in the burning down of the Excelsior Hotel, Cerberus, Cerberus and Cerberus the funeral directors and the Burger Royale Diner, and the subsequent firing of houses belonging to Anubian residents in the dog end of Otteridge.

The report has established that the bullet was fired from the same Webley service revolver used in the murder of Sergeant Oxter and PC Jakes, the remains of whose bodies were recovered from the Otteridge Meat Company's cow incinerator, along with the bullets used to kill the two policemen, but that while those bullets were of recent manufacture, the single bullet which impacted with the head of Mr Maw was of a earlier provenance. Indeed, analysis of the bullet has established that it was manufactured in 1916 and that it was fired from the Webley revolver as long ago as 1917. It had apparently been travelling around the surface of the earth for over eighty years, always managing not to hit anything in the course of its eight-decade trajectory before finally impacting with the head of Mr Maw on the night of February 15th of this year. The Webley revolver is said to have been stolen from former Superintendent Nicholas Goodman the week before the three policemen were murdered, but in 1917 it was registered in the name of a Captain Nicholas, an officer in the Royal Loamshire Infantry, who deserted his regiment in 1918 after the Battle of Amiens, when he was to have faced a court martial for dereliction of duty resulting in the deaths of a whole battalion of Loamshire soldiers, and who afterwards disappeared without trace. How this gun came to be in Superintendent Goodman's possession was a question I would have wanted to ask in the course of this inquest had he been well enough to attend these proceedings.

We thus have a situation in which Mr Maw, having suffered considerable loss of blood in the course of the two attacks, first by Mr Sirloin, and then by the group of employees and police, loses control of his vehicle because the brakes had been tampered with, and is then shot in the head the instant before he begins to drown. The post-mortem report introduces further complications, in that not only was Mr Maw inebriated, he had also suffered poisoning, from the trout, the water and the beef he had consumed that evening. Analysis of the contents of his gut revealed that the flesh of the trout contained exceedingly high concentrations of mercury and polychlorinated biphenyls. We have heard that these PCBs are synthetic chemicals manufactured by Eurochimique UK for use in electrical insulation material. They are present in tiny concentrations as a pollutant in sediment in the River Otter but they accumulate by a process of biomagnification as they move from animal to animal up the food chain, the concentration of PCBs in the trout being approximately three million times greater than that in the original Eurochimique pollutant, and thirty million times greater in the gut of Mr Maw. The water drunk by Mr Maw was mains tap water supplied to the town by the Loamshire Water Board, but malfunctions in that company's purification procedures resulted in local water supplies on the day in question being adulterated with high levels of the pesticide dieldrin, another pollutant present in effluent discharged into the River Otter by the Eurochimique plant at Loamfield. This has been the subject of recent reports in the press, and as everyone present today is aware, irregularities in the Loamshire Water Board's filtration procedures are now to be the subject of a public enquiry. While many other Loamshire residents have suffered the effects of the dieldrin poisoning, including myself I am sorry to report, none, I think, is likely to have been subjected to the particular cocktail of poisons consumed by Mr Maw, nor to have had such a lethal mix applied to a constitution weakened not only by overeating and excess of alcohol but also by a Pandora's Box of ailments, illnesses and infections.

Before I turn to those, I must also report that the beef eaten by Mr Maw on the night of February 15th was beef on the bone supplied to the Otteridge Lodge of Royal Antediluvian Order of Buffaloes by his own Otteridge Meat Company, and that laboratory analysis of the remains of the joint served on this occasion has revealed the presence of Bovine Spongiform Encephalopathy in the bone marrow, and that during the post-mortem traces of the same BSE infection were found in remnants of the beef in Mr Maw's gut.

Mr Maw, as we know, died approximately three hours after eating this infected beef, so that the effect on him is not something which need concern this enquiry. However, these findings will be a matter of considerable concern for the other Buffaloes who ate this beef – and the trout – on the night of February 15th, particularly since, as in the case of the recent outbreak of E Coli poisoning in Scotland, most of those affected, being RAOB members, will be quite old. On the other hand, it has to be said that none of their other Buffaloes is likely, I would hope, to have consumed as much beef and fish as Mr Maw on this occasion, if the reports are to be believed. As the saying has it, *Many dishes make many diseases*; to which one might be inclined to add, *Much meat, much malady*. Mr Maw consumed as many as *four* trout, all of which are now thought to have contained excessively high levels of PCBs. Therefore in respect of food poisoning suffered by the Buffaloes, those Buffaloes still left alive will have a greater chance of recovery than our extinct Buffalo, although the prognosis of one scientific witness is that if there is indeed a link between Bovine Spongiform Encephalopathy and new variant Creutzfeld-Jakob Disease, as many believe, then 'some of these gentlemen should be making their wills now as they may be dead within six months'.

In considering Mr Maw's habit of excess, I am reminded of the saying, *He loves roast meat well that licks the spit*; or more pointedly, in respect of his appetite: *He loves bacon well that licks the swine-sty door*. But of what that appetite invited, it was not so much a case – as Mrs Maw has said – of *He loves well sheep's flesh that wets his bread in the wool*, as *He loved mutton well that licked where the ewe lay*; for we have heard opinion from many learned sources concerning the likelihood that one or other of Mr Maw's many ailments may indeed have been the cause of death, or a significant contributory factor in his demise.

Dr Gallstone has stated that he referred Mr Maw for treatment at a private clinic in Pigglingford in June of last year for Non-Specific Urethritis, but it now turns out that he did not seek such treatment for several months, during which time this particular infection was unchecked. The autopsy further showed that Mr Maw was also infected with the virus Hepatitis B – as Mr Sirloin has alleged – and that his liver was in an advanced state of disintegration, the cirrhosis being linked to excessive consumption of alcohol over many years. When the post-mortem was carried out, it was discovered that his liver must have burst at the moment of death, but whether as a cause or an effect of the manner of his death, we have been unable to discover.

Furthermore, as well as being pierced in two places by the bullet which entered his jaw, Mr Maw's skull was found to be holed in several places, which Dr Kettle at first believed to be caused by an attempt at trepanning with an unsteady hand. However, subsequent tests showed that these holes appeared to have been made by a parasitic worm called *Skryabingylus nasicola* which causes progressive holing of the skulls of stoats and weasels. Dr Gallstone has confirmed this diagnosis with his account of an attack on Mr Maw by a weasel he had been attempting to kill while out rabbit-hunting on Loamsley Moor in June of last year.

Dr Kettle has reported her surprise on seeing slides of tissue taken from Mr Maw's brain, since these showed the kind of sponge-like holing which is the diagnostic hallmark of transmissible spongiform encephalopathies such as Scrapie, BSE and new variant Creutzfeld-Jakob Disease, and, as she told this inquest, 'tissue deterioration resulting from an infection contracted just three hours before would be a record for any TSE'.

However, subsequent analysis of the sample showed that the most likely cause of Mr Maw's infection was a TME or Transmissible Mink Encephalopathy, which Dr Gallstone has linked to either to the attack by the weasel, which could have been bitten by a TME-infected mink, or to the later unprovoked assault on Mr Maw by his son Mr Thomas Maw, who had apparently been bitten some months before by a dog called Shuck belonging to the late Mrs Sirloin, on whose madness Mr Goldsmith might well have written:

> The wound it seem'd both sore and sad
> To Mrs Sirloin's eye;
> And while they swore the dog was mad
> They swore poor Tom would die.
>
> But soon a wonder came to light,
> That show'd the rogues they lied;
> Tom Maw recover'd of that bite,
> The dog it was that died.

The dog that died had earlier been attacked by a minkhound, which may itself have suffered an attack from a cornered TME-infected mink during the minkhunt organised by Mr Saveloy last year along the banks of the Otter following the breakout of mink from Eurochimique's experimental laboratory.

The autopsy also revealed an unusual growth in Mr Maw's brain tissue, a cyst which Dr Kettle described as 'about the size of a golfball'. Her tests identified this as a *Coenurus cerebralis* cyst formed by larvae from the tapeworm *Taenia multiceps*, the cause of the brain condition called *sturdy* or *gid* which has only previously been known to affect sheep. However, Mr Philip Hart, gamekeeper on the Maw Estate, has given evidence to the effect that Mr Maw, whose manner of perambulation had always been strange, had over the past year developed a high-stepping gait and a jerky walk, which – taken with Mr Maw's recent habit of tilting his head to one side, something which Mrs Maw had thought 'furtive' in character, for her husband often gave the appearance of talking out of the side of his mouth, an 'affectation' she attributed to his paranoia and obsessive secrecy – led Mr Hart to believe that his employer was indeed suffering from sturdy, but until this inquest he had discounted this explanation because giddy sheep lose their appetite for food and drink, and Mr Maw had not lost his interest in either of these.

As to how Mr Maw might have contracted this sheep ailment, we have heard two theories, both of which relate to the life cycle of the sturdy tapeworm, the eggs of which are eaten with contaminated herbage by sheep and afterwards burst inside the animal's gut to produce larvae which burrow through the intestinal wall and enter the poor beast's bloodstream. These larvae grow into cysts in the brain or spinal canal. When the sheep dies, its infected skull is eaten by dogs or foxes, and portions of the cyst develop into adult tapeworms in their intestines, the eggs of which are then transmitted back to the pasture in faeces, whereupon – as Dr Kettle memorably phrased it – 'some other unlucky sheep has its alfresco lunch egged on by dogshit or fox crap', and the whole cycle starts again. That Mr Maw should have interposed himself into the tapeworm's cycle along with the dog and sheep might be related, we have heard, to the bite he received from his son Thomas, who had earlier been bitten by the dog Shuck which had itself been bitten by a minkhound, in which case the transmission involved tapeworm eggs from one or both of these dogs to the man instead of to a sheep, or it might have been due to Mr Maw having eaten an undercooked powsoudie, sheep's head broth being one of his favourite dishes, in which case the transmission involved tapeworm cyst material from sheep direct to man with no assistance required from either labrador or minkhound. In Mr Maw's case, both explanations *could* be applicable – another example, one might think, of the 'double-hit' hypothesis which has run through so much of the evidence we have heard – were it for the added complication that not only was a larval cyst from a *dog* tapeworm found in the frontal lobe of his brain, but a *sheep* tapeworm of an entirely different variety, one belonging to the genus Moniezia and measuring 100 centimetres in length, was found to be brazenly disporting its long segmented chain of a body along a one-metre length of his intestines, one treatment for this parasite being Niclosamide; and traces of that drug were found in Mr Maw's blood, but this, we have been told, is more likely to have derived from the spiking of his whisky with Mansonil by person or persons unknown, because while the Mansonil might have been self-administered had Mr Maw been aware that this parasite had taken up residence in his colon, Dr Kettle believes that he would in that instance have resorted to an anthelmintic treatment because the use of benzadole products is not only considerably cheaper but would also have served to protect him against Gastrointestinal Helminthiasis, caused in sheep by roundworm.

The Reverend Devlin has also given us a pertinent text to consider in relation to Mr Maw's death, namely that *whatsoever a man soweth, that shall he also reap*, from Paul's letter to the Ephesians, and he further warned us to beware lest we also *reap the whirlwind*, as Hosea has it. As pastor of Loamfield, he was flabbergasted by disclosures which were never even vaguely alluded to during the thirty years in which he was Councillor Maw's spiritual guide, and he has given his opinion that his late parishioner's secrecy on such matters more or less guarantees that his soul must now be howling in purgatory, and that this 'wolf in sheep's clothing', as I remember him calling Mr Maw, would surely burn in hell. Miss Gizzard further elaborated upon that metaphor in drawing our attention to the fact that Mr Maw died on the day of the Feast of Lupercal, named after Lupercus, the Roman god of fertility and flocks, and derived, she told us, from *lupus*, a wolf, and from the verb *arcere*, to ward off, and that the death of a wolf in sheep's clothing with a sheep's brain condition is likely to please a god we call upon to protect our flocks. Yet be that as it may, the significance of Lupercal in relation to our wolf's death seems to me of much less import than another significant factor, namely that Mr Wolf was suffering from a February cold. This most certainly must have had an influence on his ill luck and consequent demise. Lady Olivia Prurigeaux has stated that her lack of responsiveness to his attentions the evening before, which was Valentine's Day, was influenced by his continual sneezing. Mr Maw was still sneezing on February 15th, and sneezing on a Monday bodes very ill for a sneezer, as the rhyme has it:

> Monday for danger, Tuesday kiss a stranger,
> Wednesday for a letter, Thursday for something better,
> Friday for sorrow, Saturday, see your lover tomorrow.

At the Buffs dinner, Mr Wolf's meal was interrupted several times by his sneezing fits, and Mr Sirloin indeed commented upon the possible risks of infection from sitting next to Mr Maw. Mr Sirloin, we know, was on Mr Wolf's left at the dinner. This suggests that Mr Maw had been sneezing to the left, which is unlucky. But he did not sneeze *after* the meal, which would have been a sign of good health, but rather desisted from sneezing until he began to feel ill towards the end of the evening, when he left the Buffs Hall to drive home. As is well-known, sneezing at the start of a journey is also very unlucky. When that journey starts on a Monday, the level of ill luck involved is possibly too frightening to contemplate.

Since I am now approaching the end of this summary, I hope I may be forgiven for taking a further liberty in quoting another text which seems to me relevant to what the Reverend Devlin has called the 'sins of the fathers' aspects of this case, and more specifically the sin of gluttony, which some of our witnesses have called 'the English sin', while others have said in respect of the manner of Mr Maw's demise that 'who hastens a glutton, chokes him'; and indeed it has been said more than once in the course of this inquest that 'gluttony kills more than the sword', although Mr Sirloin wished to remind us also that 'ill air slays sooner than the sword'; to which I would add, not without a passing nod – or a tilted head – to the medical evidence we have heard, that *Ill beef never made good broo' nor ill mutton guid powsoudie*, for this favourite saying of my Scottish granny links neatly with the text I was wishing to draw to your attention, namely a comment made by Francis Grose in 1787 on the subject of the Great Fire:

> The fire of London was a punishment for Gluttony. For Ironmonger-lane was red-fire-hot, Milk-street boiled over; it began in Pudding-lane and ended at Pye-corner.

As the saying goes, *He that has an ill name is half hanged.* And if Francis Grose is to be believed, we would do well to take careful note of the more oracular pronouncements made by some of our witnesses, which I was at first inclined to dismiss but whose relevance to this case I have since had cause to review. Those warnings of future conflagrations likely to affect certain installations in this County, based it now seems to me on firm evidence in respect of the actions and influence of the Swine of Gluttony, along with the Scorpion of Lechery and the Serpent of Envy, as well as persons in their thrall, are no less compelling – and as such a matter for grave public concern – than the earlier warnings given by scientists such as Professor Richard Lacey and Dr Stephen Dealler in relation to the threat posed to public health in this country by BSE, which we now know to have been well-founded although many were inclined to dismiss them at the time. We ignore such warnings at our peril, for an ill wound may be cured, but not an ill name.

There is also the question of the bat. For as we have heard, it was discovered during the post-mortem that Mr Maw had at some time during the past twelve months contracted rabies. The tests showed his particular variety to be the new rabies virus variant associated with insectivorous bats, which now account for about half the cases of rabies reported in humans. There is no mention of a bat bite in Mr Maw's medical records, but this is apparently not unusual according to the *Morbidity & Mortality Weekly Report*, which has stated on several occasions that few patients infected with rabies from a bat have reported any history of a bat bite.

While we are on the subject of bats, several of these creatures did of course have to be removed from this building during the course of this inquest. The owner of these bats, Mr Ernest Gubbins, gave evidence in which he asked us to consider one possibly further cause of death, namely that Mr Maw had thrown out a pair of old socks on the morning of February 15th. We have heard that it is Mr Gubbins' practice to examine the contents of people's dustbins on the day after St Valentine's Day, when there are apparently an abundance of discarded socks to be found, a phenomenon which he attributes to the practice of men being given pairs of socks by their wives in return for chocolates and flowers – either as a genuine mark of their regard or even their love for their partner or, conversely, as an indication of dislike and estrangement – and subsequently being forced to dispose of their existing socks, which apparently cause offence to the ladies in question. In the heat of the moment, indeed sometimes during the course of an argument which results from this practice, the socks are thrown into wastebins and then disposed of without first being washed. As Mr Gubbins has rightly pointed out, dirty socks must be washed before they are put in the dustbin, for if you throw away a sweaty sock you are discarding your own vital life force present in the sweat, and with it your power to take luck on the wing.

Mr Gubbins has kindly furnished this inquest with the pair of socks he obtained from the dustbin at Maw Hall on the morning of February 15th. Laboratory tests have confirmed that these paisley-patterned socks, originally bought at least nine years ago from Marks and Spencer, belonged to Mr Maw, and that they could not have been washed before being disposed of, since they are both sweaty and exceedingly malodorous.

Given the numerous complications pertaining to this case, it should come as no surprise to those gathered here, that I must finally enter a verdict that Mr Maw's death was due to misadventure, caused primarily by his premature disposal of the two paisley socks, and that having discarded his vital force with the sweat-impregnated socks, he was prevented from taking luck on the wing when his vehicle flew through the air, presenting the octogenarian bullet from Superintendent Goodman's gun with the once-in-a-lifetime opportunity to impact with his jaw.

In March kill crow, pie and cadow,
Rook, buzzard and raven;
Or else go desire them
To seek a new haven.

NOTICE

To all it concerns,
This notice apprises,
The Sparrow's for trial
At next bird assizes.

CHAPTER TWENTY-SIX

The Heebee Jeebies

ALL FOOLS DAY: APRIL 1ST

Farm animals should not be castrated when the moon is waning, nor should pigs be killed then, or their meat will shrink in the boiling. Fools become more foolish still when the moon is full. Sleeping in moonlight is dangerous and may cause lunacy, or blindness, or at best a swollen face. This is why the crossbill finch always wakens children it finds sleeping in moonlight, lest their mouths become as distorted as its own.

Above him, high in the branches, the black birds were massing, a murder of crows. The wind was rushing through the tree's huge head of foliage, a high rustling sound in which he fancied he could recognise some words. *Horn*, he could hear, that was it, *hooorn*, as in hunting. The word even sounded like a horn, the way the wind was playing with it. But this was no new tout on an old horn, and it prompted a chorus of barking from the laboratory block, then a series of crashing noises. The dogs had broken out, and they were yelping like crazy, they'd gone barking mad, and the creatures were tearing round the fence, past the security hut, towards the huge oak. He could not climb the tree to escape from them, the trunk was too big, and there were no branches within reach.

At the head of the pack a gigantic man thundered towards him on a massive black horse, a black-bearded fellow with great antlers sprouting from the top of his head like a deer.

– *I am here a Windsor stag*, the horseman called out, *and the fattest I think i' the forest: send me a cool rut-time, Jove, or who can blame me to piss my tallow.*

– Piss my tallow! cried Oliver de Foie, whose face was white as a sheet. And the bull's semen, yes, he gibbered. But not the tallow here. That is not good.

In his dream, Henry Sirloin watched the tiny figure of Oliver de Fois beneath the great oak like a tom-tit on a round of beef, frozen to the spot, the wild huntsman with his pack of baying hounds bearing down on him. The industrialist was beside himself with terror, fighting with his own shadow in his panic to escape.

The rider had stopped, stilling his dogs, and towered over De Foie, goading him:

> There is an old tale goes that Herne the Hunter,
> Sometime a keeper here in Windsor Forest,
> Doth all the winter-time, at still midnight,
> Walk round about an oak, with great ragg'd horns;
> And there he blasts the tree, and takes the cattle.
> And makes milch-kine yield blood, and shakes a chain
> In a most hideous and dreadful manner…

Old Kernan was really laying it on thick, Henry thought. And Oliver was quaking, he still hadn't recognised the policeman, but kept repeating *Takes the cattle, makes the milch-kine yield blood.* He had curled up in a foetal position on the ground, his hands protecting the back of his head, though Kernan's giant horse could crush him with one stamp of its great hoof.

– Hideous and dreadful, Oliver wailed. Piss the tallow. Poison the cattle. Shit in the river. His body shook as his crying took over, the words escaping from his mouth like a toxic emission.

– Makes the cattle yield blood, he cried, makes them eat meat.

– The red specks in the water, called Kernan. Is that a fish's speckle?

– No, it's blood, De Foie lamented. I put it there, the blood.

– The yellow sheen, Kernan called out, his voice rising. Is that the sunlight playing on the water?

– No, no, it's piss, De Foie gasped. I leaked it there, the piss.

– Your plant is a dandelion, it pissed in the river's bed. And that nut-brown water, is that the peat from upstream?

– No, it's shit, De Foie croaked. I dumped it there, the shit.

– You shat on us, said Kernan. On everyone, man and beast.

Now the bearded rider was holding a wheezing box-thing in his lap, like an accordion but much smaller than the lumbering instrument Oliver's grandfather had played in Germany.

– An English concertina, said Kernan, starting to swing it like a groaning animal as he spoke. And we'll sing you another tune, you false deceiver, a merry song, me and my jolly squeeze-box, with a *right fol-di-ri-do-day...*

> When all our work is done, and the sheep are all shorn
> Then home with our captain, to drink the ale that's strong.
> It's a barrel then of hum-cap, which we call the Black Ram
> And we do sit and swagger, we swear that we are men
> And yet before the night's through, I'll bet you half a crown
> That if you haven't special care, that Ram will knock you down...

– *With a too-rum-too-rum, to-me-diddy-di-do. That Ram will knock you down, tra-la, with a two-ram-ram, with a two-ram-ram, for a ram can kill a butcher. Come in number nine, your time is up!*

– Not number nine! cried Oliver de Foie. Number nine's unstable. We were going to fix it! Kuru was meant to adjust the mixture. Just give me a few more minutes and we can stabilise...

When Henry woke from Oliver's dream, he almost expected to find the reptilian industrialist lying in bed beside him. But the scaly hand clawing at the doormat of his chest was an old woman's.

– Close your eyes, Henry, she said. Time for your reward.

Sitting bolt upright in his makeshift bed in the bracken, Nicholas Goodman heard a strange rustling sound in the bushes. He froze. There seemed to be something snuffling in the undergrowth, some beast. Even in the moonlight it was hard to make out what it was, some kind of creature, bigger than a dog, but like a dog, huge, black with glowing eyes. The Barguest. Two dogs now, two black beasts. Black Shuck and Skriker, both of them. Pad-foot and Trash. No, it was him, his sickness, he was fighting with his own shadow. He shook his head, rubbed his knuckles in the pits of his shrunken eyes. One dog now, just Black Shuck.

These things should not frighten him. An old fox is not easily snared. The only person anyone should fear in Hangman's Wood was Goodman himself. And he wasn't afraid of anyone. Only Death. Death and Sickness. Death and Pestilence. Death whom he served, and if Death came for him, he would want to know why. Goodman had been doing Death's work. He had not finished.

If any man or creature came looking for him, wanting him for Death, he would kill them. Send them back to Death themselves, and Death would know he wasn't ready. Death would let him do more work. Death would let him kill for love of Death. He still had the key. He still had the revolver too, the Webley from the war. If anyone came, he would fire, never mind the noise. If anything crashed through the bushes expecting to take him, he would kill it with the gun. Anything at all.

That rat in the trench. He should have shot it. Killed Kernan with the rat. He hadn't known then how Kernan was, how he worked. Now he knew that every creature in this wood could be Kernan's. Fields have eyes and woods have ears, Kernan's eyes and ears. They all belonged to Kernan. They all served him. Any beast or bird could be Kernan himself, dead Kernan living out another life, as he had too, only he'd stayed a man, Goodman. He'd always been *man*. Good to be man not beast. Good man. Nicholas. Nick. Steal. Stealing away. Stealing a man. Stealing a man's life for himself, to be himself. Nicholas Goodman. A man, always. Devil of a job last time, with the war, but he did it. Wars were always good. Good for a change. No one saw. You got away with murder. Changed. No one knew.

Kernan's mistake. Not changing. Wanting to be the same, like father, like son. Disappearing in the war, coming back later not as someone else, like him, but as himself, the son who was the father, the grandfather even. Same man in all those wars, First, Second and Boer. Crimea even. Waterloo. Always finding him, Goodman, but Goodman changed, Goodman someone else. Kernan the Hunter, Kernan his prey. Goodman hunter then his prey. Cat and mouse, cat and dog, dog and rat. They hunted each other.

Where was Kernan now? Watching him, he must be watching him. If not himself, then he had other eyes. His shadow Herne, good to have a shadow, clever. Be in many places. Divide and rule. But Goodman was himself a shadow, as was Kernan, Cernunnos's man. Now Goodman was like Herne, the Wild Man of the Woods, hiding. The fugitive, running away, a man outside. Kernan closing in.

If Goodman had lost, Goodman must escape, but he was sick now, sick as a dog. The stricken deer withdraws itself to die. He'd killed the deer; now he was the stricken one. He shrank, a thin man, bony, stick-like. He shook, he shook all the time. Couldn't stand, but swayed, played the giddy ox, knees hurting. Sat in den for hours, gibbering, his mind gone, out for hours. Night now, but he'd sat down to rest when sun was high. Or he didn't sleep at all, his head aching, skull wanting to burst, to break like an egg, his brain hatching out, squawking, wanting food. Hungry, always hungry now. Rabbit gone. Eaten, days back. Too weak to stalk more. Only a mouse to eat now, but better a mouse in the pot than no flesh at all.

– *Who's there?* he said, suddenly alert. A noise, there was a noise. He heard it, a squawking.

Bird. Black and white. One of Kernan's. Stood there, staring. Black-headed bird, grey beak. Magpie. Magpie the harlequin watch-bird, one bird unlucky. After the key. He grabbed the key, holding it up.

– *This what you want?* he yelled, pointing the key at the bird.

The magpie dipped its head. It started to edge towards him, slowly, as if to say *Don't.* Don't do anything. Don't move. Easy now. Give me the key. Everything will be…

Goodman blasted the bird. *Bam!* he repeated after the gun had fired. *Bam bam!* His Webley, smoking now. The bird dead, harlequin feathers floating down. Food too. He would eat the bird, roast it on his fire.

– *One for sorrow*, he said, the small silver key in his hand. Make fire now, eat bird. Relight fire. Matches, where are matches?

More squawking. New bird. Black. Kernan again. Stood there, staring. Get him. Black bird, yellow beak. Crow. Single crow unlucky. For the crow. Crow the hag bird. After the key. He grabbed the key, holding it up.

– *This what you want?* he yelled, pointing the key at the bird.

The crow dipped its head. It started to edge towards him, slowly, as if to say *Don't.* Don't do anything. Don't move. Easy now. Careful. No need to move. Now give me the key...

Goodman blasted the bird. *Bam!* he repeated after the gun had fired. *Bam bam bam!* His Webley, smoking. This bird dead too, a murder of crow's jet black feathers floating down. Food too. He would eat this bird also, roast it with the other on his fire. Eat and be strong. Escape then.

– *Bye bye blackbird*, he said, the small silver key in his hand. Make fire now, eat bird. Relight fire. Matches, where are matches?

Another squawking.

Third bird. Black. One of Kernan's. Stood there, staring. Black bird, red beak. Jackdaw. Jackdaw, thief bird. After the key. He grabbed the key, holding it up.

– *This what you want?* he yelled, pointing the key at the bird.

The jackdaw hopped about like a cat on a hot bake-stone, as if feigning the dodging of a cartoon bullet. Was it sending him up, was this cadow taking the piss out of him, Nicholas Goodman, dancing like a dog in a fair, here, there and everywhere, before dipping its head like the Green Knight inviting his own beheading? Then it started to edge towards him, slowly, as if to say *Don't.* Don't do anything. Don't move. Easy now...

Goodman blasted the bird. *Bam!* he repeated after the gun had fired. *Bam bam bam bam!* His Webley, smoking now. The bird dead, black feathers floating down. Food too. Three birds to eat. And all three dead. Never more than three.

– *Bye bye jackdaw, bye bye cadow, Kernan's shadow*, he said, the small silver key in his hand. Make fire now, eat bird. Relight. Reload. Bullets, where are bullets? Three bullets gone. Kernan's trick, his birds, his pawns. Use up pawns, disposable. Private soldiers, cannon fodder.

Goodman fool. Use bullets. Lose ammunition. Noise. They will come for him.

Another bird, squawking...

– *Chee-aw, chee-aw, chee-aw... chuff.*

Kernan stood there, staring. A trick. Black bird, orange claws. Chough. Arthur's bird. He grabbed the key, holding it up.

– *This what you want?* he yelled, pointing the gun at the bird.

The chough dipped its head. It started to edge towards him, slowly, as if to say *Don't.* Don't do anything. Don't move. Easy now. Give me the gun...

Goodman shooed the bird. *Shoo!* he repeated. *Bam bam!* he pretended, waving the gun. Pull trigger. *Click click click.* Blast the bird. *Clack-clack, clackety-clack, clack-clack.* Trickster bird. *Click click click.* The key? Where was the key?

– *Chee-aw, chee-aw, chee-aw…chuff. Skiddly-idle-daddle-diddle-didle-dadle-dum…*

The chough held the small silver key in its beak. When he tried to coax it into dropping it, the bird swallowed the key. Then flew off.

Goodman howled like a wolf.

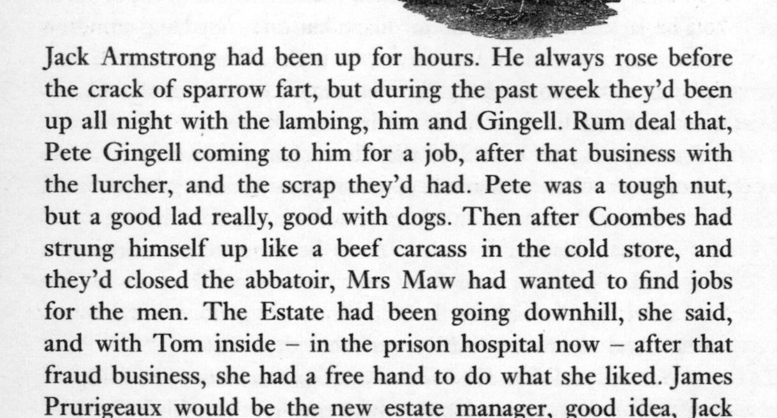

Jack Armstrong had been up for hours. He always rose before the crack of sparrow fart, but during the past week they'd been up all night with the lambing, him and Gingell. Rum deal that, Pete Gingell coming to him for a job, after that business with the lurcher, and the scrap they'd had. Pete was a tough nut, but a good lad really, good with dogs. Then after Coombes had strung himself up like a beef carcass in the cold store, and they'd closed the abbatoir, Mrs Maw had wanted to find jobs for the men. The Estate had been going downhill, she said, and with Tom inside – in the prison hospital now – after that fraud business, she had a free hand to do what she liked. James Prurigeaux would be the new estate manager, good idea, Jack thought, make the wounded hero her new broom. Then Joe Hartley and Frank Fisher had been taken on by Phil Hart to work with him on the woodland improvement scheme; and there was plenty of fencing work for Matt Hardacre.

– Look, Pete, he said, you hold the lamb down, on its back, wedged between your knees. I'll show you how it's done. It's always easier with two people.

– This is it then, is it? said Pete Gingell, fingering the elastrator. Bye bye Rambo, hello Hogg.

– That's right, said Jack. You use the elastrator pliers to open this rubber ring, sliding it over his balls like this…

– Hang on in there, my merry wether, Pete told the sheep. Hey, this beats stickin' em, Jack.

– You have to find *both* balls, Pete. You pay attention, you're not in the meatshop now. It's no laughin' matter for the sheep if it ain't done right. Never put a ring ower just one if you can't find t'other, or we'll end up wi' a rig, and rigs is trouble. So make sure you've got both bollocks in his scrotum, like this, before the ring's slipped ower and released.

– He don't seem too happy, said Pete, wincing, surprised by his own concern. Oooh! Not sure I like that. Gives me the heebie-jeebies just thinking about it.

– He'll be all right soon. If he's still playing up after he's had it on for about fifteen minutes, we'll clip it off and give him another couple of days. We dock the tails at the same time. Don't take off too much, see. Very short tailing's illegal now. You have to leave enough to cover his arse. If the elastrator's put on wi' the points forward, the ring's easily left where you want it, and the ould gadget slides away like so...

– And we always do it this soon?

– That's right. Some shepherds castrate after a day, or as soon as the ewes and lambs is turned out wi' a group, but I like to wait till I can see the lamb's all right. But if you need to wait a week, you have to use a local anaesthetic, and you can't castrate a male sheep by any method without an anaesthetic after three months. After six months, you need the vet. They're very strict about these things.

– Not like in the abbatoir, said Pete, miming the action of sticking a carcass, but with an elaborate flourish, like one of the Three Musketeers. Don't seem much point then, with the beast about to cop it anyway.

– You can tell when it's been done well, Jack added. If you're buying older sheep, you'll see it'll have a minute purse and no bollocks if it's been done wi' an elastrator. A lamb castrated by Burdizzo will be harder to judge, as they only crush the tube.

– An elastrator, there's your man, said Pete Gingell, weighing the instrument in his hand. He gripped it like a pair of secateurs, feeling for the pressure of the spring mechanism. Holding it out in front him, he jerked it back.

– This won't hurt, sir, he said, with a thin smile. Open wide.

– It's no joke for the sheep, said Jack. But we have to do it.

– Come on then, the next bugger's mine. Let me have a go.

Emma Gimmer's excavation of the mound took much longer than they had anticipated. The work had to be put off at first in deference to the two police officers who were to have begun the digging. Then they had to seek clearance from English Heritage, and much wrangling followed over the question of whether or not Alcock's Arbour was a site of special scientific interest. Diana had warned against rushing in where angels feared to tread, but once she saw the yellow JCB lumbering across the soggy field towards the smooth-grassed Devil's Nutbag, the overpowering sense of foreboding she'd had on her first visit felt like a bad dream remembered from childhood. She wanted the digger to go in now, to see the jagged-teethed shovel gouge out the mound on which Kernan had fallen, scoop out its power, exorcise his ghost. She wanted the mound erased, the cancer cut out.

As the JCB swung its great clawed arm across the mound, jamming the shovel into the bank, the giant cockerel appeared from behind the hedge and strode across the field to do battle with this metal monster. A small group gathered to watch the spectacle, including three policemen. Then a large man dressed in a blue and white butcher's apron, wearing a straw boater, interposed himself in front of the rooster, brandishing a metal cleaver. The blade flashed in the sunlight like Excalibur as he swung it through the air, severing the bird's red-crowned head with one sweep.

– *Cut!* yelled a voice from behind the JCB.

– What is it now? demanded Paddy Muttonchops, staring at his handiwork. The dead cockerel on its back with its legs in the air like vandalised trees.

– *What's that rope doing there?*

– Must be the tether, said Sergeant Oxter. From the earlier scene. Kernan must have left it here. He's taken the cow and left us the tether.

– That's one of the good things about being dead, said PC Jakes. You don't have to spend hours looking for things. I used to hate all that.

– *We'll have to shoot it again.*

– We can't, said Paddy. The cockerel's dead. If the cock dies before he's dead, he's sure to rise without his head.

– *Get another cockerel then.*

– We can't, said Oxter. There's only one cockerel this size. It's mythical, so you can't kill it again for a year and a day. We had to draft in the proverbial butcher with his evil cleaver to do the beheading. The Green Knight wasn't interested, said it was a job for a mercenary.

– *All right then. We'll keep the rope. But we'll have to work it into the rest of the story.*

– The rope has never been made that binds thoughts.

– Paddy's at it again, said Jakes, more weasel words from the butcher of language. Your proverbs are as much to the purpose as *Tomorrow I found a horseshoe*. Don't you ever let up?

– Give a thief enough rope and he'll hang himself, said Paddy.

– What does that *mean*, Muttonchops? Oxter wanted to know.

– *I like it. We'll use that on Goodman.*

– No, said Paddy. Hanging's too good for Goodman.

– He's right, PC Jakes agreed. We want him to *really* suffer…

– *I thought we'd have him hang himself in Hangman's Wood. Echo of Kernan's dream, Goodman as Odin, tie it up with the BSE business, hoisted by his own petard. Goodman dies like Judas.*

– What? Is the sheep to die as well? asked Jakes. I vote we keep the sheep.

– *No, the sheep doesn't get killed. The sheep has work to do.*

– No, no, no! cried Oxter. Goodman has to suffer. We want *revenge*.

– Where vice is, vengeance follows, Paddy insisted. Revenge is sweet.

– *Look, who's writing this story?*

– You are, said Sergeant Oxter. But you can't write it without us. It's our story, a joint effort, a collaboration if you like. And we have to be happy with what you've got planned, especially now that we're dead and can do anything we like.

– That's right, said PC Jakes. With Diana, Lambert and

Gimmer, you've got it easy. You've got them standing over by the police cars now, and they can't even see what's going on out here. They didn't even clock the cockerel.

– Not see the cockerel, spluttered Paddy, but…

– They'll do what you want them to do, said Jakes. With Muffy, Herne and Lizzie: not quite so easy, they can blur the boundaries, change shape, shift from one place to another. But with the dead, you've got trouble, mate. If we don't like what you've got in mind, we'll fuck it up for you.

– *What if I don't use you any more?*

– We won't let that happen, said Oxter.

– We can turn up any time, said PC Roger Hodge.

– And bugger up the story, said O'Scrapie.

– And right now we want revenge on Goodman, Oxter persisted, it's not much to ask. You owe it to us.

– Revenge may be wicked, but it's natural, said Becky Sharp. I'm no angel…

– See what we mean, grinned O'Scrapie, pinching the adventuress's bottom. You thought Becky had gone back to old Titmarsh when you got Kernan to do that deal with him in chapter fifteen.

– But this is the famous nightmare scenario, said Maurice Saveloy, wagging a theatrical, sausage-like finger. Everything's out of control. The whole caboodle's about to go up in smoke…

– *Stop stop! No more! You win…*

– Do we get to kill him then? asked Oxter eagerly.

– *It has to be offstage, like in a Greek tragedy. He's nearly dead, as it is. A wounded beast raving in the wood, howling.*

– A slow lingering, painful death, Hodge insisted.

– *I'm giving him that already.*

– Kill the beast, said Jakes.

– *He's been promised a cameo appearance in* The End of My Wether, *Chapter 27. Before he escapes. Now he'll get it. He'll get what was coming to him, like Maw did.*

– Only he won't escape, said Beelzebub. We've sent the Devil's Dog after him, so you'd better get moving if you want to finish him off first.

– *If you turn back to page 521, you'll find that Pete Gingell is holding an elastrator. I'm sure he'd let you borrow it.*

The iron-bound thrice-locked chest from Alcock's Arbour was lying on the big table in the incident room at Otteridge Police Station. Beside it stood a grey filing-cabinet, with two drawers marked PERSONNEL: CONFIDENTIAL, another COMPANIES, and the fourth, WORK FOR CHARITIES AND TRUSTS. They had also recovered a battered brown suitcase from the Devil's Nutbag, with brass studded corner-pieces and the inscription ARCHIE ANDREWS in faded gold letters embossed into the leather. Mrs Merkin had spent a good hour cleaning these finds before she judged them fit to be opened.

Superintendent Gimmer looked over Diana's shoulder as she fiddled with the small silver key the chough had handed in.

– Let's start on the suitcase, Lady Olivia Prurigeaux proposed. It looks like one of Johnny Jakes's theatrical props. That must be where they hid the jewels.

– It's working, said Diana. Look, the same key opens everything. And flung open the lid of the old suitcase.

A dishevelled mannequin sat up like a jack-in-a-box from inside its carrying case. As it rubbed its eyes, it dislodged a monocle from one, but quickly snatched it back, wedging it into place. It was dressed in the faded clothes of one of Bertie Wooster's chums from the Drones Club, with a musty brown-green tweed jacket shrunk down to Pinocchio size, and a yellow chequered waistcoat, a bob-watch on a chain tucked into the pocket. The pinkish paint was starting to peel off its wooden face, and there were scuff marks on its cheeks. Blinking at the bright strip-lights, and turning its head slowly in an arc, regarding each of the gathering in turn, taking in the appearance of everyone in the room, from the uniformed policemen in one corner to the aristocratic-looking woman with long fingernails whose ears were dripping with gold, the dummy first coughed to clear some dust from its throat before announcing, in Kernan's voice:

– I am the gey to by own bystery.

This is De Foie
Driving his car.
He falls asleep.
This is the sheep.
Sheep goes *Baa baa!*

Dozy De Foie
Wakes in his car.
He sees the sheep.
Car goes *Beep beep!*
Sheep goes *Baa baa!*

This is De Foie
Swerving his car
Missing the sheep.
Car does big leap.
Sheep goes *Baa baa!*

Bye bye De Foie,
You crashed your car!
Bleated the sheep.
Sheep does big leap.
Sheep goes *Baa baa!*

Watch old De Foie
Croak in his car.
Frog croaks *ree-deep!*
Sheep does not weep.
Sheep goes *Baa baa!*

No more De Foie.
Ree-deep! Baa baa!
This is the sheep.
You went *Beep beep!*
Sheep goes *Baa baa!*

CHAPTER TWENTY-SEVEN

The End of My Wether

PASSOVER: APRIL 3RD

If huntsmen chase a fine fox into a house, and find only a woman sitting quietly by the fire, she will be a witch who likes to roam the fields as a fox. When sudden drops of rain fall while the sun is shining, a fox is being married somewhere near, though some say such showers mean the Devil is beating his wife.

Stopping to catch his breath, the rider stared into the distance, one hand holding the reins while the sulphur-yellow fingers of the other rummaged nervously through a matted, tobacco-stained beard, as if searching for clues, but finding only scabs. It was no wonder the fox was getting away. He watched its reddish brush disappear into a thicket by the riverbank, the raggletaggle hunt straggling across the field behind, none of the fine mounts you used to see but this pitiful bunch of scrawny nags and jades; the huntsmen a hotchpotch of clashing colours, a motley crew of farmers on revving motorbikes and spluttering quads bringing up the rear. Over they went, down the rough slope into the ravine, the black dogs yelping as they ran headfirst into the scraggy thorn-bushes.

There was some kind of ruin down there, the Green Chapel, that was where they'd find him. He scanned the valley, a wild place strewn with great jagged boulders fallen from the crags above and rocks carried downstream by the floodtime torrent, but could see no sign of a building. Then he halted, held in his horse, searched every side for the fabled chapel, but saw nothing in that wilderness except some kind of mound, a smooth-grassed barrow on the slope by the fast-flowing stream, which foamed and frothed as if in a fever.

He hurried his horse, hied to the hillock; dismounted, tying the mare's reins round the jutting branch of a lime tree. Approaching the barrow, he paused, listened, then walked round the whole mound, found a hole at each end and one on either side, all four entrances overgrown with nettles, grass and thistles. Inside, an old cavern, or was it the crevice of an ancient crag?

Was this mound the Green Chapel? The place was deserted; damp inside and bitingly cold, it cut him to the bone. It felt less like an ancient place of worship than somewhere cursed, forsaken.

Hearing a noise then, a scuttering, he looked round, hoping to glimpse the cornered fox; not a man, or worse. And heard his name called, an eerie, echoing bass growl.

– Sir Peter Prurigeaux?

– Yes, he said meekly, hesitant.

– Where are the rest?

– I'm sure they'll be here soon. My mare is tied up outside.

As he heard their horses, the hooves clattering on the rocks, splashing through the stream in a riot of voices, it came to him that all the others in the wild hunt were dead as well, Morton, Maurice, Oliver, Harold, all violently killed; and being dead, should have nothing to fear, for what else could be in store for them? Or had they somehow to answer for their lives? Could that help the living? Was that the meaning of redemption for the truly damned?

– Don't tarry, said their host, emerging from the depths of the earth chapel, urging the others to enter, to account for themselves. Even in the dark cavernous barrow, his green skin shone; he moved towards them purposefully, a great stooping figure, grassy hair spilling in a silky fan from his shoulders, his beard a tumbling nest of leaves. Stilling their instinct to back away, the green axe held out like Excalibur, all powerful.

– Welcome, he said. You know the pact we pledged. We made our covenant, I bared my neck like Barleycorn to take your blade. Now take off your headgear, bow your heads that I may give you answer with my axe.

– There must be some mistake, stammered Oliver de Foie.

– It's Kernan you want, surely? said Hockle. He struck off your head off, he took what was yours.

– No mistake, he responded. Kernan is a part of me, and I of him. My head was his head, he took it and I took it back, a twelvemonth gone, a year ago today. But you men took what was not yours, you killed my country; what you've done has cost the earth, my plants and people, my birds and beasts who were not yours to take. No general good was served, no one's interests but your own.

– Where are we? asked Maw. Who are you, in God's name?

– I am the Green Knight and the Green Man, Cernunnos and Kernan. I am foxglove and fleabane, cat's-ear and cowslip, hogweed and cow parsnip. I am harebell and hare's-foot clover, stork's bill and bird's-foot-trefoil. I am dove-foot crane's-bill and mouse-ear chickweed. I am bee orchid and dog-violet, dog-rose and dog's mercury. I am toad and toadflax.

He moved towards them.

– I am the linnet and bullfinch, the whistling lapwing. I am the spotted flycatcher, the song thrush and tree sparrow. I am the barn owl and the grey partridge. All these you killed.

I am the cornflower, the corn buttercup,
corncockle, corn gromwell, cornsalad,
corn parsley and lamb's succory.
I am fumitory and pheasant's eye,
shepherd's needle and thorow-wax.
I am the pink bindweed in the cornfield,
the bright red poppy, yellow corn crowsfoot,
broad-leaved spurge and red hemp-nettle.
I am the purple knapweed in the meadow,
bryony in the hedgerow, I am finch and warbler
darting among the dog roses.

I am weed knotgrass in the wheatfield
with six pink flower-spikes, food
for the red-yellow leaf beetle, no more.

I am the larvae of the leaf beetle, food
for farmland bird chicks, no more.
I am the weevil and rove beetle,
the larvae of moths and sawflies, food
for songbirds, not now, all killed,
bindweed, beetles, birds, all gone.

I am seed of weeds. I am seed-eating birds.
I am corn bunting, cirl bunting, yellowhammer.
I am the insects. I am the insect-eaters.
I am the hovering lark and fieldfare.
I am the vole, the shrew and the fieldmouse.
I am the owl and the kestrel.
I am marshes and wetland, all drained,
moorland and water meadows, all gone.

I am the cowslip on the chalk down,
the dropwort, the devil's-bit scabious,
dwarf sedge, burnt orchid and toadflax.
I am the clustered bellflower.
I am the chalk hill butterfly
feeding on the horseshoe vetch.
I am the marbled white, the chequered skipper,
adonis blue, pearl-bordered fritillary.
I am hay-rattle yellow in the hayfield,
the black knapweed, the wild daffodil.
I am the cowslip and the meadow buttercup,
the adder's tongue fern, the green-winged orchid.

I am the silent field of ryegrass too,
the silage field of ryegrass, no grass
but ryegrass, no plant permitted
but ryegrass, nothing but ryegrass.
No ploughman treads this empty space
where all the air a solemn stillness holds,
no beetle wheels his droning flight,
no drowsy tinklings lull the distant folds.
Where are the owls and insects?
Where are the finches and cornflowers,
mice and moths, beetles and butterflies?

Where are the people, the farmers
who lived off the land, who gave us our food,
people and plants, birds and beasts all one?
All gone, all gone, all driven from the land.

And why, you men of greed?
Your cash crops killed us off,
your fertilisers forced us out,
you poisoned with pesticides,
you looted the land, and why?
You pulled up the hedgerows,
made big farms bigger, rich men richer,
small farms fail, money out of misery.
You turned our land into badlands
where nothing grows but money.
When money fails, nothing left,
nothing left to grow. You took it all.
There's nothing, nothing, nothing left.

With Strimmer holed up in De Foie's office, where he had been engaged since the accident in the complicated task of organising the transfer of the company's UK assets to Gerstmann Holdings using an offshore trust, Dr Jabez Kuru was hoping to be left alone. He needed to complete his most important experiments before Eurochimique's inevitable collapse, the results of which he could take with him to De Foie's rival, the mammoth chemical giant Rupert Moloch International, from which he had hopes of a research appointment and a laboratory. Only one more week of tests and he would know the ideal composition of the magic compound which could be used to identify transmissible spongiform encephalopathies through the detection of a urinary metabolite.

But the widow had not even completed the arrangements for Oliver's funeral when he found she had established her own office in the laboratory block, where she was giving interviews to investigative journalists. This would wreck all his plans for the completion of the tests and the covert removal of the most expensive pieces of diagnostic equipment.

Dr Kuru resolved to take matters into his own hands, and it was with the intention of instructing Security to refuse entry to any more television crews that he made his way across the compound towards the gate, casting a concerned eye as he did so in the direction of the number 9 tank, the emissions from whose side vents were now so unusually pungent as to give him cause for concern. He would need to check the stabiliser levels again.

On entering the gate office however, he found himself in the company of that obnoxious fellow Gubbins, who sat slumped with his great filth-caked boots propped cross-footed on the reception desk, mud jigsaw shapes from the treads scattered across the vehicle records; he hoped it was mud.

– Hello, Jabby, said the cross-eyed sweep. How are tricks in the Strangelove department? If you're looking for Gus, he's raiding the canteen. He should be back soon with the sausages. And some *croissants* for the sheep, he added, the sheep likes *croissants*, indicating the presence of a large two-shear tup in the corner of the room. The animal seemed to be watching a news programme on one of the television monitors.

– He likes the news, said Gubbins. Didn't used to get TV in the slaughterhouse.

– Slaughterhouse?

– My cousin Gus used to look after him before they all got laid off. Mickey was the Judas sheep, led all the others to that great mint sauceboat in the sky. Gus was nightwatchman, and now he's Wild Bill's deputy here. Oliver fixed it for Izzie Maw before he copped it on the bypass. You know, jobs for the boys. We know all about that here, don't we?

– I will need to speak with this Gus, Dr Kuru said, looking about him with sudden concern. I am not sure we should have a sheep in the security area. Our visitors...

– Oh, they're here already, said Gubbins. Gus thought they were journalists at first, after more scandal. But apparently they're animal rights protesters, and they've heard about the laboratory animals and want to free them.

When Dr Jabez Kuru turned and ran outside, the sheep slipped out the door behind him, heading up the ramp in search of the stunning-pens. Hearing shouts, Kuru stopped in his tracks, raising his arms to call the group of protesters to a halt. Their leader was the troublesome MP.

– We seem to have caught you red-handed, said Sirloin.

– Is that one of your animals? a duffle-coated woman demanded.

– Yeah, said a rough-voiced man in a donkey jacket. What do you do with animals here, you white-coat bastard?

– We heard about the mink, said another.

– But you have sheep too, said the Donkey Jacket. A sheep ran past us just now, trying to escape no doubt.

At that moment, they heard a short bang from across the compound, nothing very loud but an abrupt noise, like the sound of a blown-up paper-bag being burst, or the snap of a party-popper being let off. Kuru knew immediately what it might foretell, and turned to see his worst fears confirmed as a blazing ram shot out of the side door of the number 9 tank building and zigzagged around the compound like a jumping jack.

– Quick, said Donkey Jacket. Let's save the sheep. Send it towards the pond. Come on everybody, spread out and save the sheep!

The Angel of Death had completed its third circuit of the world when it found itself above the village of Loamfield in England. This was not a place it had visited often, but if the two huge flaming fingers next to the river were any indication, it was likely that black souls were waiting to be taken.

He was soon appraised of the significance of the infernal V-sign by the Morrigan, whom he had not encountered for some centuries. Thinking it best to give her a wide berth, he agreed that she should be left to her own devices in respect of the chemical plant. The Morrigan thanked him, stating her intent to force the reversal in an uncontrollable chain reaction of all the chemical processes at present active in the ten round tanks which crowded around the main compound of this establishment. He was never happy to see these piecemeal metal constructions of tank, tube and chimney next to the towns of the people. These places always boded ill, and delivered death indiscriminately, not like the Angel of Death, who struck down sinners in their pride, overreachers and men with blackened hearts. The Morrigan's explanation seemed far fetched, the use of a bat as a long burning fuse not being a method used by one who preferred to carry out his yearly scourging in the course of a single day. The rat too, that was novel, using a rodent to transport a bat whose metabolism had been altered by its immersion in one chemical to a tank containing another, contact with which would result in a highly inflammable vapour being given off, this gas then being ignited by a single spark caused by having a sheep trip over the escaping rat, banging its hoof on a metal rail in the process.

The reversal mentioned by the Morrigan was also impressive in its simplicity, guaranteeing not only the complete destruction of the whole chemical complex but also its return to a virgin, green field site. The foul plant could not be brought back to life, except if the no.9 tank were encased with a giant concrete sarcophagus, and the people would not swallow that one again. This time it would disappear for good.

It remained for him to investigate the howling and cheering he could hear from the direction of Hangman's Wood, whether the cries were from man or beast he was unable to tell at first. He thought the latter but found the dying creature to be no less an infernal being than the Goodman himself, with a Barguest on the scene, tearing him limb from limb as a group of dead policemen stood watching the spectacle, the fat one holding an object which appeared to be a pair of pliers.

– But I told you it would be a cameo part only, a wraith-like novelist was telling the flailing demon. You don't even need to say anything in Chapter 27.

A technical fault had rebounded upon the devils in the torture unit. The damned couldn't be tormented in the Cardboard Room unless the attendant demons could endure listening to the She-Devil as well. They were threatening a walkout.

– *U*-turn if *you* like, went the voice.

– The old hag's right, said Satan. All these U-turns are buggering up our system. The whole caboodle's in reverse.

– The *lady's* not for turning. *The lady's*...for turning. For turning. For turning...

– She's going haywire, changing the words, too, said Beelzebub. Now it *was* sailing away from the Falklands.

– What *was*? snapped the Devil, impatiently.

– The internal enemy? suggested Moloch.

– I thought it was her instinctive antennae, said Beelzebub.

– *You* burn if *you* like, the voice was telling the sinners now. *The lady's* not for burning. I hope that doesn't sound too arrogant.

– Can she just change the script like that? asked Moloch.

– Of course, said Belial. The more she changes the words, the more she tortures the damned. They hate hearing their language abused. It's the one thing they have left, and she shits all over it. They aren't all her words, anyway, he added. That U-turn speech was by Ronald Millar.

– All these famous lines by ghostwriters, said Belial. Nothing is real here, remember. And listen, now she's started lobbing in her minnenwerfers. They're terrified. The demon whistled as her deadly words came over.

– Not the moaning minnies? asked Mammon.

– Not only that, said Belial gleefully, but she's giving them the *whole* speech...

– The edited highlights were bad enough, said Beelzebub.

– And then after *hours* and *hours* of the *same speech*, she'll start scrambling it, running it backwards, turning it back on itself.

– *You burn if you like. You burn if you like...*

– Wait for it, lads, whispered Belial.

– *You burn if you like...*

– Ready? asked Moloch.

– *You burn if you like...*

– Now! cried Belial.

– THE LADY'S NOT FOR BURNING! all four demons yelled in chorus, clapping their hands. They whooped and swung their tails like lassoos. The Arch-Fiend was not amused.

– The bitch *will* be for roasting if she carries on like that, he said. Come on Belial, we can't put up with that indefinitely. It may be all right for the damned, but *we* have to listen to it now. Get rid of her. Where's Black Shuck? Let him sort her out.

– The Devil's Dog is unavailable, said Beelzebub. He's away from his desk at the moment. Can anyone else help you?

– No, I want to speak to the Barguest. Where is he?

– He's bringing Goodman in. Our earthly policeman needs to be recycled if we're to have any chance in the next match.

– Right, said Satan. He has to go back to the factory. His body systems and sensory data need updating. No more bullet-head either. He needs a complete reshape for the new millennium.

– Just look at our scorecard, Beelzebub added. It's not very impressive, is it? And we were doing so well.

– Though Maw got out to a spectacular dismissal, said Mammon. But he was taking too many risks, should have kept his eye on the ball, played within himself.

Satan started to screech with demonic laughter.

– We'll need a new captain now, *haw haw haw.* Look at those bowling figures. He's very expensive. *Haw haw haw*. Two no-balls in his last over. I call that a poor show. We'll have to drop him.

– But he's your prodigy, your shadow, said Beelzebub. He's even stood in for you at massacres. How can you be so cruel?

– If you think I'm being cruel *now*, roared Satan, just you wait till Goodman gets here and I'll show you what *real* cruelty's like. He was meant to have made sure half the population got wiped out by that cattle disease, and he cocked it up. Got the disease himself: how naff can you get?

– Yeah, agreed Beelzebub. What a tosser. He was lousy at networking, too full of his own importance. But he managed to keep the cover-up under wraps, didn't he? No one's twigged the whole tale, it's still too big for their little minds to grasp.

– But Kernan knows the story now, said Moloch, and he's left the strands hanging. Someone's sure to pick them up and put 2 and 2 together. We have Goodman to thank for further botching an already botched job.

– He should have been more devious, said Belial, too much demonology, not enough epidemiology.

– Too right, said Beelezebub. You have to be a good team man to pull off a stunt like that now.

INSPECTOR KERNAN'S XI *v.* THE OTHER SIDE

Played at Loamfield

THE OTHER SIDE: 2ND INNINGS

1. Sir S.P. Prurigeaux, c. Gangrene b. Muffy	62
2. Sir S.H. Hockle, c. Coronary b. Muffy	60
3. M.J.K. Saveloy, c. Fire-Fart b. Hodge	41
4. P. O'Scrapie, c. & b. Nicholas (Rev.)	34
5. M.W.R. Maw, c. Hepatitis (B), b. Goodman	88
6. N. Goodman *(capt.)*, c. Beefburger (BSE) b. New Variant (CJD)	147
7. B.O. Tucker, c. Appendix b. Leadshot	32
8. M. Oxter *(wkt.)*, run out (Goodman)	35
9. O. de Foie, c. Sheep (MJ), b. De Valéra	99
10. J.F. Kuru, st. Gubbins b. Sirloin	44
11. L. Clegg, c. Red-Handed b. Devil	14
Extras (b4, lb4, nb2)	10
Total	666

– Who's coming in now, then? asked Satan.

– That's my man Maw, grinned Mammon, arrowing his name on the screen and double-clicking it with the computer-rat. Now let's see what we've got on him. Didn't hang around in Limbo, Green Knight's sent him down on the fast track. We don't get many that way, he must be pretty bad. Look, damning figures. Example:

MORTON MAW, FINAL YEAR PROFITS

EU arable subsidies, one year

2000 acres wheat @ £109/acre	£218,000
2000 acres oilseed rape @ £193/acre	£386,000
2000 acres set-aside @ £138/acre	£276,000
	£880,000

– Nearly a million pounds in one year, Mammon went on, courtesy of the Common Agricultural Policy. Quarter of a million for doing nothing with those set-aside fields. Not bad going, eh? Come on then, tell us Maw, what did you do with it all?

– Spent it of course, said Maw. Income's up, but so's the cost of land and inputs: sprays, fertiliser, animal feed, machinery, contractors. You have to keep up, raise output, keep the profits up. Can't lose ground to pests and disease. Or they close you down, call in the loans.

– Like when you had that plague of orange wheat blossom midges in '94. Green Knight says you drenched the land with OPs, chlorpyrifos and triazophos. You couldn't risk waiting for the ladybirds and rove beetles to kill off the midges.

– Bank wouldn't let us. They had to protect their investment, couldn't rely on a bunch of insects for that.

– So you nuked the midges, and everything else as well. Following year, same thing again. Cereal aphids move in, you waste the wildlife. No more insects, no more beasts and birds.

– Plenty of game birds to shoot. Those are the birds we need.

– Partridges? Plenty of those?

– No, now you come to mention it, the old partridge was becoming a bit scarce. Blamed it on Hart the gamekeeper. Lazy fellow. Said there weren't enough beetles around for the game chicks. I've heard some excuses in my time but...

– No buts, interrupted Satan. I'm sorry to say your time is now at an end, Mr Morton Maw. We're going to close you down, call in your debts.

– But I'm dead, aren't I? Maw protested. If I'm dead, you can't kill me.

– Your soul's alive. Normally we'd just torture your soul, but I really don't see the point in your case. Your soul is meant to be eternal of course, but in special circumstances we can apply for an obliteration order. Killing people's neither here nor there in our book, but we take a different view where the earth's concerned.

– Yeah, said Beelzebub. Owls, voles, bugs, and all them plants. Your fucking awful farming's fucked up the ecosystem.

– All those sheep and cows you breed to kill, said Belial. Superior creatures to man. Pigs too.

– And the yellowhammer, said Satan. And the devil's-bit scabious. *Succisa pratensis*. Mauve flowers, all over the Loamshire hills once. Not now, thanks to you. That's my plant, Maw. You shouldn't have done that, killed my plant.

This is the big plant
De Foie built.

This is the chimney
That stood by the big plant
De Foie built.

This is the chimney
That stood by the chimney
That stood by the big plant
De Foie built.

This is the tank
That always stank
That stood by the chimney
That stood by the chimney
That stood by the big plant
De Foie built.

This is the bat
That burned in the vat
Inside the tank
That always stank
That stood by the chimney
That stood by the chimney
That stood by the big plant
De Foie built.

This is the rat
That ate the bat
That burned in the vat
Inside the tank
That always stank
That stood by the chimney
That stood by the chimney
That stood by the big plant
De Foie built

This is the sheep
Brought by the sweep
Tripped by the rat
That ate the bat
That burned in the vat
Inside the tank
That always stank
That stood by the chimney
That stood by the chimney
That stood by the big plant
De Foie built

And this is the spark
That jumped in the dark,
The hoof of the sheep
Brought down in a sweep
Igniting the rat
Exploding the bat
That burned in the vat
That burned in the tank
Whose deadly fumes stank
That blew up the chimney
That blew up the chimney
That blew up the big plant
De Foie built

BOOK VII

BELTANE

MAY – JULY

Little lad, little lad, where were you born?
Far off in Loamshire sir, under a thorn,
Where they sup buttermilk
From a ram's horn;
And a pumpkin scooped
With a yellow rim
Is the bonny bowl they breakfast in.

CHAPTER TWENTY-EIGHT

The End of My Tether

BELTANE: MAY 1ST

A child born after the death of its father will have healing powers by virtue of the peculiar circumstances of its birth. Posthumous children can cure certain ailments, particularly thrush or whooping-cough, usually by breathing down the throat of the sufferer, while still fasting, on nine successive mornings, or by taking a hair from his head, wrapping it in red cloth, and giving this to the patient to wear round the neck until the illness goes.

Oh God, she didn't want to have it now, not here in the woods. She had to keep running. But the baby wouldn't let her. The baby told her to stop. And slowing down, pushing back a branch, she found a path, and remembered her mother's words, *Don't stray from the path or the wolf will gobble you up*. The path looked familiar. Was this the Forest of Otter? Or was it the copse above Hoggett's Field, where Kernan had fled as a stag with the hunt in pursuit. Or Long Wood, where he had been an angel?

Hearing noises through the trees, Diana crouched behind a bush, squatting in the undergrowth over a small black mound of fresh earth, a molehill. Yet these were not loud crashes like those of an animal in flight, these suggested steady movement, and not just one beast but two – or possibly three, the third lighter on its feet than the others. She kept her head down and did not see them, the beasts passing at some distance.

She returned to the path, and could soon see more light between the trees. Expecting to reach a clearing, she was surprised to find herself in someone's garden. She looked in at the window of the cottage, whose green door was almost obscured by a riot of buddleia; then peeped through the letterbox. She knocked and called out, but there was no response. No sound but the ticking of a grandfather clock on the other side of the door. So she turned the handle, knowing the door would not be fastened, because people never locked their doors in the country.

On the kitchen table, there were three bowls set out on a blue gingham tablecloth, a large bowl in front of the largest of the chairs, a middle-sized bowl with a smaller chair drawn up to it, and a little bowl with a child's chair. In each bowl was a serving of porridge, which must be hot because it was still steaming. Unless they had been spirited away like the crew of the *Marie Celeste*, the people of the house must have gone out for a short walk while their porridge was cooling, for it had probably been much too hot to eat. She was sure they would let her have some porridge too, and it would not be long before they returned, but she suddenly felt so ravenous that she could not wait for them. She had the baby to feed now, she was sure they would understand when they saw her state; her large belly, the red-flushed face of a woman about to go into labour.

So first she tasted the porridge in the large bowl, but that was still too hot for her. And someone had added salt, which she didn't like in porridge. Then she tasted the porridge in the next bowl, but that was too cold, and someone had added a sprinkling of brown sugar, which lent it a sweet gritty taste that she disliked. And then she turned to the smallest bowl, and tried this porridge, which was neither too hot, nor too cold, but just right; and someone had stirred a spoonful of honey into this porridge, and it was so smooth and delicious that she ate it all up, telling her invisible hosts she was sure they couldn't mind, her baby was due and needed feeding. Her baby must like honey too.

Then the baby started to kick again, so she sat down in the largest chair, thinking she needed to splay her legs, but the chair was too hard, her bottom felt uncomfortable, even with the cushion for her back. She knew she could not sit there for long, so tried the middle-sized chair, but that was too soft for her. And something was trickling down her legs. Then she sat down in the little chair, and though it was a child's chair it was neither too hard nor too soft, but just right. As she spread out her legs, and let the little chair take her full weight, she felt it give. The chair collapsed, and down she went with it, hurting her bottom. The baby started to kick again.

If the people didn't return soon, she would have to get help. She tried her police radio, but couldn't get a signal. She tried her mobile, but it just said SEARCHING FOR NETWORK and didn't find one. She looked around her a phone, but couldn't see one, and so went upstairs to the bedroom where there was a telephone on an oak dressing-table. It gave a reassuring purr when she picked up the receiver. She dialled 999.

– Thank you for calling the emergency services, said the slow deliberate voice of the woman from *Jackanory*. If you have a touch-tone telephone with a star button, please press it thrice now.

She pressed it three times.

– You have *three* options. If you want to report a fire, please press 1. If you need the assistance of the police, press 2. And if you need an ambulance, press 3. If the emergency is of some other nature, please keep holding until an operator answers.

She pressed the 3 button. And felt the baby kick again.

– Thank you for calling the ambulance. You have three options. If you are calling for someone else who needs our help, please press 1. If you need the ambulance yourself, press 2. And if your request relates to an accident involving several people, for which more than one ambulance will be required, press 3.

With some force and irritation, she pressed the 2 button.

– Thank you. We are sorry if you are distressed, but would ask you to remain calm and follow these instructions carefully. You have three more options...

– *Kernan, help me!* Diana called out; pressing the 3 button.

– Thank you for keeping calm. You should not have much longer to wait. Your call is held in a queuing system, and there are currently *beeeeeep* other calls in the queue, *beeeeeep* other calls in the queue, *beeeeeep* other calls... The line went dead.

She needed to lie down. The bed was king-size, with three pillows, each on a bolster: a large pillow nearest the door, which felt too hard for her; a softer down-filled pillow nearest the window, but this wasn't firm enough; however, the smaller pillow in the middle seemed just right, so she slipped under the duvet, laid her head on it and fell fast asleep.

By this time her hosts thought their porridge must be cool enough, and returned to eat their breakfast. Diana had left the big spoon in the salted porridge in the largest bowl on the table.

– Somebody has been at my porridge! boomed a Great Huge Bear, his offended voice rough and gruff. And when the second Bear saw her spoon lying on the table, smeared with brown sugared porridge, she declared that someone had been eating her porridge too, in her Mummy Bear voice, which though gentle was still an offended voice. Then the Little Bear looked at his little spoon, left lying in his empty bowl.

– Somebody has been at my porridge, he said in his little flutey voice, and has eaten it all up!

At this, the Three Bears, realising that someone had been in the house and eaten the Little Bear's breakfast, began to look about them. And Diana had not put the cushion straight in Daddy Bear's chair after trying it out.

– Somebody has been sitting in my chair! he roared in his great rough, gruff, offended colonel's voice. And when the Mummy Bear saw her chair, she almost exploded.

– Someone has been sitting in my chair, she cried, and they've done a wee-wee in it!

The other bears gasped. And you know what Diana had done to the Little Bear's chair.

– Somebody has been sitting in my chair, the Little Bear said in his squeaky wee voice, and it's been smashed into smithereens!

The Three Bears decided to investigate further, and seeing that the wee-wee trailed out of the room and up the stairs, they followed its scent to the bedroom. Now when Diana had tried out the pillows, she hadn't plumped them up again afterwards or straightened them on the bolster, and looking at his big pillow, the one nearest the door, Daddy Bear knew right-away that someone had been using it.

– Someone has been lying on my pillow, he grunted, and they've left it all askew, like a turbot's face.

Diana had also squashed the soft pillow nearest the window, and had left it flat as a Dover sole.

– Somebody has been lying on my pillow, cried Mummy Bear, and they've left it flatter than a flatfish.

And when the Little Bear went to look at his pillow, there was the bolster in its place; and the pillow in its place on the bolster; but upon the pillow was a redheaded lady's head – which was not in its place, for she had no business there.

– Someone has been lying on my pillow, declared the Little Bear detective, and she's still there!

Diana had heard in her sleep the great rough gruff voice of Daddy Bear; but in her exhaustion was so deeply sunk in sleep that it was no more to her than the roaring of the wind outside, or the distant rumbling of thunder, or a low-flying Harrier from RAF Otteridge on a sheep-scaring exercise. And she heard the gentle but cross voice of the Mummy Bear, but it was as if she had heard someone speaking in a dream; either that, or she had left the radio on downstairs, and *Woman's Hour* was on. But when she heard the squeaky, flutey wee voice of the Little Bear, it was so sharp, and so shrill, that it woke her at once; and she sat bolt upright in the Three Bears' bed. And when she saw the Three Bears standing between the bed and the door, she tumbled out of the other side and ran to the window.

Now the window was open, because the Bears, being good healthy Bears, liked to have a fresh breeze in their bedroom, especially if Daddy Bear had been farting in the night (bears' guffs are far worse even than dogs'), and Mummy Bear always opened the window when she got up to make the tea. And Diana would have jumped then from the window, but as she clambered onto the window-ledge, the baby kicked again, this time really hard, and the shock sent her reeling back onto the floor, whereupon Daddy Bear seized her with his great bear's paws, and breathed hot fetid bear-breath into her face. She recoiled.

– Not so fast, Goldilocks, he boomed in his great rough gruff voice. But Mummy Bear pulled at him.

– No, she said, can't you see? She's going to have a *baby*.

– I think you may be right, the big bear agreed, his voice softening. She has a tympany with two heels from the beast with two backs. That's why she needed to eat Little Bear's porridge.

– And why she was too heavy for my chair, squeaked the Little Bear.

– And why she needed to sleep in our bed, said Daddy Bear, releasing his grip on her. We'll have to help you then, girlie.

– But how do I know you won't just gobble up my baby as soon as it's born? Diana asked.

– Like she gobbled up my porridge, the Little Bear added.

– But bears don't eat people, said the Daddy Bear, trying to lower his voice and make it less threatening. It's people who eat animals, not the other way round, not unless you're a crocodile or a Big Bad Wolf; and the wolves have all gone, there was no food left for them, their prey disappeared when the land was poisoned with pesticides, the cattle poisoned with the offal of dead sheep, the hedgerows uprooted, the copses, spinneys and thickets chopped down, and all the fields given over to intensive farming of cereal crops and genetically modified oilseed rape.

– Still, I'm not sure I like the idea of my baby being delivered by three bears.

– By two bears. Little Bear will run and fetch for us, said the foul-breathed Daddy Bear, who was not the reassuring doctor she'd hoped would deliver the baby. In fact, she'd wanted Herne to help her with a natural birth. A birth assisted by two bears couldn't be more natural, but she was worried they might hurt the child with their big blundering paws.

– I don't think I need the help of a big smelly bear with huge, awkward paws and rotten breath, said Diana, and immediately regretted it, for Daddy Bear groaned like a bear with a sore head, and stormed from the room telling her to have her precious baby on her own. He would eat his porridge instead, which she'd nearly made him forget.

– We'll need plenty of hot water and towels, said the Mummy Bear, ignoring him, but her breath too was also quite stinky, and her paws looked less than delicate.

– I don't think I need the help of a smelly bear like you with your blundering paws and bad breath, said Diana, whereupon Mummy Bear too ran from the bedroom, calling her an ungrateful wretch. She would eat her porridge instead, which she'd nearly made her forget. The baby started kicking again.

Then the Little Bear appeared at the foot of the bed with a kettle of hot water and a pile of freshly laundered towels.

– Where shall I put these? he asked brightly, like a young

bear with all his troubles behind him. And what do you want me to do?

– Oh God, cried Diana, why don't you just go away you silly little bear, you don't know anything about childbirth or anything! And the Little Bear ran off crying, sobbing to the Mummy Bear that Diana had made him feel inadequate and he would surely be afflicted with problems of self-esteem for the rest of his life, especially now he had no porridge to cry his tears into. And Diana burst into tears too.

When the Three Bears heard her crying, they crept back up the stairs. Hearing a gruff voice trying to offer her comfort, Diana decided she had been too harsh on them, and paws or no paws, bad breath or rotten breath, she would gladly accept the Bears' offer of help, whereupon she wiped the tears from her eyes, looked up and saw Herne with a towel in his hand, Muffy putting on her apron, and Lizzie Gizzard holding the steaming kettle, a large white jug and a porcelain bowl.

Although her waters had broken, the baby was not inclined to follow, preferring to bide its time. Diana lay back exhausted in the great bed as Muffy inveighed against trying to rush, for nothing should be done in haste except gripping a flea, the bairn would make itself known to them its own good time. Haste is from the devil, she said, the hasty bitch brings forth blind whelps. It was only when evening came on, and it grew darker outside, that Diana's contractions started again, with renewed vigour.

– I thought as much, said Muffy. A baby born at twilight, or at the chime-hours, will be conscious of the unseen. It will see the ghosts and spirits, and it cannot be bewitched itself. It will have second sight. The baby knows this. And you must help it now. You must push. Count and push. The best way of counting is the sheep method, trying to remember the sheep numbers distracts you from the pain. And once you get going, it becomes a sheep mantra, it helps you move into a rhythm.

– Right then, said Diana. Yan, tan, tethera, pethera, pimp. *Push!* Sethera, lethera, hovera, covera, dik. *Push!* Yan dik, tan dik, tethera dik, pethera dik, bumfit. *Push!* Sethera dik, lethera dik, hovera dik, covera dik, figgit. *Push!*

– More quickly now, with a steadier rhythm, said Muffy. Try the other way, *onetherum*...

– Onetherum, twotherum, cocktherum, qutherum, setherum. *Push!* Shatherum, wineberry, wigtail, tarryfiddle, den. *Push!* Onetherum, twotherum, cocktherum, qutherum, setherum. *Push!* Shatherum, wineberry, wigtail, tarryfiddle, den. *Push!*

– Faster. Change to Welsh sheep.

– Un, dau, tri, pedway, pum. *Push!* Chwe, saith, wyth, naw, deg. *Push!* Un, dau, tri, pedway, pum. *Push!* Chwe, saith, wyth, naw, deg. *Push!* Un, dau, tri, pedway, pum. *Push!* Chwe, saith, wyth, naw, deg. *Push!*

– Slow down now. It's coming. I can see the head, it's got a caul. That's lucky. It won't be long now. Back to *yan tan*...

– Yan, tan, tethera, pethera, pimp. *Push!* Sethera, lethera, hovera, covera, dik. *Push!* Yan dik, tan dik, tethera dik. *Yes*...

The child was not bald, as Diana had feared, so could not be Lambert's, but when she looked up and saw Muffy holding a creature with a hairy body, its hirsute head covered with a strange translucent, papery hood, her heart missed a beat as she tried to take in the diabolical implications. But the hood was a sillyhow, said Muffy, a birth-caul; she must keep it safe for the child, for a child delivered in a caul will be protected throughout its life, and will never drown or be killed by fire. The caul must be carefully preserved, kept in a drawer, and neither she nor the child should be tempted to sell it, even if a sailor offered a high price, for if ever the caul were lost or taken by someone else, its life-saving and luck-bringing powers would go with it, leaving the true owner exposed to many dangers.

The baby was not only hairy, Lizzie said, it was a lovely little wolf cub, which was why it had been kicking her so much. And it continued to kick its little paws about as Muffy passed it three times across the Beltane fire in the hearth, then carried it sunwise three times around the fire, a circling deasil movement, before Lizzie washed it in the porcelain bowl in which Herne had placed a gold sovereign beforehand.

When Diana took her child, she saw that the creature had changed from a tiny wolf into a wiry-haired civet with impish eyes and speckly-pink gums. It licked her face with its long tongue, before diving down to feast on her breasts. Diana held its snout to her nipple while it supped greedily, first on the right breast then on the left, and when it emerged having drunk its fill of both, it had changed again, into a little green-eyed baby boy.

– No doubt then about who the father is, said Herne, glowing with pride.

– He hath as many tricks as a dancing bear, observed Lizzie.

Muffy called upon them to bless the new soul incarnate in the child with her Prayer of the Nine Waves:

A little wave for your changing form,
    A little wave for your growly voice,
A little wave for your man's speech.
    A little wave for your earth's share,
A little wave for your protection.
    A little wave for your earth's wealth,
A little wave for all your creatures,
    A little wave for your healing.
May nine waves of grace be upon you,
    Nine waves from the seven seas.

The child also needed to be empowered as an earth warrior, said Herne, in the name of Cúchulainn and the legendary hosts of Fionn Mac Cumhaill, the Fianna, that he protect us all:

Power of lynx's eye upon you,
    Power of the earth's elements upon you,
Power of my heart's desire.

Power of my life's ebbing shadow upon you,
    Power of your life's surging flow upon you,
Power of our three-in-one fellowship.

Power of Kernan and Cernunnos upon you,
    Power of the Earth Mother and the Green Man,
Power of the Great Goddess upon you.

In that instant, Diana remembered the angel's words, that speech she'd thought was Kernan's extravagant joke, him showing off his powers. How his lord would be reborn through her in his Second Coming, and she should call the child Cernunnos, which meant Lord of the Forests. But whatever powers he might have, no child would thank her for being given the name Cernunnos. Had not Kernan himself always stressed the need to be circumspect, to use his powers quietly, without drawing attention to his methods.

– You could always call him Kernan Oswald, said Herne. Or Kernan Oz for short.

– You read my thoughts, said Diana.

– Your thoughts are my thoughts, said Herne. Otherwise you would not know how those two names bring together Angle, Saxon and Celt, Pagan and Christian, for it was Oswald who brought the Christian gospel in its pure form from exile on Iona to Northumbria, where he defeated Cadwalla at Heavenfield, installing Aidan as his bishop at Lindisfarne. When King Penda had him chopped into pieces eight years later, his head, body, legs and arms ended up in all different parts of England, and miracles and powers of healing were attributed to them.

– I hope our little Kernan doesn't end up that way, said Diana. But tell me, Herne, is he actually Kernan himself, is he Kernan reincarnated through me? I'm not sure I like the idea of that; being used as someone's vessel, even though the boy is lovely.

– You still don't know, do you? Herne answered. The boy is both your child and Kernan's. He is the new Green Man, the Green Man for the millennium. And I will be his shadow, as I was Kernan's before.

Startled, Diana looked at the shadows cast by the lamplight, and realised that only she of those in the room had a shadow. Herne had moved towards the child, his outline against the fire seeming to grow diffuse until his body appeared somehow to transform itself from solid flesh to smoky shadow, shrinking as it did so, to a smaller shadow, and finally to an even smaller one, the boy's shadow.

She looked at Muffy and Lizzie, scared.

– Herne's gone, she cried.

– Herne's gone back into himself, into Kernan, into the boy, said Muffy. They are all three of them parts of the Green Man, consort of the Great Goddess, just as I am Hecate the Crone and the Hag; Lizzie is the Whore Mother, Hera and Demeter; and you were the Virgin.

– Diana, Artemis, Persephone, said Diana, and Cybele and Phoebe, all my moon names.

– And we are all one, three-in-one, said Muffy. We are the Goddess and Cernunnos is our son and lover. The Bible has its Father, Son and Holy Ghost, but they re-wrote their Trinity to fit their patriarchal scheming. Ours is unrevised, the Earth's Trinity. We are Gaia.

What a complicated life the boy would have, thought Diana,

hearing the sounds of animals and birds gathering outside in the garden, and someone knocking at the door downstairs. The chough was back, perched on the window-ledge, giving out its repetitive, unvaried call of *cheeaw, chee-aw, chee-aw…chuff.*

– It's Bill Jarman from next door, Muffy called up. He's brought us three sheep for the boy, a Bluefaced Leicester gimmer, a Swaledale theave and a Suffolk tup. You have to choose between them.

– There's nothing to choose between a gimmer and a theave, Diana called back, they're both the same in my book, and even if a Gimmer did carry on Kernan's work, helped by a Theave; so it has to be the ram. And if it's a sturdy Suffolk, perhaps it will let me use its broad back as an ironing-board.

– Especially if the same ram brought down the infernal chimneys in the Great Fire, said Muffy, for I do believe it's Mickey. And Bill says you made the right choice, she continued, and because you chose correctly, you may have all three sheep, the gimmer and theave as well as the tup.

– Well don't bring them up here. I've had more than enough beasts today with your bears, said Diana, hearing someone else at the door, and the sounds of more creatures assembling outside, including the Angus bull, who was subjecting some other poor beast in the garden to an Aberdonian monologue.

– *Ah'm telling ye, ah kenned Immanuel Kant's granfaither, so ah ken what ah'm tarking aboot. More than can be said for a moose wi' nae tail…*

– Don't worry, said Gubbins, entering the room in a flurry of bats and protestations, I've left the big beast tethered outside, for I've come to grant you three fishes for the boy. And if you choose correctly for him, his fish will turn into a wish, which will always come true. If wishes were horses, beggars would ride.

– If wishes were butter-cakes, said Muffy, beggars might bite.

– Won't the wish start to smell after a while? asked Diana.

– Of course, said Gubbins. The fish will have a lovely haddocky, buttocky smell. The best fish stay near the bottom. But the fish turns into a wish before then, as it makes its way up the river to spawn. So what is to be then, what will be his fish? I have a dace, a tench and a salmon.

– The dace is full of surprises, said Diana, so a wish like a dace might be worth having, especially if the child keeps its power of fath-fith, but wants to shape-change at will. But then the tench is the doctor-fish, the healer and thorn-in-the-side. Though it was killed, the tench started the trail which led us here, so the tench is a strong candidate for a wish-fish. But taking everything into consideration, I think the boy has to have the salmon, for the Salmon of Knowledge knows everything. Kernan sought it like Finneces, but he never completed his quest…

– But he *did* complete it, said Muffy. Not as the earthly policeman you loved, but from the other side, still working in his mysterious ways.

– Then the salmon is even more fitting, said Diana. For it was the youth Fionn Mac Cumhaill not the old man who received its wisdom when cooking the fish for his teacher, the hot fish-juice spurting onto this thumb, which he thrust in his mouth to cool, so receiving all knowledge. Now it shall pass to young Cernunnos. For the salmon's powers are all-embracing, and must include healing and fath-fith among many, and a large salmon could easily swallow a tiny dace or even a small tench. And because Muffy was sired by a salmon-man, I choose it as Cernunnos's fish.

– You have chosen well, said Gubbins. A pint of salmon is your man.

– Nevertheless, said Diana. I'd still be grateful if you could just pop it in the fridge downstairs, and not leave it with the boy, just now. He's started to wrestle with it already, and I don't want him getting too many strange ideas too early. So we've had sheep and fish, there must be something else? A third gift?

– Love-bites, said Flea, who had stumbled breathless up the stairs, with Lucy Saveloy in tow. You have to choose one of three love-bites. First this one on my neck: this is Tom Maw's which he gave to Lucy while James was away, and she gave it to me…

– I don't like the sound or look of that one, said Diana. The kiss of betrayal, with two previous owners. No, I don't think so.

– Then there's this one on Lucy's neck, he continued, pulling back her green scarf to reveal a freshly drawn strawberry bruise.

– Are you two courting? Muffy asked.

– That's right, said Lucy, I'm a one-man woman now, and I bestow my love-bites only on Flea and Flea bites me and no one else, which is a good thing for a Flea…

– For a Flea who only bites a willing woman will never be squeezed by others, said Flea, singing

> A funny thing is a flea.
> You can't tell a he from a she.
> But *he* can... And *she* can...
> *Whoopee!*

– A ragged colt may make a good horse, said Diana.

– She is better than she is bonny, said Flea, for

> She's gi'ed to me my winter's beef
> Beside my winter fuellin'
> Far better than that she's gi'ed to me
> Was a stable for my stallion.
> *For she's a rum one*
> *Fol-the-diddle-di-do-day,*
> *But a bonny one*
> *Fol-the-diddle-di-do.*

– And you must never bite the hand that feeds you, but only the neck, said Diana. What is the third love-bite?

– The baby has the third bite already, but you may choose to take it away. I know this because I saw it in a dream. If you look, you'll see he has a snake-bite on the back of his neck...

– That must be the bite I gave Kernan as a snake, as his wolf-head swelled in my mouth. He must have passed it on, so Cernunnos must keep that love-bite it as my son-lover. Your second bite was tempting, Flea, the love-bite of innocence, but the blood you drew was less than innocent, even if the tainted flesh be reformed now. That must be all then, for we have had three lots of gifts, including sheep from a shepherd, and only lack our three kings.

– No king but a King Henry, said Henry Sirloin, for I have acted as such with women and witches, meddlesome priests and poison dwarfs, and was for ever clinging so blindly to life's conveyor-belt that I never saw where it was taking me, where I went wrong, till Lizzie drained all the sourness from me, and Muffy supped at my teats like a hare. I bring no gifts but just the belt, stretching back to the Year Dot, that speck where the belt looks so thin you might think it a rope tethered there, the pull of the past. Whatever you can recall from it in one minute, you may have for the child to take with him.

– A tall order, said Diana. But I'll try, for the child. Let's see then. The blue-marbled notebook. The key. The blue-arsed fly. The Everyman edition of *Vanity Fair*, inscribed by my grandmother. The dried toad's heart to ward off evil. The captive-bolt pistol and the Webley service revolver, both of which we'll decommission. The sieve and shears, to find a liar. Kernan's small bannock with his mother's blessing. Becky Sharp's rouge pot, and Olivia's panties, smelling of *1881, Escape* and three-in-one oil mixed with Biethylenetripropethyl-6 lubricant. The poultice of poppies. The pretty kettle of fish. One of the sun-dried rabbits. The goose from the phone box. The packet of Hobnobs, because we're hungry as well as nobbled, and my breasts need a refill. Kernan's piece of knotted string, its two halves retied. His grimoire too, he must have had one and I'd like to read it. The Durex I found in Goodman's pocket, if any are left, because I want to know if I really did put those pin-holes in them...

– You must have done. You're still here. He didn't run you over.

– Not like a rabbit. A rabbit dead to the world, a closed book. Forget the johnnies then. When you're thinking about the belt or the rope, you remember how one thing, one decision, one meeting, leads to another, but you could equally have gone the other way, or met someone else.

– I'll have to hurry you now. Only ten seconds left. What else?

– The sign reading CAUSALITY from the hospital...

– But it said CASUALTY...

– You can make it read CAUSALITY though, can't you? I want that version of the sign, the one he imagined he saw. What else? Kernan's warrant for the arrest of O'Scrapie in 1830, his *Book of Shadows*, and Thomas Browne's *Pseudodoxia Epidemica*, the 1646 edition...And Kernan's tether of course.

Sergeant Cobb knocked at the cottage door with his knuckles, three raps. He whistled under his breath, while DC Cora Theave stood beside him, sniffing at the buddleia trailing from a hanging-basket above the rain-butt. The door was green, slatted, with a horse-shoe above the letterbox. Eventually, they heard footsteps creaking down the stairs, and the door was opened.

– Excuse me, sir, said DC Theave, we're sorry to disturb you. We appreciate that this may not be a good time...

– How can I help you?

– It's like this, said Sergeant Cobb, looking through the porch into the kitchen. I won't beat about the bush...

– Yes?

– Well then... Cobb began again. We have reason to believe that you are the author of this book, and if you don't mind, we'd like to ask you a few questions.

– Of course.

– I think it would be better if we came inside, said Cora Theave, pleasantly but with an edge to her voice. Would that be all right?

– By all means. Do come in.

Sergeant Cobb sighed, and gestured for his colleague to go before him; taking off his helmet, he stooped to enter the low doorway, looking around to take in the present appearance of a familiar room. The two police officers sat down on two wooden chairs, slightly away from the kitchen table on which the remains of an unfinished breakfast were still to be seen, the sergeant placing his dark blue helmet with its gold otter-star emblem on the blue gingham tablecloth where it was free of crockery. DC Theave smoothed her skirt, and looked to her colleague to initiate the interview.

– We appreciate your cooperation, said Sergeant Cobb. This is a difficult situation, not one which I would wish to have been placed in myself, but I have to follow my instructions...

– Which are?

– First, said Cora Theave, smiling, we would like to ask you to clarify a few points for us.

– I'll try to help in whatever way I can.

– Thank you, she said, with a slight squeak to her voice. We would like to ask you first about the murder of Bernard Tench. We know – or we think we know – that Dr Tench was killed by a group of police officers from our force?

– That's right.

– And we think that former Superintendent Goodman was

in charge of this group, and that he may even have had a rôle in the killing of Dr Tench. Who else was there?

– Sergeant Oxter, PCs Hodge, Clegg and Jakes, and Mr Maw, with some Anubian helpers. I think you know that Dr Tench was stunned with a captive-bolt pistol borrowed by Mr Maw from his slaughterhouse, and that it was Mr Maw who used the weapon on Dr Tench, firing it into his forehead at point-blank range.

– You're very sure about this, interrupted Sergeant Cobb. He did this himself, of his own volition, without prompting from anyone else? Not even from Superintendent Goodman?

– No, it was Maw's idea to stun Tench. But when the four police officers had hoisted him up onto the rafters of the barn, it was Goodman who first ripped his clothes off, using the knife to assist in this when he grew impatient with the buttons. He disliked buttons. And it was Goodman, of course, who did the sticking. I don't think Tench will have been killed by the stunning, that would only have paralysed him. He was probably conscious of pain, but not of what was happening to him.

– You're saying that Goodman stuck the knife in?

– I thought that was obvious. It didn't really need to be spelled out. If one of the others had done the actual killing, that would have been reflected in how they behaved after the event. They were accomplices only.

– And Goodman stabbed Tench without prompting from anyone else, not even from Maw? asked the sergeant.

– No. It was his own idea. But he and Maw would of course have discussed the plan beforehand, and agreed that Maw would stun and he would stick. They had the idea that this was, how shall I say, *appropriate*. Tench had been a thorn in their flesh, and was about to name names. They wanted to protect their interests. They wanted him out of the way. And clearly they thought the manner of his death, as well as satisfying themselves, would act as a warning to others.

– And yet Goodman sought to cover up what happened? said Cora Theave. At first he blamed an unknown attacker…

– That was his bait for Brock, to draw him into a trap in which Brock would be killed, and would afterwards be blamed for killing Tench. Goodman thought that Tench had probably talked to Brock about what he knew, as a safeguard perhaps. They had gone on the fishing-trip to Lough Erne remember, and Goodman himself had questioned the two men at Enniskillen.

– But we can't be sure that Brock *did* know anything.

– Goodman wasn't prepared to risk that.

– I don't know how we can know that, said Cobb. There are many inconsistencies which we find worrying. Like, for example…

– Yes?

– O'Scrapie's murder. How he existed, or didn't exist, in two periods, two places…

– I think you'll find it was three places…

– You're telling me that, said Sergeant Cobb. But how do we know that? And who carried out the two murders in 1830?

– You can't expect a definite solution for those, it was so long ago, but Inspector…Superintendent Gimmer's theory seems plausible to me, that O'Scrapie killed Alcock, probably after an argument of some kind, or when drunk, and stripped his body. His own soldier's clothes were immediately identifiable, and there was a warrant out for his arrest.

– Alcock's clothing, which O'Scrapie took, was also described in the warrant, added Cora Theave.

– Then he probably headed down the hill to Dealchurch…

– Probably, said Sergeant Cobb. That word again.

– Where he might have been disturbed in the act of trying to rob the poor-box at St Belial's. Or he could have attacked the incumbent, the Reverend Nicholas. He and Alcock had already attacked the Reverend Prurigo at Loamfield remember…

– So who killed O'Scrapie? asked Sergeant Cobb.

– The implication, surely, is that it was the Reverend Nicholas.

– That's only one possible reading, said DC Theave.

– The coincidence of the names? The fact that he was buried on the north side of the church. That the church itself was in Dealchurch, and named, not after a saint, as is usual, but a demon… *a spirit more lewd fell not from heaven, or more gross to love vice for itself*, as Milton said. Those are pretty strong clues. The devil is a busy bishop in his own diocese. There were also no other relevant suspects in that part of the narrative.

– All that seems to be conjecture to me, said Cora Theave. *Your* conjecture. I don't see why we should believe anything you've said.

– That's right, said Sergeant Cobb. And I would like to put it to you that your assertion that no one prompted Maw and Goodman to murder Tench is completely untrue, as is your suggestion that the Reverend Nicholas, a man of the cloth, killed O'Scrapie. And if they did indeed commit those murders, it was you who made them do these killings. You put the idea of murder into their minds, and they did what you told them to do, what you wanted them to do.

– The same applies to the alleged murder by Goodman of Sergeant Oxter and PC Jakes, said Cora Theave. You made him do it. He may have thought it was his idea, but it wasn't, was it? Goodman couldn't exist but for your actions, your intervention.

– But that's preposterous... You can't possibly blame me for Goodman's actions any more than you could hold God responsible for what Man's done.

– You created Goodman, said Cobb. And now here's the nub. You killed Goodman too, you had him killed.

– He had Creutzfeld-Jakob Disease.

– That's right. He was dying, but he wasn't dead when you sent Oxter and his ghoulish crew to finish him off with the elastrator...

– We don't know that they actually castrated him, that he then bled...

– No, said Cobb. We don't know that, but we do know that the Angel of Death saw him being torn apart by Black Shuck. And who sent in the Devil's Dog?

– Beelzebub. Try asking him about that bit.

– You may have created Goodman, but you had him killed, and that makes you guilty of murder.

– But I'm the author. I'm allowed to create people and kill them off.

– So if you had a son, said Cobb, and killed him – that would be all right, would it? That wouldn't be murder, because you had created him?

– Of course it would be murder. But that's different.

– We can't see any difference between the two, Cora Theave retorted.

– That's because you're my characters. You're not real.

– You be careful of what you're saying, now, said Sergeant Cobb. Cora's right. You're as much a murderer as Goodman, and as police officers it is our job to make sure that the law is obeyed, regardless of who is involved, author or no author.

– And in your case your involvement must be counted culpable, because you made yourself part of the story, said DC Theave.

– I am therefore cautioning you, warned Sergeant Cobb. And I am arresting you for the murders of former Superintendent Nicholas Goodman, Sergeant Malcolm Oxter, PC Johnny Jakes and Mr Patrick O'Scrapie.

– You can't be serious.

– We are also looking into whether you might be charged with the murders of Mr Morton Maw, Mrs Candida Sirloin (whom you killed with cancer), Sir Peter Prurigeaux (gangrene), Sir Harold Hockle (heart attack), Mr Oliver de Foie (car accident), Mr Brucellosis Tucker (poisoned), Chief Constable Maurice Saveloy and PC Roger Hodge (explosion), and the two people who perished in the fire you started at the Eurochimique plant, namely Dr Kuru and Mr Strimmer.

– I didn't invent the diseases.

– You made that sheep stand in the middle of the dual carriageway, insisted Sergeant Cobb. If you'd put him anywhere else, Mr de Foie would not have had to swerve to avoid him.

– I can't control a sheep. Anyway, De Foie had fallen asleep at the wheel. More accidents happen as a result of tiredness than from drunken driving. You should know that, being police.

– You made the Chief Constable fart when Hodge was in the next cubicle, said Cobb. You knew the methane would ignite when that happened.

– I can't prevent my characters from farting. The bear farts too, remember. *With me room-rum-ra fal-the-diddle-a star-vee-upple-al-the-di-dee-do.* Books are full of people farting...

– Are they? said Cora Theave. I don't know of any other books in which characters fart... Does Becky Sharp fart in *Vanity Fair*? You don't even read of Jos Sedley farting, the Collector of Boggley Wallah, and he ate as much as our Chief Constable. Nor does Thackeray himself fart in Mr Carey's critical biography, and you'd expect a critical biographer to be exacting in his recall of detail in such a warts-and-all portrait of the artist. So where are all these farting characters? They're another fiction, admit it.

– They do it all the time, just as people do, but authors don't always mention when their characters fart. Scenes usually involve different characters interacting, and obviously they don't fart until they're on their own, after they've left the room...

– More conjecture on your part, said Cora Theave sniffily.

– Other possible charges may follow, added Sergeant Cobb, relating to deaths in the war...

– But there you have rules of military engagement.

– But you made Captain Nicholas kill Lieutenant Lambert, Cobb persisted. And you fixed it so that Brock was executed after his court martial. You could have saved them both.

– I...

– As well as other charges, DC Theave continued, under the Wildlife Protection Act and the Cruelty to Animals Act relating to your treatment of rabbits, rats, weasels, squirrels, dogs, mink, horses, sheep, cattle and pigs.

– Charges of conspiracy to pervert the course of justice are also possible, said Sergeant Cobb. We're throwing the book at you, all six hundred pages of it. And in respect of all these charges, especially those for which you have now been placed under arrest, I must caution you that you do not have to say anything, but anything you say may be taken down and used in evidence against you in a court of law. You are entitled to make one telephone call now, to a solicitor if you wish, after which we must ask you to accompany us to Otteridge Police Station.

– Very well. I shall phone Mr Merino. The phone's upstairs in the bedroom. I'll just make this one call and collect my things.

– And don't try anything, warned Sergeant Cobb. We haven't come alone. There are officers waiting behind the house, as well as down the lane. You won't be able to escape.

When five minutes had elapsed, Sergeant Cobb called upstairs, but received no response. He decided to investigate.

Entering the attic room, he saw an old dressing-table next to the window with a round oak-framed mirror which someone had draped with a green silk scarf. This bedroom had a sloping ceiling, and occupied the roof space of the cottage. It was empty. There were no other rooms.

He called to Cora Theave to join him, to witness the scene, and walking slowly across to the dressing-table, she lifted the silk scarf from the mirror. What she saw, or glimpsed rather, for it was that fleeting, made her face whiten. Since the room was empty, she had not expected to see in the glass, standing behind her at the window where the white curtains were ghosting in, the man they had been talking to downstairs. She had not seen him before, he had died, or disappeared, before she had joined Emma Gimmer's team, but the face she saw in the mirror was also very like the pictures of Inspector Kernan in the file; not that these had been good likenesses, Diana Hunter had assured her, because Kernan had never liked being photographed, but the resemblance was unmistakable.

What was stranger still was that the face in the glass was green in hue, and the man's hair seemed to be made from leaves. There were leaves coming out of his mouth, like a green cry. But when she turned from the mirror to look behind her, he had gone, of course.

It was then that she saw the end of the rope. The rope had been secured from a manger ring fixed to the window frame, no doubt in case of a fire. She went to look out of the window to follow the rope, but knew that it would end in nothing but air.

– You knew, she said, turning to Cobb. You knew it was him, didn't you? You let him pull the wool over our eyes.

– His thread is spun, Sergeant Cobb answered. He told us all we needed to know. I wanted him to escape. He was at the end of his tether.

GLOSSARY OF NAMES & DISEASES

Adidasitis: See *Hilfiger's Disease*.
Albert: Illustrious, nobly bright, as ALBERT JARMAN, trooper with the King's Own Loamshire Hussars, killed when a troop train was shelled in Ypres station. Diminutive: BERTIE, Albert's horse.
Alcock: *Alcock's Arbour*, the *Devil's Nut Bag* or *Devil's Night-Cap*, is a conical hill between Stratford and Alcester, near the Haselor-Temple Grafton crossroads in Warwickshire. Its Loamshire twin is much smaller, and has gathered an additional association with DAN ALCOCK, a cobbler from Sussex.
Alpers: Company involved in research and development of chemicals, a subsidiary of Gerstmann Holdings. *Alpers Disease* is a rare transmissible spongiform encephalopathy affecting humans, causing progressive degenerative disorders of the central nervous system; like the histologically similar *Creutzfeld-Jakob Disease*, Alpers can be easily transmitted to hamsters but not to guinea pigs by intracerebral inoculation, but unlike CJD, it is also characterised by fatty degeneration of the liver.
Anubis: Egyptian god with a human body and a jackal's head. The son of Osiris, he took the souls of the dead before the judge of the infernal regions. The dog-headed ANUBIANS take their name from him.
Archer: Contemporary English slang for £2000, the amount which Jeffrey Archer said he did not give to a prostitute.
Armstrong: JACK ARMSTRONG, tenant of Long Wood Farm on the Maw Estate; his grandfather BILL was killed at Arras.
Becky: Diminutive of Rebecca, an ensnarer; name chosen by W.M. Thackeray for Miss Sharp.
Belinda: A serpent. Name chosen for Nicholas Goodman's wife.
Bella: Kernan's Newfoundland bitch, short for Bellatrix, shoulder star with Betelgeuse of Orion, the great hunter slain by Diana.
Bernard: Bold as a bear. Name chosen for TENCH.

Bovine Spongiform Encephalopathy (BSE): Also known as Mad Cow Disease, this transmissible spongiform encephalopathy (TSE) was first discovered in UK cattle in 1986, possibly caused by feeding herbivorous cattle with scrapie-infected sheep's brains in a "protein feed" made from an offal paste called MRM (mechanically recovered meat). Another possible cause or "trigger" is exposure to organophosphorus chemicals present in various agricultural products such as sheep dip and insecticide used for treating warble fly in cattle; another is mutation of a rogue protein, possibly triggered by environmental factors. All these causes can be related to mismanagement by agribusiness and government during the 1980s involving short-term cost-cutting and long-term disaster. In this book, the scientific and business background to the BSE epidemic are figured through the case of Bernard Tench.

Brock: Badger. The Brocks have always lived at Oakwood: MIKE BROCK, his son JOHN and wife RACHEL; his grandfather JACK was wrongly accused of cowardice and executed by firing squad in 1916, and his son later hung himself.

Bruce: Short for *Brucellosis*, an animal disease, also called *contagious abortion*, communicable to man as *Malta*, or *undulant fever*. The shortened version is a popular first name in Australia, as adopted by BRUCELLOSIS TUCKER in this book.

Bunty: Affected by *stink-brand*, or *bunt*, a disease of wheat. Name chosen for the wife of Maurice Saveloy.

Candida: Parasitic yeast-like fungus. *Candidiasis* is an infection of the skin or mucous membrane caused by a Candida, usually *Candida albicans*, which causes thrush. Name chosen for Mrs Sirloin (*née* Yeats).

Cerberus: Three-headed dog which guards the gates of Hell, its fable possibly linked with the ancient Egyptian custom of guarding graves with dogs. *Cerberus, Cerberus & Cerberus:* firm of funeral directors in Otteridge.

Cernunnos: Celtic earth god often identified with the *Green Man* (*Le Feuillu* in French folklore) and *Herne the Hunter*, and as son-lover of the Great Goddess.

Chawdron: An animal's entrails. Also CHAWDRON, an official in the Department of Health who removed Tench's milk licence.

Clegg: A gadfly or horsefly. LEE CLEGG: paratrooper acquitted of the murder of 18-year-old Karen Reilly, a passenger in a stolen car who was shot dead by British soldiers in Belfast on 30 September 1990. PC LEE CLEGG (no relation): a pusillanimous weasel-faced constable with Loamshire Police stationed at Otteridge.

Clio: The Muse of History. The car of Kernan.

Cobb: From *cob*, a big or notable man; a thump on the buttocks. SERGEANT COBB: Otteridge's stout desk sergeant.
Coombes: From *coomb*, a wooded valley. COLIN COOMBES: abbatoir manager for the Otteridge Meat Company; his grandfather was disembowelled by machine-gun fire at the Battle of Arras.
Creutzfeld-Jakob Disease (CJD): Transmissible spongiform encephalopathy affecting humans, its new variant linked with BSE in the recent epidemic, although world distribution of CJD does not correspond to that of scrapie in sheep. First described in 1920, the disease takes hold rapidly, with muscular spasms, dementia, loss of higher brain function and behavioural abnormalities.
Daglock: Or *dag*, a shit-clotted tuft of wool on a sheep, hence the Australian expression, *Don't rattle your dags* (Don't get flustered). Name chosen for DS DAGLOCK of Loamshire Police.
Damian: The tamer. Phoebe Hunter's husband.
Daube: A stew, hence INSPECTOR DAUBE, who is always stewed.
Davis: Loamshire farming family, all the men born on St Joseph's Day and christened Joseph, including FLEA, his father Joe and his great-grandfather who was shellshocked but not killed in the Great War, for a St Joseph's child will never be shot in battle.
De Foie (Gras): Of liver (goose), as in OLIVER DE FOIE, the Franco-German industrialist, and PATTY DE FOIE, his wife. His grandfather Hans Gans changed the business of the family firm from sauerkraut to mustard gas to assist the German war effort in 1914. When Alsace was returned to France, the company was renamed De Foie-Gras, and later, when it switched from poison gas to pesticides, to *Eurochimique.*
Devlin: Short for deviling, secret vice of the REV. KEVIN DEVLIN, vicar of St George's, Loamfield.
Diana: Moon-goddess (identified with Artemis), chaste goddess of hunting and woodlands, associated with fertility and worshipped by women. Name chosen for DC DIANA HUNTER, daughter of CYNTHIA, granddaughter of PHOEBE, all Hunters with moon names.
Doddypoll: Blockhead. DOCTOR DODDYPOLL: proverbial name for preachers used for Dr Gallstone's medical colleague.
Dogbreath: Friend of Ernest Gubbins.
Dragon: Fire-breathing monster with a snake or crocodile's body covered with scales and with the forelegs and head of a lion, eagle or hawk, which must be propitiated by human sacrifice. MARGARET THATCHER, who takes the form of the she-devil Sin in Chapter 23, is a recent version of this creature, a dragon slain by a sheep. However, in Christian legend, the Dragon is the Devil or his servant, and when St George slays the Dragon, that's a good thing, although

if the Dragon represents the Old Religion and George is fighting the good fight, that's a bit suspect. Dragons have been linked with matriarchal Goddess cults, turning George into a jackbooted champion of patriarchy, but that's rather unfair on England's later hero and saint, a Palestinian who lived in the third century AD.
Eurochimique: Jolly ungreen chemicals giant. See *De Foie*.
Felcher: One who licks anuses. RICHARD FELCHER, MP for South Loamshire, a character removed from this book for legal reasons.
Fisher: Fisherman. FRANK FISHER, a slaughterman; his grandfather KEN FISHER drowned in a shellhole in the Third Battle of Ypres.
Flea: A person of diminutive stature, like FLEA, our student of woodcraft and spellcraft.
Fraser: Family of Loamshire Scottish exiles: WILD BILL FRASER, a security guard at Eurochimique; his grandfather CSM FRASER was killed leading a raid in No Man's Land in May 1917.
Gallstone: A concretion in the gall-bladder. Name chosen for the Otteridge quack.
Gans: Goose. See *De Foie*.
Gawain: A hawk. Nephew of King Arthur, who beheaded the Green Knight and went on the Quest for the Holy Grail.
George: Land-holder. England's hero ST GEORGE (d. *c*.303) defeated the dragon after the beast was offered the king's daughter in place of its usual diet of two sheep a day when sheep had become scarce, but George's services to sheep did not prevent his being struck off the Church's list of approved saints in 1969. GEORGE KERNAN's name unites England with the earth god Cernunnos. See also *Dragon*.
Gerstmann: *Gerstmann-Straussler-Scheinker Disease* (GSS) is similar to CJD, but with a tendency towards cerebellar ataxia as the initial predominant neurological sign, and a large number of amyloid plaques present among the spongiform encephalopathic changes of the brain; GSS has been transmitted from a human source to monkeys and rodents by intracerebral inoculation and to hamsters merely by the insertion of the human abnormal PrP gene from chromosome 20 into the hamster genome. GERSTMANN: A holding company with interests in petrochemicals, agribusiness and leisure, the parent company of Eurochimique, Alpers Pharmaceuticals, Braxy UK, the Otteridge Meat Company, Straussler and Scheinker.
Gimmer: An unshorn ewe. INSPECTOR EMMA GIMMER: policewoman with long hair.
Gingell: PETE GINGELL, a dog-loving slaughterman; his grandfather JIMMY GINGELL, killed in No Man's Land in May 1917.
Gizzard: A muscular stomach, especially a bird's. Name chosen for LIZZIE GIZZARD to encourage false assumptions.

Goodman: A husband or master, a name often used confusingly for the devil; so chosen for SUPERINTENDENT NICHOLAS GOODMAN.
Green Man: Mysterious and ambiguous archetypal figure whose pagan image survives in numerous European churches, often linked with CERNUNNOS (*q.v.*) and various other earth deities and forest folk, and seen as a symbol of Life in Death and of Death in Life. In churches he is perhaps a threshold figure whose pre-Christian image serves both to honour and contain the forces of Nature.
Gubbins: A trivial object or rubbish. ERNEST GUBBINS: Retired chimney sweep, thief, hartshorn addict and heretical olfactologist, married to THE COOT; his cousin GUS, the ram-loving nightwatchman at the abbatoir in Otteridge.
Hackerton: Proverbial lawyer who when told his heifer had been gored by an ox, claimed the ox in recompense, but when told the reverse had happened replied 'The case alters there.' Hence the phrase *That is Hackerton's cow*, spoken of those who alter their opinions for reasons of expediency. The Sirloins bought *Hackerton Manor* from the proceeds of the Yeats land sale.
Hardacre: MATT HARDACRE: oddjob man and erstwhile burglar; his grandfather was blinded in a German gas attack in 1917.
Hart: A male deer usually over five years old, when the antlers or hartshorn (see *Gubbins*) appear. The Harts have always been gamekeepers, latterly for the Maws and before that for the Loamsleys.
Hartley: A maker of jam. JOE HARTLEY: Otteridge slaughterman whose grandfather WILF was killed at Arras in 1917.
Henry: This book has many Henrys, not all interchangeable, and including: HENRY SIRLOIN, MP for North Loamshire; HENRY OF POITOU, infamous Abbot of Peterborough; HENRY I (1068-1135), whose later reincarnations include Éamon de Valéra and several sheep; HENRY II (1133-89), who wanted rid of Thomas à Becket; and the eponymous KING HENRY of the ballad sung by Lizzie Gizzard.
Herne: Mythical hunter figure linked with CERNUNNOS and the GREEN MAN (*q.q.v.*), and thus Kernan's shadow; *Herne the Hunter* haunts Windsor Forest in winter, in whose guise Kernan appears to Oliver de Foie in Ch.26 as Falstaff did in *The Merry Wives of Windsor*, taunting him with Shakespeare's description of the ghostly woodsman. Herne also appears in Harrison Ainsworth's novel *Windsor Castle*, and in the 1980s TV series *Robin of Sherwood.*
Hilfiger: A false or stolen name. *Hilfiger's Disease* or *Adidasitis* is a highly infectious disease affecting impressionable humans who pay large sums to sportswear companies under the delusion that plastering themselves with other people's names expresses non-conformity. Since sufferers pay the companies for the supposed privilege of

advertising their products, this vicious circle accelerates the spread of branding to others, with the result that only 20% of sportswear sold in Britain is used for sport. See also *Nike*.

Hodge: A countryman, a rustic; pejorative corruption of Roger; ROGER HODGE, a police constable in the Loamshire force noted for his low intellect and unsophisticated sexual technique.

Hogg: A yearling sheep not yet shorn; formerly slang for a shilling; also a low filthy fellow, a greedy person, an inconsiderate boor, a person of coarse manners, or a brush used to clean a ship's bottom. DOUGLAS HOGG, Agriculture Minister in the Conservative Government during Britain's BSE Crisis in the 1990s.

Hoggett: Variant of *Hogg*. The Hoggetts were sheep farmers in Loamfield until the 18th century, when the last son died without issue, his name surviving in Hoggett's Field.

Hunter: See *Diana*.

Isabella: As in ISABELLA MAW, from *belle amour.*

Jabez: Sorrow (Hebrew); literally, he will cause pain; first name of DR KURU.

Jake: a country lout, a yokel; *conversely*, honest, correct, first-rate, which just shows you can't assume anything where names are concerned. GINGER JAKE: A headache remedy, the cause of an epidemic of delayed neuropathy in the USA in 1930, due to contamination with triorthocresyl phosphate; in this book, a toxic demon created from organophosphate pesticides.

Jakes: A toilet. JOHNNY JAKES, a police constable in the Loamshire force, noted for his comic manner and jolly japes; also owner of Benny Hill Farm, notable for breeding police horses.

Jarman: BILL JARMAN of Hoggett's Farm is Kernan's neighbour at Loamfield. See also *Albert*.

Johnson: BILLY JOHNSON, a Gulf War veteran suffering from the supposedly mythical Gulf War Syndrome; his grandfather was killed in a no less mythical No Man's Land in 1917. 'Billy Johnson's Ball' is a lilting, tongue-twisting ballad in which we play *la, la-di-da, row-di-dow-di-diddle-um* on the fiddle, *up and down the middle*, jolly girls, pretty girls, *enough to pl'ase us all, and a regular jollification spree was Billy Johnson's Ball.*

Kernan: See *Cernunnos, George, Green Man* and *Herne*.

Kesteven: A bad dream, after LADY THATCHER OF KESTEVEN. See also *Dragon* and *Thatcher*.

Kuru: This disease is not named after DR JABEZ KURU, Eurochimique's Chief Research Scientist, an erroneous attribution made by certain misinformed journalists. *Kuru* is a condition of the Fore tribe of the Okapa district of Papua New Guinea, resulting from

ritual cannibalism which survived in the Eastern Highlands until 1956. Kuru was almost exclusive to women and children, due to the practice of giving the brain of a dead tribe member to them, while the men ate the muscle tissue. Clinically, the disease is of a progressive cerebellar ataxia leading to uncoordinated movements, neurological weakness, palsies and decay in brain cortical function. Unlike CJD sufferers, most people dying of Kuru are not demented.
Lambert: Illustrious land-holder, but when shortened the word describes a young sheep. LAWRENCE (always Lawrence, never Larry) LAMBERT: Assistant Chief Constable of Loamshire Police who takes one step forward and two steps back; his grandfather, LIEUTENANT ARCHIBALD LAMBERT, was killed in the assault on Eagle Trench in September 1917.
Leech: Blood-sucking parasite, a branch of the Chaetopod worms, of the class *Hirudinea*. Leech saliva contains the anticoagulant hirudin, used by surgeons during the First World War; HENRY LEECH, Adjutant in the Royal Loamshire Light Infantry, responsible for recruitment in the county at the same time; his granddaughter, MARY LEECH, a nurse with the Loamshire Blood Transfusion Service.
Lionel: Young lion. LIONEL TENCH, son of Bernard.
Lucy: Light-bringer. Once Flea-bitten, LUCY SAVELOY becomes this.
MAFF: Ministry of Agriculture, Fisheries and Food, government department responsible for the BSE cover-up, later renamed DEFRA (Department for the Elimination of Farm-Reared Animals).
Mansonil: Niclosamide drug used to treat sturdy in sheep.
Marshall: As in the martial CORPORAL JACK MARSHALL, killed in an attack on a German bunker in 1917; and grandson, JACK MARSHALL, an aggressive slaughterman.
Maw: Stomach; the fourth stomach of ruminants; a bird's craw; any insatiate gulf or receptacle (a mawbound cow is constipated by impaction of the rumen). MORTON MAW, MBE, Chairman of the Planning Committee of Loamshire County Council, a glutton who eats all in his path; married to ISABELLA, with one son, THOMAS.
Merkin: A hair-piece for the pubic area; formerly the name of a greengrocer's used by the author (who can thus vouch for the name's authenticity). MRS MERKIN is the cleaner at Otteridge Police Station.
Merino: Sheep of a fine-woolled Spanish breed; in Spanish, also a governor; in this book, PAUL MERINO is an attorney, a chicano or Mexican American sheep.
Morrigan: Great Queen or Queen of the Demons in Irish myth, one of the wives of the war-god Nét with the scald-crow Badbh, who haunts the battlefields, and Nemain, goddess of panic. In the *Táin Bó Cuailnge*, she takes the form of an eel and tries to drown

Cúchulainn at river-crossings where fights take place.
Morton: Unsatisfied; insatiable more like, as in MAW.
Muffy: Female pudendum. MUFFY, the wise old woman, identified with Hecate, crone part of the triple goddess.
Nicholas: Old Nick, the Devil. NICHOLAS GOODMAN, his servant.
Nike: Victory, an attribute or daughter of the goddess Athene; a stolen name used for overpriced shoes and ground-to-air missiles. See also *Hilfiger's Disease*.
Oliver: Of liver. See *De Foie*.
Olivia: Female liver with an appetite for sex and meat.
Openshaw: JOHN OPENSHAW, petty criminal; his grandfather was killed in a German gas attack in 1917.
O'Scrapie: Of scrapie. O'SCRAPIE, a Loamfield family of thieves, including PADDY MUTTONCHOPS, the proverbial village butcher, and his grandson/grandfather (PATRICK) O'SCRAPIE. See also *Scrapie*.
Oxter: Armpit. SERGEANT MALCOLM OXTER: Bulky police sergeant with two oxters.
Pagan: Rustic. Word used by Christian missionaries for country people, from the Latin *paganus*, from *pagus*, village or country folk.
Patty: A small flat cake of minced beef; an English corruption of the French pâté, a paste made of blended meat and herbs, as in *pâté de foie gras*, made from the liver of a goose which has been force-fed to achieve fast, artificial fattening; a diminutive of Patricia, as in PATTY DE FOIE.
Peter: To fart (*French*), as in SIR PETER PRURIGEAUX (*q.v.*).
Phil: Short for Philip, a lover of horses, as in PHIL HART (*q.v.*).
Prurigeaux: Frenchified version of PRURIGO (*q.v.*) adopted by the *nouveau riche* Prurigo family to disguise their origins. SIR PETER PRURIGEAUX: Yellowbeard leader of Otteridge District Council killed by gangrene and witchcraft; his wife LADY OLIVIA (*q.v.*) and son JAMES, a peacekeeping hero.
Prurigo: An itchy skin eruption.
Rachel: A ewe. RACHEL BROCK looks after ewes.
Roger: A goose; police radio shorthand for received (and understood); *verb*, sexual intercourse (slang); see also *Roger Hodge*.
Saveloy: A sausage, as in MAURICE SAVELOY, Chief Constable of Loamshire, killed in a botulist conflagration; see Ch.2 for his sausage genealogy. His wife BUNTY (*q.v.*); and daughter LUCY (*q.v.*).
Scheinker: Sportswear company responsible for the spread of *Hilfiger's Disease* (*q.v.*). See *Gerstmann.*
Scrapie: Naturally occurring sheep disease known for over 200 years but implicated in the spread of BSE after sheep's brains were fed to cattle in so-called "protein feed".

Sheeder: Female lamb. SGT SHEEDER: Pigglingford policeman.
Shuck: Black demon dog or Barguest with glowing saucer eyes, also known as Skriker, Padfoot and Trash in various parts of England. Name chosen for Candida Sirloin's black labrador.
Skryabingylus nasicola: Parasitic worm which causes progressive holing of the skulls of stoats and weasels.
Sirloin: Loin of beef. HENRY SIRLOIN: MP for North Loamshire.
Snell: Keen, sharp, severe. Otteridge's NURSE SNELL and Ambridge's LYNDA SNELL share these traits. A snell is also a short piece of gut or hair used to attach a hook to a line. See also *Dragon*.
Spermwail: HAMISH SPERMWAIL, manager of the Excelsior Hotel.
Straussler: Hotels group. See *Gerstmann*.
Strimmer: Grass-cutting machine. JAMES STRIMMER: Marketing Director of Eurochimique UK.
Tench: Freshwater fish (*Tinca tinca*) of the carp family, reputed to have healing properties (see Ch.6). BERNARD TENCH: Murdered owner of Hogsback Hill Farm, a disaffected boffin, formerly with Eurochimique; an archetypal maverick scientist, his research combining strands from the work of several similar figures who have fortunately been spared his fate. His son, LIONEL TENCH.
Thatcher: One who roofs houses, usually with straw but with excrement in the saying *She that thatches her house with turds shall have more teachers than reachers*. MARGARET THATCHER, notorious British Prime Minister deposed by a sheep called Sir Geoffrey. Her early political career was supported by a small fortune made by husband Sir Denis out of the manufacture of pesticides and paint products, from a family business originally set up in New Zealand to sell sheep dip. See also *Dragon* and *Kesteven*.
Theave: Ewe between first and second shearing. DC CORA THEAVE: policewoman with short hair.
301: Not the name but the number of a Bluefaced Leicester ewe from Long Wood Farm, one of Kernan's informants. Had the action of Chapter 10 taken a different turn on page 238, this ewe would have played a significant role in the action, straying onto the road and causing Goodman to swerve, so saving Diana's life.
Tomkins: Turncoat *Loamshire Chronicle* editor; his grandfather, a poison gas casualty in 1917.
Twinter: Two-year-old ewe. DC TWINTER: Young policewoman.
Tucker: Australian slang for food. See *Brucellosis*.
Yeats: Anagram: see *Candida*.

ACKNOWLEDGEMENTS

The main sources of this book are such as should need no acknowledgement, but since the English folk tradition is commonly misunderstood, denied or denigrated at the same time as those hostile or affecting indifference to it actually honour its wisdom and forms or their modern equivalent in their own speech, writings and thought, I will make no bones about declaring my indebtedness to that common English inheritance, which embraces myth, folklore, folksong, nursery rhymes, superstition, bawdy and all those English proverbs and age-old idioms which still enrich the speech of the good folk of Loamshire. Cervantes called proverbs 'short sentences drawn from long experience', and if Bacon was right that the 'Genius, Wit, and Spirit of a Nation, are to be discovered by their Proverbs', this author would rather see an expression of England in what James Howell in 1659 called 'the People's Voice' than in the debased modern currency of the cliché, slogan and sound-bite.

Since this novel is likely to be charged with the crime of magic realism, I ask the court to believe that its upbringing was not unduly influenced by the modern masters of that exotic genre but was rather schooled by the ancients; the book's territory, resources and myths come from England itself, and if it is sometimes guilty of an addiction to animal fables, miracles and transformations, then an unhealthy association with Greek and Biblical myth, Celtic and English folklore, medieval literature and the Lives of the Saints should be taken into account before sentence is pronounced.

With the exception of correctly named historical personages, the characters in this novel are all fictional and entirely the product of the author's imagination, bearing no relation to any person in "real life". The folklore and superstitions drawn upon in the book are, however, entirely genuine, including the one about dogshit in chapter 23; and likewise the Hellfire speeches of Sin, as well as the scientific research discussed by various characters in the book, are genuine and may be checked by the reader, with the exception of the Anubian flight of fancy in Dr Kuru's report (although his bibliography and account of the effect of oestrogenic chemicals on fauna and flora draw on actual papers published in scientific journals). While Eurochimique and its web of companies is a fabrication, its research portfolio has an impeccable scientific pedigree, including the production during the First World War of poison gases at the Bayer Chemical Works in Leverkusen (for which I am indebted to Otto Hahn's account). But no other connection is intended in this book with Bayer or any other company, with the exception that the Niclosamide drug used to treat sheep with sturdy, referred to in chapter 25, is a product marketed by Bayer under the name Mansonil; while Beelzebub's rainbow mission statement expounded in chapter 23 was "borrowed" like a customised bar of perfumed hotel soap from Moat House Hotels. Although the Royal Loamshires are mythical, the accounts of actions and incidents on the Western Front in 1916–17 are historically based, as are the descriptions of the moon (the source of the book's calendar) at all times in the narrative.

While the main sources of this novel lie in a diverse oral tradition, it could not have been written but for the work of numerous collectors, editors and commentators, and I would like to acknowledge my debt to their publications, and to those of other writers on mythology, history, natural history, literature, science, agriculture and war, including farmers and soldiers, and in particular the work of William Anderson, Anne Baring, Margaret Blackwood, Katharine M. Briggs, Joseph Campbell, Jean-Luc Caradeau, John Carey, Angela Carter, Jules Cashford, Theo Colborn, Quentin Cooper, Joseph Cundall, Stephen Dealler, Cécile Donner, Dianne Dumanoski, George Ewart Evans, David Farmer, Edith Hamilton, Charlotte Hardman, both Graham Harveys (on paganism and agriculture), Harold Hillman, Eric Hiscock, E.J. Hobsbawm, Christina Hole, Prudence Jones, Sean Kane, Peter Kennedy, Richard Lacey, James Lovelock, A.L. Lloyd, Lyn Macdonald, Caitlin Matthews, 'Muck-spreader', John Peterson Myers, Iona & Peter Opie, Roy Palmer, Hans & Audrey Porksen, Mark Purdey, E. & M.A. Radford, George Rudé, Nicholas J. Saunders, Cecil Sharp, Robin Skelton, Eddie Straiton, Paul Sullivan, Carol Thatcher, Edwin Campion Vaughan, Barbara C. Walker, Marina Warner, Ralph Vaughan Williams, Denis Winter, Leon Wolff and Hugo Young; and I am especially indebted to those people whose words and versions of stories and songs were recorded by several of those authors, including many singers and storytellers (in particular Charles Boyle, Edgar Button, Seamus Ennis, 'Shepherd' Haden, Dicky Lashbrook, Alec McNichol, Cyril Poacher, George Spicer, Davie Stewart, John Strachan and Mr Trump of North Petherton), and soldiers from the Western Front whose stories were collected by Lyn Macdonald (in particular Privates W.G. Bell and J. Bowles, Rifleman B.F Eccles, Troopers Sydney Chaplin and G. Huggins, Corporals H. Bale, Harold Diffey, John Lucy and C.R. Russell, Sergeants S.V. Britten and Bill Hay, 2nd Lieutenants J. Macleod and Ewart Richardson, Captains A.F.P. Christison, R.A. Macleod and W. Grant Grieve, and Major J. Cowan).

The rhymes, poems and songs sung in the book are mostly traditional, but some are my own or bastard versions. The war poems quoted include 'Anthem for Doomed Youth' and 'Insensibility' by Wilfred Owen. The epigraph by Thea Gilmore is from her song 'Gun Cotton' on *As If* (Shameless/Flying Sparks Records, 2001). Excerpts from 'I Know an Old Lady' by Rose Bonne and Alan Mills are used by permission of Peermusic (UK) Ltd, 8-14 Verulam Street, London WC1X 8LZ, copyright © 1952 Peer International (Canada) Ltd. The poem at the end of chapter 14 is stolen from *Biting My Tongue* by Neil Astley (Bloodaxe Books, 1995), inspired by 'The Twa Magicians' from Peter Buchan's *Ancient Ballads and Songs of the North of Scotland* (1828). Parts of chapters 9 and 27 owe an unbeheadable debt to the 14th-century Middle English poem *Gawain and the Green Knight*, while my Green Knight's lament was in turn inspired by incantations attributed to the 10th century Irish poet Amergin Glúngel in *Lebor Gabála*, the pseudo-historical 'Book of Invasions' (with a sideways nod to Gray's *Elegy*).

For help, inspiration and information of various kinds I am grateful to Lorna Black, Helen Dunmore, the English Folk Dance and Song Society, Kate Fitzpatrick, Linda France, Brendan Kennelly, Caradoc King, the Imperial War Museum, *The Lancet*, Peter and Margaret Lewis, Martha Lishawa, Loamshire Antiquarian Society, the National Sheep Association, *The Observer*, *Private Eye*, David Scott, the Scottish play, Steeleye Span, William Makepeace Thackeray, Uncle Tom Cobbley and all at www.mad-cow.org.

My special thanks go to Dr Lewis Routledge: the few hours I spent in his company pulled the trigger of this book, and set off its double-hit chain of reaction to his provocative bombardment of facts and insights, although with results he probably won't have anticipated.

The pictures come from a variety of sources. They include a number of woodcuts by Thomas Bewick and his school taken from his books *A General History of Quadrupeds* (1790), *A History of British Birds* (1797 & 1826), *Select Fables* (1820), *Vignettes* (1827) and *A Memoir of Thomas Bewick, Written by Himself* (1862), as well as studies by John Trusler (1791), Robert Robinson (1867), Thomas Hugo (1870), Julia Boyd (1886), William Mavor's *English Spelling Book* and the Leadenhall *1,000 Quaint Cuts*. Others come from various toy books, chapbooks and nursery rhyme broadsheets (the woodcuts in these often borrowed from each other), including *Food for the Mind; or, A New Riddle-Book* (1758), *Juvenile Sports and Pastimes* (1776), *A Curious Hieroglyphick Bible* (1783), *The Looking-Glass for the Mind* (1792), *Vocal Harmony, or No Song, No Supper* (1800), *Tom Thumb's Song-Book* (1815), *The Cheerful Warbler, The Courtship of Cockrobin and Jenny Wren, An Elegy on the Death and Burial of Cock Robin, The House That Jack Built, Jack and Jill and Old Dame Gill, Jack Horner's Pretty Toy, Jumping Joan, The Life and Death of Jenny Wren, The Life of Jack Sprat, Old Dame Trot and Her Comical Cat, Old Mother Goose, Poetic Trifles, or Pretty Poems for Young Folks, The Silver Penny, Tom the Piper's Son,* and *The World Turned Upside Down* (all 1820), *The English Mother's Catechism for Her Children* (1824), *Æsop's Fables* (1824), *The Little Woman and the Pedlar, The Temple of Fancy*, and *Tom Thumb's Play Book* (all 1825), *Tales of Animals* (1833), *Puzzle-cap's Amazing Riddle Book* and *Tom, the Piper's Son* (both 1835), *The Amusing Riddle Book, Nursery Rhymes, Poetic Trifles, for Young Gentlemen and Ladies*, and *The Riddle Book* (all 1840); from 19th-century books of natural history, including *Wild Nature Won by Kindness* (1890), *The World of Animal Life* and *The Boy's Own Book of Natural History* (undated), and the periodical *Pictorial Museum of Animated Nature*; and from *Sear's Stereotype Ornaments* (1825).

The animal initials used to begin each chapter are from an 18th-century wood-engraved alphabet, reproduced from *Les Fonderies de Caractères et leur Matériel dans les Pays Bas du XVe au XIXe Siecle*, printed and published in 1908 by Joh. Enschedé en Zonen, Haarlem.

As well as being dedicated to the memory of the animal and human victims of the recent BSE epidemic, this book was written out of kinship with many animals, and with two cats in particular, Malcolm, who persuaded me to stop eating animals while continuing to eat meat himself, and the much missed Cairo, a highly vocal seal-point Burmese who sat on my shoulder during six months of its writing, as well as three bitches, Dido, Rosie and Raiker, and numerous unnamed sheep, cows, horses, deer and birds of my acquaintance, especially the herds at Dargues Hope, Moses the bull, Jim Scott's and Bobby Anderson's Swaledales and Scottish Blackfaces at Otterburn, and my nineteen muses, the noble and boisterous Suffolk tups I used to watch from my window, who were murdered by DEFRA assassins on New Year's Day 2002 along with 2100 other sheep in Martin Weeks's flock who did not have Foot and Mouth Disease, the last animals in England to be massacred in the recent conflict.

GK

NO ANIMAL WAS HARMED IN THE MAKING OF THIS BOOK